ALIX JAMES

Everbound

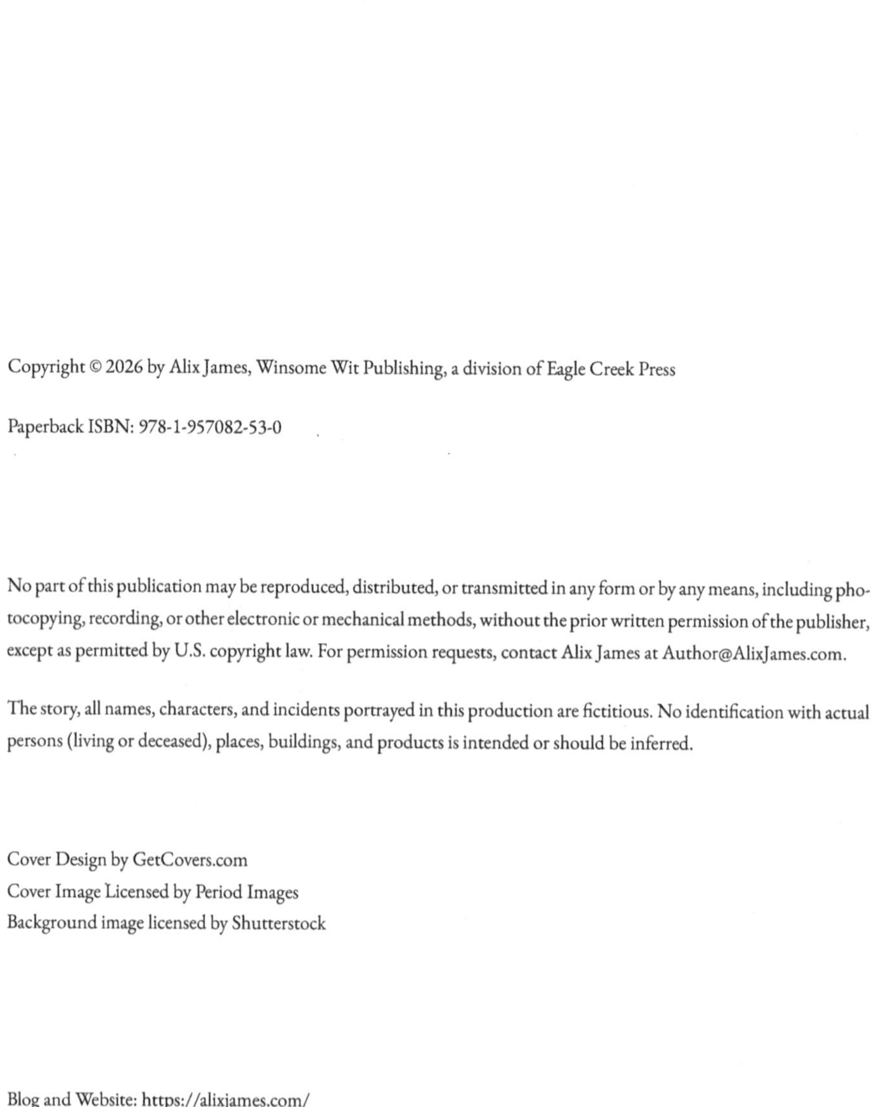



Paperback ISBN: 978-1-957082-53-0



Cover Design by GetCovers.com
Cover Image Licensed by Period Images
Background image licensed by Shutterstock

Blog and Website: https://alixjames.com/
Newsletter: https://subscribepage.io/alix-james
Book Bub: https://www.bookbub.com/authors/alix-james
Facebook: https://www.facebook.com/ShortSweetNovellas
Twitter: https://twitter.com/N_Clarkston
Austen Variations: http://austenvariations.com/

# Contents

# Chapter One

*Pemberley*
*August, 1811*

THE AFTERNOON HELD A rare stillness. The sort that hovered only in the last days of summer, when the air was heavy with ripened green and the shadows, though short, had begun to lean eastward with a kind of anticipatory gravity.

Darcy rode alone, as he preferred, save for Brutus, who trailed a pace behind him with ears alert and tongue lolling in pleasure. The path he took, curving southward through the lower wood, was not the most direct, nor even the most scenic, but it was the one he had followed since boyhood. It pleased him to take it in the same direction, at the same pace, marking the same hedgerows and glens and half-fallen stone wall near the streambed as one might reread a volume long-memorised. The satisfaction lay not in discovery, but in reaffirmation.

Bellerophon moved beneath him with the same comfortable swagger he always had, tossing his dark head whenever the bridle felt too much like instruction. The horse was older now, and moody, but retained that proud edge which Darcy could not entirely dislike. There was an understanding between them: neither suffered fools, and neither pretended patience to be a virtue when it was not sincerely felt.

The sunlight filtered warm through the canopy, dappling Darcy's coat and hands, and catching at Brutus's shaggy back whenever he darted ahead to nose a scent or leap a stone. The wolfhound was a brute in name only—he had a soldier's caution and a scholar's solemnity, and his loyalty, once earned, was irrevocable. At present, he chased shadows and rabbit smells, his tail a metronome of quiet joy.

Darcy's own mind was pleasantly empty. There had been no troublesome correspondence at breakfast, no new accounts to concern him, and Georgiana had smiled, not nervously, but simply—with that fleeting expression he remembered from their childhood summers, before their father's illness had pressed gravity upon her shoulders. It had struck him, that smile. Not for its rarity, but for its ease.

Everything was in its place.

The land was in good order—the tenant farms reported a lower yield than expected, but nothing that could not be managed through the winter. The river was low but clean, and the beekeepers had brought a second round of honey that was less than hoped for, but the quality was rich and dark with linden. The new hedgerows were taking root near the eastern edge, and even the kitchen garden, prone to temperamental patches, had at last begun to yield its late crop of beans.

Darcy let the rhythm of the ride lull him. Bellerophon's gait was smooth, and the sound of hoofbeats mingled with the burr of insects and the distant, overlapping calls of wood pigeons.

There was, he thought, a certain moral clarity to land. It was not a sentiment he shared aloud—too sentimental by half—but he felt it all the same. One need only look well, tend what required it, and keep faith with the natural rhythms. The land would tell a man what it needed. And when it thrived, so did he.

He took the lower fork in the path without thinking. It led toward the elder grove—dense and slightly marshy, but not impassable—and if the light held, he might make a wide circuit and return behind the stables.

Brutus darted ahead, tail high, nose to the wind. Darcy let him go, content to follow at a stroll.

He did not notice the silence at first. The birdsong faded gradually, the way candlelight dims with dusk. The wind quieted. Even Bellerophon's hooves began to sound strangely muted against the earth.

Darcy frowned—not at any conscious alarm, but at the sensation that something had fallen out of joint. He tightened the reins slightly. The horse did not respond. His ears had gone back, and his breath came faster, more shallow.

Brutus stopped. The dog stood still at the edge of the copse, one paw lifted, head lowered. He made no sound.

Darcy eased Bellerophon to a halt. "What is it, then?" he murmured, though he did not expect an answer.

The light had changed. It was not cloud—there were no clouds. The sun still shone somewhere above, but it did not reach the forest floor. The shadows had thickened, and the air smelled strange. Not foul—just foreign. A sweet, overripe tang, like cut flowers left too long in their vase.

He dismounted, more to settle the horse than from any wish to investigate, and Brutus gave a low, uncertain huff but did not move. The trees here were older, twisted. That was not new. The grove had always been a place of denser growth, thornier hedges, roots that curled up from the ground as though trying to speak.

But now, there was something else. Darcy stepped forward. The earth beneath his boots was dry—not cracked, but not moist as it should have been in this low place. A few leaves scattered, and he noted their colour—not golden with the season, but dulled and spotted.

Sick.

Ten paces more, and he saw it. An ancient hawthorn stood at the centre of a shallow rise. Its bark was blackened. Not entirely, but in long, creeping streaks, as if fire had licked along its branches and changed its mind. The leaves, what remained, hung limp, curled inward, brown at the veins.

At its base, a ring of earth had turned to dust. Not churned soil, not erosion—simply... dust. Grey and fine. A breath might scatter it.

Darcy did not move closer, though his boots were halfway there. His eyes narrowed, not from disbelief, but calculation. There had been no lightning. No blight in the orchards. No sign of illness among the hedges or trees further down the slope. And yet here stood this—the ruin of a single tree in the middle of his woods, untouched by weather, marked by... what?

Brutus whined.

Darcy turned his head slightly. The dog had crept forward, just enough to press his flank to Darcy's boot. Not cowardice—he knew the difference—but unease. Waiting for instruction. Waiting for sense.

There was none.

Darcy rose slowly, brushing his hand on his coat without realising it. He looked around—not quickly, not in panic, but with a careful sweep of the trees. Nothing moved.

"Come," he said to Brutus, more command than comfort.

The dog obeyed, but kept close.

Bellerophon snorted as he approached. His nostrils flared, and his ears remained pinned. Darcy mounted and turned the horse toward the open path. He did not look back.

By the time he reached the ridge, the sun had returned. The wind lifted. Brutus shook himself and barked once, as if to clear the moment from his memory.

Darcy did not speak the rest of the way home.

Elizabeth Bennet did not take the path home directly.

It was not out of defiance—though her mother might claim as much when she arrived late to breakfast. It was simply that the hedgerow along the eastern rise had begun to bloom a second time, as if the coming autumn were merely a good joke, and Elizabeth could not resist it. The air was warm but not close, the sun shifting through early cloud in hazy gold bands, and the faintest breeze pressed the leaves into a kind of trembling applause.

She paused by a patch of dogrose, pale and insistent against the bramble. It was odd, their timing. The petals should have been gone by now, but here they were again, fragile and new.

She reached out and touched one with the back of her knuckle. It shivered under her touch.

Elizabeth blinked. She had not felt a breeze. No hare or fox was stirring under the bramble. But still, it seemed to quiver at the brush of her fingers.

She swallowed and drew her hand back. A bird trilled nearby, louder than it ought to have been. She turned, half expecting to see it perched within reach, but nothing stirred in the branches. Just a flutter of feathers, retreating through green.

How very charming. The afternoon seemed determined to please her. Elizabeth smiled faintly to herself and continued on.

The house came into view just as the bell rang—late enough to rouse Mama's nerves but not her tears. Elizabeth dusted her boots at the threshold and stepped inside to the familiar sound of chattering voices, clinking porcelain, and Lydia arguing over jam.

"I told you I meant the raspberry," Lydia groaned. "Why must Jane always take what I was thinking of?"

"You were thinking of sleeping through breakfast," Jane replied. "Which is why I poured yours before you came down."

"I would rather choose my own." Lydia slumped into her chair. "Besides, it is dreadfully warm. I think raspberry spoils faster."

Elizabeth kissed Jane's cheek in passing, exchanged a raised brow with Mary, and accepted her tea from Hill without comment. Mama, however, noticed the bonnet she was still wearing.

"Good heavens, Lizzy, not again! Out before breakfast, your hems a fright before anyone can even come calling. If you have come back with burrs in your hair, I shall scream."

Elizabeth removed the bonnet and placed it on the peg. "Only petals this time, I believe."

"That is worse! Petals stain. You will have that ridiculous brown dress looking like a rag by Michaelmas."

Elizabeth sat. "Perhaps I will embroider it to disguise the evidence."

"You are too clever by half, Lizzy. No man likes a woman always turning words on end."

Elizabeth laughed. "I shall keep that in mind."

Jane's smile tilted just slightly at the edge. "You might as well ask her not to breathe, Mama."

Mama sniffed. "Well, when she breathes like that, it is no wonder she has not yet had a serious offer. Always off wandering. Always reading books about people who never existed. Why not take a turn about Meryton for once and speak to someone with proper prospects?"

Elizabeth lifted her cup and met Jane's eyes over it. "Because the people in books, at least, do not snort or have greens in their teeth when they speak."

Jane pressed her lips together to suppress a laugh. Lydia giggled openly and Kitty gurgled her tea faintly as she tried to swallow. Only Mary looked up with something like censure.

The conversation turned to the rumours of a new neighbour taking Netherfield, and Elizabeth let herself drift quiet again. The tea was strong, if slightly over-steeped, and the breeze had begun to rise. Through the open window, the curtains lifted just so, and a flicker of motion caught her eye—a leaf, still green, spinning in the air, circling once before vanishing.

The odd thing was that she could not see where it fell. She blinked, sipped, and turned back to the table.

THE DRAWING ROOM WAS unusually cold.

It was not a matter of the fire—it burned low but hot on the hearth, and the coals had been properly turned. Nor was it the windows; the draughts had long since been sealed, and Darcy himself had seen to the replacement of the mullioned panes the previous winter. And yet, when he passed beneath the central arch toward the west wall, a cool blast struck the back of his neck. A draft where there should be none.

He paused, brow furrowed, but said nothing.

Georgiana looked up from the pianoforte. "Is it too loud?"

He shook his head. "No. Only... now that you mention it, the tuning is odd."

She touched a key again, testing. "I had it looked at not a fortnight past."

Darcy moved toward the instrument. The note had sounded well enough just now. But when she had been playing earlier—he could not explain it. The resonance had seemed... wrong. Too thin. Or too high, but not enough to ruin the melody. The sort of imbalance that pricked at the edges of one's hearing but vanished upon inspection.

He gave a short shrug. "Never mind. Likely, I imagined it."

Georgiana smiled and returned to the final passage of her étude, her fingers moving with cautious elegance. The notes cascaded, even and pure. Still, Darcy found himself stepping back from the hearth. He turned instead to the escritoire and sorted through the correspondence his footman had brought earlier. A note from Bingley, predictably cheerful. A circular concerning some minor estate commission, dense with figures and already familiar. Nothing that required immediate thought.

One envelope remained.

The seal was plain, impressed with his uncle's crest. Darcy slit it open at once.

*My dear Darcy,*

*I wonder if you might indulge a moment's curiosity on my behalf. Do you still have the old transcription of some odd ballads—the one your grandfa-*

*ther kept among his papers and later passed to you? A green binding, if I recall. A strange fancy, of course, but something I read last week called it to mind, and I find I cannot recall when last I saw the volume myself.*

*There is no urgency in the matter. I merely wish to know whether it remains in your possession.*

*Yours,*
*M.*

Darcy read it again, slower this time.

*The Harrowe Ballads.*

The name rose at once, unbidden and unwelcome. Why would his uncle be asking after that? It had been years since Darcy last thought of it. But he did not need to search his memory, nor the library shelves. The order of the household had always been too deliberate for that—certain books were placed where they would not be mistaken for accident. Where they could not even be misplaced or lost on high library shelves.

Darcy crossed the room and reached for the closed cabinet beside the drawing room window. The volume came away easily, and Darcy opened the book where his thumb fell, more from habit than intent. The pages were thin, the margins crowded with the neat, angular hands of at least two or three Darcys before him. He skimmed without interest—place names, half-Christianised invocations, the sort of antique verse that mistook obscurity for depth.

Then his eye caught on a line set apart by a faint mark in the margin.

*He stood where water meets with land,*
*And sware no troth unbound;*
*Yet held his hand where first it lay,*
*And so the bound unwound.*

He read it again, slower, against his will.

The book shut with a decisive snap.

Darcy stood there for a moment, hand still resting on the cover. Whatever irritation stirred was sharp-edged and immediate, leaving no room for reflection.

He returned to the escritoire and took up his pen. The reply to his uncle was brief.

*My dear Uncle,*

*I do have the book you mention. If it is required, I shall bring it with me when next I am in London. Or I may send it with Richard, if he should arrive soon, as he claims he will.*

*Yours,*
*F. D.*

He sanded the page, folded it, sealed it, and set it with the others to be sent.

Only then did his gaze return, unbidden, to the desk.

The *Harrowe Ballads* lay where he had left them, the cover dark and unassuming, as though it were nothing more than any other relic of family excess. Darcy picked it up again—not to open it—but to move it. He slid it onto the back shelf, behind a folio of surveys and a stack of legal abstracts, where it would not catch the eye.

There.

He did not look at it again.

# Chapter Two

*One week later*

THE MORNING MIST HAD not yet burned away when Darcy sighted down the barrel of his fowling piece. One breath—then the muffled crack of shot as a pheasant burst from the underbrush, scattering in a wild flurry of feathers.

"Well shot," Richard Fitzwilliam called from behind. "I swear the poor creature gave you a bow before it fell."

Darcy lowered the barrel and turned. "Your jealousy does you no credit."

"Jealousy? Hardly. I am simply concerned for the local pheasant population. At this rate, Derbyshire will have to import from Hertfordshire just to fill its tables."

Richard's grin spread as he strode forward, kicking through frost-hardened grass, his gun resting carelessly across his shoulder. His jacket, though tailored, bore faint scuffs at the cuffs, a reminder that the man had spent more hours in bivouacs than ballrooms these past years.

"You might consider aiming before firing," Darcy said, breaking the barrel to reload. "I thought you were taught marksmanship in the line of duty."

Richard swung his gun down, not bothering to check the powder. "I aimed at the sky. The sky remains. My duty is done."

Darcy shook his head and walked on. Brutus padded at his heel, nose twitching as they neared a cluster of cottages nestled in a shallow valley. Smoke curled from chimneys in tight columns.

"Your valley looks well enough," Richard said. "It's good to see something thriving. God knows the villages I passed through in Spain would make this look like Versailles."

"You were near Salamanca last, were you not? You never named the place in your letters, so I was left to guess."

"Was never *permitted* to name it, but I knew you would put it together. Salamanca, yes. Then we pushed further south. I do not recommend it as a holiday destination. Mud up to your knees, lice in your hair, and French cannon fire to rattle the nerves." He grinned. "Still, the wine is tolerable. When we could get it."

They crested a rise, and Darcy raised a hand to a man mending a low stone wall. "Good morning, Mr Telford."

The tenant straightened, wiping lime-stained hands on his apron. His face, weathered but alert, broke into a cautious smile. "Good day to you, sir. Fine morning for it."

"Indeed. How is Mrs Telford recovering?"

"Well enough, sir. The little one's come through the fever, too. She still tires quickly, but Mr Barnes says there's no lingering harm."

"If there is any further need of the apothecary, send word. I will see him sent for."

Telford's eyes shone with quiet gratitude. "We're obliged, Mr Darcy. Truly."

"Not at all. How is your root cellar? I recall some trouble last year."

Telford touched his cap. "Dry as a bone, sir. Danny helped me with the mending. All it wants is some stores. My potato crop were fair-middling this year, sir."

Darcy grunted, his gaze flicking over to the little door built into the earth. "You were not alone, Telford. I will have Granger inquire whether there may be barley or oats yet to be had from the next market town. And salt pork, if it can be secured at a reasonable rate."

"Aye, sir. There were talk at Lambton fair that the southern fields did not yield as hoped. Too much wet in June, then that sharp heat in July. Blighted some of the late potatoes outright."

Darcy's expression altered by a degree. "And your wheat?"

"Short in the ear, sir. Not empty—but lighter than we'd wish. Mr Granger says we must not count on the winter as kindly as the last."

A wind moved low across the yard, lifting the dust along the path. Darcy glanced toward the hedgerow beyond the cottage. The leaves had turned early at their edges, a faint rusting where there ought still to be strength.

"Has the miller remarked upon it?" he asked.

"He has, sir. Grain's coming in thinner. He says he's had to set the stones closer to make good flour of it."

Darcy inclined his head once. "Then we will not wait upon Providence alone. I shall see what may be purchased before prices rise further. Keep careful account of what remains in your cellar. If your stores run low, you will inform Pemberley at once."

Telford swallowed. "Aye, sir."

Darcy gave a final look toward the low, earthen door set into the bank. Sound construction. Proper drainage. But construction would not conjure abundance where the fields had withheld it. He tipped his head in brief farewell to the tenant and turned down the slope. A moment later, Richard's boots caught up beside his, the rhythm of his stride quickening to match.

"You know," he said, brushing his glove against a low-hanging branch, "you are wasted on London society. Striding about dispensing medical care and cellar stores and justice, too, no doubt—one might mistake you for a minor deity."

Darcy brushed a fleck of mud from his cuff. "It is mere responsibility."

"Call it what you like. That man will speak of you in the village with the reverence of a saint."

"I prefer to be spoken of not at all."

"Modest as ever. Meanwhile, my men in the regiment would have given a year's wages for half your management skills. You would have had supplies landed at Cadiz and rations distributed before breakfast."

"Perhaps. But I doubt I would have been as popular with your officers."

Richard gave a bark of laughter. "True enough. I won them over with my magnanimous smile and my willingness to lose at cards." He slowed his pace. "It was all a sham, you know. There were days I thought we would never see England again."

Darcy glanced toward him, but his expression did not shift. One hand closed loosely around his walking stick, the knuckles whitening just slightly.

Richard looked away. He kicked a stone from the path, watched it tumble into the brush. "Still. One survives. One finds amusement where one can." He cleared his throat and nudged Darcy with his elbow. "Speaking of amusement—have you endured Aunt Catherine lately?"

"I have not," Darcy said. "I take it I should be grateful."

"That depends on your tolerance for repetition. But I passed through Kent after we came ashore at Dover, thought I would call on our dear aunt. A handsome bed and full table, only a handful of miles from port? I daresay not one in a hundred lads had such a proud welcome back to England. But it did not come free of cost, I am sorry to say."

"Let me guess. She enlisted you to work upon me for some scheme that involves marriage and duty and family dignity. Did I get it all?"

Richard laughed. "She has not altered her opinion in the slightest. Only her volume."

"How original."

"She spoke of duty, naturally. Of legacy. Of matters long deferred and now—apparently—pressing." He shook his head. "It was the same old argument, only delivered as though time itself had grown impatient."

Darcy's mouth curved. "I suppose it did not occur to her to consult the intended."

Richard shrugged. "She prefers proclamations to conversations. Easier to win those."

They walked on. A pheasant rustled in the underbrush but did not take flight.

"Still," Richard went on, as though idly turning over the matter, "you cannot fault her consistency. She has believed you and Anne inevitable since we were all in shortcoats. Do you recall the old justification? Something about bloodlines aligning at last."

Darcy made a dismissive sound. "I recall being bored."

Richard laughed. "Ah. Then you will be pleased to know she has not confined herself to memory. She has been rummaging. Asked after the Harrowe folio, of all things. I told her you still had it."

Darcy stopped short.

The pause was brief—no more than the time it took him to adjust his grip on the gun—but it was enough.

"That book is nonsense. Antiquarian indulgence. Your father asked about it, too, and I offered it only as a courtesy. He never answered, and I had quite forgot about it."

"Of course," Richard said easily. "I thought as much. Still, Aunt Catherine has never been one to distinguish between myth and mandate. She speaks of it as though it were evidence of something."

Darcy resumed walking at once. "Then she is welcome to her fancies. I have no intention of conducting my life by half-remembered verse."

"Just so," Richard chuckled. "Now—are we likely to find any decent game, or have your tenants scared it all off with their cheerful greetings and visible affection?"

Darcy gave a low huff that might have passed for agreement. He glanced toward the tree line ahead, where the path narrowed, and the sun flickered low between the branches.

"We shall try the south ridge," he said. "There is a clearing near the stone fence—last year it was full of partridge."

"Excellent," Richard replied. "I have every intention of shooting something today, if only to justify the state of my boots."

They walked on, boots breaking through dry grass and the occasional brittle patch of heather. The dogs ranged ahead, vanishing and reappearing like thoughts that would not settle.

Richard's gaze swept the landscape with the ease of long habit. "It is a good stretch of country. You have done well with it."

"I have tried to do right by it."

"You have. Most of the old families are hanging on by their teeth or courting heiresses in town." He nudged a stone with his toe. "You do not court anything, and yet the place still breathes."

Darcy did not answer at once. His gaze tracked a kestrel overhead, then dropped again to the fields beyond.

"Pemberley is not meant to be impressive," he said finally. "Only enduring."

"Well," Richard said, adjusting his coat, "it certainly endures your company with greater grace than I do."

That earned him a faint smirk, and they fell into a comfortable silence that had nothing to prove.

When they reached the ridge, Richard paused to scan the horizon, shading his eyes more from habit than hope. "Do you suppose there is news from the front today?"

Darcy followed his gaze. The fields lay open and untroubled, the sky pale and unremarkable. "If there is, it will reach us a week too late."

"A week too late is better than not at all." Richard shifted the gun on his shoulder and exhaled. "In any case, I do not expect much to concern me just now. I have been warned—unofficially, of course—that I am to be kept in London after Christmas. Reports. Committees. Endless questions from men who have never heard a cannon fired in anger."

Darcy turned his head slightly. "And how do you receive the news?"

Richard considered it. "With gratitude," he said at last. "And a certain amount of dread. I have grown used to mud and marching. Ink may prove the greater trial. Still, it will be agreeable to sleep in the same bed two nights running. And to know, more or less, where I am meant to be."

"That seems a reasonable ambition," Darcy said.

"So I thought. One does one's part, and then one is set aside for a time. The machine turns. Others take the strain." Richard glanced at him. "It is how things are meant to work, is it not?"

Darcy did not answer at once. He shaded his eyes again, though the light had not changed. "In general," he said finally, "yes."

Richard nodded, satisfied, and swung the gun back into a more comfortable position. "Come on, then. Let us go startle something innocent."

ELIZABETH STEPPED LIGHTLY ALONG the lane, her boots striking the dew-softened earth with a muffled clop. Jane walked beside her, her bonnet ribbons dancing in the mild breeze, one hand tucked in her sister's arm.

The countryside held that peculiar stillness which often preceded autumn storms—not ominous, but alert. Overhead, a handful of swallows circled in a frantic spiral. Too soon for their migration, Elizabeth thought absently. And no direction at all, as if they had forgot the way.

"Mrs Long says they have had no tea from London in three weeks," Jane remarked. "She fears the ships are delayed again."

"Or swallowed whole by the Channel," Elizabeth replied. "Perhaps it is not French cannon but sea serpents that have put the merchantmen off their course."

"Even so, Mama will grieve for her breakfast pot."

"She might discover the merits of barley water instead. Surely an adventure for her palate."

They reached the edge of Meryton and stepped aside for a cart rattling past, the driver muttering to his companion about the "scarcity of good timber" and "foreign distractions." Elizabeth caught none of the particulars but felt the weight in his tone—the same weariness she had heard in Mr Bellweather's voice last week when he spoke of rising prices for muslin.

At the market square, neighbours called greetings—Mrs Gould remarking on the fine weather, Mr Pratt tipping his hat with a cheerful observation about harvest yields. Elizabeth returned their courtesies easily enough, yet some part of her remained half turned inward, tracing the flight of those restless swallows now darting above the apothecary's roof.

"...so, I thought we might send her one of Mary's essays," Jane was saying, her tone tickling with amusement. "Though I am not certain our aunt will understand it any more than the last. Lizzy, are you even listening?"

Elizabeth blinked. Jane's gentle look reminded her that she was not alone in her reverie.

"I was," she said, though she had lost the thread.

Jane squeezed her arm. "You have been elsewhere all morning."

"Only halfway elsewhere," Elizabeth admitted. "The other half is firmly tethered to my boots. Though whether they tread on earth or air, I cannot always say."

Jane shook her head and glanced at the bookseller's shop. "Well, come on. We might as well do a little daydreaming together."

They ducked into the bookshop, its dim interior cool and faintly scented of ink and dust. The shelves leaned at comfortable angles, and the floor creaked in protest of their tread. A cat slumbered on the windowsill, indifferent to commerce or conversation.

Elizabeth let her fingers drift over the cracked spines, drawn toward the history section out of long habit. A slim volume on Anglo-Saxon etymology tempted her, followed by a curious pamphlet on the migration of swans in the Scottish isles. She flipped a few pages, lingered on a marginal note written in a cramped feminine hand, then returned it to the shelf.

Nothing she needed, but much she wanted.

"Are you looking for something in particular?" Jane asked from the next row, where the bindings were more brightly coloured.

"Only a glimpse of distraction," Elizabeth murmured. "Or perhaps a forgotten treasure."

Her gaze caught on a battered book with a green leather binding and no title printed on the edge. The spine was sun-bleached, the gold lettering on the cover mostly worn away. She tilted it free, feeling the dry whisper of its weight shift in her hands.

"Not another ballad book," Jane teased. "Last time, Papa put Mary up to setting one of them to music, and we heard nothing else for a week."

"I shall only peek."

The pages crackled faintly as she turned them. A ballad about St. Melangell—protector of hares. A sailor's lament for a lost bride. A curious charm for mending broken ploughs ("Best read aloud," someone had scribbled in pencil). She smiled. None of it useful, all of it delightful.

*Confess thy sins by river's side,*
*And turn thee not again;*
*For what the running waters take*
*The wise recall not then.*

Another page, another curious entry:

*When orchard wights abroad do roam,*
*Then bar both gate and door;*
*Set milk without upon the step,*
*And call the fruit no more.*

Elizabeth gave a soft laugh under her breath. "Nonsense," she whispered fondly.

Then, nestled in a corner of a brittle page, almost as an afterthought, her eyes caught a final fragment—scrawled in a different hand, darker ink, the lines cramped and slightly slanted:

*Love vaunteth not, nor envieth,*
*Nor seeketh for her own;*
*It suffereth long,*
*it thinketh no ill,*
*Nor counteth what is done.*

*It beareth cold,*
*it hopeth still*
*When earthly light is low;*
*For what two hearts in troth do keep*
*No storm shall overthrow.*

*But what one heart would guard alone*
*And make its charge apart,*
*Shall wither though it yet endure—*
*For love requireth heart.*

Her fingers paused on the edge of the page.

The rhythm tripped her for a moment—not in meaning, but in cadence. She found herself rereading the lines without knowing why, her attention snagging as if she had missed something just out of reach.

It was not recognition. Only a brief hesitation, the way a phrase sometimes lingered after sense had passed.

Jane peered over her shoulder. "That sounds like a hymn."

"Or a children's rhyme," Elizabeth said. "Perhaps it was once."

She read it again, slower this time, as if something might rearrange itself into clarity. But it did not. It only lingered—the words slipping past her understanding but clinging to her thoughts.

Papa would have laughed at this one. Or pretended to—and then read it twice when no one was watching. She closed the book and set it back on the shelf, brushing a faint layer of dust from her fingertips.

On their way out, Mrs Brampton, the shopkeeper's wife, reached out to adjust a stack of ledgers, then paused to smile at them.

"Storm's coming, Miss Bennet," she said lightly, glancing toward the cloudless window. "You wouldn't know it to look, but I've seen the signs. The starlings were flying low this morning, and Mr Brampton's knees have been aching something dreadful."

Elizabeth returned her smile. "Then we shall defer to the true authorities."

Mrs Brampton chuckled. "Oh, I don't mind the rain. It's the hush before it that sets one's teeth on edge. Like the land is holding its breath."

Elizabeth smiled politely. "Then it is fortunate we do not all listen too closely," she said, and turned toward the door before the notion could take hold.

"Well," the woman said, with a fond shake of her head, "you always were one for pretty notions."

Back in the sunlight, Elizabeth glanced once over her shoulder. The swallows had vanished, and she paused, listening. Perhaps the weather truly was changing; birds noticed such things long before people did.

"Odd. It *feels* like stormy weather, but it does not *look* like it," she murmured.

"What was that?" Jane asked.

"Nothing." Elizabeth shook off the thought and tucked her arm through her sister's again. "Only that I have the strongest craving for tea—and perhaps a proper cloudburst to make the afternoon interesting."

THE TABLE WAS SET with its usual care—silver gleaming, linen crisp, the low candlelight catching at the rim of Georgiana's glass as she reached for the salt. Across from her, Darcy carved a slice of roast and passed it without comment. They dined as they often did—companionable, unhurried, the conversation light and occasional.

"I saw the pigeons today," Georgiana said, selecting a spear of asparagus with careful grace. "Three of the white ones came back."

Darcy looked up. "Only three?"

She nodded. "Tomkins thinks a hawk took the fourth."

"A reasonable guess."

"Perhaps." She tilted her head. "But I do not know. They circled twice before landing—as if they were not quite certain this was the right place."

He raised a brow, amused. "You think they have forgot where they live?"

"I think..." She smiled faintly. "They seemed a little agitated. Broken feathers, and they fought over their boxes. But that may only be my fancy."

He glanced toward the window, where the last threads of twilight clung to the horizon. "Changing of the seasons. Everything is restless this time of year. Were you in the gardens long today?"

She nodded. "And I played after. A new piece. Something Miss Bingley sent me in the last parcel."

Darcy dabbed at the corner of his mouth. "The Allegretto?"

"No. The other one."

"The adagio?"

"The one in G minor."

He gave a wry smile. "That explains the long faces among the roses."

Georgiana laughed, quiet and genuine. "It's meant to be cheerful, I think. But it feels like snow."

Darcy only nodded. When supper ended, Georgiana moved to the pianoforte, lifting the lid as if she were peering in on an old friend. The notes fell clear and light, but somewhere in the middle registers they caught, briefly—a breath of hesitation in an otherwise faultless performance.

Darcy poured a modest glass of brandy and opened a letter from Bingley that had arrived that afternoon, letting the paper rest flat on the table beside his plate. Georgiana was still at the pianoforte, her fingers drifting through a light Italian air—something crisp and cheerful, more habit than performance.

*I have now nearly settled at Netherfield. It is just as I left it before the contract was completed—though the west field was wetter than expected, and the kitchen garden overrun with herbs I do not remember seeing before. Mrs Nicholls has taken it upon herself to introduce 'seasonal flair' into everything, so I've had three courses with mint this week, and I fear it's turning me virtuous.*

*I trust you are well. Come visit if your affairs allow. I could use your opinion on the stables, and the company would not go amiss.*

Darcy smiled faintly and refolded the letter. Bingley's notions of "seasonal flair" had always bordered on botanical anarchy. He set the paper aside.

Georgiana, having finished the piece, trailed a hand along the keys and stood. "Do you ever feel," she asked idly as she crossed to the sideboard, "that September has too many endings in it?"

He glanced over, brow raised.

She shrugged, pouring herself a small glass of watered wine. "It is nothing. Just a thought. The light changes. The trees shed. Everything pulls back."

"Nature's economy," Darcy said. "It spends freely in spring, then counts its pennies in autumn."

"Spoken like a true landowner."

He inclined his head. "I am told the habit suits me."

Georgiana reached for the teapot and poured herself a second cup, more out of habit than desire. The fire crackled softly.

"Mrs Reynolds says the bees have grown sluggish," she murmured, watching the steam rise. "She blames the cooling weather. But I think they're just tired of being bees."

Darcy gave a short breath of amusement and reached for the letter still folded beside him.

"Bingley writes," he said, as though it had only just occurred to him. "He asks if I will visit."

She looked up from her cup. "Will you?"

"I expect I ought to. He grows restless without company."

"You say that as if it is a failing."

"It is a tendency." Darcy's mouth twitched, and he tapped the edge of the letter against his fingers. "I have not yet decided."

"Then go," she said, without hesitation. "Before the roads freeze and the excuses multiply." She glanced at the dog lying at Darcy's feet. "And take Brutus. He's grown bored of my company and has taken to sulking under the piano."

"I assumed that was commentary on your playing."

She gave him a look. "You wound me."

He did not smile, not exactly, but the corner of his mouth shifted in that rare, reluctant way it sometimes did.

"Good night, William."

"Good night."

She slipped from the room with a rustle of silk, and the house settled into stillness.

Darcy turned back to the letter, not to reread it, but to place a hand over it for a moment—grounding something that did not quite need grounding. Then he finished his brandy and rose to bank the fire.

# Chapter Three

Elizabeth turned the corner of the lane just ahead of Charlotte, the hem of her walking dress brushing through damp grass and wild thyme. The sun had not yet burned off the silver in the hedgerows, and the morning air clung to her skin in a way that felt oddly personal, as though it remembered something she had forgotten.

"I do think Mama is near to despair," she said. "Lydia accused Kitty of stealing her bonnet, and then Kitty threatened to dip Lydia's hair ribbons in beet juice. Jane tried to mediate and was accused of 'always taking sides.' You may imagine the outcome."

"I can," Charlotte said drily. "I have dined with you all more than once."

Elizabeth smiled but did not laugh. A pair of crows passed overhead, their wings silent as they turned toward the east wood. She paused and craned her neck to watch them.

"I suppose," Charlotte continued, "you will never escape your mother's campaign. But if she begins speaking of eligible clerks and shopkeepers again, I may intervene on your behalf out of sheer mercy."

Elizabeth made a noncommittal sound. Her attention had shifted to a cluster of hawthorn trees that pressed close to the path just ahead. The branches had grown in strange angles there—twisting inward over a fresh sprig of new rose buds. Imagine it! Rose buds in September!

She stepped forward, parting a thin veil of leaves, and a branch snapped back just enough to catch her wrist. A thorn—not large, but sharp—scratched the skin below her glove. She gasped, but did not cry out. It was not pain so much as surprise.

She looked down. The scratch was thin, like a seam drawn in red thread. But the blood did not rise. The skin beneath remained dry, even as the mark darkened faintly, like ink settling on paper.

Her fingers hovered over it, then dropped. Charlotte was already walking ahead, talking again, the words trailing back toward her without shape.

Elizabeth glanced once at the branch. The leaves looked duller here, the green slightly too grey, as if caught between seasons. And the rosebuds were fresh as any May blossoms.

She shook herself and stepped back onto the path. "I think," she said, raising her voice slightly, "we ought to go by the mill road. I have no wish to be caught in Mrs Long's inquiries."

Charlotte said something agreeable—Elizabeth did not quite catch the words.

As they walked on, she touched the inside of her wrist once more. The mark was still there. Not bleeding. Just... there. Pulsing with offended dignity.

She kept her hand at her side and did not look back.

THE LONG TABLE IN the south study bore no trace of its former use as a card table in their grandfather's day. Now it was neatly lined with ledgers, seasonal accounts, and a fresh pot of ink.

Darcy stood at the window, arms folded behind his back, gazing out at the rising mist over the south fields. A pair of jackdaws hopped across the lower lawn, their black eyes bright in the slanted light.

Behind him, the door opened. "Am I early for the shoot," said Richard Fitzwilliam, "or late for the War Council?"

Darcy glanced over his shoulder. "You are early."

"And this is the council?" Richard stepped in and eyed the table. "Ledgers, supply rosters, and Granger with his battle maps. Very medieval, I should say. Shall I fetch a bugler?"

The steward, Mr Granger, gave a polite nod from where he stood, setting out a folio. "Shall I withdraw, Mr Darcy? I should not like to interrupt."

"No, no, Granger. Richard, you are welcome to stay and take notes," Darcy offered without turning.

"God forbid," Richard muttered. "I'll be in the morning room. Alert me if the estate revolts or you run out of ink." He vanished through the opposite door, almost at the same moment the main door opened again to admit the others.

Darcy stepped to the table as Granger and Mr Tait, the head groundsman, took their places. Mr Orme, the tenant liaison, was already seated, his cap in his hands.

Granger began. "First: the hedgerows near the east pasture. They've rooted well enough, but the gap near Cressfield's boundary will need reinforcing. Tait recommends staking it now, before the frost sets."

Darcy nodded. "Use the ash from the orchard clearing. It is seasoned."

"Yes, sir." Tait made a mark in his notebook. "Also—the north spring has dropped again. Not more than a foot, but enough the cattle noticed. The overseer's watching it."

"It's likely runoff," Orme offered. "The rains in August were heavier than usual. Cut the banks more than we expected, especially near the mill stream."

"We will keep an eye on it," Darcy said.

Granger adjusted his spectacles. "On the matter of the harvest—yields are coming in lower than anticipated. Not disastrously so, but enough that I thought it best to mention."

Darcy looked up. "Yes, I have been hearing something of that. Is it the same across the estate?"

"Unevenly," Granger said. "The barley in the west fields recovered after the late planting, but the oats nearer the ridge did not fill as they ought to have, even after the weather turned fair."

Tait shifted in his chair. "It was a wet spring," he said. "Cold, too. Everything started late."

"Late, yes," Darcy agreed. "But once it started, it should have made up ground."

Granger inclined his head. "That was our expectation, sir."

"And the tenants?"

"Concerned, but not alarmed," Orme replied. "They remember lean years. This does not yet feel like one of them."

Darcy nodded once. "Very well. We proceed as planned. Adjust where we must, but no retrenchment yet."

Granger turned a page. "The only oddity—and I hesitate to call it that—is the chalk by Thorn Holt."

Darcy's gaze sharpened, though his tone did not. "Explain."

"It's likely some local child, or a courting couple feeling poetic." Granger produced a small folded sketch. "Marks in a circular pattern around the base of the old hawthorn. No damage to the tree, but the grass is dry within the circle. Not trampled. Just... faded."

Tait scratched his beard. "Like something leeched the colour out."

"Could it be lime from a mason's barrel?" Orme asked. "Or old ash?"

"No residue," Granger said. "And nothing nearby to explain it. Besides that, the tree itself appears to be dying."

Darcy took the sketch. The markings were faint—rough, but deliberate. No symbols he recognised. The tree was noted on Pemberley's older maps as part of a glade long left to its own devices.

"Leave it be for now," he said. "We are entering a season of dormancy. If any disease appears to spread, I will ride out myself."

Granger inclined his head. "Very good, sir."

They moved on. Tait reported favourable numbers from the gamekeeper, who had noted strong nesting near the southern copse—more, in fact, than usual for the season. The mill repairs were finished. The tenant at Bell Hill had recovered from his fever. There was some minor complaint from a new ploughman who did not like the thatching of his stable loft, but Granger dismissed it as nonsense.

When the ledgers had been reviewed and the last of the notations made, Darcy dismissed the men with a quiet word of thanks. Tait and Orme rose and tipped their heads. Granger lingered a moment longer.

"I did find something else, sir," he said. "From the old drawer in the steward's desk. I meant to show you sooner."

He held out a parchment—thick, discoloured with age. "It was tucked behind the old land-use maps."

Darcy unfolded it. The script was cramped, but familiar—his grandfather's hand.

At first glance, it appeared to be a soil analysis: regions of clay, limestone, loam. But the annotations... curious. Not scientific. Phrases like *spotty light* and *growth without seed*.

"Is this part of the weather notes?" Darcy asked.

"I do not believe so," Granger replied. "There's no date. No title. I'm not even certain he meant it for record. I do not believe this is Pemberley's land at all, but somewhere else. The river lines are not familiar to me, and there is no marking of the county, even."

Darcy refolded it. "Leave it with me."

Granger bowed and left the room.

After a moment, the opposite door opened again, and Richard reappeared, tossing a cushion from hand to hand.

"You look as though you've just read a summons from the Tower."

"Just harvest figures," Darcy said, setting the paper aside.

"I'm telling you, cousin, you give these estate meetings the same expression you wore at your father's funeral."

Darcy reached for his coat. "The two are not dissimilar. One leaves you with more responsibilities than you wished, and the other with guests who outstay their usefulness."

"Which am I?"

"That remains to be seen."

They exchanged faint smirks, and Richard gestured toward the terrace. "Shall we find something to shoot?"

Darcy nodded—but before he moved, his eyes fell again on the sketch Granger had left. The ring beneath the hawthorn. The ash circle in the woods. The thin yield from fields that ought to have recovered.

Coincidence, he told himself. Coincidence—and a season that had asked more patience than usual.

THE DOGS WERE RANGING wide again—Brutus tracking the brush line with disciplined focus, while Leo thrashed through a patch of dead bracken with more enthusiasm than sense.

Darcy adjusted the strap on his powder flask and scanned the low ridge ahead. "They will not flush here. It's too open."

Richard lifted a hand to shade his eyes. "Then your pheasants are idiots. I nearly stepped on one."

"Perhaps you should have aimed lower."

They moved on, the dogs catching a fresh scent and tearing ahead. Below, a cluster of partridge scattered with a start, too far out of range.

Richard made no effort to follow. "We'll go hungry yet."

"I doubt it. Mrs. Reynolds rarely trusts us to provide."

"Wise woman."

They crested the hill together, boots grinding over frost-cracked stone. The breeze had shifted since dawn, carrying with it a scent of mouldering wood and the distant smoke of a brush fire. Nothing alarming—yet it made Darcy glance westward, toward the slope where Granger said the old ash circle stood.

He had not ridden that way in some time.

"You are brooding," Richard observed, swinging his gun to rest over his shoulder. "Is it about Aunt Catherine's marriage campaign, or are you simply composing your next estate report?"

"Neither." Darcy slowed to a halt. "I am considering a ride south."

Richard raised a brow. "London?"

"No. Netherfield."

"Ah." Richard let the word hang, thoughtful rather than amused. "So, Hertfordshire has claimed you at last."

Darcy did not look at him. He crouched beside Brutus, checking the dog's paws for burrs. "Bingley writes that the house suits him. The land, he swears, is the best in all England. And he wishes for company." He rose again. "He always does."

"Hertfordshire is not short of company," Richard said mildly. "Nor of old boundaries."

Darcy straightened. "If you are about to quote my aunt, spare me."

Richard smiled, but did not retreat. "I only mean that she has been saying for years that when certain things begin to go wrong, they do so first on ground that has been argued over before. Borders. Old holdings. Places people stopped naming but never stopped minding."

Darcy shook his head. "Coincidence dressed up as foresight. I am not riding south in pursuit of a parable."

"Of course not," Richard said easily. "You are going because Bingley asked, and because it costs you nothing to oblige him."

"That is reason enough."

"Well," Richard said, stretching, "I only thought the location curious, whether you care for that fact or not."

"Our aunt mutters about everything," Darcy said shortly.

"True," Richard conceded. "But she mutters louder when she thinks timing is involved."

Darcy gave a low, humourless laugh. "Timing, place, lineage—she selects whichever suits the argument of the moment. Last year, it was Kent entire. Before that, the Thames corridor and every acre south of there. If I recall correctly, she once suggested this puzzle she obsesses over lay somewhere between Rosings and nowhere at all."

"Kent is not nowhere," Richard said mildly. "And she does at least have *one* justification, however strained."

Darcy glanced at him. "And?"

"Well, if you ask our aunt, the difficulty lies in other people not reading carefully enough. Or else in refusing to accept what seems obvious to her."

Darcy did not look up. "Which is?"

"Why, Kent, of course. She has said it often enough, and with such confidence that one might suppose the matter settled." He paused, then added, more mildly, "She claims there are old writings to support it. Copies, she calls them. My father, however, has never seemed inclined to discuss them."

"And what does he say?"

"Very little," Richard admitted. "Which, in this family, usually means he says nothing at all." He shrugged. "I have never seen the texts myself. Nor, I think, has anyone who speaks of them so freely."

Darcy only grunted.

Richard glanced at him, then away again. "In any case, it has long been treated as a question best left alone—except by our aunt, who has never found restraint much to her taste."

Darcy's mouth thinned. "So, a blot of ink decides an inheritance."

Richard smiled. "Or a smudge. Or a monk with a fondness for geography he half remembers. One ancient 'boundary' is the same as another's 'gateway.' You know how these things go—one scribe copies what he thinks he sees, the next copies him, and by the third generation everyone is prepared to swear to it."

"And to build obligation upon it," Darcy said. "Remarkable."

"And what did your father think?" Richard asked. "Surely George Darcy had an opinion on the matter. Aunt Catherine would have made sure of that."

Darcy hesitated—only long enough to be truthful without inviting speculation. "My father regarded it as invention compounded upon invention. A handful of half-remembered Roman names, some unfortunate Saxon lore, a monk with too much patience and not enough discipline, and a family unfortunate enough to preserve what ought to have been forgot."

"That is one way of settling the question," Richard said.

"It was the way he preferred," Darcy replied. "He allowed that such things made passable stories, and that they might amuse antiquarians with time to spare, but he would not hear of obligation being built upon them. Particularly not obligation that required sacrifice beyond sense."

Richard glanced at him. "Sacrifice? Wait, I never heard that bit."

Darcy gave a brief, dismissive motion of his hand. "It does not matter."

"Oh, it sounds like it very much does. Speak, cousin. What has your father told you?"

"That part came from Lady Catherine, so treat it with the gravity it deserves—which is to say, not much. She was always quoting odd things to him that seemed to change with the color of her gown. My father believed," he continued, "it indulgent to contradict her, and safer to teach his son the truth—that none of it deserved serious consideration."

Richard was quiet for a moment. Then, with a faint edge of humour, he said, "And yet everyone seems remarkably eager to tell you where you ought to go."

Darcy did not answer at once. He had the sudden, unwelcome sense that his father's certainty had been less dismissal than protection—and that what had been dismissed had not vanished, only waited.

"That does not oblige me to do so."

"He is already handsomer than anyone expected," Lydia declared, kicking her heels in the air as she plopped into a seat.

Elizabeth threaded her needle and did not look up at her sister. "Are we talking about little John Lucas, age twelve? Yes, he is rather a handsome young chap."

"How can you be so vexing? I mean the new neighbour, Mr Bingley! And he brought *horses*, Lizzy."

"I rather expect he did. How else was he to arrive, by sledge dog?"

"No, I mean the most beautiful matched four in hand anyone ever saw. Jane said they were black. That always means something in a novel."

"I doubt a horse's coat colour is a reliable indicator of his quality," Elizabeth replied, taking her seat by the window with a small embroidery hoop she had no intention of using.

Kitty chimed in from the settee. "Papa went to call this morning, you know. Mama insisted he wear his best coat, and he actually did."

"I helped pick the cravat," Lydia added proudly.

"I'm sure that made all the difference."

Across the room, Mary looked up from a battered copy of Fordyce's Sermons, her tone mild but pointed. "We might concern ourselves less with a man's tailoring and more with his character."

"Yes," said Elizabeth, "but that would spoil all the fun."

Before Mary could reply, Jane entered with her arms full of linens and a warm flush in her cheeks. "Mama says we must air all the tablecloths and polish the silver, just in case there is a dinner party. Mr Bingley has two sisters, and Mrs Long says he will also have a friend staying with him."

"Did she say what kind of friend?" Kitty asked with glee. "Gentleman friend? Handsome friend?"

Elizabeth smiled behind her stitching. "Perhaps a reclusive philosopher or an amateur botanist. Mama will be devastated."

"Mrs Long says—" Lydia lowered her voice and leaned forward dramatically, "—that he is very rich, and very tall, and very melancholy."

Jane raised a brow. "You heard no such thing."

"I could have!" Lydia grinned, unabashed. "And if he is melancholy, we shall simply have to cheer him."

Elizabeth shook her head, but it was all fondness. "Did Papa say anything of Mr Bingley gentleman himself?"

Jane thought for a moment. "Only that he seemed amiable. A little anxious to please, perhaps, but eager to make the acquaintance of the neighbourhood."

"And what of the others?" Elizabeth asked.

"I do not know," Jane said. "Mr Bingley did not say much of his friend, and Papa had no occasion to meet his other guests."

Mama wandered into the drawing room then, looking lost and only half-minded about what she was doing. "Where is that lace? I told you it must be ready if Mr Bingley comes to dine." She began rooting through the drawer, then tumbled over her sewing basket.

Elizabeth reached for the bonnet box on the side table and lifted the lid. "Perhaps it sought refuge here," she said, extracting the length of lace with a small flourish.

Mama turned, hands on her hips. "Exactly where you left it. You see? If you would only keep to my system—"

Elizabeth passed it to her without comment, her eyes bright with amusement. "How remiss of me, to fail the system."

"Well, it's a mercy we have it now. If there's to be company, everything must be perfect."

"Of course," Elizabeth said. "Nothing impresses a man like properly catalogued millinery."

Lydia threw herself back onto the settee the moment their mother swept out of the room. "Well. That was exhausting. I'm certain she meant to shout at Kitty and just got the names mixed again."

"She never confuses my name," Kitty said. "Only yours."

"Because I am more memorable."

"Because you are louder."

"Because I am the heroine," Lydia declared, tossing a cushion in the air. "Which means the melancholy stranger is meant for *me*!"

"He is not melancholy," Kitty argued. "He is mysterious."

"Everyone is mysterious until they are revealed to be utterly ordinary," Elizabeth laughed.

"What if he's secretly a duke?"

Elizabeth resumed her seat by the window. "With amnesia, I suppose."

"And a vendetta," Lydia said eagerly. "He's come to Netherfield to unmask the man who wronged him, only he doesn't remember who it is."

"He just knows it was someone... tall," Kitty added, nodding with solemn drama.

"I do not think Mr Bingley's guest is tall or wronged. But he is coming to dinner while he remains in Hertfordshire, if Mama has anything to say about it."

"Soon?" Elizabeth asked. "We have yet to meet Mr Bingley, and now his whole party is looked upon as our rightful property."

"I suppose that depends upon when we are introduced. If Papa can be prevailed upon to call on him again, it will be soon. Otherwise, I suppose we will meet them ourselves at the Assembly."

Lydia gave a sigh and rolled over. "I shall die of suspense before then."

"You will not," Elizabeth said, amused. "You have a robust constitution."

Jane crossed to her side. "Will you go walking today?"

Elizabeth glanced toward the window. The sky had cleared, and a warm edge had crept into the light. She nodded slowly. "Yes. I think I will. After I help with the account sheets. Papa has refused to touch them since March."

"Why?" Kitty asked. "They're so boring."

"Exactly," Elizabeth said. "And yet he persists in believing someone else will enjoy them more."

She threaded the needle and made a single stitch before setting it down again.

Across the room, Lydia gave a delighted squeal and leapt up from the chaise. "Mama's putting on her gloves in the hall! She must be going to town! Come, Kitty, don't dawdle."

Elizabeth gave Jane a look that was all silent affection and bone-deep weariness.

"You should walk," Jane said again, gently. "I'll help Mary."

"I might." Elizabeth stood and stretched, then crossed to the window and looked out at the pale sun rising above the hedgerow. "It seems a very fine day to walk somewhere that is not here."

# Chapter Four

*Hertfordshire*
*Michaelmas*

The road narrowed as Darcy's carriage turned off the main coaching way and onto the lane that wound toward Netherfield. The hedgerows here ran tall—untidy, overgrown in a manner that suggested neither neglect nor diligence, only a kind of haphazard enthusiasm. He could see why Bingley found them charming. Charles had always preferred abundance to order.

The afternoon light slanted across the road in pale gold sheets, warm but thinning. Autumn was settling over Hertfordshire with a softness Derbyshire never attempted; the hills in the distance smoothed themselves into gentle humps, their edges blurred by a lingering haze.

Brutus trotted alongside the carriage for a short stretch, tongue lolling, fur catching the light. He was too intelligent to exhaust himself following for miles, but he enjoyed these last furlongs of a journey, inspecting new scents and periodically glancing up as if to confirm that Darcy was noting everything properly.

Inside the carriage, Darcy shifted slightly, one gloved hand resting on the window frame. Nearly there. The journey had been mercifully uneventful. A brief conversation at the market town where he exchanged news with an officer escort riding north—grim tidings of blockades in the Channel, of rising prices and merchant delays—but otherwise nothing to occupy the mind. And yet Darcy's thoughts had refused to cease their rolling. A restlessness had hounded him since they left the Pemberley stables, like a question forming behind a closed door.

He pushed it aside. The matter of disease in his hedges and orchards still gnawed, though he had spoken of it to no one. He would not bring ghosts of Derbyshire into Hertfordshire. Bingley deserved better than to host a man preoccupied with groundskeeper's business and half-formed impressions.

The carriage rounded a bend where the hedgerow dipped low, giving a clear view across a stretch of open field. Brutus suddenly paused—head lifted, ears sharp.

Darcy followed the line of the dog's attention.

A figure moved in the distance—too far for features, but unmistakably a young woman. She was crossing a narrow footbridge that spanned a shallow ditch, but rather than walk the length of it, she vaulted lightly over the last plank, landing with quick, easy balance before striding on.

Through the carriage window, Darcy watched as she wandered closer to the small copse that bordered the lane. She carried something under one arm, a parcel or satchel by the look of it, though the distance made it impossible to be certain.

Reaching a low-hanging branch of an old oak, she paused only long enough to toss the parcel up onto a higher limb—an action so practiced it could not have been her first attempt—before gathering her skirt and climbing after it with quick, nimble confidence. Not a scramble. Not quite decorous either. Simply efficient.

Brutus huffed an approving sound, tail giving one slow wag. He had frozen entirely still, and was falling some distance behind the coach.

Darcy's brow ticked upward, more in curiosity than any real surprise. "Leave her be," he said. Brutus whimpered—a discordant sound for a dog of his size, and then resumed his easy trot beside the carriage. The trees closed in again, and the figure disappeared as though the land had swallowed her whole.

The house appeared at last over the rise—Netherfield Park, cream-stone and wide-shouldered, sitting with all the assurance of a gentleman who has just taken off his coat and declared himself comfortable. Smoke curled from two chimneys; the stable roof glinted; and somewhere beyond the gardens, faint voices carried on the air.

Brutus barked once, the sound sharp and echoing too far. Darcy frowned. The echo returned a half-second late, as though the hedgerow had caught the sound and released it reluctantly.

The shape of the land, surely. A hollow. A damp pocket of air.

As he approached the front of the house, the door was thrown open in a manner that would have startled any footman trained within thirty miles of Darcy's aunt.

"Darcy!" Bingley bounded down the steps, coat unbuttoned, hair wind-ruffled, and entirely himself. "I thought you'd arrive tomorrow—I told Mrs Nicholls to expect you, but she insisted the ducks needed glazing—good God, you brought Brutus. Excellent. He'll terrify the poachers."

Darcy dismounted with a laugh. "Have a care, my friend! I have not even removed my hat. Good afternoon, Bingley."

"Afternoon? It feels like morning here. Hertfordshire has its own time entirely. Do you know, the kitchen garden insists on growing mint everywhere? The housekeeper calls it 'a blessing.' I call it an invasion."

Darcy allowed the corner of his mouth to tilt. "Your letter said as much. You are being outmanoeuvred by herbs."

"Repeatedly. And without mercy." Bingley clapped him on the back. "But Caroline is pleased that the flower garden is still something to look at. Come in. Everyone will want to greet you—but don't worry, one of them is Hurst, who is barely awake after his luncheon, so that doesn't count."

Darcy's gaze flicked over the façade of the house. The shadows cast by the columns were long—longer than they ought to be for the hour. A trick of the sun, no doubt. Southern counties had different light.

He followed Bingley through the entry. The hall was bright and pleasant, if slightly too warm. A cluster of flowers sat on a side table, their scent richer than most—overripe roses, edged with something sharper. Linden? No. Thorn blossom? Impossible. They were out of season.

Bingley was still talking. "—and the west field drains terribly, but I've had men working since last week. You must see it tomorrow. Oh, and there's talk of militia movement in the next county—nothing dramatic, but enough to stir the taverns. My groom says half the village expects French spies in the hedges."

"Villagers often do," Darcy said, removing his gloves. "War makes imagination a national pastime."

"Yes, but Hertfordshire imagination is a special breed." Bingley leaned closer. "Someone swore the birds have been flying strange patterns. 'Not natural,' they said. I daresay it is only talk to cover up a bit of poaching, eh? But the talk is all over. You'll see."

Darcy schooled his expression. "Birds do as they please. They require neither excuses nor reasons."

"Exactly what I said." Bingley turned back toward the drawing room. "Come along. Caroline is in a mood to be impressed."

Darcy followed him, but his mind lingered—unwelcome—on the kestrels circling over Pemberley's ridge, the jackdaws hopping strangely near the south fields.

Bingley pushed open the drawing-room door with the confidence of a man who had never once doubted the warmth of his reception. Inside, the scene was pleasantly chaotic. Caroline Bingley rose from a settee near the window, a volume of Cowper closing between perfectly gloved fingers. Darcy doubted she had actually been reading it. She was dressed for admiration—pale amber silk, an embroidered hem, and a posture that suggested the room itself had been arranged for her convenience.

"Mr Darcy! How fortunate. We had begun to expect you tomorrow."

Darcy bowed. "Miss Bingley. It is a pleasure."

"It always is," she murmured.

On the opposite side of the room, Mrs Hurst lifted her head from a genteel recline. "Mr Darcy, how very good to see you again. Do come and sit. The journey must have been fatiguing."

Her husband, Mr Hurst, acknowledged Darcy with a brief incline of his head before returning his attention to a plate of almonds on the table beside him.

"Were the roads very dreadful?" Miss Bingley asked.

"I assure you, it was quite a comfortable journey," Darcy replied.

She crossed the room in such a way that the light from the window cast her figure into sharp relief. "Charles has been quite determined to have you here. I believe he has half the county prepared to celebrate your arrival."

"That is not the case," Bingley protested cheerfully. "Though I am delighted he came sooner rather than later. "You will help us make sense of this place, Darcy," Bingley said. "Caroline has already declared war on the draperies."

His sister gave him a look. "I declared no such thing. I merely observed that the former tenant had a rather puzzling affection for mustard-coloured damask. It has all been removed."

Darcy smiled. "A mercy to everyone, I am sure."

Mrs Hurst sniffed lightly. "A considerable mercy."

Darcy's mouth tightened, but only slightly. "It seems pleasant enough to me."

Miss Bingley brightened again. "Then we must show you everything. The library is smaller than you are accustomed to, of course, but the view from the south windows is charming. My sister has already claimed it for her morning room."

Mrs Hurst smiled faintly. "The light is agreeable. And the roses look rather pretty near the window."

Bingley clapped Darcy again on the shoulder. "Come, let me fetch you something to drink. Mrs Nicholls says the wine has been settling just long enough. And we have a few matters about the stables I want your opinion on."

Darcy allowed himself to be steered toward the sideboard. Brutus came to sit neatly at his heel, drawing a mild sound of surprise from Miss Bingley. "You brought your dog, I see."

Darcy glanced down at the hound. "He is well-mannered."

"I am sure he is," she said sweetly. "And I daresay the country will suit him."

The room settled into an easy conversation—Bingley discussing repairs, Mrs Hurst offering opinions on the upholstery, Miss Bingley inserting herself into every topic. It was, on the whole, precisely what he expected of Netherfield. And precisely what he needed.

"Well," Bingley said, handing him a glass, "what do you think? Will you stay long?"

Darcy considered the question only briefly. "As long as is useful."

And Bingley beamed, as though Darcy's presence alone guaranteed a season of prosperity.

KITTY BURST INTO THE parlour before the door had fully opened. "He is here!" she cried. "Maria and Charlotte are right behind me. You will never guess their news."

Lydia jolted upright, nearly upsetting her embroidery frame. "What news? Do not stand there. Tell us!"

Kitty pressed a hand to the doorway. "Sir William called on Mr Bingley yesterday. He met his friend, whose name is Mr Darcy. And he said"—she paused for effect— "that Mr Darcy is the tallest man he has ever seen in a drawing room."

Lydia gasped. "Taller than Mr Purvis?"

"Much."

The declaration hung in the air as if it were of national importance.

Elizabeth exchanged a look with Jane. They both adopted the same unbothered posture—steady hands, composed expressions, the picture of mild interest and nothing more.

Footsteps sounded in the passage, then Maria Lucas hurried in, cheeks bright and hair escaping her bonnet. Charlotte followed at a calmer pace, shawl clasped neatly, eyes already sparkling.

"Kitty outran us," Maria announced. "We tried to keep up."

Charlotte laughed. "Papa has opinions to share, and he wished them spread with all due speed."

Lydia leaned forward. "Is it all true? About how tall he is?"

Charlotte gave a thoughtful nod. "Papa seemed quite certain."

Jane's needle hesitated a moment. "Tall or not, I hope he is amiable."

Lydia barked a laugh. "Amiable? What a dull hope. I wish him to be a good dancer who is interesting to talk to. Perhaps he has a mysterious past. Perhaps he abandoned a betrothal. Perhaps—"

"Perhaps," Charlotte interjected, calm as water, "he is simply a man who travelled here by coach and now wishes to enjoy his stay in peace."

Lydia ignored her. "I wager he has a scar. All interesting men have a scar."

Kitty nodded vigorously. "Sir William did say he had a very serious countenance."

Elizabeth kept her expression smooth, eyes lowered to her work. "Serious men may yet be agreeable."

Jane glanced at her. "You do not sound convinced."

"Do I not? Then I must apply myself more diligently."

Charlotte's lips curved. "Lizzy, your interest is showing."

Elizabeth lifted her chin. "I have no interest."

Charlotte reached for another spool of thread. "Of course you do not. You simply blushed when you said he might be agreeable."

Elizabeth scoffed. "I was giving a stranger the benefit of the doubt."

"Indeed. And when Kitty declared that he was tall as an oak tree, you pricked yourself with your needle."

"I did no such thing."

"Then what is that mark on your hand?" Charlotte insisted, turning Elizabeth's wrist over.

Elizabeth tugged her hand free. "Nothing. I scratched it last week. It must have a bit of thorn still in there."

Charlotte studied the mark with a small frown. "You ought to draw it out, whatever it is. Soak it in warm water and salt, or steep a cloth in vinegar. You will invite trouble if you leave it."

"It does not trouble me."

"Not yet," Charlotte said. "But you know how thorns are. They hide more stubborn pieces than one expects."

Elizabeth closed her hand. "I assure you, it will fade."

Charlotte gave her a look that suggested she doubted it very much, but she had no opportunity to say more.

Lydia bounced in her chair. "Come, enough about Lizzy's thorn. You said Mr Darcy hardly spoke? Then he must be profound. Men who think deeply always speak little. That is what novels say."

Kitty scoffed. "No, that is what Mama says whenever she wishes Papa to be interesting. And speaking of interesting, what do you care for a stuffy old man like that? I thought you liked officers better."

"Oh, I do! But do you see any in Meryton? I say we must take our gentlemen where we can find them."

Mary looked scandalised. "Lydia, you cannot say such things."

"I can and I will," Lydia replied. "If no officers appear soon, I refuse to sit at home stitching hems until I am grey."

Elizabeth bit back a laugh.

Charlotte clucked and wagged a finger. "Lydia is plain enough, but I still say that you, Lizzy, are more intrigued than you will say."

"Not a bit of it!" she protested.

"I have known you for many years, Lizzy, and I assure you I can spot the signs. A certain stillness. A certain tilt of the head. A certain way in which you pretend to be wholly uninterested in a gentleman until the subject is exhausted."

Elizabeth gave her a long, level look. "You are mistaken."

"I seldom am."

Jane's soft laugh betrayed her. "Lizzy is more curious than she admits. But that does not mean anything beyond simple curiosity."

"Oh, certainly," Charlotte said, threading her needle. "One must always maintain reasonable curiosity. Especially when the gentleman in question has already been seen climbing out of his carriage with a dog the size of a large pony at his heels."

Elizabeth's head snapped up before she caught herself.

Charlotte's eyebrows lifted. "Ah. There it is."

Jane pressed her lips together, eyes shining. "Lizzy may not love horses, but she adores dogs, the smelly things. The bigger and louder, the better."

Elizabeth set her work aside with deliberate calm. "Curiosity, Charlotte, is the mark of a lively mind. If you cannot distinguish that from admiration, I despair for your future."

Charlotte laughed. "Then consider me thoroughly chastened. Still, if Mr Darcy proves dull, we may all be honest and put him quietly aside."

Kitty shook her head. "I hope he is not dull. That would be so disappointing."

Lydia clapped her hands. "He cannot be dull if Sir William called him impressive."

Elizabeth rose and crossed to the window as if to escape the rising cacophony. Sunlight fell across the fields beyond, pale and sharp, the way September light often was. Somewhere out there, she imagined, stood a tall, serious man who had already provoked entirely too much conversation for someone she had not yet met.

She inhaled slowly.

Charlotte's voice drifted after her. "Lizzy, if you stare at the horizon any harder, we shall conclude you are waiting for him to call."

Elizabeth did not turn. "I assure you, I am waiting for nothing."

Charlotte's amused hum made Jane cover another smile.

Elizabeth lifted her chin one fraction higher, aware her composure was slipping in ways Charlotte saw too clearly.

"Nothing at all," Elizabeth repeated.

# Chapter Five

Bingley plunged straight into the crowd the instant they crossed the threshold. "Look at them, Darcy—half the county turned out. Meryton thrives on gossip and speculation. We have given them both."

Darcy followed because there was no place to stand without blocking someone's way. Bingley was already clasping hands and offering cheerful bows, exclaiming over people Darcy had never seen in his life. Names flew past him with no faces attached—Long, Goulding, Purvis—each greeted as if Bingley had known them for years.

A woman in a plum-coloured gown dipped in a curtsy, and Bingley returned it warmly. "Good evening, Mrs Long. Yes, yes, I have brought my friend with me. Darcy, this is Mrs Long."

Darcy inclined his head. Mrs Long seized the opening at once.

"Such a pleasure! I declare we have heard so much about you. I have two nieces here this evening, Mr Darcy," she said, lifting her hand toward a pair of young ladies lingering near the punch table. "Both accomplished, both eager for dancing. You shall meet them, I am sure."

Bingley beamed. "Mrs Long hosts the most charming gatherings. Her nieces are quite the favourites."

She gave another quick curtsy—nothing like departure, everything like anticipation. "You are welcome among us, sir, most welcome, indeed! Hertfordshire is always improved by new faces."

Bingley moved on before Darcy could summon a polite reply, and Mrs Long drifted after them with purposeful slowness, clearly waiting for a better moment to resume the introduction.

Darcy surged ahead, if only to avoid becoming the centre of a small circle at once.

Bingley caught him by the elbow. "You will like it here. They are eager to know us. At least—to know *you*. You will be besieged in a moment. Best to meet it head-on."

Darcy doubted that, but he closed the distance anyway.

Bingley stopped to greet another neighbour, and Darcy's attention slipped past the crush of unfamiliar faces. Someone called out a name—*"Lizzy"*—and the group of young women near the far wall broke apart for a moment.

Darcy meant only to glance at the commotion. Instead, his vision narrowed.

A young woman stepped into view with a riot of dark curls pinned into a haphazard display. She was speaking to a girl who bounced at her side, and her voice carried just enough to reach him without forming clear words. Something about the way she stood—balanced, alert, ready—caught at him before he could explain why.

He had seen countless young women in countless rooms. None had ever struck him like this: not with admiration, nor surprise, but with a jolt so abrupt it made the air wad up in his throat, as if someone had suddenly grabbed his cravat. Another instant and it seemed like a nauseous fever had brushed up the back of his neck and over his crown.

He drew a slower breath, annoyed by the sensation. It was nothing. The room was warm, the day long, his thoughts still largely back in Derbyshire. His body was merely reminding him that he had not eaten since midday.

Still, his gaze returned to her before he permitted it.

The young woman turned at that moment. Her eyes—dark, joyful, unflinching—caught his without the slightest hesitation. She looked at him as if she were assessing a stranger in a crowd, nothing more.

Yet some inner part of him lurched, as if his balance had shifted a hair too far forward.

He looked away at once.

Bingley called across the room to some acquaintance. "Sir William! There you are! I hope you will introduce us all."

A man with animated limbs and courtly enthusiasm hurried forward. He bowed to Bingley, attempted a bow to Darcy while still finishing the first, and then swept toward the same pair of young women Darcy had just been studying.

"Miss Bennet! Miss Elizabeth!" Sir William exclaimed. "Fortune smiles. You must—yes, indeed—you must meet our new neighbours."

Darcy had no time to compose a polite expression. Sir William had already placed the two ladies before him as if arranging pieces on a chessboard.

The shorter one—Elizabeth—studied him rather openly. Up close, she was even more arresting, though not in the glossy, ornamental way Miss Bingley prized. Her face held a quickness, a readiness, the same charged poise he had noticed across the room. She met his eyes without the slightest trace of modesty, but there was nothing brash in her look.

Darcy felt the odd fever-surge again, sharper this time, as though his pulse had skipped in the wrong direction. He tamped down his breathing, refusing to acknowledge it.

"Mr Darcy," she said.

He returned her greeting with a bow. "Miss Elizabeth."

She offered her hand with the ease expected in such an introduction. He reached to acknowledge it, but just as his fingers met hers, she gasped and withdrew—so swiftly and with such apparent intention that the gesture settled between them like a closed door.

He could not pretend he had imagined it. She disguised the motion at once by smoothing the edge of her sleeve—an adjustment without purpose, save to conceal the first.

What could have occasioned that? It might have been nothing more than a misjudged angle, or some sudden twinge of pain—her sleeve had shifted as if she concealed an awkwardness there. Or perhaps she disliked the formality of such greetings. Some young ladies cultivated little gestures of mystery in public rooms; he had seen that often enough.

Yet the movement had lacked any trace of coquetry. If anything, she seemed intent on denying notice, not inviting it.

Or perhaps the fault lay with him. His height often put people off, and his reserve was seldom misread kindly.

He dismissed each idea as quickly as it came. None satisfied. None aligned with the directness he had seen in her gaze from across the room. He bowed again, falling back on courtesy because it required no interpretation. "A pleasure."

She dipped faintly. "Likewise, Mr Darcy."

A sudden cry of "Mind the line!" rose behind them, followed by the unmistakable shuffle of feet losing their place. Before Darcy could turn, a pair of dancers veered off the figure and brushed hard against Miss Elizabeth's back.

She tipped a fraction, and he reached without thinking to draw her away from calamity. His hand met her wrist—lightly, only enough to keep her from stumbling—but at the instant of contact she gasped, then jerked as if burned. The movement snapped through her arm so quickly that he let go at once.

Miss Bennet gave a little cry of alarm. "Lizzy, what is it?"

"I am well," Miss Elizabeth said, though her breath caught on the word.

Darcy stood still, more startled than either of them. He had touched hundreds of hands in polite society, never provoking such a reaction. Had he injured her? Had he grasped too firmly? He replayed the moment in his mind and could find no fault except the simple fact of his hand on her arm.

"I beg your pardon," he said. "I meant only to keep you from falling."

She did not look at him directly. "The dancers gave more of a push than I anticipated. Pray, think nothing of it."

Bingley laughed. "These rooms do grow lively, do they not? I fear they were built for quieter generations."

Darcy glanced at Miss Elizabeth. Her composure had returned, but a faint line remained about her mouth. "You need not remain in the midst of it, Miss Elizabeth," he said. "The hall is crowded. If the movement is troublesome—"

She studied him briefly, the smallest tilt of her head. "I was only surprised, sir. Nothing more."

He inclined his own head. "Then I misunderstood."

"So it seems."

ELIZABETH WOULD HAVE GIVEN much to disappear for five minutes—just long enough to cool her cheeks and reorder her thoughts—but the crowd surged directly toward the punch table, carrying her with it. Jane kept close, her arm warm against Elizabeth's.

"Lizzy, you gave such a start."

"I tripped. Or someone trod on my gown. Or the floorboards creaked—really, someone ought to see to them before the next Assembly, or we will all fall through one day." Elizabeth reached for the ladle before Jane could wonder her further. She could feel that traitorous pulse still fluttering in her wrist.

Mama descended upon them at once. "Girls! There you are. I have been trying to reach you for an age! Mrs Long would not release me, though I told her I must see how Jane fared with Mr Bingley. Oh, Jane! You looked delightful together. Quite delightful. And Lizzy—" she turned abruptly, breathless— "Lizzy, I saw you speaking to his friend. What did you think of Mr Darcy? Is he as fine as they say? Does he dance? Did he—oh! Kitty, move aside and let your sister breathe."

Jane coloured but smiled. "Mr Bingley was very amiable, Mama."

"Amiable? He was enraptured," Mama declared, turning in triumph from one daughter to the other. "Even from across the room, we could see it. And Lizzy—my dearest girl—*you* spoke to his friend. Mr Darcy. Tell me everything."

Elizabeth lifted her cup, hoping to hide behind it. Jane, whose composure never deserted her at such moments, answered instead.

"Mr Bingley introduced him very handsomely. Mr Darcy seemed a gentleman of excellent manners."

Mama clasped her hands. "That is precisely what I hoped to hear! Imagine it—both of you making such impressions. Oh, this is the best evening—"

"Well, Lizzy made *some* impression on Mr Darcy," Kitty blurted. "Though not the one she hoped, I am sure."

Mama froze, half-beam, half-gasp. "What sort of impression?"

"The sort where she was *fighting* with him," Kitty said, clearly delighted to have the superior tale.

Mama let out a soft shriek. "Fighting? Lizzy!"

"I beg your pardon?" Elizabeth nearly sloshed the punch.

"Oh yes," Kitty said. "Aunt Philips said you flashed at him. And Mrs Goulding said she saw him look most offended. And Lydia says—"

"I do not wish to hear what Lydia says."

"She says you nearly leapt out of your skin."

"It was no argument. That," Elizabeth said crisply, "was a shock."

Kitty leaned in as if this were delicious. "A *shock*?"

"The merest sting. From the carpet or the air. Something in the room." Elizabeth sipped her punch, grateful for the cool. "Mr Darcy must drag his feet. Or his valet failed to air his coats properly. Static clings to neglect, you know."

Jane pressed her lips together, fighting a smile.

Charlotte appeared at Elizabeth's elbow, folding herself neatly into the circle. "Is that the latest theory? A poorly-aired coat?"

"It is the only rational one. And what do you mean, 'latest theory?' Half the room cannot already be talking of it."

Charlotte's eyes glimmered. "I assure you, they are. Mama says you took against him for something, and you say it was some sort of shock. I think it far more romantic than that—a *spark*."

"Romantic?" Elizabeth nearly laughed. "Being jumped like a cat startled from a nap? I assure you, Charlotte, nothing in it resembled romance."

"Still," Charlotte said, "it *is* unusual."

"So is Mr Darcy," Kitty chimed in. "He stared at you a great deal."

"He did not."

As if summoned by the remark, she caught sight of him across the room. Mr Darcy stood a little apart from Mr Bingley, half in shadow, as if studying a sconce with the grave attention of a man judging a work of Greek statuary. He looked every inch a gentleman who wished to be left alone, and Elizabeth was more than inclined to oblige him.

"Lizzy," Mama urged, fluttering her fan, "pray tell me you admired him. I must know—"

"Mama, I have nothing to tell."

"But you *did* speak to him!"

"We exchanged the customary phrases."

"And then you startled so!" Kitty said.

"Because of a shock," Elizabeth repeated. "If a gentleman's garments are so poorly brushed that he carries half the carpet with him, the blame cannot lie with me."

Charlotte hid a laugh behind her cup. "Poorly brushed garments. That is your final answer?"

"It is the only answer that preserves my dignity. The alternative is that Mr Darcy's manners are so ill-assembled that even a touch from him sets one on edge. And that, I believe, is entirely possible."

Elizabeth glanced again toward the far side of the room—and froze.

Mr Darcy had turned his head. He was not studying the sconce.

He was looking directly at her.

And she remembered, all too late, that she had spoken the last sentence aloud.

His posture altered—not a step, barely a breath, but something in the angle of his shoulders changed. A brief tightening, as though a string had drawn him upright. Then he moved away from the column and into the deeper crowd, disappearing behind a line of dancers.

The heat scalded her cheeks again, and not from any spark.

"Oh, Lizzy," Charlotte murmured, "he heard you."

"I know," Elizabeth muttered. "And now I shall certainly never meet that great dog of his."

LYDIA BURST THROUGH THE front hall first, laughing as she shook the night air from her sleeves. "I danced every set, every single one. Wally Purvis said he had never seen such spirit!"

Kitty followed at her heels, nearly colliding with Jane as she called, "And Jane danced twice with Mr Bingley! Twice! Mama was fit to swoon over it!"

Mama was, indeed, swooning. She swept in behind them, breathless and triumphant, her ribbons askew from the crush of the carriage. "Jane, my darling girl, you were perfection. Your papa must hear of it immediately—Mr Bennet! We have had the most *delightful* evening—"

Jane tried to smooth her gown, still glowing from the dancing. Elizabeth stepped aside to untangle her cloak from Kitty's elbow, but the hallway was too crowded, too noisy, everyone talking at once.

Papa looked up from his chair as his family descended upon him. "Well," he said, dryly surveying the flushed faces and swirling gowns, "I see the Meryton Assembly retains its reputation for noise."

Mama clutched at her heart. "You have no notion of it, Mr Bennet. Jane was the toast of the evening! Mr Bingley could scarcely remove his eyes from her. Did you not hear me? They danced *twice*, and everyone observed how exceedingly pleased he was."

"Was he, now?" Papa mumbled.

Jane coloured. "He was very obliging, Papa."

Lydia spun once in the middle of the room to make her point. "And I danced every single dance, Papa—every one! Wally Purvis said—"

Kitty interrupted, "Lizzy would have danced nearly all of them, too, if—"

Elizabeth shot her a look, but Kitty's excitement outran Elizabeth's caution.

"—*if* she had not been fighting with Mr Darcy."

Papa's gaze sharpened over the edge of his book. "Fighting? With someone named 'Mr Darcy,' you say?"

Elizabeth closed her eyes briefly. "Kitty is exaggerating."

Lydia giggled. "Not at all, Papa. She quite *sprang* away from him. Like he slapped her, but he only touched her. Half the room saw."

Papa's brows lifted. "Touched my Lizzy, did he? Well, well, that is, indeed, something worth fighting over."

Elizabeth drew herself up, coat still unfastened. "I did *not* fight with Mr Darcy."

Papa set the book aside. "And yet you sprang?"

"I started," Elizabeth replied. "There is a difference."

Kitty popped up behind her. "Mrs Long says she believes Mr Darcy offended you. Mrs Long's cousin says *you* offended *him.* I told her you never offend anyone unless you wish to, and then you take care to do it properly so it could not possibly—"

"It was *nothing*. A spark. The rooms were close, the air dry. The dancers collided with us, and—"

"And Lizzy flew back as though she had been pricked with a pin," Lydia finished.

Papa regarded Elizabeth with a flicker of seriousness. "You are unhurt?"

"Hurt! No, not at all," she said. "Why did everyone make such a fuss over such a little thing? It was nothing."

He nodded, the brief shadow of concern passing. Then his expression shifted into the familiar dry amusement. "I see. So, Mr Darcy's touch is enough to send young ladies leaping about the room. A powerful man indeed."

Mama pressed a hand to her cheek. "Oh, Mr Bennet, do not tease! Lizzy would never leap unless she had good reason. Though I must say," she added, turning suddenly toward Elizabeth, "you might have handled the matter with a little more grace, my dear. Mr Darcy is a man of consequence, and it does no harm to appear agreeable."

Elizabeth opened her mouth, but Kitty got there first.

"She *was* agreeable, Mama. And then she said—"

"Kitty," Elizabeth warned.

Kitty ignored her entirely. "—she said Mr Darcy must drag his feet, or else his valet forgot to brush his coat, because the spark—"

Mama gasped and clapped a hand over her heart. "Lizzy Bennet! You said that?"

"Not to him," Elizabeth muttered.

Jane raised a hand to conceal a smile. Lydia gave a delighted squeal and spun again.

"I should like to see his face if he heard that," Lydia declared. "He is as tall as a church steeple and twice as solemn."

Elizabeth felt heat rise to her temples. "Lydia, pray stop."

"Oh, let her have her merriment," Papa said. "A household must take its entertainment where it may. If Mr Darcy cannot bear a spark—or a remark—he is hardly fit for a country assembly."

Mama fluttered. "Oh, Mr Bennet, you do not understand. If Mr Darcy is Mr Bingley's intimate friend, then any slight, any offence—real or imagined—might influence Mr Bingley's opinion of Jane. Lizzy, my love, tell me you were perfectly civil."

Elizabeth drew a slow breath. "I said nothing *un*civil, Mama. And the rest... was said in jest."

Mama squinted at her. "A jest that half the room may repeat."

Elizabeth winced.

Papa chuckled. "Then I expect Mr Darcy will recover admirably. He is like enough a sturdy fellow. A good night's rest may restore him."

Kitty flopped onto the nearest chair. "Well, I think he deserved it. He stared at Lizzy so dreadfully, like he was trying to decide whether she was peculiar."

Elizabeth felt a prickle at the back of her neck. She had noticed that odd look of his, too.

Mama put a hand to her mouth. "He stared? *Stared?* Oh, Jane, do you hear? Mr Darcy took notice of Lizzy. This bodes exceedingly well. If Bingley admires Jane and Darcy admires Lizzy—oh, Mr Bennet, do say you are pleased!"

Papa stretched his legs toward the fire. "I will be pleased when the house regains its quiet."

Elizabeth narrowed her eyes at him, half-amused despite herself. "You might show a morsel of interest in your daughters' happiness, Papa."

He tilted his head. "My dear, your happiness is my constant concern. And if dancing twice with Mr Bingley makes Jane happy, I applaud it. If leaping away from Mr Darcy makes you happy, I applaud that as well."

Elizabeth huffed a laugh. "I did not leap."

"According to Lydia," Papa said, "you took flight."

Lydia bobbed in agreement. "Like a startled cat."

Elizabeth groaned into her hands. "I shall never hear the end of this."

"Of course not," Papa said cheerfully. "That is the delight of daughters."

Mama waved him off. "Enough, Lizzy. You must tell me—did Mr Darcy show the least inclination toward you? Any admiration at all?"

Elizabeth shook her head. "None worth mentioning, Mama."

Not quite true, but she would sooner swallow her glove than admit it.

The faint sting at her wrist pulsed again as she unfastened her cloak. She rubbed at it absently, annoyed it had not yet faded.

Nothing but a spark. A spark and a misunderstanding.

And a very tall man she had no wish ever to encounter again.

# Chapter Six

The guns had been brought down before sunrise, and the smell of oiled metal hung in the entrance hall as Darcy fastened the last button of his shooting coat. Brutus circled impatiently at his heels, nails clicking on the tiles, pausing now and then to stare up the staircase as though expecting someone.

Darcy tugged his gloves into place. "Leave it," he murmured to the dog. "The ladies will not be coming down merely at your pleasure."

Brutus ignored him and paced to the door again.

Bingley strode in, bright as if he had slept twelve hours and dreamt of nothing but roses. "Fine morning for sport. A bit misty out, but I daresay it will clear. Hurst, are you ready?"

Hurst, adjusting his waistcoat with more resignation than enthusiasm, gave a grunt. "Ready enough."

Bingley laughed and slapped him on the shoulder. "Hurst does not wake so early for anyone but me, Darcy. Consider yourself favoured."

Darcy managed a faint smile. Anything more would have required real cheerfulness, which he did not feel. His sleep had been fitful; the memory of Miss Elizabeth's recoil kept intruding at the edge of consciousness, accompanied now and then by that odd sickening heat he had felt the instant he first saw her. Foolish. Entirely foolish.

Bingley reached for a cartridge case, speaking as he checked the latch. "Caroline had much to say last night after we returned. She declared the Assembly a trial, of course, but even she could not deny that the Bennet sisters made an impression."

Darcy stilled a fraction. "Did she."

"Oh yes." Bingley grinned. "She said Miss Bennet was perfection in every respect. And as for Miss Elizabeth—well—Caroline noticed that you and she held a rather spirited exchange."

Darcy set his jaw. "Spirited?"

"That was her word. Though Caroline insisted she did not hear what was said."

Darcy checked the strap of his gun case for the second time. "Nothing of importance."

"Caroline claims otherwise. Something about a rebuke." Bingley laughed again. "Though I told her she must have misunderstood."

Darcy felt the memory of Elizabeth's voice strike him again—her quick wit, her mockery of his grooming, her casting-off of him as though he were an inconvenience. Entirely undeserved. Entirely... vexing.

He tightened the strap. "Miss Bingley is mistaken."

"Possibly," Bingley said, fastening his gaiters. "But truly, Darcy—Caroline insists Miss Elizabeth looked at you with a rather curious sort of interest."

Darcy reached for his gloves. "Women look. It means nothing."

Bingley laughed. "Yes, but they do not usually look... like *that*."

"I observed nothing of the kind."

"Of course you did not. You never do."

Darcy had no intention of pursuing the subject further. He checked the clasp of his powder flask with unnecessary care. Brutus pressed his shoulder against Darcy's leg, impatient for the door to open.

Hurst finally took up his gun. "If we are to shoot today, let us shoot. Standing about while Bingley speculates on romantic nonsense is no way to start the morning."

Bingley only laughed again, undeterred. "Very well, very well. Darcy, shall we?"

Darcy nodded once. Ordinary movement. Ordinary conversation. The predictable morning routine would clear the remnants of last night from his thoughts.

The grass was heavy with last night's rain, bending under their boots as they crossed into the lower meadow. Brutus ranged ahead in wide, eager arcs, nose sweeping the ground. Hurst muttered that the dogs ought to be kept closer this early, but Brutus ignored him entirely.

Bingley adjusted his stride to match Darcy's. "We ought to try the northern covert this morning. The keeper swears a good covey settled there after the harvest."

Hurst snorted. "That man says a good covey settles anywhere he wants an easy day."

"True," Bingley said cheerfully, "but we cannot shoot the same ground every week. *Variety*, Hurst. One must give the birds a sporting chance."

Darcy lifted an eyebrow. "I had not realised you were so humanitarian."

Bingley laughed. "If I cannot bring down a bird without feeling like a villain, I shall blame you entirely."

They crested a slight rise, the earth soft beneath them, the smell of damp soil rising with each step. Brutus checked suddenly, tail rigid, then plunged into a patch of rushes. A pair of partridge burst from the cover, beating hard for open air. Hurst swung first and fired; Darcy took the second shot half a heartbeat later. The birds fell almost in tandem.

"Now *that* was neat work," Bingley called, already trudging forward to watch Brutus retrieve. "We shall have a fine dinner this evening."

Darcy reloaded, wiping a smear of damp earth from the barrel with his glove. The morning mist began to thin by degrees, revealing the undulation of the fields beyond—ridges and hollows dotted with late-autumn scrub.

Bingley shaded his eyes with one hand. "Fine ground today. If the weather holds, we ought to follow that hedge line eastward and circle back through the stubble."

Hurst grunted approval.

Only once they turned east, once the slope stretched out long and uninterrupted, did the distant horizon begin to clarify. A pale line of rooftops edged into view far beyond the undulations of field and meadow.

Bingley straightened, breath visible in the chill air. "Ah—look there. Do you see it?" He pointed with the barrel of his gun. "That roofline. That must be Longbourn. Lucas Lodge sits farther west. We ought to see it a little closer soon, eh?"

Darcy lifted his gaze, following the angle of Bingley's gesture. The houses were still faint through the thinning mist, but the shapes aligned with the map Bingley had sketched out last evening.

"Likely so," Darcy said. Hurst squinted. "You mean to call on them so soon?"

"Of course I do," Bingley said. "We are introduced; what is the point of being sociable if one does not behave as such?"

Darcy gave a noncommittal sound and adjusted the angle of his gun.

Bingley stopped speaking long enough to fire. A grouse burst from the grass; Hurst took the second shot and brought it down neatly. Brutus bounded off to retrieve it, tail spinning with pride.

"Fine shot," Darcy said.

Hurst shrugged. "Luck." He reloaded.

They waded through another stretch of boggy ground, the water sucking at their boots. A farmhouse sat crookedly to the east; Darcy caught the scent of woodsmoke from its chimney.

"I must ask Mrs Nicholls about hiring again," Bingley said as they skirted another boggy patch. "When we returned from the Assembly, the fires were low, the lamps half-trimmed, and the cold supper laid out as if the staff had abandoned it midway. Caroline swears Netherfield has not seen proper management in years."

Hurst grunted. "You will never find good help."

"Well, that is why one asks for references." Bingley brushed a reed from his coat. "I may inquire at Longbourn. Mrs Bennet knows everyone in the parish. She would have ten names for me by the end of the visit."

Darcy lifted his gun as Brutus froze near a patch of rushes. "Hold," he said quietly.

Another bird rose; Darcy fired cleanly. Brutus tore through the grass to retrieve it, shaking water from his coat as he returned.

Bingley beamed. "Very good. I shall put that one down as yours. Now—ah, yes—before I forget: Darcy, did you receive your post last night? I told them to place it in your room before we went out."

Darcy's grip tightened slightly on his gun. "I received it."

"Nothing urgent, I hope?"

"A steward's report," Darcy said. It was the simplest way to end the subject, though the words settled heavy in his throat. "I will attend to it in due course."

Bingley nodded, already scanning the fields again. "Well, if you require assistance with any estate matters, you know I will help however I can. Now—Brutus! Leave that hedgehog alone, you menace."

The dog abandoned his quarry and dashed on ahead, sending a flock of small birds wheeling up in alarm.

Darcy watched them rise, disappearing into the pale morning sky.

THE BREAKFAST TABLE AT Longbourn was already in commotion when Elizabeth entered. Mama darted between chair and sideboard with a level of agitation usually reserved for calamity—or advantageous courtship.

Lydia plopped into her chair with an exaggerated groan. "I shall be tired all day, I know it—but it was worth it. If autumn brings half as many assemblies as Mrs Long predicts, I shall never have a quiet evening again."

Mary sighed over her book. "One wonders whether a quiet evening might be of use now and then."

Lydia ignored her. "Mama, we must ask at once when the next ball will be. I intend to dance every set of the season."

Kitty giggled. "Miss Goulding said she had never seen a girl so determined to burn through her slippers."

Elizabeth reached for the jam to hand it down the table. "Then you had best pace yourself, Lydia, or you will be carried home before the first reel begins."

Lydia laughed. "I never tire. You know that."

Kitty frowned. "I danced almost as many as she did, you know, but no one says a thing about it. Should not I be tired, too?"

Elizabeth passed the jam toward her... and her sleeve dragged across her wrist.

A sudden sting lanced up her arm.

She caught her breath and drew her hand back sooner than she meant to, the jam pot tilting in her grip.

Jane caught it at once. "Lizzy?"

Elizabeth forced a smile and shifted the pot into her other hand. "My sleeve snagged. I suppose I shall have to mend it."

She dropped the offending wrist under the table, hiding it from Jane's gentle scrutiny. Beneath the cloth, the skin throbbed once, warm and insistent. The urge to push back her sleeve and inspect the mark rose sharply—but Kitty was already asking her for the butter, and Mama was bustling behind her chair.

Elizabeth lifted the butter dish with her free hand, nodding at Kitty's chatter as though nothing at all had occurred.

"Mrs Long says Mr Bingley will surely call today."

"Of course he will!" Mama gushed. "I shouldn't wonder if he is nearly at the door already."

"Oh, there is a very fine thing," Papa grunted. "The gentlemen come to the country for a bit of sport, but instead of taking advantage of a fine morning in the fields, they come to inhabit my drawing room."

"Mr Bingley told me himself that he planned to go shooting this morning," Jane supplied.

"Oh, never mind whether Mr Bingley is shooting or riding or whatever," Kitty protested. "I was talking about Mrs Long. You know she never hands out compliments she does not have to, but even *she* thinks Jane made the finest impression of the whole room. There, what do you all say to that?"

Mama caught up the teapot and nearly overfilled her cup. "Naturally she did, my love! And if Mr Bingley has the sense I hope he possesses, we shall hear the front bell before noon."

Jane caught Elizabeth's eye with a gentle smirk and a soft chuckle, then lowered her eyes, smiling into her tea.

Mary glanced up again. "There is such a thing as excess of spirits, Kitty."

Lydia tossed her hair. "Only in sermons."

Elizabeth tried again for the jam, more carefully this time. The movement tugged faintly at the scratch—nothing serious, but enough to keep her thoughts too focused on her wrist. It was absurd to mind a scratch at all. Absurd to feel it now. It should have healed days ago.

"Lizzy, you must wear your muslin today—the one with the embroidered hem. Mr Darcy will come with Mr Bingley when he calls, you may depend upon it. Surely, he regrets his conduct and will wish to make amends. Men of fortune are always eager to redeem their manners when beauty is concerned."

Elizabeth made the mistake of swallowing tea at that moment. She coughed, the cup rattling in its saucer. "Mama, I—"

Kitty giggled. "There, Mama, you made her choke! I told you she despises the man."

Lydia kicked her under the table as Elizabeth sputtered to clear her airways.

Mama patted her back with unnecessary vigour. "There now! Compose yourself. Nothing is more unbecoming than appearing flustered. I am sure Mr Darcy will find you quite agreeable. You must try to keep him talking, for Jane's sake. Who knows that they will not overstay the quarter hour? Oh, I shall have Hill make some fresh cake. And plums! Who has better plums than Longbourn, I ask? Come, Lizzy, compose yourself, or Mr Darcy will think you terribly odd, indeed."

Elizabeth's spine went rigid. *Talk* with Mr Darcy? For an entire call?

*No.*

The word struck through her so sharply she did not realise she had thought it—only that her pulse surged and something in her demanded refusal.

At that instant, the spoon beside her cup gave a quick, clear tap against the saucer. A single sound, light but crisp—loud enough to cut through Lydia's bragging and Kitty's chatter.

Mary looked up at once. "What was that?"

Elizabeth pinned the spoon with her fingertips before it could tremble again. "The table shifted," she said. "Lydia is kicking her feet again."

"I was not," protested Lydia. "Not just then, anyway."

"There was no movement," Mary said.

Elizabeth reached for a roll she did not want. "Then Hill must take care to sweep the floors better because something has got under the leg and it is sitting unevenly. Think nothing of it."

Mary returned to her breakfast with evident scepticism.

Elizabeth sat straighter, schooling her expression. Breakfast at Longbourn did not allow for private unease. And she would rather endure a dozen of Lydia's embellishments than let anyone suspect she fretted over something as foolish as a scratch or a spoon tapping itself.

Mama clasped her hands. "Now—all of you—eat quickly. Mr Bingley may arrive at any moment, and we must not appear unprepared."

Elizabeth lifted her cup again, more carefully this time. *Prepared.*

She doubted very much that she was.

ELIZABETH SLIPPED OUT AS soon as the breakfast things were cleared. Mama was already issuing orders for Hill to air the drawing-room curtains and polish the silver, and Kitty had begun rehearsing what she would say if Mr Bingley complimented her lace. Lydia had countered with plans for her next gown.

Jane alone noticed Elizabeth reaching for her shawl. "Will you be long?" she asked.

"A quarter hour. Perhaps two," Elizabeth murmured. "You know how it is."

Jane's smile held understanding. "Do not stay out if it starts to rain."

Elizabeth promised she would not and stepped into the pale morning light.

The air did not warm as the sun climbed; it sharpened. The wind carried the faint scent of turned earth and distant woodsmoke as she walked the familiar path toward Oakham Mount. Each rise steadied her thoughts; each patch of dry bramble felt like a small claim of solitude.

At the foot of the Mount, she paused to catch her breath and looked east. The fields rolled wide and open toward the distant line of trees. Something moved there—a cluster of figures cresting a lower rise. A dog bounded ahead of them, dark against the pale grass.

A *large* dog.

She shaded her eyes. The creature ran with a heavy, confident gait, tail sweeping once before plunging into a tangle of brush. Even at a distance, its size marked it apart from every farm dog in the parish.

"That must be Mr Darcy's," she muttered to herself before she could stop the thought. The Irish Wolfhound Mrs Long had mentioned.

The dog burst out of the brush again. For a moment, he stopped, head lifted, facing the slope where Elizabeth stood. The distance was too great for certainty, yet she had the odd sense that the dog had fixed on her.

She stepped back behind a jut of stone, annoyed with herself. "Nonsense," she whispered. The sun was behind her; any dog would stare into a shape on a bright ridge.

Still, her wrist pulsed again. She rubbed it once, more firmly, and climbed the last incline.

At the summit, the wind met her in a steady rush. She breathed it in, clearing away the remnants of breakfast clamour—and something else. A heaviness that had settled along her ribs since the Assembly.

She stepped toward the familiar outcropping and set her hand on the stone to lower herself. The moment her palm touched it, a warmth met her skin—not from her wrist this time, but from the rock itself, as if some small glow had gathered there beneath her hand.

Elizabeth yelped and pulled back at once.

"What now?" She pressed her fingers to the stone again, cautiously. It was warm — undeniably warm—though the air bit with cold everywhere else. She moved the tip of her littlest finger an inch to the left: the stone was chilled at the first instant... then suddenly it was warm as her teacup.

A prickle ran up her spine. Impossible. Stones did not warm themselves for company.

She lifted her hand a final time, and the heat faded instantly, leaving only the ordinary autumn chill.

Elizabeth jumped back to lean on a branch, annoyed with herself. "Nonsense," she muttered. "A fever... it must be a fever."

The twig beneath her hands changed at once.

Not warmth this time—*movement.* The dry bark softened under her touch, supple as fresh growth, and a pale green point forced its way through a crack in the wood.

Elizabeth jerked back so quickly she scraped her glove. "Oh, absolutely not!"

The twig hung motionless. Lifeless. A dead thing, just like all branches in autumn ought to be.

She stared at it, pulse thudding in her throat. "You were grey a moment ago," she told the branch, as if accusing it of mischief. "I refuse to believe otherwise."

But the image of that tiny, impossible bud hovered before her eyes, undeniable.

She folded her hands against her shawl. "This is what comes of going out without my plum jam at breakfast," she muttered. "Next, I shall imagine the rocks reciting poetry."

Elizabeth straightened and stepped back from the outcrop. She refused to indulge a fancy about thorns or scratches or spoons tapping themselves. She had too much sense for that.

She turned her face toward the fields again. The hunt had moved farther west; the figures were smaller now, merging with hedgerows and shadow. The wolfhound—if it was a wolfhound—could no longer be distinguished from the darker patches of brush.

She let out a breath and sagged, just a little.

Enough. She had walked long enough to quiet her thoughts, if not her wrist.

# Chapter Seven

Bingley declared, shortly after the early dinner hour, that the weather was "too fair to waste indoors" and that a call upon Longbourn that afternoon would be the very thing. Darcy had hoped the morning's sport might excuse him from further society, but he knew the obligations of a neighbour as well as Bingley did. Refusal would only excite remark. He therefore submitted to changing coat and cravat once more, as if outward order might secure inward composure.

Miss Bingley elected to accompany them—ostensibly to offer her civilities, though Darcy had observed too often where her attention truly inclined to be deceived on that point. Mrs Hurst joined her, as she always did, and thus the party set out in Bingley's carriage a little after two.

Darcy took his place opposite the sisters and turned his gaze to the fields beyond the window. The sky lay clear and pale, the light keen upon the hedgerows and stubbled fields. Within the carriage, the air seemed thicker than the season warranted. He attributed it to the closeness of company rather than any defect of ventilation.

His thoughts slid, whenever they were not forcibly engaged, back to Derbyshire—to the steward's letter folded in his desk, to the second ash along the boundary line whose crown had thinned so notably, to the unpleasant knowledge that no degree of reluctance would excuse him from examining the matter in person when he returned.

Nor, it seemed, from this call.

When Longbourn's chimneys rose beyond the last turn in the lane, he schooled his features into the neutrality expected of a guest and braced himself for half an hour of noise, colour, and Mrs Bennet's unchecked satisfaction.

THE HOUSEKEEPER ADMITTED THEM without delay, and the Bennet parlour rose at once to receive them—warmth and bright upholstery, the flutter of ribbons, the clatter of chairs, and Mrs Bennet advancing with such earnest welcome that Darcy instinctively set his shoulders before she quite reached them.

"You are all so very kind to call," she cried, hands clasped as if greeting old friends rather than near strangers. "Pray be seated, do. Mr Bingley, you must sit here—yes, by my Jane. And Mr Darcy, I insist upon your taking the chair nearest the fire. Lizzy, move half a place for Mr Darcy. Miss Bingley, if you please, there by Mary. Mrs Hurst, you will be quite comfortable opposite the fire."

There was no graceful way to object without drawing more attention than the arrangement deserved. Darcy took the place indicated. Miss Elizabeth shifted just enough to allow it, the soft rustle of muslin marking the narrow space between them. He caught the faintest hint of lavender as her gown moved—a mere impression, and gone.

"Such a pleasure to receive you," Mrs Bennet continued, already reaching for the teapot. "We are quite delighted. Kitty, do not stand gaping. Sit, child, sit."

Miss Kitty dropped into the nearest chair with a hurried curtsy. Miss Lydia perched at once upon its arm until Mrs Bennet snapped, "On the seat, Miss Lydia Bennet, if you please. We are not in the orchard now."

Bingley appeared only more gratified by the bustle. "Your house has a very cheerful aspect, Mrs Bennet," he said. "I cannot conceive a warmer welcome."

"I always say there is no use in keeping one's comfort to oneself," Mrs Bennet replied, glowing at the compliment. "If a house cannot be cheerful, what is it for? Lizzy, pour for Mr Darcy. Jane, give Mr Bingley a slice of cake. Hill, bring the other plate. Mr Darcy, I trust you do not object to country cake?"

"I do not, madam."

Miss Elizabeth reached for the teapot. Her hand was steady, her manner unhurried. "Sugar, sir?"

"None, I thank you."

She passed him the cup. Their fingers did not meet. Yet as porcelain crossed the narrow distance between them, the air near his sleeve warmed, as if the fire had shifted its breath in that direction alone. He was no nearer to the grate than before; there was no sensible alteration in the room. He dismissed the notion, took a cautious sip, and set the cup upon the small table at his elbow.

Bingley accepted his own tea with delight. "Miss Bennet, you must allow me to say how much I enjoyed the Assembly. I can scarce recollect when I last danced so often."

"I am glad you were pleased, Mr Bingley," Miss Bennet answered, her voice as gentle as her countenance. "The neighbourhood was very curious to meet you."

"Curious and excessively kind," he said. "Every face was new to me, yet I felt as if I had stumbled into a room of acquaintances. Sir William Lucas could not have been more attentive. Mrs Long is all civility."

Miss Kitty brightened at once. "Mrs Long says we shall certainly have another ball if you stay long enough, Mr Bingley. She told me so herself."

Miss Lydia kicked her foot against the rung of her chair. "And there will be officers by then, Kitty. Papa heard it from Sir William."

"Oh, Lydia, do not tease us so!" Mrs Bennet declared—with a full smile at Bingley. "You know how your papa insists on tormenting my nerves with little fancies like that."

"But it is true, Mama," the younger girl insisted. "I am sure Maria heard it, too. Imagine a room full of red coats! I declare I shall never sit down."

Miss Mary cleared her throat with the air of one who introduces a solemn truth. "A young lady who never sits exposes herself to vulgar observation."

Miss Lydia rolled her eyes. "I would rather be observed than sit in a corner with Fordyce."

"That is an uncharitable reflection," Miss Mary said, though she coloured as she spoke.

Miss Bingley, who had been examining the room with polite attention, chose that moment to address their hostess. "I confess, Mrs Bennet, I had not expected Hertfordshire to be so..." She paused, selecting her word with care. "...animated. One hears of the country as if it were all hedgerows and turnpikes, yet your Assembly had quite the air of a little town."

"We do very well," Mrs Bennet replied, brisk and satisfied. "Meryton may not be London, but we have our share of visitors. Lizzy, my love, pass that plate to Mr Darcy. Mr Darcy, you must try the plums; they are from our own trees."

Darcy accepted the plate because refusing it would only draw notice. But as Miss Elizabeth's hand neared his, the china gave a tiny, unnatural twitch—nothing that ought to be possible, a mere brush of motion beneath his fingertips—yet his stomach lurched as if he had missed a step in the dark. A sharp prickle raced up his wrist; the air tightened around his skin, too warm, too near.

He pulled back before he meant to, the movement abrupt enough to betray him.

Her eyes jumped to his—quick, sharp, catching far too much—and then dropped again at once. No laugh, no apology. Just the quiet acknowledgement that she had seen something he wished he could explain, or deny, or ignore.

And he could do none of it.

"I assure you," Bingley was saying, oblivious to everything but his own contentment, "Netherfield could not be better situated. The views toward Oakham Mount are very charming."

"Oh, are they not?" Mrs Bennet cried. "Our girls walk there often. Lizzy was there only this morning. Lizzy, tell them how fair the prospect is."

Miss Elizabeth looked as though she would rather bite out her own tongue, but replied dutifully. "The air was remarkably clear, ma'am. One could see as far as Lucas Lodge in one direction and Netherfield in the other."

"Did you not say, Miss Elizabeth," Bingley asked, "that Longbourn has some land in that direction?"

"We have a few fields to the east," she replied. "My father walks there most mornings."

"Mr Bennet is very fond of his walks," Mrs Bennet said. "He knows every hedge and gate within three miles. I say he knows them too well; he is never in the house. But men must have their fancies."

Darcy took another sip of tea. The heat broke across his tongue with a sudden flare, fierce enough to jolt him. He returned the cup to its saucer, fingers pausing there as the sensation settled. A prickle ran up the back of his neck—brief, but unmistakable.

His breath snagged on its next rise—not from pain, but from the unsettling certainty that someone had marked his reaction. The familiar hum of conversation resumed around him, unaltered, yet the instant still hung between his thoughts like a question he could not dismiss.

Miss Bingley turned toward him, her smile arranged with the care she devoted to every social manoeuvre. "I have often observed Mr Darcy's fondness for a well-situated estate," she said brightly. "He cannot resist a property with fine woods. Pemberley is renowned for them. Netherfield must seem quite modest beside such grandeur."

Her tone slid neatly into the room, but to Darcy it felt like a hand closing around a thought he had not meant to display. He had no inclination to discuss Pemberley in a parlour already too full of voices and impressions, nor to entertain comparisons that invited every listener to picture his home.

He straightened slightly in his chair, forcing his attention back into order. "Netherfield possesses its own merits," he said. "One cannot set two such places side by side as if they were entries in a ledger."

But even as he spoke, a part of him strained toward the earlier oddness—the twitch of china, the heat of the cup, the feeling that the air itself had shifted without warning. And beneath all of it, the unwelcome thought that Miss Elizabeth Bennet had noticed far too much.

Mrs Hurst nodded. "Quite so. A more modest estate may be very elegant, if properly managed."

Mrs Bennet nodded vigourously. "Netherfield will do very well when Mr Bingley is fully settled there, I am sure. It is a fine house. It only wants a mistress to put it perfectly in order." Her smile encompassed the room and yet rested, unmistakably, upon Miss Bennet. The intention was so open that even Bingley, who seldom perceived what he did not wish to see, looked for a moment uncertain.

"I am persuaded it will be difficult to leave it," he said quickly. "I grow more attached every day."

Miss Bennet coloured and bent her head over the plate of cake she held.

Before Mrs Bennet could enlarge upon so promising a declaration, a new voice sounded from the doorway.

"More callers? I see I shall be driven to take my book out of doors."

Mr Bennet stepped into the room, spectacles in hand. He bowed towards the Netherfield party. "Mr Bingley, you are most welcome."

Bingley half rose from his chair out of sheer goodwill. "Mr Bennet, we could not be in the neighbourhood and fail to pay our respects."

"Then my parlour is honoured, Mr Bingley," Mr Bennet replied. His gaze travelled around the room, taking in daughters, guests, and tea-tray with equal composure. "This must be your friend Mr Darcy we have heard so much about. You find Longbourn tolerable, I hope, sir?"

"It is very comfortable, sir."

Mr Bennet's mouth twitched at one corner, though no full smile emerged. "Comfort is a precious commodity in any house. I hope my daughters have not overwhelmed you with it. They collect callers the way some men collect broadsheets—every day brings a fresh edition."

Bingley laughed at once. "I assure you, sir, your daughters offer far better conversation than most printed matter."

"That may be," Mr Bennet allowed, "though broadsheets seldom talk all at once."

Mrs Bennet let out a sound that might have been a laugh or a scold. "You are determined to make us look foolish, Mr Bennet."

"I would never dare," he replied, bowing slightly. "Your household makes its own impressions without my assistance."

Bingley chuckled aloud. "I confess, sir, I envy you. A morning spent in such a lively house must be very cheerful indeed."

"Cheerful, yes," Mr Bennet said. "Quiet, no. That is why I take my walks. A man who wishes to hear himself think must look outdoors for the privilege."

Bingley leaned forward, eager. "Miss Bennet tells me you walk the estate every day."

"Not every day," Mr Bennet answered. "Only on the mornings when the house is awake before I am—which is to say, most of them."

There was a ripple of amusement around the room.

He went on, more lightly still, "I was out at the eastern boundary today. A pleasant stretch, though my poor trees there are nearly broken from all the fruit they bore this autumn. I tell Mrs Bennet we must teach them better manners, but they resist improvement." He turned his gaze toward Darcy, curious rather than pointed. "A gentleman with such woods as Pemberley must have a way of keeping his oaks in line. A veritable army of groundskeepers, I shouldn't wonder."

The words landed with a jolt he had not braced for. A flicker of warning travelled across Darcy's thoughts, too swift for reason to overtake it. "We attend to planting and pruning," he said. "There is no method beyond that."

"Ah. Attention." Mr Bennet nodded once. "I am persuaded that is the rarest commodity in any household." His gaze rested on Darcy an instant longer, curious rather than intrusive, and then he turned toward his wife. "My dear, I leave our guests in your capable hands. If you require my company further, you know where I am not to be found."

"You are a strange creature, Mr Bennet," Mrs Bennet said, half fond, half vexed. "Always running off. Pray do not mind him, Mr Bingley. He pretends indifference to company, but he is very glad you are here."

Mr Bennet inclined his head again to the visitors and withdrew. The sound of his retreating steps faded down the passage.

Conversation did not cease; the parlour at Longbourn did not allow such a thing. Yet there was a slight readjustment among the company, a shifting of shoulders and cups, as if everyone sought a new place after his departure.

Miss Kitty broke the moment. "Mr Bingley, will there be hunting again tomorrow? I heard you say you saw a great many birds."

"If the weather holds, I shall try that way again," Bingley said. "The cover near the rise looks promising."

Miss Lydia brightened. "Oh, that way! Lizzy, is that not where you walk? You will wander too close to the guns and be deaf before you are thirty."

"I shall take care to avoid both shot and conversation," Miss Elizabeth replied, the slightest glint of humour in her eyes.

Darcy's mouth compressed before he could prevent it. The remark was general; it was delivered to her sister, not to him. To suppose she had meant him was unreasonable. Yet his thoughts turned upon the words longer than their lightness merited. Conversation with whom did she intend to avoid?

Miss Bingley, perhaps sensing an opportunity to display her refinement, spoke into the space that followed. "For my part, I cannot admire these rough country expeditions. Mud, dogs, damp air—Louisa, you recall that horrid morning in Yorkshire when the carriage could scarcely reach the house for ruts?"

Mrs Hurst shuddered with delicate exaggeration. "I remember my shoes. They never recovered."

"Mr Darcy enjoys the sport," Miss Bingley added, turning the subject toward him, "but he is used to a very different style. The shooting parties at Pemberley are quite celebrated, are they not?"

Darcy had no wish to have his habits displayed for the amusement of the room. "The day was pleasant enough," he said. "Netherfield offers all that is needful."

Miss Elizabeth did not look at him, yet he had the distinct impression that her attention sharpened then. Her hand moved, almost unconsciously, toward the cuff of her sleeve, fingers pressing lightly at a raw-looking scratch that she took care to turn under her sleeve. The motion was small, easily overlooked, but the fire gave a low crack at that instant, sending up a brief shower of sparks that died as swiftly as they leapt.

The visit could not last forever. At length, after another exchange or two upon the neighbourhood and the hope of future assemblies, Bingley glanced towards Darcy with the look he wore when he knew at last that propriety demanded retreat.

"We must not trespass on your hospitality, Mrs Bennet," he said. "I have already prolonged our call beyond a quarter hour."

"Nonsense, Mr Bingley, you are no trouble at all," Mrs Bennet protested, though her eyes shone with satisfaction. "We are always glad to see you. Jane, my love, ring for Hill. They must not go without their cloaks."

Darcy rose with the rest. The room appeared to widen at once, as if the walls had drawn back with the movement of so many bodies. He bowed to the ladies in turn. When he reached Miss Elizabeth, she curtsied, her gaze level and entirely composed.

"Miss Elizabeth."

"Mr Darcy."

Nothing in her manner betrayed offence, interest, or any alteration from the first moment of his entrance. It ought to have relieved him. Instead, some contrary part of his mind resented that his presence could leave so little trace.

# Chapter Eight

Elizabeth escaped the house under the pretext of fetching a book she had "forgot" in a tree crotch in the orchard, though she carried another book in her hands. Mama had been especially triumphant all morning—hovering over Jane, praising every word Mr Bingley had spoken, and recounting the visit at such length that even Jane had blushed and begged her to stop. Kitty and Lydia darted through the sitting room with their usual commotion, interrupting each other constantly, and Mary practiced a hymn with such earnest force that Elizabeth feared the piano might rebel.

She did not resent any of them for it. She merely felt unequal to the noise.

The air outside was cool enough to sharpen her thoughts. Frost clung to a few blades of grass where the sun had not reached; her boots left faint marks behind her. She followed the familiar path beyond the garden wall and let her shoulders loosen as the quiet settled.

She did not wish to think of Mr Darcy, yet her mind kept circling back to him by some involuntary logic. Not the awkwardness of their first meeting—she could laugh at that, if she tried—but the strange pulse that had run through her arm when their hands had neared the same plate. The almost-imperceptible jump of the china. The way he had drawn back so quickly that she felt more confused than offended.

It must have been an illusion. A trick of the hand. Nerves on her part, perhaps; or an odd tremor of heat from the fire. If she repeated the argument often enough, she might come to believe it.

Her wrist throbbed again beneath her sleeve—an insistent, needling pulse that refused to be ignored. She stopped with an irritated breath and pushed back the cuff. She had looked at it so many times already that she half expected it to vanish out of sheer embarrassment, but the scratch remained: reddened, uneven, and far more inflamed than any simple scrape deserved.

"I told Charlotte it was nothing," she grumbled, scowling at the mark. "And it *ought* to be nothing."

She touched the edge lightly. The sting leapt at her finger at once. There had been no splinter left behind—she had checked the first night, and dozen times since. She had even tried a little oil of lavender, which usually calmed any small injury. Instead, the skin had grown angrier by the hour, almost as if the remedy had offended it.

This was absurd. She had spent days pretending she felt no discomfort, telling Charlotte, telling Jane, telling anyone who wondered that it barely troubled her. But here, alone, she could not escape the question forming in the back of her mind:

*What was this?*

It was a foolish question, and she shoved the thought aside, tugging the sleeve back into place as if that would finally hide it from her mind. She was not fanciful. She was merely... tired. Overset. Irritated by too much company and too many odd impressions.

She resumed walking more slowly, her fingers hovering near the sleeve as though unwilling to leave the matter entirely alone.

The field opened before her in a long sweep of pale stubble and winter-brown grass. A few crows picked along the far hedge. The sky, thin and bright, gave everything a washed colour—cold, but honest. She paused to watch a small flock of sparrows rise from a tussock of dried weeds. Their bodies caught the light in arcs of soft brown, and she felt a familiar lift of spirit. Nothing could be very wrong in a world that still offered sparrows in winter.

She walked on, letting the rhythm of her steps quiet the remnants of last night's unease. She counted the fence posts ahead without thinking, observed the angle of the sunlight along the hedges, wondered briefly whether Jane would enjoy a walk later if Mama could be convinced to release her from the house.

Only when the old boundary ditch came into view did her pace ease. Not out of fear—nonsense—but something in the look of the ground tugged at her attention. The ditch was as shallow as ever, no more than a soft fold in the earth, and the rise beyond it had never qualified as a hill. Yet today the line cut sharply across the field, as though someone had drawn it with a deliberate hand.

Fanciful notion. She refused to indulge it. Still...she did not step forward. The air on this side lay perfectly ordinary, touched by a faint stirring of grass and the last thin breath of morning chill. But just beyond the ditch, the quiet thickened, a stillness that did not match the rest of the field.

"Walk on," she muttered. "Or you will think yourself into a fever."

She dropped into the dip, boots sinking into softer soil. Damp earth lifted around her, cool and familiar. Better. She climbed the rise.

And stepped into something that was not the morning she had left behind.

The change did not strike; it unfolded. The light thinned, as if a high cloud had drifted between her and the sun—only no cloud moved across the sky. The colour of the grass dulled, not uniformly, but in patches, as though sections of the field belonged to different hours of the day. The hedgerow directly before her seemed to draw back a fraction, narrowing into a shape she could not immediately parse: not hedge, not shadow, something between.

Elizabeth blinked. Her thoughts attempted to arrange themselves into objection, but the scene refused to sharpen. A fine trembling sensation ran along her fingers, as though the air itself carried a low current.

And her wrist burned.

The heat was so abrupt, so focused, that she staggered without meaning to. She clutched her forearm at once, startled by the sensation—hot, sharp, pulsing between the edges of the scratch as though a coal had been pressed against her skin. She tried to draw a steady breath, but her lungs seemed to misremember the process, producing only a thin shiver of air that did nothing to steady her.

"What—"

The word broke. She sank into a crouch to keep from falling outright.

The field blurred. A shimmer appeared at the base of the hedges—pale, glasslike, shifting with a faint suggestion of movement. Water? Impossible. But the impression lingered stubbornly in her senses, refusing to be dismissed.

Her pulse hammered in her ears. She lifted her head to regain orientation, and for an instant the entire line of hedge re-formed into a curve of dark thorn—arched, repeating, an impossible rhythm laid over the winter branches.

Her mind recoiled. Her body followed.

She dropped to her knees.

The silence came next—not a sudden absence, but a withdrawal, as though the world around her stepped back. The faint rustling of sparrows, the breeze riffling the grass, even the warmth of her own breath seemed to recede. She felt suspended inside a hollow moment, one that had no clear border between where she ended and the field began.

She tried to speak, to say anything that might ground her, but the words clung uselessly to her throat. The pain in her wrist pulsed again, stronger this time, flaring upward until her eyes stung. Her left hand groped instinctively for support, but the ground beneath her palm felt altered—firmer in one place, grainy in another, as though the soil carried the memory of another season.

She jolted upright, a sharp, instinctive flinch, though nothing in her limbs answered properly. A cold ripple swept through her chest. Her hand scraped up her arm for balance, fingers catching the trembling fabric of her sleeve.

"No!" The word rasped out before she knew she meant to speak. "No, I am...walking. That is all. Only walking!"

The light faltered. Her sight pinched inward as if the edges of the field had drawn toward her. The hedges wavered between their ordinary winter tangle and that unfamiliar, thorned geometry, shifting with each blink. Cold seeped through the ground into her knees, meeting the fierce heat beneath her sleeve in a surge that tipped her stomach, as though the earth itself had given a single, deliberate heave beneath her.

She tried to crawl backward toward the ditch. Her palm slipped in the damp grass; her balance tilted. She felt a wave—heat, then cold, then a peculiar lightness, as though her body no longer held entirely to the ground.

The sense of being watched swept over her—not by a person, but by the place itself, a recognition she could neither prove nor escape.

Her thoughts scattered. Shapes blurred. The thin strip of sky above her folded in and out of focus. She reached for breath and caught only fragments. Her wrist flared. Everything dimmed.

And the world dropped away.

BINGLEY URGED HIS HORSE up the rise at an eager clip. "Look at this morning, Darcy. Why, it might as well be June for all the sunshine and green grass! One could almost believe the entire county contrived it for our benefit."

Darcy kept his own mount to a steadier pace. "If Hertfordshire begins arranging its weather to please you, we shall never see you in London again."

"Every encounter has been entirely pleasant," Bingley said as they reached the rise. "Miss Bennet especially—the fairest creature I ever beheld. One could not wish for a kinder introduction to the neighbourhood."

Darcy guided his horse toward firmer ground. *Too quick,* but he kept his expression even. Bingley's admiration had grown with alarming ease. Miss Bennet was agreeable—anyone might acknowledge as much—but her family was unknown to them, and Bingley's openness made him vulnerable to hopes others might mistake for promises.

Mention of the Bennets unnerved him more than it ought. Too many unknowns, too much eagerness in Bingley already. And behind all of it lay the one Darcy preferred not to revisit: Miss Elizabeth.

None of it bore examination. He kept his attention on the hedgerow and added only, "She carries herself well."

The words felt safely neutral, though his mind refused to agree.

Behind them, Hurst reined in with a sigh that could have been mistaken for a groan. "Gentlemen, I believe this incline is designed to humble mankind. I will go no further. Mrs Nicholls promised broth at eleven, and I intend to find it."

Bingley glanced back with a laugh. "You have not been out half an hour!"

"Exactly my point," Hurst replied, already turning his horse. "You will forgive me if I choose sense over valour."

He executed a lazy salute and trotted off toward Netherfield, leaving Bingley shaking his head. "I suppose that leaves the true sportsmen to continue."

Darcy nudged his horse forward. "If we wish to see the coverts before midday, we should keep on."

Bingley leaned forward in his saddle. "Come—there's excellent cover near the eastern line. Williams swears he saw at least a dozen birds rise there yesterday."

They continued along the narrowing path. Bingley drew a deep breath and let it out with satisfaction. "There is something remarkably civil about this neighbourhood. Everyone greets one another, and even the roads appear to approve of visitors."

Darcy allowed a faint smile. "You will credit the roads next with opinions."

"Why not? Miss Bennet said much the same—that Hertfordshire prefers to welcome rather than impress. I like the notion."

Darcy tipped his head in acknowledgment. "She has a sensible manner, though far too agreeable to my taste."

"Why, Darcy, you speak as if that is a bad thing! And the countryside itself—look at those trees." Bingley pointed with his riding crop toward a distant stand of ash beyond the hedgerow. "They make a better canopy than anything in London."

Darcy studied the line. Pemberley's trees were nearly bare by now, but the leaves here were hardly even turning, though they were fully into October. Perhaps the unseasonably warm weather accounted for that. Still, his mind returned—unbidden—to Pemberley's weakened harvest. He doubted very much that Hertfordshire had seen any such ill luck this autumn.

Bingley nudged his horse a little closer. "Darcy, if you stare at those trees any harder, they will pick their leaves back up out of sheer modesty."

"Only considering whether those in Derbyshire are faring as well," Darcy grunted. "After last week's storms, we ought to be watchful."

"Well, the groves at Netherfield seem perfectly content." Bingley gave a little flourish of the reins. "No reason we cannot enjoy a morning without improving the world's forests, Darcy."

"True enough."

The hedgerow ahead opened slightly, offering a view of the lower slope. Darcy glanced at the field out of habit. A man accustomed to managing a vast estate rarely walked anywhere without taking stock. The ground here appeared even, the rise gentle, the colour of the grass unremarkable.

Bingley pointed toward a patch of scrub. "Williams swears he saw partridge there yesterday. If we circle round that way, we may flush a few."

Darcy nodded. "Lead on."

Bingley glanced over. "Are you brooding already? It is barely ten. Smile, man. The countryside is good for you."

"I am not brooding," Darcy said.

"You are," Bingley replied cheerfully. "If you brood any further, the pheasants will surrender out of pity."

Darcy offered no answer. His gaze lingered on the line where the hedges met the field, a faint tremor of instinct drawing him forward faster than reason could account for.

Bingley slowed first, lifting a hand to signal the change. The ground ahead dipped toward a narrow copse—thin trees pressed together in a way that suggested shelter for birds. If they rode straight in, they would scatter whatever game hid there.

"Wind's turned," Bingley said, glancing at the angle of the branches.

Darcy felt it too—the faint shift of air brushing the right side of his face. Coming from the copse toward them. Any approach on horseback would be folly.

"We go on foot," Darcy said.

Bingley nodded. "Downwind and quiet, then."

Darcy looped his reins over a low branch, testing it with a brief pull; the horse stood quietly at the end of the rein. Bingley tethered his own mount beside it. The cover ahead offered a clear line through the undergrowth if approached carefully.

Darcy stepped forward first, boots sinking into the softer earth beneath the trees. The air grew stiller here, muffled by the cluster of trunks—a good sign for game, though something about the silence prickled faintly against his awareness.

Bingley followed close behind, keeping enough distance to avoid breaking twigs or rustling brush. "Birds might lift from the far edge," he murmured. "If we circle, we may see them rise."

Darcy inclined his head and continued toward the opening between the trees, prepared to scan the ground for movement. They rounded a bend in the rise, and Darcy stumbled to a halt.

A shape lay in the grass ahead—small, still, and out of place.

Bingley's steps carried onward, light and untroubled, but Darcy only stared. That was no fallen branch. The outline was wrong; the colour did not belong to the field. Fabric, not bark. A figure, not debris.

His heels hit the earth in a rapid staccato before he formed any conscious decision. The distance between them and the shape closed too slowly for his liking. Something in him had already leapt to recognition, though he could not yet see enough to name it. He dropped his fowling piece and ran.

"Darcy—?" Bingley began, but he had already quickened his pace to keep up.

The form resolved as they neared. A woman's gown, the skirt rumpled, the figure half-turned toward the earth.

*Elizabeth Bennet.*

Cold went through him—not a chill, but a clarity that jolted every thought into sharp order. He dropped to one knee beside her while Bingley called her name in alarm.

She lay curled upon her side, one hand slack in the grass, the other tucked near her chest. A smear of damp earth darkened her glove; her sleeve had slipped back enough to expose the tender skin above her wrist he had seen yesterday—flushed and angrily inflamed.

"Is she hurt? Darcy, is she—good heavens, what happened? Did she fall from a horse?"

Darcy knelt and touched her shoulder lightly. The contact drew a sharp, unwelcome sensation through his chest, as though his breath had misjudged its own depth.

"Miss Elizabeth?"

No response. Her breathing came shallow and disordered, not the soft rhythm of a simple faint.

He shifted to support her, turning her carefully to rest against his arm—and had to pause. A brief wave of vertigo passed through him, swift and disorienting, the world narrowing to the press of her weight and the heat of her skin against his sleeve. He set his jaw and continued, adjusting his hold until her head rested more securely.

Her head lolled, a faint crease between her brows as though some discomfort still gripped her even in near-unconsciousness.

"No sign of hoofprints," Bingley mused, shading his eyes up and down the lane. "What could have brought her out here alone? She must have stumbled—though there is nothing to trip her. You do not suppose she was attacked, do you?"

Darcy scarcely heard him. The field around them held an odd quiet. Not absolute stillness, but a pause in the natural sounds he expected—the wind seemed to have forgotten its movement. The hedges almost seemed to lower themselves to a more modest height, as if they had bowed to watch the woman on the ground.

The earth seemed less reliable beneath his feet, not enough to alarm, but enough that he adjusted his stance without thinking. "We must take her back at once." His voice sounded easy, confident, though he had to apply somewhat more effort than usual. "Fetch my horse. Quickly!"

Bingley sprinted toward the small copse where they had tethered the animals.

Alone, Darcy adjusted his hold on Elizabeth. Her skin felt warm through the fabric of her gown—overwarm—and the slight tremor in her fingers washed a wave of weakness through his arm that did not belong to him alone. For an instant, his stomach turned sharply, as though his body had mistaken her distress for its own.

He gritted his teeth and brushed a fallen strand of hair from her cheek. Her eyelids fluttered with faint distress.

"Miss Elizabeth," he murmured, though he did not expect her to wake. "You are safe now."

The effort of speaking left him briefly light-headed, as though he had given away more strength than the words themselves required.

Her lips moved. A fragment of sound escaped—no more than a breath, but it carried the shape of a word.

"...wrong...place..."

His body went still—not from fear, but from the sudden, undeniable sense that in coming to her aid, he had crossed something of his own. He bent slightly, straining to hear, but the rest dissolved into an indistinct murmur.

Her brow creased; a shudder passed through her shoulder and into his arm, faint but unmistakable.

Darcy adjusted his hold without thinking, drawing her closer to keep her from slipping, and felt again that quiet draining sensation, as though the strength required to steady her had been taken from him rather than summoned. He set his jaw and bore it, unwilling to loosen his grip even by a fraction.

Bingley returned with both horses, breathless from haste.

"Is she worse?"

"She is insensible, nothing more," Darcy said, keeping his voice even. "We must take her back to Netherfield."

He gathered her in his arms and rose. She felt light, far too light, and when her head fell briefly against his shoulder, a sharp flicker of protectiveness shot through him—unwelcome, unbidden, but impossible to ignore.

"Netherfield!" Bingley cried. "Would not her family be better—"

"Longbourn is three miles from here. Heaven only knows how she got so far on her own, but she needs a doctor at once. I can take her if you will ride ahead for help."

Bingley nodded. "Right."

Mounting with her proved difficult until Bingley lent a hand. Darcy felt the delay keenly, not from impatience but from the way his arms protested the effort, strength answering more slowly than habit promised. He dismissed it at once and swung up, settling Elizabeth before him, his arm secure around her to prevent any slip.

She stirred once, a faint sound of protest or confusion, then fell quiet again.

For a brief instant, the thought crossed his mind that it would be simpler to send her with Bingley. Safer. He could not have said why the idea felt wrong, only that it did. Before he could examine it further, he tightened his hold and gave the word.

Bingley urged his horse into a gallop, the sound of hooves striking the cold earth fading quickly along the rise. Darcy set his own mount in motion at a more cautious pace, every shift of Elizabeth's weight requiring adjustment, each correction demanding more attention than it ought. The effort of keeping her steady drew upon him steadily, as though the act of bearing her diminished what remained.

She lay against him without resistance, her head tucked beneath his chin, her breath warm but uneven. The warmth did not comfort him. It only made him more aware of the strange heaviness gathering through his chest and arms, the sense that his body was lending itself where it would not easily be reclaimed.

A long strand of hair had come loose from her bonnet and brushed against his sleeve in a slow, dragging arc that unsettled him more than any cry would have done. A conscious woman protested, complained, demanded release. This utter quiet screamed louder in his thoughts than protests ever could.

The field blurred past them, hedgerows dipping and rising, but he scarcely marked it. Her earlier words—half-formed, unmoored—returned again and again without sense. *Wrong place.* No coherence, only distress. As the distance between them and Netherfield shortened, he adjusted his seat once, then again, annoyed to find that balance now required care. He looked down at her face—pale, drawn, lashes resting motionless against her cheek—and felt a colder thought intrude, uninvited and unwelcome.

Whatever had overtaken her in that field was not exhaustion, nor injury, nor anything he had known how to remedy.

And though he continued to ride on without faltering, Darcy was conscious, for the first time in years, that his strength was not equal to his resolve.

# Chapter Nine

DARKNESS POOLED AND THINNED in turns, like ink stirred through water.

A shape at the edge of her mind kept reforming—hedge, hill, ditch, hedge again—never holding still long enough for her to grasp it. The world blinked white once, then slipped sideways. Something throbbed behind her eyes, a steady pulse she could neither name nor ease.

"Miss Bennet?"

A man's voice, too close, too real to be part of the dream.

The light changed. A thudding grew louder—her own heartbeat? Footsteps? The rise of wind along the field? She tried to turn her head, and the sound stuttered, splitting into two uneven beats.

The wrongness surged again—cold earth rising toward her, the hedge tilting—and she flinched, or thought she did.

"Her pulse is stronger now," someone murmured. A different voice. Female.

Elizabeth tried to open her eyes; one lid obeyed, the other sagged as if held down by a thumb she could not see.

Blur. Firelight? A lamp? Her vision rippled, and for an instant the flame elongated into the shape of the boundary hedge, needle-thin and shivering. She gasped. Or tried.

"Easy, my dear," the woman said. "You are quite safe."

*Safe*. The word rang oddly, as though echoed back at her from the wrong direction.

A hand touched her wrist. She jerked, the movement weak but sudden.

"Forgive me, Miss Elizabeth," the man said again. His voice floated somewhere above her shoulder—familiar yet somehow distorted against familiarity. Was it... Mr Jones? No... Something cool brushed her swollen wrist, smelling faintly of spirits and crushed leaves. "That should help with the inflammation. Can you open your eyes?"

She attempted to answer, but her tongue felt thick, clumsy. What came out was a dry whisper: "Not... here..."

The woman clucked her tongue. “Poor lamb. She is wandering. Shock does strange things.”

Shock. Yes. That might have been it. Fainting from exertion or hunger—some innocent explanation. She clung to that idea with both hands.

The man pressed a palm lightly to her forehead. “Her fever appears very slight. She may simply have overtaxed herself. A fall, perhaps. Miss Bennet? Do you recall anything of your morning?”

Morning. Yes. She had gone walking. Clear skies. The far hedgerow like a line of stitching through the field. Her wrist—

Her eyes fluttered wide at once.

The world swam, but she managed to rasp, “The... ground.”

“Gently, Miss Elizabeth,” he said. Yes—surely it was Jones. She knew that voice. Had known it since her childhood. But the room tilted, and the certainty dissolved almost at once. “Give yourself a moment.”

Elizabeth’s gaze caught on a fold of brown wool near her shoulder—someone standing beside the bed, though she could not yet place them. Pillows held her upright, blankets arranged with a care that did not feel like home. The air carried a faint scent of wood polish and something sharp from the herbs. Beyond the half-open door, two voices murmured—low, deliberate, neither of them familiar.

*Not home.*

The thought flickered and died.

“Where—” Her voice cracked. She swallowed. “Where am I?”

“Netherfield, miss. Mr Darcy and Mr Bingley found you on the east rise. You were quite unwell. Mr Bingley brought Mr Jones and then rode to Longbourn himself. Mr Darcy waits in the hall for word.”

Netherfield?

The name dropped into her consciousness like a stone into dark water. Memory rippled outward: Mr Darcy’s face bending over her, the hollow sway of a saddle beneath her, the dull roar of hooves. His voice—steady, unnervingly calm—telling someone to fetch help.

Mr Jones lifted her hand and turned it toward the lamplight. “What happened here? It looks as though it has been festering some while.”

Elizabeth snatched her hand back before thought could intervene.

“No,” she said at once. Too quickly. “No, it is nothing.”

He exchanged a brief glance with the housekeeper but did not ask more.

She swallowed and lay her head back on the pillow. She was lying in a guest chamber—she could see now the fine plaster moulding, the pale curtains drawn against the afternoon light, the unfamiliar quilt draped over her legs. The room spun once, gently, as though nudged.

She brought a hand to her temple.

Mr Darcy had carried her here. And she had been... babbling? Her mouth tasted of cold air and uncertainty. She opened her eyes.

"Netherfield," she whispered.

Mr Jones adjusted the blanket at her shoulder. "Just so. And I think it time Mr Darcy came in to see you for himself. He will be relieved to see you awake."

Mrs Nicholls opened the door only a hand's breadth before slipping away, leaving it ajar in clear invitation.

Darcy stepped inside.

The room was warmer than the passage, a small fire crackling low in the grate. Mr Jones stood beside the bed, frowning down at his leather satchel; Mrs Nicholls moved to occupy a chair near the foot, upright as a sentinel. Elizabeth lay propped against pillows—still, pale, her lashes faint shadows against her cheek.

He had seen her only moments before, carried in his arms and laid out on the bed until Mrs Nicholls had huffed in to take charge of her. But the sight of her now—quiet, reduced to stillness—struck him with a sharper unease. This was not merely illness. It was absence. As though something essential had been interrupted.

Mr Jones looked up. "Mr Darcy. I thought it best you hear the particulars at once."

Darcy moved nearer, keeping to the opposite side of the bed from Mrs Nicholls. He kept his hands behind his back; even so, he felt conspicuous, an interloper where he had no formal right to stand. Improper, perhaps—especially as he had heard her voice through the door only moments earlier, and now her eyes were closed again. "Tell me."

Jones cleared his throat and consulted the small ledger in his hand. "Pulse irregular but not dangerously so. No evidence of injury save for an old scrape at her wrist—no bruising, no contusions. Her breathing is sound, though shallow from exhaustion." His brows drew together. "Her pupils respond, but somewhat sluggishly. I confess myself puzzled."

Darcy's attention drew, unbidden, to Miss Elizabeth's hand lying open upon the coverlet. There was earth beneath her nails, a faint dark crescent at the edge of each finger. He felt the question form before he could stop it—*how long had she been there alone?*

Jones went on, "One possibility is exposure. She may have wandered farther than she intended, lost her way, succumbed to chill—"

Darcy shook his head before the sentence was complete. "She was not lost. Not in any ordinary sense. She walks those fields often."

"Even the eastern rise?" Jones asked mildly. "I have known Miss Elizabeth for many years, and I have never heard of her being incautious."

Darcy hesitated. He could not explain why that detail lodged so sharply—the memory of that stretch of ground, the way the hedgerow thinned, the quiet that did not feel like quiet at all. "I cannot say," he replied at last. "But she would not go there without purpose."

Jones nodded, indulgent rather than convinced. "Very well. Another possibility is strain of the nerves. A fright, perhaps. A sudden shock can sometimes bring on faintness of this sort."

"No," Darcy said at once. "She does not seem the sort to be given to fancies. She would not collapse because of a startled bird."

Jones shifted, his tone lowering. "There are... more prosaic causes. Some ladies, after certain unwise associations—"

"No." The word cut cleanly across the room.

Jones stopped short, colour rising in his face.

"I do not know her well," Darcy continued, his voice even now but leaving no space for retreat, "but Miss Elizabeth Bennet is a gentlewoman of sense and character. You will look elsewhere for your explanation."

"Of course, of course," Jones murmured, chastened. "I merely list the possibilities. But none seem to fit the evidence. She took nothing poisonous that I can detect. There is no fever. No sign of illness. Merely..." He spread his hands helplessly. "A collapse without cause."

Darcy drew a slow breath. *Without cause.* The phrase rang false the moment it was spoken. There was always a cause. He had felt it on that rise—an awareness he had dismissed at the time as fancy, fatigue, anything but what it had been. The memory resisted examination. He let it. Some impressions were best ignored.

Mrs Nicholls rose quietly from her chair. "She tried to speak, sir, just before you entered. A word or two. But they made no sense."

Darcy's attention snapped back to the bed. "What did she say?"

Nicholls hesitated. "It sounded like... 'Not here.' Or perhaps 'not near.' I could not be certain."

The words settled into him with unwelcome precision. *Not here. Not near.* As though the distinction mattered.

"And she lost consciousness again?" he asked.

"Not entirely, sir," Jones replied. "She hears us, I am sure of it. She will wake soon enough."

Soon enough.

"May I—?" Darcy checked himself. The request was improper; he knew it the instant the words formed. And yet the conviction remained, stubborn and unaccountable, that there was something she might say—if she could say anything at all—that would render sense where none yet existed. "May I speak with her a moment? Alone?"

Jones looked up sharply, then exchanged a glance with Mrs Nicholls. "It is irregular," he said after a pause. "But I see no harm in it. We will remain by the hearth. Speak quietly, sir—and take care not to startle her."

Darcy inclined his head.

Jones and Mrs Nicholls withdrew, their voices lowered at once to practical murmurs—poultices, broth, warmed bricks—leaving the space beside the bed suddenly, conspicuously his.

He stepped closer.

The movement brought about a curious slackening, as though the strength in his legs had momentarily forgotten its purpose. He adjusted his stance, slow and deliberate, until the sensation passed enough to be ignored.

He did not touch her; he would not presume to do that. He stood only near enough that, should she open her eyes, he would be within her sight.

Her breathing was uneven but steady. A loose strand of hair lay against her cheek, displaced by nothing more than her own movement. He noticed it—and found, to his quiet irritation, that his hand had flexed before he stilled it again at his side.

"Miss Elizabeth," he said softly, unsure whether he wished her to hear him or not. "Can you hear me?"

Her eyelids stirred—once.

Then again.

Darcy held himself motionless. The faint weakness returned to his calf muscles, accompanied now by a dull heaviness through his shoulders, as though standing had become a conscious effort.

Her lashes trembled, and her mouth shifted, as though shaping a word that had not yet found its way free.

Darcy's breath shortened despite his will. "Miss Elizabeth?" he said gently. "If you can hear me, try to open your eyes."

She stirred... and wide brown eyes fluttered open to him.

Elizabeth became aware of light before sound.

Not the blaze of it—only a pale intrusion through her lashes, as though the day had found a way in without asking leave. She opened her eyes and closed them again at once, fortifying herself against the faint tilt that followed.

When she tried again, the room was quite right again.

A bed. A familiar ceiling. The small fire in the grate, reduced to embers. And beside her—

Mr Darcy.

He stood near enough that she did not need to turn her head to see him. Not looming. Not withdrawn. Simply there, as if he had been so for some time.

Her mouth was dry. "I... beg your pardon," she said, the words soft and uncertain, but her own. "I fear I am very ungracious company."

"You are awake," he said. The relief in his voice was unmistakable—and instantly checked. "Do not trouble yourself to speak if it costs you."

She tested the instruction by drawing a breath. The ceiling wavered, then flattened again. "I am not hurt," she said. It seemed important that he understand that much. "Only... unsteady."

"So I was told." He paused. "You were found alone. On the eastern rise."

The words stirred something sharp behind her eyes. Not pain—memory. The hedges. The quiet that had not been quiet at all.

"I went walking," she said slowly. "The morning was very fine." She frowned, annoyed by how thin the explanation sounded even to her own ears. "I did not mean to go so far."

"And yet you came more than three miles from Longbourn. On foot."

"Yes." Her fingers tightened against the coverlet. "I do not know why."

He did not contradict her.

"There was a place," she said. "Just there—where the path bends. I have passed it a dozen times. But this time..." She faltered, searching for language that would not slide away from her. "It felt wrong. As though I had stepped where I ought not to have done, though I could not say how I knew."

Darcy's hand moved—then stopped. He clasped it behind his back instead.

"Were you frightened?"

Frightened? She considered the word. Then shook her head, faintly. "Only... wrung out. As though the air had decided to leave me." Her gaze lifted to his face. "And then I remember nothing more."

The silence that followed was not empty. It was held—carefully, deliberately—by the man standing beside her bed.

"You are safe now," he said at last.

Elizabeth closed her eyes briefly, gathering herself. When she opened them again, the room remained steady. Darcy had not moved.

"Mr Darcy," she said, quietly. "Why are you here?"

For a moment, he did not answer. His thumb brushed unhappily against his fist, and his mouth reshaped itself two or three times. "Because I was nearest," he said at last.

Elizabeth forced another breath, heavy as a stone lifted from the earth. "I am..." She meant to say well. Or grateful. Or something that would send them away so the room would stop spinning. But the word dissolved the moment it left her tongue. "I am..."

She never finished it.

Sleep caught her mid-syllable, pulling her under so swiftly she did not feel her head sink back into the pillows.

Miss Elizabeth drifted back into shallow sleep, her breathing evening into a rhythm that was gentler than before. The room settled with her, not into rest, but into a watchful stillness that closed in upon Darcy from every side.

Seeing her so unmoving maddened him beyond reason. He had met her only twice before; he had no claim upon her, no history that justified the tightness in his chest or the restless pull to remain where he stood. And yet the longer he stayed, the more pronounced the weakness became, subtle but persistent, as though something in him were being drawn outward and spent.

This was not propriety. Nor concern alone.

He took a step back, then another, compelled less by thought than by the certainty that lingering would cost him more than he was prepared to examine.

Darcy turned and left the chamber.

The corridor received him with cooler air and a welcome distance. He drew a steadying breath just as footsteps sounded at the far end. Bingley came toward him at a brisk pace, colour still high from exertion. Close behind followed Mr Bennet, one hand on the banister as though he had taken the stairs too quickly, and Miss Bennet—her bonnet crooked, her face pale with worry.

"Darcy," Bingley panted, "how is she?"

Mr Bennet did not speak. He simply watched Darcy with a stillness so grave that Darcy felt every word he shaped must be exact.

"She wakes for moments only," Darcy said. "Not clearly. Her thoughts wander, and she drifts away again. Mr Jones finds no injury to the body, but he believes she may have fallen or taken a sudden fright."

Mr Bennet swallowed, the sound audible. "May I see her?"

"Of course." Darcy stepped aside at once. "But gently, sir. She is—" He searched for the right word. "Easily overwhelmed."

Mr Bennet did not wait for more. He pushed open the chamber door and went directly to his daughter's bedside. Darcy followed only far enough to be out of the way. Miss Bennet crossed the room quickly, her composure cracking only when she reached her sister's side.

"Lizzy," she whispered, gathering her sister's hand between her own. "We are here, and you are safe."

Miss Elizabeth stirred faintly, her brow tightening, though she did not wake.

Mr Bennet lowered himself into the chair beside the bed. His hand hovered over his daughter's on the coverlet before finally resting upon it with a care so tender it seemed almost unrecognizable in the man. Gone was the playful sarcasm, the easy indolence—what remained was a father nearly undone.

Darcy turned away from the intimacy of that moment, his own unease sharp in his chest.

Miss Bennet glanced toward him then. "Papa," she said softly, "perhaps... perhaps Mr Darcy and Mr Bingley might tell you how they found her. I will stay with Lizzy."

Mr Bennet did not move.

Miss Bennet tried again, her tone very mild. "Papa, I shall not leave her. Not for an instant. But you must hear all that they know. Please, Papa, at least until she wakes and we can take her home."

A long moment passed. Then Mr Bennet nodded once—short, jerking, as though agreeing cost him something—and rose. His eyes never fully left his daughter.

Before he could step back, Mr Jones cleared his throat. "She must not be moved today. Not until we understand what brought on this collapse. A journey in a carriage would be ill-advised; the jostling alone could cause harm."

"Yes," Miss Bennet said at once. "Of course. She will remain here until she is stronger."

Bingley straightened with immediate resolve. "Then her comfort must be secured. Miss Bennet, may I send for your things? We shall have a room prepared for you adjoining this one."

Her eyes softened with gratitude. "You are very kind, Mr Bingley. Thank you."

At that moment, footsteps clipped sharply in the passage, and Miss Bingley appeared in the doorway, one hand pressed to her chest as though she had run the entire length of the house.

"Is it true?" she said, breath quick. "I am told Miss Elizabeth Bennet is taken ill, and that I am just now hearing of it?" Her gaze flicked at once to Bingley, then to Darcy, as if they had conspired to keep the news from her.

Miss Bennet rose slightly from her seat. "My sister had a fall, I believe. We are not entirely certain what occurred. But she is resting now."

Miss Bingley swept forward, arranging her expression into something poised and sympathetic. "Then allow me to sit with her. It is the least I can do as hostess. Miss Bennet, you must be exhausted—pray let me relieve you."

Miss Bennet blinked at her, too polite to challenge her outright but not yielding an inch of ground. "You are very considerate, Miss Bingley, but I cannot leave her."

A faint crack appeared in Miss Bingley's smile. "Indeed. Well. If you require anything, I am at your disposal."

Mr Bennet exhaled shakily and stepped toward the door. Darcy moved at once to assist him, though the gentleman waved him off and steadied himself against the jamb.

"Mr Bennet," Darcy said quietly, "if you will come with us, we shall tell you everything we know."

Bingley offered his arm. "This way, sir."

Mr Bennet nodded but glanced back once more at his daughter—his gaze raw with a fear he could not disguise—before he allowed the two younger men to lead him from the room.

# Chapter Ten

Elizabeth drifted upward through layers of sleep—slow at first, then abruptly, as though some sound had nudged her from very far away.

Cold air brushed her cheek.

Not Longbourn.

Not her room.

Too still. Too ornate. And the door—was that... open?

She blinked against the blur clouding her sight. The ceiling wavered, then steadied. Her pulse gave one uneasy skip.

Where—

A whisper of movement. Soft. Close.

She turned her head, sluggishly, and froze.

A dog sat only a few feet from her bed. Not some gentle, hearth-side creature—this one held himself the way men did when bracing for command. Broad-chested, dark-eyed, stone-still but for the faint rise and fall of breath.

He watched her as though she were the one intruding.

Her throat balled up into a dry, scratchy thing. "...Hello?"

A single thump of his tail. Nothing more.

She swallowed. Her tongue felt thick, useless. "Where... where did you come from?"

Another blink, slower this time, and she recognised the slope of his muzzle. The rangy wolf-hunting lines. Had she seen him once—at a distance? At... Netherfield?

The name stumbled into her mind and hung there, unanchored. Yes, Netherfield. She remembered now. She had been brought to Netherfield.

But that... that was a dream. Was it not?

Her wrist warmed beneath the covers, a small, disquieting pulse she did not examine. Not with that creature staring as if waiting for her next move.

The dog's ears flicked toward the hallway.

Voices. Low. Two of them. A man's tone she half-knew, tugging at recognition.

The dog rose—not quickly, not with enthusiasm, but with purpose. He stepped to the threshold, gaze fixed outward, muscles taut.

"Brutus? Brutus, what are you doing?"

The sound itself barely touched her. What caught her attention was the dog's pause—the alert way his ears shifted, the way he *considered* the doorway, then her, as though choosing between two duties. He looked torn—watchful—almost protective, and far too aware of *her* for a creature she had never met.

Then Mr Darcy appeared in the doorway.

He looked first at the dog, confusion written plainly across his features. Then his gaze shifted—too fast, too intent—straight to her.

She had not expected the jolt of embarrassment that followed. Her hair—she could feel it tangled across her temple. Her gown—where was her gown? What about her pelisse, her stays, her petticoat? She was not even decent!

And Mr Darcy stared at her as though he had not planned on seeing her awake.

"Miss Elizabeth," he said quietly.

Her lips parted, but nothing coherent followed. The room sat strangely crooked for a moment, tilted and skewed as if reality itself had bent. She caught one breath, thin and unsteady.

Darcy stepped forward—and halted at once, as though suddenly aware of proximity, propriety, every rule that governed sickrooms and young ladies.

"Forgive the intrusion," he said. "Brutus slipped away from me. I—I had not meant..." His voice trailed when she blinked too slowly.

"Lizzy?"

Elizabeth startled. Jane was there, crossing the room toward her. "Lizzy, you are awake!"

Her whole body flinched. Jane's voice wasn't a memory this time—it was real, and she was rushing past Darcy, dropping to her knees beside the bed. Her hands fluttered—one brushing Elizabeth's hair back, another cupping her cheek with the gentlest caution. "Oh, my dear girl. I stepped out only for a moment—they told me you would be sleeping for hours yet—I never meant to leave you alone."

Elizabeth tried to smile. It felt crooked. "I am... awake now."

"Yes." Jane laughed a small, trembling breath. "Yes, you are. And quite yourself again, I see."

Elizabeth held the expression, though her limbs still felt as though they belonged to someone else. *Quite yourself* suggested a comparison, and the idea of what she must have been moments before stirred unease. "What happened?"

Jane's fingers tightened around hers. "You were tired. Very tired. You frightened us, Lizzy, but that is past now. There is no need to trouble yourself with it."

"But I caused a deal of fuss," Elizabeth said. It was not a question. She glanced past Jane, toward the doorway she had not quite dared to look at again. "Did I not?"

Mr Darcy had not moved from his place. He stood just inside the threshold, one hand resting on the doorframe, the other loosely at his side. Brutus waited behind him, alert and silent.

"You were unwell," Darcy said. He did not soften it. "Disoriented."

Jane shot him a look—quick, warning.

Elizabeth's gaze returned to him at once. "In what way?"

Darcy hesitated. Not long. Only long enough to seem as though he had considered evasion and rejected it. "You spoke. Not always to those in the room."

Jane leaned closer. "Lizzy, truly—"

Elizabeth did not look at her sister. "What did I say?"

Darcy's mouth opened. Closed again. For a moment, she thought he would tell her regardless of Jane's disapproval.

Then Jane's look hardened—Elizabeth had almost thought her sister incapable of such an expression.

Darcy exhaled with a grimace. "Nothing of consequence," he said, though the words did not entirely convince. He straightened. "You should rest. Mr Jones will wish to see you again shortly." He turned toward the dog. "Brutus. Come."

The dog rose at once and came to heel, though his head turned back once, gaze lingering on Elizabeth before he followed.

Darcy paused only long enough to incline his head. "Miss Elizabeth."

"Mr Darcy."

He withdrew, the door closing softly behind him.

Elizabeth lay back against the pillows, the space he had left feeling oddly bare. Jane brushed her hair away from her temple with gentle insistence.

"You need not worry," Jane said. "You are safe now."

Everyone kept telling her that. Elizabeth sighed and stared at the ceiling. *Spoke. Not always to those in the room.*

She shut her eyes, dizzy with memory.

DARCY DESCENDED THE STAIRS slowly, as though his footsteps on the carpet might carry upward and disturb the fragile order that had finally settled in the bedchamber above. The house felt altered—no longer merely Netherfield, but something temporarily rearranged around the presence of a guest who had not arrived by invitation.

Bingley was pacing the length of the drawing room, turning sharply at each end as if he meant to wear a path into the carpet. He stopped short when he caught sight of Darcy.

"Well?" he asked at once. "Is she—did she wake again?"

"For a moment," Darcy said. He took the chair nearest the window without quite meaning to. "She is clearer than before. Still weak."

Bingley let out a breath and dragged a hand through his hair. "Thank heaven. I thought—when Jones shook his head like that—" He broke off, then resumed his circuit. "I cannot abide waiting. It feels heartless to sit when a friend and neighbour is upstairs—"

"It would not serve her for the house to turn itself inside out. She requires quiet."

Miss Bingley, who had been seated at the escritoire with an air of injured patience, rose at once. "Of course she does," she said. "Though I cannot imagine what possessed Miss Elizabeth Bennet to walk so far alone. It is scarcely prudent behaviour."

Mrs Hurst nodded. "One hears so many cautionary tales. A young lady wandering without escort—"

Darcy did not look at either of them. His gaze fixed instead on the far wall, where the light fell evenly and refused to waver. "She did not wander," he said. "She was walking, as many do for exercise. There is no impropriety in it."

Miss Bingley's brows lifted. "I meant no offense. Only that the household must now manage a delicate situation. Her mother will certainly wish for her to remain here, and for goodness knows how long."

Bingley stopped pacing. "As long as she needs. Jane Bennet will stay with her. Nicholls is perfectly capable of managing the maids for her care. And if there is anything more to be done, it shall be done."

Darcy's attention shifted then—to the foot of the stairs, where Brutus lay stretched across the rug, head lifted, eyes trained upward. The dog had not moved since they returned. Not even at the sound of voices, which was strange enough, for he usually listened to conversations as if he could comprehend them.

Miss Bingley followed his look and frowned. “Must he lie there?”

“He will not stir unless called,” Darcy said. He did not add that Brutus rarely chose such a post without reason.

Mrs Hurst folded her hands. “It will look odd, you know. Two Bennets staying on, and for no cause Mr Jones could determine. People talk.”

“Let them,” Bingley said, already turning away again. “They talk whether invited or not.”

Darcy listened to the exchange with only half his mind. The other half remained upstairs, replaying a question Miss Elizabeth had asked—*What did I say?*—and the look she had fixed on him while waiting for an answer he had chosen not to give.

Then there were footsteps in the hall. A servant appeared at the door, holding out a small tray. “A letter for Mr Darcy, sir. Just arrived.”

Darcy rose at once. He took the letter from the servant with a brief “Thank you.” Richard’s seal caught the light.

Bingley halted mid-stride. “News from Pemberley? I hope your sister is well.”

“From Fitzwilliam. He was in London last week,” Darcy said, and turned away before the question could widen.

He broke the seal standing, unfolding the page with controlled movements while Miss Bingley resumed speaking—something about accommodation, about whether Mrs Bennet would insist on bringing the younger sisters, about how exhausting it must be for Miss Bennet to sit up so long and for so little cause. The words washed past him.

Richard’s hand was brisk, the lines tight.

> *Darcy,*
>
> *You will be pleased to know that I have been deemed indispensable once again. Evidently, England cannot be defended without my presence in a place no one has thought worth occupying for the better part of thirty years.*

Darcy snorted. Typical.

*The post is temporary, they say. Everything is 'temporary' when one is being sent somewhere unpleasant. I am to leave within the week, and I am assured—very earnestly—that this is not a punishment, nor a test, nor a correction of any sort. You may imagine how reassuring that is.*

Miss Bingley was speaking behind him—something about Mrs Bennet's nervous tendencies, Bingley retorted with something about sending word to the apothecary that Miss Elizabeth was now alert—but Darcy did not turn. He read on.

*The official explanation involves altered conditions, re-evaluated trade routes, and the need for a steady hand where men have begun to complain of dwindling supplies. You will be amused to hear that the complaints are not about the enemy, but candle wax. Candle wax! And ale, naturally. I daresay they have been overrunning their rations, for the matter was well in hand when I left. I told them soldiers have been sneaking into the troop stores since Agincourt, and that this hardly constitutes novelty.*

Darcy's jaw set.

*Still, someone higher up has decided this discomfort requires a Fitzwilliam to observe it. I drew the short straw, apparently. Do not trouble yourself. I have endured worse than a few reluctant supply lines and an inconvenient posting.*

A pause in the writing showed where Richard had hesitated—only briefly.

*The name of the region is wretchedly poetic. You would recognise it. I laughed when I heard it and was told, very politely, that I need not. I am bound again for Ciudad Rodrigo. I expect I shall be bored, cold, and irritated, but otherwise intact. Give my love to Georgiana. Do not allow her to read between the lines—I have taken pains to make them dull. Write when you can.*

*Your affectionate cousin,*

*R.F.*

Darcy folded the letter once. Then again. He could picture Richard perfectly—smiling as he delivered the lines, shrugging as though the matter were of no consequence, already shouldering the burden so no one else need protest.

It was not right.

Not the posting. Not the timing. Not the way Richard had circled the truth without naming it.

Darcy crossed the room and set the letter down on the escritoire, his movements controlled only because he forced them to be. This was not how assignments were made. Not for officers of Richard's experience and standing. Not without cause.

And yet, cause had been supplied. Supplies running short. Shipping lanes blocked, perhaps? Or was there something amiss with the acquisition and production of those supplies?

He thought of the steward's earlier letter, folded and ignored too long. Of exposed roots where no rain had scoured them. Of markers turned up as though the land itself had shifted.

Of Miss Elizabeth Bennet, pale and insensible on the grass, her presence there inexplicable by any sensible measure.

The world had acquired an irritating habit of placing obstacles at his feet and demanding he step over them without explanation.

Darcy pressed his fingers briefly to the bridge of his nose. This was not superstition. He would not have it so. There were answers for everything—misjudgements, coincidences, human error.

Weather. Coincidence. Misfortune. He had been taught those answers before. He had learned young how often they were used to smooth over neglect.

Unbidden, an old cadence rose in his mind—something his grandfather had once recited with infuriating solemnity, about land held in trust and lines drawn not for ownership but for keeping. About vigilance. About what happened when watchfulness lapsed.

Utter superstition.

Elizabeth woke again to the quiet creak of a chair and the soft brush of fabric.

Jane sat beside the bed, her bonnet laid carefully on the table, her gloves folded with exaggerated neatness in her lap. At the sight of Elizabeth's open eyes, she smiled at once—then stopped herself, as though afraid of encouraging too much.

"You are awake again," Jane said. "Properly awake, I think."

Elizabeth shifted, discovering at once the truth Jane had not spoken. Her limbs felt distant, obedient only after consideration, as though they belonged to someone else who had to be consulted before movement was allowed. She managed a nod.

"I do not seem... very impressive," she said, and was faintly startled by how dry her own voice sounded.

Jane's smile wavered. "You need not be impressive. You only need to rest."

Elizabeth studied her sister's face, the careful composure, the way her hands had folded and refolded in her lap. "You have been saying that all day," she said slowly. "I wonder if anyone believes it."

Jane hesitated. "Of course. You only had a bit of a strain of some sort. Why even Papa was perfectly assured that another day or two would see you right."

Elizabeth's brows drew together. "Papa was here?"

Jane exhaled, the breath half a laugh and half something else. "Yes, quite the surprise. He sat in the chair by the window and pretended to read. He did not turn the page once."

Elizabeth's mouth curved despite herself. "That bad?"

"He told me—quite seriously—that you were not to be hurried for anyone's convenience, including your own. And then he asked whether you preferred essays or histories when you were feeling unwell."

Elizabeth blinked. "Papa? Asking after my preferences?"

Jane nodded.

Elizabeth lay back against the pillows. "That sounds suspiciously like him attempting to look cheerful and failing."

Jane laughed. "He sent these." She reached for the small stack of books arranged at the edge of the table and brought them nearer.

Elizabeth recognised her father's taste at once: the selection was unmistakable. Humorous essays. A history she had once remarked upon and never found in the house. Two volumes still stiff at the spine, their pages uncut. And at least two books that had certainly not come from Longbourn.

"He went into Meryton himself," Jane said. "This morning. He said the shopkeeper was very obliging, though he did not approve of being forbidden to recommend anything 'improving.'"

Elizabeth stared at the books. For a moment, she could not think what to say.

"Papa?" she said at last. "Went into Meryton? And he purchased these just for me?"

Jane nodded. "He would not hear of sending anyone else."

That did not fit. Her father was many things—observant, indulgent, quietly fond—but he was not given to displays or expenditures. Elizabeth had expected concern, yes, and perhaps a wry remark delivered afterward to reassure himself that the world remained sensible. She had not expected effort.

"He was... upset, then," she said, more question than assertion.

Jane's expression softened. "Very."

Elizabeth looked away, unsettled by the word. It sat oddly beside her image of him, as though someone had spoken of a familiar landscape under an unfamiliar light.

"And Mama?" she asked, bracing herself.

Jane hesitated.

"Jane?"

"She was delighted." Jane cleared her throat. "Quite delighted, in fact. She said it was the best possible arrangement, that Netherfield was far superior to Longbourn for recovery, and that she had always maintained you would benefit from a change of air."

Elizabeth shut her eyes briefly. "Of course she did. I shouldn't wonder that she will be here herself to oversee my 'recovery' as soon as I can stir from the bed."

"Not at all, for Papa forbade her to come," Jane added quickly. "Very firmly. He said—" She paused, then smiled despite herself. "He said that you wanted quiet, not fresh lace."

Elizabeth's lips curved, despite her fatigue. Surprise flickered beneath it—her father setting his foot down so decisively—but relief followed close behind. The thought of her mother sweeping into the room, voice raised with concern and satisfaction in equal measure, was more exhausting than the faint ache still lingering behind her eyes.

"I am grateful," she said. "For once, I believe Papa and I are of precisely the same mind."

Jane reached out and touched her hand. "Indeed. And if you did not hear me before, I shall repeat it—Papa asked me to tell you that you are not to hurry yourself on his account. Or Mama's. Or anyone's."

Elizabeth absorbed that in silence.

"I should like to go home as soon as I may," she said finally. "Not because I am uncomfortable here. Everyone has been exceedingly kind. But I would rather be ill at Longbourn than well anywhere else."

Jane's eyes shone with understanding. "I know."

Elizabeth's gaze drifted back to the books. The thought of reading—of losing herself in familiar argument and voice—was tempting. Comforting, even. But as soon as she imagined opening one, the weight behind her eyes deepened, heavy and insistent.

"I should like to read," she admitted. "But I do not think I should make it past the first page."

"Then do not attempt it."

"You need not stay and watch me stare at the walls," Elizabeth added gently. "Go downstairs. Mr Bingley is beside himself with the desire to be useful, and Miss Bingley will no doubt be relieved to have someone sensible to impress."

Jane hesitated. "Are you certain?"

Elizabeth nodded. "I am. I shall sleep better knowing you are not hovering."

Jane laughed softly at that, rose, and bent to press a kiss to her sister's temple. "Very well. But I shall not be far."

"I know," Elizabeth said.

When Jane had gone, the room settled again into quiet.

Elizabeth closed her eyes, the weight of sleep already pulling at her, and wondered—distantly, uneasily—how much worse she must have been, to inspire such effort from her father, such restraint from her mother, and such careful kindness from everyone else.

The thought did not trouble her long, for sleep claimed her first.

# Chapter Eleven

Elizabeth had reached the place where reading ceased to be an occupation and became a kind of penance.

She had finished the same paragraph three times without retaining so much as a phrase. The words lay politely on the page, offering themselves to her attention, and she refused them with equal politeness. Her eyes slid away. Her thoughts drifted. The book—one of those her father had newly bought in Meryton, rested open in her hands.

She shut it.

The room was quiet in the particular way of a house that was too large for its occupants. Longbourn had its own sounds even when empty: a floorboard that never quite held its peace, the distant clatter of the back stairs, a cough from the library that might or might not be Papa. Here, everything was orderly. Even the silence seemed arranged.

Elizabeth shifted against the pillows, then swung her legs over the side of the bed and stood. Then she buckled from an odd softness in the knees. A delay between thought and action. She waited it out, hands braced lightly on the coverlet, until the room steadied and her annoyance returned in full force.

She was not an invalid. She had fainted, yes—but fainting was hardly a declaration of permanent incapacity. And she would not remain upstairs like some delicate ornament while the household proceeded below her without explanation or apology.

Dinner would be taken soon. Even if she did not hear Jane next door, retired to dress, she would know the hour by instinct alone. Her body still kept its own clocks, at least.

Elizabeth crossed to the looking glass and examined herself with a critical eye. Pale. Thinner than she liked. But her eyes were clear enough, and there was no reason—no reason at all—that she should not present herself, smile calmly, and put an end to the whispered concern that had settled over her like a fog.

She chose her gown carefully. Not the one Mama had clearly sent along with hopes of securing a bachelor's notice. One of her older favourites, no doubt secreted in the trunk by Jane. Something that would not invite comment. She pinned her hair with more care than usual, her fingers slower, more deliberate, until the familiar shape returned her to herself.

There. Respectable. Ordinary.

She opened the door. The passage beyond was empty. The house breathed quietly around her, a low, even sound that made no demand upon her notice. She stepped out and drew the door closed behind her. The stairs lay ahead. She placed her hand on the rail and began her descent.

The first steps passed without remark. The carpet was firm beneath her slippers; the banister smooth and cool beneath her palm. She told herself—absurdly—that she had been foolish to hesitate at all.

Then something... happened.

It was not her footing. Not her balance. The world itself seemed to tilt, just enough to make her pause. The depth of the next step was wrong. The distance between her and the wall skewed oddly, as though the space had been rearranged while she was not looking.

Elizabeth stopped.

She set her foot down again—and the world slipped.

Not a stumble. Not a sway. The stair did not move, yet her stomach lurched as if it had. The banister crept sideways at the edge of her vision, the angle of the steps subtly wrong, as though the house had shifted its opinion of her weight. Her pulse jumped, hard enough to throb in her ears, and a sour heat rose beneath her ribs.

Elizabeth froze. "No," she whispered, more in irritation than fear. "That is ridiculous."

The space before her felt *closed*. Not blocked—*refused*. The air pressed back faintly, like water against a palm. When she turned her head, just a little, the sensation eased at once. Facing the stairs again brought it rushing back, sharper now, decisive, impossible to mistake.

She knew, with a clarity that stole her breath: if she took another step forward, she would fall.

Not trip. Not faint.

*Fall*—because the house would no longer hold her.

She withdrew her foot and straightened, her heart beating harder now, though she could not have said why. The moment she turned upward, the feeling eased. The stair returned to itself. The space behaved.

Elizabeth stared at the steps below her, then behind her, then below again. This was the same wrongness she had felt two days earlier. Not the fall. But the instant before—the moment when the world had ceased to agree with her understanding of it.

She backed up a step. At the base of the stairs, something moved.

A large dog sat squarely on the rug, dark head lifted, his body aligned with the stair as though placed there with intention. *Darcy's dog.* Brutus.

"Oh," Elizabeth said faintly.

His tail struck the floor once. Almost like a salute.

She tried a smile, because she had always believed it best to greet animals as one would sensible people. "Good evening, Brutus," she said. "I was hoping you and I might be on friendlier terms than the house and I currently are."

The dog did not blink.

She descended one more step. The sensation returned immediately—stronger now, unmistakable. Her body recoiled before her thoughts could catch up, a refusal so swift it left her breath shallow and her hand tight on the rail.

The dog did not move aside.

Elizabeth swallowed. "I am not attempting escape," she told him, though the words left her before she had quite decided to speak. "Only dinner."

For a heartbeat, nothing happened. Then Brutus rose.

He unfolded himself to his full height and stepped forward, placing his body squarely between her and the stair. His chest filled the narrow space, broad and solid as a gate. A low sound left him, not a growl exactly, but something deeper, more deliberate. A warning shaped without anger.

Elizabeth's breath left her in a short, involuntary rush. "Oh," she said again. "Blast, where is your master?" She craned her neck to see what she could of the hall below the stair.

The dog's ears flicked toward the corridor below. His head angled slightly, not toward her, but past her—as if attending to something she could not see.

Voices drifted upward from below. Human voices. Familiar ones. Mr Bingley's laugh. A woman's reply. Perfectly ordinary sounds, and yet the knowledge of them pressed against her skin in a way she could not explain. *Where* was Mr Darcy? Any gentleman ought to keep a better watch on his dog, particularly one as big and as... *odd*... as this one.

Her foot slid back without conscious instruction.

The dog did not advance. He did not need to. He held the line as though it had always been there, and she was the one who had forgot it.

Elizabeth retreated another step. Brutus's head lowered a fraction—not toward her, but toward the stair—until she stood fully clear of it. Only then did he sit.

The corridor behind her felt suddenly safer, though she could not have said why. She reached the top of the stairs and leaned her shoulder briefly to the wall, the stone cool through her sleeve.

Elizabeth went quietly back to her room and closed the door with care. The silence returned at once, complete and watchful. She crossed to the bed and sat, hands folded in her lap, heart still beating too fast for rest.

She could not go home yet.

The decision formed without effort, as though it had been waiting for her to catch up to it. Whatever had checked her steps on the stair had done so with too much certainty to be dismissed as fancy or lingering weakness. It had not frightened her so much as corrected her.

Until she understood what lay beneath that correction—what had placed its hand upon her path and turned her back—she would have to remain where she was.

"I always find," Miss Bingley was saying, as she adjusted her embroidery frame, "that evenings are best enjoyed when one resists the urge to fill every silence."

Bingley laughed and shifted his chair closer to the fire. "I do not know that I have ever found silence difficult to endure, provided the company is agreeable."

Miss Bennet stood near the window, one hand resting lightly on the curtain as she looked out into the darkened garden. "I think I shall go upstairs presently," she said. "Elizabeth has been resting for some time, and I would like to see whether—"

"Oh, she will ring if she wakes," Miss Bingley replied, her needle flashing as it dipped. "Mrs Nicholls is quite attentive. You need not keep watch every moment."

Miss Bennet turned back with a polite smile that did not quite conceal her unease. "I know. Still—"

"You must take your comfort while you may, Miss Bennet," Bingley said warmly. "You have scarcely had a moment to rest since you arrived."

She hesitated, then resumed her seat, though her gaze lingered on the doorway as if already half gone.

Darcy had taken possession of the small escritoire near the wall, where the candles threw a steady light upon paper and ink. He wrote with intent concentration, aware of the room only as a murmur at his back.

He had opened Bingley's modest bookcase earlier—agricultural treatises of uneven quality, a county history, two volumes of sermons—and extracted what little might serve him. It was not much, but it was something. He wrote steadily, his pen scratching out instructions to his steward: drainage channels to be cleared, a survey of older plantings along the boundary, a request—carefully phrased—that inquiries be made of neighbouring estates without stirring alarm.

Darcy paused at the end of the line, the pen hovering while he considered how much authority he might reasonably claim without provoking resistance. The margin of the page had begun to fill with small, precise adjustments—practicalities, contingencies, the kind of measured response that calmed the mind by occupying it.

Beside the paper lay Richard's letter, folded once, then again, as if its contents might be reduced by compression. Ciudad Rodrigo had lodged itself in his thoughts regardless, its name incongruously lyrical for a place that demanded men be sent where they were most easily lost.

He set the pen down, drew a breath, and returned to his work. Whatever his cousin had been ordered to do, fretting would not alter it. What could be altered—what must be—was everything else still within his reach.

Miss Bennet rose from her chair once more. "I am so sorry, but I still feel I ought to look in on my sister. She has been quiet a long while."

Before Miss Bingley could agree with her, Bingley protested. "Nonsense, you must not vanish just yet. Let us give you a bit of enjoyment before you retire. Come—Caroline, will you not play something? A reel perhaps? It would do Miss Bennet good to be diverted."

Miss Bingley looked down at her hands as though noticing them for the first time. "I would, if I could," she said regretfully, "but I have quite ruined my nail. See? It caught during dinner. I doubt I could manage a proper touch."

"I am sure no one would mind a slight imperfection," Bingley said earnestly. "And Darcy does not require perfection to be entertained."

Darcy did not look up from his writing. If he had, he would have denied the charge.

Miss Bingley's voice tightened. "Even so, the room has grown very warm. Dancing would only make it worse. Miss Bennet ought to be resting as well—surely we have done enough to excite her spirits for one evening."

Miss Bennet hesitated, her hands clasped loosely before her. "I should only be a moment—"

"After you have sat," Bingley insisted, drawing out a chair with easy good nature. "Five minutes. I promise not to detain you longer."

She yielded, though her gaze strayed again toward the door.

Darcy's pen slowed, irritation stirring not at the exchange itself, but at the familiar pattern of it: good intentions pressed into service of delay, comfort offered where none was wanted, and all of it circling the very thing no one seemed inclined to address directly. Darcy's pen paused.

Miss Bennet hesitated, caught between inclination and courtesy. "Very well," she said at last, and allowed herself to be guided back toward her chair.

Darcy returned to his letter, though the line he had meant to complete dissolved beneath his eyes. Brutus should have been asleep by now, stretched before the hearth or stationed obediently at his heel. Instead, the dog had chosen to sit at the base of the stair and would not be moved. Darcy had called him twice. The second time, Brutus had looked at him deliberately, and remained where he was.

Ill-trained behaviour. Unacceptable.

Miss Bingley set down her embroidery with a sigh designed to be overheard. "It is quite admirable of you to keep such close watch over your sister, Miss Bennet. One would hardly expect it in a household with so... *many* sisters."

Miss Bennet inclined her head. "Elizabeth has always been her own keeper," she said. "I only assist when she allows it."

"A charming arrangement," Miss Bingley said. "Though I imagine it must be a relief to have her *here*, where one may be certain she is properly attended."

Darcy's jaw tightened. *Properly attended*. As though Miss Elizabeth's collapse were a consequence of mismanagement rather than... well, he did not know what. The blank space where an explanation ought to be troubled him more than any faulty one offered in its place.

Miss Bingley had resumed her embroidery, the soft pull of silk through linen marking time. Mrs Hurst lounged beside her, idly turning her bracelet so that the firelight caught each link in turn. Bingley, restless in his concern, crossed the room and back again, pausing near the window before drifting toward the hearth, as though movement itself might resolve what conversation would not.

Mrs Hurst spoke first, her tone even and incurious. "If Miss Elizabeth wakes, she will hardly be alone. Mrs Nicholls is in the house, and the servants know where to find her."

"Yes," Miss Bingley added at once. "And Miss Bennet has already done everything that could reasonably be expected. One does not improve matters by hovering."

Bingley's chair creaked, and his voice sounded a little uncertain. "Quite right. Still, Miss Bennet's instincts are laudable. I should not like her to feel as if she cannot go—"

"Miss Bennet is patience itself, but brother, you must not let her tire herself," Miss Bingley said, lightly decisive. "It is far more sensible that Miss Bennet rest while she may. This has been quite an exerting day."

Darcy's pen slowed.

*Hovering. Exertion.* Words chosen not to comfort, but to conclude.

Miss Bennet made a small noise in her throat.

Bingley nodded, though without conviction. "I should hate to see you made uneasy, Miss Bennet. Truly, we enjoy your company, but if it will ease your mind to go upstairs—"

Miss Bennet had been listening with a politeness that grew more strained by the moment. She rose again, this time without apology.

"Yes, sir, I appreciate your hospitality. Very much, in fact, but I have been away from her two hours already," she said. "If she wakes and finds herself alone—"

Darcy set his pen down, then hesitated with his hand still resting on the desk. Rising now would draw notice. Remaining seated after she left, and the party called on him for entertainment would draw more. He weighed the balance and found neither side comfortable.

"I shall retire as well," he said at last. The words were ordinary enough to pass without comment. He paused, then added, as though the thought had only just occurred to him, "I mean to take an early ride. I will see Miss Bennet to the stair."

It was the smallest courtesy. Entirely defensible. And yet he was aware, even as he spoke, of the faint resistance in himself, as though some other part of him had hoped the moment might pass without requiring decision.

Miss Bennet turned toward him, surprise giving way to gratitude. "Thank you, Mr Darcy. I should not wish to trouble anyone."

Bingley brightened immediately. "That is very kind of you, Darcy. Miss Bennet, you see? We all wish your comfort, whatever you require. Do let us know if we can do anything, please."

Miss Bingley's reply came a fraction too quickly. "You need not inconvenience yourself," she said. "The stair is hardly perilous, and you have had a long day."

Darcy rose. The chair legs marked the floor with a soft complaint. "It is no inconvenience."

He did not look at her as he spoke it. He did not need to. The justification was sufficient; the form was observed. If his patience had worn thin, that was his own affair.

Darcy offered his arm, and Miss Bennet accepted it with quiet relief. They passed into the hall together, the warmth of the drawing room giving way to cooler air and the hush that followed evening's retreat. The lamps had been lit along the passage, their light steady, unremarkable. Nothing in the house appeared out of order.

He told himself this twice.

Brutus was still guarding the stair. The dog sat squarely on the rug before the first step, his great head lifted, his body aligned with the stair as though he had been placed there deliberately. He did not rise at Darcy's approach. He did not wag. He watched.

Darcy halted.

Miss Bennet's hand tightened briefly on his sleeve. "Oh," she said, and then, more softly, "I did not know he was here."

"He should not be," Darcy replied.

"He is a very *large* dog, sir. Is he quite safe?"

"Quite safe." Darcy snapped his fingers. "Brutus. Here."

The dog's ears shifted, but he did not move. Darcy felt the faintest stir of irritation. "Come *here*."

Brutus looked at him—held his gaze a moment longer than habit allowed—then turned his head slightly, not toward Darcy, but toward the stair.

Darcy's mouth tightened.

"Brutus," he said again, with more authority. "Heel."

The dog remained where he was. His tail struck the floor once, a single heavy sound, neither greeting nor defiance. He merely extended one paw and licked it as if in meditation.

Miss Bennet drew a breath. "Perhaps he is injured?"

"He is not injured," Darcy said, and then stopped himself. He could not say what the dog was, only what he was not.

He stepped forward. Brutus did not bare his teeth. He did not growl. But the dog rose to his feet, slowly and deliberately, and placed himself fully between Darcy and the stair.

Darcy froze.

This was wrong. Brutus had never barred his path. Never. The dog had been trained to yield, to obey, to trust instruction over instinct. Darcy had raised him with care, with consistency, and he had never needed to test this.

Miss Bennet shifted beside him. "Mr Darcy—"

"Stay," Darcy said quietly, though he did not know whether he meant the dog or the lady.

He studied Brutus more closely now. There was no agitation in him. No alarm. Only attention. The kind of attention a sentry might give to a gate.

"This is absurd," he said under his breath, and tried again. "Brutus. Away."

The dog's head lowered a fraction—not in submission, but in acknowledgment. He did not retreat.

Darcy glanced up the stair. The passage above lay empty, perfectly ordinary. No sound. No movement. Nothing to justify—

Brutus's gaze followed *him*.

Not Miss Bennet. Not the stair itself. Darcy. The dog's attention did not waver as Darcy shifted his weight or turned his head; it tracked him with a steady, unblinking focus that raised the fine hairs along his arms.

Darcy let out a slow breath. "Wait here," he said to Miss Bennet. "One moment."

He stepped aside, breaking the line between the dog and the stair. Brutus did not follow him. He held his position—still aligned with the steps, still watching Darcy, as though the space mattered less than the man approaching it.

A brief, unwelcome calculation followed. Calling the dog again would look foolish. Lifting a hand to collar him would require explanation. And Miss Bennet—already weary, already strained—stood waiting for him to decide what to do about a very large, very stubborn animal.

Darcy stepped back instead.

He paused, then added, as if only just considering it, "Brutus is not attending to you, Miss Bennet. He has taken some private objection to *me* this evening. I shall answer for it. Like enough, he has it in mind to oblige me to procure him another bone from Mrs Nicholls."

She looked doubtful. "He is that clever?"

"Absolutely. See how his eyes never leave me? Take a step toward the stair, Miss Bennet."

She nodded and did so. Brutus never even glanced at her.

"Ah, you see. I have him fairly, the old criminal." The corner of his mouth lifted—barely. "You need not concern yourself."

Miss Bennet hesitated, then inclined her head. "Good night, Mr Darcy."

"Good night." He waited until she had turned away before looking back at the dog.

Brutus remained where he was.

And Darcy turned back for the servant's staircase.

# Chapter Twelve

Sleep came to him unevenly, as it often did when his mind refused to relinquish its hold upon the day. He lay aware of the bed, of the hangings stirred faintly by a draught he had not noticed before retiring, of Brutus shifting once at the foot of the mattress before settling again. It should have been enough. He had known harder nights than this.

Yet when the dream took him, it did so without even a hint of warning.

He was walking—no, inspecting—a stretch of land that ought to have been familiar. By the view of a low hill in the distance, the river cutting across the valley below, it was the same land he had stalked with Bingley only yesterday.

The lie of the hedge, the thinning grass where water gathered, the shallow descent toward lower ground—all of it answered to expectation. His attention moved as it always did, measuring, noting, arranging what he saw into habit and record.

One moment, he was filling his lungs, marking breaks in the grass where a hare had flushed, trees in the stand still green and full, listening to Brutus ranging on ahead.

Then his stride shortened.

Not by intention. Not by misstep. His foot lifted and set down again, but the distance it carried him had diminished, as though the ground itself had subtly altered its measure. The next step required attention. The next, effort.

He stopped and drew breath.

The breath came, but without force behind it. His chest rose; the air reached him thinly, as though some deeper correspondence had failed. A faint tremor passed through his legs—not pain, not alarm, but enough to set his nerves on edge.

He waited, but the sensation did not pass. Fatigue, he told himself. A residue of poor sleep. Of long days. Such things left impressions even in dreams.

Perhaps there was a slight incline here, gradual enough that he had not marked it. He adjusted his stance and went on.

The weakness deepened with the next step. His sight remained clear; the world did not reel. Yet something essential drained from him with each attempt to advance, as though the effort of standing upright were no longer fully his to command. His arms hung heavier. His knees answered him by degrees so small they might have gone unnoticed, had he not been watching himself so closely.

He stopped again, his heart pounding as if he had run a mile.

The ground ahead was broken.

Not by hedge or ditch or any deliberate boundary, but by a long, jagged fissure torn through the earth itself—as though floodwater or tremor had split the land open and never been mended. The edges were raw. The soil beneath lay exposed, dark and uneven, falling away into a depth he could not sound.

Beyond it, the land continued.

He knew it at once—not by detail, but by recognition. Hertfordshire lay beneath his feet, but what rose on the far side belonged to another order of knowing. In the distance, that same mountain lifted against the horizon, its shape unmistakable. He had seen it before, surely! From afar. Never like this.

At the edge of the rupture stood a thorn tree. It did not mark a boundary in the common sense—neither hedge nor orchard nor fence—yet it claimed the place with an authority that halted his gaze. He could not have said why. Only that his attention fixed upon it and would not be persuaded elsewhere.

At its base stood a woman, turned from him.

Her cloak hung loosely from her shoulders, hair snarled free of its pins by wind or neglect. He could not see her face, and the absence did not feel accidental. As though to look upon her directly would require more than he yet possessed.

But he knew her.

Not by feature or dress, not by any detail he could later name, but by the certainty of her presence. The line of her shoulders struck him with a familiarity that burned, like the sudden recall of a name learned long ago and never spoken since.

"Madam," he said, meaning only courtesy.

She did not turn.

"I am not—" He faltered. Whatever ought to follow refused coherence. The words he reached for—explanation, entitlement, insistence—collapsed before they could take form, as though they did not apply here.

"You are not real," he said instead, the words brittle, offered as resistance rather than belief.

She turned.

Not all at once, but enough that he knew her utterly. Her face would not resolve—featureless in that peculiar way of dreams—yet recognition struck him with a force no clarity could have improved. She lifted her hand toward him. Not imploring. Not urgent. Simply held out, as one might indicate the only course that exists.

The ground between them yawned open. A raw break in the earth, torn wide by water and upheaval, its edges crumbling still. He saw at once what no courage could alter: there was no bridge, no footing, no leap to be made. Not by a man. Not by a horse. Not by any means he had ever trusted. His breath staggered, sharp and panicked, and the old instincts rose in him—measure, retreat, command.

"What is this?" The words scattered even as he spoke them—Netherfield, the morning, duty, the ordinary course of things—each excuse failing the moment it touched the air. "I want nothing to do with any of this!"

Her hand did not withdraw.

Something in him broke loose then—not fear, not pain, but the last, desperate motion of assent. He stepped forward without ground to receive him, reaching for what could not yet be reached—and the strength that had held him upright, intact, certain of himself, simply ceased.

His arms pinwheeled as he stumbled backward, but no power of man could save him now. Whatever had held him together—muscle, balance, the habit of standing—gave way all at once. He did not feel himself fall. There was simply no ground left to meet him.

There was no suffering in it. Only the certainty that Fitzwilliam Darcy had ended—not because he failed, but because he had answered.

DARCY BOLTED UPRIGHT IN his bed.

The chamber lay in darkness, the familiar lines of it momentarily strange. His heart beat hard against his ribs, not from terror but from a furious need to *understand*. He dragged in a breath that felt sharper than it ought, and pressed his hand against the mattress as if to reassure himself of its substance.

Brutus stirred, rising halfway before settling again at a wordless sound from Darcy's throat.

It was only a dream. A wild one—one that was already fading from memory.

Yet even as he told himself so, the image of the stone—newly uncovered, cold beneath his hand—was a sliver that refused to fade. He swung his legs over the side of the bed and rose, crossing to the window, though the night beyond offered nothing but darkness and the faintest suggestion of movement in the trees.

He stood there longer than he meant to, his thoughts circling restlessly, seeking purchase.

*Utter insanity,* he told himself again, with more force this time.

And yet sleep did not return.

Elizabeth snapped awake with the curious conviction that sleep had abruptly withdrawn from her, leaving her behind.

The chamber lay as she had last known it: the fire reduced to a steady glow, the curtains fallen into their proper folds, the air neither chill nor close. Nothing ached; nothing pressed upon her. And yet, remaining where she was felt impossible, as though rest had reached its limit and left some necessary motion unfinished.

She sat up.

The effort brought a brief wave of delirium—not pain, but a faint thinning of strength that required patience rather than alarm. She waited until it passed, then set her feet upon the floor and rose.

Once upright, she crossed the room, turned, and crossed it again, the narrow space between hearth and window marking her pace. With each circuit, her breathing eased, her pulse settling into its usual rhythm. She was not restored, precisely, but she was awake in a way she had not been since before the field—before that inexplicable yielding of ground which she could recall only as sensation, not event.

She opened the door.

The corridor beyond was empty, a single lamp burning at its far end, its flame steady and untroubled by her movement. Elizabeth stepped out and closed the door behind her with care, the soft click of the latch sounding louder than she liked in the quiet.

She walked on somewhat randomly. She was conscious of the floor beneath her feet—where the boards answered firmly, where they dipped by degrees scarcely worth remarking. She noted the faint current of air near the window recess, the thinning of the carpet runner along the wall. Everything was orderly, familiar, and unremarkable in the way of places one knows well enough to stop observing closely.

At the head of the main staircase, she halted. She was stronger now. Perhaps this time, she would not be beset by delirium.

Her foot lifted—and remained suspended. There was an unmistakable check, as though some inward balance had been disturbed by the direction itself. She lowered her foot again.

At once, the resistance... or whatever it was... eased.

Elizabeth stood for a moment, her hand resting lightly upon the banister. She tried again, more deliberately, as though a slower approach might make some difference.

It did not.

Facing the stairs produced a quiet but insistent wrongness that turning away did not. The distinction was immediate, beyond persuasion, as if she were attempting to begin where no beginning lay.

She stepped back. She had long since learned that the body sometimes refused co-operation without offering explanation, and that such refusals were rarely improved by argument.

Turning away from the staircase, she resumed her walk along the corridor, allowing the measured pace to restore her composure. Near the far end, beside a linen press she remembered only dimly, a narrow passage opened to the side. It was plainly not intended for guests: the ceiling dipped, the air carried the clean, faint scent of soap and starch.

Elizabeth turned into it and went on.

The servants' stair curved back upon itself, narrow and steep, turning away from the main body of the house before descending. Elizabeth set her hand to the wall as she went, steadying herself by habit rather than need. The plaster was cool beneath her palm.

Here, nothing barred her.

She went down a little way, then further, attentive not to the steps but to herself. There was no resistance. At the turn where the passage bent toward the lower floor, she slowed.

Light rose from below. Voices, too—low, indistinct, the familiar murmur of servants settling the house for the night. The sound ought to have reassured her. Instead, it brought back that faint inward pressure, not sharp enough to stop her, but sufficient to suggest that she had reached her limit.

*Enough.*

She turned, gathering her skirts to climb back.

"Miss Elizabeth?"

She started violently. Her shoulder struck the wall; her foot slipped on the stair. A breath tore from her before she could check it, sharp and humiliating, and her hand flew to her chest as though her heart required anchoring.

Mr Darcy stood a few steps below her.

One hand rested on the rail. The other held a book, forgotten. His expression was not alarmed, precisely, but intent, drawn in a way that made her suddenly, acutely aware of the narrowness of the stair and the closeness of his presence.

"I beg your pardon," he said. "I did not mean to startle you."

"I—" She drew another breath, forced it steady. "I could not sleep."

"I see."

His gaze lingered. Not searching her face so much as taking her in as she stood there—barefoot, shawl about her shoulders, her pulse still too near the surface.

"You have found the back stair? Not... er... avoiding anyone?" he asked.

"No." Her fingers tightened briefly in the wool at her throat. "I was walking."

"You seem to take a great deal of pleasure in walking."

There was no rebuke in his voice. Nor ease. He looked as though he were listening for something she could not hear.

She swallowed. "I... Mr Darcy, please do not tell them."

"Them... who?" His brows drew together. "That you are out of your room?"

"Not because I am well," she said quickly. "I am not—not entirely. But I needed to know whether I could move about without..." She stopped, vexed by the failure of words. "Without *it* returning."

He studied her then, openly. "'It?'"

Elizabeth cleared her throat. There was a sudden, unreasonable heat rising beneath her skin, a discomfort that had nothing to do with modesty and everything to do with being seen too clearly. She did not care to explain herself further.

"I will return to my room, without putting anyone out," she said. "I promise. I only wished to test myself."

"And you have done so. With... positive results, I trust?"

"Yes."

He opened his mouth, closed it again, and looked instead at the book in his hand, adjusting his grip as though it required attention. Elizabeth followed the motion without meaning to, then caught herself and looked away.

At last, he inclined his head. "Then it would be best to go back the way you came. Miss Bingley claims that steps as light as a cat would rouse her if too close to her room."

Relief loosened her all at once, sharp enough to leave her faint. She did not trust herself to speak again. She turned and climbed, conscious of him behind her until the passage curved and his presence fell away.

At her door, she paused only long enough to ease it shut. The quiet of the room rushed back upon her, too sudden after the stair, and she stood there a moment with her hand still on the latch, drawing breath as though she had climbed farther than she had.

She pressed her forehead briefly to the wood, willing the sensation down, irritated by its persistence. This was foolish. She was not ill. She had not imagined what she felt. And yet—

Longbourn rose in her mind at once: the familiar rooms, her father's voice, her mother's anxious attentions. The thought brought no comfort. Only a sharp, unreasoning certainty that if she went home now—if she placed herself again within those walls—whatever had begun to impose itself upon her would not lessen, but worsen.

She swallowed hard.

From the adjoining room came the faint rustle of movement—Jane turning in her bed, perhaps, or stirring toward wakefulness. The sound decided her. Elizabeth crossed the room at once and slipped beneath the covers, drawing them close as though they might hold her in place.

THE DOOR SHUT BEHIND him with enough force to make him jump in his skin.

Darcy halted, hand still on the latch, listening for any sound that might follow—footsteps, a startled voice, the scrape of a servant roused by the disturbance. Nothing came. The corridor remained hushed, the house settling back into its accustomed quiet as though it had not noticed him at all.

He released a breath and crossed the room in three long strides.

The candle on the escritoire guttered as he passed, stirred by the wake of his movement. He caught it, steadied the flame, and only then became aware that his heart had not yet resumed a sensible pace.

*Not fear*, he told himself sharply. Irritation. Startlement. The natural consequence of being roused from uneasy thoughts and encountering a young lady wandering where she ought not to have been.

Brutus padded in behind him and stopped. Darcy glanced back.

The dog did not go to his cushion. He did not circle before settling. He stood just inside the threshold, broad head lifted, gaze fixed—not on Darcy, but on the closed door.

Darcy frowned. "Enough," he commanded. "There is nothing there."

Brutus did not move.

Darcy turned away first. He knew better than to start a battle of wills with an Irish Wolfhound he could not win.

He set the book down upon the desk with deliberate care. It had come from the lower library—a slim, unassuming volume of county surveys, its leather rubbed thin by age and long neglect. He might have reached for any number of more engaging works, but had passed them all by without pause.

This one had promised certainty. Predictability.

Field boundaries. Parish lines. Measurements fixed to paper by men who understood land could be rendered obedient through ink and scale. No speculation. Nothing that trafficked in imagination.

He had taken it up because the dream had troubled him, though he would not have phrased it so even to himself. Because Brutus's conduct had demanded explanation that did not involve superstition. Because if something in the ground had *felt* wrong—if distance and direction had seemed briefly unreliable—then the sensible response was to consult what had been recorded when such things still behaved.

If there was nothing there, he would find nothing. And if there was something, then it would be named, dated, and properly accounted for.

He opened it now, standing rather than sitting, one hand braced against the edge of the desk. The pages yielded a faint, dry scent—dust, ink, something vegetal long pressed flat and forgotten.

Parishes. Acreage. Watercourses.

Orderly. Comfortingly dull.

Darcy read a paragraph without absorbing it, then another. His attention slipped, returning instead—unbidden—to the narrow stair, to Elizabeth Bennet standing there with her shawl drawn close, insisting she was only walking.

*Please do not tell them.*

The words pricked at him anew. Not fear. Resolve. She had known something was amiss, and she had chosen silence over spectacle.

He turned the page. A marginal note caught his eye—not in the same hand as the text, but cramped, angular, written with a pen sharpened to severity.

*Boundary altered after the great frost. Marker re-set by custom, not measurement.*

Darcy squinted and read it again.

Custom, not measurement.

He scanned the following lines more closely. A reference to a stand of hawthorn not aligned with any recorded hedgerow. A remark—dismissive, almost irritated—that local tenants avoided the ground "out of habit," though no impediment was visible.

Superstition, the author concluded. Nothing more. Darcy shut the book with a snap and paced toward the rug.

Brutus moved. Not toward him, but closer to the desk, placing himself between Darcy and the window now, body angled, watchful.

Darcy stared at the dog. "This is becoming tiresome."

Brutus's tail waved once. No jubilant wag. No rigid agitation. Simply acknowledgement.

Darcy passed a hand over his face and forced himself to think. He returned to the edge of the desk and stood there, one hand braced against the wood.

Elizabeth Bennet had not been on the main stair.

That, at least, was certain. No guest—no *lady*—wandered the servants' passages without reason, particularly not one already under scrutiny for her health. And yet she had been there, alert, composed, and determined enough to ask him not to betray her wandering.

Why?

He had no answer for that.

Nor could he account for Brutus's conduct.

The dog had barred *him* from the main stair earlier. Not with threat or agitation, but with a calm insistence that defied training and habit alike. Brutus did not guard capriciously. He did not invent dangers. And he had never, in all his years, placed himself bodily in Darcy's path without cause.

Had the dog done the same with her?

Darcy did not know. He had not asked. He had been too intent upon removing her from notice—and removing himself from her proximity—to examine the matter further.

And yet the fact remained: she had been using the servant's stair… and so had he, and all because of a blasted dog.

He frowned, irritated at the way it refused to resolve into sense. Fatigue muddled the edges of thought; conjecture bred conjecture. Whatever Brutus had perceived—whatever had drawn both master and guest away from the ordinary paths of the house—it would bear examination.

Tomorrow.

He would think more clearly tomorrow.

Darcy returned to the desk and opened the book again, this time with intent. He read more carefully, noting every reference to altered ground, every passing mention of boundaries observed by tradition rather than deed. The entries were scattered, unconnected, never lingered over—but they were there.

Always there.

Brutus lowered himself at last, settling beside the desk, head resting on his paws—but his eyes did not close.

Darcy straightened slowly.

He did not think of curses. He did not think of magic. He did not think of half-remembered ballads fit only for antiquarians and children.

He thought of stewardship. Of land held in trust.

Of rules established so long ago that forgetting them felt like progress.

"No," he said under his breath, not to the dog, nor to the book, but to the rising unease he refused to indulge. "I will not be made a fool of."

Brutus's ears flicked.

Darcy closed the book with care this time and carried it to the mantel to place it beside a few other volumes full of nonsense. He extinguished the candle, one deliberate pinch of fingers, and crossed back to the bed.

# Chapter Thirteen

Elizabeth woke before the house had fully agreed to morning.

The light lay pale and undecided upon the ceiling, caught between night's retreat and day's arrival. For a moment, she remained where she was, eyes open, breathing shallowly, taking stock not of her surroundings but of herself.

No dizziness. No trembling. No sense of *wrongness* darkening the corners of her thoughts. That was promising.

She sat up. The movement brought a brief rush of warmth to her face, a delay between intention and action that irritated her more than it alarmed her. Elizabeth waited it out, hands resting lightly upon the coverlet, gaze fixed on the far wall until the room settled back into proper proportion.

Very well, then.

She rose, crossed to the washstand, and splashed cool water upon her face. The mirror above it reflected a young woman pale enough to invite remark, but not so altered as to provoke alarm. Her eyes were clear. Her mouth firm. She would do.

Except, perhaps getting up was a mistake.

The thought had barely formed when sound reached her—footsteps, easy and unhurried, not the brisk purpose of a servant but the lighter, familiar tread she knew too well. Jane. Coming down the corridor, humming under her breath.

Elizabeth crossed the room in two quick strides, the hem of her nightgown brushing her ankles as she reached the bed and slipped beneath the coverlet, tugging it into place. Her bare feet were still chilled when she turned onto her side, schooling her breath, softening her posture, letting the moment of motion drain from her limbs as though it had never occurred. She had no wish to explain herself half-dressed and fully alert.

The door handle twisted.

Elizabeth wormed under the blankets, slowly, deliberately, letting her breath deepen as if drawn from sleep. She turned her face toward the pillows and allowed her shoulders to slacken a fraction. The door opened.

"Lizzy?"

Jane's voice carried relief tempered with caution, as though she were afraid of startling something fragile back into breaking. Elizabeth waited a heartbeat longer before answering.

"Mmm?" she murmured, pitching it low and unguarded. "Is it morning already?"

Jane crossed the room at once. Elizabeth felt the mattress dip as her sister sat beside her, felt the familiar weight of Jane's attention settle over her like a coverlet.

"You are awake. How do you feel?"

Elizabeth considered the truth, then set it carefully aside.

"Tired," she said instead. "Not ill. Just... heavy."

"That is to be expected, I'm sure."

Elizabeth opened her eyes at last and managed a faint smile. "You make it sound official."

Jane returned it, though her gaze searched Elizabeth's face closely. "Mr Jones said you might find the mornings the most difficult."

Elizabeth turned her head slightly, as if the light were too bright. It was not. But the gesture cost her nothing, and Jane noticed everything.

"I had the oddest dreams," Elizabeth added, lightly, before Jane could ask more. "They have left me feeling as though I have been awake all night."

Jane reached for her hand, fingers warm and familiar. "You need not trouble yourself about anything today. We can read, if you like. Or simply rest."

Elizabeth's pulse ticked up—not with fear, but calculation. If Jane stayed, Elizabeth would have to be careful. Jane noticed too much. She listened too well.

"I should like that," Elizabeth said. "Though every time I attempt it, the words seem determined to climb off the page."

Jane smiled. "Then you shall not read."

Elizabeth let her eyes close again, trusting Jane to interpret the gesture as fatigue rather than choice. In the darkness behind her lids, her thoughts sharpened.

At Longbourn, she would be expected to recover briskly. Mama would fuss and prod and pronounce her cured within hours, and Papa—Papa would watch her too closely, his humour edged with something quieter and more unnerving.

Here, she was permitted to linger. Here, she could build herself time to think.

Jane adjusted the blanket at her shoulder. "Mr Bingley asked after you before breakfast," she said. "He was quite earnest."

Elizabeth hummed, noncommittal.

"And Mr Darcy—" Jane stopped herself. "He asked whether you had slept."

Elizabeth kept her eyes closed. "Did he?"

"Yes." Jane hesitated. "He seemed... concerned."

Elizabeth made a small, incredulous sound. "Mr Darcy? Concerned?"

Jane smiled despite herself. "He did."

"Well, I am gratified to have inspired such unprecedented feeling," Elizabeth said. "Do assure him that I slept most soundly—at least in the sense that I was horizontal for several hours."

Jane laughed softly. "Lizzy—"

"I am quite serious," Elizabeth added, opening one eye. "If Mr Darcy begins taking an interest in my rest, we shall have to alert the neighbourhood. Do you think Miss Bingley will send out a notice?"

"Very funny, Lizzy," Jane rose with a chuckle. "I will bring you some tea. Do not move until I return. No overtaxing yourself."

"I promise," Elizabeth said.

There was the briefest of knocks, then before Jane could even rise to answer, the door opened again upon a small procession.

Miss Bingley entered first, all gracious concern and elegant composure, and Mrs Hurst, who paused just inside the threshold to survey the room with mild curiosity before taking a seat without waiting to be asked.

"My dear Miss Elizabeth," Miss Bingley said, crossing the room with a smile so perfectly arranged it might have been styled in the mirror. "How pleased I am to see you sitting up! Miss Bennet told us you were feeling quite yourself again, and I declared we must bring tea at once. One cannot recover properly without it."

Elizabeth blinked. *Quite yourself* was not the phrase she would have chosen.

"That was very kind of you, Miss Bingley."

"Oh, but it is the *very* least we could do. Now, I do hope we are not disturbing you, my dear Miss Elizabeth. We shall not stay if you had better entertainments." Her gaze slid pointedly to the stack of books beside the bed.

"Not at present," Elizabeth said, unable to keep the regret from her voice. She rested her hand on the top book. "Papa sent these from Meryton, but I confess, my eyes are still not cooperating with the print."

Miss Bingley clicked her tongue. "How thoughtful of him. Well, more is the pity. I have heard that you prefer reading above all things, and we want you perfectly content while you recover. Is that not right, Louisa?"

Mrs Hurst poured herself tea and stirred it lazily. "Truly. You are fortunate to have such an attentive family," she observed. "Not everyone can rely on sisters to sit vigil."

Jane flushed faintly and busied herself with the cups. "Elizabeth is much improved today. Truly. I think she might manage the drawing room later."

Miss Bingley's smile brightened. "How delightful! Then you must be nearly ready to return home. I am sure Mrs Bennet will be eager to have you back under her own care."

*Ah*, Elizabeth thought. *There it is.*

She did not answer at once, reaching instead for her teacup. "I imagine Mama will have many opinions on the subject," she said mildly.

Miss Bingley laughed—a light, approving sound. "A most sensible mother. Still, it must be a comfort to dear Jane to know she will not be required to remain away from home much longer."

Jane looked up, startled. "Oh. I do not mind staying—"

"Nonsense," Miss Bingley said quickly. "You have been exceedingly generous with your time. And my brother has been quite restless all day—walking the rooms, consulting the windows, asking every quarter hour whether Darcy has returned. It would do him good to have his house restored to its usual order."

Elizabeth's brows rose a fraction.

Mrs Hurst nodded. "Indeed. Charles is beside himself. And with Mr Darcy saying he will be out for the better part of the day—well, we have all been at loose ends."

Elizabeth took a sip of tea she did not want and considered this new arrangement of facts. Jane, drawn upstairs and kept there. Mr Bingley pacing below. Miss Bingley managing the distribution of her brother's attention like a puppet master.

"But you must not trouble yourself with any of that," Miss Bingley continued. "The only thing that matters is your recovery. You look so much stronger already."

Elizabeth smiled at her. Not brightly. Not weakly. With clarity. "Appearances," she said, "are often very encouraging."

Miss Bingley inclined her head, as though in agreement. "Indeed. Which is why one must be careful not to mistake improvement for strength." She rose at once. "You must be eager for quiet again, Miss Elizabeth. Rest is quite essential."

"Naturally," she agreed.

"And yet," Miss Bingley continued, already turning the matter to her liking, "it would be a shame for your sister to be drawn away to pointless amusements just when she is most useful to you. Nothing comforts an invalid like familiar company." She smiled at Jane. "I would not blame you if you chose to remain upstairs with her the rest of the day, Miss Bennet."

Jane blinked, surprised—and then relieved. "If Lizzy wishes it, I should be glad to stay."

Elizabeth met her sister's eyes. There was no space here for protest, no graceful way to redirect without inviting exactly the attention she meant to avoid.

"Of course." Miss Bingley was already moving. "Come, Louisa. We shall leave the sisters to their tea and see whether our brother has at last ceased his pacing."

Mrs Hurst rose, scarcely glancing back at Elizabeth as she followed.

Miss Bingley paused only long enough to add, "Do ring if you require anything, Miss Elizabeth. Anything at all."

When they were gone, Elizabeth glanced at the teacup cooling beside her, then at Jane.

"I was just beginning to understand that argument," she said, with a rueful little smile.

Jane returned it, though her eyes were thoughtful. "Some arguments are clearer once one party has left the room."

"DARCY, THERE YOU ARE."

Bingley caught him just beyond the drawing-room door, quick enough to suggest he had been watching for him. "I was beginning to think you had slipped back to London."

"I have not," Darcy said, slowing despite himself. "Only stepped away."

"Ah." Bingley smiled. "That is what you always say just before vanishing for hours at a time." He glanced back toward the drawing room. "Caroline wishes to know whether you intend to sit by the fire or the window. She is convinced it matters."

"You may tell her that I am equally ill-suited to both."

Bingley laughed, then fell into step beside him as Darcy turned toward the hall. "You are being evasive."

"I am being practical."

"Since when has practicality required this much pacing?" Bingley asked. "You have crossed or circled the outside of this house more times today than the servants combined."

Darcy paused at the threshold, one hand resting briefly on the doorframe, as if considering how much explanation was owed. "I find I am unable to sit just now."

Bingley studied him—not intrusively, but with the easy concern of long habit. "Is this about Miss Elizabeth?"

Darcy's gaze flicked to him. "It is not about—" He stopped, exhaled. "Not directly."

"That is not an answer. But I will accept it for the moment. Only do not let my sisters imagine you have taken fright at their hospitality. Or, God forbid, an interest in our guest upstairs."

"I have taken neither fright nor interest. I only require a little air. And perhaps a book."

Bingley's brows rose. "A dangerous combination. I have seen you brooding at your very stormiest, and I daresay my library is not up to the task. Very well." He stepped aside with a half-bow. "I shall distract Caroline as long as I am able. But if you return with county maps or a ledger, I reserve the right to mock you."

*Maps...* Darcy inclined his head, the corner of his mouth lifting at last. "I should expect nothing less."

He reached the small morning room adjoining the library—a space rarely used except for sorting correspondence—and shut the door behind him. The quiet inside was immediate and complete.

Good.

He crossed to the sideboard and drew open the shallow drawer where Bingley kept odds and ends of estate interest: a ruler, a length of twine, sealing wax, and—after a moment's searching—a rolled survey map bound with a faded ribbon. Darcy loosened it and spread the paper across the table.

The map was serviceable rather than elegant. Hedgerows carefully marked. Elevations noted in an indifferent hand. Boundaries drawn and redrawn as property had changed hands. Darcy leaned over it, bracing one palm against the table's edge, scanning for a particular stretch of land.

There. The eastern rise.

He studied it longer than the rest. The notation was old—his grandfather's era, perhaps earlier. Boundary stone indicated. Thorn hedge recorded only as "existing growth," with no symbol to suggest enclosure or special consideration.

Nothing unusual. That was the point.

A knock sounded at the door, brisk and unceremonious. "Darcy?"

Bingley did not wait for an answer. He came in, then stopped short when he saw what covered the table. "Ah. So that's where you went."

Darcy's attention remained on the map beneath his hand. "I said I would be a moment."

"You did," Bingley agreed. "I did not believe you."

He leaned in, scanning the spread of papers. "County surveys? You know, I was joking about the maps."

"And drainage records," Darcy said. "Where they exist."

Bingley gave a low hum. "That sounds... absorbing. Also, faintly alarming."

"It is neither. Yet."

Bingley glanced at him sideways. "This would not happen to have anything to do with why you vanished mid-conversation."

"No."

Bingley smiled faintly. "That was not convincing."

Darcy grunted, the closest he came to a concession. "I am confirming a certain detail."

"Only one?" Bingley grinned. "You are improving."

Darcy straightened and reached for the ruler, aligning it precisely along the marked boundary. "Do you know when the waterways were last redug?"

Bingley blinked. "Good heavens—years ago. Before I took Netherfield, certainly. Why?"

"No reason," Darcy said at first, rolling the ruler once between his fingers before setting it down again. He hesitated only a moment, then added, more deliberately, "I am looking for any record of disturbance. Slips in the ground. Alterations in drainage that were not made by design. Anything that suggests the land has ever broken... irregularly."

Bingley stared at him. "Disturbance?" A grin threatened. "You do realise this is Hertfordshire, not Sicily."

Darcy did not smile. "Ground settles. Springs shift. Old works collapse and are forgotten. It does not require catastrophe. Only time, and the natural fractures of the terrain."

"And this sudden interest has nothing whatever to do with why you vanished mid-conversation?" Bingley asked.

Darcy met his look. "Nothing I can yet prove."

Bingley laughed and shook his head. "Walk it, then. We have guests, my friend—two anxious sisters, one very vocal hostess, and a household convinced you are indispensable to morale."

Darcy folded the map again, tightly. "The land will not object to waiting."

"That depends entirely on the land," Bingley said lightly. "But if you insist, at least take your coat. The air has turned."

Darcy reached the door, then paused. "Has anyone altered the eastern fence since you arrived?"

Bingley frowned. "Not that I know of. Why?"

Darcy opened the door. "Then the maps should read from there. Or I shall know whether to be annoyed with others, or with myself."

Bingley stared after him. "That sounded ominous."

Darcy stepped back into the corridor, where the life of the house resumed its quiet authority—footsteps passing, a door closing somewhere below, the low cadence of voices untroubled by anything beyond the next hour. Whatever unease the night had conjured, whatever distortions fatigue and disturbed sleep had lent his thoughts, daylight would have the advantage of them.

Land did not deceive without cause. It bore what it had always borne, unless men had mismeasured it, neglected it, or chosen—conveniently—to forget what had once been noted.

If something had been overlooked, then the error was not in the ground itself, but in the confidence with which it had been declared understood. And that failure belonged not to the present moment alone, but to whoever had last decided the matter settled—and ceased to look again.

Darcy took Brutus by the collar as they crossed the threshold, more force than affection in the gesture, and set off across the park at a pace that discouraged interruption. The air carried the damp edge of early autumn, sharp enough to clear the mind—or so he told himself.

"This is absurd," he muttered, though to whom he could not have said. Brutus's ears flicked, but the dog made not a whimper, which Darcy perversely found worse.

They left the formal walk almost at once, angling across the rougher grass toward the eastern rise—the shallow swell of ground where Miss Elizabeth Bennet had been found two mornings earlier. Darcy had not needed a guide to bring him back. The place had lodged itself in his memory with unwelcome clarity: the curve of the hedge, the slight hollow beyond it, the manner in which the ground dipped where continuity ought to have held.

Walking had always steadied his thoughts. Motion imposed order. Figures resolved themselves. Boundaries were marked as they were meant to be.

Here, they were not.

He slowed near the rise and stopped beside the hedge, turning in a deliberate circle. If there had been a shift deep in the earth, it would not announce itself grandly. It would show in small cracks: uneven settling, a crumbled place where water trickled, ground worn thin where it should have borne weight evenly.

Brutus sniffed at the base of the hedge and sat.

Darcy stepped off again, following the same line he and Bingley had ridden before. He began to count his paces—habit, drilled into him young and never quite abandoned. One. Two. Three.

He reached the hollow exactly where he expected it. He reached into his coat and drew out the map. He unrolled a portion of it and read again, his lips shaping the words despite himself.

...a shallow run, long since dry...

...set between the hedge and the stone, marked upon older surveys though no water now appears...

Darcy lowered the page and looked again at the ground.There was no watercourse here. There never had been, not within memory, not within any living account. And yet the land bore the quiet signature of one: a faint gouging, a long depression too regular to be chance, too slight to attract notice unless one knew to look for it.

"A run without water," he murmured. "Or a line mistaken for one."

He did not say the rest aloud. In older records, such features were sometimes named streams for want of better language—where the earth had cracked, or sunk, or parted once and never quite recovered its former firmness. A weakness, not a passage. A place where strain had been released, and the ground remembered it still.

He turned back toward the hedge and paced again, not to test distance, but alignment—hedge to hollow, hollow to where the old boundary stone was said to lie buried. The measures agreed too neatly to dismiss.

Darcy stopped.

This—precisely this—was where Elizabeth Bennet had lain. He could see it now: the scuffed grass, the faint compression where a body had pressed the soil, the gentle fall of the ground—enough to draw one off balance if one were already weakened, enough to give way without ever seeming treacherous.

He lowered his gaze.

The grass here was unlike the rest of the field. Not worn as by frequent passage, nor scorched by the end of summer, but kept short in a way that suggested long habit rather than recent use—as though growth had never properly taken hold. Beneath it, the soil showed faint, parallel ridges, softened by time yet still legible to an attentive eye.

Darcy bent and pressed the toe of his boot into the surface.

The earth gave easily—cool, dense, retaining moisture where the surrounding ground had already begun to harden for autumn. He withdrew his foot and crouched, brushing aside a little of the grass with his hand. The soil beneath was darker, finer, settled into itself rather than layered.

A filled channel, then. Or the remnant of one.

He straightened slowly. This was not proof, but at least it began to make sense. It was no more than a collection of small indications, each harmless in isolation: a shallow run, an old notation, ground that held water differently than it ought. Such things occurred. Fields were altered. Land was pressed into service and forgotten again.

And yet—

Darcy's gaze lifted, following the line of the depression toward the hedge beyond.

There, a thorn grew thicker than the rest, its trunk older, its lower branches long trimmed back. Not planted as part of the hedge's later work, but allowed to remain—marked, perhaps, rather than removed. He approached it and examined the base. The surrounding growth had been cut and recut over the years, but the thorn itself bore no sign of having been set aside by accident.

A marker, then. Not ornamental. Not useful. Simply permitted.

Brutus came nearer, settling at his side, the great dog's presence watchful and fixed on nothing Darcy could see. Darcy rested a hand briefly against his shoulder without looking down.

"Do not start that again," Darcy told him. "You are a dog, not a—"

Not a sentinel. Not a warder. Not...

"This is how nonsense begins," he grumbled. "By mistaking neglect for intention, whimsy for meaning."

He took a few steps farther along the hedge, then stopped. The line held true: thorn to hollow, hollow to where the old stone was said to lie buried. Nothing here contradicted the records. If anything, the land confirmed them.

Darcy turned back toward Netherfield, setting his pace with care and refusing the impulse to revisit the measurements. There was nothing more to be gained by lingering.

# Chapter Fourteen

Miss Bennet had excused herself not long after the ladies withdrew from dinner, pleading her sister's fatigue with gentle insistence and a smile that admitted no argument. Bingley had protested—briefly, earnestly, and without effect—and soon the door had closed behind her, leaving the room altered in a way no one remarked upon aloud.

The fire crackled. Mrs Hurst reclined with her eyes half closed, her attention fixed nowhere in particular. Mr Hurst had surrendered entirely, his head tipped back, breathing slow and untroubled. Miss Bingley sat with a book open in her lap, the page unmoved for some time.

Darcy crossed the room to the small writing desk near the window.

A servant had intercepted him as they left the dining room, murmuring that a letter had arrived during the meal—addressed in a hand Darcy recognised at once. He had acknowledged it with a nod and said nothing more. He did not wish for an audience.

He seated himself, broke the seal with care, and unfolded the page.

*Grosvenor Square*
*October, 1811*

*My dear Darcy,*

*I trust this letter finds you well settled in Hertfordshire and enjoying, if not repose, at least a change of scene. Though I would ordinarily spare you correspondence on matters that can wait until your return, circumstances have persuaded me that delay would serve no one.*

*You will have heard, no doubt, that Richard has been ordered back to the*

*Peninsula. The summons came with a haste I did not expect and an explanation I do not find entirely satisfying. I am told—very earnestly—that his presence is required owing to "altered conditions" and a need for "continuity" and "experience" among the men. Such phrases are admirably flexible, and I have learned over the years how often they are employed to conceal inconvenience or someone else's incompetence rather than danger. Still, the manner of it troubles me more than I care to admit.*

*I do not mean to burden you with a father's unease, but this redeployment is not the only irregularity that has come to my attention of late. I have received a number of small reports—trifling in themselves—from estates and holdings not my own. Trees failing without obvious history of blight. Pigeons not returning where they ought. Men complaining, half in jest, that the harvest was not a third what was expected. All of this has been dismissed, quite sensibly, as weather, ill luck, or imagination. I have dismissed it myself.*

*Yet it has been suggested to me—quietly, and not by those inclined toward legend—that certain irregularities have been remarked upon beyond Derbyshire. My steward, in the ordinary course of correspondence, has noted reports from several quarters that echo what I have heard nearer home. Autumn advancing even as early as July, and winter falling long before the first snow. Nothing dramatic. Nothing that cannot, taken singly, be attributed to chance or neglect. But enough, in their accumulation, to warrant attention.*

*It is for this reason that I write to you now. You are, at present, removed from your own lands and from the habits of ground you know as well as your own hand. Hertfordshire is not governed by the same soil, nor the same weather. And yet, if the reports I have received are accurate, it is precisely there that certain expected signs have failed to appear. While elsewhere the season asserts itself with increasing insistence, Hertfordshire appears, oddly, to have been spared the worst of it. I do not offer this as proof of anything. I merely observe that absence may be as instructive as decay.*

*If, in the course of your stay, you have noticed anything that strikes you as inconsistent, I would ask that you note it carefully. Not with an eye to explanation, still less to significance, but simply as fact. I do not wish to encourage conjecture. Nor do I think it prudent to dismiss patterns merely because they suggest conclusions we would rather avoid.*

*Your aunt Catherine has, as you might expect, formed her own interpretation of these matters. She is firmly persuaded that they point toward a personal resolution, and has been unrestrained in advancing her views regarding what she terms the proper completion of certain family expectations. On this point, I must be plain: I consider her reasoning unsound, her confidence misplaced, and her interference deeply unwelcome. Whatever is amiss, and I do not yet concede that anything is, it will not be remedied by matrimonial enthusiasm.*

*What concerns me more is the question of timing. Your cousin's orders were altered with an abruptness that admits of no satisfactory explanation, and I do not care for coincidences that arrive in clusters. I am not prepared to say that these things are connected. But neither am I content to pretend that they are not.*

*Write to me when you are able. Say what you see, and no more. Above all, do not allow yourself to be hurried into anyone else's conclusions. I write because I trust your judgment, and because you have always possessed the rare ability to observe without haste and to act without noise. If there is nothing to report, I shall be content to hear it so. If there is something—however small—I would rather know it plainly than have it softened by good intentions.*

*Give my affection to Georgiana when next you write. I hope you will forgive the length of this letter; it has been composed with more care than ease.*

*Yours ever,*
*M*

He read once, straight through, his expression giving nothing away. He read again more slowly, his attention catching on certain phrases—*altered conditions*; *suggested quietly*; *observe without dismissal*. By the third pass, he had ceased to see the words as correspondence at all and began to read them as one reads a ledger whose sums do not reconcile.

His uncle's hand was almost artistic. The phrasing was careful—his uncle was a politician, after all. There was no alarm in it—no claim, no declaration.

Which was precisely what made his stomach turn.

Darcy folded the letter once, then again, and set it beside the inkstand. He did not reach for pen or paper immediately.

Across the room, Miss Bingley turned a page that made no sound. "How gratifying," she said lightly, "to receive letters from town when one is buried so far from civilisation."

Darcy did not look up.

"I take it Lord Matlock writes on business?" she asked, as though merely curious. "Or family matters? One never knows which will prevail with gentlemen."

He uncapped the ink and examined his quill tip. "My uncle writes rarely without cause."

Miss Bingley smiled, closing her book at last. "I hope it is nothing tiresome. You have looked positively distracted all evening."

Darcy dipped the pen and tested it against the paper. The first line he wrote was bland, formal, entirely unremarkable.

"I am rather occupied than distracted. It concerns matters beyond Hertfordshire," he said.

"Ah." Miss Bingley leaned back, studying him with renewed interest. "Then it must be important indeed."

Bingley, who had been stirring the fire into needless enthusiasm, glanced over his shoulder. "Good news, I hope? Your uncle does not write merely to complain about the weather, does he? I declare, he ought to come to Hertfordshire. Best autumn weather in the country, or I will eat my hat. We shall have a crisp day tomorrow with not a cloud in sight."

Darcy paused, pen hovering. For a moment, he considered offering the easy answer. Instead, he lowered his head and wrote, the reply forming with care.

He thanked his uncle for his confidence. He acknowledged Richard's orders without comment. He addressed the question put to him directly—whether he had observed anything out of the ordinary in Hertfordshire—and found himself choosing his words with uncommon deliberation.

Miss Bingley's gaze had not left him. "So very studious you are, Mr Darcy," she remarked. "One might suppose you and the earl were plotting something grand!"

He did not lift his eyes from the page. "If I were, I should hardly do so at Bingley's escritoire."

"That is true," she conceded. "You would prefer privacy for such things."

The pen paused.

Darcy finished the sentence he had begun, then set the pen down. He read what he had written with a critical eye, weighing omission as carefully as inclusion.

*I have observed nothing that cannot be accounted for by season, circumstance, or coincidence,* he had written.

It was almost accurate. It was also incomplete. He folded the letter without sealing it and rose. "You propose an excellent idea, Miss Bingley. I will finish this in my room and shall send it down in the morning."

Bingley crossed the room. "Is everything... quite all right?"

"Entirely."

It was true, in the narrowest sense. No illness. No loss. No crisis demanding immediate remedy.

Nothing urgent at all, in fact.

ELIZABETH HAD NOT INTENDED to leave her room.

That, at least, was what she told herself as she crossed to the wardrobe and drew out a gown. It was not the one Jane had laid ready the night before—too neat, too expectant—but an older favourite, plain in cut and forgiving in colour. One that suggested comfort rather than recovery, and would invite no comment should she be seen in it.

She dressed with care that bordered on caution. Not haste, exactly, but an awareness of every fastening, every small exertion. When she reached for her shawl, she paused, testing herself without movement. Her head was clear. Her limbs answered her without protest—too easily.

She froze and glanced at the open door leading to Jane's room, then slowed her movements.

Jane must not suspect—not because there was anything to hide, but because she did not yet know how to name what she felt. Until she did, it was simpler to let her sister believe the illness lingered.

Elizabeth crossed to the looking glass and adjusted her hair with deliberate imperfection. A pin left slightly loose. A curl allowed to escape. She looked—if not unwell—then at least not perfectly restored.

It would do.

Elizabeth had just finished fastening the last pin at her shoulder when the door moved. Not a draft. Not the soft complaint of settling wood. It opened—slowly, with unmistakable pressure from the other side—until the latch yielded and the door swung inward by a careful hand's breadth.

The dog stood in the passage, one great paw braced against the panel as if he had pushed it there and was now considering whether further effort was required. He did not cross the threshold. He did not lower his head. He simply looked at her, dark eyes intent, his stillness so complete it felt deliberate.

"Well," she said faintly. "That is exceedingly improper."

Brutus withdrew his paw and sat.

"You have the wrong room, sir. No doubt your master is downstairs. Shoo!"

He only blinked at her.

Elizabeth did not move. Nor, she realised a moment later, did she feel the least inclination to shut it. The dog's presence filled the narrow space without urgency, without threat. He was not asking. He was not waiting for permission. He was simply guarding her.

"Go on," she told him, summoning more firmness than she felt. "I am quite capable of managing my own whereabouts."

He did not stir.

"Lizzy?" Jane's voice came from the adjoining room. "Are you dressed? I thought I heard—" Jane appeared at the threshold just as the dog rose.

Brutus stepped back into the passage, clearing the doorway entirely, then turned and sat again, this time angled toward the corridor beyond, as if the matter had been resolved.

Elizabeth looked from the open door to the dog and found, to her own irritation, that the answer had arrived before the question was finished.

Jane glanced between them, smiling faintly. "I suppose he has decided you are presentable at last."

Elizabeth did not answer at once. She took one step toward the door. Brutus pricked his ears, and his tail fanned slowly in welcome.

Jane put a hand on her arm. "Wait... Lizzy, are you quite sure you are well enough?"

Elizabeth nodded, very carefully. "I am."

The dog rose again, tail moving once, then turned down the corridor; unhurried, confident they would follow when ready.

The drawing room was warm with lamplight and conversation. Bingley, who had been standing near the hearth with his back half-turned, looked up first and brightened as though someone had struck a match behind his eyes.

"Miss Elizabeth!" he exclaimed. "Well! This is a victory indeed. I had nearly resigned myself to another evening of worrying in silence." He crossed the room at once, all animation and concern. "You look vastly improved—vastly. Pray, sit—do sit. Caroline, will you not—?"

Miss Bingley had already risen. "Miss Elizabeth, how very glad I am to see you," she said, advancing with hands lightly extended. "You quite astonish us. I hope you have not been persuaded downstairs against your better judgment?"

Elizabeth returned the smile. "I persuaded myself. Which I find generally answers better."

Bingley laughed outright. "Spoken like a woman restored! Come, the sofa at the centre—it is by far the most comfortable. You must tell us how you feel."

"I feel," Elizabeth said, as she was guided forward, "remarkably surrounded."

Brutus entered last.

He did not bound, nor linger uncertainly at the threshold. He walked in with purpose, paused just inside the room, and sat—not near Elizabeth, but near Darcy, who had been standing by the writing desk with one hand resting upon it, as though he had been about to take his leave.

He inclined his head to Elizabeth, but his eyes moved—not to her face, but briefly, to the dog, then back again. He was staring, nearly open-mouthed, before he clamped his jaw.

"Well," he said, in a tone of dry civility, "it appears Brutus has decided we all require supervision."

Elizabeth glanced at the dog, then back at Darcy. "I had not realised I was in need of it, but he is a very gallant companion."

His mouth firmed as he gave a very slight inclination of his head. "I am very glad you were able to join us, Miss Elizabeth."

Miss Bingley laughed lightly. "Your dog is quite devoted tonight, Mr Darcy. One would think Miss Elizabeth had secured a noble escort."

Darcy's mouth curved—barely. "He has been known to choose his own company."

Elizabeth nodded and chose her seat. Or rather, she was about to when Miss Bingley intervened with graceful urgency, one hand already extended.

"Here, Miss Elizabeth—by me," she said, indicating the chair nearest her own, angled carefully towards the hearth and away from the writing desk beyond. "You must not be exposed to drafts, and I insist you be comfortable. Louisa, you will agree—this seat is far better for one who has been unwell." She cast a look over her shoulder towards Mrs Hurst, one that plainly requested reinforcement.

Mrs Hurst, however, had sunk back into her chair with a look of placid detachment, her attention apparently fixed on the fire. If she noticed her sister's appeal, she gave no sign of it.

Bingley, meanwhile, had already pulled forward another chair—this one even nearer the hearth—and was ushering Jane into it with cheerful solicitude. "Here, Miss Bennet—this will be warmer. Darcy, do move that table, will you? There. We shall all be quite snug."

Miss Bingley's smile tightened by a degree almost too small to be seen.

Elizabeth accepted the seat offered her, because refusal would have turned courtesy into contest. She settled herself with an air of obedience that concealed amusement, noting the careful distance Miss Bingley had achieved—not merely from the hearth, but from Darcy as well.

Brutus remained where he was, seated near Darcy, his broad back angled toward the room, as though the arrangement of persons required no further comment.

"Truly, how are you feeling this evening, Miss Elizabeth?" Miss Bingley asked. "You look remarkably restored. I trust the quiet upstairs has done you good."

"I am much improved, thank you. The house has been very obliging."

Miss Bingley gave a light, musical laugh at once. "Obliging! The house? Such an enchanting turn of phrase, Miss Elizabeth. Netherfield prides itself on being comfortable, but I did not know the walls had cultivated manners as well."

There was a polite ripple of amusement. Elizabeth smiled, neither apologetic nor corrected.

"Well," Miss Bingley continued briskly, as though tidying the moment she had just unpicked, "that is excellent news. Nothing is so fatiguing as prolonged confinement. One does begin to long for one's own comforts again."

Elizabeth heard it clearly enough. Jane met her eye with a look of anxious questioning.

Bingley, who had been hovering near the card table with a deck already half-shuffled, brightened at once. "If Miss Elizabeth is feeling better, we must celebrate it properly. A little loo, perhaps? Or commerce? Though I confess my enthusiasm for cards wanes without sufficient competition."

Mrs Hurst murmured something agreeable without conviction.

"I doubt Miss Elizabeth should be overstimulated," Miss Bingley said, with a quick glance toward the sofa she had so carefully selected for her. "Recovery must be managed sensibly. A short visit to the drawing room is one thing. An evening of play quite another."

Elizabeth inclined her head. "I should not wish to exhaust anyone."

Bingley laughed. "You could hardly do that, I assure you. Well, perhaps a bit of conversation?" He glanced toward Darcy. "You were out this afternoon, were you not? Did you find anything of interest? Any new coverts worth our attention?"

Darcy, who had remained near the escritoire with his hand resting on its edge, did not answer at once.

His very silence struck Elizabeth's notice, and she turned her head. He was not distracted—he was too still for that. While Bingley waited and Miss Bingley arranged her patience into something decorative, Darcy's attention had slipped elsewhere, downward somehow, as though the question had missed him entirely and landed beneath the room instead.

"Nothing conclusive," he said at last.

Elizabeth smiled faintly. "That suggests you *expected* something conclusive. May I ask what you were looking for?"

Darcy seemed to catch himself. "I was verifying something I had read," he said, then stopped. "Which proved unnecessary."

Miss Bingley waved a hand lightly. "There, you see. Nothing to detain us, save to prove it was a fine day for walking. Which is why I think it would be wisest for Miss Elizabeth to return home tomorrow, while the weather holds. She is in such excellent spirits now, but would it not be a pity if we delayed and her carriage were caught out in a storm? One recovers best among one's own things, I always say."

Jane opened her mouth, then closed it again.

Elizabeth felt the pull of the idea keenly. *Longbourn*. Familiar rooms. Her father's library. Chaos and noise and expectations, to be sure. But no need to interpret the meaning of staircases or dogs or glances that lingered longer than courtesy required.

"Yes," she said slowly, glancing at the dog who was still ignoring her. "Home would be *most* welcome. If I am... able."

Darcy looked at her then with an attention that made the word "able" feel provisional, as though it had been placed upon the table for examination rather than accepted at face value.

Miss Bingley saw the look and moved at once to claim the moment. "Excellent. Then it is settled. We shall send word to Mrs Bennet first thing tomorrow and arrange—"

"Perhaps," Darcy said quietly, "it need not be decided this evening."

The interruption was mild. Perfectly civil. And utterly unexpected.

Miss Bingley turned toward him, her smile intact but strained at the edges. "I merely meant—"

"I know what you meant." His tone remained even. "I only suggest that Miss Elizabeth's comfort be considered without haste. She has done very well today. There is no need to undo that by hasty provisions."

Bingley glanced between them, clearly uncertain whether a decision had been made or avoided. "Indeed! There's sense in that. No reason to rush anything. We may leave it till morning, when everyone is refreshed."

Miss Bingley's smile had failed utterly. "Well! There we have it." She rose at once, smoothing her sleeves as she turned toward the bell. "Shall we have tea brought in? The room has grown quite dull without it."

Brutus, who had moved to settle himself some minutes earlier near the hearth, rose and crossed the room with unhurried purpose. He did not return to Darcy. He did not go to Elizabeth.

Instead, he moved toward the door, then glanced back with a look that somehow encompassed them both.

Elizabeth glanced away swiftly, her gaze accidentally blundering across Darcy's as she did so. "I think," she said, rising, "that I shall go upstairs again. This has been... quite enough for one evening."

Jane was on her feet at once. “Of course, Lizzy. I will come with you.”

A chorus of polite dismay met their ears, with Mr Bingley rising in offer of escort, Miss Bingley promising to send up tea.

But it was Darcy who stepped across her path with a simple bow. “Good night, Miss Elizabeth.”

She met his gaze briefly. There was nothing remarkable in it—only the unmistakable sense that he had seen her choose, and had chosen not to contest it.

“Good night, Mr Darcy.”

# Chapter Fifteen

DARCY SHUT THE DOOR of his chamber with care and stood for a moment where he was, hand still on the latch.

Brutus crossed the room at once and dropped heavily at the foot of the bed, turning a slow circle before settling with a sound of contentment that Darcy did not return.

"Yes," Darcy said under his breath. "You have done very well indeed. What the devil is with you and Miss Elizabeth?"

Brutus only stretched and offered a low groan as his eyes closed.

Darcy shook his head and crossed to the writing desk, then drew out the letter he had begun earlier. One page only. A careful opening. Polite. Circumspect. Entirely unsatisfactory.

He read it once, lips pressed thin, then folded it decisively and crumpled it for the fire.

He took a fresh sheet and seated himself, pen poised. For a moment, he stared at the blank page as though it might offer instruction. When it did not, he wrote, anyway.

*My dear Uncle,*

*Your letter reached me this afternoon, and I would have answered at once had I not wished first to consider it properly. I thank you for your candour—*

He stopped.

That was already untrue. He had wished first to *dismiss* it properly.

Darcy crumpled that paper, too, and began again.

*My dear Uncle,*

*I received your letter today and am obliged to you for writing so plainly. You will not be surprised to hear that I have spent the better part of the evening attempting to determine whether you are correct in supposing that recent oddities of weather or herbage are anything more than coincidence.*

He paused, considering the word "disturbances."

It was serviceable. Vague. Noncommittal.

*In Hertfordshire, I have observed nothing that cannot be explained by weather, neglect, or the ordinary inconveniences of rural management. That said—*

His pen hovered.

"That said."

Always the pivot to something unpleasant.

Brutus shifted at the foot of the bed, nails rasping faintly against the floor as he rolled upright and swivelled his head to stare at the wall as if he could see through it. Darcy glanced up despite himself. "What is it now?"

The dog gazed, unblinking. Darcy twisted in his seat. Either Brutus had suddenly taken an interest in the portrait of someone's departed grandmother on the wall, or he sensed someone moving in the room beyond.

Darcy watched him for another moment, then returned to the page.

*That said, I have lately encountered a number of small irregularities which, taken separately, would merit no attention at all. Taken together, they have proven more resistant to easy dismissal.*

He read the sentence twice, then nodded once. Acceptable.

*Several features recorded in earlier surveys do not answer to their stated purpose. A minor watercourse appears never to have carried water, and nearby growth remains unusually green for the season, despite no corresponding advantage in soil or drainage.*

He stopped again.

So, what did any of that matter? It seemed a trivial thing to bring to his uncle's notice. Lord Matlock was grasping at straws, and it was likely foolish to give him more meaningless notes to fret over.

He considered striking it through, but decided to add a clarification instead.

> *I am inclined to wonder whether some irregularity beneath the surface—an old shift or settling of the ground, long since stilled—may account for both observations.*

Better.

Safer.

He continued for several lines—about hedgerows, about drainage, about a warmth in the soil that had no business being there so late in the season, with no proper frost yet. He kept his tone dry, professional, almost bored.

Only then did he hesitate.

There was one more matter.

Darcy sat back in his chair, the pen balanced loosely between his fingers, the page before him no longer quite in focus.

He had not intended to write of it. He had been perfectly resolved not to. And yet the room refused to supply him with anything else to consider.

Miss Elizabeth Bennet had come downstairs under her own power.

The thought arrived without invitation and lingered, resistant to dismissal. Not carried. Not urged. Not pale in the manner of one determined to prove fortitude at the expense of sense. She had been tired, yes—but present, alert, with that quick turn of expression that suggested she was already measuring the company she found herself in and finding it wanting in small, amusing ways.

She had spoken lightly. Too lightly, perhaps. As though careful words were an inconvenience rather than a necessity.

*The house has been very obliging.*

It was an odd phrase. He had noticed that at once. Too precise to be accidental, too casual to be deliberate. The sort of remark one made without fully examining why it had chosen itself.

He turned the pen between his fingers, gaze dropping to the desk, then lifting again without his quite noticing the movement. There had been colour in her face. Not the flush of fever, nor the brittle rosiness of false cheer, but something brighter. Awake.

Her eyes had been...

Darcy stopped.

This was pointless.

He drew a sharp line beneath the half-written paragraph and leaned forward again, forcing his attention back to the page. Elizabeth Bennet's eyes were of no consequence to county surveys, nor to weather patterns, nor to dogs behaving badly at staircases. Whatever he had thought he observed was merely the aftereffect of a day too long and a mind insufficiently occupied.

He resumed writing at once, his hand firmer, his letters more compact.

> *There was also an incident here involving a young lady taken ill without evident cause while walking the grounds. No injury was discovered, nor could any clear explanation be supplied at the time. I mention it only because the location coincides with a portion of the park where the dry watercourses were noted.*
>
> *I have heard of certain individuals who seem particularly sensitive to terrestrial fissures. Perhaps Hertfordshire is to expect convulsions of the ground soon? Or perhaps that is merely folk fancy, I cannot be sure.*

Darcy read it once.

That was factual. Temperate. Entirely reasonable.

He hesitated, then added a line beneath the last.

> *I do not infer cause from this, nor do I ascribe any particular significance to it. I note it only because you once advised me that repeated coincidence deserves at least the courtesy of attention, particularly where that coincidence concerns the instincts of beasts who seek no conclusions of their own.*

He set the pen down.

For a moment, he did nothing at all.

The letter lay before him, incomplete and imperfect, saying more than he wished and less than he knew. He folded it once, then again, and placed it beside his uncle's letter, aligning the edges with deliberate care.

Brutus rose and crossed the room, placing his head briefly against Darcy's knee before settling again.

Darcy rested a hand between the dog's ears without looking down. "Yes," he said quietly. "I am aware."

He did not seal the letter.

Instead, he stood, tucking both papers into his coat pocket, and crossed to the window. The night beyond offered nothing—only the dark outline of trees and the suggestion of movement where there should have been none.

ELIZABETH STACKED HER FATHER'S books with care and placed them at the top of her trunk, though she had already packed them once. She checked the ribbon Jane had insisted upon, then set it aside again. She straightened the shawl she had folded only moments earlier, then left it where it lay. Each task had a reason. None of them required haste.

Downstairs, voices drifted faintly upward—Jane's, unmistakable, and Mr Bingley's brighter tones beside it. The house was awake. The carriage would be announced any moment now. Elizabeth paused with her hands resting on the edge of the trunk, listening.

Nothing.

She glanced toward the door.

She did not expect to see the dog there. That would be ridiculous. And yet she found herself waiting for the sound of nails on the floor, for the quiet assurance of his presence in the passage beyond, as if he were some sort of custodian. When nothing came, irritation stirred where unease might otherwise have settled.

Very well, then.

Elizabeth took up her reticule and turned toward the door before she could reconsider. She opened it and stepped into the corridor.

The passage lay empty. She stood there a moment longer than necessary, then moved on, setting her steps with care that was not caution so much as attention. She reached the stair.

For an instant—only an instant—she hesitated, expecting that subtle resistance she had felt before, that quiet refusal she could not have named if pressed. Nothing answered her pause. The stair remained as it always had been.

Elizabeth frowned faintly and placed her foot on the first step.

It held.

She took another.

Still nothing.

Her pulse quickened, not with alarm but with something closer to disbelief. She descended another step, then another, her hand brushing the banister more out of habit than need. The space behaved. The house offered no objection at all.

Halfway down, she became aware she was not alone.

Darcy stood at the foot of the stair, one hand resting on the newel post, a book open in his hand as though he had been interrupted mid-thought. He looked up as she descended, surprise flickering across his features before discipline smoothed it away.

"Miss Elizabeth."

"Mr Darcy. I have not yet thanked you for finding me in the fields. Your kindness has not gone amiss, for I am well enough to go home today."

"So I had heard." His gaze shifted briefly—up the stair beyond her, then back to her face. "You appear quite recovered."

She smiled, a little. "Appearances are having a very successful morning."

The corner of his mouth moved, almost despite him. "I am glad to see it."

Elizabeth took the remaining steps, watching him now with a curiosity she did not trouble to conceal. He had not offered his arm. He had not moved to bar her way or hasten her passage. He simply stood there, present, as though that were sufficient.

She reached the bottom of the stair without incident. The moment she stepped onto the hall carpet, the awareness she had carried with her—the quiet expectation of correction—slipped away entirely.

Elizabeth drew a breath and gave a small, incredulous laugh. "Well," she said, "that is settled, then."

Darcy's brows drew together—not sharply, but with the faint crease of someone who had not reached the same conclusion. "Is it?"

She met his look squarely. "I appear to have alarmed myself unnecessarily. A habit I am determined to break."

"One I should not have attributed to you," he said, after a moment. His gaze flicked—briefly, unmistakably—toward the stair behind her. "You do not strike me as prone to it."

"Not even after that incident at the Assembly? I beg to differ sir, for I alarmed myself right and proper."

"An incident I am assured had less to do with your character and more to do with some peculiarity in the room."

She smiled. "Well, I should be sorry to disappoint."

Before he could answer, footsteps sounded from the drawing room.

"Lizzy!" Jane appeared, relief written plainly across her face. "The carriage is waiting. I was just coming to fetch you."

"I am quite ready," Elizabeth said, with a composure she felt she had earned.

Darcy stepped aside to make room for them. As she passed him, his attention followed—not boldly, not with any claim upon her, but with a quiet awareness that made itself felt all the same.

At the door, Elizabeth paused and glanced back once more at the stair she had descended without effort.

"Good morning, Mr Darcy," she said lightly. "Thank you for keeping me company in such an... accommodating house."

Something in his expression stilled, then eased—amusement, perhaps, or recognition. "I shall take that as encouragement rather than instruction."

"I recommend it," she said, and this time did not trouble herself to look away as she left.

# CHAPTER SIXTEEN

THE DOOR HAD SCARCELY closed behind her before the house rushed to meet her.

"...and I said as much, Jane, for it is perfectly obvious to anyone with eyes that matters are advancing, and I cannot imagine why anyone should pretend otherwise—Lizzy! There you are at last."

Elizabeth barely had time to set her reticule down before Mama swept her into her arms.

"You look very well," her mother declared, inspecting her with swift approval. "Quite refreshed. I told everyone you would be, of course. Fresh air, good food, and proper attention—that is all that was ever required."

Elizabeth smiled and stepped aside before she could be steered fully into the centre of the room. "I am glad to have satisfied expectations."

"Oh, they are most satisfactorily exceeded," Mama declared. "And now that you are home, we may speak freely. Jane, my love, tell your sisters what Mr Bingley said last evening."

Jane protested at once. "Mama, there was nothing to tell."

"There was quite enough," her mother returned briskly. "Dining with the family, walking out every day, music in the evenings—why, they danced, Lizzy. A reel. In the drawing room!"

Elizabeth turned to Jane, one brow lifting. "You did not mention that."

Jane laughed, flustered. "It was nothing formal. Only a little diversion. Mr Bingley insisted, and after some persuasion, Miss Bingley was prevailed upon to play for us."

"He is so very good," Mama declared. "And some things besides. Oh, so terribly clever of you, Lizzy, to fall ill at Netherfield, and how good you were, Jane, to make the best of it. Always thinking of your poor family, you are!"

Elizabeth caught her father's eye across the room. He closed his book at last.

"So," he said mildly, "Netherfield survives the Great Bennet incursion. I trust you did not exhaust them entirely."

"I did my best," Elizabeth said. "But I was outmatched."

"That is always the danger," he replied. His gaze lingered on her a moment longer than usual. "You are quite restored, then?"

"I am. At least, I appear to be."

His mouth twitched. "Appearances are a great comfort to the anxious."

"Oh, what about that enormous dog everyone talked about?" Kitty burst out suddenly, turning a chair for Elizabeth to take a seat. "Did you see him? Mrs Long said he was enormous. Was he as big as the table? Did he bark? Did he—"

"He did not bark," Elizabeth said. "At least, not at me."

Kitty looked faintly disappointed. "Well. That is dull."

Elizabeth accepted the chair Kitty dragged out for her and let herself sink into it with more relief than she meant to show. The room was loud—voices overlapping, her mother already in full speculation, Lydia laughing at something only she found amusing—and Elizabeth allowed it to wash over her while she adjusted her shawl. "Not when the creature's shoulder is as high as my elbow. Truly, Kitty, he is the largest dog I have ever seen, but he was quite..." Her brow creased. "Chivalrous, I suppose. I found it comforting."

Lydia groaned. "How very boring, Lizzy."

Elizabeth smiled, but as she reached to accept a pillow Mary passed her, her wrist stabbed her movement in a way it had never done before.

She froze—not enough for anyone else to remark upon—but long enough to twist her wrist about in shock. The sensation faded almost at once when she shifted her grip, leaving behind nothing more than a faint awareness, localised and precise, like a fingertip pressed lightly to the inside of her arm.

Elizabeth lowered her hand to her lap and frowned at it.

Jane was still speaking, earnest and glowing. "...and Mr Bingley was so attentive to everyone, Mama. He asked after you twice and sent his regards. Miss Bingley, too, though she said nothing about accepting your invitation to dine."

"Oh, no fear of that," Mama said at once. "Surely, now that you have caught Mr Bingley's notice so thoroughly, everything may proceed sensibly. He can hardly do otherwise, you see?"

Elizabeth rose before she had quite decided to do so, the motion arriving a half-second ahead of the explanation. "I believe," she said, while Mama was still in full possession of the conversation, "that I shall go up to my room."

Mama waved a hand, already turning back to Jane. "Yes, yes—do not overtire yourself, my love. You have done quite enough for one day."

Jane's eyes followed her, but Elizabeth smiled once—quick, reassuring—and slipped away before concern could gather momentum.

The noise thinned as she reached the hall. She paused at the foot of the stairs.

It had become a habit now, this hesitation. A small accounting taken before motion. She placed her hand on the banister, half-expecting—she did not know what.

Nothing answered her. No barrier. No strange insistence. The stair stood exactly as it always had.

Elizabeth mounted it without effort, then another step, and another, her stride settling into its familiar rhythm. Whatever had troubled her at Netherfield did not follow.

In her room, she crossed first to the trunk Mr Hill had brought up, still half-latched where it sat at the foot of the bed. She knelt and lifted the lid.

The books lay where she had packed them at Netherfield, wrapped carefully against one another. It was thoughtful of Papa to send these, and she had meant to read them all. Unfettered access to some of his books, including some new ones bought just for her? What a treasure! But she had not opened more than one all the while she lay at Netherfield. Intention, it seemed, could substitute for action longer than one might expect.

Now she drew them out, one by one, setting them on the coverlet and noting their titles properly at last. History. Essays. A slim volume of sermons she dismissed at a glance.

Then her hand paused, and she smiled.

A narrow book, plainly bound, its pages uneven with age. Not one she remembered from his library, and not one she had bothered to examine while at Netherfield. She knew it—not by title, not by reason, but with the quiet certainty of recognition, the sort that arrives before explanation.

"Well," she murmured, lifting the book, "so you did listen, after all."

She turned it over in her hands, amused. This was the one—the small, oddly charming collection she had noticed in the shop at Meryton and mentioned only in passing. Essays, certainly, but of a lighter sort: observations, fragments, reflections collected and translated from older hands, perhaps with more affection than ambition. The kind of book one dipped into, not studied.

She opened it at random and read a few lines. Her mouth curved. Not profound. Not improving. But clever in its way—and oddly familiar in rhythm, as though it brushed against a half-remembered rhyme from childhood. She read another paragraph, then another, entirely untroubled.

Charming.

Elizabeth closed the book and set it atop the others. For now, they would all go back to the safety of Papa's shelves.

DARCY DID NOT BEGIN with walking the land again.

He began, instead, with tea.

Bingley had only just settled himself at the small table near the window, cheerfully resigned to a second cup, when Darcy took the opposite chair without comment and unfolded a sheet of paper he had brought with him.

"You look ominous again," Bingley observed, brightening rather than recoiling. "Should I send for reinforcements, or is this merely one of your thoughtful silences made visible?"

Darcy glanced up. "Did you have the boundaries of Netherfield surveyed when you took the lease?"

Bingley laughed. "Ah. That sort of ominous. Yes, they have been—well—no. Not by me, at any rate. The place has been standing comfortably for years. I saw no reason to unsettle it."

Darcy accepted this without visible reaction. "What about before you took possession?"

"I believe my predecessor had it done once. Or perhaps his father. Someone sensible, certainly." Bingley sipped his tea. "Why? Has the house been quietly annexing Hertfordshire while I slept?"

"No," Darcy said. "But I am curious."

That earned him a look. Bingley leaned back in his chair. "You are never *just* curious."

Darcy did not dispute this. He glanced toward the door. "Is your steward engaged?"

Bingley followed his gaze, then shrugged with easy good nature. "Mr Bixby is somewhere about the place, no doubt heroically preventing chaos. If you wish to consult him, I shall summon him at once. But I warn you, he will be earnest."

"I should expect nothing less."

Mr Bixby arrived promptly: a man of middle years, composed manner, and an expression shaped by decades of orderly service. He bowed to both gentlemen and waited.

"Mr Bixby," Bingley began, with the air of a host relinquishing responsibility, "my friend has developed a rather... morbid fixation on Netherfield's land history."

"An interest," Darcy corrected, politely.

The steward inclined his head. "Very good, sir. In what respect?"

Darcy laid his paper on the table between them. It held no drawings, no flourishes—only a neat list of questions. "I should like to know whether any portion of the eastern rise has ever been remeasured, adjusted, or remarked upon in the course of the estate's keeping."

The steward blinked once. "The eastern rise, sir?"

"Yes."

"Well." Mr Bixby considered. "Not to my knowledge. It is not especially notable ground."

"Has it ever been enclosed?"

"No, sir."

"Cleared?"

"Not in my tenure."

"Divided? Possibly purchased or sold off to a neighbour?"

"No land sales have taken place in more than a century."

"Marked? In any way at all—a stile, perhaps, a fence..."

The steward hesitated. "There are old boundary stones, sir. Or were. Many were set deep. Some are no longer visible."

Darcy's pen moved. "And not uncovered?"

Mr Bixby glanced at the paper. "Forgive me, sir, but this is an unusually precise inquiry."

"It is," Darcy agreed. "That is intentional."

Bingley, who had been watching with affectionate bemusement, rose. "I think this is my cue to vanish. You have that look, Darcy—the one that suggests ledgers will soon appear, and I shall be made to regret my fondness for you."

Darcy did not look up. "You will regret nothing."

"That alone gives me pause." Bingley clapped Bixby lightly on the shoulder. "Answer whatever he asks. If he requests parchments from the reign of Henry VIII, humour him. There's a good fellow."

Darcy shook his head as the door closed and returned to the map. "Have there ever been complaints regarding that ground in years past?"

The steward frowned. "Complaints, sir?"

"Poor growth. Unaccountable cold. Captured pockets of frost, or perhaps even fissures from spring run-off—that sort of thing."

Mr Bixby paused longer this time. "No complaints of that nature have ever been formally lodged."

"Informally, then."

The man considered his words carefully. "There have been... remarks. Shepherds do not linger there. Game does not take to that stretch readily. But such superstitions are common enough. One learns not to give them undue importance."

Darcy made a note. "And the harvest?"

Mr Bixby blinked. "Sir?"

"This year's yield," Darcy clarified. "I am aware that the season was not ideal—late planting, thin heads, sluggish summer weather. How has Netherfield fared?"

The steward's expression changed at once—not to caution, but to something like pride. "Exceptionally well, sir."

Darcy looked up.

"In truth," Mr Bixby continued, "it has been our strongest year in recent memory. Wheat above expectation by nearly double. Barely clean and heavy—why, I daresay we had to sell a great deal of it merely for lack of space in the barn. No loss worth remarking upon. I laid the figures before Mr Bingley last month."

Darcy's mouth tightened slightly. He did not comment on that. Bingley would have accepted the statement with pleasure and asked no further questions; of that, Darcy had no doubt. No comprehension of the true bounty in his lap. The failure was his own, then, for not having insisted earlier upon instruction where instruction was plainly needed.

"You have those figures still?" he asked.

"Of course, sir. I can have them brought at once. As well as the previous years, if you wish."

"Yes." Darcy paused, then added, "And any older field notes. Tenant records. Drainage plans."

Mr Bixby hesitated. "I believe you have already seen the extent of what we possess. Netherfield's papers are... serviceable, but not especially deep. Anything earlier than my predecessor's time was not preserved with care."

Darcy inclined his head, accepting the answer without satisfaction. "Then I may need to look beyond this house."

"Sir—may I ask—are these inquiries prompted by some recent concern?"

"I prefer to understand what I am responsible for. While this land is not *my* responsibility, per se, my friend has taken up its stewardship, and he is inexperienced in certain matters."

Mr Bixby frowned, then nodded. "Of course. If you are seeking older context—records beyond the estate accounts—some matters were once noted in the parish books at Meryton. Land use. Enclosures. Boundaries that no longer exist as such. Not everything was preserved here."

Darcy's pen stopped. "Meryton," he repeated.

"Yes, sir. The clerk there keeps older materials. Dusty things. Rarely consulted."

Darcy folded his paper with care. "Thank you, Mr Bixby. You have been most helpful."

Mr Bixby nodded, though his expression had grown thoughtful. "I will have the harvest figures sent up directly."

Darcy turned back to the table. "Please do."

What troubled him was not that Netherfield prospered.

It was that it did so alone.

THE SITTING ROOM AT Longbourn had regained its usual volume.

Teacups clinked. Lydia laughed too loudly at something Kitty had not quite finished saying. Mama was explaining—at length—why Netherfield china was superior in weight and finish to anything that could reasonably be expected in a country neighbourhood, and Jane was smiling in the manner of one who had learned that resistance only prolonged the discussion.

Charlotte had been listening for some time before she spoke. She set her cup down carefully, as though concluding an internal reckoning, and looked from Jane to Elizabeth with a small, deliberate smile. "Well," she said, "Netherfield, then."

Jane laughed softly—not quite in amusement, not quite in embarrassment. "It was... very pleasant. Everyone was exceedingly attentive."

Elizabeth tilted her head. "That is one way of putting it."

Charlotte's brows rose. "I take it there is another?"

Jane glanced at her sister, colour touching her cheeks. "They were kind," she said again, more firmly this time. "And generous. I do not wish it to sound as though we were imposed upon."

"No one thinks that," Charlotte said, mild but keen. "One only wonders what sort of impressions were made."

Elizabeth lifted her cup. "I made mine horizontally, in a field."

Charlotte laughed. "I had heard your visit was eventful," she said. "I did not realise it involved geography."

Elizabeth sipped her tea. "I assure you, the ground was very determined."

Jane shook her head. "Lizzy—"

"Oh, do not look so concerned," Elizabeth said lightly. "I survived it, so I shall laugh about it. I should hate to be remembered as the Bennet sister undone by a mole hill."

Charlotte's mouth curved. "You always did have a talent for finding yourself in unusual situations."

"Or for unusual situations finding me," Elizabeth returned. "I cannot decide which is more troublesome."

Charlotte nodded, as though conceding the point. "If it is any comfort, the account circulating in Meryton is far less dramatic."

Elizabeth glanced at her. "Circulating?"

"Only mildly," Charlotte said. "Meryton has not spoken of anything else for a fortnight. Half the town is convinced you were struck down by a tragic constitution. The other half insists it was romance."

Lydia leaned forward at once. "It was Mr Darcy, wasn't it? There, I told you, Kitty. She had to make up for the Assembly."

Elizabeth reached calmly for her tea. "I just... fell. Or something. It had nothing to do with Mr Darcy."

Charlotte's gaze flicked, briefly and almost absently, to Elizabeth's lap.

"You're guarding that hand again," she said. "Does it still ache?"

Jane looked down at once. "Lizzy, does it?"

Elizabeth glanced at the pillow over her wrist, then smiled. "Only when it wishes to be noticed."

Charlotte huffed a quiet laugh. "That is not an answer."

"It is the truest one I have," Elizabeth said. "It has been perfectly well behaved all morning."

Jane relaxed. "I told you it would be well healed by now."

Charlotte tipped her head, studying her friend with the same practical calm she always employed. "It looked worse when I saw it last—quite the festering bother, as I recall. I only wondered."

"As did everyone," Elizabeth said. "I was quite the object of medical enthusiasm. No, Charlotte, it is quite healed now."

Charlotte accepted that, lifting her cup again. "Then I am satisfied."

Mama broke in, bright with conviction. "And very right you are, Charlotte—very right indeed. Nothing could have been better for Elizabeth than a few days at Netherfield. Such air! Such company! I always say that a change of scene does wonders, especially when there are agreeable young gentlemen involved."

Jane shifted, gently. "They were exceedingly kind, Mama."

"Kindness is quite beside the point. It is opportunity that restores one's spirits. And I am sure it did you good as well, my dear—walking, dining, dancing—why, I have no doubt Mr Bingley was in constant attendance."

Elizabeth hid a smile behind her cup.

"As for Elizabeth," Mrs Bennet continued, waving a hand in her direction, "she was never truly ill. A little faintness, nothing more. I told Mrs Long as much myself. Still, it is very proper that she should come home now, having been so very much admired."

Charlotte's mouth twitched. "Naturally."

Jane flushed, but smiled all the same.

Charlotte set her cup down at last. "How did you find Miss Bingley, then?"

Jane hesitated, colouring. "She is—very accomplished."

"And very invested," Elizabeth supplied. "In comfort, order, and the proper placement of guests."

Charlotte laughed. "That sounds like a study in itself."

At that moment, the door opened. Papa entered with a letter in his hand and an expression of mild, anticipatory resignation—the look of a man about to inflict news upon his family and prepared to enjoy it despite himself.

"My dear girls," he said, "I trust I am not interrupting a critical examination of wealthy gentlemen, dogs, or the moral character of Hertfordshire society?"

Elizabeth brightened. "Only its entertainment value."

"Excellent. Then you will all be pleased to know that we are shortly to receive another visitor for your amusement."

Mama sat up at once. "A visitor?"

"Yes. A cousin, my dear."

"A *male* cousin?" Mama demanded. "Is he single?"

Papa unfolded the letter with deliberate care. "He is one Mr William Collins, and no, my dear, I gather there is no Mrs Collins. He is newly ordained, and presently residing in Kent. He proposes to arrive tomorrow, to make our acquaintance, survey our domestic arrangements, and no doubt secure the happiness of the family in some manner yet to be determined. He writes with great enthusiasm and very little punctuation."

Mama clapped her hands. "Mr Collins! Oh, I should hate the very sight of the man but... You *did* say he was single? A clergyman, too—how respectable."

Charlotte leaned forward, suddenly alert. "How very interesting. Mr Collins of—?"

"Hunsford," Papa supplied. "Under the patronage of Lady Catherine de Bourgh."

Jane looked between them. "That sounds... formidable."

"Oh, it will be educational," Papa said pleasantly. "I trust we shall all survive it."

Charlotte lifted her teacup again, smiling into the rim. "Well," she said, "I should very much like to be present for that."

"That makes one of us," Elizabeth laughed.

# Chapter Seventeen

Meryton was busy in the late morning, carts edging past one another in the narrow street, voices overlapping in the practiced disorder of a market day. Darcy crossed it with purpose, coat buttoned, hat low, Brutus pacing at his side with unaccustomed restraint. The dog drew glances, but Darcy pretended to ignore them.

The clerk looked up as Darcy entered, surprise flickering into recognition and then sharpening into something closer to uncertainty.

"Mr Darcy. Good morning." He glanced instinctively toward the door, as though expecting explanation to follow.

"Good morning." Darcy removed his gloves with unhurried precision. "I was told the parish records are kept here."

The clerk blinked. "They are, yes—but—" He broke off, clearly recalibrating. "May I ask, sir, the nature of your request? You do not reside in Meryton."

"No." Darcy folded the gloves and set them aside. "But I am conducting inquiries relating to land use and boundary history in the neighbourhood."

That earned him a longer look. "I see," the clerk said, though it was clear he did not. "Most gentlemen apply through the steward at Netherfield, or else consult their own family papers."

"I have done so. I was advised there may be older references here."

"Well." The clerk hesitated, then nodded, already half overmatched by Darcy's manner. "Yes. Quite possibly. The earlier books are not often requested."

At that moment, Brutus stepped forward, intending to follow.

"Stay," Darcy said quietly, without turning.

The dog halted at once, then sat just inside the threshold.

The clerk glanced at him, then back at Darcy. "Is—will he—?"

"He will not interfere," Darcy said. "Nor move."

Brutus did neither.

After a moment, the clerk cleared his throat and gestured toward the back room. "If you will follow me, sir. The records are... thorough."

"I prefer it so."

The room beyond was a collection of clutter and piles of books, folios, and papers—a mountain of accumulation rather than neglect. Shelves lined the walls in uneven ranks, ledgers thick with age and habit, some spines cracked, others stiff with long disuse. Darcy removed his coat and laid it carefully over the back of a chair.

"Where would you wish to begin?" the clerk asked.

Darcy did not answer at once. His gaze had already settled on a particular shelf.

"Enclosure records. Agricultural surveys. Land grants, perambulation records, removed markers, or quitclaims and fines. The older the better. Have you anything copied in the Tudor period or earlier?"

"Tudor! Indeed, Mr Darcy, you are something of an historian." The clerk paused, then nodded slowly. "That would be... here. And here. Manorial court rolls, certain marginalia. Even some Jacobean era scribblings." He pulled out one volume, then another. "You may find some duplication."

"I will manage." He took the first ledger, opened it, and began.

He worked methodically. Rental agreements. Old surveys. Boundary disputes long settled and never revisited. Names repeated. Names vanished. Notations grew sparse the farther back he pressed, as though the land itself had grown less talkative with time.

Brutus settled near the doorway, watchful.

Darcy traced a finger along a margin, pausing at a note half-crossed out—*old stone removed during replanting*—with no date and no explanation attached. He turned the page. The next entry referred to a hedge realigned "for convenience."

He made a note. Then another. He did not allow himself to connect them until he had time to look over them all.

A burst of laughter from the street cut across his concentration. Boots passed the window—heavy, careless, unmistakably martial. The militia, then. He had heard they were to be quartered nearby; Bingley had spoken of little else since it had been announced.

Darcy did not look up at once. When he did, it was only because Brutus had risen.

The dog's attention fixed on the glass, posture alert but contained. He emitted a small "whuff," and the hair at his scruff lifted slightly.

Darcy followed the line of his gaze. A man stood across the way, half-turned, speaking to one of the shopkeepers. Darcy saw only his back, the careless angle of his shoulders, the easy confidence with which he occupied the space. He laughed again—an unremarkable sound, indistinct through the pane.

Darcy's hand stilled on the page. Was that...?

*No.* That was absurd.

The coat was wrong. The height uncertain. Any number of men walked with that loose assurance. Memory was not proof, and he would not be led by it.

The man followed his fellows, stepped out of view. Brutus remained where he was, but there was the faintest rumble in his deep chest.

Darcy closed the ledger and drew the next one toward him. His attention returned to ink and margin, to lines that could be measured and verified.

By the time he finished, the clerk hovered with polite unease.

"Find what you were seeking, sir?"

Darcy considered the question. "For now." He gathered his notes, replaced the ledgers precisely where he had found them, and reached for his coat. "Thank you for your time."

THE DECANTER MADE A soft, decisive sound as Bingley set it down.

"Now then," he said brightly, rubbing his hands, "we are agreed that the pheasants cannot possibly have all fled the county at once. I refuse to believe it. Darcy, you will back me up—won't you?"

Darcy looked up a moment too late. "I beg your pardon?"

Bingley laughed. "There! You see? Proof already. You were not listening."

"I was listening," Darcy said. "I was not, however, listening to the pheasants."

Miss Bingley closed her book with a snap that suggested she had never been reading in the first place. "He has been like this all evening. Present in body, absent in spirit. One would think he had left something unfinished."

Darcy reached for his glass. "I assure you, Miss Bingley, nothing of consequence has been neglected."

"Nothing *you* consider of consequence," she said sweetly. "Which is an entirely different standard."

Mrs Hurst reclined a little more deeply on the sofa. "Charles, you were saying something about a ball? I do hope it shall not be too tiresome."

Bingley seized upon the rescue with enthusiasm. "Ah, yes! A ball. I am convinced it is precisely what the neighbourhood requires. The weather is bound to keep us all indoors soon, and one cannot hunt forever."

"One can try," Darcy said.

Miss Bingley laughed. "Oh, Mr Darcy, you are a marvel of encouragement."

"I was not aware encouragement was my assigned role."

Bingley waved that away. "We should host it here, of course. Netherfield has not been properly animated in years—that is what the steward said. A fortnight from now, perhaps? Long enough to spread the word, not so long that everyone grows anxious."

Mrs Hurst nodded, already imagining it. "With proper music."

"And the very latest dances," Bingley added. "I shall have the most fashionable musicians brought from Town to ensure it."

Miss Bingley's gaze slid back to Darcy. "You are remarkably silent on the subject. Are you not in raptures at the notion, sir?"

"I see no objection," he said. "If you wish to host a ball, you certainly may."

"That is not an opinion," she said. "That is permission."

He inclined his head. "Then you have it."

She smiled thinly. "How generous."

Bingley leaned forward. "Darcy, you must agree it would be pleasant. New friends, good food for the season, a little gaiety—"

"A great deal of observation," Miss Bingley put in lightly. "We shall all be quite the spectacle, I daresay."

Darcy met her look. "If one attends a ball, one expects to be observed."

"Ah," she said. "But you were *observing* rather keenly two evenings ago, were you not?"

Bingley blinked. "Was he?"

Darcy set his glass down. "I have no idea what you are referring to."

Miss Bingley's smile widened by a fraction. "Miss Elizabeth Bennet's recovery was quite the evening's entertainment. One could hardly miss it."

"I fail to see how concern for a guest's health constitutes entertainment."

"Oh, concern," she echoed. "Yes. Of course."

Bingley laughed again, a little awkwardly this time. "Caroline—"

"I only mean," she continued, "that you seemed unusually attentive. Brutus too. One might almost think the household had adopted her."

Darcy's expression did not change. "My dog behaves as he sees fit. He is a dog."

"And yet," she said, tapping her book against her palm, "he does not follow *everyone* about the house."

Darcy's jaw tightened. "Nor did he follow Miss Elizabeth."

"No," Miss Bingley agreed. "He merely escorted her like a knight errant."

Bingley poked the fire with a stick. "Dogs are excellent judges of character. That is what they always say, is it not?"

Darcy's gaze lifted. "Dogs are creatures of habit who know which persons are likely to pet them or feed them."

Bingley cleared his throat. "Well! In any case, she did look improved. Quite herself again."

Darcy stood abruptly. He moved away from the hearth, crossing to the window as though the darkened grounds might offer something the room did not. The conversation resumed behind him at once—arrangements, invitations, the certainty that Mrs Bennet would be delighted, the question of whether the militia ought to be included.

Darcy did not turn.

"You will attend, of course," Bingley said.

"I attend events I am invited to," Darcy replied.

"That is a yes," Bingley declared. "Now, then, what of the guest list? Caroline, I trust you are keeping note of everything?"

Miss Bingley was watching Darcy in the glass. "Indeed. Mr Darcy, I cannot help but notice that you are rather restless."

He turned back at last. "If we are done speculating upon my disposition, I would be grateful to return to matters of substance."

"Oh, but that is the matter of substance," she said lightly. "You are rarely so… elsewhere. Meditating on.. What was it? I declare I recall some mention of 'fine eyes…'"

Darcy held her gaze. "You mistake distraction for reflection."

"On what?"

"On the dangers of overinterpretation."

Bingley chuckled. "You see? Perfectly himself, Caroline."

Darcy nodded once, as if to seal it. "Exactly."

He took up his glass again, posture composed, expression schooled—every inch the man at ease among friends, engaged in the pleasant business of an evening well-spent.

And if his attention strayed, if his replies came a heartbeat late, if his thoughts refused to settle—

Well.

No one could be blamed for that.

Miss Bingley's voice drifted across the room—some speculation about what she might wear, a remark on the tiresome habits of neighbouring families who thought calling weekly was the norm—and Bingley, who was now canvassing the subject of a menu for the ball with such enthusiasm that it required no effort at all to let it pass around him rather than through him.

Darcy stood near the mantel, one shoulder braced against it, glass untouched in his hand. He nodded when expected. He smiled when politeness demanded it. He even answered once or twice, briefly, with enough presence of mind to avoid remark.

The knock at the door was sharp enough to cut through conversation without apology. Bingley turned at once. "Good Lord—what now? We are not besieged, are we?"

The footman entered with unusual haste, crossing directly to Darcy without waiting for invitation. "A letter for you, sir. By express."

Darcy set his glass aside. "From whom?"

"Your steward, sir. At Pemberley. The messenger did not stay for a reply."

He did not open it at once. He turned slightly away from the hearth, unfolding the page with deliberate care, his posture composed even as his eye moved rapidly across the hand he knew as well as his own.

*Sir,*

*I beg leave to trouble you with a matter that has arisen in the ordinary course of estate management, and which I would not press upon your attention were it not, in my judgment, time-sensitive.*

*Our stores remain sufficient for the present, though they have begun to draw down more quickly than anticipated. In seeking to supplement them, I have made inquiry among our usual correspondents in Derbyshire and the neighbouring counties, only to find that many report shortages comparable to our own, and some far worse. Requests that in other years would have been answered readily have met with delay, apology, or refusal.*

*It has been mentioned to me—indirectly, and with some caution—that*

*Hertfordshire did not suffer the same deficiencies this season. I do not know whether this is mere optimism born of rumour, or a fact grounded in account, but the suggestion has arisen more than once.*

*As you are presently in that county, and in company with Mr Bingley of Netherfield, I thought it prudent to ask whether there is any truth to the report, and if so, whether it might be possible—discreetly—to ascertain whether a limited arrangement could be made before wider notice is taken. I would not wish to invite attention where none is needed, nor to impose upon hospitality, but it seems wise to consider the matter while the opportunity remains quiet.*

*I await your direction, and remain, as ever,*

*Your obedient servant,*
*Nigel Granger*

Impossible.

Darcy read the letter again.

Then again.

Miss Bingley's voice intruded faintly. "Is everything quite all right, Mr Darcy?"

Darcy folded the letter, but his gaze had grown muzzy, distant.

Bingley had risen now. "Darcy?"

He looked up. For a moment, he considered saying nothing. Of treating the matter lightly—of dismissing it as a steward's over-caution, the sort of anxious accounting that always followed a middling harvest. It would be easy enough. Comforting, even.

Instead, he found he could not.

"A matter for tomorrow, I daresay. No doubt some accounting error—Bingley and I may investigate it tomorrow."

Miss Bingley tilted her head. "You cannot mean here at Netherfield? I assure you, Mr Darcy—"

He slid the letter into his pocket. "My steward writes that supplies are drawing down faster than expected. He has been attempting to secure additional grain and finds that very few counties have any to spare."

Bingley's expression sobered at once. "I had heard the harvest was poor in places, but—"

"So had I," Darcy said. "I did not suppose it was so general."

"And yet," Bingley said slowly, "you speak as though this concerns us."

Darcy met his gaze. "It may. There are... reports now circulating abroad that Hertfordshire did not suffer in the same way. And there is truth to it, for Mr Bixby told me that your stores were nearly overrun this year."

Miss Bingley laughed. "Really, Darcy, one would think we were sitting on a dragon's hoard."

"I would prefer," Darcy said, "that we not discover whether that is how it will be described."

Bingley frowned. "Do you mean to suggest—"

"I mean only that attention, once drawn, is not easily redirected," Darcy replied. "And that generosity, when misunderstood, can become obligation."

Bingley was silent now, considering. At last, he said, "You think people will come asking."

"I think," Darcy said, after a moment, "that they already are."

"My dear Mr Hill, are you certain? Oh! Mr Bennet, he is here! Mr Collins... oh, look at that carriage—why, he must have a wealthy patroness, indeed. You said nothing of that, my dear. Jane! Where is Jane? Kitty, stop hovering—Lydia, do not run—Elizabeth!"

Elizabeth looked up from the book she had been pretending to read and exchanged a glance with Jane.

"That," Jane said mildly, "sounds decisive."

"That," Elizabeth replied, closing the book, "sounds inevitable."

Papa appeared in the doorway at that moment, eyes alight with the quiet delight of a man who sensed excellent sport approaching. "Ah, there he is. Two minutes early, for I should have expected no less."

Mama was already at the door, peering through the glass nearby. "There he is! Mary, my dear, put down that book, for you must be ready to receive him. Elizabeth, you will attend as well. Kitty—Lydia—where are you?"

Lydia skidded into the room, nearly colliding with Kitty. "Is he young?"

"Is he handsome?" Kitty demanded at the same time.

Papa smiled benignly. "He is, I believe, neither. But he is quite determined to be admired nonetheless."

Mr Collins entered as though making a presentation to a committee. He was tall, solemn, and dressed with conscientious respectability, his coat brushed smooth and his expression arranged into something he clearly believed conveyed humility. He bowed—deeply—then straightened with a faint air of relief, as though pleased to have executed the manoeuvre without mishap.

"Mr Bennet," he said, advancing a step as he drew off his hat. "It affords me the greatest satisfaction to make your personal acquaintance at last."

Papa inclined his head, amused already. "Mr Collins. You are very welcome to Longbourn. I trust your journey was tolerable."

"Entirely so, sir. Entirely. I am most grateful for your willingness to receive me, particularly given the long interval that has, regrettably, passed between our families."

Mama leaned forward, glowing. "We are delighted, I assure you. A cousin! And in holy orders! Pray, let us have your coat and come into the drawing room. You must sit—Jane, Elizabeth—"

Mr Collins turned then, evidently becoming aware that the room contained additional persons. His gaze passed over the assembled Bennets with careful neutrality, as though unwilling to hazard a guess.

"These," Papa said mildly, "are my daughters. I shall spare you the trouble of learning all their names at once."

Mr Collins bowed again, slightly less deeply, but with renewed solemnity. "Ladies. I am honoured."

Jane returned the courtesy, and Elizabeth followed—though a faint pressure stirred just behind her temple, brief and unwelcome. She dismissed it at once as the lingering consequence of too much movement too soon. Mary inclined her head gravely. Kitty and Lydia performed something between a nod and a stare.

"I hope," Mr Collins continued, folding his hands, "that my arrival does not impose upon your arrangements. I am most anxious that my visit should be conducted with perfect propriety."

Papa gestured toward the chairs. "You find us at leisure, Mr Collins. Pray, sit."

Mr Collins did so carefully, as though seating himself were a moral act requiring deliberation.

Mama clasped her hands. "And you must be quite fatigued after your journey. Tea shall be brought at once."

"Tea would be most welcome," Mr Collins said earnestly. "Lady—"

He stopped himself, coughed lightly, and resumed with visible effort. "That is to say—refreshment is always restorative after travel."

Papa's eyebrow rose a fraction.

Elizabeth, watching closely now, felt the distinct sensation of a sentence postponed rather than abandoned.

Tea arrived in a flurry of cups and polite fussing, Mama presiding with particular satisfaction as Mr Collins accepted his cup as though it were a sacrament.

"I am much obliged," he said gravely. "Nothing fortifies the constitution so reliably as a properly conducted domestic table."

Papa murmured something agreeable and leaned back in his chair.

Mr Collins cleared his throat. "I ought, perhaps, to begin by explaining the circumstances under which I have undertaken this visit," he said. "Not merely as a relation, but as one whose position places him in a certain—ah—responsibility toward the family."

Elizabeth's spoon paused halfway to her saucer. A faint pulse stirred at her temple again—there and gone before she could do more than notice it. She resumed the motion at once.

Mama brightened at once. "Responsibility! How very considerate."

"Yes. Indeed." Mr Collins inclined his head, pleased to be encouraged. "I am, as you know, in holy orders—and it is in that capacity that I enjoy the singular advantage of serving as rector to a most distinguished patroness."

Papa lifted his teacup. "Ah."

Mr Collins's chest expanded. "Yes, I had the honour of writing of her to you, Mr Bennet, but I would very much like to indulge your family with the magnanimity of Lady Catherine de Bourgh."

Elizabeth tilted her head. The name meant nothing—and yet Collins had spoken it as though it ought to. The pressure returned, no stronger than before, and she shifted slightly in her chair, attributing it to the stiffness of sitting so long after illness.

Mama, never one to leave a silence unused, leaned forward. "And Lady Catherine is—?"

"A lady of rank, fortune, and the most elevated sense of propriety," Mr Collins supplied at once. "She resides at Rosings Park in Kent, where her benevolence is felt far and wide. Her interest in the moral improvement of those beneath her care is both constant and comprehensive."

Papa's mouth twitched. "Indeed! And such a person has taken an interest in your humble self, sir? Why, that is indeed a boon."

"I am fortunate," Mr Collins continued, warming to his theme, "to enjoy her guidance in all matters of conduct. Few men are so privileged as to receive instruction so... personally delivered."

Mary leaned forward. "Does Lady Catherine take an interest in theological discourse?"

"Oh, most ardently," Mr Collins replied. "Indeed, she frequently condescends to offer suggestions—not merely upon sermons, but upon household arrangements, decorum, and the proper regulation of family life."

Mama looked faintly awed. "How very kind."

"Yes," Papa said. "Condescension is a rare gift."

Mr Collins nodded and set down his cup carefully. "Precisely. It was at her encouragement that I resolved to renew acquaintance with my cousins. Family harmony is a subject she esteems greatly."

Papa inclined his head. "A noble sentiment."

"Quite." Mr Collins hesitated—just a moment too long—then continued with visible restraint. "There are... connections, you see. Associations of some significance."

Elizabeth's eyes flicked to his face. The faint ache returned once more, sharper only in its persistence, and she pressed her lips together, determined not to indulge it.

Connections to what?

Mr Collins seemed to feel the question pressing upon him from all sides—and resisted it, with a very great flourish. "But," he concluded briskly, "such matters are best discussed when all parties are properly present. It would be quite premature to speak at length."

Elizabeth hid a smile behind her teacup.

Mama, however, was already nodding. "Of course. One must never be premature."

Mr Collins relaxed, satisfied. The explanation—postponed, not abandoned—settled into the room like a wrapped parcel set carefully aside. Tea was not going to be the most exhausting part of his visit.

# Chapter Eighteen

Papa did not so much suggest the walk the next morning as seize upon it.

"Mr Collins," he said, rising with an alacrity that startled the table, "you must excuse me. I have promised myself a turn about the grounds before the day escapes me entirely."

Collins was already on his feet. "How gratifying! I find that walking, when undertaken in sober reflection—"

"—is best accomplished alone," Mr Bennet finished cheerfully. "Do enjoy the morning."

And with that, he vanished through the door.

There was a brief silence.

Elizabeth felt it first—not awkwardness, precisely, but a faint foggy sensation, as though the very air in the room had grown less accommodating.

"Well," Collins said, clasping his hands. "Perhaps the ladies would care to accompany me into Meryton? It would be quite improper for a gentleman newly arrived in the neighbourhood not to make himself visible."

Lydia was already reaching for her bonnet. Kitty followed. Jane hesitated only long enough to glance at Elizabeth with a question in her eyes. Elizabeth smiled reassuringly—indeed, she would go, because refusal would have required explanation. They set off at once.

Mr Collins took the place beside Elizabeth with an air of decision, as though the arrangement had been settled in advance. His stride refused to find a common measure—too brisk for Jane, too lingering for Elizabeth—so that she was obliged either to hasten or be left a half-step behind. He corrected for this constantly, edging closer as he spoke, his shoulder nearly brushing her sleeve.

"And it is my firm conviction," he was saying, "that propriety, once established, must be upheld with consistency. One cannot allow uncertainty to creep in where duty has already been so clearly defined."

Elizabeth murmured what courtesy demanded and fixed her gaze ahead.

He continued without pause. Of obligations. Of family arrangements. Of... nothing of substance, really. The full summary of any actual points he made could have been voiced in a handful of words, but he chose instead to ladle them on rather more generously.

But it was his voice that grated the most. It had a particular quality when he warmed to a subject—flat, yet earnest, and unyielding, each sentence laid atop the last as though he were building toward a conclusion that permitted no alternative.

She listened. Or tried to.

The difficulty did not announce itself at once. It began as a faint compression, deep behind her ears, as though the space around her head had grown subtly smaller. His words reached her clearly enough, yet seemed oddly displaced—too near and too far at once.

She shifted her attention to the road. The hedgerow. Jane's profile a few steps ahead.

The sensation persisted. Similar to yesterday's faint headache, but worse. She shook her head experimentally, and the pressure branching across her forehead grew no worse, no better.

Mr Collins leaned nearer, lowering his voice with confidential gravity. "In matters of inheritance, especially, one must be prepared to act decisively. Hesitation serves no one."

The pressure sharpened—not pain, not dizziness, but a firm internal protest that had nothing to do with her thoughts or temper. Sound hollowed. His voice dulled into vibration rather than meaning, each word arriving with uncomfortable force, as though striking a single point just inside her skull.

Elizabeth slowed without intending to. She brought a hand up, fingers pressing instinctively to her ear, and turned her head away from Mr Collins.

As if he were to blame for her sudden earache! How Papa would laugh at the notion. Why, that was preposterous. She was overtired. Should not have undertaken such a long walk so soon. That was all.

Yet when she straightened, and he fell briefly silent, the pressure eased at once—retreating, not gone, but diminished enough to breathe.

Elizabeth frowned.

Voices did not behave like this. Proximity did not produce sensation. Words did not create screaming pain in one's ear all on their own. And yet the moment he resumed—earnest, uninterrupted—the nerve-biting pain crept back again, clear and unmistakable.

"...a duty I have long considered with the utmost seriousness," he was saying, hands folded before him as he walked, his tone warm with self-approval. "One must, after all, look beyond personal inclination when Providence has laid out one's responsibilities so plainly—"

"Naturally," Elizabeth said, digging a finger against the side of her neck just below her ear. Perhaps the pressure could be shifted...

"It has always been my belief," he continued, "that a proper sense of obligation, once embraced, is a source of great comfort. There is relief in knowing one's course has been determined—arranged, if you will—by wiser authority than one's own—"

Something twinged behind her left ear this time.

Elizabeth frowned faintly and shook her head. The sensation persisted—narrow, insistent—like a finger pressed too firmly just out of reach.

"—and that personal happiness, while not insignificant, must always be understood as secondary to the greater structure of—"

The sound wavered. His voice did not grow louder, but it lost shape, flattening into a single, grating thread that vibrated against her skull. The words no longer arrived as sentences—only as pressure.

"I beg your pardon," she said quickly, though she could not have said what she was interrupting. "Would you—would you allow me a moment?"

"Certainly, certainly," he replied, sounding pleased rather than concerned. "I was only remarking that once a young lady understands the advantage of a suitable arrangement, she is spared the inconvenience of—"

The ringing spiked, almost like an explosion inside her ears.

Elizabeth yelped and clasped the sides of her head with a hiss. But her foot came down late, her balance tipping just enough to force her hands out into the empty air. She caught herself at once, but the world had narrowed unpleasantly, the sound pressing inward until there was nowhere left for it to go.

She could not have said what he was saying now. The words no longer mattered. The sound pressed in on itself, crowding the narrow space of her attention until there was no room left to endure it.

Elizabeth turned away from him abruptly—not as an act of will but writhing, ignorant evasion.

And the ringing eased at once.

Not vanished—but receded, like a tide withdrawing the moment one stepped back from the shore. Air rushed in where pressure had been. The world righted itself.

She stood very still, heart beating harder than the exertion warranted.

This was not faintness. This was not some inflammation of the ear, as she used to get when she was a child. Whatever had protested had done so vehemently, selectively—and with far too much precision to be ignored.

Elizabeth narrowed her eyes and decided to put it to the test. A little distance might... She slowed.

Collins slowed to match her, and the pressure in her ear rang down her spine until she was grating her teeth.

She angled left to admire a hedge.

Collins angled with her.

The sensation sharpened—through her core as much as through her ears. Not alarm, but an unmistakable urging to move away. She quickened her pace without quite knowing why.

They had nearly reached the first houses when a burst of laughter carried toward them—easy, unrestrained, utterly unconcerned with being overheard. Two officers came into view first, walking abreast with the unselfconscious ease of men who had nothing to prove to one another.

Kitty gave a small, excited sound. "Oh! That is Lieutenant Denny. We met him last week—Lydia, do you see?"

"I do," Lydia replied, already quickening her pace. "And the other must be—oh, I do not know him. But he is wearing regimentals, so we must meet him!"

The two men slowed, then halted altogether as Denny turned, his expression brightening. "Ah—Miss Lydia Bennet! I thought that was your voice."

Lydia all but bounced forward. "We knew it! Kitty, I told you."

Kitty smiled at once. "*I* told *you*, Lydia. Good afternoon, Lieutenant Denny. Oh, you haven't met our sisters. This is Jane and Lizzy, and... oh, dash it all, Mary did not come. She never does."

"Good afternoon to you, ladies," Denny replied with a bow. "May I present my friend and newly appointed brother officer, Mr Wickham."

Mr Wickham inclined his head easily. "Ladies."

"Well now, this is most fortuitous," Mr Collins said, his voice carrying with it a tone of instant proprietorship. "Gentlemen, allow me to introduce myself. I am Mr William Collins, cousin to these young ladies and a clergyman entrusted with the moral welfare of a respectable parish. It affords me the greatest satisfaction to encounter officers of His Majesty's forces engaged in the worthy task of preserving order in our county." He smiled upon them—not warmly, but approvingly—like a man conferring acknowledgment rather than seeking it.

Elizabeth's ear sent a painful shiver down the cords of her neck. A thin, narrowing sound that pulled her focus inward despite herself.

Denny blinked at Collins' speech. "That is very good of you, sir."

Mr Collins gesticulated broadly. "I have long held that discipline and moral instruction, when properly aligned, serve as the twin pillars of social order. One must admire the uniform, of course, but it is the character beneath it—"

Elizabeth shifted her stance and crossed her arms tightly over herself—she could hardly help it. Her eyes were starting to water.

Mr Collins shifted with her. "—that ensures the stability of our communities."

Jane glanced sideways. "Lizzy, are you well?"

Elizabeth lifted a hand to her ear, fingers pressing lightly. "Perfectly. Pay me no mind."

Denny laughed at something Mr Collins had said. "Most amusing, sir! You catch us at an opportune time, for we were just returning to our barracks. I was giving Mr Wickham a tour and introducing him around town."

Wickham inclined his head. "Ah, yes, I am indebted to you for introducing me to Mrs Morris and her excellent larder, as well as Sir William and his equally splendid cellars. I very much look forward to meeting more of Meryton's fine residents if they are all so welcoming."

The sound in Elizabeth's ear did not vanish. But it... well, it shallowed somehow. The ringing, which had tightened to something like a snapped violin string, loosened just enough that she could distinguish his words again from the noise that had been riding them. Her head felt... less compressed. Not clear—no, not comfortable. Merely tolerable.

Mr Collins resumed at once, encouraged by the attention. "How generous of you, sir! I am certain that I, too, shall find the good neighbourhood excessively welcoming when I—"

The sound sharpened again, quick and unwelcome. Elizabeth's jaw tightened. She turned her head slightly, as though angling away from the sun, and the pressure eased by a fraction. Enough to breathe. Enough to think.

It had to be the cold. The walk. The lingering effects of her illness. Or possibly a new ailment altogether. Perhaps Hill still had some drawing salve she could apply when she returned home.

Wickham, to his credit, listened with courteous patience, his expression easy, unstrained. When Mr Collins paused for breath, he remarked mildly, "You must find the county quite pleasing compared to… Kent, was it? Ah, yes, I have been there a handful of times. Lovely country, but somewhat rocky soil, as I recall."

Elizabeth lowered her hand, the better to hear Mr Wickham, when she became aware that the screaming pain in her ear had eased somewhat rapidly.

The relief was incomplete. Unreliable. It came and went with her attention, with the cadence of voices, with the way the group stood arranged upon the road. She could not have said why it improved when Wickham spoke, only that it did.

The idea was… well, it was obscenely convenient. How clever she was to develop some sort of allergy to an odious man while the agreeable-looking ones brought relief! Indeed, Papa would laugh rather heartily at her contrivance. She scoffed and rolled her eyes at herself. If only she could claim such a selective malady!

And yet, when Mr Collins spoke again, the agony crept back—only for a moment, but still… Curious.

Hooves sounded on the road behind them, and Elizabeth turned more from instinct than curiosity. Mr Bingley reined in with an audible laugh, already half out of the saddle.

"Well! This is a fortunate meeting, indeed," he called. "We were just thinking of calling on you at Longbourn, Miss Bennet. And Miss Elizabeth, how very pleased I am to see you looking so well."

Mr Wickham turned at once, recognition lighting his face. "Bingley?"

Bingley blinked, then broke into a broad smile. "Wickham! Upon my word—I had no notion you were anywhere near Hertfordshire." His gaze dropped to the uniform, then lifted again, quick and incredulous. "Darcy, did you know of this?"

Mr Darcy was already dismounting, but he seemed to freeze in place as his eyes found the man in question. His jaw flickered—just once, then his boot found the ground, and he shook his head. "I did not."

Wickham laughed lightly. "The regiment keeps its own counsel, it seems. I enlisted only two days ago. Good to see you again, old boy."

Darcy hardly even inclined his head. But he did glance at Elizabeth, his eyes scarcely touching hers before his gaze retreated again.

Mr Collins drew himself up, his expression brightening with renewed purpose. "Mr Bingley, you say? How exceedingly fortunate. I have had the pleasure of hearing your name spoken with the highest regard in the neighbourhood. Your hospitality at Netherfield is already quite the subject of admiration."

Bingley laughed, a sound as easy as his dismount had been. "You are very kind, sir. I am always glad to make new acquaintances."

"And your companion," Mr Collins continued, turning with deliberate ceremony toward the other gentleman, "Did I hear you name him as—" He paused, eyes sharpening with a kind of anticipatory reverence. "Mr Darcy? I trust that is... *the* Mr Fitzwilliam Darcy of Pemberley in Derbyshire, son of the late George Darcy, esquire, and nephew to Lord Matlock?"

Darcy inclined his head. "I believe you have me at a disadvantage, sir."

Mr Collins' hands clasped together as though the word itself had completed some long-prepared sentence. "Indeed. Indeed! How gratifying—how truly gratifying to encounter you here, sir, and under such circumstances! Why, truly, fate has smiled on me. I am Mr William Collins, at present residing with my cousins at Longbourn, and entrusted with the spiritual guidance of a most respectable parish in Kent."

Darcy acknowledged this with a second, briefer bow.

"I need hardly say," Mr Collins went on, warming at once, "that your name is known to me through channels of the utmost propriety. Your estate, sir—your family—your connections—" He smiled, full and confident. "My noble patroness, Lady Catherine de Bourgh, speaks of you often."

Elizabeth felt a flicker of something like dread, though she could not have said why. She watched Darcy closely now, half-expecting him to bristle, or withdraw, or—she did not know what. Instead, he remained still, his expression composed to the point of severity.

"I am honoured," he said after a moment.

Mr Collins nodded, as though this reply had confirmed something long anticipated. "Her ladyship takes a most active interest in the preservation of proper order," he continued. "Indeed, she has often remarked upon the uncommon responsibility borne by certain families—those whose inheritance is not merely a matter of property, but of continuity."

Darcy's expression remained unchanged.

"It is a rare privilege," Mr Collins pressed on, "to observe such a convergence of stewardship and descent. There are names, after all, which carry obligations beyond the ordinary—threads laid down long before our present arrangements, yet still... still discernible, if one knows how to look."

*Threads?* What in the world could that mean? Elizabeth glanced at Jane, but her sister's expression remained politely blank.

"One does not often see them align so clearly," Mr Collins concluded, with utter satisfaction, "as they do in your family, sir. I am, you see, something of an authority on the matter, having done extensive studies on the family histories. Sir, I would count it the *highest* honour if you should desire for me to lay out the lineage and—"

"That will hardly be necessary," Darcy cut in. "I am quite familiar with my own circumstances."

Mr Collins faltered—only for a moment—before recovering with a deferential smile. "Of course. Of course. I merely meant—"

"I understand what you meant," Darcy said. "I do not care to have my family or my affairs discussed." His gaze shifted away, signalling the end of the matter.

Elizabeth glanced at Jane, who met her look with a faint crease of confusion. Lydia, for her part, had already turned her attention back to Lieutenant Denny, who appeared deeply engaged in recounting some small adventure of the previous evening.

Wickham stood a little apart, hands loosely clasped behind his back, observing the exchange with mild amusement. "Darcy is rarely tempted by ceremony," he remarked pleasantly. "Even when it is offered with the very best intentions. Pray, do not be put out, Mr Collins."

Darcy shot him a brief look—more acknowledgment than reproach—and Wickham's smile deepened just slightly, as though pleased to have smoothed the exchange without drawing attention to the act.

Nothing more followed. The space between the two men felt oddly taut, as though something unspoken had been set down between them and neither wished to be the first to move it. But Mr Bingley, at least, could be relied upon for genial conversation, and Mr Denny held his end admirably well.

She lost the thread of what was being said because, all at once, her ears no longer hurt. The change struck her so sharply that she nearly looked about her, as though something in the air had shifted without warning. She listened again, cautiously, half-expecting the pressure to return, but the voices reached her plainly enough now, no longer forcing themselves upon her attention.

She drew a slow breath, irritation flickering at herself for having noticed at all. She must have been dwelling on it—worrying at a discomfort until it grew teeth. It would ease, naturally, the moment she stopped attending to it. There was no mystery in that.

Mr Collins brought his hands together with brisk satisfaction. "Well! This has been an encounter of the greatest interest. I shall certainly write to her ladyship at once. She will be exceedingly gratified to learn of it."

Elizabeth let out a short, incredulous breath before she could stop herself. "I am sure Lady Catherine receives a great many letters."

"Ah, but not of this nature," Mr Collins replied, undeterred. "Such meetings are not mere coincidence. They signify—"

"Mr Collins," Jane said, stepping in without raising her voice, "we were just about to continue on to Meryton."

"Yes, yes—of course," he agreed at once, turning on the word as though it had been his idea all along. "I would not think of detaining these gentlemen further. Duties call us all in different directions." He inclined his head toward Darcy and Bingley with formal approval, already gathering himself for departure.

Bingley swung back into the saddle with a cheerful wave. "We shall see you all again soon, I hope."

Darcy lingered a moment longer. His gaze passed over Elizabeth without pause, then returned to Wickham. "If you will excuse us," he said. He mounted his horse without further comment. Bingley followed at once, already speaking as they turned their horses back toward Netherfield.

Lieutenant Denny laughed. "Come along, Wickham. If we do not return by dinner, the colonel will have us scrubbing boots for a fortnight."

Wickham cast one last, polite glance toward the ladies. "My apologies. Duty insists." The two officers turned off down the road toward the barracks, their conversation already rising into laughter as they went.

Elizabeth watched them go, her attention lingering longer than she meant it to, until the curve of the street carried them out of sight.

"Well," Lydia declared at once, "that was diverting! Officers, estates, titled ladies—what a very excellent morning."

The little party gathered itself again without ceremony, and Mr Collins resumed his place at Elizabeth's side as though nothing at all had intervened.

She did not register the change immediately, but when she did, it was hard to think of anything else.

They had gone no more than a dozen steps when the faint compression returned, just behind her ear. Whatever it was had returned, just as sharply as before.

# CHAPTER NINETEEN

TWO DAYS HAD PASSED since the walk to Meryton, and Darcy had already learned how little time a neighbourhood required to draw conclusions. Refusing Sir William Lucas's invitation would have been read as withdrawal; attending it, at least, allowed him to hear what was said in his presence rather than beyond it. He therefore came to Lucas Lodge as expected, with Bingley beside him and his own intentions held firmly in check.

Sir William received them in the entry with a warmth that required no encouragement. "Mr Bingley, Mr Darcy, how very good of you to come. We are delighted, quite delighted." He ushered them forward at once, speaking as he went of the pleasure of company and the fortune of such an afternoon.

The drawing room was already arranged for the purpose. Several neighbours were present, seated in small clusters that suggested conversation begun and paused rather than concluded. Miss Lucas stood near the tea table, conferring quietly with her mother. Mrs Philips occupied a chair by the window, her attention divided between the room and the door. Darcy took the chair indicated and tried to speak as little as possible. Tea had not yet been poured.

"But where are the Bennets?" Sir William wondered, glancing toward the hall. "Why, Mrs Bennet is always here first of everyone. Charlotte, my dear, did you not speak with Miss Elizabeth only yesterday?"

"I did," Miss Lucas said. "Lizzy said they were surely coming. She did say she had been troubled with a rather persistent headache, though. Nothing serious, I am sure—but enough to delay them, perhaps."

Mrs Philips shook her head. "Dear Lizzy is forever doing too much. Out walking without her bonnet again, no doubt. I daresay she has taken a cough, and she will not rest when she ought."

"Quite so, quite so," Sir William said. "But she is young and hearty, and what good is youth if one does not have a bit of gaiety?"

Darcy did not join in the speculation. The explanation was taken up and set aside with equal ease, and the room turned its attention to safer ground. Mrs Philips resumed her account of a recent party elsewhere; Sir William responded with approving exclamations; Lady Lucas moved between the chairs, greeting everyone, calling for a fresh cup, murmuring that tea was already cold and a fresh pot would be brought directly. Bingley accepted a biscuit he did not eat. The talk settled into the mild, circulating pattern of people filling time while waiting for others to arrive.

A burst of laughter sounded in the hall, and Sir William broke off at once. "Is that the Bennets? Oh! Why, no, but those fine fellows I met yesterday have come. Jolly good!"

The door opened before anyone could answer. Lieutenant Denny entered first, two officers close behind him, their voices still trailing the end of some private jest. Wickham followed last, his expression easy, his step unhurried as his gaze crossed the room and met Darcy's without hesitation.

"How exceedingly welcome you are! Pray, come in, come in." Sir William bowed and scraped to make himself amenable. Chairs were shifted, names exchanged, connections supplied with enthusiasm that required no encouragement. Wickham turned at once to answer a question put to him, his manner easy, his replies pitched to be heard without demanding attention. He laughed when expected to laugh, spoke when addressed, and gave no sign that anything lay between him and Darcy that was not entirely civil.

It was only a matter of time before Sir William got round to "introducing" Darcy to all the militia members, and Heaven only knew what he would say. No less, surely, than what was probably already circulating all Meryton about him, thanks to Collins.

It would not take much. A remark repeated with a flourish. A hesitation filled in by someone else. Collins had a talent for speaking with certainty where none was required, and Wickham—standing there so comfortably, answering when asked, declining to explain nothing at all—gave the room precisely the shape it needed to begin filling the gaps.

Bingley bent toward him. "It seems Sir William is a prodigiously welcoming host."

Darcy did not reply. He watched Wickham accept a cup and thank the lady who offered it, watched the officers draw closer together, watched attention collect and redistribute itself in small, decisive movements. Whatever was said next would not remain contained. It never did.

The talk had drifted toward the window when a new rush of voices finally carried in from the passage. Mrs Bennet swept into the room still speaking, her flustered apologies—complete with one or two barbs toward her second daughter—tumbling over one another as she crossed the threshold. Her daughters followed close behind her and were already scanning the company for interest. Miss Elizabeth came in last.

She halted just inside the room, and Darcy marked it at once—not a pause of uncertainty, but the reflex of someone meeting resistance. Her smile came late and did not quite settle; a faint line appeared beside her eye, as though she were bracing against something she had learned to expect. There was nothing languid or coy in it. If anything, she looked prepared for endurance.

The recognition stirred sharply in him. Not curiosity—something nearer to alarm.

Mr Collins advanced at once beside her, his manner already shaped for possession, his smile fixed as though the moment belonged to him by right. Whatever he said did not carry across the room, but Miss Elizabeth's response did. She recoiled—not backward, but inward—a quick, unmistakable withdrawal. Her hand lifted to her ear, fingers pressing there as though a sound had struck too near or too suddenly.

Darcy's hand tightened around his glass before he was aware of the movement. It was an absurd response. He told himself so at once. And yet he could not look away.

She mastered herself quickly. She lowered her hand and spoke brightly to their host, with a smile that did not look like her own.

"Oh, Sir William, what is that I see on your mantel?" She turned her head decisively toward the far wall. "Is that a new volume of Fordyce?"

Sir William brightened. "Ah! You have an excellent eye, Miss Elizabeth. Pray, allow me—"

Mr Collins seized upon the opening with joy. "Indeed, sir, quite so—that volume is most instructive, most instructive indeed. One cannot but admire the care with which his words have been selected, particularly when they speak to—"

Sir William beamed and drew the book from the shelf. "Ah, you must allow me to show you—this one, for instance—"

Miss Elizabeth did not wait for the sentence to finish.

She moved quickly—too quickly to be accidental—her attention fixed solely on the narrow space that had opened before her. A chair clattered as her foot caught its leg; she checked herself with a sharp breath and a murmured, "I beg your pardon," already past the lady she had nearly collided with.

"Lizzy!" Mrs Bennet called after her.

But Elizabeth did not turn.

Darcy found himself following her course across the room without conscious choice. As she passed out of the press near the mantel, something sharp flickered at the corner of his eye—a brief, involuntary spasm that vanished the moment he tried to still it. He blinked once, then again, annoyed, and fixed his attention back upon her.

At first, she did not look where she was going, only away—away from the mantel, away from Mr Collins. After several steps, her pace altered, her shoulders lowering by small degrees, as though something had loosened its hold. Darcy felt the answering pull at once: not pain, not weakness—only a persistent irritation, like a muscle refusing to settle no matter how carefully he adjusted himself.

Her gaze passed over Darcy—swiftly, without either visible pleasure or disdain—and fixed instead upon the officers standing a few feet to his left. She went to greet them at once.

When she stopped, she drew in a breath that lifted her chest fully, one hand touching her temple for the briefest moment before falling again. The strain that had carved itself about her mouth eased; the line at her brow softened, as though she had crossed some invisible threshold.

At the same instant, Darcy's eyelid betrayed him again—once, twice in quick succession—an absurd, persistent twitch that refused command. He clenched his jaw and let his gaze drift, unwilling to be seen fussing over such a thing.

"Well!" Wickham said, turning to Miss Elizabeth as she came to a halt near them. "This is an improvement upon the afternoon. I was beginning to think the Lucases meant to overwhelm us with propriety before allowing a single agreeable face into the room."

Miss Elizabeth let out a breath that was almost a laugh. "You have my sympathy. It appears propriety has been in robust health of late."

Denny grinned. "You should hear Wickham complain when he is truly afflicted."

"I do not complain," Wickham said mildly. "I merely observe."

"And endure?" Miss Elizabeth returned.

"Endurance is not my strongest virtue," Wickham admitted. "I prefer variety. Conversation, for instance, that does not insist upon instructing me."

Denny laughed again. "Then you are well placed. Miss Elizabeth has a talent for discouraging instruction."

"I make no such promise," she said. "Only that I listen selectively."

"Wisely," Wickham replied. He shifted his stance slightly, opening the small circle without breaking it. "Some subjects do suffer from being listened to too closely." His gaze lifted then—not abruptly, but as if the thought itself had widened—and found Darcy where he stood nearby.

"You have been subjected to it longer than any of us, Darcy," Wickham said, making a brief, careless gesture. "That rot Mr Collins was discoursing upon yesterday. I hope you did not suppose any of us took it seriously."

Darcy did not answer at once—not because he had nothing to say, but because Miss Elizabeth had already spoken.

"Oh, I should hope not," she said. "I have found that the more confidently a subject is explained to me, the less likely it is to improve my understanding of it."

Her tone—dry, exact—caught his attention. He found himself watching her mouth as she spoke, the faint emphasis she placed upon *confidently*, the quiet satisfaction of a thought well landed. The rest of the room receded. He was aware of Wickham again only when he resumed.

Wickham smiled. "Exactly my thought. A great many words expended to prove what requires none. One would think the matter settled generations ago, and yet it resurfaces whenever someone wishes to feel important."

Wickham's ease unnerved him. He spoke as though the matter were safely abstract, when Darcy knew too well how quickly such talk acquired shape once repeated aloud. Darcy felt the faint tug beneath his right eye again—irritating, insistent. He forced his mouth into stillness, held it there until the twitch subsided.

"Generations! My, that is an impressive talent," Miss Elizabeth returned. "To say everything at once and nothing in particular and to never let old bones rest."

Darcy's attention sharpened further. She was engaged now—not merely teasing, but probing—and the knowledge set him on edge. He did not want her encouraged in this line of thought. He did not want Wickham entertaining her curiosity at all. The muscle along his cheek tightened without permission; he masked it at once by shifting his jaw, as though easing a stiffness that did not exist.

Denny grinned. "That sounds like half the men I've met since joining the regiment."

"And all the sermons," Miss Elizabeth added. "Though I am told one must be charitable."

"Charity," Wickham said, "need not extend to listening without end. Especially when one is reminded, again and again, of obligations attached to certain unwilling people."

The words struck too near. Wickham was opening a door Darcy had spent years keeping firmly shut, and doing so before an audience he did not trust himself to disregard. A thin, crawling sensation traced the inside of his right arm, from elbow to wrist—nothing painful, merely intolerable. His fingers curled and uncurled once at his side before he stilled them.

Miss Bingley, who had drawn near enough to hear this, paused beside Darcy. "How very philosophical," she said lightly. "One would almost imagine you speak from experience, Mr Wickham."

He inclined his head. "Only from long acquaintance with the subject. Some families acquire expectations as naturally as others acquire furniture, and are told it would be ungrateful to question either."

Miss Bingley smiled. "Expectations are rarely without foundation."

"Nor are they always welcome," Wickham replied, just as pleasantly.

Darcy became acutely aware—too late—that he had been positioned within the circle without volition. Wickham had done it deftly, as though Darcy's participation were a foregone conclusion. He had not spoken. He had not assented. And yet Elizabeth was now looking toward him, however curiously, as though waiting to see whether he would.

A brief spasm caught at the corner of his mouth. He forced a breath through his nose and let his expression settle into composure by sheer habit.

"You never cared for that sort of talk, did you, Darcy?" Wickham went on, his tone pitched easily, publicly. "I remember you could scarcely keep a straight face when such subjects were raised at Pemberley. Old trusts, family obligations, and the like."

Darcy felt irritation rise—swift, sharp, and threaded with something more dangerous. Wickham had no right to summon those words into the open. Not here. Not where *she* could hear them and begin, in that incisive way of hers, to wonder. The twitch returned, sharper this time, drawing a faint line along his cheek. He turned his head slightly, presenting his profile, as though the angle alone might subdue it.

"I do not recall finding it amusing."

"No," Wickham said at once, conciliatory. "Perhaps not amusing. Tiresome, then. A burden laid on you without your consent."

Miss Elizabeth's mouth curved. "A most considerate assessment. One might think consent a useful element in many arrangements."

Darcy glanced at her despite himself—and was caught. Her expression held a challenge lightly worn, curiosity sharpened by wit rather than suspicion. The sight of it unsettled him far more than Wickham's provocation. The sensation in his arm deepened, concentrating itself with malicious precision in the middle finger of his right hand. It twitched once. He pressed the offending finger against his thigh and kept his posture perfectly still. He had already allowed too much.

"And yet," she continued, "I find it endlessly fascinating how certain topics manage to recur, no matter how decisively one declines to encourage them. It does tend to excite curiosity, despite my better judgment."

She was not circling idly; she was closing in. The ease with which she articulated it, the care of her phrasing, stirred a cold unease beneath his ribs. She spoke as though the thing itself had already begun to yield to her attention.

"You see, Darcy? Declining encouragement is rarely sufficient," Wickham said. "One must appear to entertain them, or they return with greater enthusiasm."

Darcy barely heard him. His awareness had narrowed to her—her tone, her concentration, the way her mind moved forward even as her manner remained easy. He had known she was clever. He had not anticipated how dangerous that cleverness might become when turned toward this.

"Like a cold," Miss Elizabeth chuckled. "Or an unwelcome relative."

Miss Bingley's laughter rose like a bubbling brook. "Both topics with which you are intimately familiar, Miss Elizabeth?"

Elizabeth levelled a cooler smile at Miss Bingley, and Darcy's unease deepened. The muscle beneath his eye flickered again, stubborn as a pulse. He smiled immediately—an old, reliable reflex—hoping the motion concealed it. The effort made his jaw ache.

Miss Elizabeth continued to regard Miss Bingley for a moment, her head tilted slightly, as though considering a line of argument rather than a jest. "And yet intimacy does imply attachment," she said.

And then her eyes turned to Darcy. "One does not revisit unhappy subjects so persistently without being forced to acknowledge that they retain *some* power—whether to instruct, to warn, or merely to remind."

Darcy felt a sharp, unwelcome recognition. She was not guessing. She was reasoning. And worse—she was enjoying it. The notion that this might matter to her, that she might feel the pull of it as something worth understanding, filled him with a sudden, irrational need to stop her at once.

Miss Bingley smiled, her eyes bright with interest. "How very philosophical. I should not have thought the matter so complicated."

"Nor should I," Miss Elizabeth replied. "Which is precisely why I find it so engaging."

That did it.

Darcy's restraint frayed—not from temper, but from urgency. The twitch in his hand broke free again, a quick, traitorous movement he subdued by curling his fingers hard into his palm. He could not allow her to follow this thread any further. Not with Wickham present. Not with half the room listening. Not when she had already come so close without knowing it.

Wickham's brows lifted, amused. "You would have made a formidable auditor, Miss Elizabeth. Few endure such discussions long enough to inquire into their persistence."

"I doubt endurance is the issue," she laughed. "One listens because one suspects there is something beneath the repetition that has not yet been said."

Darcy spoke then—not loudly, but with a firmness that surprised even him.

"There is not."

The words came out cleaner than he felt, edged with an authority he did not entirely possess. He had not decided to speak; the moment had forced him to it. The tick in his face ceased at once, as though chastened by the sound of his own voice.

He did not trust himself to say more. Already, he had said too much.

Wickham smiled, as though amused by the exchange rather than checked by it. "You see, Miss Elizabeth? A question answered before it is fully asked."

"And a very efficient answer," she returned. "Though I confess I am not yet persuaded."

Darcy felt that confession land like a challenge, though it was offered with perfect civility. His hand twitched again, once, sharp and unmistakable.

"You are not required to be."

He inclined his head and stepped away from them—not in haste, but with unmistakable finality. He could not remain. Not while she was still looking at him as though the matter were unfinished. Bingley, speaking with Sir William near the window, turned in surprise as Darcy joined him.

Behind them, Denny laughed at something Wickham said; Miss Bingley's voice followed, quick and animated, seizing upon the thread Darcy had abandoned. The space he had occupied filled itself almost at once, the conversation bending and reforming as though it had never paused.

Darcy did not remain to hear what was made of it.

# Chapter Twenty

The candles had been lit, and the servants dismissed when Mr Collins began again.

"Her ladyship has always maintained," he was saying, "that a household prospers best when each member understands his or her proper sphere."

Elizabeth kept her eyes on her plate and applied herself to the small, manageable business of eating. The scrape of knife against porcelain gave her something firm to hold. She matched her motions to it deliberately, as though the rhythm itself might keep the rest of the room at a tolerable distance.

"...a principle her ladyship herself has often impressed upon me, particularly where families of established consequence are concerned."

The sensation broke over her at once.

It gathered behind her ears, narrow and insistent, not pain yet but unmistakable pressure, as though the space around her head had been drawn a fraction too tight. Elizabeth adjusted in her chair, turning slightly away from him, and bent her attention to her plate. She cut her meat into pieces smaller than necessary, precise to the point of absurdity, and waited for the moment to pass.

"Indeed, Mr Collins, Lady Catherine's guidance is most valuable. How very fine for you, sir, to have the patronage of such a splendid lady."

The pain sharpened.

Elizabeth's fork paused halfway to her mouth. The room felt closer suddenly, the space around her head reduced by degrees she could not measure but could certainly feel.

"Oh, yes, truly! And it is precisely this attention to lineage and responsibility that renders her counsel so indispensable. One cannot disregard such authority, particularly when it is exercised with such benevolence—"

Benevolence pressed like a hot poker just behind her ear.

Elizabeth swallowed without tasting anything and set her fork down with care. The words reached her clearly enough, but they no longer arranged themselves properly. They arrived as emphasis without content, weight without distinction, each syllable landing in the same narrow place until she found herself bracing for the next.

Papa's voice cut in, a dry chuckle. "I should think authority is often exercised whether one invites it or not."

Mr Collins laughed. "Ah! Just so, sir. And yet her ladyship would argue—and has argued most persuasively—that guidance freely offered is a gift, not a burden."

The pressure tightened further, sliding upward now, as though something were drawing a line from the base of her skull toward her temples. Elizabeth lifted her hand under the table and pressed her fingers lightly against the side of her neck, searching for some place to shift it.

"Lizzy," Mama said sharply, "pray do not fidget. You will make yourself nervous."

Elizabeth dropped her hand at once.

Mr Collins never even paused for breath. "Lady Catherine herself has often remarked that the misfortunes of society arise not from hardship, but from a failure to accept the arrangements that Providence has so wisely set in place—"

The sound thinned.

Not quiet—never quiet—but narrowed, as though all other noises had been filtered away, leaving only his voice, flattened and relentless. Elizabeth blinked and found she could no longer quite separate one word from the next. *Arrangement, Providence, duty*—they struck the same internal note, each one reverberating against the last until she could feel it along her jaw.

She set her glass down—though when she had picked it up, she could not recall. "Must we discuss Lady Catherine at supper?" The words escaped her before she had fully considered them. "It is difficult to digest instruction along with mutton."

There was a pause—not silence, but a distinct hitch in the flow of conversation.

Mama turned toward her at once. "Elizabeth!"

Jane's hand brushed her arm, a warning more than a comfort.

Mr Collins blinked, then smiled, indulgent rather than offended. "My dear cousin, I assure you I speak only from admiration. Her ladyship's example is—"

The pressure flared, sharp enough this time to make Elizabeth draw a breath through her teeth. She looked down at her plate again and said nothing further.

Papa cleared his throat. "I believe Elizabeth has had enough of edifying discourse for one meal."

"Edifying, indeed," Mama said, with a look that promised later reproach. "I daresay she could do with a bit of edifying."

Mr Collins inclined his head. "Oh, pray, Mrs Bennet, do not give yourself the slightest concern over the matter. I have often observed that sensitivity is not uncommon in young ladies of refinement."

He continued speaking—of something else now, perhaps of the parish or the weather—but Elizabeth could not have said what. The pressure receded by a fraction, enough to endure, if not enough to ease. She folded her hands in her lap and fixed her attention on breathing evenly, on counting the spaces between words she no longer followed. Until, suddenly, they came to make sense again.

Elizabeth noticed it not because she followed the words, but because the pressure eased by a measurable degree. Someone laughed—Kitty, perhaps—and the sound did not strike her like a blow. Her shoulders loosened without permission. She drew a fuller breath and tasted salt again, which seemed a small mercy.

Mr Collins had turned, at last, from Lady Catherine herself to matters adjacent. "...and it is quite remarkable," he was saying, "how a family so long established continues to exert influence in the county. Pemberley, of course, has always stood as an example of continuity—"

Elizabeth lifted her eyes.

Darcy's name was not spoken, but she heard it all the same, implicit in the careful reverence with which Mr Collins shaped his sentences. For now, nothing worsened. The sound remained tolerable. His voice was merely a voice again, not an instrument pressing against her skull.

Papa made a small sound of interest. Jane glanced at her, perhaps expecting a reaction. Elizabeth returned her attention to her plate, cautiously encouraged.

Mr Collins went on. "—and Mr Darcy himself bears the weight of that inheritance with admirable seriousness. One cannot but respect a gentleman who understands the importance of stewardship—"

Still nothing.

Elizabeth's brow furrowed despite herself. The pressure did not return. She could follow him now, word to word, sense to sense, even if she disliked the tone. *Darcy. Pemberley. Responsibility.* All of it irritating, certainly—but not painful.

Then Mr Collins smiled, pleased with his own direction. "And of course," he added, "her ladyship has always taken the keenest interest in her nephew's conduct. She has long held expectations for him—not merely as a landholder, but as a figure of influence, one whose decisions must reflect the dignity and authority of his position—"

The room narrowed violently.

The pressure returned at once, no longer gradual but abrupt, a tightening band that snapped into place behind her ears and sent a sharp line of sensation down her neck. Elizabeth's breath caught hard in her chest and refused to complete itself. Sound flattened again, Mr Collins's voice collapsing into a single, insistent vibration that seemed to strike the same point again and again.

"...and it is only proper," he continued, "that such expectations be met with due consideration. Lady Catherine's guidance—"

*Guidance* pressed. *Authority* rang. *Expectation* burned.

Elizabeth's chair scraped backward before she had fully decided to stand. "I beg your pardon," she said, though the words arrived thin and oddly distant to her own ears. She rose too quickly, and the room tilted, not enough to unseat her but enough to demand attention.

Mama's voice snapped, sharp with disapproval. "Elizabeth—what is the matter with you now?"

Jane half-rose as well. "Lizzy?"

"I am quite well," Elizabeth said, because it was the only answer available to her. The pressure surged again as Mr Collins drew breath to speak.

She did not wait for it. "If you will excuse me," she added, already moving, one hand brushing the back of her chair as she passed it to keep herself aligned. The edges of the room blurred as she stepped away from the table, the sound of voices chasing her for several paces before thinning, loosening, releasing.

By the time she reached the doorway, the pressure had retreated just enough for her to draw a full breath again. She fled and did not look back.

Elizabeth woke with the distinct impression that she had not meant to.

For a moment, she lay quite still, uncertain whether she had only closed her eyes or surrendered to something deeper. The room felt altered—not different in substance, but in proportion—as though time had slipped while she was not attending to it. It might have been five minutes. It might have been two hours.

She lay on the bed fully clothed, one slipper kicked loose, the coverlet caught awkwardly beneath her knees. The position answered the question well enough. She had not intended to rest. She had simply ceased resisting it.

Her head felt... quieter.

Not well—she would not claim that—but the sharp compression had withdrawn, leaving behind a dull, cautious awareness, like the memory of a sound after it had passed. She turned her head a fraction, testing the pain. Nothing flared. No sudden sharpening followed. That, at least, was a relief.

Elizabeth exhaled and stared up at the underside of the tester, letting the room reassert itself by degrees.

A knock sounded at the door.

Elizabeth closed her eyes.

"Lizzy?" Jane's voice followed, already edged with worry. "May I come in?"

"If you must," Elizabeth said, and immediately regretted her tone.

The door opened, and Jane crossed the room to sit on the edge of the bed, her hand hovering for a moment before settling lightly at Elizabeth's wrist, as though she were unsure whether contact would be welcome.

"You left supper so suddenly," Jane said. "Mama is quite vexed—and Mr Collins was—well, *very* attentive afterward."

Elizabeth huffed, then winced faintly at the sound. "I am sure he was."

Jane studied her face. "Is it your head again?"

Elizabeth considered denying it. The effort required seemed greater than the truth. "Only a little," she said. "It is nothing."

"You said that at Netherfield."

"Yes, and I was correct. I survived the experience."

"You look pale. And you have been so quiet these past days. I thought you were better."

"So did I." Elizabeth turned onto her side, propping her elbow beneath her. "Jane, truly, there is nothing to be done. I am tired. That is all. Supper was long."

"And Mr Collins?"

Elizabeth rolled her eyes... carefully. "Is eternal."

Jane's lips curved despite herself. "Papa asked me to come and see you."

She pinched the bridge of her nose, then dug her fingers into her eyes. "Did he?"

Jane nodded. "He would like you to come down when you feel equal to it."

Elizabeth sighed and let her head fall back against the pillow. "I suppose I am to be set down for my behaviour at dinner."

"I doubt it. He did not seem displeased. Only... concerned."

Elizabeth sat up. The movement brought a faint echo of pressure, but nothing like before. She pressed her fingers briefly to her temple and then dropped her hand, determined not to invite further scrutiny.

"I am quite able to go downstairs," she said. "I do not require a tribunal."

Jane smiled, though her eyes remained watchful. "It is only Papa."

"That," Elizabeth said, swinging her legs over the side of the bed, "is precisely the difficulty."

Jane rose to give her room. "Shall I come with you?"

Elizabeth shook her head and reached for her shawl. "No. If I require an audience, I shall request one."

Jane hesitated, then nodded. "Very well. But if you feel unwell again—"

"I shall retreat with dignity," Elizabeth said, standing. "Or at least with speed."

Jane laughed softly and stepped aside as Elizabeth passed her, though she did not look away until Elizabeth had reached the door.

The corridor beyond was quiet. Elizabeth paused there a moment, letting the air out of her lungs. The pressure behind her ears, under her eyelids, did not return. She drew a careful breath and made her way downstairs.

PAPA'S LIBRARY HELD A haze of dust and something faintly resinous from the fire. Elizabeth had always liked the room best in the evenings, when it seemed to withdraw from the rest of the house and become its own quiet territory.

He was standing at the shelves when she entered, with one hand braced against the bookcase, and several volumes already pulled free and stacked on the table behind him. She recognised them at once—not by title, but by association. The books he had sent to Netherfield. The ones she had returned with thanks and no questions. She had not realised until this moment that he had kept them together.

"Shut the door, if you please," he said mildly. "Your sisters are inclined to believe any conversation behind a threshold belongs to them by right."

Elizabeth did as he asked. The latch clicked softly into place.

"Sit," Papa added, nodding toward the chair by the desk.

She obeyed, though she did not settle easily.

Papa turned then and regarded her over the rims of his spectacles. Not with alarm. Not with indulgence. Simply with attention.

"You left the table in some haste," he said. "Was that deliberate, or did you miscalculate?"

Elizabeth considered the question. It was framed as though either answer would be acceptable.

"I miscalculated," she said at last. "The conversation proved… longer than I had anticipated."

"Hm." Papa reached for one of the books and opened it without looking at the title. "You have endured worse."

"I have," Elizabeth agreed. "But not recently."

That earned a faint lift of his brows. "Was it fatigue? Or merely irritation?"

Elizabeth hesitated. She disliked both options equally. "I thought it was fatigue. At first."

Papa nodded, as though she had answered a different question entirely. He closed the book and set it aside, then picked up another, this one thinner, its spine creased from age rather than use.

"You were unwell at Netherfield," he said. "And then you were not."

"Yes."

"And now you are again."

Elizabeth frowned despite herself. "I did not say that."

"No. You did not." He gestured toward the stack of books. "These were gifts, but you returned them to me."

"I did."

"Did you read them?"

"I only cracked one of them. I was not equal to reading. But there was another I fancied very much, and I should like to attempt it again if you do not object."

Papa chuckled. "My dear, I never asked you to return them. I would rather you read them all, many times if you pleased."

Elizabeth's brows rose. "Indeed? Then I shall start with that small one, the one with the silly rhymes and ballads that you found in Meryton."

Her father passed her the book and watched her thumb the pages without comment. After a moment, he asked, "What was that about at supper?"

Elizabeth shifted in her chair. "Tonight was... a little conversation-heavy."

He smiled then, briefly. "Yes. Your cousin has that effect."

She exhaled. "It is not merely him."

"Is it not?"

She shook her head. "He speaks of other people's importance as though it were his own. He repeats things—about Mr Darcy, about Lady Catherine—as though repetition itself grants authority."

"And does it?"

Elizabeth thought of the way the pain had sharpened. Of how abruptly it had arrived. "No," she said. "But it demands attention."

Papa's mouth puckered a fraction, but then he seemed to dismiss some notion or other. He returned one of the books to the shelf, then stopped, his hand resting there as though he had misplaced the next thought.

"Forgive me," he said lightly. "I may be misremembering. Supper conversations tend to blur into one another." He glanced toward her. "When Mr Collins spoke this evening—before you left—do you recall what he was saying?"

Elizabeth frowned. "He was saying a great many things."

"Yes," Papa agreed. "But which of them proved intolerable?"

Elizabeth scoffed. "What did not? And why are you asking?"

Papa shrugged. "It is only that sometimes you appeared scarcely able to abide your own skin. Other moments, you looked rather engaged in the conversation. I was only wondering if the conversation itself was the cause for your discomfort or if it was something more transitory."

"When have you ever heard of such a thing as the topic of conversation causing someone physical pain?" she retorted.

Papa chuckled. "Humour me, if you please. What was Collins saying when you were in the greatest discomfort?"

She considered. The question was uncomfortably precise.

"He spoke of Lady Catherine," she said at last. "Of her views. Her guidance." She paused. "And of Mr Darcy."

Papa's brows lifted a fraction. "At the same moment?"

"No," Elizabeth said slowly. "Not at first."

He waited, tapping his thumb on a book spine.

"When he spoke of Mr Darcy's estate," she continued, "or of Pemberley itself, I was... irritated, perhaps, but no more than usual."

She searched the memory again, unwilling to trust it too easily. "I could still follow him."

Papa nodded once, encouraging without approving. "And then?"

"And then," she said, feeling suddenly foolish for the care with which she chose her words, "he began to speak of what Lady Catherine *expected* of Mr Darcy. Of how his conduct ought to reflect her authority." Her fingers tightened together in her lap. "That was when I could no longer sit there."

Papa was silent for a moment. He slid the book back onto the case, then paced round his desk. "At Lucas Lodge," he said finally, "you were already unwell before we arrived, and displayed some considerable discomfort until you had situated yourself in the room."

"Yes."

"And Mr Collins was speaking then, too."

Elizabeth nodded.

"Do you remember what he was saying *immediately* before you put your hand to your ear?"

She hesitated. The memory sharpened against her will.

"He was speaking of Lady Catherine again," she said. "At least... I think so. He speaks of little else."

"What about her?"

Elizabeth squinted. "Of her interest in certain important affairs. Of how fortunate it was that such influence was exercised so... attentively."

"So..." Papa's brow furrowed, and he began to pace. "I wonder if it is not Mr Collins himself."

"I beg your pardon?"

"... Nor his voice, grating as it is. Nor even his personal manner, though I do wonder at his welcome in the home of anyone of sense." He tapped the spine of the booklet once against the desk. "It is expectation, voiced as authority."

Elizabeth stared at him. "That is absurd."

"Quite possibly," Papa replied. "But it is at least a consistent absurdity."

She laughed. "I do not see how my head could possibly object to such a distinction."

"Nor do I. Which is what makes it interesting."

"Oh, come, now!"

"You did not leave the table because Mr Collins was tedious," he continued. "You endured him long past that point. You left because something in his manner crossed a line you could not ignore—even if you did not yet know where that line lay."

Elizabeth leaned back in her chair, unsettled not by the conclusion, but by how closely it matched her own unarticulated experience.

"I am not imagining this, Papa."

Papa met her gaze. "I should be very surprised if you were."

He moved to the sideboard and poured a small glass of wine, which he set within her reach without comment. "Elizabeth," he said gently, "you are not prone to dramatics. You do not retire from supper lightly. And you do not complain of headaches as a rule."

She wrapped her fingers around the glass, trying to soothe herself with the cool of it. "And what am I to do?"

Papa considered her for a moment, then said simply, "Pay attention."

"I can hardly do otherwise," she snorted as she lifted the wine glass.

"And do not allow anyone else," he added, "to tell you what a thing means before you have decided whether it exists at all."

Elizabeth nodded slowly. That, at least, was advice she could trust.

Even if it still made no sense.

# Chapter Twenty-One

Elizabeth left the house before anyone thought to look for her.

The morning had not yet gathered itself into calls and visits; the air held that pale, undecided quality of late autumn, cool without being sharp, the light thin but serviceable. She took her shawl from the peg by the back door and went out as though she had done so a thousand times before—quietly, without announcement, without destination.

The door shut behind her with a soft, final sound. She drew a breath and found it went where it was meant to go. That alone decided her pace.

She walked at first, briskly, as though she merely meant to turn about the garden before breakfast. The house was already receding behind her. When Mr Collins's voice reached her through an open window, earnest and unrelenting even at this hour, she turned without hesitation and followed the line of the hedge instead.

The sound did not follow.

Her steps lengthened as her skirts brushed damp grass. She moved faster—not from alarm, but from the unshakable certainty that stopping too soon would invite something she did not wish to test. The path narrowed, then vanished altogether, leaving only ground she knew by habit rather than sight.

Elizabeth broke into a run.

Not recklessly, not far, but with the focused urgency of someone seeking space rather than escape. The morning air cut clean across her face. Her breath deepened, full and unimpeded, each one arriving without effort or warning. The farther she went from the house, the more the world seemed to resume its proper dimensions.

She slowed only when the rise came into view—the low bank beyond the meadow where the land dipped inward, sheltered from the path and the house alike. She had liked the place since childhood for reasons she had never bothered to examine.

Elizabeth stopped there and bent forward, hands braced against her knees.

Nothing clouded her brain.

No sound crowded the edges of her attention. No sense of strain followed her out into the open. She straightened cautiously, half-expecting the reprieve to prove temporary.

It did not.

She lowered herself onto the bank and drew her shawl closer, though she was no longer chilled. The bank was clammy, but the grass was oddly green for November. Somewhere nearby, a bird called once and fell silent again.

Elizabeth leaned back and let her eyes close.

For the first time since she had begun paying attention, there was nothing she needed to endure.

DARCY WAS STANDING BEFORE the glass while his valet finished fastening the final buttons of his coat when the whining began in earnest.

It had started earlier as a low sound at the door, easily ignored while soap was worked into lather and the razor drawn with practiced care. Brutus had been accustomed to waiting his turn. Today, however, patience appeared to have deserted him entirely.

The dog pushed the door open with his nose and entered the room as though invited.

Darcy did not look round at once. He was watching his own reflection with habitual severity, noting the fall of the collar, the precise alignment of linen. The whining continued—closer now, accompanied by the unmistakable scrape of claws upon the floor.

His valet paused.

"Sir," the man said, with a hint of strained politeness, "shall I remove the animal?"

Darcy's gaze shifted at last. Brutus had seated himself squarely between the bed and the window, head lifted, eyes fixed upon his master with unwavering intent. His tail thumped once against the floor.

"No," Darcy said. "Leave him."

The valet inclined his head and resumed his work, though the tightening of his mouth suggested he did not approve of the arrangement. Brutus took this as encouragement and rose at once, pacing the length of the room with deliberate exaggeration. He paused near the door, looked back, and let out a short, reproachful sound.

Darcy sighed as the valet finished his shave and he rose from the chair. "You have already been fed," he said, adjusting his cuffs. "And no doubt you have already had a morning airing."

Brutus stopped pacing and sat again, posture rigid, ears alert. The tail thumped twice this time.

"I am not going fowling," Darcy added, more firmly. "It is too early, and I have no intention of—"

The whining resumed, louder now, edged with insistence rather than complaint.

The valet stepped back at last. "If there is nothing further, sir?"

"That will be all," Darcy said. "Thank you."

The man gathered his things and departed with visible relief, casting one last disapproving glance at Brutus as he closed the door behind him.

The moment they were alone, Brutus rose and crossed the room again, placing his head against Darcy's thigh with a persistence that bordered on accusation.

Darcy looked down at him. "You are acting rather uncouth today. You know better than to demand."

Brutus met his gaze, unrepentant.

Darcy reached for his gloves, hesitated, then let his hand fall. He regarded the dog for a long moment, as though weighing a matter of consequence rather than inconvenience.

"A short walk," he said at last. "That is all. No wandering. No nonsense."

Brutus bounded toward the door with a joyful bark.

Darcy shook his head, though he did not smile. "You are entirely too confident."

He took up his hat and followed the dog from the room. Brutus paused on the landing, gave a low, unmistakable grumble, and fixed Darcy with a stare that admitted of no negotiation.

"Yes," Darcy said under his breath. "I know."

The sound came again, sharper this time.

Darcy continued down. The breakfast room lay open ahead, already bright with morning. Bingley stood near the sideboard, halfway between pouring coffee and engaging his sister in some animated discussion that Darcy had not been attending to closely enough to follow.

Bingley turned at once. "Ah! There you are. I wondered if you meant to sleep half the day away."

"I did not," Darcy replied. "I had originally intended to attend some correspondence."

Brutus took this as encouragement and moved forward, nails ticking briefly before Darcy checked him with a look.

Bingley laughed. "He appears to have formed other plans for you."

"He has," Darcy said. "And he is not accustomed to being gainsaid."

Miss Bingley glanced over her shoulder. "Surely you are not proposing to take him out now? You have not broken your fast."

"I have no intention of lingering," Darcy said.

Bingley hesitated, disappointment flickering across his face. "But I had hoped—well. Never mind. I suppose you may as well go, if you must. I am to meet with Mrs Nicholls directly after we are done."

Darcy paused. "For what purpose?"

Bingley looked surprised. "The ball, of course."

"The—" Darcy checked himself. "You have decided upon that, then."

"I mentioned it to Sir William yesterday," Bingley said easily. "It seemed past time, and everyone expects it. Mrs Nicholls has very strong opinions about the ordering of things, and Caroline insists she must be consulted."

Miss Bingley smiled without warmth. "Someone must ensure the affair does not descend into chaos."

"But why am I to be included in this discussion? The matter ought to be your own to determine."

"Oh, come, Darcy," Bingley said. "You have attended more balls than I."

"But I have never hosted one."

"You are our guest, though—a rather distinguished guest, though you refuse to admit it. Caroline will wish to know your preferences."

Darcy glanced at Brutus. The dog's tail struck once against the side of a chair. "No doubt. But I am sorry, Bingley, I believe I shall withdraw."

Miss Bingley lifted her brows. "You will not absent yourself entirely, I hope."

"I shall return," Darcy replied. "Before you have exhausted yourselves."

Bingley laughed again. "Very well. Do not be long."

Darcy did not answer. He turned instead, the decision already made, and Brutus moved at once, satisfied now that motion had been conceded.

Elizabeth sat with her hands folded loosely in her lap, not so much resting as paused.

The air lay still. The distant sounds of the house had fallen away, and even the usual small movements of thought seemed to have loosened their hold. Her eyes rested on nothing in particular—the pale reach of grass, the curve of a low bough—and her mind drifted without purpose, not asleep, not properly awake either. It was the same half-state she sometimes fell into when a book slipped from meaning into cadence, when words became sound, and sound became something softer still.

She drew breath. Let it out... and it was wonderful. It felt almost like forgetting.

A sharp bark split the stillness.

Elizabeth lurched upright with a gasp, her heart leaping before her mind had caught up. The sound came again—closer now—and the brush behind her parted with sudden energy. Something large and dark burst through the undergrowth, moving too quickly to be anything but alarming.

She squeaked—an undignified, involuntary sound—and sprang upright, skirts gathered clumsily in her hands as she lurched back a pace.

A large, hairy dog reached her and stopped as though he had struck the end of some invisible lead.

He dropped neatly into a sit no more than a step away, chest lifting with exertion, ears forward, tail still. His head tipped slightly as he regarded her, alert and intent, but making no move to advance.

Elizabeth's heart hammered once, then slowed. "Oh," she said faintly. "Brutus? Out for a little ramble on your own?"

The dog remained where he was, panting with a pleased canine grin that flashed his long white teeth. She let out a careful breath and lowered her skirts, her pulse still quick but no longer quite so wild. Whatever else he was, he did not appear inclined to leap.

Then the brush behind him burst apart.

Elizabeth did not wait to see what emerged. Instinct sent her retreating at once—two quick steps back, blind and hurried—and her heel caught hard against a root that she could have sworn was *not* there a moment before. The ground tilted beneath her, sudden and absolute.

She gasped and pitched backward.

"Miss Elizabeth!"

Darcy broke through the brush at speed, branches snapping against his coat as he crossed the remaining distance in a stride and a half. His hand closed on her arm and drew her upright with a force that left no room for protest, his grip firm, certain, and gone almost as quickly as it came.

She found her footing again, breath stuttering.

He stood close—too close—his chest rising sharply, his coat tugged awry by thorns, his hair disordered, his face stripped of every careful reserve.

Only then did colour climb his cheekbones, as though awareness had arrived a heartbeat late. "I beg your pardon," he said, releasing her. "I feared he had startled someone."

"I *was* startled," Elizabeth managed, still watching the dog, who continued to sit as though awaiting further instruction. "More by you than by him. But I do not appear to have suffered lasting harm."

Darcy exhaled. His shoulders lowered a fraction. "He should not have run ahead of me. I hardly know what has come over him of late."

Brutus glanced back at his master, then returned his attention to Elizabeth, ears flicking as though he were listening for something only he could hear.

Elizabeth's heart began, belatedly, to resume its proper pace. She released her skirts and straightened, newly aware of the space between them. Her hand, where his had briefly closed about it, retained a faint, lively warmth, as though some quick current had passed and left her more wakeful than before.

Not a shock this time. Not a painful warning. Merely... a notice.

"No harm done. He did stop and sit. I had expected... well. Some sort of excitement."

Darcy almost smiled. The expression did not complete itself, but it altered his face enough that she noticed. "He has his own mind, but is usually not inclined to mischief."

"As I am relieved to discover." She hesitated, then added, "He looks as though he expects me to say something."

"He often does. Sometimes I think he speaks the King's English."

Elizabeth looked down at the dog again. "Good morning, then," she said. "You gave me quite a fright."

Brutus's tail thumped once against the ground.

Darcy cleared his throat. "I am truly sorry to interrupt your walk, Miss Elizabeth. I had not realised anyone would be here."

"Nor had I expected I would be discovered in so dramatic a fashion," she replied. "We are even."

He inclined his head, accepting the truce. "If you would prefer not to be disturbed further, I shall take him another way."

She surprised herself by answering too quickly. "No—please. I mean—there is no harm done. And you may as well know that I have a particular fondness for dogs. The larger the better." She smiled—small, reflexive—and let her hand fall to Brutus's head before she had quite decided to do so.

The dog accepted the attention gravely, as though this were the proper conclusion to their meeting today. His ears flicked once; he leaned, just perceptibly, into her fingers.

Darcy watched the exchange with an expression of polite reserve that did not quite mask relief.

"He will take that as encouragement," he said. "You may find him following you home."

"I should be flattered," Elizabeth replied. "Though I imagine he already has a home superior to anything I could offer."

"He has nothing to complain of," Darcy said, after a pause. "But he is... discerning in those he chooses to bestow his affections on."

Elizabeth glanced up at him. "Then I am honoured," she said, and bent again to the dog. "You see? I pass inspection."

Brutus's tail answered with another dignified thump.

Darcy cleared his throat. "If you were seeking solitude, I fear we have intruded upon it."

"I was seeking air," she said. "Solitude was merely its most agreeable companion." She straightened and brushed her hands together. "Besides, I find interruptions less objectionable when they arrive on four legs."

"Yes, well... as I have said, he is ordinarily better behaved."

Elizabeth bent again to the dog, smoothing a hand along his neck as though this were the most natural continuation of the exchange. "I should hate him if he were. Perfection is tiresome in any creature. You walk him often?"

"When I can," Darcy replied. "Today he was terribly... insistent."

"So I observed."

"He disapproves of prolonged confinement. And of certain kinds of company."

Her hand stilled on Brutus's head. "How very discerning indeed. If only we ladies could afford to be as discerning as a giant wolfhound!"

Darcy's gaze sharpened, though his tone remained even. "You have been distressed by certain company? Shall I hope it was not my own?"

She tilted her head. "Yours? Not necessarily. But as for others... let us say I have learned to value distance."

"Distance?"

"And silence," she added. "In judicious measure."

Darcy's mouth screwed down to an unhappy frown. "You did not appear to value silence yesterday," he said at last. "At the Lucases'."

Elizabeth smiled. "Yesterday was an exercise in endurance."

He scoffed. "Indeed, it was."

"And one is tempted, after such exertion, to ask why it is so often demanded."

Darcy looked away, toward the line of trees beyond them. "Some subjects," he said, "are revived not because they merit attention, but because someone *wishes* them to."

"Ah." She considered this. "Then the fault lies not in the subject, but in the persistence."

His eyes returned to her. "You sound as though you have been listening."

"One cannot help overhearing when a gentleman speaks with such conviction, and another denies with even more vehemence."

"It is nonsense, Miss Elizabeth," he retorted quickly. "The vain and silly wishes of those whose minds have nothing else to engage them."

"Ah. So, comforting nonsense, then?"

He snorted. "If one is inclined to be comforted by it."

She tilted her head. "I should think nonsense loses its charm when so many people insist upon taking it seriously."

His expression tightened a fraction. "Mr Collins is fond of... consequence."

"He is devoted to it," she agreed. "Particularly when it can be borrowed from someone he envies." Then, because the thought would not let her alone, she added, lightly but not casually, "He spoke as though your family were burdened with some antique charge—something weighty, venerable, and entirely inconvenient."

Darcy's jaw set. He did not look as if he meant to answer her.

Elizabeth waited. She did not look at him. She busied herself instead with Brutus, who had resumed a thorough examination of her gown as though convinced a secret might be stitched into the hem.

"I have heard it called many things," Darcy said at last. "Most of them imaginative."

"So, it is not true?"

"It is old superstition," he replied. "Which allows people to treat it as important, regardless of its substance."

She glanced up at him then. "Well, if it is nothing but a folk tale fit for children and old women, perhaps you may indulge me. I have a fondness for silly things."

Darcy's jaw fairly rippled with reluctance, as if the words were simmering forth and he was still trying to clench his teeth against them. "I remember being told," he said carefully, "that there was once a story attached to my family. The sort that acquires embellishment simply by surviving long enough to be repeated."

"A legend?"

Mr Darcy made a face of distaste. "If one insists upon the word. The kind of tale that encourages people to speak of duty as though it were an inheritance one might accept without question."

"Indeed, what a horror! Why, it sounds perfectly scandalous, sir. A ruinous tale, to be sure."

"It was never presented to me as truth," he corrected her, his tone controlled, dry as toast. "Only as something one was meant to admire politely when dusting the library shelves. To acknowledge, and then put aside."

"Put aside?" she echoed. "And yet it seems determined not to stay there."

His mouth tightened. "Others have always found it more engaging than I ever did."

"Because the old... tales, if you will... are false?" she asked.

"Because they invite interpretation."

She smiled, but it did not soften the inquiry. "Interpretation is hardly a crime."

"No," he said. "But it does tend to produce expectations. Particularly in those who interpret with an eye toward self-interest."

"Ah." She nodded, as though that explained everything—and nothing. "Then it is expectation, not facts themselves, that troubles you. You, Mr Darcy, do not appreciate being fodder for the gossip of those who presume to know you better than you wish to be known."

He only frowned.

Brutus chose that moment to wedge his head firmly beneath her knees, insistent, irrepressible. Elizabeth laughed under her breath and pushed him back, then obliged him with a good scratching as her fingers found the silky softness of his ears.

"You see," she said, glancing at Darcy, "even he resists being told what he must be."

"He seems to resist being told *anything* these days," grumbled the gentleman.

She straightened, pushing the dog back at last. "I shall ask no more, since it is clearly a subject you do not enjoy. But you must forgive me if I find it difficult to ignore a mystery that everyone else insists upon parading."

"I would expect nothing less."

That answer surprised her. Enough that she laughed. "Well," she said at last, "Good day, Mr Darcy. I do hope your handsome dog will remember me fondly if I should have the good fortune to encounter him again."

Darcy inclined his head. "I suspect he will make that determination for himself."

As she turned back toward the path, Brutus glanced after her, then looked up at his master with unmistakable reproach.

Darcy exhaled. "Come along," he said, his tone dropping in command. "No more nonsense from you today."

# Chapter Twenty-Two

DARCY HAD WRITTEN HIS sister's name three times before he allowed himself to continue.

*My dear Georgiana,*

He paused, pen hovering. Brutus lay at his feet, chin on his paws, eyes half-lidded but alert enough to register the slightest shift of movement. The library windows stood open to the afternoon; voices drifted faintly from elsewhere in the house, the murmur of activity that Netherfield never quite escaped.

*I hope this letter finds you in good health and spirits. I trust Pemberley remains much as I left it, and that you have not been overburdened by visitors or correspondence in my absence.*

That would do for civility. He read it once, then continued, more cautiously.

*I write to ask after a matter which has occurred to me of late, and upon which I find my own recollection insufficient. Do you remember, among Father's books, a small volume kept apart from the others—bound plainly, without title upon the spine?*

He stopped. The phrasing felt clumsy. Too abrupt.

He crossed out *kept apart* and rewrote the line above it.

> *a volume he did not often bring out, but which you may recall seeing inside the cabinet in the drawing-room.*

The pen dragged slightly at the curve of the dash. Darcy set it down and pressed his fingers to his brow.

The door opened without knock or permission. "Oh, Mr Darcy, there you are!"

Miss Bingley entered as though she had been expected, though he had not summoned her. She carried a folded paper and an air of decision.

"I wondered where you had gone. Mrs Nicholls has settled the matter of the menu, and Sir William has been most obliging about a referral for the musicians. Though I do hope that one flutist we had the dubious pleasure of hearing at the Assembly will find himself indisposed for the occasion. We must decide whether the supper will be laid in two courses or three."

"I am occupied," Darcy said, without looking up.

"Oh, yes, but this will only take a moment. Now, I understand the, ah… the *locals* are still quite satisfied with two courses, but I fancy three, in the French style. It has become quite the fashion in London, of course, but shall the provincials of Meryton think us unpatriotic?"

"Have two, then."

"Two! I daresay Netherfield can bear the expense of a lavish party, Mr Darcy!"

He shook his head, his eyes never leaving his letter. "Then amuse yourself by having a third. I must beg your pardon, Miss Bingley." He dipped his pen again.

> *If it is still there, I should be obliged if you would send it to me. But not to Netherfield, as I anticipate I shall stop in London some while this Season.*

That was too much. He struck through *obliged* and replaced it with *glad*.

Miss Bingley glanced at the page. "Writing to Miss Darcy?"

"Yes."

"How conscientious of you." She moved closer, peering with open curiosity. "I hope you are not alarming your sister with tales of militia officers and provincial excitements."

He angled the paper away. "I am not."

"Good. Dear Georgiana is far too sensible to be troubled with unnecessary speculations."

The word struck too close.

Darcy's jaw tightened. He continued writing, his hand firmer now.

> *You need not trouble yourself to search for it if it is no longer at hand. I ask only because a reference was made recently that put me in mind of it, and I find I dislike not knowing whether my memory has embroidered the thing beyond recognition.*

He stared at the sentence. The word *reference* sat there like a lie. And he knew very well that the book was certainly "at hand," for it was precisely where he had told her to look.

He drew a line through the entire paragraph.

Miss Bingley cleared her throat. "Mr Darcy, I should dearly like to know your opinion—truly, do you think a third course—"

"I have no opinion on the matter," he said, evenly.

She laughed. "You always say that, and yet you always do. Mrs Nicholls insists the supper must follow the dancing without delay, or the room will lose its air. I told her you would know best."

"I care little for the matter."

Miss Bingley watched him a moment longer, then sighed. "Very well. I shall tell them you are being inscrutable again." She turned toward the door, then paused. "You will join us shortly?"

"In time."

She left, but not until she had hovered in the still-open door, as if waiting for him to call her back. Darcy did not look up until the door closed and her footsteps faded outside.

He looked down at the letter.

The page bore his sister's name, the opening civility, and then a confusion of crossed lines and half-erased intentions. What remained read like the work of a man attempting to approach a subject without admitting it existed.

He added one final line, smaller than the rest.

> *And tell me, if you would, how the grounds fare. Whether the lower walk has altered at all since Michaelmas, or if the old markers near the beech stand as they always have.*

That, at least, was harmless.

He folded the paper once. Twice.

Then unfolded it again.

The questions, laid bare, looked worse than foolish. They looked suggestible. He imagined Georgiana reading them, her brow knitting, her voice cautious as she sought to answer without understanding what he had failed to explain.

Darcy tore the sheet cleanly in half. Then again.

He gathered the pieces and dropped them into the fire, watching until the edges curled and the words vanished entirely. He would have to write a clean draught.

Brutus shifted at his feet, as if dissatisfied with the conclusion.

"Yes," Darcy said quietly. "I thought so too."

He rose, pushing back his chair, and left the library without looking again at the desk.

Darcy left the library by the side passage, taking the stairs two at a time more from irritation than haste. The upper corridor lay quiet, the afternoon light stretching long across the carpet. He had gone no farther than the turn toward his chamber when he nearly collided with a footman ascending with a small stack of letters balanced upon a salver.

"Mr Darcy, my apologies." The man halted at once. "I was just coming up with the post. This arrived for you."

Darcy stopped. "Thank you."

The footman offered the salver. Darcy's eye passed over the familiar hands and seals without interest until it reached the last.

Rosings.

The crest was unmistakable. The wax had been impressed with decisive force, as though hesitation itself were a fault to be corrected.

He took the letter. "Please lay the others on the writing desk in the drawing room. I will attend to them later. That will be all."

"Very good, sir." The servant withdrew.

Darcy did not open it at once. He turned the letter over once in his hand, then again, as though the seal itself might yield something before he was obliged to break it. The corridor felt suddenly exposed. Too open. He folded the paper against his palm and continued on toward his chamber, shutting the door behind him before he allowed himself to pause.

Only then did he look at it properly—the familiar crest, the decisive press of wax, the unmistakable weight of expectation it carried.

He broke the seal.

*My dear Nephew,*

*It has come to my attention, through channels I need not name, that you are presently established at Netherfield in Hertfordshire, and yet have not thought it necessary to apprise your family of this circumstance. I find this omission remarkable, given the proximity of events which have, for some time now, required attentiveness rather than absence.*

Darcy rubbed the bridge of his nose and read on.

*Mr Collins has written to me with an account of his recent introduction to the neighbourhood, and of the conversations which have naturally arisen therefrom. I am pleased to learn that he has comported himself with the propriety I have always encouraged, and that he has taken it upon himself to speak with appropriate seriousness on matters of inheritance and responsibility. Such subjects ought not to be treated lightly, particularly at a moment when long-standing arrangements are due for consideration.*

He stared at the words harder as his thumb pressed more firmly into the edge of the paper.

*I cannot suppose that your presence in Hertfordshire is accidental. If you imagine that silence will delay what has long been in preparation, you mistake both the nature of obligation and the patience of those who have preserved it. Certain arrangements do not lapse simply because one chooses not to attend to them. There are places, Darcy, where duties must be acknowledged, whether or not one finds the subject agreeable.*

The pen nib had pressed harder here; the strokes grew darker, less ornamental.

*You are, of course, aware that your own position presents a convergence of duty and heritage such as not been seen in a dozen generations. Mismanaged though it was, it shall not now be squandered through inattention or misdirection. I had hoped that the advantages of your birth, so carefully aligned, and at no small cost, would have produced a more immediate understanding of what is now required.*

Darcy's teeth met hard enough to ache. He read the line again, then a third time, as though repetition might render it less offensive.

It did not.

*Anne's constitution has improved sufficiently that there can be no further excuse for delay, and it would be folly to pretend otherwise. The suitability of her situation has never been in question; indeed, it was precisely this suitability that was once expected to answer a deficiency elsewhere. That it has not done so as fully as one might have wished does not render the design void, only incomplete.*

*I had expected you at Rosings by now, that we might speak plainly and determine the proper course while discretion could still be maintained. Your continued absence obliges me to be explicit. There is work to be done, Darcy, and it is work that admits of neither delegation nor evasion. The moment does not belong to the idle, nor to those content to be acted upon rather than to act.*

*If you have allowed yourself to be diverted by provincial concerns, I trust you will correct the error without delay. Matters of this gravity must not be subjected to casual interpretation—or, worse, to the curiosity of those not equipped to understand their significance. I expect to hear from you at once, and to receive your assurance that you comprehend both the necessity and the propriety of what is required.*

*Your affectionate aunt,*
*Lady C. de Bourgh*

Darcy lowered the letter.

*Work to be done,* she had written.

He folded the paper and set it aside on the bedside table. The presumption of it set his teeth on edge; the confidence with which she spoke of nonsense as though it were account-keeping made his blood run quietly hot.

And yet—he stood at the window a moment, staring out at ground that ought to have been ordinary, and was no longer entirely certain she was mistaken.

ELIZABETH DID NOT GO down to the sitting room.

She made the excuse before anyone could press her for one: a headache, one branching behind her eyes and over her brow, detailing her discomfort without emphasis or apology. It was not untrue.

Mama protested, of course—as if Elizabeth was somehow in the habit of claiming discomfort when there was company to be entertained—but Jane met Elizabeth's eyes across the room, and it seemed that she, at least, understood.

Elizabeth climbed the stairs with one hand on the banister, pacing herself as though she had learned a new method of navigation. Each step away from the sound of voices loosened something behind her ears—not relief, not yet, but space. By the time she reached her chamber, the pressure had retreated to a dull awareness, present enough to be watched, distant enough to endure.

She sat on the edge of the bed and closed her eyes.

This was ridiculous. She had never been delicate. She had walked miles in poor shoes with soggy petticoats and laughed at it afterwards. She had endured sermons, lectures, her mother's anxieties, and her aunt Philips's inexhaustible commentary without once needing to flee a room like a startled animal.

She opened her eyes again and looked at the door, as though she might still hear him through it.

Thank Heaven for Jane.

Elizabeth crossed to the small escritoire by the window and stopped there, one hand resting on its edge. She did not sit. Sitting suggested waiting, and she had no patience for that just now. She remained standing, listening—not for voices, but for the absence of them—measuring the quiet with the same care she had learned to apply to sound.

Jane knew what to ask. Elizabeth had been very clear about that.

"You must ask him for me," she had said when they had been dressing for dinner. "Not everything. Only a few things."

Jane had regarded her curiously. "What things?"

"What Lady Catherine believes," she had said. "Not what she hopes, or wishes, or praises herself for believing—but what she treats as fact."

Jane had nodded as she put the last pins in her hair. "Very well. What else?"

Elizabeth had frowned. "Whether she speaks of it as something past, or something expected. Something finished, or something yet to be done."

Jane had hesitated. "Lizzy—"

"I cannot be in the room when he answers. You know that I cannot, and I wish I could explain. But I need to know what he thinks he knows."

"But why? What does any of it matter? You never cared about a word Mr Collins said, and now suddenly you want me to interrogate him?"

"Jane, I…" Elizabeth had pressed her fingers into her eyes. "I cannot say *why*. I only feel that there is something to do with…" She had bitten her lip then, and simply shaken her head. "Never mind. I will only sound crazy."

Jane had studied her for a moment longer, then inclined her head. "Very well."

Now Elizabeth waited.

Time passed unevenly. She lay back on the bed at last, one arm flung over her eyes, listening to the house rearrange itself below. Cups. Chairs. The cadence of Mr Collins's voice, mercifully distant, its edges dulled by walls and floors. Even that carried a faint echo, but it no longer ached.

A knock came at the door, and Elizabeth sat up. Jane entered with a tray—tea, bread, a little dish of butter.

Elizabeth watched her sister's face rather than the tray. "Well?"

Jane set the tray down and exhaled softly. "He was very pleased to be asked."

"Of course he was."

Jane smiled faintly. "I asked what you suggested. About Lady Catherine. About whether she has always spoken of these matters as… ongoing."

"And?"

Jane considered. "He spoke at great length," she said honestly. "But I am not certain how much of it meant anything."

Elizabeth closed her eyes. Not from pain—anticipation.

"He believes there is something," Jane went on. "Something important. Something connected to old families and proper order. He spoke of stewardship. Of inheritance. Of responsibility."

"Those are his favourite words, but was there any substance to it, or mere pontification?"

"He was rather short on specifics. And when I asked whether Lady Catherine spoke of it as a thing accomplished, or still expected, he became vague. He said such matters were 'not always suited to public articulation.' That they were preserved through understanding rather than record."

Elizabeth opened her eyes again. "So, he does not know anything useful."

Jane shook her head. "Not really. He knows that Lady Catherine believes herself involved in some great legacy. And, rather oddly, he claims that Mr Darcy is, in some way, central. But everything else was... impression. Repetition. Reverence."

Elizabeth groaned and set down the teacup she had absently picked up. A dead end, then. Or worse—a noisy one.

"And did he say anything else?"

Jane hesitated. "Only that Lady Catherine has been displeased of late. That she believes matters have been delayed unnecessarily."

Elizabeth's fingers rose, unthinking, to her ear.

Jane noticed at once. "Lizzy?"

"It is nothing," Elizabeth said, lowering her hand. And it was, now. Or near enough. "Thank you."

Jane hesitated. "It is *not* nothing. I can hear and see that much. I have never known you to flinch from company or complain of headaches. I only wish I understood what to do with it."

Elizabeth shook her head. "I do not understand it myself."

"If it is pain, I can fetch Hill again. She can make you some tea. If it is worry..." She stopped herself, a faint crease appearing between her brows. "I know you do not always wish to speak of such things. I only mean that I will help. Listen, if that is all I can do."

Elizabeth's mouth curved. "I know. Go on, you needn't hover over me. Mama will be looking for you."

When Jane left, Elizabeth did not follow her down to the drawing room.

She waited until the sound of her sister's steps had descended the stairs and faded, then rose and followed. But she did not go to the drawing room, where her family were gathered, but the other way—barefoot and careful—toward her father's library.

The books were where she had left them. Some were familiar—volumes Papa had always kept, their spines worn by his idle reach—others newer, their bindings still stiff, the shop-scent not yet worn away.

What she did not know was whether the collection was deliberate or haphazard. Grouped for pleasure, variety, or some other reason. If Papa had gathered them with intention, he had done so without comment—and she suspected that no question of hers would alter that silence.

She pulled one from the stack at random. Then another, and another, until her lap was full.

Elizabeth opened one at random and was rewarded with three pages of agricultural speculation that managed to say nothing at all. Another offered a cheerful catalogue of Roman remnants—coins, broken tiles, a road whose course could no longer be traced with confidence. She closed it with a soft thud.

"What am I meant to do with you?" she muttered, low enough that only the shelves could hear.

She tried again. Ballads this time—fragmentary, moralised beyond usefulness, every verse footnoted into submission. Papa's hand, she thought suddenly. This was exactly the sort of thing he read when he wished to pretend he was not looking for something else.

Elizabeth set that book aside and took up another, thinner, its title promising a *History of Ballads and Tales as Translated by Rev Josias Harrowe* and delivering instead a collection of observations so cautious they scarcely qualified as conclusions. Most claimed to be translations, transcriptions, or a consolidation of earlier writings of irregular spelling and composition.

She skimmed, impatient now, her thumb running down the margin as though the page might confess under pressure.

Why these? Why her?

She turned another page. And another. Each passage slipped past without catching—until one did not.

It was buried in a paragraph so hedged and qualified that it nearly escaped notice altogether, offered as a reflection rather than a claim, framed with the careful distance of someone unwilling to be held responsible for what they recorded.

*They set her where the land was first made known,*
*At the far verge where water meets with stone.*
*No crown was laid upon her brow,*
*Nor sceptre put within her hand;*

*She was but given to the ground,*
*As fire is given unto the hearth—*
*Not to command,*
*but keep the land.*

*She wandered not,*
*nor was she borne away;*
*She stood as first she there was set.*
*Yet in due time the keeping waned,*

*And more was asked than first was met.*
*What further charge was laid that hour Is not in any song declared;*
*Or else the singers lost the verse*
*And left the burden unrepaired.*

*Of him that stood in bond with her*
*But little now is writ.*
*His name is once remembered there,*
*And after that is silent kept.*

*He fled not from the hallowed ground,*
*Yet neither did the ground him hold;*
*And from that hour the border dimmed,*
*And what was knit grew faint and cold.*

*Those that came after wrote but this:*
*No charge is borne in secret long;*
*What one alone was made to keep*
*He keepeth till it break him strong.*

Elizabeth read it once.

Then again.

There was no thrill. No chill. Only the unmistakable sense of recognition—clean, immediate, and entirely without metaphor.

This might be lightly poetic... but it was not allegory.

Her body knew this.

She did not ask why. She did not ask how. She understood only that it had happened before. That it happened still. That it was not imagination, nor accident, nor fancy born of fatigue.

She let the book fall open once more and read the sentence again, her eyes stopping this time on a later phrase she had not noticed before.

*The Lady perished not by wrath,*
*Nor by false dealing driven;*
*But lacking that which should her guard,*
*She was as one unwoven.*
*And once the border crossed alone,*
*No man might cross it then.*

Elizabeth's finger stopped.

She drew the book closer and read the stanza again, slower this time. There was only the distinct awareness of having seen her own experience placed neatly into language.

If only she understood what it all meant.

# Chapter Twenty-Three

Elizabeth had already put on her boots when the rain began in earnest.

It came down in slanting sheets, the kind that rattled against the windowpanes and made the yard beyond them shine darkly. She stood with one foot braced against the bedpost, pulling her laces until they strained nearly to breaking, listening to the sound with an impatience she did not attempt to disguise.

This would not do.

She had meant to be gone by now—out before anyone thought to ask where she was going or why she required her cloak so urgently. A turn along the hedgerow would suffice for an explanation. "A short walk." Nothing that invited remark. Nothing that suggested purpose beyond air and motion.

She straightened and crossed to the window, pushing it open a fraction despite the cold. The wind met her, sharp and damp, carrying with it the smell of soaked earth and leaf rot. The path beyond the garden gate had already softened into a slick ribbon of brown. One misstep there, and she would not only be wet but questioned.

Behind her, the door opened, and her mother fisted a hand on her ample hip. "Elizabeth, where are you going dressed like that? I thought you were fitting your ball gown today!"

Elizabeth watched the rain for a moment longer, as though it might change its mind if ignored. "For a walk."

"In this?" Mama advanced into the room and halted at the window, drawing back as a gust sprayed the sill. "You will do no such thing. You were ill only a few weeks ago, and I will not have you missing the Netherfield ball through sheer obstinacy. Really, Lizzy, you have no consideration—"

"I am quite well," Elizabeth said, too quickly. She reached for her cloak. "I only wished for air."

Jane had stepped into the room now, and she folded her arms with an arched brow. "Lizzy."

Elizabeth sighed. Jane was shaking her head slowly, frowning and glancing at their mother. She did not scold. That, somehow, made it worse.

"You have scarcely been still since breakfast," Jane said. "And Papa mentioned the ground was already slick and treacherous by the lower field."

Elizabeth's fingers tightened on the clasp of her cloak. She had not told Jane where she meant to go. She had been careful of that, but Jane had guessed her intention, anyway.

"I will not go far," she said.

Mama snorted. "You never do—and yet something always comes of it. I cannot imagine what possesses you to choose *today* of all days—"

Elizabeth closed her eyes for the space of a breath. She let her cloak fall back across the chair. "Very well. I shall stay in."

Mama looked immediately satisfied. Jane looked as if she were waiting for a "*However...*"

Elizabeth turned away without another word and sat at the small table by the window, folding her hands together as though that had been her intention all along. The rain continued its steady assault, indifferent to her surrender.

She had not wanted mere *exercise.*

She had wanted to stand somewhere specific—somewhere quiet, open, unoccupied—and see whether the strange sense she had felt before would return. Whether it would sharpen, or soften, or do anything at all.

Now, the weather had made the decision for her.

Elizabeth stared out at the blurred line of the lane and felt a sharp, restless frustration settle in its place. If she could not go to the answer, then she would have to make it come to her.

Darcy brought his horse down to a walk as the posting house came into view.

The morning had offered no obstacle to a ride—clear enough skies, firm ground despite yesterday's heavy rains—and the exercise gave him a reason to be elsewhere without requiring explanation. He dismounted near the posting house, looped his reins at a nearby post, and went inside.

At the counter, he drew the letter from his coat, the direction visible for the space of a breath as he placed it down to be weighed and entered. Ink, ledger, the muted scratch of pen upon paper. He kept his attention fixed upon the clerk's motions, not upon the small awareness that he would prefer not to be standing there at all.

"Darcy! Out early today, I see."

Darcy turned. Wickham stood only a few paces from the doorway, hat in hand, his gaze moving—not to Darcy's face first, but to the letter on the counter as though the name upon it had drawn his attention of its own accord.

"Forgive me for staring," Wickham said, with easy cordiality, "but I believe I glimpsed your sister's name."

Darcy did not answer. The clerk took the coin he offered, stamped the paper, and moved the letter aside with the rest. Only when it was done did Darcy step back from the counter.

Wickham's expression remained open, almost companionable. "You must be writing to dear Georgiana. I do hope nothing is amiss."

"Nothing urgent," Darcy said. "I asked her to locate a particular volume of verse among my father's effects and have it sent on to the London house. It is one I recall with some fondness."

Wickham smiled, as though the explanation had confirmed something agreeable rather than deflected suspicion. "Ah. Poetry. That is reassuring. I had half-feared you were assembling more academic authorities."

Darcy glanced at him. "On what subject?"

"Oh—anything that inspires people to speak with confidence when none is warranted." Wickham adjusted his grip on his hat and turned back toward the door. "What luck to find you here, for I came on the same errand, as it happens. Just posted a letter of my own."

They stepped out together into the street. Wickham fell easily into stride beside Darcy, matching his pace without effort.

"Speaking of letters," Wickham went on, "I should think that you will have heard from your aunt Lady Catherine by now."

Darcy's expression did not change. "On what grounds?"

Wickham's brows lifted, mild amusement returning. "On the grounds that Mr Collins has found himself in possession of an audience. A dangerous condition for any man inclined to explanation."

"He explains what he does not understand," Darcy said. "And he does so loudly."

Wickham's smile thinned—not unkindly. "Then Lady Catherine will already be in receipt of a very complete account."

"There appears to be little I can do on the matter."

"Oh, but you know how she is," Wickham added. "Once a notion reaches her, it rarely improves with repetition."

Darcy only grunted.

"You have my sympathy, Darcy. Truly. It is no small thing to have one's movements weighed and measured by people who mistake expectation for entitlement."

"That is not my concern."

"No? Then you are fortunate. Most men I know would find it exhausting."

Darcy stopped at the corner where his horse was tied. Hopefully, this was where their paths would part. "I do not concern myself with my aunt's speculations. Nor with the inventions of those who repeat them."

Wickham smiled faintly. "A sensible resolution." He hesitated a moment, then went on, as though recalling something long dismissed. "Though—if one were inclined to indulge the nonsense for a moment—I once heard your uncle say to your father that such matters, if they were ever to be finished at all, were best finished on the ground that gave rise to them. Not discussed from afar. Settled, as it were, by standing where the talk began. My memory on the matter might be faint, but I recall something... I believe it began with a 'C,' did it not?"

Darcy sighed in exasperation. "Ambiguous nonsense. I have heard it a thousand times, and never with any confidence in its veracity."

"Ambiguous it may be, but I doubt it is nonsense. Is that not why you came to Hertfordshire just now?"

Darcy's eyes narrowed. "I am here because Mr Bingley invited me."

"Come, Darcy, even you cannot be so obtuse! You were a fair Classic when we were in school. Dredged up odd little old things our beaks never even cared to learn about, did you not?"

Darcy looped the rein over his horse's neck. "I fail to see how my academic interests ten years ago have any bearing on the present."

"Well, if even *I* recall it, then surely your memory is a fair sight more exact. One must look away from the Roman road. The places that were never quite claimed by one authority or another. Hertfordshire has been pointed to often enough in that context—close to the lands of the ancient Celts, close to old Londinium, but never properly either."

Darcy's expression cooled. "That is geography made to serve superstition."

"Or gossip," Wickham returned easily. "Plenty of that these days, particularly with the unseasonably warm autumn—unique, I daresay, to Hertfordshire this year."

Darcy ground his teeth. This was all becoming rather tiresome. "*If* it ever meant anything at all, which is doubtful, it could have referred to any point between Northumberland and Kent."

"Ah, yes... Kent. Collins has been repeating that notion with great conviction, but I daresay he has got it all wrong, circulating the idea that *Kent* holds all manner of answers, and Lady Catherine... or rather Anne... keeps the key."

Darcy gathered his reins into a gloved fist. "You know as well as anyone there is nothing in it," he growled.

"In Kent? Of course! I thought Collins' weak intelligence on the matter as good a reason as any to dismiss the whole business. But I wonder if the same ought to be said for—"

Darcy swung into the saddle, intentionally letting the heel of his boot brush Wickham's elbow in the process. "There is nothing to be done," he said. "Here or in Kent or Derbyshire or on the dark side of the moon. The sooner that is understood, the better."

Wickham inclined his head. "Indeed. Well! Good day, Darcy."

Darcy put his heel into his horse and did not look back.

ELIZABETH AND JANE WENT to Lucas Lodge the following afternoon, armed with their sewing baskets and a purpose respectable enough to pass without scrutiny.

Mama had approved it instantly. Charlotte Lucas had sent word that she had acquired more trim than she required—something pale and fine, suitable for evening wear—and Elizabeth's gown for the Netherfield ball would benefit from attention. It was precisely the sort of domestic errand that pleased her mother: economical, social, and entirely uncontroversial.

The weather had repented of that one day of rain, and now the sun made it feel almost as pleasant as a May afternoon. By the time they were shown into the Lucases' sitting room, she felt more composed and relaxed than she had in days.

Charlotte greeted them warmly and looked from one sister to the other with open curiosity. "You look better, Lizzy," she said at once. "Much better than you did when we last met."

Elizabeth paused, the remark catching her unprepared. "Do I?"

"You had quite the headache, if I remember," Charlotte replied. "You scarcely spoke two sentences together."

"The remnants of a cold, I believe. Nothing more."

Jane glanced at her with the sort of quiet attention that suggested she did not accept the explanation quite so readily. Elizabeth pretended not to notice.

They sat, and the lace was produced at once: a length of delicate patterning, carefully folded, finer, even, than Elizabeth had hoped. Charlotte spread it across the table between them, and the three bent their heads together, comparing it against Elizabeth's gown with small exclamations of approval.

"It will do very nicely," Jane said. "Especially here, along the hem."

Charlotte nodded. "And the bodice, perhaps, if there is enough. I thought of you at once when I saw it. I hope you will not mind that my gown has some of the same."

"Mind? I should count it an unmerited dignity to be dressed like you," Elizabeth laughed.

The conversation moved easily then—stitches, colours, the likelihood of rain holding off for the evening of the ball. Tea was poured. Cups were lifted and set down again.

Only then did Elizabeth ask, as though the thought had occurred to her in passing, "Have you had many callers today?"

"Not many. The roads were still damp this morning, and that kept most people close, apart from a few of the more intrepid sort."

Elizabeth kept her eyes on the lace. "Anyone of interest?"

"That depends upon one's definition. The officers called earlier—Lieutenant Denny and one or two others. They did not stay long."

Jane looked up. Elizabeth did not.

"How lively of you," Elizabeth said mildly. "I hope they were not disappointed."

"I believe they were on their way elsewhere," Charlotte replied. "Mr Wickham, in particular, seemed in haste."

Elizabeth's fingers paused for a fraction of a second against the cloth. She resumed smoothing it at once. "How unfortunate," she said. "I should have liked to meet him again. He seems... agreeable."

Charlotte's smile turned knowing. "I am surprised you say that."

Elizabeth lifted her head. "Why?"

Charlotte shrugged. "Oh! Only that last we spoke of gentlemen in general, you claimed utter disinterest. In fact—Jane, am I not right?—You were far more interested in Mr Darcy's dog than any gentlemen, officers or otherwise."

Jane chuckled. "Charlotte remembers everything."

Elizabeth rolled her eyes. "I maintain that a large dog is a far more compelling introduction than its owner."

Charlotte laughed outright. "I shall be sure to remember that when next I see Mr Darcy."

Elizabeth waved the notion away. "Pray do not. I should hate to be thought ridiculous."

They returned to the lace then, measuring and folding, making small, sensible plans for its use. Elizabeth found that she had nothing further to ask that could not be made to sound deliberate, and so she asked nothing at all.

When they took their leave, she carried the extra trim carefully wrapped, exactly as intended.

It was the only thing she had come away with.

Darcy returned to Netherfield with the sense of having outridden nothing at all.

The horse was warm beneath him; the exercise should have done its work. Instead, the impressions of the morning clung—Wickham's tone, the ease with which he had spoken, the casual confidence of a man who had never been required to prove that a thing was false in order to dismiss it. Darcy handed off the reins at the steps and mounted them with less deliberation than usual, as though momentum might carry him past the point where thought intruded.

The housekeeper appeared from the morning room. "Oh, welcome back, Mr Darcy. Shall I have luncheon brought in? Mr Bingley waited for you, sir, but when you did not return—"

"He rode out," Darcy finished, removing his gloves. "Did he leave word?"

"He did, sir. He said you would forgive him, but he could not be still another quarter hour. Something about needing to see if the road toward Chesterton fares after the recent rain. He was in excellent spirits."

Darcy inclined his head. Bingley's spirits rarely failed him; it was one of the qualities that had first commended him. "Thank you. I shall take luncheon later."

He crossed the hall toward the stairs and was intercepted halfway by a familiar rustle.

"Oh! Mr Darcy, there you are." Miss Bingley swept out of the drawing room with a flush of triumph that suggested a morning very well spent. Mrs Hurst followed at a more stately pace, offering Darcy a brief nod before returning to the papers inside.

"Everything is arranged," Miss Bingley said. "I have taken it upon myself to ensure that the guest list is... judicious. One must think not merely of numbers, but of *effect*. I have spoken personally to the Lucases, the Philipses, and Sir William has been quite obliging about the order of introductions."

Darcy inclined his head, neither encouraging nor resisting.

"And I have made certain," she continued, lowering her voice as though confiding something of real consequence, "that no one of questionable consequence will be given undue prominence. A ball reflects its hosts, after all—and its guests. One cannot be too careful." She smiled at him, clearly expecting approval.

"I am very glad to hear it, Miss Bingley," he said, stopping short enough that she nearly collided with him. "Forgive me. I am not fit company at present."

She blinked. "Not fit?"

"I have letters to attend to," he continued. "And a matter of business that will not improve by delay."

Her expression sharpened at once, curiosity quickening. "Oh, but surely, that can wait!"

"It cannot. And..." He paused, then forced a smile. "I would not wish to offer you half congratulations where the full measure is warranted."

That, at least, she seemed to appreciate. She drew back a pace, studying him with renewed interest. "Very well. But perhaps you will come down early before dinner?"

He nodded. "If I am able."

Miss Bingley smiled, the sort of smile that promised she would hold him to it. "Of course."

Darcy inclined his head and took the stairs two at a time, conscious of her gaze upon his back until the turn of the landing put it from him. Only then did his pace falter. Not stop—never that—but ease, as though his body had recalled something his mind had not yet named.

It was nothing more than a place on the stair. An ordinary turning. He had passed it a hundred times without thought. And yet, as his foot struck that tread, a chill went through him—quick, involuntary. A remembered moment, unbidden and clear as crystal.

Brutus, planted there like a small, immovable sentinel, forcing him to go around, take another path.

The next day, Elizabeth, standing at the top staring down as though the stair must be haunted—until she had looked further and found him instead.

The recollections struck and passed in the same breath. Darcy frowned faintly at himself and continued upward, irritated by the persistence of it.

At the upper hall, he slowed again at the door that had been hers.

He stopped.

The passage was empty. No servants within sight. No sound but the distant tick of the clock below. After a moment's hesitation—brief, irrational—he stepped inside and closed the door behind him.

The room was bare of her.

Too bare.

The bed had been stripped and remade. The chair drawn back into its proper place. The washstand cleared, the fire cold. No shawl forgotten over the rail, no book left awry. Even the faint disorder she had introduced by mere occupation had been erased by the efficiency of the maids.

And yet, the air felt altered. Not crisp, like a room freshly aired. Not charged or dense, as a place holding its breath before a storm. Simply expectant, in a way that made his stomach turn with a sudden, inexplicable unease. The sensation was not dread. It was nearer to anticipation, like the moments before a door is opened upon something long imagined.

Darcy crossed the room without quite knowing that he had decided to do so. He stopped at the foot of the bed and laid his hand upon the post.

The memory came at once. Her weight, slight and searing in his arms, doing unholy things to his conscience. The heat of her skin through linen and wool. The way his arms had tightened without instruction when she stirred in his embrace.

His knees weakened—just enough that he felt it.

Darcy drew his hand back as though he had been burned.

That was enough.

He turned sharply and left the room, closing the door behind him with a decisive click. He did not look back as he strode down the hall, nor pause again at his own door.

By the time he tossed his coat over his own bed, the resolve had settled into him with grim clarity. Hertfordshire was no place for him any longer.

Whatever had been awakened here—by chance, by proximity, by some magic he did not yet understand—it was not something to be endured. And if he lingered, he suspected he would not choose wisely.

He would remain through the ball. Duty required that much. After that, he would leave Hertfordshire.

As fast as his carriage could drive.

# Chapter Twenty-Four

The company had withdrawn to the drawing room, but the evening had not yet found its feet.

Chairs were drawn into loose formation; the fire had been stirred; Mama was speculating aloud upon the rumours that Miss Bingley had secured a stag for the feast at Netherfield.

Elizabeth meant to give the evening her best efforts. She despised running from her own drawing room, so she chose a seat at the edge of the grouping—far enough to appear disengaged, near enough the door that retreat would not be remarked upon. She folded her hands and fixed her eyes on the hearthrug, counting the pattern without truly seeing it.

Mr Collins remained standing.

"If I might beg the indulgence of the family," he said, rising halfway from his chair, "I have lately received correspondence of such distinction, such consequence, that I feel it would be remiss not to share it—particularly as it bears upon matters already, ah, familiar to us all."

Papa rose and crossed to the sideboard with an air of casual deliberation, lifted the teapot, and poured a single cup. Elizabeth did not look at him until it was set beside her hand.

"For fortification," he murmured. "The evening threatens the endurance of the rational."

Elizabeth blinked. When had Papa ever poured tea for someone? She watched in awed silence as he wandered casually away.

Mr Collins cleared his throat. "The letter is, of course, from my greatly esteemed patroness, Lady Catherine de Bourgh. I have, quite naturally, taken the liberty of reading it myself, but she desired that its contents be shared and comprehended by all."

Papa did not return to his seat. He leaned instead against the mantel, one arm braced, the other folded across his chest. His gaze rested on Mr Collins with an interest Elizabeth had not seen before—not amusement, not indulgence. True curiosity.

Mr Collins unfolded the letter. "Written in her own hand, no less."

*"'My dear Mr Collins,*

*I have received your recent account of the state of society in Hertfordshire and must confess myself less surprised than concerned by what you relate. It is not unexpected that a neighbourhood unaccustomed to proper distinctions should entertain conjecture where none is required, yet I cannot approve the conditions under which such conjecture has been allowed to arise.*

*You will therefore oblige me by attending closely to the manner in which certain matters are spoken of, particularly where my nephew, Mr Darcy, is concerned. His present situation is, in my view, ill-judged, and his continued residence in that quarter serves only to invite confusion, curiosity, and improper expectation. There are places in which one may reside without consequence, and others where presence alone is sufficient to provoke misinterpretation. Hertfordshire is, quite clearly, of the latter kind.'"*

Mr Collins read with emphasis rather than fluency, pausing often to savour phrases he clearly considered exemplary. Elizabeth found herself counting breaths—not to soothe herself, but merely to remain seated.

But at the mention of Hertfordshire, something in her stomach turned outright.

She lowered her gaze to the cup, tracing the faint groove in the handle left by years of wear. The sound of Mr Collins's voice seemed to drive inward, not upon her ears, but somewhere behind them—like standing too near a bell that still trembled long after being struck.

*"'It has always been understood that responsibilities of long standing are not subject to personal inclination, nor altered by temporary associations. They persist until acknowledged and addressed in their proper sphere, and it is neither prudent nor becoming to allow them to be discussed as though they were matters of opinion rather than position. I should regret exceedingly any circumstance that permitted idle speculation to obscure what has been settled by inheritance and arrangement alike.*

*You will recall the arrangements regarding my daughter, Anne, and the necessity of proceeding with due seriousness where her interests are involved. I must insist that nothing be said or done in Hertfordshire that might encourage false hopes or unseemly conjecture on the subject of my nephew's marital prospects. Silence, in such cases, is not neutrality. It is invitation.'"*

When Anne de Bourgh's name was spoken, Elizabeth's vision dimmed at the edges—not darkness, but a soft blur, as though the room had slipped half an inch out of alignment. She took another sip of tea and found it helped less than before.

Papa stiffened, and his gaze found her. A faint narrowing of his eyes as their gazes crossed, then his expression eased, and he seemed to chuckle as he dropped his attention to the floor.

*"'I trust you will understand that I rely upon your discretion, judgment, and loyalty in these matters. It is essential that those within your influence are guided toward a proper understanding of what is—and is not—to be expected. Should my nephew require reminding of where his duties properly lie, I do not doubt that he will receive such guidance from the appropriate quarter without delay.*

*You will keep me informed of any developments that touch upon this subject, and you may assure yourself that I shall not regard neglect lightly where clarity has been so plainly afforded.*

*Lady C. de Bourgh'"*

Mr Collins folded the letter with satisfaction. "I trust," he said, "that my esteemed patroness's views will be received in the spirit intended—one of clarity, propriety, and the preservation of established order."

Silence followed. Mary appeared to be pondering the letter deeply. Kitty coughed, and Lydia snickered.

Papa regarded Mr Collins for a long moment, his head tipped slightly to one side, as though considering a specimen whose function remained uncertain. He made a small sound in his throat—not assent, not dissent. Curiosity.

"And this order," he said at last, mildly. "You find it so very fragile?"

Mr Collins stiffened. "Not fragile, sir. Merely vulnerable to... distraction." His gaze flicked, just once, toward Elizabeth. "Society cannot indulge every personal inclination when greater obligations are at stake. One must be vigilant, lest sentiment interfere with duty."

The words landed like a misjudged step—too close, too deliberate, and a shiver shot down her spine.

"Well," Papa said at last, "how very generous of Lady Catherine to concern herself so fully with affairs at such a distance. One might almost suppose she feared something might occur without her approval."

Mr Collins blinked. "I—I assure you, sir, her ladyship's concern is entirely appropriate—"

"Undoubtedly," Mr Bennet agreed. "Though I confess I admire her confidence. To know so precisely where a man ought *not* to be, without troubling herself over where he actually is."

"Sir!" Mr Collins shook his head with a dismissive smile. "You misinterpret her intentions. My reasons for sharing her words are merely to... *instruct* my fair cousins that certain comportment may be unseemly. Why, I understand that there was some disturbance recently, requiring prolonged intimacy with the party residing at Netherfield. While such an incident certainly must reflect well on the hospitality of our neighbours, to *encourage* further such encounters would be..." He smiled again. "*Most* unwise."

Elizabeth lifted her head.

Papa's gaze flicked to her—briefly, carefully—then away again.

"I think," he continued, "we have been thoroughly instructed for one evening. Mr Collins, you must be fatigued after such earnest reading. Pray allow the rest of us the comfort of digestion. And if you will all excuse me, I believe the hearth in my library is currently boasting a fire that no one is enjoying."

ELIZABETH LEFT THE DRAWING room without waiting for anything else to be said. She clipped the doorframe with her shoulder and barely registered it. Someone said her name behind her—Mama, she thought—but she did not slow to answer. The passage seemed longer than it ought to have been. Her stomach turned hard and fast, warning her with an urgency she did not question. If she stopped, she would not keep her composure. She set her jaw and kept going.

She was close on Papa's heels now, as he opened his library door. But before he went inside, he turned. "Lizzy?"

She reached for the door and fled inside with him. The door shut behind her with a force she did not moderate.

The change was immediate. The air inside the room felt different—cooler, still. The sick surge ebbed as swiftly as it had risen, leaving her shaken but upright. She stood where she was, one hand braced against the door, counting nothing at all until the worst of it passed.

Only then did she turn.

Papa stopped just short of the desk. He was watching her closely now, not smiling, not speaking.

Elizabeth crossed the room and planted her hands on the edge of his writing table. "You are going to tell me," she said, without preface or softness, "what that letter meant."

He regarded her for a moment longer, pulled a handkerchief out of his pocket, then tucked it back in without using it. "I had hoped," he said mildly, "that my exit might be taken as a general dismissal rather than an invitation to interrogation."

"You poured me tea," Elizabeth said. "You stood between him and me. You watched me the entire time he was reading. You do not do those things without reason. So? What do you know?"

He crossed to the chair by the hearth and sat, one leg extended, hands folded loosely. "I know," he said, "that my cousin is a fool who has an unshakable faith in other people's opinions. I know that my daughter does not enjoy being made an audience for them."

"That is not an answer."

"Can a father not show a bit of concern without provoking inquiry?"

Elizabeth stepped to the desk and pulled one of the books from the neat stack there—thin, brittle, its spine repaired with careful thread. She laid it open, turning to a marked page with no hesitation. "Why this book?" she demanded, tapping the margin. "And why this one beside it, and the one beneath? You have had some of them for longer than I have been alive, and others you seemed to have purchased with a purpose of some sort. You gave them to me when I was ill, and you did not say why. You let me read them as though they were harmless." She lifted her gaze. "They are not."

Mr Bennet's mouth curved, not in amusement. "They are paper and ink, Lizzy."

"Do not," she said sharply. "Do not make sport of this. Not now."

He frowned and drew the handkerchief back out of his pocket, and this time, he slowly wiped his spectacles. "Very well."

He eased himself into the chair opposite her, the desk between them. For a moment, he did not speak. Then he reached out and turned the book a fraction, so the light fell more cleanly on the page. "I do not know what it means."

Elizabeth crossed her arms. "That is not possible. You cannot be entirely ignorant."

"It *is* entirely possible," he replied. "It has been my chief talent, these many years."

She shook her head. "You gathered them."

"I inherited some. Acquired others. When something seemed to echo what I already had, I added it to my collection." He shrugged. "A habit, perhaps. Or a failing."

"A pattern, you mean."

"Yes," he admitted. "That, too."

"You meant something," she said. "When you put those books into my hands. You do not do anything by accident, Papa."

Papa glanced up from the page he had been pretending to read. The pretence fell away at once; he folded the paper neatly and set it aside.

"I do a great many things by accident," he said mildly. "I merely prefer not to advertise them."

"That will not do."

"No," he agreed. "It rarely does."

He leaned back in his chair and regarded her over steepled fingers, his expression thoughtful rather than amused. "You are unwell," he said at last. "Not dangerously so, despite your mother's enthusiasm. And you are observant enough to notice patterns where others might be content with convenience. That does not oblige me to invent explanations."

"I am not asking you to invent," Elizabeth said. "I am asking you to tell me what you know."

He smiled faintly. "Ah. That is a different thing."

She waited.

Papa rose and crossed to the shelves behind her. He did not take anything down at first. He only ran his fingers along the spines, as though reacquainting himself with old friends he had not meant to call upon.

"What I know," he said, "is that books are safer than conclusions. They permit one to be curious without being committed."

Elizabeth turned toward him. "That is not an answer."

"It is the only one I am prepared to give you just now."

She frowned. "You have noticed it."

"I am old, not blind. But pray, elaborate, in case I have missed something."

"The headaches. The way I feel when Mr Collins speaks. And—" She hesitated. "When Mr Darcy is mentioned. I know you saw that."

His brows lifted. "Did I?"

"Do not trifle, Papa. You pointed that coincidence out before I had even made the connection."

He sighed and dropped his hand from the shelf. "Very well. I have no explanation about Mr Darcy, but I have noticed that you are more yourself when Mr Collins is not imposing himself upon the room. I have also noticed that you appear less so when he is. I require no philosophy to account for that."

"That is not fair."

"Nor is Mr Collins," her father said dryly. "And yet he persists."

Elizabeth crossed her arms. "Then you do not think there is anything... particular about him?"

Mr Bennet hesitated. Just long enough.

"I think," he said slowly, "that he is a man who arrived pre-equipped with certainty and has never misplaced it since. Such people are tiresome. Occasionally harmful. Rarely interesting."

"That is not what I mean."

"Well? Be more specific, Lizzy."

She pressed her lips together. "What do you know of his family?"

That did it.

Papa's mouth curved—not in amusement, but in something more reluctant. He returned to his chair and sat, folding his hands upon the desk as though arranging his thoughts before allowing them speech.

"Very little," he said. "And most of that second-hand."

Elizabeth waited again.

"His mother," her father went on, "was a cousin of my own, once removed and twice regretted. She was thought... delicate. High spirits, they called it at first. A less charitable description was 'troubled.' She was married young to a man with a keen eye for property and a temper equal to it."

"And she was well?"

Papa shrugged. "Define well. She disappeared from family life with remarkable efficiency. Letters arrived. Perfectly sensible ones. Polite. Domestic. She seemed, on paper, entirely reconciled to her circumstances."

"And in truth?"

"That was less clear. There were whispers. Accusations. A quarrel between her husband and Collins' father—my cousin—that ended all communication. Collins insists she died. Others believed she was... placed somewhere quieter." He waved a hand. "It is many years past. No one saw fit to pursue the matter."

Elizabeth stared at him. "You say this as though it were nothing."

"I say it as though it were no longer actionable," he replied. "One cannot rescue a woman twenty years too late, nor indict a son for accepting the version of events most convenient to him."

She swallowed. "And you think it has no bearing on me."

"I think," Papa said carefully, "that families are full of unhappy stories if one is inclined to look for them. I do not propose to burden you with every skeleton rattling about in our relations' cupboards."

Elizabeth turned away, restless now, crossing the small distance to the window and back again. "Then why the books?"

Her father rose once more, selected a slim volume from the shelf, and placed it in her hands.

"Because," he said, "you will not be satisfied with being told there is nothing to see. And because if you must worry, I would rather you do so with poetry than with conjecture."

She looked down at the cover. "You are evading."

"I am postponing," he corrected. "There is a difference."

Elizabeth met his gaze. "Do you think I am in danger?"

Papa chuckled. "Mr Collins is a danger to no one, least of all himself."

"Do you think I am imagining things?"

"No. You would conjure something more inventive."

She wagged the book in his face. "Papa, I am being serious. Do you think there is something wrong with me?"

He smiled then—softly, unmistakably. "Absolutely not."

She exhaled, trying to pass back the book she was holding. "And your advice, the best you have to offer, is for me to just... read."

"I advise you," he said, pressing the book gently back into her hands, "to be curious without being frightened. To observe without concluding. And to remember that discomfort is not prophecy."

She hesitated. "And if the books suggest otherwise?"

"Then," he said lightly, "we shall discuss them. Over tea. Preferably after you have slept."

Elizabeth did not smile, but she nodded. "Very well. I shall read."

"I thought you might."

As she turned toward the door, her father spoke again—almost casually.

"And Lizzy?"

She paused.

"If any book makes you feel worse rather than wiser," he said, "bring it back down. We shall put it away."

She inclined her head and left him there, the book held carefully in both hands.

# CHAPTER TWENTY-FIVE

NETHERFIELD WAS ALREADY ALIVE when they arrived.

The carriage scarcely halted before the door was opened, voices spilling out to meet them—laughter, music tuning itself into order, the bright clatter of shoes upon glowing marble floors. Mama surged forward, issuing greetings before anyone had quite finished alighting, Lydia and Kitty close behind her, darting glances toward the lights and uniforms beyond the threshold.

Elizabeth followed more slowly… hesitantly.

Inside, the entry had been transformed. Candles burned in ranks along the walls; greenery framed the doors; the air carried warmth, perfume, and the promise of too many people gathered into too little space. A receiving line had formed near the foot of the stairs, guests pausing to offer their bows and compliments before being absorbed into the crowd.

Mr Bingley stood at its centre, radiant with pleasure and wholly unequal to the task of regulating the flow. Miss Bingley flanked him, attentive and vigilant, her smile brimming with eagerness to impress. A pace behind them—deliberately behind—stood Mr Darcy.

Elizabeth did not look at him directly, but she could feel his gaze, nonetheless.

She moved with her family through the line, offering her curtsey, accepting Mr Bingley's welcome with genuine warmth, submitting briefly to Miss Bingley's cool appraisal. Darcy inclined his head. Their eyes met only for a moment—long enough to acknowledge one another, no more.

She passed on.

The room beyond was already a riot of sound. Musicians struck into their first set; officers gathered in bright knots near the edges of the floor; gowns brushed past one another in constant motion. Charlotte Lucas was barely visible near the far wall, deep in conversation with Maria and Lady Lucas. Elizabeth caught her eye and smiled. Charlotte smiled back, a flicker of relief crossing her face, as though she had been waiting.

Mr Collins was less eager to lose her company.

He had entered with them, of course—attached to her mother's elbow one moment, then loosed upon the room the next—his voice rising above the first swell of conversation as though the evening required instruction before it could proceed. Elizabeth felt the onset at once: not pain, but the first unmistakable warning, the sense of pressure gathering before it declared itself.

While her mother paused to greet an acquaintance and Lydia darted ahead in search of uniforms, Elizabeth lengthened her stride, letting the movement of the crowd carry her forward and away. Each step put more bodies between her and that voice. The warning receded to something manageable.

She took in the room as she moved: the pattern of traffic between doors, the way the music drew people forward and released them again, the press of bodies near the floor, and the pockets of relative calm beyond it. She noted where conversation gathered and where it thinned. Where sound collided. Where it slipped past.

Netherfield offered much tonight. Noise. Movement. Witnesses everywhere.

And freedom, if one used it carefully.

Elizabeth paused near the wall and let the current of guests pass her by, her head finally clear enough to think. Mr Wickham had not yet appeared, but surely he would. Officers did not miss such free meals and entertainment, nor did men who enjoyed being observed. She would speak with him when the moment allowed.

She noticed Darcy again only when he crossed her path, when a turn of the set or the angle of the room placed him briefly in view. There was nothing remarkable in that. He was near enough to be noticed by anyone, and tonight he lacked even the excuse of his dog.

Elizabeth adjusted her gloves and stepped aside to allow a passing couple through. The last time she was in this house, it had erected invisible walls and dictated her movements. Hopefully, nothing… odd… would yank the rug from under her feet tonight.

DARCY HAD NOT MEANT to speak to her that evening.

He had already erred in watching her as closely as he had. To approach her now—before the supper interval, when the room was still lively with expectation—would invite notice. He knew the patterns of such evenings too well. A request made at the wrong moment acquired weight. It gathered inference.

Still...

Elizabeth Bennet stood near the edge of the room, her posture composed but alert, as though her attention were divided between the figures of the dance and something gathering just behind her. Darcy was passing when Mrs Bennet's voice rose—bright, eager, and entirely unrestrained by discretion.

"Oh, it will all come right," she was saying to a small knot of ladies clustered near the refreshment table. "Mr Collins has been most patient, and I have told him as much. Elizabeth is merely—well—she likes to be persuaded. But of course, she will dance the supper set with him this evening! One cannot refuse such an offer indefinitely, not when it has been so properly proposed. Goodness, where is that girl? I have hardly seen her all evening. Perhaps Mr Collins is asking her even now."

There was a murmur of approval. Someone laughed. Another voice chimed in with a remark about propriety and gratitude.

Darcy slowed.

"...and really," Mrs Bennet continued, "it will be quite a relief to have it settled. These things must be arranged, after all. Elizabeth will see the sense of it soon enough. Why, I am sure Mr Collins is only waiting to catch her between partners."

Elizabeth did not turn, did not look.

But something in her changed. Not a movement—she remained perfectly still—but a tension drew through her shoulders, fine as a thread pulled too tight. Her hand, which had been resting lightly at her side, curled once, then stilled again. For an instant, her head dipped, as though she were bracing herself against a sound she could not escape.

Darcy halted altogether.

He had seen embarrassment before. Mortification, even. This was neither. It was quieter, more grotesque—a look that passed too quickly to be claimed as reaction, but not quickly enough to be missed.

Mrs Bennet's voice sounded again. "Mr Collins understands these matters exceedingly well. He is quite certain it will all be resolved as it ought."

Elizabeth's chest rose, enough that Darcy saw the flicker of it from several feet away. She shifted her weight, just barely, as though seeking to draw herself apart without drawing attention. He saw her eyes flickering to the hall, as if she might escape out that way.

Darcy did not think of intervention at once.

He thought of impropriety. Of notice. Of the strange personal consequences of placing himself where expectation already strained the air.

Then he thought of her face—composed, silent, absorbing some sort of discomfort or terror that was not of her making.

The sensible course would have been to continue on. To let the evening arrange itself as it would. He disliked interference. He disliked gossip even more.

He found himself speaking all the same.

"Miss Elizabeth."

She turned, surprise flashing across her face before settling into polite attention. "Mr Darcy."

He inclined his head. "Might I speak with you a moment?"

She hesitated—only a breath—then stepped aside with him, just far enough that conversation might pass without performance.

"I had wondered," he said, choosing his words with care, "whether you were already engaged for the supper set."

Her expression changed at once—not into gratitude, not quite, but into something like relief held in check.

"I... perhaps." She clenched her jaw, then winced and sniffed. Then, after a pause, "At least—that is, I am *meant* to be."

Darcy waited.

She drew a breath, quivering slightly. "My mother has been kind enough to announce it for me," she added lightly. "With a generosity that leaves little room for correction."

"I see," he said. "Well, if you are already engaged—"

She looked up at him then, more directly. "If you would be willing," she said, "I should like to beg a small indulgence."

That word—*beg*—sat ill with him at once.

"I would... appreciate it if... a belief could be made to circulate," she went on, carefully, "that you asked me for the supper set several days ago. Just after the ball was announced."

Darcy stiffened. "I did no such thing."

"I know." She offered a quick, apologetic smile. "That is the difficulty."

He drew back a fraction. "Miss Elizabeth, I cannot—"

"I would not ask it," she said, more urgently now, "if it were not for certain extenuating circumstances."

Darcy swallowed. He was acutely aware of how such a story would sound—how readily it would be repeated, embroidered, examined. He had spent the evening resisting exactly this: the impression of intention, of preference.

And pretence, above all, offended him.

"I do not care to encourage invention," he said. "Nor to supply it with evidence."

Her gaze did not waver. "Nor do I," she replied. "But I care even less to be cornered by it."

Something in her voice—controlled, but not light—gave him pause.

"You have found Mr Collins... oppressive," he said, before he had quite decided to.

Her mouth curved, briefly. "That is a charitable description."

Darcy considered her then—not as she moved among the company, but as she stood now, deliberately composed, asking him for something he did not wish to give, and yet she clearly needed.

The lie troubled him.

So did the look in her eyes.

"Very well," he said. "If the arrangement can be easily assumed, I will not contradict it."

Her shoulders eased—only fractionally, but enough that he noticed. "I am obliged to you," she said. "I promise not to entertain fancies beyond the inescapable."

"I should hope not. Very well, Miss Elizabeth. I shall come to claim your hand after two dances for the supper set."

She curtsied, then turned away soon after. Darcy remained where he was, telling himself—firmly—that the matter was settled.

It was only when the officers entered, laughter preceding them, that he noticed Elizabeth glance back over her shoulder. Not toward him. Toward the room itself.

Her eyes moved—swift, eager—from Mr Collins to the space beside Darcy, then onward to Wickham as he joined the circle.

Darcy stiffened. No, it was not jealousy. Not alarm.

Surely.

He looked away before he could consider it further.

ELIZABETH SMILED WHERE SMILES were due, answered easily when addressed, and allowed herself to be drawn into conversations that required nothing deeper than agreeable attention. If her laugh came a moment too quickly, if she inclined her head with more care than usual before committing herself to a direction, no one remarked upon it. A ball rewarded animation. It excused movement. It permitted a lady to circulate without appearing restless.

That, at least, was her intention.

She kept a careful sense of the room as she moved through it—not in any deliberate fashion, but with the same instinct that guided her steps in a crowded street. She noted where the officers clustered, where the matrons had claimed the safer seats along the wall, where her mother's voice rose and fell in tones of energetic satisfaction.

And she noted, with a vigilance she would have denied if asked, the shifting position of Mr Collins.

He was never quite where she expected him to be. At one moment, he appeared firmly engaged near the refreshments, expounding to Sir William on the advantages of proper ventilation for a greenhouse; at the next, his voice carried from behind her shoulder, closer than she had judged, already winding itself toward some declaration of duty or improvement. Each time, Elizabeth adjusted her course without appearing to do so—accepting a remark from Mrs Long, stepping aside to admire a ribbon, turning neatly into another circle before he could quite lay claim to her attention or approach near enough to send a bone-numbing shock of pain through her ear.

It was exhausting work, made more so by the necessity of appearing entirely at ease.

She had just extricated herself from a discussion of the musicians—conducted largely by her mother, with Elizabeth cast as approving audience—when she became aware, too late, that Mr Collins had begun to angle in her direction, his expression fixed with purpose. The sound of his voice reached her before the words themselves, and with it came the familiar constriction that warned her she had misjudged the distance.

Elizabeth did not hesitate. She retreated—not backward, but sideways—allowing the press of guests to carry her toward a quieter corner near the windows, where George Wickham stood with two of his fellows.

"Miss Elizabeth!" he greeted, "you have been quite lost to us. May I say, you look particularly radiant this evening."

Elizabeth had time enough to notice two things at once: the angle of Mr Collins's approach from her left, and the first sharp tightening that warned her she had waited a moment too long.

She turned brightly back to Wickham. "What a pretty compliment. Did you intend to follow that with asking me to dance?"

The question was direct enough to earn a blink of surprise from him—quickly followed by laughter. "Indeed, I did," he said, offering his arm with exaggerated readiness. "And I should be grievously disappointed to be forestalled."

"Then I am very glad you arrived when you did," Elizabeth replied, already moving.

They passed Mr Collins at a decisive angle, Wickham's presence creating just enough interruption to prevent a claim from being made. Elizabeth did not look back. She did not need to. The moment his voice fell behind them, the pressure receded, leaving her clear-headed enough to breathe easily again.

She told herself—without much conviction—that it was merely the relief of motion.

They joined the forming set near the centre of the room, not far from where Mr Darcy stood apart from the dancers. Elizabeth became aware of him without seeking him out, as one becomes aware of a fixed point in a shifting crowd. His gaze was already upon them.

The music began.

She did not think about the steps. She had danced often enough for them to require no attention. Wickham spoke rather constantly, some comment about the press of the room or the merits of the musicians, but his words passed her with little impression. What she noticed instead was the relief—the absence of strain, the ease with which she turned and moved.

Across the floor, Darcy did not look away.

Elizabeth caught the fact of it more than once as the figures carried her round, his attention following with an intensity she did not pretend not to notice. She did not smile at him. She did not acknowledge it at all.

But when the dance ended, she was certain of two things. First: that Wickham's timely intervention had spared her more than a dance.

And second: that Darcy had remained within a dozen paces throughout, watching every moment.

The supper tables were already being claimed when Darcy entered with Elizabeth after their dance. The atmosphere had transformed from the ordered brightness of the ballroom into a looser, louder arrangement of appetite and opinion. The air itself felt heavier—warm with exerted bodies, sound, and the sharp edge of hunger.

Darcy was aware, acutely, of the distance between his own breath and the strength he required of it.

The dance had been a late one—graceful, restrained, chosen by the musicians as much out of courtesy as necessity. Fewer turns. Longer figures. The sort meant to carry a room gently toward a respite. It should have spared him.

Instead, it had demanded more.

Her hand in his—light, exact, responsive—had sent the now-familiar sensation through him in uneven waves: a twitch behind the eyes, a faint hollowing beneath the ribs, as though something essential were being drawn away and returned out of order. Each time she stiffened—each moment her attention snagged elsewhere—the feeling sharpened. When she relaxed again, it eased, but never fully released him.

He had held her through it. Smiled when required. Counted the measures. Let no one see how many times his toes dragged or his vision swam.

Now, as he guided her forward, his fingers tingled where they had rested at her back, not with heat but with a strange, echoing chill. He was faintly aware of his own pulse—too quick, then oddly slow—of the floor rising and falling by degrees so slight they might have been imagined.

He ignored the eyes upon them. He could not afford to spare attention for anything but remaining upright.

Elizabeth did not.

She took her seat with composure, but it was the sort that required effort. Her shoulders remained square; her hands folded neatly in her lap. Only the quick glance she cast along the table betrayed her attention to something beyond the place set before her.

Darcy drew back his chair—and had to pause before sitting, his hand resting a moment longer than necessary on its carved back, waiting for the faint rush in his head to pass.

It did. Mostly.

Mr Collins appeared only a short distance down the table, holding a chair for Charlotte Lucas. Collins was speaking already—apologizing profusely for the delay, congratulating himself upon securing such an advantageous position—and as he moved down the line toward his place, Darcy saw Elizabeth squirm in discomfort.

Not sufficiently to invite notice. But enough.

Her head angled away from Collins; her gaze dropped as though to inspect the napkin she had already arranged. One hand lifted briefly—not quite to her face, but near enough to suggest the gesture had been checked midway, as though she had remembered herself just in time. Then she blinked, drank in a breath, and the tension in her shoulders eased. She looked up, around, and smiled at him before he pulled out his own chair.

A pulse of nausea rose and fell again, sharp enough that he briefly considered—quite seriously—whether he might beg indulgence and withdraw. A breach of etiquette. An unpardonable one. And yet the thought clung, insistent, until he felt Elizabeth shift beside him.

She was not looking at him now. But her spine went rigid again, and with it, so did the pressure in his chest.

Darcy narrowed his eyes and frowned as he took his seat beside her.

Collins settled into his own chair two places down, still talking, still pleased. Charlotte Lucas inclined her head politely, her expression composed in the way Darcy had come to recognise as endurance rather than interest.

Elizabeth's posture altered, her breath drawn as if to speak—but instead she startled, visibly, and turned her head. Staring… across the room.

Her gaze travelled past the nearer tables, past the press of gowns and uniforms, and came to rest—briefly, searchingly—on the far side of the hall, where the militia officers were being seated together. Wickham stood among them, laughing at something said by Denny.

Elizabeth's eyes lingered there.

Then confusion crossed her face—not alarm, not distress, but a clear, unguarded uncertainty, as though the thing she had expected to find had failed to present itself. Her hand tightened once on the edge of the table.

The pressure in Darcy's chest eased—just enough to be unmistakable.

She looked away again, this time more slowly, and straightened in her chair as if correcting herself. When her gaze returned to the place before her, it held no relief—only calculation.

Darcy swallowed and glanced away. He had not intended to attend to her so closely. He had resolved, in fact, upon quite the opposite. Yet the effort of *not* noticing her now required more attention than simply allowing himself to see what was plainly there.

"Miss Elizabeth," he said quietly, leaning just enough to avoid being overheard, "are you well?"

She looked back to him, a forced brightness returning to her expression as though it had never left. "Perfectly," she said. "Why do you ask?"

"Because," he replied, choosing his words with care, "you appear less at ease than you were a moment ago."

She hesitated—only a fraction of a second. "I am only observing," she said lightly. "One must, in such company."

Darcy drew his chair back only a fraction, enough to shield her from the worst of the room's traffic without making a show of it. The motion left him faintly light-headed—nothing alarming, merely an odd swim at the edge of his sight—but it passed when he fixed his attention upon her.

He did not look toward Mr Collins again.

"You seem rather sensitized to the general—may I say, entirely expected—speculation of the room this evening," he said mildly. "I should recommend ignoring at least half of it."

Elizabeth's mouth curved. "Only half? How generous."

He flicked his eyes toward another corner, where Mrs Bennet was fluttering her handkerchief and holding forth with unmistakable animation. Elizabeth's name surfaced even at a distance. Then there was Collins, whose glances in their direction were too frequent to be accidental.

"At least," Darcy continued, "the remainder may safely be dismissed as invention. I have already heard three incompatible accounts of your prospects, my intentions, observed six hands covering indiscreet mouths, and we have been seated less than five minutes."

She laughed—softly, but with unmistakable relief. The sound settled something in him. The faint queasiness that had dulled his appetite eased, replaced by the simpler pleasure of watching her speak without caution.

"Then I am glad of it," she said. "I was beginning to fear I had been living a double life without noticing."

"If you have," Darcy said, "you conduct it with admirable discretion."

Her eyes brightened at that, and she leaned back in her chair. "You see? That is precisely the sort of encouragement one requires. If I am to be misrepresented, I prefer it done with elegance."

He found himself smiling before he could check it. The room still pressed close, the noise still rose and fell in uneven waves, but seated beside her, it all seemed manageable—background rather than assault.

"I shall endeavour to correct the record where possible."

"I should be grateful," she said. "Though I warn you—my mother will only improve upon any correction you offer."

"That," Darcy said dryly, "does appear to be a talent."

She laughed again, more freely now. "It is rather astonishing how pleasant an evening may become when one is no longer obliged to listen for one's own name. Do you not find that the success of any evening depends almost entirely on whether one is permitted to choose one's own companions?"

"A dangerous doctrine," Darcy replied. A brief blur crossed his vision; he blinked it away and went on. "Society would collapse."

"Only the duller portions," she said sweetly.

He huffed a quiet laugh before he could stop himself. "Then I shall consider myself warned."

They ate for a moment in companionable ease, the clatter of the room receding to a tolerable murmur. Darcy found he had little appetite for what lay before him, though he made a show of it—lifting his fork, taking a few careful bites—more for the sake of appearances than hunger. The effort cost him more than it ought, but he ignored that as well.

"You danced well," he said at last. "With attention and skill, I mean. Not merely with energy."

She glanced up, amused. "That sounds suspiciously like praise."

"I intended it as an observation," he replied. "And perhaps gratitude from my toes, though I am aware the distinction is rarely convincing."

"I shall allow it," she laughed. "You strike me as someone who notices *how* things are done, not merely *whether* they are done."

"That is generous," he said. "And perhaps unwise."

"Why?"

"Because it invites questions," he said. "And I find myself ill-equipped to deflect them."

Her smile turned curious. "I should have thought deflection a practiced skill of yours."

"Only when necessary," he answered. He reached for his glass, then set it down again untouched. "I prefer candour when it is... safe."

She considered that. “I suspect we differ there. I find candour most useful when it is inconvenient.”

He shook his head, a quiet huff of amusement escaping him despite the faint tightening beneath his ribs. “Then I am glad not to be your adversary.”

Her smile hovered between deliberate flirtation and calculation. “Not at present.”

Warmth answered that—quick, dangerous—and with it a slight tremor at the corner of his vision that made him blink once, hard, before it passed. He did not look away from her.

“May I inquire,” he said, more softly now, “what occupies your time when you are not enduring the attentions of half the county?”

She blinked, then smiled. “Reading, mostly. Walking, when I can escape supervision. Observing people when neither is possible.”

“Reading,” he repeated, pleased despite himself. “What sort?”

“Varied,” she said. “Though lately I have been quite taken with something unexpected.”

“Oh? Anything worth reciting? I daresay it would make more agreeable fodder than most of the other conversation we might overhear tonight.”

She hesitated—only a fraction—then shrugged. “It is a collection of old ballads and fragments my father procured while I was unwell. Nothing fashionable. Odd, really. But strangely compelling.”

Darcy’s fingers stilled against the stem of his glass.

“Ballads,” he said carefully. The word itself seemed to settle wrong in his mouth. “Of what sort?”

She pursed her lips, thinking. “Legends, mostly. Folk tales. Inconvenient places. Unwise promises. The sort of thing sensible people pretend not to believe in.”

A faint pressure gathered behind his eyes. He shifted in his chair, the movement precise, controlled, and found his gaze drawn—of all people—toward Mr Collins before he could stop it.

“Have you a favourite?”

“I do. Though I doubt it would suit you.”

“Try me.”

“Well. I only recall the first two stanzas.” She smiled, then recited—softly, with a thoughtfulness that stripped the verse of any pretension:

*"When Avalon in mist was bound,*
*And noble steel undone,*
*The thorn abid upon that ground*
*Till reckoning were begun.*

*She bore no sword, nor carried shield,*
*Nor rode in silver mail*
*Her voice alone the grove did bind,*
*Her oath the thornwood vale."*

"There," she finished with a faint lift of her shoulder. "That is all I remember at the moment."

Darcy remembered.

His lips parted without his consent, the next words pressing forward—not as recollection, but as something that had never loosened its hold on him. He had learned them young. He had been instructed, just as firmly, never to give them voice.

A sharp, visceral awareness went through him—like misplacing one's footing and discovering there is no ground beneath. This was not a fragment. Not a curiosity. This was the ballad as his father had kept it, intact and unromantic, meant to be endured and dismissed, not spoken aloud by anyone who had no right to it.

And she had spoken it.

Elizabeth Bennet's eyes were still upon him—bright, attentive, waiting.

She could have no notion of what she had just touched. Darcy forced his attention back into himself, into the room, into the harmlessness of the moment. Some recognitions, once admitted, could not be lived with. They altered the terms of everything that followed.

"That," he said, managing a faint, dismissive smile, "is a remarkably earnest choice for light reading. Were there dragons and faeries as well? A black sorcerer, no doubt. I hope the volume offers something that does not hinge quite so heavily upon doom."

Elizabeth laughed. "You object to a story that asks something of its characters?"

"I object to stories that make demands at all," he replied easily, though his appetite had quite abandoned him. "I read to be educated or entertained, not enlisted."

"Ah! Then you must avoid half the best poems and legends. They are forever insisting that one thing must follow another."

"Yes," he said, lifting his glass and taking a measured sip. "A most tiresome habit."

"And yet people keep repeating them." She pursed her lips, brow arched in quiet challenge.

"People repeat many things they do not intend to believe," Darcy answered, a shade too quickly. Then, as if it were of no consequence at all, he added with a smile, "That does not make them true."

She laughed, conceding the point with a tilt of her glass, and glanced away.

For a moment, he allowed himself to think the matter settled. Then he noticed the direction of her gaze—deliberate, wary—down the length of the table.

Toward Mr Collins.

Her mouth tightened, only briefly, before she smoothed the expression away.

"May I ask," Darcy said quietly, "whether your cousin has given you cause for discomfort beyond his... conversational enthusiasm?"

Her brows lifted. "An odd question for a ball supper, sir."

"I am observant," he replied. "Occasionally, to my regret."

She stiffened. Her smile now held a question. "What concern is it of yours?"

He met her gaze and chose his tone with care. "Call it a general dislike of seeing anyone cornered against their will."

She laughed softly, as though to dismiss the matter. "You are very kind, but I assure you my cousin's chief offense is endurance. One grows weary of being improved at."

Darcy did not return the smile. "That is not what I asked."

Her expression shifted—sobering, then brightening again. For a moment, she seemed poised to parry. Instead, she hesitated. The hesitation was slight, but he had been watching her too long to miss it.

"You flinch," he said quietly. "Not merely from tedium. When he approaches. When you are forced into proximity with him." His voice lowered. "I do not believe that is nothing. Has he harmed you?"

She drew a breath and released it more slowly. "You observe too much for your own comfort, sir."

"So I am often told."

Her fingers tightened about the stem of her glass. "It is not his voice," she said at last. "Nor even the manner of his address. It is... what he insists upon saying."

Darcy leaned a fraction closer. The movement sent a faint, unwelcome pressure through his chest, which he ignored. "What does he insist upon?"

She met his eyes now, and all levity fell away. "He speaks of arrangements. Of expectations laid out long before anyone had a voice in the matter. He speaks as though repetition itself might grant authority." Her mouth tightened. "And when he speaks of them, it is as though he believes I ought to listen—ought to accept—as if such things concerned me personally."

"That… makes no sense."

"No," she agreed. "It does not. And I doubt he is intelligent enough to perceive any fault in it."

She frowned, then tilted her head, studying him with a curiosity that had sharpened into something more exacting. "But if we are to be candid," she continued, "the conversations that trouble me most do not begin with myself at all."

"Oh?"

"They begin," she said evenly, "with one Lady Catherine de Bourgh. Your aunt, I understand."

The name fell like a tolling bell. Darcy blinked, a brief tightening passing through him.

"And they end," she added, "with you."

His hand closed against the edge of the table. "My aunt has a talent for presuming," he said. "You need not trouble yourself with her suppositions."

"And yet she troubles the room with them," Elizabeth replied. "And my cousin repeats them as though they were already settled." Her gaze searched his. "What is it Lady Catherine expects of you, Mr Darcy?"

The question struck too near. Habit rose at once to shield him.

"I do not think this is a suitable subject for—" He pushed back his chair.

He did not know what he meant to do. There was no proper excuse for leaving the table mid-course.

But the instant he rose, Elizabeth startled.

The reaction was immediate, unguarded. She gasped—not loudly, but sharply—one hand shot to her temple, and the other flew out as though to stop him, closing around his wrist without thought.

The contact was unmistakable.

Not pain. Not shock.

Something else entirely.

Heat flared where their skin met—swift, certain—as though recognition itself had taken form. Darcy froze. The pressure in his chest deepened, breath caught high and shallow, every instinct arrested.

The room did not vanish. It simply ceased to matter.

Elizabeth stared at their joined hands, then up at him, her expression caught between surprise and something perilously close to understanding.

Darcy did not move. Could not.

For the first time, the old stories did not feel distant or absurd. They stood before him, embodied and undeniable—looking back through her eyes.

And in that instant, he knew—beyond sense, beyond any chance of saving doubt.

This was the thing he had been fleeing. A lifetime spent in dismissal and reason, laughing off a heritage so buried beneath habit that its shape had nearly been lost.

It had found him out at last.

# Chapter Twenty-Six

"Jane, my dear, you have scarcely touched your tea," Mama said for the third time, pressing the cup nearer as though appetite were a moral obligation. "You must keep up your strength! One never knows how much conversation the day may require."

Jane smiled faintly and complied, though Elizabeth could see the effort behind it. She looked tired in a way that had nothing to do with the hour or the way they had passed the night.

"I should not be surprised," Mama continued, lowering her voice with a theatrical air that failed to diminish its reach, "if we were to receive a *visitor* before luncheon. Indeed, I should be quite astonished if we did not. Such attentions are not paid twice without intention, and Mr Bingley is nothing if not decisive."

Elizabeth paused with her spoon halfway to her mouth. She set it down again. She would rather not eat, if this was to be the course served.

Mary nodded from across the table. "It would be the natural progression," she said. "Affection, when properly guided, seeks resolution."

Kitty almost knocked over her poached egg as she reached for the tea. "Do you think he'll bring flowers?"

"I think," Mama replied, "that he will bring a *question*. A most important question, indeed! Is that not right, Mr Bennet? Oh, for mercy's sake, that man has gone off to his library again. Kitty, darling, do stop coughing! Jane, go upstairs and put on your pink gown. It does so much for your complexion. Yellow only makes you look ill, and we cannot have Mr Bingley fearing the Bennet girls are forever taking to their beds for the least little thing."

Elizabeth pushed her chair back a fraction. "Really, Mama," she said, "it seems premature to speak as though—"

"Premature?" Her mother turned. "My dear Lizzy, one must be practical. Nothing is gained by pretending ignorance when everyone can see what is before them. Jane is admired. Mr Bingley has been constant. We must make of it what we can!"

Mary glanced at Elizabeth over the rim of her teacup. "It is unwise," she said, "to resist conclusions that recommend themselves so plainly. Excessive doubt is as much a failing as rashness."

"I am not resisting anything," she said. "I merely think it best not to decide matters before—"

"Before what?" Mama demanded. "Before opportunity passes? Before misunderstandings arise? Heaven knows we have had enough of those."

The words struck with uncomfortable accuracy. Elizabeth pushed the rest of the way out from the table and rose.

"And where are you going now? Sit down, child. You are forever darting about, as if motion itself were a virtue."

Elizabeth resumed her seat, frowning down at her still-full plate and cold tea. She felt watched—not with hostility, but with expectation. As though her role were already written, and deviation would require explanation.

Mr Collins chose that moment to enter the breakfast room. When he paused and no one looked up with rapt anticipation, he cleared his throat.

"I had hoped," he said, folding his hands upon his ample middle, "to speak with you this morning, Cousin Elizabeth. A matter of some importance has weighed upon me."

Elizabeth looked to her mother. Mrs Bennet inclined her head at once.

"By all means, Mr Collins. I am sure Lizzy will be most eager to hear what you have to say."

She turned to her mother, eyes wide in horror. Oh, no, no! Mama could not be suggesting... *No!*

Mary set her cup aside with interest.

Elizabeth did not trust her voice. She stood again, this time with purpose. "I am sure Mr Collins and I have nothing in particular to speak of. If you will excuse me, I wished to speak with my father."

Mr Collins moved to block the doorway, bowing with a strange, self-contented little chuckle.

"Indeed," he said, with a smile that suggested correction rather than consent, "that may wait. It is precisely this habit of withdrawing—of placing oneself at inconvenient angles to one's family—that I wish to address."

Elizabeth stopped. So... this was not... what she had feared? "I do not withdraw," she said carefully. "I remove myself when—"

"When you ought to listen," Mr Collins supplied. "There is a difference, Cousin, which I fear you have not yet learned to distinguish. You are fortunate in your relations, and it is only proper that you attend to their guidance."

Mary nodded. "Instruction, when offered in good faith, should be received with gratitude."

Mama waved a hand, as if to dismiss any suggestion of severity. "Mr Collins means only your good, Lizzy. You have a way of putting yourself forward, and it leads to misunderstanding. You must see that."

Elizabeth's mouth opened, then closed again as a sharp agony went winging through her head. She had learned not to wince outright, but she could hardly smother the grunt of pain as she stepped backward. She had the sudden, unwelcome sense that whatever she said would confirm the very charge laid against her.

"I... only wished to find Papa," she said. "Has anyone seen him this morning?"

Her mother shook her head. "Oh! I daresay he is nursing an aching head this morning. He certainly drank enough punch last night. Surely, he is keeping company with his books again."

"He was not in his study when I came down," Elizabeth said.

"Well, then," Mr Collins replied, "this conversation is all the more timely. One cannot rely upon indulgence forever."

"Excuse me, Mr Collins, but it is improper for you to impose upon me with this so-called instruction of yours when my father has not been advised of your complaint. I beg you will excuse me," she said, and stepped toward the door.

Mr Collins moved with her. Not blocking her way, precisely, but close enough that she could not pass without a spike of discomfort shooting behind her eye. She pushed past him anyway.

She moved through the house with the same careful steps she had learned as a girl, when the day's temper might be read by the sound of her mother's voice alone. The doors stood open. The sitting room lay abandoned, chairs set at odd angles from the night before. Her father's book lay face-down upon the small table near the window, its ribbon marker crushed between pages.

"Papa?" she called, lightly at first, as though he might answer from habit rather than presence.

Nothing.

His library was empty. The chair stood pushed back from the desk, the ink dried in its well. No fire. No scent of his favourite tobacco.

She crossed the passage to the back stairs. "Mrs Hill?" she asked, finding the housekeeper sorting linen with brisk indifference. "Has my father been down this morning?"

Mrs Hill glanced up. "Not that I saw, Miss Elizabeth. He did not ring."

"Did he breakfast?"

"No, miss."

Elizabeth nodded, thanked her, and moved on. In the passage by the pantry, she encountered one of the kitchen maids, then the other. Each shook her head. Alice suggested, cheerfully, that Mr Bennet might be enjoying a quiet morning walk. Sarah supposed he was having a long lie-in after so much merrymaking the night before.

Elizabeth did not answer either conjecture. She passed through the back door instead. The yard was damp from last night's rain. The stable boy was sweeping near the threshold, his boots leaving dark marks on the stone.

"Tom," she said. "I do not suppose you have seen my father this morning?"

He looked up at once. "Yes, miss. Early."

"Early? Where?"

He touched his cap. "I saddled the horse, miss. Just as he asked. But he didn't say where he was bound."

Elizabeth stared at him. "The *horse?* Did he... Well, did he take his fowling piece?"

"No, miss."

"A book, perhaps?"

Tom shook his head. "No."

She thanked him and turned away before he could ask why she looked as she did.

Her father did not go out early. He did not ride without remark. He did not leave without a word when the house was in such a state of expectation and strain. He avoided mornings altogether when he could.

Elizabeth crossed the yard again, then climbed the stairs to her room and closed the door behind her—not to sleep, not to think, but to gather herself into a space private enough to block out the clutter of people.

She began to pace—three steps from the bed to the window, three back again. She pressed her palms together, then dragged them through her hair and abandoned the effort. Nothing would settle. Nothing would line up.

Last night refused to stay where it belonged.

After the supper table—after that instant when he had stared at her like he had seen a ghost—there had been no... no ease or gaiety for her. No return to civility disguised as comfort. Darcy had placed himself elsewhere, then farther still. When the room shifted, he shifted with it, until the distance between them felt arranged rather than accidental. Once—only once—he had paused near her, then altered course so abruptly that she had wondered whether she had imagined the moment at all.

What the devil had she done to offend him? He did not speak to her. He did not even look at her again.

Instead, he had stationed himself where Mr Collins was thickest in his attentions, as though proximity itself might be used as cover. Elizabeth had noticed because the relief she expected never came. She had waited for it—waited with the patience of habit—and found only the same tightening, the same internal recoil, sharpened now by the absence of something she had not known she relied upon.

She stopped short, turning back toward the bed.

Mr Wickham.

That *had* been her certainty. It still wanted to be. She *had* felt easier near him—lighter, almost—and she had accepted the feeling without question. But memory, once disturbed, would not lie still. Darcy had been nearby then, too. Always somewhere at the edge of the room, never quite out of reach. She had not noticed because she had not been looking for him.

She pressed her hand to her middle and turned again.

It had grown worse this morning. That was the part she could not reason away. She knew—*knew*—precisely where Mr Collins was in the house. Not by sound, not by sight. By a faint, sour wave that moved through her without warning, leaving her oddly queasy and alert. When he crossed the passage outside her door, she felt it behind her eyes. When he lingered below the stairs, it reached her even there.

Elizabeth stopped pacing and leaned her forehead against the window. The glass was cold, and she welcomed it. It brought some relief to the insistent throbbing that had become a part of her existence of late.

Outside, the garden lay stripped and damp, the lawn darkened by recent rain. Beyond it, the rose hedge climbed the side of the house in its usual disorder—bare stems, thorns exposed, leaves long since fallen.

Except...

She leaned closer.

Along one length of the hedge, tight knots had formed at the joints of the stems. Small. Green. Unmistakable.

*Buds.*

In November.

Elizabeth turned away at once, pressing her fists against her eyes as though she might blot out the image by force. Frustration surged, hot and useless. Nothing fit! Nothing agreed. People caused pain they should not, the foliage around her seemed to forget which season it was, and her own body insisted on meanings she could not understand.

If there were answers to be had, they did not lie here. The thought arrived whole and unwelcome.

If she were to understand anything at all, she must begin with Mr Darcy.

The conclusion did not comfort her. It did the opposite. Because after supper last night, he wanted nothing to do with her and had already made himself unreachable.

The door opened.

Elizabeth dropped her hands and turned, schooling her face by instinct rather than intention. Jane stepped just inside the room, her colour uneven, her composure strained. She held something in her hand—a folded sheet, gripped too tightly.

"Jane? What is it?"

Jane's mouth trembled. "This just came from Miss Bingley." She did not explain further. She held out the paper instead.

*Netherfield Park*
*Tuesday Morning*

*My dear Miss Bennet,*

*I hope you will permit me the freedom of writing to you so soon, but the events of this morning have left me in a state of such vexation that I find I cannot rest until I have spoken, at least to you, upon whom I can always count for sensible counsel.*

*You may already have heard that Mr Darcy quitted Netherfield at a very early hour, with scarcely more than a word to my brother before his departure. I need not tell you how unexpected and mortifying this was to us all, particularly after the attentions he was at such pains to show our party last evening. That he should have been driven to such a step speaks, I think, to the degree of discomfort he must have experienced.*

*I will not pretend to understand how so regrettable a misunderstanding arose. Certain freedoms, taken without reflection, can place even the most forbearing gentleman in an impossible position, and Mr Darcy is, as you know, scrupulous in all matters of conduct. He bears embarrassment badly, and when once offended, prefers removal to remonstrance.*

*It grieves me to think that anything should have occurred under my brother's roof to occasion such an insult. I am sure you, at least, will appreciate how delicate such situations are, and how easily a single ill-judged moment may undo the harmony of an entire evening. Your own manner, always so quiet and considerate, only throws the contrast into sharper relief.*

*I trust you will understand my anxiety to see this matter set right, insofar as it may yet be possible. I rely upon your good sense—and your influence within your family—to prevent any further unpleasantness arising from what I can only hope was an error of judgment rather than intention.*

*Pray believe me when I say that my regard for you remains undiminished, and that I should be loath to see our friendship suffer on account of circumstances so entirely avoidable.*

*Yours most sincerely,*
*Caroline Bingley*

Elizabeth read the letter again.

Not from the beginning. From the middle—where the courtesy thinned and the meaning sharpened. Where the words ceased to pretend at concern and began to lean, ever so delicately, in one direction.

Jane came to stand over her shoulder so she could read the lines again as well. "Lizzy... perhaps she only means... Well, you know, she attended that fine London seminary, and she can be very particular about manners. It may have nothing to do with you at all."

Elizabeth lowered the page. "It has everything to do with me."

Jane looked stricken. "No—surely not. She speaks only of misunderstanding, of discomfort. That could be any number of things."

Elizabeth gave a short, incredulous laugh. It surprised her as much as it did Jane. "She does not accuse," she said. "She has no need. She only arranges the room so that blame may fall where she prefers."

Jane frowned. "But she does not name you. She speaks kindly of me, certainly, but—"

"That is precisely how I know. Do you see how carefully she distinguishes?" she pointed out the lines, paraphrasing them. "You are prudent. You are discreet. You are to be relied upon. And I—" She stopped, pressed her fingernail hard against the paper. "I am the omission. The unspoken correction."

"Lizzy, you are reading far too much—"

"No. I watched her last night. I saw where her attention lay. I saw where her stares were directed."

Jane hesitated. "You mean... Mr Darcy?"

Elizabeth did not answer at once. She could still see him across the room—too distant to be chance, too deliberate to be coincidence. Could still feel the way the space between them had been kept, measured, enforced.

"She believes," Elizabeth said slowly, "that I offended him. That whatever drove him away began with me."

Jane shook her head. "But you did nothing improper. He seemed rather pleased when you were dancing the supper set—indeed, I am sure I saw him smiling, and once or twice he looked almost close to a laugh."

"Oh, no, the dancing was rather pleasant. We got on quite decently, though he did seem a bit tired, even slightly clumsy in some of the figures, which I found odd. But he was… I was…" Elizabeth looked down at her twisting fingers. "I came perilously close to enjoying myself."

"Yes, I saw," Jane said with a suspicious grin. "In fact, I daresay you were flirting rather shamelessly."

Elizabeth's mouth dropped. "I did no such thing!"

Jane laughed. "I was only teasing, Lizzy. But you did both appear rather agreeably engaged. So, what did happen?"

She frowned. "I really do not know. It was over supper, that…" Elizabeth stopped. "Well, it was only a bit of a misunderstanding, I suppose. Surely, not enough to run a man out of the county, but Miss Bingley would not know that. She only assumes that *something* occurred, and I am the most convenient cause."

Jane was quiet now, studying the letter anew.

Elizabeth rose and crossed the room, the restlessness returning at once. "She had hopes," she said. "You know she did. Hopes she did not trouble to conceal. And now he has gone—without explanation, without a cause anyone can fix—and she must place the fault somewhere."

Jane's voice was small. "She would not be so unkind."

"She would be *exactly* so unkind, and in exactly this manner."

Elizabeth turned away and moved back to the window, though she did not look out again. She rested her hand against the frame and stood there, breathing through the ache that had settled behind her eyes.

"So," she said at last, with an attempt at lightness that convinced neither of them. "That is that, then."

"Lizzy…"

"He has gone," Elizabeth said more quietly. "And I am to be the reason for it, whether I consent to the distinction or not."

Jane crossed the room and stood near her, close enough that Elizabeth could feel the warmth of her presence without turning. "We do not know that he has gone far," she said gently. "Nor that he intends to be absent long. Such departures are sometimes made in haste and repented just as quickly."

Elizabeth shook her head. "No. He does nothing by halves. Not when he has decided."

Jane hesitated. "Lizzy... if you fear that something which *might* have been—"

"No!" she blurted abruptly, then checked herself. "No. That is not it. I have no romantic designs on Mr Darcy. At least, I..." Her brow furrowed. "Well, clearly there is *something,* but I am not sure what it is."

She looked away again, searching for words that would not betray her into false ones. "It is not the loss of what was never promised that troubles me," she said at last. "It is the removal of the only person who might have told me plainly *what* occurred. What is *still* happening to me. And why."

"Lizzy, I do not pretend to understand, but surely Mr Darcy is not the only person you can speak to. What of Papa?"

Elizabeth shook her head. "He understands less than I do. Look, Jane, we shall not improve matters by standing about. If I am to be blamed, I may as well do so from a position of dignity."

Jane smiled at that. "And what would that be? Mr Collins is still downstairs, you know."

"It hardly matters today. He seems to give pain no matter where he is. Come, let us walk to Lucas Lodge and see how Charlotte fares today after drinking so much punch."

# Chapter Twenty-Seven

Darcy arrived at his London house without warning anyone of his coming. The servant had scarcely time to register who stood before him as Darcy stepped inside, his coat still fastened, his gloves carried loose in one hand.

"Sir! Mr Darcy," the footman said, recovering himself. "We were not apprised—"

"Has a parcel arrived from Pemberley?" Darcy asked.

The man hesitated, caught between duty and recollection. "Yes, sir. Yesterday afternoon. Miss Darcy's hand was upon it."

Darcy inclined his head once. "Where is it?"

"In your study, sir. I thought—"

"That will do. Will you see Brutus walked and settled, please?"

The footman's eyes dropped to the massive dog standing at Darcy's side. "Yes, sir."

"Thank you." Darcy went toward the study without further explanation. The house lay quiet in the manner of a place only partially occupied, its rooms kept in order rather than use. The sound of his passage echoed like a whisper of empty spaces.

The study was as he had left it. The desk stood cleared. The chair was drawn in. No fire had been laid. Upon the table, precisely centred, rested a brown-paper parcel tied with twine.

Darcy closed the door behind him. He set aside his gloves, drew out his knife, and cut the string. The paper fell back to reveal the book beneath—always smaller than memory suggested, but heavier in the hand, its leather darkened and worn smooth at the edges, the spine bearing the marks of frequent consultation.

*Rev. Josias Harrowe.*
*1605. Revised in 1769.*

The pages were thick and irregular, the margins crowded with a careful, persistent hand. Lines had been corrected, words altered, phrases reconsidered and set down anew. This was not a fair copy. It was a working one.

He read standing, the book resting against the desk.

The bell rang somewhere in the house—a summons from the kitchen no doubt. Darcy's stomach rumbled in reply, but he scarcely looked up.

The ballad—the book contained many, but there was only one that interested him—did not announce itself. It began without flourish, as though assuming the reader's patience. The beginning, he knew like his own heart, but this time, he heard it in *her* voice.

*When Avalon in mist was bound,*
*And noble steel undone,*
*The thorn abid upon that ground*
*Till reckoning were begun.*

Darcy read more slowly after that, his attention drawn not only to the verse but to the notes that flanked it. Corrections had been made with care, not to beautify the language but to attempt to explain it.

His eyes lingered there. This… *this* was the one that came directly after Elizabeth Bennet's recitation.

*The knight who swore to keep her safe*

He paused. The word "swore" was underlined in the margin, once, firmly. A later hand had added a notation beside it, smaller, more cramped, but it was too smudged to be legible.

Darcy turned the page.

*Came late upon the fen.*

Late.

Not absent. Not faithless. *Late.*

His fingers rested against the paper as though it might answer him if he only stared long enough.

*In his stead, the silence fell.*

Silence? Not death. Not ruin. Silence—an absence that remained.

*On field and hill and glen.*

Only the word "Where?" and a question mark in the margin.

A voice sounded beyond the door, lowered, cautious. Someone spoke his name, and a moment later, a tea cart was wheeled in. But the maid hesitated at the threshold, and Darcy heard the housekeeper advising her to just leave it there and not disturb the master further.

He read on.

*Yet still the thorn unseen abides*
*Where river meets the lane;*
*And they who keep their plighted faith*
*Shall call her forth again.*

The annotations grew denser toward the latter pages, as though Harrowe himself had begun to understand, too late, the shape of what he was translating. Words circled. Passages were reconsidered. One line bore three successive attempts at typesetting correction, none entirely satisfactory.

Darcy reached the end at last and remained where he was, the book open before him, his attention fixed not upon the page but upon the space just beyond it.

What lay before him was not explanation. It was corroboration without clarity—meaning dispersed across hands, centuries, and intentions, none of them sufficient alone. Harrowe had translated faithfully; that much was plain. But Harrowe had not resolved what he copied, and perhaps had not dared to.

Darcy moved around the desk and set the volume aside. The room felt smaller for having held it open so long. He stood for a moment, his hand resting against the back of the chair, and considered what remained to him.

If the ballad spoke truly, then memory alone could not answer this. If the records existed—as he had long suspected—then they would not be here. They would be in the keeping of someone who had guarded confusion as carefully as others guarded certainty.

He rang the bell.

When the servant appeared, Darcy was already reaching for his coat. "Have my carriage brought round at once," he said. "I am going out. And tell Cook not to trouble herself over a formal supper. I will be late."

"Yes, sir. Shall I send for some hot bricks or a basket?"

"No," Darcy replied. "That will not be necessary where I am going."

And with that, he left the study dark behind him, the questions he carried no longer waiting to be read, but answered—if they could be—only by those who had kept them alive.

Darcy was announced into his uncle's study with less ceremony than usual, for the simple reason that Lord Matlock was already crossing the space before the servant had finished speaking his name.

"Darcy?" He looked genuinely startled. "I had a letter from you scarcely a week ago. I had thought you would be in Hertfordshire through Christmas."

"So had I," Darcy said, stopping just inside the room. "But circumstances dictated otherwise. Has there been any further word from Richard?"

Matlock did not answer at once. He turned back to the desk, drew a letter from beneath a folio, and held it there without unfolding it. "He has arrived safely."

Darcy's shoulders eased by a degree. "And?"

"And he writes... cautiously," Matlock replied. "Which is unlike him."

Darcy crossed the room. "But he is well? Not near any fighting?"

"So far as he says. He is quartered away from the line for the present. His concern is not the enemy."

"So why the urgency? Does he detail why he was recalled?"

Matlock took up the letter again, unfolding it at last. "When he went on leave back in September, his superiors believed the season sufficiently provisioned. There were shortages, yes, but nothing beyond the army's ability to manage. Arrangements were made accordingly."

"And now?"

"And now," Matlock said, "what was expected has not arrived."

"Not at all?"

"Not where it was to have gone. Some shipments were delayed. Others diverted. A few were lost to weather. Nothing remarkable in isolation."

"But enough, together, to strain what remains."

"Enough to make winter planning uncertain." Matlock hesitated. "Enough that they no longer trust their assumptions, and they wanted an experienced officer, with knowledge of the local resources, ready to hand."

Darcy moved toward the window, then stopped short of it. "So, Richard has been asked to go from house to house, as it were, buying grain and meat for England's soldiers."

"They have not said so plainly," Matlock replied, "but that is the substance of it. He has been asked to secure provisions by whatever means prove expedient. To smooth delays. To press local stewards. To make arrangements where arrangements have failed."

Darcy scowled. "As though diligence might conjure stores that are not there."

"As though influence might persuade the land to yield," Matlock said. "He is to do what can be done quickly, without troubling London with causes."

"And what does he report?"

Matlock unfolded the letter once more. "That some houses comply readily. Others cannot. Not from refusal, but from want. He writes of granaries already drawn down, of contracts fulfilled on paper and empty in fact. Of promises made in good faith that cannot now be kept."

Darcy considered this. "Everywhere?"

"So far as the reports extend. Not ruin all at once, but sparse across regions that ought to sustain themselves. Stores drawn down faster than expected. Replacement slow, or insufficient, or absent altogether."

"Then it is not a local failure."

"No."

"But neither is it sudden."

"Not... precisely." Matlock frowned. "The recognition of it has come rather unhappily, and it seems, by some surprise. But I daresay it has been gathering quietly—slowly enough that it might have been borne, had nothing else gone amiss."

Darcy nodded. "And they have sent Richard to stave off the reckoning. This is not the first season in which provision has proved thinner than expected. Derbyshire has felt the strain for some months now, and we'd nothing held over from last year, either."

Matlock inclined his head in acknowledgment. "Yes. My steward wrote to yours in September. At the time, it appeared no more than the ordinary consequence of an uneven yield—nothing to provoke alarm. But now, I understand, matters are somewhat worse than first believed."

"I had word of the same while I was in Hertfordshire," Darcy said. "Enough to warrant grave concern. There is little to be had elsewhere, and Pemberley's stores are the lowest they have been in ages. No one, it seems, has anything to sell. But now, my steward reports having heard rumours to the contrary."

Matlock sat up straighter. "What rumours, Darcy have you heard?"

"It is no rumour, Uncle. I have seen it with my own eyes, in Hertfordshire."

His uncle appeared taken aback. "So, it is true? Why, that is but half a day's ride! How should we all not have known of it? Are you sure, Darcy?"

Darcy paced, staring at the rug. "I did a little investigating, and the local farmers are boasting the best year they have ever had. Cabbages the size of Brutus. Wheat, barley, and potatoes such as they have never seen. Bingley's garden still had mint overgrowing the lanes in October. Even the rose hedges are still in bloom!"

Matlock's first response was immediate and instinctive. He turned partway toward the bell-pull, already calculating the distances, the contracts, the speed with which such an opportunity might be secured.

"If there is grain to be had—" He stopped himself and turned. "And... you are *quite* sure? This is not mere fancy, Darcy. Not some single farm with a particular sort of miracle soil or a fool with a fantastical bent to his storytelling?"

"I made extensive inquiries, sir."

Matlock considered this, his gaze intent, his thoughts evidently running ahead to questions of supply, transport, and discretion. "If there is indeed provision there, it ought to be secured," he said. "Quietly, if possible."

His hand moved again toward the bell, and again he checked himself. "*Hertfordshire*?" he repeated slowly, as though tasting the name for some quality not at once apparent.

Matlock turned then to face him fully, and in his expression there was a twisting of his countenance—subtle, but unmistakable—from the calculation of stores and routes to something more inward, more wary, as though an older map had been laid atop the newer one in his mind.

"You did not come here merely to speak of grain," he said.

Darcy met his gaze without evasion. "No."

Matlock swallowed. "I see."

"I want to see it," Darcy said. "Urgently. I know you have it."

Matlock did not ask what he meant. He paled, drew a shaken breath, and heaved it out slowly. "I suppose there is no more putting it off."

Then, with a grim set to his shoulders, he crossed to a cabinet set into the panelling. The key came from his pocket, not his watch-chain, which told Darcy more than any explanation might have done.

When he returned, the book lay cradled in both his hands, wrapped in a length of linen that had long since lost any pretence of cleanliness. The cloth was worn thin at the folds and darkened where fingers had handled it again and again, as though the act of uncovering it had become habitual long before it became reluctant.

Beneath it, the volume itself was plainly bound in cloth, faded to a colour that might once have been blue or green, the spine rubbed soft by age and use. It looked less like a relic than a thing that had survived by being consulted and put away, consulted again, and never fully set aside.

Darcy's eyes went to the cover at once, trying to make out the faded title.

"The *Liber de Terris et Finibus.* 'The Book of Lands and Boundaries.' Said to have been first written in the eleventh or twelfth century. Who knows how old this copy is, but it was never intended for hurried reading," Matlock said, offering it. "It is not a narrative. It offers no patience to those who seek one."

Darcy accepted the volume and turned it in his hands, feeling the give of the cloth beneath his fingers, the unevenness of the boards, the way the spine resisted being flattened, as though it had learned to close itself against too much attention.

"You will find what you are looking for before the middle," Matlock said, his thumb resting against the linen where the page beneath lay marked by a faint crease. "There is a place where the hand changes. The Reverend Harrowe is said to have spent so much time with that page open that the book would never close properly again."

Darcy glanced up. "Harrowe himself?"

Matlock lifted a shoulder. "Well! It strains credulity a bit. This *might* have been the very copy he referenced. Although... well. Less said on that for now, the better, I suppose."

Darcy lowered his gaze again. "I should like to keep it," he said quietly. It was not a request for which he would accept refusal. "For a short time."

Matlock did not answer at once. He moved away instead, crossing to the window and standing there with his back to the room, his hands clasped behind him as though the posture might steady something internal.

"I wondered how long it would take you to say that."

Darcy looked up. "You object?"

"No." Matlock's voice roughened a little on the word. "I would object only if you skimmed it, or if you believed it would explain itself readily. The book is not dangerous because of what it contains." He paused. "It is dangerous because of what it refuses to do for the reader."

Darcy closed the cover, careful, deliberate. "Then I will take the time it demands."

Matlock turned back at last. There was something like resignation in his look, tempered by a grim affection. "If you make sense of it," he said slowly, "if you truly understand what is being described and not merely what is written, then you are a better man than I ever managed to be."

Darcy frowned. "You have read it."

Matlock gave a short, humourless breath. "More than once. Enough to know where I lost my footing." His gaze rested on the book in Darcy's hands. "Read it where there is quiet, and no one to interrupt you with sensible objections. But understand this, Fitzwilliam—what you find there will not ask whether you wish to know it."

Darcy inclined his head. "I have not found that knowledge ever does."

Darcy bent again over the table, the lamp drawn closer, its flame trimmed down to a steady core of light. He had not intended to be up so late. He had not intended to pull half the shelves bare. And yet the study now bore the marks of a mind unravelling, writhing with truths it did not like, and unwilling to be contradicted: books stacked open on the floor, others laid face-down across chairs, slips of paper marking places he meant to return to and could not afford to lose.

He found the crease in the *Liber* without difficulty. The book opened to it as though taught. The page itself bore the history of that habit—worn thin at the fold, darkened where fingers had lingered, the margin softened beyond what time alone might have accomplished. The hand here was not uniform. The script shifted from careful to compressed, from authority to urgency, as though the act of recording had become more difficult the longer it continued.

The text had changed its purpose. Earlier pages marked and referenced. This one concerned itself instead with relation.

*From þe þorn hegge set afore þe ford,*
*þe saide erthe is holden in perpetuite,*
*neyther demesne nor waste,*
*and schal not be enclosed by hegge nor banke,*
*ne taken into severaltie by any lord as it was holden in elder tyme,*
*and so shall remayne.*

Darcy read it again, silently this time, his finger tracing the line as though the meaning might yield to pressure. *Held in perpetuity.* The phrase appeared nowhere in his father's legal volumes, nor in any charter he had ever studied. It belonged neither to conveyance nor inheritance. It assumed obligation without naming authority, duty without benefit.

He reached for another book, then another. A collection of medieval annals copied by monks whose names were long since reduced to initials. A slim volume of regional ballads—not Harrowe's—his mother had once given him, amused at his fondness for what she had once called harmless antiquities. He laid them open beside the *Liber* and began to compare.

The words were not the same. The shapes of the letters differed. And yet...

Here, in a marginal gloss half-erased by time, the same hedge. There, in a verse dismissed as metaphor, a crossing named only by what stood before it. In one ballad, a keeper mentioned only once and never again, not praised, not mourned, simply... absent.

Darcy's breath slowed. The room had gone very quiet, not with peace, but with concentration so complete it excluded everything else. These were not stories elaborating upon one another. They were records circling the same absence from different angles, each careful not to say too much, each assuming knowledge that had once been common and was now lost.

He turned back to the *Liber* and read on. The later hand crowded the margin, tighter, darker, impatient with restraint. The tone altered again—not to explanation, but to warning.

Darcy leaned closer, the lamplight catching the uneven edge of the page. What troubled him was not what the text claimed.

It was how many different voices, across centuries, had agreed on what could not be owned—and what could not be abandoned—without ever daring to say why.

# Chapter Twenty-Eight

Elizabeth woke to light already upon the wall.

She knew it without turning her head—the angle was wrong. Morning had advanced without her. That recognition pricked sharper than the light itself, and she lay still, displeased, as though the bed had betrayed her by keeping her too long.

She did not rise at once. She waited, gauging herself by degrees, as she had learned to do after long walks or late nights. Only then did she become aware of the pressure gathering behind her eyes, a muted insistence that pulsed when she shifted her gaze.

She drew a breath and let it out slowly. Cold air last night. Too much noise—mostly from Collins. Too little rest since the ball four days earlier. The body was entitled to its complaints.

Elizabeth pushed herself upright. The movement required her to pause—only a moment, only enough to let the room finish circling around her—before she swung her legs over the side of the bed and placed her feet upon the floor.

Dressing took longer than usual, though she could not have said why. Her fingers fumbled at the buttons, and she had to pause again at the washstand, one hand braced against the wood until the faint swimming passed.

"A trifling cold, no doubt," she murmured, and was faintly irritated to hear how unconvincing it sounded. It would have been lovely to have a blocked nose to accompany the sentiment, but there was no such concurrence.

By the time she reached the breakfast room, she had composed herself sufficiently to pass without comment. Jane looked up, her expression brightening with relief that softened into scrutiny the moment Elizabeth took her seat. "You slept late."

"So did you, or you would not be still breakfasting," Elizabeth replied. "Do not attempt to make a case of it."

Jane's eyes widened, and she turned away.

Elizabeth managed her tea, though she found she did not want it. The warmth was too much; the steam made her head throb more insistently. She set the cup aside and reached instead for the book Papa had bought her from Meryton.

Reading helped. It always had. The lines unfurled, for a time, and the rambling nonsense unfolded as it ought. She read more slowly than usual, but with care, and by the end of the page she had nearly convinced herself that the discomfort had been exaggerated by inattention.

The house, however, felt oddly hollow.

Not quiet—there were the usual sounds of Longbourn in the morning: footsteps, the clink of dishes, Kitty's voice somewhere upstairs—but hollow all the same, as though a door had been left open to a space that was not meant to be empty. Elizabeth frowned at the thought and turned the page.

"Mr Wickham is expected to call later," Mama announced. "He called yesterday to inquire after you, my dear, and seemed quite disappointed to have missed you."

Elizabeth looked up. "Did he?"

"Indeed. Most attentive. He said he hoped you were not unwell, though I cannot think why he would fret about that nonsense. I told him you were, but wool-gathering again. I hope, Lizzy, you will make yourself presentable today."

Elizabeth shook her head and turned back to her book. The ache behind her eyes pulsed once, faint but insistent, and she pressed her fingers briefly to her temple before catching herself and lowering her hand. "I shall be glad to see him."

The words were true enough. Wickham's company was easy. Uncomplicated. He brought with him a sense of gaiety that she found restorative. If she was overtired, if the remnants of the ball had lingered longer than expected, an hour's conversation would surely set her right again.

And yet, even as she settled herself more firmly into the chair, she could not shake the peculiar impression that something essential had been mislaid—not lost, precisely, but removed without notice, leaving the rest of the day to adjust around the absence.

She dismissed the thought at once.

Fatigue, and perhaps a touch of winter malaise. Nothing more.

"Lydia, do sit down this instant—Kitty, you are blocking the light," Mama said, clapping her hands once in emphasis. "Mr Collins, pray take that chair. Yes, that one—no, not with your back to the door."

"I am quite content to stand, Mrs Bennet," Mr Collins replied solemnly, though he shifted anyway, aligning himself where he might be seen to advantage. "Indeed, it is most agreeable to remain active when in company. It sharpens the mind."

"That is very true," Mama said, beaming. "Jane, you may pour—Mary, do not hide behind the pianoforte, child."

Elizabeth paused just inside the doorway, taking in the scene as Kitty darted toward the sofa and Lydia followed, whispering fiercely about who ought to sit nearest the window. Mary adjusted her book with deliberate care and lowered herself into a chair as though preparing for examination.

Mr Collins turned at last, his expression brightening with unmistakable satisfaction. "Ah! Miss Elizabeth. You are just in time."

She inclined her head and crossed the room, aware as she did so of how closely the air seemed to smother—of how every sound arrived a fraction later than she expected. She dismissed the sensation at once and took the seat Jane drew out for her.

"You are well?" Jane murmured.

"Perfectly," Elizabeth said, and smiled because it was expected.

Mr Collins cleared his throat, folding his hands with intent. "I was remarking, only moments ago, upon the singular harmony of your family arrangements. One feels, upon entering this room, a most improving atmosphere."

Lydia rolled her eyes with minimal discretion.

A stir near the door preceded the announcement, the brief murmur of a servant's voice carrying across the room.

"Mr Wickham, Mr Denny, and Mr Saunders, madam."

Mama rose, her expression arranging itself into cordial animation as the gentlemen were shown in. Mr Wickham entered with his companions close behind, hats in hand, his manner already attuned to the room—easy without presumption, attentive without haste.

Wickham's gaze crossed the room and found Elizabeth's. But he tore it away to perform the expected pleasantries. "Mrs Bennet," he said, bowing when he was presented. "I feared we might have intruded upon an established assembly."

"Oh, not at all, not at all! Come, Mr Wickham, Mr Denny... and you, Mr Saunders. Girls, make room, make room. Oh, Mr Collins, a little space if you please."

Mama busied herself directing the officers toward the seating nearest the hearth, eager that they be both visible and comfortable, while Kitty and Lydia hovered close enough to require only the slightest encouragement to be included. Mary relinquished her place at last, though not her book, and withdrew to a straighter-backed chair with visible resignation.

Mr Collins cleared his throat.

"Sir," he began, drawing himself up with an air of conscious importance, "permit me to extend my welcome, not merely as a relation of this family, but as one entrusted with certain—ah—duties of moral regard."

Wickham inclined his head at once. "You are very good, sir."

"It is always a satisfaction," Mr Collins continued, "to receive gentlemen whose conduct reflects credit upon the circles in which they move. Propriety, I need hardly say, is the foundation of all harmonious society."

Wickham inclined his head with commendable seriousness. "I should expect nothing less, sir." He waited for the pause that followed—polite, inevitable—and then turned.

"Miss Elizabeth," he said, as if the rest of the room had only just resolved itself around her. "I was sorry to miss you yesterday. I am glad we did not arrive too late."

"Only just," she answered with a smile. "But you are so well attended that you must be forgiven."

"I came armed," Wickham replied, a glance toward his companions making the excuse lightly. "One never knows what claims may be made upon a gentleman in such company."

"And most wisely so," Mr Collins said, inserting himself with a pleased air, "Society, when rightly ordered, is both a pleasure and a responsibility."

Elizabeth's fingers tightened in her skirts. The throbbing pulsed—not sharply, but insistently, as though something were knocking from the inside.

Wickham inclined his head. "I shall endeavour to conduct myself with due caution, sir."

"Quite so. Quite so." Mr Collins smiled, encouraged. "One must always be mindful of propriety, particularly in households blessed with—" his gaze swept the room, lingering a breath too long "—*so* many young ladies."

The words might well have been a physical presence. She shifted in her chair, then immediately wished she had not; the room tilted a fraction before righting itself.

"Miss Elizabeth?" Wickham said quietly, his voice pitched so that only she might hear. "You look unwell."

"Only tired," she replied. Too quickly. The effort of shaping the words sent another throb through her temples. She dropped her voice to a bare whisper. "I fear Mr Collins has exhausted us all with his... enthusiasm."

Wickham smiled, but it faltered when she cleared her throat and pinched a furrow of her brow.

Lydia laughed too loudly at something Mr Denny had said. Kitty echoed her, half a sentence later. Wickham glanced between them, then back to Elizabeth.

"You are usually quicker than this," he said, gently. "I was counting on your wit and merriment to sustain me today, Miss Elizabeth."

She tried to answer. Something clever. Something easy.

What came instead was a blur of sound—Collins continuing, Mama murmuring approval, the officers laughing—and the sensation of heat gathering at the base of her neck.

"I beg your pardon," she said, missing the cadence of the room entirely. She pressed her lips together and tried again. "What assistance did you require?"

Wickham's brows drew together, but he gave a short chuckle. "Only your conversation. I was saying the weather has turned."

"It has," she agreed, though she could not have said how. The words twisted wrong, too flat, and she knew it even as she spoke them.

Mr Collins nodded solemnly. "A salutary reminder of the need for moral vigilance. Seasons of change are most instructive."

The pain spiked—sudden enough that Elizabeth swayed in her chair. Jane's hand was on her arm at once.

"Lizzy?"

"I... I believe I have a megrim," Elizabeth said, the excuse tumbling out before she could weigh it. She stood, the movement blurring the edges of the room. "Pray, forgive me. I fear I shall be poor company if I remain."

Mama made a protesting sound. "Elizabeth, really! You cannot be taken ill now. We have the party from Netherfield coming to dine this evening!"

"I shall be well by this evening," Elizabeth insisted. "But for now, I should do better lying down."

Wickham watched her closely now. "You must not exert yourself merely for the pleasure of others."

"I assure you, I shall recover admirably," she said, and managed a small, apologetic smile that felt like it belonged to someone else entirely.

Mr Collins rose halfway. "If your constitution is unequal to extended discourse, Miss Elizabeth, rest is certainly advisable."

She did not trust herself to answer him. Elizabeth inclined her head to the room, took Jane's offered arm, and let herself be guided away—every step an effort, every sound behind her receding as though she were walking out of a tide.

The candles had been placed closer together than usual. Someone must have thought the evening dim. The flames wavered as the door opened again, sending a brief, unwelcome shimmer across her vision. Elizabeth blinked and fixed her attention on the pattern in the rug until the room eased into its proper proportions.

"Mr Bingley!" Mama welcomed. "How very good of you to come, and your sisters as well—Mrs Hurst, I am delighted, quite delighted. Do come in, do come in. Mr Hurst, mind the step."

Elizabeth did not look up at once. She had already accounted for them—the pause before Mr Bingley crossed the threshold, the way Miss Bingley's gaze would travel the room before she moved at all, Mrs Hurst's unhurried step behind her. It was a pattern she knew well enough to picture without seeing.

Only when they stood before her did Elizabeth glance up.

Mr Bingley's eyes were on Jane. They always were, now. He smiled when Jane met his gaze, a look so open it would have been impossible to mistake. Jane rose, and Elizabeth followed a moment later, slower than she intended but still in time to offer a proper greeting.

"Dinner is quite ready," Mama announced, clapping her hands. "We shall not keep that splendid roast duck waiting. Jane, my dear, Mr Bingley will escort you. Yes, that will do very well."

Mr Bingley looked momentarily startled, then pleased, and offered his arm. Jane accepted with what passed for composure, though the faint colour in her cheeks betrayed her.

The procession moved through the passage, past the sideboard polished to an ambitious shine, into the dining room where the long table waited under the glow of too many candles. The room felt close tonight. Or perhaps it was only that the light pressed in from all sides.

"Jane, here, beside Mr Bingley. Yes. Lizzy—there. Mary, you will sit opposite Mr Collins. Kitty—no, not there—Lydia, for heaven's sake, you are blocking Hill with the wine."

Elizabeth took the chair indicated and set her hands neatly in her lap. The scent of roast meat reached her a moment later, rich and heavy. Her stomach declined it at once.

Mr Collins settled near her with evident satisfaction, smoothing his napkin as though the arrangement itself confirmed something he had long suspected. His gaze flicked toward Elizabeth, then away, then back again, lingering just long enough to make her aware of it.

She fixed her eyes on the rim of her plate and waited for the room to arrange itself properly again.

"Well," Papa said pleasantly, "this is an excellent assembly. One would hardly suspect the world beyond Longbourn continues to exist."

Mr Bingley laughed. "If it does, sir, it is doing so with very poor manners. The weather alone suggests a conspiracy."

"Indeed?" Mama said at once. "We have been quite fortunate here."

"So you have," he agreed. "Remarkably so, in fact. My steward insists we are the envy of three counties."

Miss Bingley dismissed the matter with a small, elegant flick of her wrist. "Country houses are forever discovering new inconveniences. A chill in the hall, a draught by the stairs—it is the same every winter."

"Perhaps," Mr Bingley countered easily. "Though it has been an uncommonly gentle season so far. One can hardly call it winter at all. My coachman, however, insists we are tempting fate. He is quite convinced we shall have a storm before long, and urges us not to linger tonight."

"A storm?" Kitty repeated with interest.

"So he says," Bingley replied. "I told him he sees portents in every cloud, but he would not be persuaded."

Miss Bingley sniffed. "Coachmen delight in foreboding. It gives them importance."

"Still," Bingley went on, "I cannot help thinking Darcy would have had some opinions on the matter. He was always inclined to notice such things—soil, air, the way a season turns." He laughed softly. "A farmer at heart, I daresay. Would that I had half his experience in these matters."

Elizabeth's sight dimmed for a breath, the candles blurring into pale halos before resolving again. She set her glass down with care, though she had no clear memory of lifting it.

"Oh, but you have been very busy entertaining without him," Mama said. "A credit to the neighbourhood, I am sure."

"I like to hope so, Mrs Bennet," Mr Bingley replied, and for a long second, he let his eyes drift to Jane.

That suited Mama well enough that she did not bother to ask him anything else until the soup was served.

Mr Collins, however, was not built for tolerating silences, so he determined to fill it himself. "Indeed, I do fear we are bound for a particularly hard winter. It is in seasons such as these," he said, addressing the table with careful projection, "that one is reminded how greatly Providence rewards those households governed by foresight. Economy, moderation, and a proper submission to order—these are not merely virtues, but safeguards."

Papa sipped from his glass with dry interest. "Oh, indeed, quite right, sir. I shall take such economy into consideration, but everyone does insist on entertaining." And then he returned to his soup.

Mr Collins shook his head. "I have always found, in my own modest experience, that preparation forestalls not only want, but anxiety. One may sleep more soundly, knowing that one's larder reflects one's principles."

Elizabeth's spoon paused above the bowl. The scent of the soup—onion and pepper, too warm, too near—made her stomach turn unpleasantly. She set it down again, careful not to spill. "A comforting thought," she mumbled, only half answering Mr Collins.

Jane glanced at her then, just briefly.

"Still," Miss Bingley observed, "there has been an uncommon amount of talk in London about the season—how disrupted it has been. Why, the letters from my friends in Town are full of little else. One never knows whether to expect a mild evening or something altogether more disagreeable. It plays havoc with one's arrangements."

"Speculation thrives where discipline does not," Mr Collins replied at once, turning slightly in his chair. The movement brought his sleeve nearer Elizabeth's arm. "In well-ordered families, uncertainty finds little purchase."

Elizabeth's teeth ground. The room seemed louder—not suddenly, but steadily, as though each voice had gained timbre and volume.

"It is my firm belief," Mr Collins continued, "that much suffering arises not from misfortune, but from moral laxity. When one neglects one's duty—"

Her head gave a sharp, unwelcome throb. She pressed her fingers lightly against the edge of the table, willing the sensation to pass.

Papa had stopped eating. His gaze rested on her, intent now as his eyes narrowed. Jane, too, was dabbing her mouth and staring at Elizabeth, but she was not near enough to offer any inconspicuous comfort.

Miss Bingley had resumed tasting her soup, though her expression left little doubt of her opinions of it. "Miss Elizabeth, I fear you are looking rather diminished of late. Are you quite well, my dear?"

Elizabeth drew herself up. "Nothing of any consequence, I assure you."

Miss Bingley hummed with a faint smile. "Nonetheless, I imagine you might prefer to exchange the country for town before the winter deepens. London has its inconveniences, of course—but one is never truly uncomfortable there."

Elizabeth inclined her head. "I have no such plans at present."

"No? I had thought you might be tempted. You have relations there, do you not? Cheapside, if I remember correctly."

"I do," Elizabeth said. The effort of keeping her tone even was greater than it ought to have been. "And they are very well, I thank you."

"How fortunate," Miss Bingley purred. "It must be a comfort to know one has a refuge, should the country grow... trying."

Elizabeth returned the smile she was given, though it felt oddly delayed, as though she were answering from a short distance away. "If you are asking whether I intend to pursue... diversions in Town, I shall answer in the negative. The country has always suited me."

Mr Collins, encouraged by what he took for Elizabeth's attentiveness to the conversation, leaned nearer to continue his point—on economy, on gratitude, on the dangers of excess. His voice grated against her like wool too thick for the season. She followed it as one follows a sermon whose cadence is familiar enough to predict the end without quite hearing the middle.

By the time the plates were changed, the conversation had taken on a new shape. Someone was speaking about prices now. Grain. Coal. Elizabeth caught only pieces of it, as though the talk had broken into manageable shards.

"—no one prepared—"

"—extraordinary demand—"

"—only temporary, surely—"

Her head ached—sharply. Insistently. She winced and pinched the bridge of her nose, hoping it would drive the pressure back somewhat.

The voices continued, overlapping politely, rising and falling with the passing of dishes. Someone laughed—Kitty, perhaps. Someone else murmured assent. Elizabeth followed none of it with any certainty. Each sentence reached her as an isolated thing, stripped of its beginning and end, demanding effort simply to place. She kept her gaze lowered, fixing upon the pale curve of her plate, the edge of the tablecloth, anything that did not move.

She became aware, dimly, that she had not eaten. Or had she? The question felt unimportant. The soup had been taken away; that she remembered. What followed after was uncertain.

Elizabeth caught her name once—only once—and then lost the rest to the dull roar gathering behind her temples. She answered when spoken to, or believed she did. Her replies sounded clumsy to her own ear, as though spoken through water.

Papa had gone quiet. That, at least, she noticed.

She did not look at him directly, but she felt his eyes on her all the same—the pause in his eating, the way his attention had settled, uncharacteristically fixed. He said nothing. He would not—not with company watching their every word and move.

Elizabeth straightened, then immediately regretted it. The room tilted—not enough to alarm, but enough to make her still. She folded her hands in her lap and waited for the sensation to pass, counting her breaths as though that might impose order.

The conversation moved on without her.

That was the strangest part of it. Ordinarily, she would have steered it, brightened it, found amusement even in solemnity. Tonight, it flowed around her as though she were no longer quite within its bounds.

By the time the last dish was removed, she could no longer follow a word that was said, and what little she had tasted of her food threatened to unmake her precious dignity.

She lifted her eyes at last, and across the table Papa met her gaze. Then his eyes dropped back to his wine, and he said nothing.

ELIZABETH DID NOT REMEMBER choosing the corner.

One moment she was standing, the next she had found her way to the far end of the drawing room, half-hidden by a tall screen and the shadow of the bookcase. The lamps had been moved for tea, but little of the light reached her. The quiet there was fresher, easier to bear.

Miss Bingley noticed at once.

"Well," she said, glancing across the room as she accepted her cup, "if this is not a familiar posture. Miss Elizabeth, you are quite in the Darcy manner this evening—removed from the bustle, observing rather than engaging."

Elizabeth's fingers tightened around the arm of the chair.

*Darcy.*

The name itself seemed to draw the warmth out of her. Not pain—something worse. A sudden hollowness, as though a door had been shut somewhere deep inside her and left the space behind it unheated. She swallowed and inclined her head.

"I am only economizing my spirits," she said. The effort it took to form the sentence surprised her. "They have been overused."

Miss Bingley smiled as though that pleased her. "How very prudent."

Across the room, Mama was already in motion. "Jane—Jane, my love, come here, do not sit so near the fire. You will be flushed. Mr Bingley, if you would be so kind—yes, there, that chair is quite comfortable, I am sure. Mr Hurst, you will not mind shifting just a little. Oh, and dear Mrs Hurst, I have left you the most comfortable seat, beside me."

Chairs were claimed. Cups rearranged. Jane was placed precisely where Mama wished her to be, her chair angled just so, Mr Bingley beside her, his expression open and faintly startled, as though he had been swept into position by a tide he did not entirely resist.

"There," Mama said, surveying her work with satisfaction. "Now we may all be comfortable."

Elizabeth watched Jane smile—gentle, patient, hopeful. Mr Bingley leaned closer, saying something low that made her laugh. For a moment, the sight was a balm to Elizabeth.

Then Mr Collins cleared his throat.

"I beg the indulgence of the company," he said, rising from his chair with deliberate care. "For a moment, if you please."

Papa lowered his cup.

Mr Collins clasped his hands before him, his expression arranged into solemn triumph. "It is my duty, as both a man of the cloth and a near relation, to proceed with openness in matters that affect the harmony of the family." He paused, as though to allow the weight of this principle to settle upon them all. "Accordingly, I am happy to announce that earlier this day, I tendered an offer of marriage to one of your daughters."

Elizabeth nearly dropped her cup, and her head immediately swivelled about the room. Who...?

Mary was sitting up a little taller than usual, a faint smile tickling the corner of her mouth.

Mr Collins moved through the room towards her, gesturing magnanimously. "I am gratified to inform you that Miss Mary Bennet has, with becoming seriousness and gratitude, consented to make me the happiest of men."

For a moment, no one spoke.

Papa blinked. "Indeed?" he said mildly. "This is the first I have heard of it."

Mary's cheeks flamed, and her mouth opened faintly, only to close again. She dashed a look of reproach to Collins before smoothing it away, then folded her hands together, her lips pressed in an expression of solemn resolve.

"Oh! My dear sir, you must forgive me," Collins protested. "I can only plead the impetuousness of ardent love, and the necessity of preparing to receive your most—" he broke off to bow gallantly toward Mr Bingley— "*excellent* guests. I am afraid the usual forms were not observed; however, I flatter myself, the joy of a public announcement to the entire family at once was not without its charms, and therefore, I comforted myself in the knowledge that such a confession might bring joy to the entire family at once."

Mama made a sound that might have been surprise or might have been calculation, then clapped her hands together. "Oh, yes, yes, Mr Bennet shall make no protests, no protests of the kind! How wonderful! Mr Collins, this is—this is quite excellent. I always knew Mary would make an excellent partner for a clergyman. And what a comfort it will be to have her so advantageously settled!"

Papa opened his mouth. Mama spoke over him.

"Do not look so doubtful, Mr Bennet. A proposal in the morning, an acceptance by afternoon—it is perfectly efficient. We shall need to speak of gowns at once. New ones, of course. Nothing old-fashioned. And a wedding before Twelfth Night would be quite suitable."

Mr Collins beamed. "I was confident, Mrs Bennet, that you would perceive the wisdom of the arrangement. Miss Mary's seriousness of mind, her devotion to improvement, and her aptitude for moral influence render her an ideal partner." He hesitated, then added with benevolent emphasis, "And I trust her example will prove... salutary to the household at large."

Elizabeth felt it then.

Not gradually. Not as a warning.

The pain struck behind her eyes and spread downward, sharp enough to steal her breath. Her stomach turned violently, the room tilting so that the edges of the furniture blurred and doubled. Cold sweat broke along her spine.

She gripped the arm of the chair, but it was not enough. The world narrowed to the sound of her own pulse, loud and erratic.

"Lizzy?" Jane's voice echoed distant, alarmed.

Elizabeth stood too quickly. The movement sent a wave of nausea through her, and she swayed, her hand reaching blindly for the screen beside her.

"I beg—" The words failed her. She pressed her lips together and shook her head once, sharply, as if to refuse the entire room.

Papa was on his feet at once. "Make space," he declared as he moved toward her. "Elizabeth is unwell."

Mama protested, of course. "But we were just—Lizzy, do not be dramatic! Not everything must be about you, and I daresay a little envy for your sister's good fortune—"

Elizabeth did not hear the rest. She made it only as far as the door before the strength left her legs entirely, the pain cresting at last into something she could not master. The room dissolved into sound and shadow as she clutched the frame, her breath coming in shallow, broken pulls as her stomach violently betrayed her.

This was not a megrim. Her body knew it now.

And it would not be reasoned with.

# Chapter Twenty-Nine

*One week later*

THE FIRE HAD BURNED low without his noticing it.

Darcy stood at the table where the *Liber* lay open among a disorderly ring of other volumes—chronicles, ballads, marginal compilations whose bindings had softened with use long before he had thought to value them. He had been on his feet for hours, shifting between texts, comparing phrasing, marking concordances with slips of paper torn from a correspondence ledger he would regret later.

Candle wax had dripped onto the desk in long, careless lines. He was reading a passage again—one he had already read twice—when the knock came.

"Sir," his man said, "a packet. Just arrived."

Darcy took it without comment and set it aside unopened, his attention already pulling back to the page. It took him a moment to realise what he had done—to recognise the restlessness in his own hand, the way his fingers had closed over the folded paper as though it might escape.

Still, he did not open it at once. Instead, he read the line again.

*Holden neyther by ryght ne by enheritaunce,*
*but by þe aunswering þat is not withdrawen.*

"Answering?" What the devil did that mean? He closed the book with an exhausted sort of reverence and turned at last to the packet.

Two letters.

The first bore his aunt's hand: unmistakable, bold, every line pressed into place as though the paper itself had been obliged to submit. The second—lighter, hastier—was addressed beneath it, folded smaller, almost apologetic in its presence. Bingley.

Darcy separated them. He would save Bingley's little note to cleanse his palate after whatever edict his aunt had decided to send today.

He broke Lady Catherine's seal and unfolded the letter.

*My dear Nephew,*

*I trust you will forgive the directness of my address, but circumstances no longer permit delay. Matters in Kent have progressed to a point that requires immediate and decisive attention—your attention, to be precise.*

*The season has turned ill. You will hear foolish talk of weather and chance, no doubt, but I assure you this is no ordinary inconvenience. The grounds at Rosings, which have been managed with unimpeachable care, now show signs of upheaval that cannot be attributed to neglect. The lake has receded without cause. The lower orchard has suffered losses that defy expectation.*

Darcy paused and read that paragraph again.

Not because of the damage described, but because of what was absent from the account. No mention of remedy. No curiosity. Only certainty that the cause lay *elsewhere*—and that she had already identified it.

He read on.

*I have consulted the appropriate records. I have spoken with those whose families have held this land for generations. I am not misled. There are moments in which duty must be assumed, not debated. You are at the edge of such a moment.*

*You need not fear for Pemberley, nor for your sister. All that concerns them will be secured once matters are properly aligned. Indeed, much that now appears uncertain will resolve itself the instant you cease to hesitate.*

His back stiffened, and he frowned.

She was not reassuring him. She was *excluding* him—quietly, deliberately—from the list of those whose safety... whose *future* required consideration. Why the devil would she talk like that?

Darcy had a sinking feeling that he understood more than he wished, but he forced himself to continue.

*Anne is prepared. She has always been prepared. The arrangements require only your concurrence to proceed as they ought. But do not delay, for every moment of your indecision causes suffering and blight. It is an historic fact, and entirely within your power to set right.*

*I would remind you that destiny is not a thing to be avoided, Darcy. It is fulfilled or it is resisted, to the detriment of all concerned. The cost of refusal is rarely borne by the one who refuses. Would you be so self-serving? I think not.*

That last line, he could not read smoothly.

It sounded very much like what his father had once dismissed as fancy, half-remembered, and laughed away—that some duties ended not in service, but in loss, and that she had already chosen *who* should bear it.

Why, she could hardly... it truly sounded as if she *believed* all this rot! Not as a tool by which to make him act according to her bidding, but as part of some greater crisis, with herself as the benevolent tyrant orchestrating the demise of some sacrificial lamb.

*I trust I may expect you at Rosings without delay.*

*Your affectionate aunt,*
*Lady Catherine de Bourgh*

Darcy lowered the letter slowly. For a moment, he did nothing at all.

Then he folded it—slowly, deliberately—and set it aside on the table, not atop the books, but apart from them, as one sets aside a blade.

One thing, he could understand. She had observed the same irregularities as he had this season.

Not understood it—he refused to grant her that—but noticed enough to mistake recognition for mastery. She reached at once for lineage and inevitability, for conclusions that required no examination, as though order were something that could be restored simply by placing the right person in the right position.

And she spoke of an end she believed acceptable. Someone or something *else's* end, naturally. Certainly not something that might inconvenience her.

Darcy drew a quaking breath and reached at last for the second letter. Indeed, he had need of a bit of Bingley's ease and cheer.

Bingley's hand ran a little uphill across the page—a little crowded, a little uneven, as though written in haste and reconsidered twice before being sent.

*My dear Darcy,*

*I must begin with an apology, for the enclosed letter from Lady Catherine de Bourgh arrived for you several days ago, and I ought to have forwarded it at once. A brief but determined snowstorm intervened, however, and the roads were impassable for two days and a half. I trust you will forgive the delay, as I assure you it was not occasioned by neglect.*

*I hope London agrees with you, though I cannot pretend not to wish you back in Hertfordshire. Netherfield has felt rather empty of late, and I find myself missing our walks and discussions more than I should have expected. My sisters send their regards, though Caroline insists she has already written to you herself.*

Darcy's mouth tightened faintly. *Insists* was precisely the word.

*Before the snow fell, we had the pleasure of dining at Longbourn, which was—as always—lively in the extreme. Mrs Bennet was in excellent spirits, and I need hardly say how very glad I was to see Miss Jane again. She was all kindness and good cheer, and I continue to admire her exceedingly, though*

*I fear I do not always do justice to my admiration when I attempt to express it.*

Darcy paused there, letter lowering a fraction.

*Admire her exceedingly.*

Well. That, at least, was no surprise.

He read on.

*You will scarcely believe it, but a most unexpected announcement was made during the evening—one which took us all quite by surprise. Mr Collins declared himself engaged to one of the Bennet girls, and not a soul present had suspected his intentions beforehand.*

Darcy straightened sharply.

Engaged?

His eyes jumped ahead, skimming, hunting for the name that mattered—

*Elizabeth*

The words blurred for a moment before he forced himself to slow, to read.

*Indeed, I was quite astonished to learn that he had not even consulted Mr Bennet prior to making his proposal, which struck me as irregular in the extreme. The bride-to-be, as I am sure you are eager to learn, is Miss Mary Bennet.*

Darcy closed his eyes briefly. Relief—real, undeniable—passed through him, loosening something he had not known was clenched so tightly. Mary Bennet. Of course, it was the falsely modest one for Collins. It made a dreadful sort of sense.

He drew breath and continued.

*I confess myself pleased for the happy couple, and yet slightly mortified on Mr Bennet's behalf, as the announcement was made with great solemnity and very little warning. Mrs Bennet required some moments to reconcile herself to the change in her expectations, but she recovered admirably, as I am sure you might expect.*

Naturally. Darcy's lips twitched despite himself.

*I regret to say, however, that the evening did not conclude as agreeably as it began.*

His eyes narrowed.

*Miss Elizabeth was taken unwell shortly after the announcement and was obliged to leave the room. The matter appeared suddenly, and though she attempted at first to make light of it, she could not be persuaded to remain. Indeed, she collapsed before she had quite gained the threshold, and while still in our presence, she was taken violently ill, in the most indelicate sense. I was greatly concerned for her, and Mr Bennet not less so.*

Darcy's gaze fixed on the page, unseeing.

Taken unwell.

*Again?*

*I sent to Longbourn early the next morning, before the snows came, to inquire after her, and was told only that she had slept, was awake, and was keeping to her rooms. Mrs Bennet assured my messenger that there was no cause for alarm, though Caroline is of a different opinion and has hinted at explanations I refuse to entertain, as they would be unjust to the lady and unworthy of repetition.*

Darcy's fingers tightened on the paper. His mind supplied images he did not permit himself to examine too closely: Elizabeth pale, stubborn, insisting she was well enough...

...and failing.

*We have not had liberty to be in company with the family since then, owing to the weather. Indeed, today was the first day of any clearing whatever, and so you see, I wrote immediately. I intend to call on the family soon, if I may. I hope sincerely that this was nothing more than fatigue or a passing malaise, though I confess the recurrence after last month troubles me. Louisa believes Miss Elizabeth to possess a delicate constitution, but still, I am not persuaded. She has always seemed to me spirited rather than fragile.*

Darcy swallowed.

*Spirited.* Yes. That was the word.

*Matters of the estate weigh on my mind as well, though I hesitate to burden you with them. The harvest, as you know, was excellent—better than any my steward has ever recorded—but there have been odd reports of spoilage in certain bins, and my steward cannot account for it. I have begun selling modest quantities of grain to those who have applied, thinking it wiser to move it while it is sound, though I cannot help wishing for your counsel in this.*

Darcy barely saw the words. What cared he for grain stores against the more urgent news? He even turned the letter over, seeking some sort of update, more information, but there was only a single paragraph remaining, and a signature.

*Pray forgive the length and disorder of this letter. I write as things occur to me, and fear I have made a muddle of it. I hope you will write soon and tell me how you fare, and whether you mean to return to Hertfordshire before the year is out. We should all be very glad to see you, particularly myself.*

*C. Bingley*

Darcy lowered the letter slowly to the desk. For a long moment, he did not move. Then he reached for the edge of the table, as though the room itself required anchoring.

Elizabeth Bennet had collapsed.

Again.

And this time, he had not been there to help her.

THE HOUSE HAD NOT quieted since Mr Collins's departure.

Elizabeth learned this by degrees. By the way doors were opened and shut with purpose. By the sound of Mama's voice—never raised in panic these days, but commanding, as though the air itself must be kept moving lest it encourage doubt. By Mary's movements through the house that never carried her to her beloved piano. No, she was fitting gowns and trying bonnets and already packing a trunk to take with her to Kent.

Elizabeth lay awake and listened.

She had meant only to rest. To give herself an hour. The worst snowstorm Hertfordshire had experienced in memory had dulled to a low howl two days before, leaving behind a sky of thin winter blue and drifts of ice-hardened snow that piled against the windows as though testing their resolve.

The house, however, seemed determined to behave as if nothing had been interrupted. Breakfast had been taken later than usual, but with uncommon cheer. Wedding plans were spoken aloud—lists named, letters dictated, small domestic triumphs anticipated with confidence.

Elizabeth turned her face into the pillow and waited for the pressure behind her eyes to ebb.

It did not.

She rose at last, more from stubbornness than strength, and dressed, pausing between each movement as though the intervals themselves might be counted against her. By the time she reached the stairs, the house was already in motion. Mama's voice carried from the breakfast room, directing Hill to fetch paper, to bring the good pen, to see whether Mrs Gardiner had replied yet with a promise of silk from Uncle Gardiner's warehouse.

"—and we must consider gowns at once," Mama was saying. "December is no time to delay. A winter wedding requires foresight."

Elizabeth placed her hand upon the banister. The wood felt colder than it ought.

She descended slowly.

Mary sat at the table, her back straight, her expression composed in a way Elizabeth had never quite seen before. There was a letter before her, carefully folded and refolded, as though it had already been read enough times to require reinforcement. She looked up when Elizabeth entered, her eyes bright with a restrained solemnity.

"Good morning, Lizzy," she said. "Mama has asked me to draft a reply to Mr Collins's last note. He is eager that matters proceed with propriety."

"I am sure he is," Elizabeth replied. She cleared her throat and reached for the chair nearest the window, grateful to sit where the light was less direct. Jane glanced at her at once—only a glance.

"Did you have a nice lie-down?" Jane asked.

"Pleasant enough," Elizabeth said, which was not quite true, but near enough to pass.

Papa lowered his paper. He did not speak, but his gaze rested on her face longer than usual before returning to the column he pretended to read.

Mama, meanwhile, had not paused. "Mary, my dear, we must also consider whether it would be proper to invite the Lucases to dinner now that the announcement is made public. And the Philipses and Longs, of course. One does not wish to appear secretive."

Mary inclined her head. "Of course, Mama. Mr Collins expressly desired for us to make our joy known in Meryton, though he is not here at present to share in it."

Elizabeth closed her eyes for a moment. Each sentence seemed to arrive before the last had finished fading, as though the air itself were impatient. She reached for her tea and found her hand unsteady enough to require both fingers and will.

It was not pain just now. Not quite. It was the waiting for it.

She tried to follow the conversation. To make some contribution that would mark her as present, attentive, herself. But the words slid past without anchoring. Dates. Names. Distances between houses she had walked a hundred times without thinking. The effort of holding them all at once felt suddenly... excessive.

"Elizabeth?"

She looked up to find Jane watching her again, concern no longer concealed.

"Yes?"

"You have not eaten."

Elizabeth glanced down at her untouched plate and laughed softly. "I must have forgot how."

Mama waved a hand. "Nonsense. You have always had a delicate appetite in winter. It will improve."

Elizabeth did not answer. The pressure behind her eyes flared, no longer content to wait. She pressed her fingers lightly to her temple and found that even the smallest touch sent a ripple of dizziness through her.

"I think," she said carefully, "that I shall lie down for a little."

Mama frowned. "Again? Lizzy, you have been half the day abed this past week, at least!"

"Only briefly, Mama."

Papa folded his paper. "Let her go, my dear. The house will not collapse in her absence."

Elizabeth caught his eye and managed a smile in return. She did not make it far.

The corridor tilted—not sharply, not enough to provoke alarm, but enough that she stopped short and leaned against the wall until the world agreed to behave. From behind her came the sound of Mama's voice again, brisk and satisfied, already turned back to arrangements. Mary's reply followed, earnest and assured.

Elizabeth closed her eyes.

This was worse than Netherfield.

But why? Mr Collins had gone back to Kent as soon as the roads cleared—Mr Collins, whose very voice caused ripples of agony down her spine. The air should have eased. The strain should have lessened. She had told herself as much with quiet confidence the day she had watched his carriage depart before the storm.

Instead, her troubles spiralled on without him, and her body seemed determined to collapse into the space he had vacated.

She reached her room at last and sat upon the bed, waiting for the nausea to pass. It did, eventually, leaving behind a weakness so complete she could not have said where it began. She lay back and stared at the ceiling, listening to the house move around her.

Below, a door closed. Mr Hill was chopping more firewood. Someone laughed.

Elizabeth turned her face toward the window. The light had faded again, though the hour had scarcely changed. Outside, the garden lay under a thickening coat of snow that was so deep only the most intrepid spikes showed through. The rosemary, once so stubbornly green, sagged beneath it.

She did not know when she began to cry. Only that the tears came without effort or sound, slipping down into her hair and vanishing there, as though even that small evidence of distress were unwilling to remain.

Whatever this was, it had not left with Mr Collins.

And whatever it required of her, it was no longer content to wait.

# Chapter Thirty

The break in the weather lasted three days.

Long enough for the roads to turn to slush, then harden again with frost. Long enough for Mama to declare the worst of winter past and drag Mary back to Meryton to admire lace. Long enough for Papa to walk the perimeter of the fields once more and pronounce himself cautiously satisfied.

Then, on the fourth night, the wind came.

It did not announce itself properly. There was no long warning, no gradual thickening of cloud. It arrived late, sharp, and furious, rattling the shutters with a violence that suggested long-checked impatience rather than the natural teeth of winter. Freezing rain followed first—hard, slanting pellets of ice, driven sideways so that it found every weakness the house had not yet discovered. Only after that did the snow fall, wet and heavy, clinging to what the rain had already slicked into a frozen glare.

By morning, nothing moved.

No carts on the road. No messengers. Even the servants ventured out only in turns, quick and unwilling, returning with cheeks stung raw and boots soaked through. The world beyond Longbourn had narrowed to what could be seen from the windows, and even that changed by the hour as the wind worried at drifts and stripped branches bare.

Papa said little at first. He stood at the window longer than usual, his hands clasped behind his back, watching the line of the barns through the blowing snow. When he did speak, it was to ask after roof tiles, then shutters, then whether the grain bins had been checked again since dawn.

"They were sound yesterday," Mr Hill reminded him. "The doors held through the stoutest of the gusts."

"Yes," Papa replied, gazing out the window. "Yesterday."

By the second day of the storm, he could not be kept indoors. He pulled on his boots and coat and went out with two of the men, returning an hour later with water on his cuffs and a look Elizabeth did not care to see upon his face. He said nothing at dinner, but he did not eat much either, and when Mama began to complain of the inconvenience of being cut off from society, he waved her off without humour.

"The inconvenience," he said, "is not the point."

When the storm broke after several days, it did so almost grudgingly. It would be some days more before the roads were passable by anything but the most intrepid. Papa bundled himself in as many layers as could be found and went out to his barns, with ledger and pencil in hand.

He came back slower. Frozen from beak to boots.

The harvest had been sound. Of that, there was no question. The bins had been dry, the roofs intact. And yet, grain that should have kept dry and sound for years at a time had begun to heat in places.

Not everywhere. Not evenly. One bin untouched, another only lightly spoiled along one edge. Damp where there had been no leak. Warmth of spoilage where there should have been cold.

"It makes no sense," Papa said that evening, more to himself than to anyone else. "If it were water, it would spread. If it were rot, it would be predictable, would smell foul. This is... just dry and black. I have never seen the like. It is almost as if..." He trailed off, then shook his head. "We will know more tomorrow."

Elizabeth listened from her chair by the fire.

She had been unwell for more than a fortnight now. Long enough, she should have recovered from any mild complaint several times over. The illness that had struck her down at Netherfield—whatever it had been—had come upon her suddenly and released her just as cleanly. This did neither.

There was no fever. No single point of pain she could name and address. Only a weakness that ebbed and returned without pattern, a general agony that refused to be dislodged. Some mornings, she could sit up and read a page or two. Others, she could scarcely bear the light.

DARCY LEFT THE HOUSE with a list folded neatly into his pocket and every intention of crossing each item off before dusk.

The air had turned sharp overnight. Snow lingered in the seams of the street—pressed into corners, dulled by soot—while the paving stones held a thin, treacherous glaze. His boots found purchase by habit rather than care. London moved around him with its usual insistence: carts rattling, porters calling, the early bells still echoing faintly between buildings.

He reviewed the list as he stepped into his carriage. For Georgiana, something chosen, not merely bought. For Richard, something useful enough to survive campaigning. For Mrs Reynolds, Mrs Hodges, and the senior staff, the customary acknowledgments that marked the season without extravagance. Practical kindness, properly ordered.

Nothing on the list required urgency. Nothing ought to be difficult. That, he reflected as his carriage turned onto a familiar street, was the advantage of preparation.

THE BELL ABOVE THE shop door jingled as he opened it.

Darcy paused just inside, letting his eyes adjust, expecting—without thinking of it—a particular arrangement of light and colour: bolts of cloth stacked in their accustomed places, the long counter polished to a soft sheen, the small display near the window reserved for finer pieces set aside for established patrons.

The counter was there. The shelves were there. They were simply... rather bare.

"Mr Darcy," the proprietor said at once, emerging from behind the counter with more haste than courtesy. "A pleasure, sir. What can I do for you today?"

Darcy inclined his head. "I require very little. Something suitable for a young lady—my sister. And something for my housekeepers, possibly."

"Of course. Of course." The man gestured toward the shelves, then hesitated. "You may find our selection somewhat... reduced."

Darcy stepped closer. He did not need the explanation. Where there should have been stacks upon stacks of samples, bolts, ribbons, there was bare wood. Where a certain shade had once been plentiful, there were only two lengths left, both set aside with paper tags tied to their corners.

"Delayed shipments?" Darcy asked.

"Yes. Well—partly." The man's hand moved, then stopped. "Some diverted. Some promised and not delivered. It is all most irregular."

Darcy examined a bolt of fabric, running its edge lightly between his fingers. Serviceable. Not what he had intended. This was to be a gift, not a necessity.

"And this?" he asked, indicating a bolt of pale silk.

"Already spoken for, I'm afraid. A standing request, my best customer, sir. I cannot possibly—"

"No, no. I would not ask it," Darcy interrupted. He selected the first bolt instead. This might not do for Georgiana, but his housekeepers would think it very fine, indeed. When the shopkeeper named the price, Darcy had to cough to smother his shock. Nevertheless, he signalled his approval and waited as it was measured and wrapped.

As he turned to leave, the proprietor added, almost apologetically, "One hopes matters will settle after the season, sir."

Darcy did not answer at once. He took the parcel and adjusted it under his arm. "One hopes," he said, and stepped back into the street.

The market lay only a few streets on, and Darcy altered his course without deliberation. If one shop had been thinned, another might compensate. That was the advantage of London: redundancy, abundance, alternatives.

The noise reached him first. Voices overlapped in argument rather than commerce. A cart stood half-unloaded in the street, its driver shouting back at two men who had seized the same sack by opposite ends. Someone laughed, but it carried an edge that did not belong to amusement.

Darcy slowed.

At the nearest stall, baskets that should have been heaped were filled barely to their rims. Apples with bruises set carefully outward. Roots still clotted with frozen soil. A chalkboard leaned against the counter with prices written twice—one crossed through, another added beneath in a darker hand.

"Is this all?" a woman demanded.

"For today," the vendor replied, not looking at her. "I told you—come earlier."

"And tomorrow?"

The man shrugged. "Ask me tomorrow."

Darcy moved on. He heard the same exchange repeated with minor variations: assurances hedged, tempers shortened, promises made with the air of men who expected not to keep them.

He stopped at a butcher's stall that he recognised. "Mr Darcy," the butcher said, wiping his hands. "You have chosen a lively morning."

"So I see," Darcy replied. "Is the supply delayed?"

The man snorted. "'Delayed' implies it is coming."

Darcy tilted his head. "Then where—"

"Bought up," the butcher said. "Or spoiled before it ever reached me. I cannot say which."

Darcy glanced at the hooks above the counter. Too many were bare.

"And your winter contracts?" he asked.

The butcher hesitated. "Being honoured. As far as may be."

Darcy inclined his head and moved on, but the answer followed him. *As far as may be.* Not utter refusal. Not panic yet. Rationing—but rather sudden. Should not all the papers be full of it, if matters had gone this far?

At the far end of the market, a man had mounted a crate and begun to shout. "There are signs, I tell you! The land answers its own account—"

"Answers *what* account?" someone called back. "Your tab at the gin shop?"

Laughter broke out, then was swallowed by more voices. A turnip struck the crate and split; another followed, less accurately thrown.

The man ducked, straightened, and pressed on, voice rising to meet the noise. "You mock because you are comfortable, but mark me! This is the price of pride. Too much ploughing, too much forcing. We have stripped the soil to bone and marrow—"

"It's the war," a woman snapped from the edge of the crowd. "Always the war. Everything goes to the army, and we get the scraps."

"Rubbish," another voice answered. "It's the mills. Smoke spoils the rain. My cousin swears the fogs are thicker every year."

"It's God's judgment," the man insisted, thumping his chest. "You pave over fields, you pull hedges down, you think the earth will not sicken—"

Someone shouted back, "Sicken! Eh, who does he think he is? Last winter was mild as milk."

"That's how it begins," the man cried. "Mercy first, then the reckoning!"

Something struck the crate hard enough to rock it. The man caught his balance, lifted his hands again, and kept talking, his words breaking apart under the din—sin, smoke, soldiers, grain, gold—none of it landing cleanly, all of it spoken at once.

Darcy did not need to hear more. What followed him was not belief—no, not yet—but *attention*. The kind that gathers when explanations fail, and people begin trying them on regardless.

By the time Darcy reached his next intended stop—a bookseller whose stock he knew as well as his own shelves—the list in his pocket had begun to feel less like an errand and more like a test.

"Ah, Mr Darcy! You are early this year," the bookseller said, peering at him over his spectacles. "Most leave such purchases until the last possible moment."

"Habit," Darcy replied. "I prefer to avoid crowds."

The man smiled thinly. "A wise preference. You may find fewer temptations than usual."

Darcy scanned the shelves. Gaps again—here and there, but unmistakable. A space where a particular history ought to have stood. Another where pamphlets were usually stacked in careless abundance.

"Delayed printings?" Darcy asked.

"Paper," the bookseller said. "Ink. Transport. Take your pick." He tapped the counter with one finger. "Mere inconveniences, sir."

Darcy selected a volume nonetheless, one he knew Georgiana would value for its quality rather than novelty.

As it was wrapped, he asked, casually, "Do you hear much talk?"

The bookseller glanced up. "Talk, sir?"

"Of shortages. I have just come from the market, and one can hardly find a potato for sale that is not blighted."

The man's mouth tightened with calculation. "Enough to sell certain titles more briskly than others."

"Which titles?"

"Almanacs. Particularly the old ones! Never thought they would be worth anything but fodder for the fire, but there is an interest just this week in histories of poor seasons," the bookseller said. "Old winters. Hard years. People prefer to read themselves into perspective."

Darcy accepted the parcel. "And do they find comfort there?"

The bookseller shrugged. "They find precedent, I suppose."

DARCY DID NOT GO directly home.

When the carriage stopped at the kerb, he gave his direction to his driver, then checked himself. "No," he said, after a moment. "Take the long way. Along the river."

The man glanced back in surprise, but nodded and turned the horses.

Darcy settled back against the seat, one gloved hand braced against the door as the carriage lurched into motion. The streets grew rougher as they moved eastward, the buildings giving way to warehouses and yards where carts stood idle in ranks that felt too neat, too patient. He watched men gathered in doorways, not working, not idle either—waiting. For what, he could not have said.

At the docks, the air thickened, damp and metallic. Ships lay moored without bustle, their lines slack, their decks quiet. A pair of stevedores argued near a stack of crates, one gesturing sharply toward the river, the other shaking his head. Darcy caught fragments through the carriage window—*late, spoiled, should've been here by Michaelmas*—before the horses carried him on.

"Slower," he said, and the driver obliged.

They passed a chandlery with its shutters half-closed despite the hour. A cooper's yard where barrels lay overturned, unused. A line of carts waiting at a gate that did not open. Darcy's gaze moved from face to face, from doorway to doorway, measuring not hardship exactly, but something nearer to apprehension—people checking the sky, the river, one another, as though expecting a signal they could neither name nor ignore.

He told himself, again, that London was always uneasy in winter. War bred rumour. Storms disrupted trade. Nothing here was extraordinary in itself.

But nothing stood alone, did it? It was all multiplying, one thing upon another, until no denial was possible.

The carriage turned west, rolling back toward order and lamplight and stone façades that pretended permanence. Darcy did not look away from the window until the river was well behind them.

He had not seen proof. He had not seen cause.

But he had seen enough to know that the unease was not confined to his own thoughts—and that whatever was wrong had begun to press outward, testing the edges of things that had once held.

"PAPA?"

She had roused at the sound of his step, pushing herself upright against the pillows with an effort she did not bother to disguise.

Her father stopped just inside the room. "My dear child, you ought not to sit up on my account."

"You went out again," she said, glancing at the dusting of snow on his shoulders. "Did the bins hold through the night? Is there more rot?"

He sighed, and that alone answered more than she liked. "Some did. Others less obliging. It appears that surplus harvest we experienced is withdrawing itself."

Elizabeth blinked. "That is... not reassuring."

"No," he agreed. "It is not."

She sat up a bit more, drawing the coverlet closer to her chest. "If it is damp, it will spread."

"That is precisely the difficulty," he said, moving nearer. "It has not. One bin spoiled along the southern edge. Another perfectly dry not ten paces away. If I did not know better, I should suppose the blight was intentionally caused by some nefarious hand. But enough of that for now. Elizabeth."

His expression had changed—not alarmed, not yet—but grave, purposeful.

"You did not come up to talk of grain," she guessed.

"No," he admitted. "I did not. The roads are passable again. Not comfortably, but sufficiently. I sent for Mr Jones this morning."

Her fingers tightened in the coverlet. "You need not have troubled him."

"Nonsense. He is paid to be troubled." He took the chair beside her bed and sat, folding his hands loosely. "And I should like to hear him explain why my daughter grows weaker by the day while insisting she is quite well."

"I did not say I was well," Elizabeth replied. "Only that I am not ill in the usual sense."

"Ah. That distinction again."

She drew a breath. "You may tell him what you like, Papa. He will find no fever. No injury. He will recommend rest and patience, and you will pretend to be satisfied."

"And you?"

Elizabeth did not answer at once. When she did, her voice was very even. "I will listen. I always do."

A knock sounded at the door below—voices, the unmistakable murmur of arrival. Papa rose. "That will be him."

When Mr Jones was shown in, she greeted him politely and answered his questions without hesitation. He examined her with care—pulse, eyes, breath—his expression tightening by degrees.

He frowned.

Then frowned again.

"There is no corruption in the flesh," he said at last. "No fever. No sign of injury. Oh, and I daresay that old wound on your wrist has healed nicely."

"And yet?" Papa prompted.

"And yet she is plainly not herself," Jones admitted. "I can offer no better explanation than fatigue. Lingering strain. The remedy must be time. And quiet."

Elizabeth inclined her head politely. "I shall endeavour to behave myself, sir."

When he had gone, she smiled at her father. "There, see? Why, it was almost comical how well he echoed what I told you he would say."

But Papa did not find it amusing. He rose and laid a hand on her head. "I will have Hill bring you some broth. Get some rest, my child. I have some letters to write."

If Papa's letters had aught to do with business, he was likely kept very busy, indeed. Reports from about the neighbourhood began to come in as the days went on.

The accounts did not arrive all at once. They could not; nothing moved while the ice held. When they did come, they came in fragments—spoken at the door, written in cramped hands once ink would flow again, carried by men whose boots were still stiff with frozen mud.

The sheep had never thickened their fleeces properly, one tenant said, bewildered. The autumn had been too mild, the grass too rich for too long. When the cold struck, they went down where they stood. Others would not cross certain fields at all, balking as though the ground burned their hooves.

Milk cows dried up within days. Not sick—simply emptied, as though their bodies had decided there was nothing left to give. Calves dropped without warning, found stiff in the mornings despite shelter and straw.

Horses fared little better. Legs swelled hot beneath the skin, fevers that would not break. Poultices did nothing. Walking only worsened it. One mare at Lucas Lodge had gone lame in all four legs at once, and no one could say why.

The ground itself had betrayed them. It had been hard and dry when the first snow fell, sealed fast by late summer sun rather than softened by autumn rains. Now, where the thaw came unevenly, water had nowhere to go. It ran over the hard pan surface, pooled where it should not, drove against roots and posts that had held for decades.

Trees came down without warning. A barn roof sagged and split when a beam gave way beneath the weight of ice and meltwater together. Another leaned, then collapsed outright—not from age, but from something loosened beneath.

Papa listened. He asked questions. He wrote everything down.

Elizabeth watched him at the small desk by the window, his papers spread and sorted with an attention she had never known him to give anything but a book. Dates. Places. Names. He set each account beside the others, not as a list, but as one might assemble pieces of a map.

Mr Bingley's letter lay open among them.

He had sold grain, he wrote, reluctantly and too quickly. The moment the roads cleared, the requests had come—farmers, agents, men sent on behalf of others farther afield. He feared rot if he waited. His bins were failing in the oddest ways as well: one side heating, another sound; spoilage without pattern or sense. He had thought it prudent to move what he could.

Papa had snorted when he read that. *Prudent for today,* his expression said. *Starving tomorrow.*

He had not followed Bingley's example. What remained at Longbourn he had ordered sealed, shifted, covered again and again. If the family went without comfort, so be it. Hunger was not a thing he meant to invite.

Elizabeth absorbed all of this quietly, from her chair near the hearth or the bed she now occupied more often than she liked. She did not comment. She did not ask questions. Each new account pressed inward, not outward—settling somewhere beneath her ribs, tightening her breath.

The county had not failed in any sort of orderly fashion. That would have been easier to bear. Instead, it was coming apart unevenly, in pockets and fractures, like ice cracking beneath weight that had not yet broken through.

As the afternoons darkened sooner and the firelight grew harsher to her eyes, Elizabeth felt herself doing the same—drawing inward, conserving what little steadiness remained. It was not fear that drove it, nor imagination.

It was recognition.

Something that had once held—quietly, without effort—was no longer holding at all. And her body, traitorous and exact, was answering the loss as faithfully as the land itself.

# Chapter Thirty-One

Elizabeth was there already.

For one wild instant, he believed he had come home—though nothing in the room was his, and nothing in her belonged to him. The sight of her struck with the same unreasonable certainty as a name spoken aloud in a church: intimate, improper, and answered before a man had time to consider whether he ought to answer at all.

She stood with her back half-turned, not avoiding him, merely occupied—as if she had been listening for something and had heard it at last. Her hands were gathered behind her, fingers laced as though to keep them still. The lamplight caught the edge of her sleeve, the pale fall of her throat above the fichu, the dark coil of hair at her nape. A domestic figure, and yet not; his mind supplied the memory of her laughing eyes and quick mouth and made it worse, not better, for the quiet in her now.

When she turned, it was not with surprise.

It was with that even, disconcerting regard she had fixed upon him once at Netherfield—when she had thought herself unseen, when she had looked up and found him gazing at her. There was no startlement, no question of his right to stare. Only that calm knowledge of him, as if the shape of him had been kept somewhere and fitted back into place without effort.

"Mr Darcy. I thought you had gone."

His name, in her voice, did not strike like flattery. It struck like truth—stripped of ornament, impossible to contradict.

He drew breath to answer, but found he had none. Filling his eyes with her was enough.

"You have been absent," she said again, more softly—not as accusation, not as plea, but with a weary clarity that reached him before understanding did. As if absence were a thing with consequence, and he had committed that wrong without intending to.

Something in him lurched toward her at once—toward explanation, toward apology, toward that ridiculous urge to set matters right as though his will had ever been sufficient to do it.

Behind her, the fire guttered, a sudden flare licking higher than its bounds, as though the room itself had misjudged its own measure.

What had been a low, orderly fire burst suddenly, a rush of flame lifting as though caught by a draught that had no source. Sparks leapt and struck the stone, one skittering close enough to kiss the hem of her gown before dying away. The wall beside her answered with a faint, dry sound—no more than a hairline crack, shedding a whisper of dust down the plaster.

"Elizabeth!" he cried in alarm—and then again, more deliberately, as though the word itself might alter what followed— "Elizabeth, please. Come away from there."

The hem of her gown lay perilously close, pale fabric fluttering on the currents of a heat it could not withstand. Behind her, more plaster cracked loose, dusting her cloak and exposing cracked beams beyond. The sight struck him with a force that had nothing to do with reason and everything to do with some deeper instinct.

She looked behind herself—only briefly—measuring the fire, the slowly splitting wall, the narrow margin left to her. Then her gaze returned to his, level still, but threaded now with something like sorrow.

He saw the cost gather in her, not as fear but as reckoning: the careful inward accounting of strength already spent, the weighing of what obedience would require. She did not avert her eyes. She did not step back.

"I cannot."

There were no theatrics in it. No regret shaped the sound. It was the plain statement of a boundary already reached.

He drew breath to answer her, and found the air thickened, hot, as though the room itself had closed ranks behind her. The fire had climbed higher, tongues of flame worrying at the edge of the hearthstone, casting light that did not behave. It flared and bent, licking toward the hem of her gown with a hunger that was no longer patient.

"Elizabeth!" he said again, and this time the name broke its own restraint. "Truly. You must come away. Take my hand."

He stepped forward at last, not toward her place but into the space between them, his hand extended without thought or ceremony, palm open in the old instinctive pledge: *I will take the harm; you need not.*

"Please!" he urged, because the word was the only one left him.

She looked at his hand. For an instant—only one—he saw the answer she wished she could give. Her fingers twitched, the smallest betrayal of impulse, and his heart answered it with a force that left no room for doubt. Then her hand stilled at her side.

"It is not for me to take it," she said, and the sorrow in her voice was no longer distant. It had come nearer, nearer than the fire.

The flames surged, bright enough now to throw her into sharp relief, the light catching in her hair, along the line of her sleeve. The crack in the plaster had reached the ceiling, showering larger chunks now of the failing wall. But the fire—he could see how close it was. How unforgiving. How little time remained.

"Then let me come to you!"

The words tore free of him before he knew he meant to speak them, because his body had already surged forward. Every instinct drove the same command—*take her, pull her back, get her clear.*

His hand closed around hers. The contact was almost delirious—warm, real, unmistakable. Her fingers tightened in his, as though she had been waiting for his touch, as though the joining itself had always been the way of things.

Relief surged through him, sharp enough to steal his breath. He drew back instinctively, already turning his body to shield her, to pull her clear of the heat rising at her spine.

But she did not come.

Her hand had not slipped from his. But the pull went nowhere, as though the force of it had been swallowed between them. He braced, tightened his grasp, set his weight into the motion.

She swayed toward him—no more than a breath, a fraction—and stopped. Her arm stretched, the line of it taut between them, but her feet remained where they were. Planted as though sunken through the floor.

His chest burned with the effort. Confusion tore through him, wild and unreasoning. He pulled again, harder, desperate now, and felt the answer in his bones. He could take her hand, but he could not take her away.

He could only take what was meant to meet her.

"Let me," he said again, and now the words were stripped of argument or pride. Not command. Not rescue. A request shaped by necessity alone. "Let me stand behind you. Between you and the fire."

For a heartbeat, she only gazed at him, wonder in her eyes and pain on her brow. Then, wordlessly, she nodded.

He stepped—not toward her, but *into* the narrow margin she guarded. Into the place that answered only to surrender. And gave his body, the only shield he could offer her. He wrapped himself about her, cradling her back in the cave of his chest and arms, covering her tender neck with his own cheeks.

The heat struck him at once.

Flame bent toward his body as water bends toward stone, divided not by force but by presence. The air thickened, burning his breath as it entered him; his skin flared with pain so immediate it erased every other sensation. He set himself there without thought, shoulders squared, chest pressed into her, knowing with a clarity that left no room for fear that retreat was no longer possible.

This was not escape—not for her. But it was salvation, all the same. All would be right... all would be well once the flame had exhausted its wrath on him.

DARCY TORE HIMSELF AWAKE with a cry already in his throat.

It ripped free of him, raw and ungoverned, dragging his body upright as though the bed itself had rejected him. His lungs seized; breath came in a harsh, scraping rush that burned all the way down. Fire clung to him still—on his skin, in his hair, along his hands where he could *feel* it, unmistakable and alive. He clawed at his nightshirt, half-mad with the certainty that it must be smoking.

The room reeled. Darkness. The low gleam of banked coals. No flame. No wall. No Elizabeth.

And yet the heat would not leave him.

His hands shook violently as he pressed them to his arms, his chest, his face. No thick dusting of broken plaster, no burns. His skin was whole. Unmarked. Still, the sensation lingered—an echo too sharp to be dismissed, as though his flesh remembered something his eyes now denied.

"God—" The word came out hoarse, broken.

He dragged in another breath and another, forcing the rhythm back by sheer will. The air smelled wrong to him—too clean, too cold. He could have sworn there was smoke.

A shape loomed at the foot of the bed.

Darcy shouted again, the sound tearing loose before thought could intervene, and lurched back against the headboard—

Only to meet the steady, unblinking gaze of Brutus.

The dog stood with his forepaws planted wide, head lifted, ears forward, every line of him intent. He did not bark. He did not move. He only watched Darcy with an attention so focused it might have been accusation. Or vigil.

Darcy clutched the coverlet with a strangled laugh that ended closer to a sob. "Damn you," he breathed, dragging a hand down his face. "You great brute."

Brutus's tail thumped once against the floor.

Footsteps thundered in the corridor. The door flew open, and it was all Darcy could do not to scream again.

"Sir?" His valet stood framed in the doorway, half-dressed, eyes wide. "We heard—are you unwell?"

Darcy swallowed hard. His throat burned. His heart still battered against his ribs like something trying to escape.

"No!" he blurted. Then, more carefully, forcing the word into order. "No. A dream. Nothing more."

The valet hesitated, plainly unconvinced.

"I require nothing," Darcy added, reclaiming command by instinct alone. "Return to bed."

His valet blinked, opening his mouth almost as if he meant to protest. But then he closed it again and bowed. "Very good, sir."

The door closed, and silence rushed back in, thick and unhelpful.

Darcy sat motionless, hands clenched in the sheets, his body trembling with the aftermath of something it did not know how to release. The fire in his nerves faded by degrees, leaving behind a deeper cold—one that settled not in the room, but in his bones.

Brutus remained where he was. Had he even blinked? Darcy was tempted to throw a pillow at him just to provoke *some* sort of reaction.

He did not lie back down. He stared into the dark, past the end of the bed he knew so well, heedless of the random comforts beside his bed—his book, a glass, even a lantern he could reach for and light. None of them mattered now, none would bring relief. For he was certain—without metaphor, without exaggeration—that whatever had passed through him had not been a dream of fear.

It had been a rehearsal.

ELIZABETH GASPED AWAKE INTO stillness.

The house lay cool and hushed around her, the sort of quiet that came only in the small hours, when even the timbers seemed to have settled into rest. Moonlight slipped through the curtains in a pale band, silvering the far edge of the bed and the floor beyond it. For once—remarkably, blessedly—there was no nausea waiting for her when she drew breath. No urgent pressure behind her eyes. No sense of the room tilting, or her body lagging behind her will.

She lay still a moment, testing the reprieve.

Her hand drifted, absently, to her ribs. Too easy to count them now. Her fingers traced the line of her hip, sharper than she remembered, then her cheek, hollow beneath the bone. She had grown thin. She knew it without mirrors, without comment. Food had held no appeal; even the thought of it had turned against her. And yet just now, there was a faint stirring where appetite might once have lived.

Nothing hot. Nothing seasoned. Nothing that would require explanation or company.

Bread.

Mrs Hill would surely have set a loaf aside in the larder; she always did. That would be enough. More than enough.

Elizabeth swung her legs over the side of the bed and rose carefully, expecting protest that did not come. The floor was cold beneath her feet, but it grounded her, and she welcomed the small, ordinary discomfort of it. She took a shawl from the chair and slipped it about her shoulders, then eased the door open and stepped into the passage.

The stairs creaked softly under her weight as she descended, though the sound seemed loud enough to alarm the sleeping house. She paused once, listening, then continued. No doors opened. No voices stirred. Longbourn slept on, unaware.

The larder yielded its prize without complaint. She broke off a crust rather than trouble herself with a knife, the bread firm and plain and smelling faintly of yeast. She took a bite as she turned away, chewing slowly as she made her way back toward the stairs.

It was then that she noticed it.

A thin line of light lay along the edge of the passage, spilling out from beneath the door to her father's library. Not the faint ghost of moonlight—this was warmer, truer. Candlelight.

Elizabeth slowed, the crust forgotten between her fingers. The house was meant to be dark. Her father was meant to be abed. And yet the light remained, untroubled by her pause, as though it had been there some time already.

Elizabeth pushed the door open without knocking.

Her father sat on the floor. Not slumped—arranged, after a fashion—one knee drawn up, the other stretched awkwardly beneath a scatter of papers. Letters lay everywhere, some half-folded, others spread flat as though they had resisted being shut away again. Two small leather-bound diaries rested open near his feet, their spines cracked with age. A book lay face-down beside them, forgotten. He held a single sheet close to the candle, angling it this way and that, his lips moving soundlessly as he squinted at the faded hand.

He did not hear her at once.

"Papa?"

The sound of her voice struck him like a hand to the chest. He looked up sharply—and for a bare, unguarded instant, something like a whimper escaped him, half breath, half sound, before he struggled to his feet. He crossed the small space between them in two strides and took her by the shoulders, as though to assure himself she was solid.

"There you are," he said, the words coming out hoarse and nearly strangled. Then he drew back, straightened, and the familiar air settled itself over him once more, like a coat resumed. "Late rising, my dear. Quite unlike you. A pity, too—there were at least two gentlemen earlier who called to inquire after your health. And Charlotte Lucas, besides."

Elizabeth smiled faintly. "How disappointing for them."

"Oh, I should think so. Still, matters improved thereafter. Miss Bingley arrived with Mrs Hurst, which you may count as providence in your favour. You have escaped a great ordeal."

She laughed—a small sound—and he bent to gather a handful of papers from the floor, shuffling them aside to clear the window seat. "Come," he said. "Sit, before I lose track of you again."

Elizabeth obeyed, settling into the cushioned recess. Her father's gaze dropped at once to the crust of bread in her hand. He made a thoughtful sound—approval, perhaps—and returned to collecting the scattered correspondence, stacking it with more care than usual, though it was clear there was no hope of restoring order.

"Papa," she said, watching him. "What on earth have you been doing? It is the middle of the night—or very nearly the morning—and you look as though you have not slept in a week."

He paused, letter in one hand, the candle guttering slightly in the other.

"Reading," he said lightly. "Remembering. And..." He glanced at the floor, at the ring of paper and leather and ink that had formed around him. "Trying, rather unsuccessfully, to persuade the past to explain itself."

"May I see?"

Her father hesitated only a moment before handing her the letter he had been holding to the candle, as though it were no more remarkable than any other scrap in the room. Elizabeth took another bite of her bread and unfolded it carefully one-handed, the paper thin as linen and twice as fragile.

Her eyes went first to the date. She blinked, then laughed softly and looked up at him.

"This is from more than sixty years ago! I have never even heard of the writer. Is this the urgent mystery that has deprived you of sleep?"

Papa made a vague, helpless gesture and bent to gather more papers, as though order might yet emerge if he persisted long enough. "From my great-uncle to my grandfather. Read it. At least the end. The rest is rather dull."

Elizabeth lowered her gaze again. The letter was precisely as he had said—mundane, almost comfortingly so. Complaints about London lodgings. The filth of the market. The price of candles. A longing for home—Longbourn, she supposed—that expressed itself in careful sentences and domestic detail. She read a few lines, then another, her attention wandering until...

Here. The tone altered.

*"'...I regret to say that Aunt Abigail is not improved by the change to London from Longbourn. Indeed, she is rather gone-off, in both spirits and sense, and her behaviour has grown such that I scarce know how to account for it...'"*

Elizabeth's chewing slowed.

*"'...she speaks at times with a confidence wholly unconnected to her circumstances, and at others not at all. She will sit for hours and then rise in the most severe agitation, always with some warning about a storm coming, and sometimes two days before it does so. She quite terrified my mother-in-law yesterday by chasing her from Aaron's nursery with cries of pestilence. Pestilence! The very idea! The physicians have done what they can, though the bleedings have only weakened her...'"*

Elizabeth swallowed.

"'*...there is talk of confinement, though I cannot think where she might be placed. She is no longer young, but I begin to fear for the children, who are all quite frightened by her manner and questions...*'"

The candle wavered. Elizabeth angled the page and read on, her brow knitting.

"'*...I do not understand it any better than you. Father said she was so merry and quick of wit when she was young, until this nonsense took her. I wish to Heaven she had never been raised at Longbourn, for the place seems to agree with her no better than with the others of her disposition.*'"

She folded the letter and held it in her lap, the bread forgotten in her hand.

"That is—" Her voice caught, and she stopped, surprised by it. "That is dreadful."

"Yes."

Elizabeth looked up at him. "Who was she?"

"My grandfather's aunt," he replied. "Or his uncle's sister, depending on which line you trace. She lived at Longbourn for most of her life."

Elizabeth glanced back at the letter. "They speak of her as though she were a burden of some long standing. As though she had ceased to be... herself."

"They did," Mr Bennet said. "And they were not unkind people, by the standards of their time."

She was silent for a moment, then asked, very softly, "Why were you reading this, Papa?"

He did not answer at once. He gathered the remaining papers into a neater stack, though it was clear he was no longer seeing them. When he finally looked at her, the humour had not left him—but it had thinned, drawn back to something more honest beneath.

"Because," he said, "I have been telling myself for years that such tales were family nonsense. That every house has its eccentric women and its unfortunate stories, and that ours were no different. And because I am no longer certain that was ever true."

Elizabeth frowned faintly and rose, setting the letter aside. As she did, her hand brushed one of the papers her father had stacked too neatly to be accidental. She lifted it without thinking... and then paused.

"This is... a deed."

Papa cleared his throat and looked away.

Elizabeth turned the page once, then again, her brow creasing as she took in the heavy hand, the formal phrasing, the seal impressed so deeply it had left its ghost on the paper beneath.

"'*...that long southern portion of the Ashbourne holding, being the enclosed grounds and dwelling set beyond the old thorn hedge, extending east to the fallow brook and west to the standing oak, together with such yards, orchards, and appurtenances as are customarily kept in husbandry, the same being land held apart from the greater demesne,*'" she read. "'*Transferred from—*'"

She stopped. "'*From Sir Reginald Netherton.*' Who is that? And where is Ashbourne?"

There was no answer. She looked up at him at last. "Papa?"

He exhaled, a sound caught somewhere between a sigh and a laugh that never quite formed. "Ah. So. We have arrived there sooner than I had hoped. Ashbourne was the name all these lands shared before Sir Reginald separated them, and sold the lands we now know as Longbourn to my... let me see, he was my great-great-great... perhaps another great..." He shook his head and trailed off. "Some ancestor. Anyway, the land Sir Reginald kept was later named Netherfield."

Elizabeth crossed the room and perched again on the window seat, the deed spread across her knees. "You are going to have to begin properly," she said. "Because at present I feel as though I have stepped into the middle of a conversation that began before I was born."

"That," he said, pulling a chair closer and sitting opposite her, "is not an inaccurate description."

He leaned forward, elbows on his knees, fingers loosely linked. For once, he did not appear amused by his own reluctance.

"When Longbourn was first separated from Netherfield," he began, "it was not a matter of convenience or profit. Not in the way such sales usually are. The land was simply... set aside. Peeled off, as you might say. Not because it was unwanted, but because it was... difficult."

"Difficult how?"

"In ways that were never written down plainly," he said. "Which is the first thing one notices when one begins to look. The language is evasive. Purposefully so. There is a great deal of emphasis on stewardship, on suitability of residence, on continuity without explanation."

She glanced back at the deed. "It reads like a legal apology."

"Yes," he said dryly. "That is an excellent way of putting it."

He leaned back and rubbed a hand over his face, as though the words themselves were wearying. "The Bennets were not chosen for distinction, Elizabeth. Nor for power. Nor even for sense, in some cases. We were... available. Respectable enough to hold land. Obscure enough not to draw attention."

"And this... Aunt Abigail?" she asked quietly.

His gaze met hers. "There it is. You see how quickly you find it. It always was the cleverest ones. I ought to have known it would take *you*."

# Chapter Thirty-Two

Elizabeth shook her head. "'Take' me? Papa, what do you mean?"

Her father kicked one foot over the other and squirmed slightly in his seat before answering. "For more than a few generations," he said haltingly, "there have been women—never many at once, and never predictable—who grew… peculiar, as they approached maturity. Not as children. Not as girls—at least, not so far as I have been able to discover. They were all said to be clever, lively, always much admired."

Elizabeth pursed her lips. "And?"

"And then…" Her father shrugged. "Something altered. Some heard voices, even talked to no one. Some spoke too much, or not at all. Some were thought touched. Others dangerous." He snorted and scraped a hand over his face. "One was even burned at the stake for a witch. But in every case, the family did its best to contain the… inconvenience."

Elizabeth's mouth had gone dry. "Aunt Abigail."

"Yes," he said, gesturing to the haphazard mountain of old letters piled on his desk. "Collins' mother. And uncounted others before her. Sixteen that I have evidence of so far, but no telling how far back the troubles go. Oh, and from what I have read, it seems many of them had an unaccountable fondness for very large canines… but that may be coincidence."

She rolled her eyes. "What became of them?"

He hesitated. "Those who married were said to have improved. Or appeared to. Whether it was affection, distraction, protection, or simple relief, I cannot say. They settled, had children, and near as I can tell, their daughters were not necessarily affected."

"And those who did not marry?"

He spread his hands. "You have read the letter."

Elizabeth looked down at the deed again. "Do you mean to say the women in our family share a hereditary weakness? *Madness?*"

"No," he said promptly. "No, I do not believe so—it is not in the blood, for the women were not all Bennets. Some belonged to families long vanished from Hertfordshire. Others lived at Netherfield, before the division. What they shared was not a name."

She drew a breath. "But a place?"

"Precisely." Papa swallowed. "And then, I was blessed with *five* daughters."

Elizabeth's mouth tightened in an approximation of sympathy.

"I told myself," he went on more lightly, "that it had all burned itself out. Two generations passed without incident. Three, if one is generous, for my second cousin Lilith was never right from birth, so I do not think..." He sighed. "Well, I allowed myself to hope that whatever our forebears had been managing—poorly or otherwise—had resolved itself without our intervention."

"And now?"

"And now," he said, meeting her gaze with a frankness she had not seen before, "my daughter has been ill for weeks, and the land is behaving as though it has lost its anchor." He lurched to his feet and paced to the darkened window. "I find myself awake at midnight, reading letters I once dismissed as the ravings of tired men who went to their graves long before I ever held you in my arms."

She folded the deed carefully. "Why did you never tell me? Or Mama?"

A corner of his mouth lifted. "Because I value my sanity."

Despite herself, Elizabeth smiled, and then it faded. "You believe I am like these others. Running mad."

He turned to face her. "Yes... And no." He frowned. "You are not speaking to walls as if they were people, or telling us a storm or an earthquake is to arrive days before it does. You are not hearing voices in your head... at least, not that you have confessed. Indeed, whatever has afflicted you appears quite different to their sort of madness. But the other coincidences... how it was always the best and brightest young lady of her generation, how Sir Reginald complained of oddities in the land... Yes, Lizzy, I think somehow, whatever this is must have affected you in ways never seen in any other."

She swallowed, and her hand wandered through the stack of letters until her fingers touched one they liked, and she pulled it out to read. This one was about a girl named Ruth, written by the lady's mother to a sister, it seemed.

*Ruth is much improved. Marriage has done what no persuasion could. She is settled now, occupied, and far less given to those fancies that once troubled us so. The arrival of our blessed Elinor has completed her joy, and I thank God daily that she is no longer so restless in her mind.*

Elizabeth read the lines twice.

*Much improved. Settled.* The words carried relief rather than joy, gratitude rather than affection—as though what had been feared had at last been contained.

"You are searching for a remedy," she said softly.

Her father was silent for a few seconds, then he sucked in a breath and swallowed. "Can you blame me? What would you do, Lizzy, if you saw your favourite child wasting away, day by day? Would you not turn the world upside down to find an answer?"

She held the letter up to his face. "This is your answer? That marrying me off would... what? Cure me?"

He grimaced. "I believe marriage has served, in the past, as a sort of... mitigation. A shelter. Perhaps not a complete healing in the usual sense, but the only thing that is ever said to have brought any relief."

"And whom would you have me marry? The first man who walked up the steps?"

He looked at her then with something raw beneath the wit. "I would have you live," he said. "And if I thought that could be secured by the attachment of your hand to the nearest agreeable fool, I might be tempted to press the matter. Wickham, after all, seems to like you well enough, and I think it would take very little to tempt him. Why, a mere hundred pounds should suffice."

She met his gaze, understanding blooming painfully clear. "But you do not believe that will serve for me."

"No," he said quietly. "Because I have watched you. And because I have watched *him*."

Her breath caught. "If you mean—"

"I am not blind, Lizzy," he said gently. "Nor am I so foolish as to mistake coincidence for cause. But you were not unwell before *he* came. And you were not untouched by him, whatever either of you may pretend."

She looked away, the room suddenly too narrow for breath. "You mistake me," she said, and the words were careful—too careful. "Mr Darcy is—was—only a neighbour. Less than that—an acquaintance."

"A mere 'neighbour' does not leave a permanent mark on a lady's mind from the first moment," her father replied, still mild. "Nor does an acquaintance alter the weather of a household. That 'shock' you spoke of at the Assembly when you tried to shake hands?

The way you fled Collins at the ball, and the only place I ever saw you looking at ease the whole night was when you were seated beside Darcy? No, my child, I cannot pretend to understand, but my eyes tell me that he is a... a shelter of sorts for you."

She shook her head. "Papa, you cannot mean—"

"I mean only what I saw," he said. "And that is what I went to speak of."

Her eyes came back to him at once. "*Went?*"

"The morning after the Netherfield ball," he said, and his tone changed then, losing its lightness. "When the house was in an uproar, and your mother complained later that she could not find me, I had taken a horse to call at Netherfield before breakfast."

Elizabeth stared. "You never asked me!"

"I had not intended to. It was a private errand, and I was not certain of my footing. I thought to speak to him plainly. To ask what he intended. No more than that."

Her hand tightened on the letter she still held. "And?"

"And he was already gone," Papa said. "Risen early. Left word with Mr Bingley while he was still in his dressing room. Did not even stay to break his fast but was gone with the first light."

"You would have obligated him," she said slowly. "Challenged his honour. Papa, do you not see? You would have nearly forced an offer from a man who would never intend to make one!"

"I would have asked him whether he understood what he had stirred," her father replied. "And whether he meant to stand by it."

Elizabeth's throat worked. "You had no right."

"Perhaps not," he said. "But I am your father, and I have rights that do not require permission."

She placed the letter carefully on top of the others. "Well. What a mercy for him that his rights do not oblige him to answer for yours."

DARCY DID NOT RING for a light. He carried one down himself, the flame sputtering in his hand, his breath still ragged from the dream he could not yet dismiss as such.

The house lay silent around him, wrapped in that peculiar stillness that followed alarm rather than peace. Brutus padded at his heel, close enough that Darcy felt the brush of fur against his calf each time he slowed, each time his steps faltered as though the floor might yet be hot beneath them.

He set the candle down on his desk hard enough to make the flame gutter and immediately reached for another, then another, until the room took on the layered glow of necessity rather than comfort. Books lay open where he had left them. The *Liber de Terris et Finibus* rested among them.

He did not sit.

He moved from shelf to shelf, from desk to cabinet, pulling volumes down without ceremony: old chronicles his father had insisted upon keeping; a battered collection of ballads that were contemporaries or proteges of Harrowe; a Latin tract copied and recopied by monastic hands, its margins crowded with cramped corrections and faint glosses. He opened them all at once, spreading them across the table, the chair, the floor, the window-seat. Brutus settled beside the hearth and watched him with grave attention, head lifted, ears pricked, as though this, too, were a vigil.

Darcy read standing, leaning, crouching—whatever position allowed him to keep moving. The language resisted him at every turn. Words shifted their meanings under his eye; spellings changed from page to page; references assumed knowledge no longer held by anyone living. He translated, then checked himself. He cross-referenced, then doubted. More than once, he snapped a book shut with annoyance, only to open it again a moment later, compelled by something he could not quite articulate.

It was in the *Liber* that he found it—not buried, not emphasised, but placed with the unthinking confidence of a scribe who assumed the phrase would speak for itself.

> *...as it was holden and keped in þe tyme of Bedeverus.*

Darcy gave a short, incredulous laugh.

The sound rang oddly in the room, too loud, too piercing, and Brutus rose, crossing to him and pressing his shoulder against Darcy's knee.

"Preposterous!" Darcy said aloud, though whether to the book, the dog, or himself, he could not have said. "A marginal fancy. A monk's flourish. I expect this entire book, then, must be suspect."

He tossed the *Liber* aside and reached for the Harrowe volume with one hand and flipped pages with the other, still scoffing faintly, as though at a jest that had overreached itself. How could he take any of this hogwash seriously? Bedevere! It was a name for nursery rhymes and French novels. A name poets reached for when they wished to lend gravity to a tale already grown thin with repetition. No serious scholar would ever—

Then he saw it again. And again.

Not the name... not exactly. But enough references to identify the myth. "*The faithful knight.*" "*The last witness.*" "*The one entrusted with the king's sword.*"

Not mythic. Not reverent. Administrative, almost. As though it were not a story being invoked, but a point of reference. A dating. A fact assumed.

And the more pages he read, the more he suddenly saw.

The disbelieving smile did not fade. It simply stopped belonging to his face.

His heart missed a beat—no, more than that. It halted, suspended in a space where breath did not seem required. The room narrowed. The candle flames drew long and thin, stretching toward the ceiling like something straining to escape. He became abruptly aware of his own pulse, loud in his ears, uneven, as though it had forgotten its proper rhythm.

Brutus gave a low sound, not quite a growl, not quite a whine, and Darcy reached down without looking, his fingers burying themselves in the dog's ruff as though to anchor himself to something solid, something present.

The dream seemed to choke his lungs again—not its images, but its certainty. Fire. Her voice. The knowledge of what "binding" himself must have meant.

Darcy closed the ballads and heaved a sigh. "Well, Brutus? What now?"

DARCY DID NOT KNOCK so much as announce himself by the force of his fist.

The servant who answered took in Darcy's coat, unfastened, his cravat imperfectly arranged, the rigid set of his shoulders, and hesitated. "Mr Darcy," he greeted. "My lord is not yet—"

"I must see him," Darcy replied, already past the threshold. "At once."

The servant followed, protesting just enough to preserve the fiction of order, and ushered him into the small study off the eastern hall—the one Lord Matlock used before breakfast, when he wished to read without interruption. Darcy did not sit. He stood where the light fell strongest, the book tucked beneath his arm like an accusation.

Lord Matlock arrived scarcely a minute later, coat half-fastened, hair still unpowdered, surprise plain on his face.

"Darcy?" He took in the scene—the book, the posture, the air that seemed to vibrate around his nephew. "This is... early."

"I would call it rather behindhand."

Matlock blinked, then recovered himself enough to gesture toward the sideboard. "You look as though you have not slept. Tea, at least. Or—" His mouth twitched, not quite a smile. "Something stronger might better suit the morning you appear to be having."

"I will have nothing," Darcy said, and brought the book up between them.

The spine protested as it always did, and Darcy turned straight to the page that had stopped his breath in the small hours. He set his finger beneath the line and held it there, as though anchoring it to the world.

"Did you know," he demanded, "that this volume asserts—quite plainly, and I shall paraphrase a more modern tongue—that land was *kept in the time of Bedevere?*"

Matlock leaned closer despite himself. His brow furrowed, not in alarm, but in concentration. "Yes," he said slowly. "What of it?"

Darcy's hand tightened. "Then you knew it preserved this nonsense. These... ramblings. Arthurian relics dressed up as record. Fairy tales, nursery rhymes, the stuff of gothic nonsense! And yet it has been guarded, recopied, handed down for generations like some sacred trust, as though it contained fact rather than fancy!"

Matlock straightened, his expression shifting—not defensive, not dismissive, but genuinely puzzled. "You did not know?"

Darcy stepped closer, his teeth almost baring in frustration. "Know *what?*"

Matlock did not bristle at the challenge. He regarded Darcy for a long moment instead, as though weighing how much could be said plainly without losing him altogether.

"The Darcys," he began, "were not always Darcys. That name comes later—Norman, as you observe. Land, titles, even surnames have a habit of reshaping themselves to survive conquest." He moved toward the desk, stopped as if to sit, then gestured to the chair opposite for Darcy before taking his own seat.

Darcy frowned, then heaved a sigh and sank into the soft leather.

His uncle settled behind the desk and slowly drew out a mahogany cigar box and a pen knife. "Before that, the family was Brythonic. Border people, pushed north by the Romans. They were Keepers of crossings and margins—men who did not rule so much as *guard* where others passed through."

Darcy's mouth tightened. "You are describing function, not lineage."

"They were the same thing, in those days," Matlock replied mildly. "When the Normans came, the family bent rather than broke. They intermarried, took a name that would endure in court and record. Mine did the same, as you recall. Fitzwilliam—son of William—was not chosen at random. It tethered the old blood to the new order. Mine chose respectability. Yours chose endurance."

Darcy stared at him. "Endurance?"

"Yes." Matlock did not look away. "The Darcys carried the line of Bedevere forward—quietly, imperfectly, but without once letting the male line break. The old Welsh name was shed. The land was retained. The duty endured, even as its meaning diluted."

For a moment, Darcy could not speak. The room felt abruptly smaller, as though some private boundary had been crossed. "Bedevere," he said at last, the word sounding foreign in his mouth. "You are telling me that my name—the history of my blood—rests on a knight who is half legend, half monastery fiction."

Matlock's mouth curved, not quite a smile. "You may call him what you like. He can hardly object now."

"*Bedevere?*" Darcy repeated. "As in, King Arthur's last knight, *the* Sir Bedevere of myth and legend? Oh, surely not, Uncle. I came here for information, not... not ghost stories concocted by some Frenchman with an overactive imagination!"

"Indeed, that is the man, but not the version you are thinking of."

"What other version is there?" Darcy exploded. "King Arthur is a figment. A fairytale invented to sell pamphlets and novels. He never existed! And neither did his knights—that preposterous table—a sword anchored in a stone! It is utter fiction!"

"Some of it. It might truly be argued that Arthur, himself, did not exist as a single man. But Bedevere was recorded before he was romanticised. Witness before he was hero."

Darcy pinched his brow and hissed. His uncle, a respected peer of the realm and a Member of Parliament, *believed* this?

Matlock, however, was carefully trimming a cigar, his eyes on his task as if it might soften his words. "What you know, Darcy—what most people know—comes to us second-hand. Third or fourth-hand, in some cases. Yes, through French verse, through folk embellishment, through centuries of retelling that favoured romance—in the old poetic sense—over fidelity."

"You could not be more correct on that last score," Darcy snorted.

His uncle set aside the first cigar and began on a second, never even looking up at Darcy. "Bedevere was not invented by the poets, only borrowed. He appears in the older Welsh accounts as *Bedwyr*. Said to be one of Arthur's first companions—I rather fancy he was the war chief of a minor tribe—and believed also to be one of the last. A man of... er, *endurance*, if you will. Not fancy."

Darcy gave a short, incredulous breath. "And you expect me to accept that this—" he tapped the book sharply "—is a continuous account across nearly fourteen centuries? That anyone could trace such a thing with confidence?"

Matlock's expression softened into something almost amused. "My dear boy," he said, lowering his knife, "my own ancestors would take some umbrage at that objection. They maintained—quite cheerfully—that they were descended from a fellow named Peredur fab Efrawg."

Darcy narrowed his eyes quizzically.

Matlock chuckled. "The French amended his character somewhat and named him Galahad. Fine name, rolls romantically off the tongue. But I suspect the real man was much as he was portrayed in the *Mabinogion*—less perfect, more human. The kind of man who learns too late and pays for it. And my family believed this story so thoroughly that they ordered their lives around the notion."

Darcy's mouth fell open. "If I thought you were going to keep plying me with nonsense, I would never have come."

Matlock studied him a moment longer, then set the cigar he had been trimming between his fingers and held it out. "You look as though you could use this."

Darcy did not take it. "No."

"As you like." Matlock struck a light, drew once, and rose from his chair. He began to pace—not restlessly, but with the long, measured steps of a man accustomed to thinking on his feet. Smoke followed him in a thin, deliberate line. "You asked why I believe it. The short answer is that belief was never optional. It was taught as fact long before it was understood as theory."

Darcy leaned forward in his chair. "Did my father believe it?"

Matlock stopped. The pause was brief, but it told. "He believed enough," he said at last. "More than he wished to admit. Less than his mother had hoped."

Darcy absorbed that in silence.

Matlock resumed his pacing. "Tell me, did you know that the original un-looked-for arrangement between the families was not you and Anne de Bourgh?"

Darcy looked up sharply. "No." He blinked. "Then who?"

"My sister Catherine was meant for George Darcy. Arrangements made before they ever met."

He sat very still. His father and Lady Catherine? Why, they would have strangled each other on their wedding night! "I did not know that. But I do not see what—"

"It matters," Matlock cut in gently, "because you see, our two families never quite forgot each other." He took another slow draw on the cigar. "For better than a thousand years, they circled. No alliances. No shared estates. But neither line was allowed to run unchecked."

Darcy frowned. "Unchecked?"

"The old belief," Matlock said, "was that one house alone could not bear what had been broken." He stopped pacing and looked directly at Darcy. "Your line carried obligation without instruction. Ours preserved memory without authority. Over generations, each dimmed, diluted—yours into duty without understanding, ours into stories without teeth."

He tapped his cigar before continuing.

"When blood ran only one way for too long, the charge decayed. Not vanished—more like a pistol misfiring." A faint smile. "Lands that prospered and then did not. Ill ladies—like Anne... both Annes, I daresay. Failed heirs—my own son Randall, my heir, appears unable to... Well." He shook his head. "You see the troubles."

Darcy's throat tightened. "And the answer?"

"Reunion," Matlock said simply. "Not for sentiment, but correction. The belief was that what had once been divided—action and witness, vow and memory—must at last coincide in living people, or the thing itself would continue to degrade."

He gestured vaguely, as if at centuries rather than furniture. "Your ancestors acted. Mine remembered. Neither was sufficient alone. And both families understood—long before any of us—that waiting any longer would leave nothing left to restore."

Darcy's fingers tightened on the arm of the chair. "I still do not..." He cut himself off. At this point, what else could he do but listen? "Forgive me. Go on."

Matlock withdrew his cigar to puff a wisp of smoke and admire it. "When it was discovered that both houses had children of marriageable age at the same time, there was talk. Serious talk. Enough that expectations began to form again—the eldest Darcy son for the eldest Fitzwilliam daughter. There was even a settlement drawn up."

"And yet," Darcy said, his voice rasping now, "my father did not marry her."

Matlock's mouth curved, faintly. "No. Because George Darcy fell boots over waistcoat for my sister Anne the moment he set eyes on her. And once that happened, there was never any question of altering the course."

He let the smoke drift a moment between them before adding, quietly, "The union of the families still took place, but love has a way of complicating arrangements made in the name of destiny."

# CHAPTER THIRTY-THREE

ELIZABETH SURFACED SLOWLY, AS though the effort of waking required negotiation. The room tilted when she opened her eyes; the ceiling drifted, then cleared, then drifted again. She closed them at once and lay very still, counting the spaces between her breaths until the motion eased.

She had not slept so much as surrendered to exhaustion. Her mind had skidded all night between half-dreams and wakefulness, her body never quite relinquishing its vigilance. Now, in the thin grey of morning, that vigilance felt like lead in her limbs.

When she tried to sit up, the world lurched. Not pain—at least not the familiar one—but a sudden, sickening sense that her body had lost its agreement with the ground. She pressed a hand to the mattress and waited for the floor to remember where it belonged.

Voices drifted up from below. Outside, surely.

At first, she thought she was imagining them. The house had its own language—fire popping in the grate, boards, the distant murmur of servants beginning their day—and this sounded like that, indistinct and shapeless. But the sound did not fade when she concentrated on it. It gathered instead, threading through the quiet with an urgency that set her nerves on edge.

Men's voices. More than one. Raised—not in argument exactly, but in insistence. A sharper note cut through them, followed by another. The cadence was wrong for the yard, wrong for the house.

Elizabeth swung her legs over the side of the bed despite the protest that rippled through her. The floor felt oddly far away beneath her bare feet. She stood, gripping the bedpost until the spinning slowed enough to risk a step toward the window.

She had just reached the chair when the glass exploded.

The sound came first—a crack like a musket shot—then the rain of shards across the floor. Elizabeth cried out and threw her arms over her face as a stone struck the far wall and dropped, skittering across the boards. Cold air rushed in through the broken pane, sharp and immediate, carrying with it the roar of voices now unmistakably outside.

"Traitor. He's hoarding!"

"We know he's got it. Look at the bins!"

"—children are starving—"

Elizabeth staggered back, her heart hammering so violently she felt it in her throat. She pressed a hand to her mouth, breathing through her nose, the taste of fear metallic on her tongue. Below, the shouting swelled, no longer scattered but unified, as though a single will had found its voice.

She forced herself to the window again, keeping well back from the jagged edges. The yard was in chaos. Men crowded the gates—a few farmers she recognised, most others she did not. Faces red with cold and fury. Someone brandished a stick; another had climbed onto the low wall, shouting down at the rest.

"Bring it out!"

"Sell it fair!"

"You can't keep it while we starve!"

A door slammed somewhere below. She heard her mother's voice—high, alarmed—cut off abruptly. Then her father's, raised for once not in irony but command.

Elizabeth's knees weakened. She gripped the back of the chair, her vision narrowing as though the world were pulling away from its edges. The noise pressed in on her from all sides, each shout landing like a blow. She became acutely aware of her own body—how light it felt, how insubstantial, as though it might simply tip over and be done.

Another stone struck the house, lower this time. She flinched as the impact shuddered through the frame.

She turned from the window, meaning to go to her family, but the floor rolled beneath her again, violently enough that she had to catch the bedpost to remain standing. A wave of vertigo swept through her, blotting out sound and sight alike for a terrifying instant. When it passed, she was left shaking, her breath coming in shallow pulls.

From below came a new sound: the tramp of boots. Ordered. Rhythmic. Someone shouted commands, the ordering of muskets, and the crowd's noise shifted—still angry, but checked, redirected.

Jane was at the door before Elizabeth had time to draw a proper breath.

"Lizzy!" She stopped short at the sight of the broken glass. "Oh—oh my goodness." She rushed across the room to her, careful of the shards, her hands already reaching. "Are you hurt?"

"No," Elizabeth said, though the word wavered. She tried to rise and failed, the floor pitching treacherously beneath her. "Jane—wait—I am very dizzy. I cannot stand."

Jane's face paled, but she did not try to force her to her feet. She slipped an arm behind Elizabeth's shoulders, supporting her where she sat. "Then do not move. Sit quite still. I heard the glass and—"

Lydia burst in behind her, skirts gathered, her face awash with alarm and excitement in equal measure. "Oh! I told you it was the officers—did you see them? There are ever so many—Jane, move, you're blocking the view!"

"Lydia!" Jane cried sharply. "You nearly stepped on Lizzy's hand!"

But Lydia was already at the window, leaning far too close to the jagged frame. "Well, good heavens, Jane, Lizzy is trying to keep Town hours now. What is she doing still abed? She's missing all the fun. Oh, they've formed a line—look! That one with the dark coat is giving orders—oh, and there's Wickham, I am certain it's him, just there—no, wait—yes, it is, I know the way he stands—"

Elizabeth closed her eyes briefly, the rush of Lydia's words making the room sway again. "What is happening?" she demanded. "Why are they here?"

Lydia barely heard her. "Papa's in the yard now—Mr Hill, too, oh goodness—Papa is shouting! Have you ever heard—oh, the officers are lowering their muskets. I do believe they mean to fire! Oh, now they're pushing them back from the gate—"

"Girls! All of you—away from the windows at once!" Mama appeared in the doorway, pale and quaking, her cap askew with her hair unordered beneath it. "I will not have you pressed up like spectacles at a fair! You will all be shot! Come along—back of the house, every one of you. This instant!"

Kitty hovered behind her, wide-eyed. Mary followed more slowly, clutching her book to her chest as though it might serve as protection.

"But Mama!" Lydia protested, craning for one last look. "They're only just—"

"Now, Lydia! You shall be the death of us all, standing at that window!"

Jane did not argue. She bent at once and slipped Elizabeth's arm over her shoulder. "Slowly," she murmured. "Lean on me."

Elizabeth managed to nod. The noise from outside surged in through the broken window—shouts, boots, the sharp bark of command—but Jane's presence anchored her just enough to move. As they turned toward the door, Lydia was still talking, breathless and unstoppable.

"I told you it was exciting—terrifying, yes, but exciting. Kitty, did you see how fine they looked when they marched up to the house? Mama, do you think they'll stay long? Do you think there will be arrests?"

Mama ushered them into the corridor. "Oh, Lydia, I'm sure I don't know, but hurry before another window is broken!"

The door to Elizabeth's room was pulled shut behind them, cutting off the view—and the cold—but not the sense of it. Mary pointed them all, very practically, to the small storage room off the back passage—the one that usually held extra linens and preserves when the house was full. It had no windows, only thick walls and the faint, comforting smell of starch and dried lavender. Someone shut the door. The noise from outside dulled at once, not gone but blunted, like thunder heard through earth.

Mama sank onto a stool as though her legs had been cut from beneath her. "This is insupportable!" she cried. "Absolutely intolerable. To be attacked in one's own home! Mr Bennet will be killed, I know it—killed outright—and then where shall we all be? Turned out! Beggared! What a good thing Mary had caught Mr Collins, or I do not know where we would be. Oh, Mr Bennet, my poor nerves!"

Jane was beside her instantly, drawing her back, murmuring soothing. "Mama, you must sit quite still. You will make yourself ill. Here—close your eyes. Mary, the salts."

Elizabeth was guided down against a crate by Kitty's anxious hands. The floor tilted alarmingly, but she clenched her teeth and waited for it to right itself. She refused to close her eyes.

"What is happening?" she demanded. "No one has told me anything that makes sense."

Kitty was the only one who had both leisure and sense to make an answer. "It—it began early, Lizzy. Before breakfast. How did you not know? Why, it is nearly midday! I would have thought—"

Jane glanced up. "Hush, Kitty. Lizzy, two of the tenants came first, from the lower farms. They said their bins had been broken into overnight. Grain taken, sacks split. Not by wild deer, but by people. Everything taken, they said. It was only a mercy there was no violence, for everyone was asleep. Mr Hill rode off that instant to fetch the militia, and thank Heaven he did, for he had only just returned when two more tenants arrived, and they did carry reports of violence."

"And then more people came," Kitty added quickly, as though afraid the words might escape her if she did not seize them at once. "Strangers, I mean. They were already on the road when the bells began ringing. Some had carts—real carriages, Lizzy, not farm wagons—and some were strangers entirely. No one knew them."

"From London," she said, without quite meaning to speak aloud. "Their stores have run low, and they've heard we had more than we could eat."

Kitty nodded. "Papa thought so, too. He tried to reason with them. He said he would sell if he could, but that the grain was spoiling, that he did not know how much would keep. They would not hear it. Someone even cried that mouldy grain was better than none at all."

"Oh! I wish he would just sell it all and they would go away and leave us!" Mama cried. "That stubborn man. He had better let Colonel Forester handle it, that is what I say."

"Mama, please," Jane said, more firmly now, as Mama began to gasp in earnest. She pressed a cloth gently over her mother's eyes and held the salts beneath her nose. "Breathe slowly. Slowly."

Lydia, who had been pacing the length of the narrow room, stopped short at the sound of heightened shouting from without. She spun to look at her sisters. "What if they set the house on fire?"

No one spoke at first.

Jane glared, making a fierce expression. "Lydia!" she mouthed silently.

"They won't," Kitty said quickly, though her voice wavered. "The militia are here now. Right, Jane?"

"Yes," Jane said, seizing on it. "Colonel Forester will keep matters from becoming violent."

The reassurance had scarcely left Jane's mouth when a sharp crack split the air outside. Not shouting. Not the crash of wood or stone.

A rifle report—clean, sudden, unmistakable.

Elizabeth felt it first as a jolt behind her eyes, a flare of white that made the room lurch. Kitty gave a small, strangled sound. Lydia's hand flew to her mouth, her eyes bright and terrified all at once.

"What was that?" Kitty whispered.

Another voice rose outside—angrier now, too close—and then several at once, overlapping, indistinct.

Mama tore the cloth from her face. "That was a gun," she cried. "I heard it! Oh—oh—he is dead. I know it. I know it! Mr Bennet is dead in the yard, and no one will tell me—"

"Mama," Jane said urgently. "I am sure Papa is—"

But the words came too late. Mama's eyes rolled back. She slumped sideways with a soft, boneless sound, the salts scattering across the floor.

Jane caught her just in time. "Mama? Mama!"

Kitty dropped to her knees, fumbling for the bottle. Lydia stood frozen, staring at the door as though she expected it to burst inward at any moment.

Elizabeth tried to rise.

The floor tilted sharply, and she caught herself against the crate, breath coming shallow and fast. The sound of the shot still rang in her ears, louder now in memory than it had been in truth.

Outside, someone shouted an order. Another voice answered—hoarse, urgent. No one said whether the shot had been meant as a warning or a threat. No one said whether it had found its mark.

Elizabeth pressed her hand flat to the wood beside her and waited, heart hammering, for the next sound to tell them which it had been.

The tray had been pushed aside more than once. A cup stood perilously close to the book's corner, its tea gone dark and still, a skin drawn across the surface. A plate bore the remains of something once warm—now untouched, forgotten—its edge nudged back to make room for another volume opened and closed again.

Matlock shifted it without comment, sliding porcelain and bread aside with the back of his hand until the table cleared just enough to bear the weight of the book between them. He turned another page. The sound was dry—the careful rasp of vellum lifted and set down again.

Darcy leaned forward despite himself, one hand braced against the table's edge as though the surface might tilt if he did not hold it steady.

"This one is a later transcript," Matlock said, indicating the cramped hand crowding the margin. "Copied in the twelfth century from something older. You can see where the scribe was in doubt about the spelling—here, and here. He did not understand the place-names, but he preserved them anyway."

Darcy bent closer. The ink varied from line to line, dark where the quill had bitten too deeply, faint where the hand had faltered. Corrections pressed in from the margins, some careful, some impatient. This was not invention. It was labour.

"And this?" Darcy asked, tapping a different leaf. "The hand is not the same."

"No," Matlock agreed. "That is later still. Fifteenth century, perhaps. Copied from a fragment that had already lost its beginning."

Darcy turned the page himself this time, slower. He traced the line with his eye, then read it again, the words refusing to settle into sense. Names repeated. Places shifted. The same phrase surfaced more than once, always slightly altered, as though no two men had agreed how it ought to be rendered.

"You see," Matlock said, "why it was never a single book. No one trusted one account alone."

Darcy sat back. "I see a great deal of effort," he said. "I see patience. But I also see a fondness for embroidery. One man copies another, and another after him, each persuaded he is clarifying what came before. That is not history. It is accumulation."

Matlock looked up. "And yet accumulation is often all history has to offer."

Darcy huffed a short breath. "You cannot expect me to believe that this"—he gestured at the spread of pages between them— "was preserved for its narrative qualities alone."

"I never claimed as much. Quite the opposite."

"But it does not say *why*, or what we are expected to do about it. Without a reason, it is nothing more than entertainment. Worse, it has become a... a vanity! Nay, a vice, for some. If *I*, as you insist, am the... whatever you call it, the supposed heir of this... nonsense, then I must have something sensible upon which to act!"

"Sensible!" Matlock snorted. "You act as if you are waiting for Bedevere himself to step from the pages and take you by the hand."

"That would be my preference, yes. Nothing in here says what was done," Darcy said. "It only implies some sort of failure. Who or what failed?"

Matlock glanced at him. "That question," he said, "has not been answered to anyone's satisfaction in some centuries."

"Then what are we meant to make of it? That a family—two families—have spent fourteen hundred years copying riddles and calling it duty?"

Matlock's eyes warmed—not with mockery, but with something like recognition. "When you put it so baldly, it does sound a touch absurd."

Darcy gave a short, disbelieving laugh and shook his head. "We cannot even tell where fact ended and legend began. That is assuming there *was* some fact, and not merely the over-indulged pride of some medieval squires. The French accounts have so badly corrupted whatever narrative we do have that one can hardly trace the truth."

Matlock did not contradict him at once. He reached for the book instead and turned another page, slower than before, as though choosing where to place the weight of his answer.

"They *did* alter it," he said at last. "That much is beyond dispute. But you mistake their offense if you think it was invention."

Darcy glanced up. "Then what was it?"

"Preference," Matlock replied. "And it was the Benedictines long before the French. You can hardly charge *them* with romantic delusions. Though, I suspect they might have polished our ancestors' portraits somewhat, leaving less authentic material for later enthusiasts. What they found spare, they adorned. But they did not discard the tale altogether—and that, I suspect, is why anything remains to quarrel over at all. Confess it, would you even know the name Arthur if not for them?"

Darcy frowned. "I have yet to see the value—"

His uncle ignored him, indicating a passage with the tip of his finger. "Later," he said, "the story changes hands. The French wrote for courts, not cloisters. For listeners, not archivists. They made heroes of lovers and conquerors. Bedevere was kept only because he could not be omitted—because someone had to remain at the end."

Darcy crossed his arms. "The sword. Balderdash."

Matlock lifted his shoulders. "That is the story, that he was to throw it in the lake after his king's death. But the legend has it that he hesitated—that he failed, in fact, because he could not relinquish his king. If..." Here, Matlock stopped to chuckle and throw up a hand. "If one can believe any of that at all. Perhaps that is the 'failure' you are meant to set right."

Darcy's eyes scanned the crabbed text cluttering the space between what was once the elegant script of a reverent monk. "That is not clarified here, and nor would I have any notion what that could possibly mean for me. Swords in lakes, goddesses bestowing kingdoms? Why, it is perfect swill!"

Matlock laid his hand flat beside the margin, careful not to touch the ancient ink. "It may be—who knows? This is as near as the record comes. There is no account of what was asked of him. Only that he was there—and that afterward, he was not. There is mention of a Lady, certainly... but not as one would expect in a tale. She is not a creature from Tennyson's imagination. No one knows anything about her—who she is, where she came from. She is simply... bound to the land, though *what* land remains uncertain."

Darcy bent closer, following the line Matlock indicated. The word lay there—spare, unadorned—set into the text as though it required no explanation at all. He read it once. Then again.

"Not a lover," he said, though the word had not been there. "Not a temptress."

"No," Matlock replied. "Nor enchantress, nor sovereign. She is referred to only by function—the woman in whose keeping the place endured. As though her role were assumed, and required no justification."

Darcy's eyes moved back along the line. No praise. No ornament. No attempt to make her intelligible.

"And Bedevere appears only in proximity to her," he said. "Not as her guardian, nor as her lord."

"Precisely. A clear connection, but not defined."

Darcy straightened, the page blurring for an instant as a name rose—unbidden, making the flesh on the back of his neck heat—and was thrust aside as quickly as it came.

"And when he disappears from the record?"

"She does not vanish," Matlock said. "Not immediately. But she becomes more difficult to discover. The references turn oblique. The descriptions move outward—toward the land itself, until one no longer knows whether it is a reference to her ghost or just... rocks."

Darcy nodded once, slowly. "She was not destroyed, but faded. So whatever failed... perhaps was not a single act that could be recorded plainly."

"Or perhaps it was a breach that could be named without embarrassment. It appears that something which had required a knight's presence was no longer protected. The highest sort of disgrace—and, if one chooses to be inventive... possibly why the Darcy name never held a title in later generations?"

Darcy glanced up. "What?"

"They *should* have," Matlock insisted. "The family held all the power and influence necessary to secure royal favour, particularly during the reign of the Tudors. But perhaps echoes of a private humility? An honour relinquished and never reclaimed due to family shame?"

Darcy scoffed. "I fail to see how that has any bearing, since it is nearly eight hundred years since the Normans invaded. How many great families have risen and fallen in that time? I think you seek meaning long since forgot."

Matlock lifted a shoulder. "It was just a notion."

Darcy's gaze returned to the margin, to the quiet finality of the phrase. *Kept in the time of Bedevere.*

"One begins to see," he said slowly, "why later generations preferred a simple, clear moment they could dramatize over all this muddle. How many copies of this are there? Can we even be certain of its authenticity?"

Matlock laced his fingers over his waistcoat and tapped his thumbs together, a habit Darcy remembered from childhood, employed only when his uncle was displeased with himself. "There *are* others," he said. "Later transcripts. Excerpts. A few copies made in the last two centuries, once antiquarian interest took hold. As to this—" He hesitated. "I *believe* this particular copy has been in the family for as long as we have known to keep it. That is all I can say with confidence."

"You are not certain?"

Matlock cleared his throat. "I ought to be."

"Why would you be in doubt?"

"Well, er... when my sister Catherine married Sir Lewis, she believed the book might follow her as a matter of right. Not merely as property, but as inheritance. I had to go to Kent myself, in person, to restore it to the family library where it belonged."

Darcy's hand stilled on the page. "She *took* it? On what grounds?"

"She believed," Matlock said, choosing each word with care, "that the line which mattered, the one through which the families would converge once more, would pass through *her*, as the eldest. That Anne's marriage to your father had altered the course improperly, and that she might yet correct it."

Darcy leaned forward slightly. "By marrying Sir Lewis. Oh, yes, she has some idea about Kent, does she not? Even I have heard that bedtime story—could hardly fail to. So, this is where that comes into the matter."

"Indeed," Matlock grunted. "By her reading, at least, the Lady would arise in Kent."

"Ah. I suppose she thinks that *Anne* is this person? It begins to make sense now, why she thinks Anne and I are destined."

His uncle offered an unhappy scowl as he shifted in his chair until it creaked. "Your father may have thought to protect you, Darcy, but in not revealing any of this to you, he has done you a wretched disservice. Yes, I fear you have judged it rightly. My sister has... expectations of you."

"Oh, yes, she has made them plain enough, but I never understood what that expectation rests upon. What gives her the impression... nay, the certainty, however misguided, that she has wedged her way into the matter and has the right to make such demands?"

"You would know that already if..." His uncle sighed and rubbed his eyes. "Never mind. She married Sir Lewis for his land—his location, more exactly."

Darcy's eyes narrowed. "If my aunt believed Sir Lewis's lands answered to it, then the proof must be here. But I have seen no such proof, and indeed, perhaps evidence to the contrary."

"Evidence to the contrary?" Matlock observed mildly. "That is not the phrase of a man speaking in hypothesis."

Darcy did not answer at once. His gaze had drifted from the page to the window, where the afternoon light lay pale and uncommitted upon the glass.

"I mean only," he said at last, carefully, "that Kent has produced no... disturbance commensurate with the expectation my aunt insists upon."

Matlock's brow lifted. "And elsewhere?"

Darcy's jaw set. He reached for the edge of the table, not for support, but as if to anchor the thought before it ran too far ahead of him.

The names tingled on his tongue—*Elizabeth.* Hertfordshire. The hedgerow still laden with roses, the split in the ground that followed no waterway, the many unexplainable things... but he did not speak it.

Not without knowing what it would cost to say it aloud.

"Surely there are places my aunt has never thought to examine," he replied instead. "And evidences she would not recognise as proof even if they were laid before her."

Matlock studied him now, openly. There was no triumph in his expression, no alarm—only a slow, dawning interest.

"So," he said, after a moment, "you are not disputing the premise."

"No," Darcy said. "Only the conclusion."

"Hmm." Matlock reached for the book again and opened it, turning several leaves with care. "Here is your answer," he said at last, pointing out a passage midway down the page. "And again, farther on."

Darcy bent to read. The place-names were there, rendered in a hand older than the marginal text, their forms faded, their spelling irregular. He traced the line slowly, following where a later correction had been worked into the margin, the ink darker, the script more certain.

"This," Darcy said slowly, "may be read as *Cantium*. The old Roman name for..."

He did not say *Kent* at once. The word sat uneasily beneath his eye, its letters cramped and uneven, the *t* nearly lost where the ink had faded.

Matlock leaned closer. "Or *Cantiacum*," he said. "The hand is inconsistent. One could argue the scribe meant the Roman province entire, rather than the people."

Darcy followed the line to its end, then to the margin, where a later hand had crowded in a correction. "And here," he said, "the name is altered."

"Or corrected," Matlock replied. "That is the difficulty."

Darcy read again, more carefully this time. "'*The hinterlands beyond Catuvellaunorum*,'" he said at last. "Or—no—*Catuvellani*. The second *l* is uncertain, but is not one the land and the other the tribe?"

"It has been read both ways," Matlock said. "Some took it for an error and amended it. Others preserved it, believing the earlier hand knew precisely what it meant."

Darcy leaned back, the book still open in his hands. "If it is the people, then we are speaking of the old tribal territory north of the Thames. Before Londinium mattered. Before the roads made everything tidy."

"Quite," Matlock said. "The country of the Catuvellauni was never a single point on a map. It was a stretch—rolling ground, river crossings, difficult hedged land. The sort of place Rome complained of for refusing to behave."

Darcy's mouth curved faintly. "Verulamium."

"And its surrounds," Matlock agreed. "What we would now call Hertfordshire, with its inconvenient borders. Close enough to the city to be useful. Far enough away to be overlooked."

Darcy nodded slowly. How had he known that county would eventually be named here?

Matlock watched him over the rim of his glass. "A convenient coincidence? You have told me the harvest was—"

"But as you have said," Darcy interrupted, "there is too much confusion in the text to call one lucky season proof of anything."

His uncle nodded. "Just so. It is worth noting that some of the later translators resisted narrowing it to Kent. Kent was convenient. This"—he tapped the page—"was not."

Darcy lowered his gaze to the text again. "And if the passage does mean the place, rather than the people—"

"Then it points not to a county," Matlock finished, "but to a threshold. Land that has changed hands often enough to forget its first allegiance, but not often enough to lose it."

"And so," Darcy said, straightening, "when presented with the difficulty, my aunt chose *Cantium*."

Matlock inclined his head. "It was the word seen most often in certain textual copies."

"And the one that placed authority squarely in her reach."

Matlock did not dispute it. "She believed she was restoring coherence where your mother had subverted it."

"I suppose that explains why she took this with her." Darcy closed the book halfway, his fingers still holding their place. "I can hardly believe she relinquished such proof when you demanded it back."

"Well, as to that…" Matlock paused. Cleared his throat. "She returned *a* volume. It bore the same binding. The same general marks of age."

Darcy frowned. "You speak as if she might have given you a counterfeit."

Matlock's mouth turned downward. "Oh, no, I believe the book is genuine, as copies go. I had no cause to suspect it. But I did not know she had obtained another copy somewhere."

Darcy's eyes widened. "Another complete copy?"

"She claims. I knew nothing of it until after Anne was born, when she let slip that she had obtained a manuscript that she considered to be Anne's birthright. One she believed… truer. But I cannot be certain the one she returned to me was the same our family had kept since before memory. I compared what I knew, of course, but that, I am ashamed to say, was rather minimal."

Darcy looked down at the closed book, at the worn cloth and softened corners. "So even this," he said, "may not be what it claims."

Matlock met his gaze again, his expression grave. "It may be the original. Or it may be a careful hand's correction of something older. I cannot swear to it."

"But Lady Catherine is convinced she has the authority."

"Yes," Matlock said. "And she means to break you on the wheel of your fate, my boy."

# Chapter Thirty-Four

Elizabeth took the stairs slowly, one hand sliding along the banister as though it might tilt away from her if she did not keep contact with it. Her head swam when she reached the last step. She paused, counted a breath, then another, until the floor steadied enough to permit dignity.

The drawing room was nearly overwhelming before she even crossed the threshold—laughter spilling out in a bright, relieved rush, edged with hysteria rather than joy. Mama's voice rode above it, Lydia's beneath, the whole sound a jumble of triumph and nerves.

Elizabeth reached the doorway and had to catch herself there, her fingers closing around the frame until the room stopped spinning long enough for her to enter.

Mr Wickham stood near the hearth, one red-sleeved arm resting easily against the mantel, his posture relaxed in the manner of a man who had already been forgiven for everything he might ever do. Mr Denny also stood nearby, flushed and pleased, accepting Mama's effusive praise with a grin that suggested he would dine out on this story for years.

"Oh, there she is!" Mama cried, catching sight of Elizabeth. "My dear, my brave girl, you must come and thank Mr Wickham properly. Such presence of mind! Such gallantry! Why, if he had not been there—"

"If I had not been there," Wickham said modestly, turning toward Elizabeth, "Mr Hill would have been hard-pressed indeed, but no doubt would have managed well enough on his own."

His smile softened when it found her, as though the room had arranged itself expressly for that moment.

"Mr Wickham," she said, stopping at a polite distance—where she could discreetly rest her hand on the back of the sofa for support. The effort of keeping her voice even cost more than she liked. "My father tells me you acted with great courage today. I am very glad of it."

"I should say so," Lydia burst in. "He fired without hesitation! Mrs Hill told us all about it. Kitty, tell her!"

Kitty nodded vigorously. "Someone was trying to knock down Mr Hill, even as he barred the door to the house! Think of it, Lizzy—why, I daresay Mr Hill meant to save our lives, and Mr Wickham saved Mr Hill's. He did not even flinch!"

Wickham inclined his head, accepting the praise with perfect modesty. "There was little time for flinching."

Elizabeth studied him as he spoke. His coat was brushed, his boots clean again, the chaos of the afternoon already smoothed away. Only a faint scorch along one sleeve hinted that anything at all had gone amiss.

"Mr Hill... he is well? And I trust that you were not injured, Mr Wickham?" she asked.

"No more than my pride would allow," he said lightly. "Your Mr Hill is, at present, supping in the kitchen, quite sound. And even the fellow who was struck will live, so I am told. A shoulder wound. Painful, but not mortal."

Mama clasped her hands. "Providential! Entirely providential. And to think—such restraint! Such mercy!"

Elizabeth nodded, though the word mercy echoed oddly in her mind. She had not seen the shot, only felt its sound tear through her. She wondered—briefly, unwisely—how near Mr Hill had been, how narrow the margin.

Mr Denny cleared his throat. "Colonel Forster thought it best we remain the night," he said, clearly pleased with the importance of it. "Or perhaps another day or two, if necessary, until matters settle fully. I understand he has sent Saunders and Carter to Netherfield to perform the same office, and you may be assured that he has similarly remembered the rest of your neighbours."

"Yes, yes," Mama said. "How very good of the colonel! We are quite honored."

Elizabeth's gaze flicked to her father, seated apart near the window. He watched the room with the distant focus of a man counting costs rather than blessings. When their eyes met, his expression softened—but he did not smile.

"You are very kind to stay," Elizabeth said, returning her attention to Wickham. "It eases my mind to know my family is guarded."

He looked at her closely then, as though measuring something beneath the words. "That is good," he said. "Peace of mind is not to be undervalued."

Elizabeth tried to smile. The effort arrived late.

The room had begun to tilt, not violently, but enough that the edges no longer agreed with one another. Candlelight pulled apart into overlapping halos; voices lost their owners and drifted free of faces. She shifted her weight to correct it, and found the floor unhelpfully distant.

Her hand went back to the back of the sofa again. She did not remember letting go of it.

"Lizzy?" Jane's voice threaded through the noise, faintly sharpened.

Elizabeth opened her mouth to answer and discovered that the words required more breath than she possessed.

That was when Papa rose.

It was not abrupt. It was not urgent. He merely set his glass aside and stood, as though an idea had occurred to him that could not wait.

"My dear," he said mildly, crossing to her side, "I wonder if you might spare me a few moments before you retire. I fear I was, after all, obliged to sell off some grain today just to appease our visitors. The figures have been giving my eyes quite enough trouble for one day, and I should value a second opinion, while I can still tell a seven from a one."

Mama's head snapped round. "Really, Mr Bennet, you will turn the girl into a steward yet. Or a clerk! Must she always be dragged off to reckon columns when there are heroes to be thanked?"

"I assure you," he replied, already offering Elizabeth his arm, "she has a natural aptitude for both sympathy and sums. A rare combination. I should be a fool not to exploit it."

Elizabeth let him take her weight. The movement of the room eased at once—not because it had stopped spinning, but because she no longer had to manage it alone.

They reached the hall. The door closed behind them, muffling the laughter into something distant and survivable.

"Well?" her father asked softly, bending his head toward hers as though inspecting a confidence. "Are you quite recovered? Or merely too stubborn to stay in bed where you belong?"

The answer wavered. "I am..." The sentence failed to complete itself. The floor lurched, nearer now.

His hand tightened on her arm, and he leaned closer, his mouth near her ear. "Say the word," he murmured, "and I will have you married before the candles burn down. I believe there is a gentleman in that room who would leap at the chance."

She shook her head. "No. Please. Papa, just... take me upstairs."

"Of course, my dear," he said, as though she had asked for nothing more taxing than a book. He turned her gently toward the stairs, and Elizabeth let the world narrow to the steady fact of his arm beneath her hand.

And that was the last thing she knew before the world spun once, then went dark.

THE CLOCK ON THE mantel marked the quarter hour with maddening precision.

Darcy crossed the length of the room, turned, crossed it again. The papers he had taken up lay abandoned where he had set them down, the fire burning lower than he would typically countenance, but he had not permitted any disturbance to his ruminations. He adjusted the grate once, then again, though the heat in the room was already mostly gone.

Foolishness. Idle nerves. The natural consequence of too much talk and too little certainty.

The thought held for several steps—no more.

*The Lady.*

The image—the very framing of the words and the answering call on himself—rose before his eyes without invitation, and his body shuddered recognition before his mind could intercede. Heat gathered beneath his collar, then broke. For an instant, the room wavered, overlaid with the memory of flame where no flame burned: light too bright, air too thin, a sense of loss so complete it left no room for sound. He halted, one hand braced against the back of a chair until the vision loosened its grip.

Enough!

He moved again, deliberately this time, counting his steps as he went. The dream was nothing. A trick of exhaustion.

Elizabeth's face intruded without warning, clear as if she stood before him—eyes intent, mouth set with that particular resolve she wore when she refused to yield ground. The memory dragged after it another, more recent and far less abstract: Bingley's hand, unsteady on the page; the careful phrasing that had failed to disguise urgency.

*She collapsed again.*

Darcy stopped short.

The house felt suddenly slanted. The walls pressed closer than they had a moment before, the familiar order of the room offering no purchase at all. Hertfordshire lay at a remove he could not cross. Whatever was happening there—whatever strain had brought her down once more—was unfolding beyond his reach, and he was left pacing a well-appointed prison with nothing but conjecture for company.

He turned sharply, seized his coat from the stand, and shrugged into it with unnecessary force. The air beyond his door, cold and unaccommodating, promised at least movement.

That would do.

Darcy took up his hat and went out.

DARCY ENTERED THE CLUB with the expectation of order.

The hall was warm, the lamps already lit against the early dark. A servant relieved him of his coat without remark, and another stepped forward to take his hat. The familiar exchange comforted him for a moment—the small, expected acknowledgments of place and belonging.

"Good evening, sir."

"Good evening." He paused, glancing past the steward toward the reading room. "Has Mr Harcourt arrived?"

The man consulted his memory rather than any ledger. "Not yet, sir. We had word he was delayed in Norfolk."

Norfolk, then. Darcy nodded once. Harcourt would have had opinions on the weather there—on the flooding reported along the lower fields, the late frosts. A sensible conversation, the like of which he sorely needed.

"And Mr Denham?"

The steward hesitated. "Returned to Yorkshire, sir. Some emergency for which his tenants required his attention."

Indeed? Darcy's gaze shifted to the card room, where only one table had been laid. "Captain Ellis?"

"Still in Sussex, I believe. He married last month."

"Yes, I was aware. I had heard he and his bride expected... well." Darcy shook his head and let that die. Ellis would have talked of nothing but horses and household arrangements, and Darcy would have let him. There was comfort in such particulars. He had not known how much until now.

The steward lingered, as though expecting another name. Darcy supplied it. "Sir Robert Crosby?"

"Remains in Manchester, sir. Business troubles."

Darcy inclined his head and dismissed him. The room beyond lay quieter than it ought to have been, chairs neatly arranged, fires banked rather than blazing. A few gentlemen sat scattered along the walls, absorbed in their own concerns, not one of them a face he would have sought.

He crossed to the dining room, then stopped short. Only one table had been prepared. No scent of food rose to meet him, no low murmur of anticipation. A servant stood idle near the sideboard, hands folded.

"Is dinner delayed?" Darcy asked.

"No, sir," came the reply. "There have been fewer reservations this evening."

Darcy turned away before the explanation could gather shape. He had no appetite for conjecture dressed as reassurance. Instead, he made for the far corridor, where the fencing salle adjoined the club by long-standing arrangement.

The door stood open. Inside, the racks were orderly, foils polished and waiting. But the room itself felt hollowed out. No voices echoed off the walls, no staccato footfalls marked the hour. A single lamp burned, its light falling across a floor unmarred by recent use.

A familiar figure emerged from the adjoining room, sleeves rolled, hands chalked. "Mr Darcy," the master said, with evident surprise. "I had not expected—"

"Nor had I, Monsieur Armand," Darcy replied, his gaze sweeping the empty space. "Is instruction concluded for the day? A little early, is it not?"

The man gave a rueful smile. "Concluded for most days, of late. Gentlemen have been otherwise engaged. Travel delayed. Matters at home."

Darcy removed his gloves, folded them once, then again. "I am sorry to hear that. Very sorry, indeed, for I had come anticipating some company."

Monsieur Armand hesitated. "If you wish it, sir, I could oblige you with a private lesson. It would be irregular, but you find me at odd ends."

Darcy did not hesitate. "That will do."

He set his gloves aside and stepped forward, the decision made not because it promised relief, but because stillness no longer could.

DARCY TOOK THE FOIL Monsieur Armand offered him and weighed it once in his hand.

The balance was familiar. Reassuring. He adjusted his grip, tested the flex with a short, controlled movement, then stepped onto the piste as though he had never left it.

They saluted.

"Begin with footwork," the master said.

Darcy did. Advance, retreat, recover. Again. The rhythm settled into him at once. His legs burned where they should. His shoulders loosened. Sweat gathered at his temples, honest and earned. When the master corrected him—two fingers to the elbow, a brief shake of the head—Darcy adjusted without thought.

Good.

They moved into simple engagements. Parry. Riposte. Reset. The foil rang against its mate, the sound sharp in the empty room. Darcy pressed, then yielded, his body remembering its lessons with gratifying obedience.

"Again," Monsieur Armand said.

Darcy lunged. Clean. Too clean. He recovered a fraction too fast and found himself guarding against nothing at all.

The master lowered his blade. "Do not hurry the return."

Darcy inclined his head and set himself again. He advanced more slowly this time, judging the distance with care. The next exchange was brutal. Steel met steel, the familiar jolt running up his arm. Precisely what his body craved just now.

Another pass. Then another.

Heat gathered beneath his collar. Then sweat. He wiped his brow with the back of his wrist and resumed his stance.

"Once more."

Darcy obeyed. The exchange quickened. Parry followed parry without pause, the master pressing him faster than before, narrowing the space between them until there was no room for thought at all. Only reaction.

Darcy met each engagement cleanly, but the effort cost him more than it should have. His arm burned. His footing shortened. He pressed to compensate, forcing the distance rather than reading it.

Steel rang again, sharper this time. Darcy recovered too quickly, already guarding against the next attack before it had formed.

That was when the room darkened—not fully, but enough that the line of the blade wavered before his eyes. Lamplight flared too bright along the steel, then was swallowed in shadow. Heat rushed where none belonged, and the air seemed too thick for his blade. His arm moved to counter a strike that did not come.

Steel met nothing.

"Mr Darcy?"

Darcy shook himself. No more of this madness! "Again," he said, before Monsieur Armand could speak.

They resumed. The master altered the pattern—narrowed the advance, restrained the reach—drawing the exercise inward until it demanded attention without offering release. Darcy complied at once. He always had. His body answered instruction even when his thoughts would not.

At first, the correction brought him round to his old routines. The familiar measures returned: the clean press of the floor beneath his foot, the expected resistance of steel, the sequence of movements he had rehearsed often enough to trust without question. This was what he had come for. This was what he understood.

But the exertion did not gather him as it should have. Instead, it dispersed him. The rhythm he sought refused to settle, each exchange requiring more effort than the last, as though the discipline itself were slipping just beyond his reach. He found himself counting where he never had before—pace, distance, recovery—forcing order where it ought to have arisen of its own accord.

He drove into the next exchange and waited—waited—for the familiar yielding, the moment when strain tipped into command. It did not come.

He pressed again at once, too hard, breaking distance to force what should have answered him without demand.

His focus wavered at the edge of the next engagement, not enough to halt him, but enough to spoil the instinct that ordinarily guided his hand. He corrected, then corrected again, pressing forward to compensate, seeking firmness in momentum where patience would once have sufficed.

And then—without warning, without sense—*her* face was there.

Not as memory, not as image recalled, but as presence: intent, unyielding, fixed upon him with that unmistakable look of challenge she reserved for moments when she would not be moved. It came not gently, nor did it recede when he willed it to. It stood between him and the line of the blade, intolerable in its clarity.

Darcy broke distance abruptly. His foot slid where it should have held.

The master withdrew at once. "You are overreaching."

Darcy drew himself back into position with visible care, each movement deliberate, contained. "Continue."

They did. The pattern sharpened, the exchanges quickened, but Darcy no longer trusted the interval between them. He drove forward when he ought to have waited, his grip tightening until the hilt pressed hard into his palm. The discomfort grounded him. He welcomed it, leaning into the certainty of strain, as though pain honestly earned might drown out what discipline could not. Still, the pressure in his chest did not ease.

"Again," he said.

Monsieur Armand hesitated, then obliged.

Darcy lunged too soon. The master's blade slid past his guard with a neat, economical movement that would have scored him cleanly. Darcy felt it even as he twisted aside, a jolt of something like shock passing through him—disproportionate, unwelcome.

He stepped back, breath uneven now, the world narrowing to the strip of floor before him.

"That will suffice," the master said quietly.

Darcy lowered his blade but did not release it at once. Sweat ran down his spine, chilled already where the air touched it. His legs trembled—not with fatigue alone, but with something unspent.

At last, he set the foil aside.

The room offered him nothing in return. No order restored. No clarity earned. Only the knowledge that motion had failed him—and that whatever waited beyond it would not be met by discipline alone.

# Chapter Thirty-Five

She surfaced slowly, as though from a great depth, the return to herself marked first by sound and then by light. Mr Jones's voice murmured near her ear, and something cool touched her brow. She opened her eyes to the familiar ceiling of the library and, beyond it, the tall shelves that had always seemed to her a kind of quiet protection.

She slid her eyes from one side to the other, trying to make sense of the room's new aspect. The desk was gone. She was reclining where it should have been, in a narrow bed moved from Heaven knew where, but with her own coverlet smoothed over her lap.

Her father's chair sat close by, angled as though he had scarcely left it. A small escritoire had been drawn up near the window, its surface cleared except for a single candle and a glass of water.

Mr Jones straightened as he noticed her attention sharpen. "Ah. Awake now, are we?" He peered at her with mild satisfaction, as though this were the best outcome he had allowed himself to hope for. "Do not be alarmed, Miss Elizabeth. You fainted again, nothing more. Your pulse is—well, not robust, but serviceable."

Elizabeth swallowed. "How long—?"

"Long enough to frighten your family," he said, with a wry glance toward the door. "But not so long as to justify my staying further. You are to rest. Quietly. And you are not to exert yourself. I think this little arrangement here, where you need not manage the stairs, and your family may all be close to hand, is the very thing."

She did not argue. She was too aware of how little strength she had to spare.

Her father murmured something at the threshold, and Mr Jones gathered his things, promising to return if summoned. When the door closed behind him, the room seemed to exhale.

A moment later, it opened again. Jane slipped inside and came at once to her side. "Oh, Lizzy," she said softly. "You gave us such a fright."

Elizabeth managed a small smile. "I seem to have made a habit of that."

"Do not jest," Jane said, though she smiled too. "Mama has scarcely sat down since. And..." She hesitated, then added, "Mr Wickham has been asking after you repeatedly."

Elizabeth's brows lifted faintly. "Has he?"

Jane nodded, her look gently knowing. "It is only natural. Everyone has thought for some time that he favours you. A feeling, I think, that might be... mutual?"

Elizabeth let her head sink back against the pillow. She closed her eyes, obliging herself to picture him as she had known him best—smiling, animated, leaning close as they danced at Netherfield. The image would not hold. It slipped away, uncooperative, and in its place rose another: darker eyes, a stiller expression, a hand closing over hers with that inexplicable, shocking certainty.

Her stomach eased.

She drew a careful breath and opened her eyes again.

Jane brightened. "There you are. Why, Lizzy, does your head feel better? That was rather a sudden return of colour to your cheeks."

"I think," Elizabeth said slowly, testing the truth of it, "that I might sit up."

Jane reached for her instinctively, but Elizabeth waved her back and gathered herself with deliberate care. The dizziness lingered, but the nausea had retreated, as though it had been listening for something and had been satisfied.

"You look rather in need of refreshment. I shall go and call for some tea," Jane said, already halfway to the door. "You have had nothing since yesterday, and Mr Jones was quite firm on that point."

Elizabeth nodded and let her go.

Her father remained where he was, seated in the chair near her bed, his hands folded, his attention fixed not on her face but somewhere just beyond it, as though listening for something he did not entirely expect to hear. He said nothing.

Elizabeth closed her eyes.

The room darkened behind her lids, and for a moment she drifted—neither asleep nor fully awake—until a sharp, unmistakable sound cut through it.

A bark.

Not the yapping of a small dog, nor the distant echo of something outdoors, but a deep, resonant sound that seemed to belong very near, very present.

Elizabeth's eyes flew open. "Did you hear that?"

Her father looked up at once. "Hear what?"

"The dog. A large one. The sort of bark a dog makes when he is guarding something."

He listened, his head tipped slightly. Then he shook it. "There is no dog anywhere near the house, Lizzy. Although with recent events, I might take it into consideration." He lifted his book. "Perhaps Mr Bingley knows where I may find a litter of mastiffs nearby."

She frowned. Was she hearing things now? But before she could reply, Jane appeared in the doorway, a tray balanced carefully in her hands. A teapot steamed faintly; a cup rattled softly against its saucer. She hesitated, then asked, "Lizzy, do you think you might bear a visitor?"

Elizabeth had barely time to wonder who it might be before Mr Wickham stepped in behind her, reaching to help catch the tray. He relieved Jane of it at once and set it down upon the escritoire, arranging the cup and plate with a care that suggested both concern and good breeding.

"I hope you will forgive the intrusion," he said, turning to Elizabeth. His voice was low, considerate. "I heard you were awake and could not resist asking after you myself. Are you improved?"

Elizabeth smiled, genuinely this time. "Somewhat," she said, surprised to find it true. "Though I must protest at all this fuss. Really, a special bed set up just for me in the library? I would have begged for such an indulgence as a child, and now I find myself feeling a bit more conspicuous than I should like."

Wickham laughed. "There, making jokes already. I told you she would be well, Mr Bennet. All she wanted was a bit of a respite after so much excitement."

A chair was drawn up for him; another for Jane beside him. "You must not think this her usual state, Mr Wickham," Jane said with a warm smile. "Elizabeth is ordinarily the strongest among us—always walking, climbing, laughing at weather that sends the rest of us indoors. It is quite unlike her to be laid low, particularly for so long."

Wickham's brows drew together at once, his expression assuming a look of injured reason. "Then something must have occasioned it," he said. "Such a change does not come without cause. It seems unjust, somehow, that Miss Elizabeth should suffer so without explanation. How long has this gone on?"

Elizabeth shifted slightly, heat rising into her cheeks. "I am sure it is nothing one can—"

"How can you say that, Lizzy?" Jane interrupted her. "We were all so frightened for her when she was Netherfield. You must have heard of it—when she was found insensate by Mr Darcy and Mr Bingley, and obliged to remain there more than a week. We thought it only fatigue at the time, but perhaps that was when it began."

Elizabeth opened her mouth again, but Jane had already carried on, her thoughts moving quickly now that they were engaged. "And before that—oh!—the thorn. Do you remember, Lizzy? It festered so dreadfully. Nearly a month it troubled you. Perhaps there is something lingering still—some corruption in the blood? Surely you have mentioned that to Mr Jones."

Elizabeth laughed despite herself. "Jane, you make me sound as though I have been poisoned."

Mr Wickham smiled at her, sympathetic and amused. "A thorn that lingers a month is no trifling matter. I should have been quite alarmed."

"And then there was the Assembly," Jane continued. "You gave such a start that evening for no apparent reason. I thought at first you had been struck. Very unlike you, Lizzy."

"Jane, you make too much of it," Elizabeth said lightly. "I merely surprised myself."

Jane frowned. "It was most peculiar. And you have complained of odd pains and headaches since—surely it cannot be rheumatism at your age?"

Papa leaned forward in his chair, his hands clasped, his eyes intent upon Elizabeth's face. He did not speak.

Elizabeth felt their attention keenly now and raised her cup as though it might serve as a shield. "Nonsense! If we are listing my supposed ailments, we may as well include my tendency to trip over nothing and my deplorable habit of forgetting my gloves."

Wickham laughed. "Still, you must allow that a moment of surprise or intrigue at an Assembly is rather more romantic than most mishaps."

Elizabeth waved a hand. "It was only a spark. No more than one gets from dragging one's feet across a carpet on a dry day."

"A spark?" Wickham echoed. "From what, may I ask?"

She hesitated—only a fraction—but it was enough. Papa's eyes narrowed.

Elizabeth sighed, resigned. "From shaking hands with Mr Darcy," she said with forced casualness. "Nothing more than that."

Wickham's smile faded. He leaned back in his chair slightly, as though weighing that statement—not for scandal, but for sense. When he did speak, his tone was easy, almost relieved.

"Ah," he said quietly. "That does explain a great deal."

Elizabeth tilted her head in curiosity. "How does that explain anything?"

"Oh, not illness—at least, not in the ordinary way." He glanced between Jane and her father, inviting their attention without demanding it. "I have known men whose mere presence seemed to destabilise an entire room, and others who, through no fault of their own, you understand, did the same to a person. Darcy is one such man, you know. It is not always intentional. Some people carry… a sort of burden with them."

Jane frowned slightly. "A burden? What could possibly—?"

"Expectation, if you prefer," Wickham amended smoothly. "Or authority. Or simply a manner that intrudes upon those more sensitive than themselves." His eyes returned to Elizabeth, kind and observant. "Miss Elizabeth strikes me as particularly alive to her surroundings."

Elizabeth let out a small, uncertain laugh. "You make me sound fragile."

"Not at all." Wickham shook his head at once. "I should say the opposite. Those who feel keenly are often the strongest, until they are forced to bear more than is properly theirs."

Papa uncrossed his knees and shifted forward in interest. "And you believe this… burden you speak of… might manifest physically?"

Wickham inclined his head. "How could it not do so? Headaches. Weakness. A sense of being overwhelmed without any clear cause. Especially when one is young, or conscientious, or unwilling to disregard the comfort of others."

Elizabeth felt something unspool in her chest at that. Not relief exactly, but recognition.

Jane reached for her hand. "Then you do not think it dangerous?"

"I think it would be dangerous to dismiss it," Wickham replied gently. "But I do not think Miss Elizabeth is in peril from her own constitution. Quite the contrary. She has likely been exerting herself—emotionally, perhaps—without realizing the cost."

Elizabeth lowered her eyes. "I did not feel exerted."

"Few do," Wickham said softly. "Until the body insists on being heard."

Papa cleared his throat. "You speak with a great deal of confidence, sir."

Wickham smiled, modest and composed. "Only with concern. I would never presume to instruct where I have no right. But if Miss Elizabeth should wish to talk further—about anything that troubles her—I should be honoured to listen."

Jane looked visibly comforted.

"That is very kind of you," Elizabeth said. "I do find your conversation rather more soothing than overbearing. In fact… why, yes, Jane—Papa, my head is quite clear. You see? I expect I shall be quite well by supper."

Wickham bowed his head slightly, as though accepting nothing more than common courtesy. "Then I hope you will permit me to speak with you again. Not as an officer, nor as a hero of unfortunate necessity—but as a friend of this house."

Papa's gaze found Elizabeth, and he pursed his lips in thought. "You will be welcome, sir."

Wickham rose a moment later, taking his leave with careful respect. As the door closed behind him, Elizabeth leaned back against the cushions. How lovely, at last, to be in the company of a friend who seemed to understand.

THE STABLE YARD LAY half-buried beneath last night's fresh fall, the snow unbroken except where Darcy's boots cut through it. The air bit hard and clean, stinging his face as he crossed to the nearest stall and slid the bolt back himself.

The groom looked up in visible surprise. Darcy did not pause to explain.

He took the tack down with stiff fingers and worked quickly, buckling and tightening with more haste than care, as though delay itself were intolerable. The horse shifted beneath his hands, unsettled by the cold and by the unfamiliar urgency of its master. Darcy mounted without assistance and turned out through the gates before the stable had fully woken, the iron shoes slipping just a little where the ground had frozen unevenly beneath the snow.

The ride was sharp and punishing. The wind cut through his coat, worked its way into his gloves, burned at his eyes until they watered. He welcomed the pain. The cold gave him something immediate to answer—pressure that yielded when met, resistance that made sense. He urged the horse harder than the footing warranted, then pulled him back again. He would not injure his horse just for his own restlessness.

By the time he returned, his limbs ached, and his hands had gone numb, the cold biting deep enough to leave his fingers clumsy on the reins. The exertion had stripped the edge from nothing. It had driven nothing out. Whatever waited for him in stillness had merely withdrawn, patient, certain he would have to stop eventually.

Darcy dismounted and stood for a moment in the yard, one hand still at the horse's neck, the animal's breath rising in steady clouds between them. The morning was thin and colourless, the sort that followed a night too long to be measured properly. He had not slept so much as surrendered to brief intervals of unconsciousness, each broken before permitted it to take shape, each leaving him more alert, more shaken, than before. The house behind him had grown intolerable hours ago. This—cold, motion, resistance—had been the only answer he could think to give it.

It was still too early for the archives. He cast an eye over the London skyline in irritation. He had outridden the dark only to find himself waiting still. Darcy turned toward the house, but not before ordering his carriage to be made ready.

Inside, he refused the ceremony of breakfast. He took an egg from the tray set before him, ignored the rest, and ate it standing, already reaching for his coat while the cook hovered in affronted silence. The plate had scarcely been removed before the carriage was brought round.

The streets were only half-awake when he set out. Doors he knew well stood shut without their usual signals, brass knockers removed or left untended, as though the houses themselves had withdrawn from notice. Shops that should have been opening for the morning showed no sign of life—their windows dark, handbills pasted crookedly against the glass—*Delayed*, *No delivery expected*, *Inconvenience regretted*. Darcy marked each one, his gaze lingering longer than habit required.

The carriage rolled on, turning where he directed, tracing familiar routes that offered no reassurance. London felt as if it were crumbling beneath its surface order, its routines interrupted in small, accumulating ways that made no single explanation sufficient. He shifted in his seat, aware that he was circling rather than traveling, passing time he could not afford to waste.

At last, he leaned forward and rapped once against the roof. "To the archives," he said.

A CLERK ROSE FROM behind the desk as he approached. The man's manner was a part of his job title—civil without warmth, attentive without invitation.

"Your name, sir?"

"Darcy," he said. "Of Pemberley."

The pause that followed was brief but not negligible. The clerk inclined his head and reached for a ledger. "And the nature of your inquiry?"

Darcy had prepared for that. He gave it to him cleanly, without embellishment: early land records, ecclesiastical holdings prior to dissolution, custodial arrangements attached to estates no longer extant. He specified counties. He specified dates.

He did not mention legends.

The clerk listened, pen moving steadily. When Darcy finished, the man looked up again, his expression unchanged but his caution newly engaged.

"You will require a reader's ticket for several of those collections," he said. "If you have not already applied, the forms—"

"I have one," Darcy replied.

"Very good." The clerk nodded once and consulted another book. "Some of what you describe is not held here in any continuous form. Monastic records are... uneven. Many were lost. Others survive only in transcript, and those are often damaged or disputed."

"I am aware."

The clerk hesitated, then closed the ledger. "Even so, sir, such materials are not ordinarily produced without specific cause. May I ask the purpose of your research?"

Darcy met his gaze steadily. "Private."

The answer appeared to satisfy the form, if not the substance. The clerk inclined his head again. "In that case, there will be a delay. Several days, at least. Possibly longer."

"There must be some record more readily available," he insisted. "Charters. Marginalia. Correspondence."

"There are always *references*," the clerk said carefully. "Interpretations as well. Inquiries of this sort tend to generate more commentary than evidence."

"Then I will begin there."

The clerk studied him more openly now, as though determining whether this persistence would prove tiresome or merely inconvenient.

"At present," he said at last, and with little pleasure, "most of the secondary material has already been consulted and may be in some... disarray."

Darcy's fist tightened on his gloves. "By whom?"

The clerk hesitated. "There is a gentleman," he said, his pen pausing mid-stroke. "An antiquarian. He has made a... particular study of these matters. Monastic survivals. Land custodianship. Continuities that—" He cleared his throat. "—fall somewhat outside the usual frameworks."

Darcy did not move. "And?"

"He is not affiliated with this institution," the clerk said at once, as though eager to establish the point. "Nor are his conclusions generally accepted. His access—" the pen tapped once against the ledger— "is granted by authority beyond this office."

"Accepted or not," Darcy said, "he has already examined what I seek."

"Yes," the clerk replied, with a thinness that had not been there before. "Extensively. To the point of inconvenience, in some quarters."

"His name?"

The clerk hesitated again, this time long enough to be unmistakable. "Mr Aldous Harrowe," he said at last, the name shaped with care rather than approval.

Darcy's head lifted at once. "Harrowe?" The name escaped him before he had time to consider it. "*The* Harrowe who compiled the northern ballads? Surely not."

The clerk's expression darkened, as though he had not expected the recognition. "He would have you believe so, sir. A descendant, at least—or so he claims. The family has made a habit of attaching itself to such material. I regret to say, Mr Darcy, that his activities will make collecting the items you seek... difficult."

Darcy said nothing for a moment. His gaze had gone distant, fixed not on the clerk but on something older and far less orderly than the ledgers before him. Ballads. Verses that survived where records failed. Lines scholars dismissed precisely because they endured.

"Where do I find this man?"

The clerk's look darkened. "I assure you, sir, he has nothing of import—"

"His direction, if you please," Darcy insisted.

The clerk frowned. "He keeps rooms off Red Lion Square. You will find him easily enough."

"Thank you."

The clerk made a brief note in the margin, then looked up again, his mouth turning into a scowl he scarcely troubled himself to conceal. "I should add, sir, that Mr Harrowe's methods are not regarded as exemplary. Nor even reputable. He has been known to request materials beyond what his inquiries strictly require, and to leave matters"—the pen paused, then resumed— "in less than ideal order."

Darcy nodded and schooled his features. "I hope nothing has been damaged or lost as a result."

The clerk closed the ledger, then did not quite withdraw it. "Fortunately not, though not without some trouble of verification. Sir, if you intend to pursue those records independently, you may submit a formal application. Certain restricted materials require additional authorization. The review will take time. Sometimes weeks."

"Then I will submit it."

The clerk appeared faintly surprised, as though he had not expected persistence to survive the redirection. He reached for a separate folio and slid it across the desk. "Complete this," he said. "You will be notified."

Darcy took the papers without comment, already unfolding the first sheet. He had no intention of choosing between answers when he could pursue them both.

# Chapter Thirty-Six

The direction the clerk had given him stood in a street that resisted easy classification. Not poor, not respectable—brick worn smooth by use rather than broken by neglect, windows crowded close together as though privacy were an afterthought. Darcy paused once to confirm the number, then knocked.

There was a moment of silence, and Darcy knocked again. This time, the knock was followed by the thump of footsteps, then the door opened a narrow span.

A man filled the gap—broad-shouldered, thick through the chest, his shirtsleeves rolled up despite the cold. His hands were marked by old scars and ingrained dirt, the sort that did not come away entirely. He looked Darcy over without hurry, eyes unblinking, expression incurious.

"Aye?" he said.

"I am here to see Mr Harrowe," Darcy replied.

The man's mouth twitched, though not into anything like a smile. "He ain't seein' no one."

"I believe you misunderstand. I have come from the Royal Library archives."

"Have you," the man said. "That's fine."

"Yes. And I have been given this address on the understanding that Mr Harrowe would be found here."

The man shifted his weight, the door creaking faintly against the jamb. "Well, you've found *me*. An' I'm tellin' you he ain't seein' no one."

Darcy's gaze flicked briefly past him, taking in what little of the interior he could see—books stacked without order along the walls, loose papers everywhere, a chair shoved aside to make room for a table scarred by use rather than age.

"I am not in the habit," Darcy said evenly, "of being dismissed at the threshold."

"Then you're knockin' at the wrong door," the man replied, unperturbed. He stepped back as if to close the door.

Darcy's hand shot out to brace against the wood. "My business is not trivial. I am seeking information pertaining to pre-Conquest custodianship of ecclesiastical lands—specifically those preserved through monastic record and popular tradition."

The man blinked. Once. Slowly.

"Popular tradition," he repeated. "That what they're callin' it now."

Darcy glanced around at the faces in the street. More than one onlooker had slowed at the sight of a well-dressed gentleman knocking at this door. With his luck, the gossip rags would be full of his name tomorrow. He lowered his voice, but was no longer courteous. "I am acquainted with the Harrowe ballads. Or rather, with the scholarly disdain afforded them. I was directed here precisely because I understand Mr Harrowe has examined materials others have chosen to ignore. The ones I currently seek."

The man leaned one shoulder against the doorframe, blocking it entirely now. "You a scholar, then?"

"I am a man who does not have the leisure to wait upon institutional approval," Darcy replied. "And I will not be turned away by a servant who lacks the authority to do so."

The man's brows lifted at that. Just a fraction.

"A servant?"

"I am *certain*," Darcy growled, "that your master will find what I have to say interesting, at least."

For a moment longer, he said nothing. Then he reached up and pushed the door open fully, stepping back just enough to allow Darcy a clear view inside.

"You might want to watch how you say that," he remarked mildly. "Especially to the man you've come to see."

Darcy stared at him. "You—"

"Aldous Harrowe," the man said, extending one large, scarred hand as if this were the most ordinary of introductions. "Compiler of certain archaic poetry. Chronic nuisance to clerks. Occasional dockworker to put bread and ale on the table. An' at present, the only person in this house inclined to decide whether you're worth the trouble."

Darcy accepted the man's hand numbly, still staring. The cockney speech, the hulking form, the gruff ways... could this man possibly have anything of value to tell him?

Harrowe tilted his head, studying Darcy now with open interest. "Well?"

HEAT. TOO MUCH OF it—pressed beneath the skin, caught there, with nowhere to go. Then cold, sharp as pins, racing along her arms, her ribs, her spine. She tried to draw her knees closer, but found they would not answer her. The blankets weighed a great deal. Or perhaps it was only that her limbs had grown distant, untrustworthy.

Water touched her mouth. It tasted wrong. Bitter, thin, with a faint edge of leaves. Tea. She turned her head away, but the cup followed, insistent, brushing her lip again. Someone murmured encouragement, the sound sliding past without settling into sense.

Leather and dust. Books. Still the library, then. Not her room. Her father would not have allowed it. The thought pleased her dimly, then slipped away.

The air shuddered. Or perhaps the floor. She could not be certain which. A noise rose beyond the walls—voices? Shouting?—too many of them, tangled together, swelling and breaking apart again. Her heart answered it without asking her leave, hammering against her ribs until she wondered vaguely whether it might escape altogether.

Cold again. Her teeth struck once, twice, a sound she recognised only because it echoed too sharply in her head. Hands came to her arms, firm, steadying. Her father's, she thought. They had always been warm.

"Elizabeth." Her name, low, close. She tried to open her eyes. Light flared instead, white and unfocused, streaked at the edges. She shut them again at once.

Something brushed her cheek. Cloth. A handkerchief, damp. The pressure lingered too long. She turned her face away and found she could not tell why.

A bark cut through the fog—sudden, sharp, near enough to startle her fully awake for a breath or two. Brutus? The sound carried with it the cold of morning walks, the snap of frost beneath her boots, the solid comfort of a body pressed close at her side. She reached for it without knowing she had done so, her fingers curling weakly into the coverlet.

"Quiet," someone said—not to her. "She is worse again today."

The barking ceased, but the echo of it remained, pacing the edges of her thoughts.

Her mother's voice rose, broke, rose again—words tumbling over one another, all urgency and dread. Jane answered her, soft and uselessly hopeful, as though gentleness alone might persuade the world to behave itself. Elizabeth tried to smile at that and could not remember how.

Another voice joined them then. Smooth. Even. It slid easily into the spaces the others left open, as though it had always belonged there.

"—not a common fever," it was saying. "You see that, sir, do you not?"

Her father replied, but she lost the words midway through the sentence, caught instead on the cadence of the other man's speech. It carried no strain. No fear. Only assurance, laid carefully atop uncertainty like a hand smoothing wrinkled linen.

Elizabeth turned her head, seeking the source of it. The movement cost her more than it ought. The room tilted in response, bookshelves leaning inward, the ceiling pressing lower. She swallowed against a wave of nausea and tasted tea again, though no cup touched her mouth.

The voice came closer.

"It is that burden I told you about," it said gently. "External. Not of her making, but brought upon her, all the same."

Something in her recoiled at that—not violently, not consciously, but with the same instinct that had drawn her hand toward the echo of barking. She tried to speak. Her tongue felt thick, misplaced.

"Papa?" she managed, or thought she did.

A hand closed over hers at once. Her father's. Solid. Real. She clung to it, anchoring herself there while the other voice continued on, patient, persuasive, explaining things she could not follow and did not wish to hear.

The heat surged again, sharper this time, chased immediately by a chill so deep it left her gasping. The library darkened at the edges, sound thinning to a narrow thread she could barely hold.

Somewhere beyond it all, a dog scratched once at the door.

Then even that was gone.

The tea was dark, over-steeped, and smelled faintly of something burnt. Harrowe sloshed it into a chipped cup without apology and shoved it across the table as though this were the natural conclusion to any conversation of consequence.

"Drink," he said. "You look like a man who's been starvin' himself on principle."

Darcy did not touch it.

Harrowe glanced at the untouched cup, then back at Darcy, his expression shifting—not offense, but calculation, as though filing away another inconsistency.

"So," he said at last, lowering himself into the chair opposite. The chair protested, but held. "You're him."

Darcy's jaw tightened. "If you mean to be obscure, I warn you I have no patience left for it."

Harrowe barked a laugh. "No, no. Not obscure. Just… unlikely." He leaned forward, beefy forearms braced on the table, eyes alight now in a way that had nothing to do with class or manners. "I've been lookin' for you near twenty years, sir. An' here you sit, complainin' about my tea."

"I am not—" Darcy stopped, pressed his fingers briefly to the bridge of his nose, then lowered his hand with care. "You have been looking for *what*, precisely?"

Harrowe's gaze did not waver. "The heir."

Darcy's pulse jumped, sharp and immediate, as though struck. He sat back slightly, the chair legs scraping the floor. "Heir to *what*?"

There it was. Bare. Unvarnished. The question that had gnawed at him since Matlock's library, since the book, since the dreams that refused to loosen their grip. His own family had the benefit of tradition, family lineage to point to him and claim he stood to inherit some legacy or other.

But that someone else had identified that thread, discovered a hole, and concluded that there *must* be a man to fill it…

Harrowe studied him for a long moment before answering. Not with the indulgence of a scholar addressing a novice, but with something closer to reverence—tempered, oddly, by relief.

"Christ," he muttered under his breath. "You're as ignorant as a wee lad."

"No one has told me anything that survives examination. Lord… my uncle has produced certain volumes which justify further study, but offer very little in the way of answers."

"And who is your uncle?"

Darcy locked his jaw. Well, what matter if he confessed it? He had uncovered too much of himself already, and it would be the work of a moment for a curious man to discover his relations. "Hugh Fitzwilliam, Lord Matlock."

Harrowe grunted—if it was a sound of surprise, his face did not register it. "You were sayin'?"

Darcy threw one hand in the air. "I was saying that I am buried beneath conjecture and riddles and family pride dressed up as duty. I am told I stand at the centre of a history no one can explain, and I am running out of time to pretend that does not matter."

Harrowe reached for his own cup and drank, grimaced, then drank again. "That'd be the old way," he said. "Keep it tight. Keep it quiet. Guard the thing so fierce they forget why they're guardin' it at all."

"You speak as though you know them."

"I know *of* them," Harrowe replied. "Which ain't the same thing. Which line are you?"

Darcy stiffened, the hair raising on the back of his neck. "I beg your pardon?"

"Well, you must've come from one of the old knights. Bedwyr would be my bet, but there's also Peredur. Not likely to have been Gwalchmei or his younger brother Gwrgi. Bors forsook inheritance for heaven. Certainly not Cei... Nay, it's got to be one of the first two."

Darcy's hand dropped hard on the table. "How did you..."

"Which is it? Bedwyr or Peredur?"

Darcy had to clamp his mouth shut with an audible click before he could answer. "I... Both. So I am told."

Harrowe gasped, like a man beholding the sunrise after an age of darkness. "By thunder... it's happened, then!"

Darcy rubbed his eyes. "If you please, this all still sounds like madness to me."

"Nay, nay!" Harrowe was holding a hand in the air, his eyes scattering about the room as if pulling together the threads of an unravelled tapestry. "Darcy... that's the Bedwyr line. It *must* be—the male line. And the other—Peredur's descendants are now the Fitzwilliam family. Blimey, I was a blind old fool to miss that!"

Darcy laced his hands and tapped his thumbs together impatiently. "Perhaps you would be so good as to enlighten me. *How* did you surmise in a few seconds what was kept secret from me for the whole of my life?"

Harrowe laughed and poured himself more of that tar-like tea. "Simple elimination. Those are the only two lines that utterly vanished from the record."

"Vanished? Something can only vanish if you know where it began. Something that old?" Darcy shook his head. "There are perhaps two civilizations in the entire world who kept family records over a thousand years. The Chinese and the Hebrews, once. Even Rome could not manage it without mythmaking. And you would have me believe two English families achieved it in silence?"

"More than two, Mr Darcy." Harrowe leaned back in his chair and hooked one heavy boot on a nearby stool. "The Benedictines traced at least five lines they believed descended from Arthur's household knights. Two ended as most families do, within a handful of generations. One was butchered entirely when the Normans came through. Names broken, lands seized, records scattered. And Gwrgi—now he's got an interestin' tale. The king's nephew, died in the war, but not before siring a son. You'd know him as Gareth, and James I claimed, rather privately, I might add, to descend from that line."

He tapped the page with a blunt finger. "The other two did not end. They folded in upon themselves. No public annals. No marriages proclaimed for advantage. The blood runs quiet, turns inward, disappears where it ought to have been loud. You don't do that by accident or oversight."

Darcy pinched the bridge of his nose. "And you concluded from this absence that I existed."

"I concluded," Harrowe said slowly, "between the records and what I could see with my own two eyes that *someone* was still carryin' the burden. An' that whoever it was, he'd been raised not to look too close. The signs are too real to ignore now."

Darcy pushed his chair back and rose, unable to remain seated. The room was too small, the walls too crowded with paper and ink, and the very bulk of their master's physique.

"You speak of me as though I were an artifact," he said. "As though my life were an appendix to a story I did not consent to inhabit."

Harrowe watched him pace. "Aye," he said. "That's about it."

Darcy stopped short. "You find that amusing."

"No. I find it *terrifyin'*. Which is why I'm still breathin'. Anyone who treats this lightly's already dead to it."

He gestured, finally, to the cup Darcy had not touched. "Drink your tea, Mr Darcy. It won't fix a damn thing, but it'll keep you upright long enough to hear the rest."

Darcy looked at the cup.

Then, at the man who had spent decades chasing a shadow that bore his name. And against his will—against reason, against pride—he sat back down. The tea was vile.

He swallowed it anyway.

SHE SURFACED THE WAY one surfaces from deep water—without knowing she had been below.

Voices were already there when awareness returned, arranged above her like figures leaning over a well. They overlapped, separated, drew together again. For a moment, she could not place herself among them. The ceiling resolved first. The familiar crack in the plaster. The tall shelves beyond, their shadows no longer shifting.

Jane's voice reached her. "...has not truly woken since before dawn. Sir, I—"

Elizabeth swallowed. Her throat rasped in protest, dry and sore, as though she had been breathing smoke. She tried to turn her head and managed only a fraction of the movement.

"Lizzy?" Jane's hand closed over hers at once. It was cool. Close. Jane had been sitting there a long while.

Elizabeth opened her eyes. The effort sent a pulse of heat through her temples. Faces came into view—Jane, pale and intent; her father standing a little back, his shoulders drawn tight; Mr Bingley near the window, hat still in his hands as though he had forgot to set it down.

"You are awake," Jane said, the words trembling despite her care. "Oh, praise be! Papa is here, and so is Mama. Everything is being seen to."

Elizabeth tried to smile. Her mouth would not cooperate. Instead, she frowned, distracted by the absence of something she had been expecting.

"Where...?" The word scraped its way out. She swallowed and tried again. "Where is the dog?"

The question seemed to move through the room without landing anywhere. They glanced at one another until her father lowered his head and scratched his brow. "She keeps asking about some dog. It was but another dream, Lizzy."

"No." She shook her head insistently. "I heard him outside. Brutus—I know I..."

Jane blinked. "Mr Darcy's wolfhound?" She cast a helpless glance over her shoulder at Mr Bingley, who only shrugged.

"Darcy took his dog back to London with him. I've no idea what she could mean. Does Sir William have a dog that might have wandered?"

Jane shook her head and turned a tight smile back to Elizabeth. "There has been no dog here, dearest. Only Mr Wickham and Mr Denny, still guarding the house."

Elizabeth frowned harder. The library felt wrong without the weight of him at her side. She could have sworn she had but to drop her hand over the edge of the bed and it would find his nose. She searched the edges of the room, confused. "He was—"

Her father stepped closer. "Yes, yes, Mr Wickham is here." He gave a dry chuckle—hollow. "He has scarcely left the library long enough to perform his duties. I shall have to ask the colonel to send me another man."

That did not satisfy her, but the thought slipped away before she could gather it.

A wave of nausea rose instead, sharp and sudden. She closed her eyes and breathed shallowly until it passed.

When she opened them again, the room felt different. Not in shape, but in tone. The voices were quieter now, arranged, as though they had reached some shared understanding while she had been elsewhere.

"Mr Jones?" she asked hoarsely. The name surfaced with effort, dragged up from memory like a dropped object recovered from water. "Has he—"

Jane's grip tightened. "Papa sent for him again, but..." She faltered. "He would not be of use to you now."

Elizabeth frowned. "I do not—"

"What you need," her mother's voice broke in, thin and frantic from somewhere beyond Jane's shoulder, "is air. Fresh air. Anyone can see that. This place is doing you no good at all, and mercy only knows what will happen if Kitty falls ill next. She always did have the most frail health, you know. Oh, and with but a se'nnight before Mary's wedding!"

Elizabeth tried to turn her head toward the sound. The movement failed halfway, leaving her oddly adrift. "No," she murmured, or perhaps only thought it.

Her father spoke next. "Your mother is only saying what several have observed," he said. "You have been here too long, my love. The disturbance, the strain—"

"—the burden," another voice supplied gently.

Elizabeth's eyes slid toward it despite herself.

Mr Wickham stood near the shelves, hands loosely clasped before him, his expression composed in a way that felt wholly out of place beside her own unravelling body. He did not meet her gaze at once. He was speaking to her father.

"There is very little to be learned of her condition, but you must see, sir, that keeping her here is only worsening it. I recall reading of such... peculiar circumstances. You are quite right to suspect this is not of the body but something else. Perhaps Lyme—away from here, and away from any memory of certain persons."

Jane's hand patted Elizabeth's. "Yes," she said quickly. "Yes, that is what I was thinking. Only until she regains her strength."

Elizabeth's fingers curled weakly in the blanket. She shook her head, or meant to. The motion barely registered. "I do not want—" The words dribbled into nothing.

Her father bent closer. "Hush," he said softly. "No one is deciding anything without care."

But his eyes did not meet hers when he said it.

Mr Bingley cleared his throat near the window. "If there is any place that might suit," he ventured, earnest and helpless, "I would of course offer—though I fear Netherfield is scarcely quieter at present, and does not offer much in the way of distance."

"Perhaps her uncle," Mrs Bennet said at once. "Mr Gardiner has always been fond of her. Or the sea! People recover by the sea every day of their lives."

The words tumbled over Elizabeth without meaning. She felt Jane's hand tighten again, felt the faint press of her thumb against her knuckles, as though urging her to be calm, to trust.

"I do not recommend London." This was Mr Wickham's voice again. The air in winter is particularly bad."

"Yes... yes! Then it must be the sea. Why, we shall take her to Bath for the waters. Mr Bennet, it is the very thing!" her mother urged. "Of course, it must be after Mary's wedding."

Elizabeth tried to pull her hand away and could not. Panic fluttered briefly, then dissolved into weakness.

"I do not want to go," she said, or meant to say. The sound came out broken, scarcely more than breath.

Jane leaned closer. "Papa is doing everything he can," she whispered. "Everything."

Elizabeth closed her eyes.

Somewhere beyond the room, boots sounded on gravel. A voice called out, distant, indistinct. The house continued on around her, occupied, guarded, altered.

When she drifted under again, it was with the uneasy sense that she had been left behind in a conversation that would continue without her—and that whatever was decided there would not wait for her consent.

# Chapter Thirty-Seven

"This is the book?"

Darcy inclined his head as he passed the *Liber* into Harrowe's thick hands. "I brought it to the Museum Library today because I hoped to compare it with whatever I might find."

Harrowe's mouth curved—not in amusement, but in something like awe. "I've spent half my life tryin' to prove that book existed," he said quietly. "An' you walk in with it under your arm."

"It has not proved especially obliging," Darcy said. "Nor has my family."

"No," Harrowe agreed. "I wonder if that aunt of yours can be quite sane."

Darcy scoffed and shook his head. "She would have you believe she is the only one who is. And according to my uncle, she has another copy, though potentially bearing certain different wordings in crucial passages."

Harrowe nearly dropped the *Liber*. "She never does! Where did she find that?"

Darcy shook his head. "She would never tell me if I bothered to ask, which I shall not. Look here, what can you tell me about... well, about anything?"

Harrowe scratched his chin. "I'd have to read it. Study it."

"You may *keep* the bloody thing as far as I am concerned, if you are willing to help disseminate its meaning."

Harrowe weighed it in his hands instead, as though its worth were not settled by its age alone. "Easy. Before I go puttin' words in it, you tell me what it's told you first."

Darcy tipped what remained of the cold, bitter tea to his lips while he considered. "That it was not preserved so much for consequence... family pride, that sort of thing," he said at last. "But for continuity. That the record avoids instruction by design—that it names presence without explaining its cost, though it does imply that there *is* a cost."

He paused, his gaze fixed somewhere beyond the table. "And that the failure was not absence," he added. "It was attachment. Something was held when it ought to have been released—and what endured afterward was not meant to."

Harrowe shook his head slowly. "An act not finished. A thing clutched too long."

He turned the *Liber* once in his hands, as though aligning it with something he could not quite see. "But that's only half the fault."

Darcy looked up. "How do you...?"

Harrowe did not look down at the book as he spoke. His gaze had drifted instead to nothing in particular, as though the thought had found him from elsewhere and only now required words.

"There's another sort o' absence turns up in records like this," he said, slow and careful. "Don't always get named. Sometimes not at all. It ain't just what was kept that ought to've been let go—there's what wasn't kept neither." He paused, as if testing the thought against something older than the ink before him.

"Somethin' that should've been kept watch on. A vow, I'd wager. I've seen that silence before. Different records. Different ink. Same piece left out."He closed the *Liber* with care and set it flat upon the table, then pushed back his chair and rose. Crossing the room with a heavy, deliberate tread, he reached for a shelf set higher than the rest. His fingers closed around a slim, time-softened volume bound in faded calf.

"*The Ballads*," he said, bringing it down between them. "My ancestor's work. They laughed him near out o' London for printin' 'em. Said it were country doggerel. Claimed he'd taken rhyme for revelation."

Darcy watched him lay the book open. "I know the verses. I read them as a boy."

Harrowe looked up sharply. "Did you, now?"

"Often," Darcy replied. "Then, I liked the lyrical quality of them. But of late..." He rubbed his eyes. "I regret to say that they haunt my nightmares."

Harrowe grunted. "Then you've read this one." He turned the page with care and tapped a finger against the margin. "Read it again."

Darcy leaned forward despite himself. The lines were familiar—too familiar. He could have spoken them from memory if pressed.

*He stood where water meets with land,*
*And sware no troth unbound;*

*Yet held his hand where first it lay,*
*And so the bound unwound.*

"I have always taken it for lament," Darcy said. "A moralizing flourish."

"Aye. That's what they all thought. Courage or cowardice. Clean miss of it. It ain't about what love broke. It's about what stayed behind—emptied out, and no one there to tend it." His gaze lifted to Darcy at last. "That's why *she* remains. And why he does not."

Darcy swallowed. "You speak of... the Lady. No name. No lineage or duty or any other identity. She just... arises."

"No," Harrowe said. "She's there already. Been waitin', one way or another, all this while. Only she'd no equal to answer her."He bent nearer, thick finger riding the line. "'*No troth unbound*.' That's the fault. He reckoned a man could divide his troth. Keep what was done for and what was still his to keep."

"You are saying—"

"I'm sayin' Bedevere didn't fail for lovin' his king," Harrowe cut in. "He failed 'cause he wouldn't leave him when there were nothin' left to do. Couldn't step off from what was already over. And couldn't give himself over to what came after—not fully."

He paused, then spoke more slowly. "Blame him if you must. But to a knight, sir, the oath to his king weren't one loyalty among many. That was the whole of him. His oath. His purpose. Himself."

The words pierced with a force Darcy felt rather than heard. He drew himself upright, the room narrowing around him, his breath arrested hard in his chest.

Because he had seen it.

Not a dying king this time—but fire, and water, and a boundary that would not yield. The certainty that whatever was asked would not take a portion of him, or a season, or a sacrifice that could be tallied and survived. It would take the whole of him, or it would take nothing at all.

His hand closed at his side, fingers biting into his palm as though to anchor himself to the present. "You are telling me," he said at last, his voice carefully level, "that what was required was not bravery."

"Not as he wanted to shape it," Harrowe said, turning a fragile page in the *Liber* once more. "No man wants to pay that price, I expect."

Darcy bit his lips together. He could scarcely draw air. Damn it all, he had come here for reassurance! Information—a way to survive, see it all, whatever it was, done rationally and decently. But that was not sounding like an option.

"And the Lady?" he choked. "What of her? Does she... come to an end?"

Harrowe's frown pushed out in thought as he followed a line with his finger. When he spoke it sounded not as if he were reading, but postulating from memory of a different passage altogether. "What of her? Aye—what of her." He shook his head. "She ain't promised a thing. 'Cause she ain't the question in it."

Darcy's voice dropped. "Yes, she is. That much I do know. She is at the very centre of it all."

Harrowe straightened and pinned Darcy with a look of incredulity. He lowered the book and cocked his head. "You... you know who she is," he murmured. "You found her."

Darcy turned his gaze to the hearth and did not answer at once. When he did, it was barely above the level of the fire's soft collapse. "Quite by accident, yes. And not in *'Cantium,'* as some might suggest."

"Her name..." Harrowe half rose from his chair, his face alight with the awe of a child. "You know her name? And where she is? Then you must have..."

He broke off, the colour draining from his face as the implication caught up with the wonder.

"Then you've drawn it out," he said. "Not made it—no. But fetched it forward. Took what was meant to stand silent and made it answer afore its proper hour."

He stared at Darcy as though seeing him at last. "If you've stood before her—if she's known you an' you to her—then the keeping couldn't bide as it was. Not after that. You'd have set it on the road to reckonin'."

Darcy closed his eyes and scrubbed his face with his hands. "Toward collapse would be a better word."

Harrowe stared at him, something like disbelief breaking through his habitual reserve. "Then why in God's name are you sittin' here?"

The question tore loose what restraint Darcy had left.

"Because I do not know what I am meant to do!" he snapped. He jerked to his feet, the chair legs clattering behind him. "Every course I can see ends in ruin. When I first came near her, she weakened. Heaven above, *I* weaken! She drains my strength like sap from a tree, but she still collapsed in my arms. Whatever passes between us takes from me and gives nothing back to her!"

He dragged a hand through his hair, breath uneven now.

"Yet when I am absent, the world itself begins to fail. The land turns against its keepers. Markets collapse. Men riot for bread. My cousin is called back to war when he has already paid his due. And my own mind has turned against me! Day and night, I see nightmares, visions of her face... And I have had word that she is weakening still more in my absence!"

He snatched up the *Liber* and made as if to throw it against a wall, but a quick yelp from Harrowe stayed his hand. He clenched his fist around the cover and shook it in Harrowe's face.

"I am told that I must act—and yet no one can tell me how. If I pledge myself blindly, and it destroys her—"

He broke off, shaking, and released the book back to Harrowe's eager hands. "I will not be the man who finishes what Bedevere began."

"You've no choice left in it, sir. You'll either keep to it or you won't. And it's standin' before you even now."

Darcy heaved a sigh. "At the end of it... I am altered beyond retrieval." He turned to stare at Harrowe. "Am I not?"

Harrowe did not contradict him. "That's the fear," he replied. "And it is not an idle one."

Darcy's gaze drifted back to the table, to the *Liber* where it lay open between them. "And there is no other means? There must be a way... some manner in which all can be saved from ruin."

Harrowe drew a heavy breath. "What I know—and it ain't much—is this: once before, a man stood where you're standin'. Loyal past reason. Faithful near to breakin'. And when the hour came that asked the last of him... he wouldn't give it."

Darcy's fingers curled slowly against his palm. "Wouldn't? Or simply made a mistake, chose the wrong path?"

"I can't tell you the particulars. The record don't set down his precise fault." Harrowe kept his finger on the line. "But it sets down what followed. The Lady faded from the keeping. The land went wanting without its guard. And Britain—" His jaw tightened. "Britain was plunged into centuries of darkness."

Darcy sank back into his chair, resting his forearms on his knees and leaning forward to stare into Harrowe's square face. "You cannot mean to imply—"

"Your history books are rot," Harrowe said flatly. "Rome pulls out, Arthur rises, brings a spell o' peace—and when he's gone, so's Britain. That's how they tell it."He gave a short, humourless breath. "'The dark ages,' they say."His mouth twisted. "Dark. They don't know the half of that word."

He rubbed a thumb along the edge of the page. "We scraped through, mind. Raids, wars, pestilence—still we held. The old Britain's here yet."

His gaze shifted toward the window, toward the sprawl of the city beyond. "But this time... with France watchin'. The sea unsettled." His voice lowered. "I ain't certain England would weather it twice."

Darcy searched his face, desperate now for contradiction, for some sign that this was exaggeration, that history had softened the truth. "What must I do?"

Harrowe frowned and gestured to the *Liber*. "Give me a day or two with it," he said. "Might be there's a thread left to pull. Long as you don't go throwin' yourself on a blade before I'm done."

Darcy closed his eyes. The image rushed unbidden—firelight, the sound of water, a presence he could not approach without harm—and he drove it back with a well-worn sort of violence.

At last, Darcy reached for his coat and drew something out of the pocket. "Here is my card. I will instruct my butler that you are to be admitted at any time, day or night."

Harrowe's brows arched as he pinched the card between calloused fingers. "Me? Callin' at the home of a gentleman like a dandy in a powdered wig?"

"You could wear Wellingtons and reek of fish for all I care. You are the one man in all London who would take any of this seriously." Darcy buttoned his coat and took up his hat. "And pray... do not be too long in coming."

THE MOTION CAME FIRST.

Not a jolt, not a fall—only the steady, rocking insistence of it, the sense that the world had narrowed to a small, enclosed rhythm that would not stop. Elizabeth surfaced into it without alarm, aware only that she was no longer lying flat, that the air pressed close on all sides, and that something warm and woollen had been tucked too carefully beneath her chin.

The air itself felt different—cooler, thinner, carrying the faint, uncommitted light of a morning not yet decided. Wheels whispered rather than clattered, as though the road were being crossed before it quite belonged to anyone.

A voice drifted in and out of reach. "...only a few hours—yes, that's it—Lizzy, can you hear me?"

Jane. The sound of her sister's voice did not startle her; it belonged where it was, even if Elizabeth could not quite place why. She meant to answer, but the effort scattered before it reached her mouth, and the motion took her again.

At some point, a hand brushed her temple, smoothing hair back from her face. The touch lingered, light and familiar, and Elizabeth turned toward it without opening her eyes. The leather beneath her cheek creaked faintly. The scent of lavender gave way to something sharper—cold air, perhaps, or the trace of horse-sweat carried in on coats not yet dry.

Jane spoke again, too brightly. "She's warmer," she said to someone else. "I think she's warmer."

Another voice answered—lower, male, careful in its cadence. Mr Bingley? Elizabeth caught his name only because Jane repeated it, as though to check herself. There was reassurance in his tone, though the words themselves slipped past Elizabeth before they could be weighed.

The carriage slowed. Stopped. The sudden stillness squeezed oddly against her, and for a moment the effort of breathing felt deliberate, as though she had forgot how to do it without thinking. Outside, boots struck the ground. A man called out. The door opened, admitting a sharper draft that cut along her throat and made her shiver despite the blankets.

"She has not stirred," a woman said. "She is not dead, is she?"

"She took a deep breath, just now," Jane replied, a touch defensively. "Did you not, Lizzy?"

Elizabeth tried again to answer. Her lips parted. Nothing came. The world tipped, blurred at the edges, and she was carried back under before she could feel the disappointment of it.

Time lost its order.

There was water—no, tea—bitter and too hot at once, the rim of a cup touching her mouth and retreating again. A sound like barking reached her from a great distance, abrupt and insistent, then vanished as though it had never been. She frowned faintly, the effort pulling at her temples, and the sound was gone.

More voices. Jane's, always Jane's. A woman she did not immediately recognise—cooler, brisker, speaking as though the matter were already settled. Miss Bingley, perhaps. Elizabeth did not care enough to be certain.

The carriage moved again.

SHE WOKE ALL AT once.

Not gradually, not by effort, but as if a veil had been drawn aside, letting in the glaring light of day. The motion remained—the familiar rocking of the carriage—but the weight in her head was gone, the pressure behind her eyes eased to nothing. Light resolved into shape. Sound found its proper distance.

Elizabeth pushed herself upright.

Jane gasped. "Lizzy—oh, Lizzy!"

"I am quite awake," Elizabeth said, surprised to find her own voice unshaken. Her throat felt dry, but it obeyed her. She took in the carriage with a single, lucid glance: the facing seats, the narrow window, Miss Bingley opposite her with a hand half-raised in instinctive alarm. Jane's fingers were still clasped tightly around hers.

"Why," Elizabeth asked, after a moment, "am I in a carriage?"

Jane laughed and caught at her sleeve in relief. "Because you were ill, and Papa agreed it would be best—"

"In Mr Bingley's carriage," Elizabeth went on, turning her head slightly as the gentleman in question leaned forward at once. "Which suggests Papa is not here, and I was not consulted."

Mr Bingley smiled, earnest and unmistakably pleased. "You were in no condition to be consulted, I am afraid. But you are improved already—quite improved. Miss Elizabeth, I cannot tell you what a comfort it is to see you sit up so."

Elizabeth looked from one face to the next. Jane's eyes were bright with unshed tears. Miss Bingley's expression had settled into careful interest. "Where are we going?"

"Papa decided on Ramsgate," Jane said. "Only for a little while. Mr Wickham was very clear that a change of air..."

"Would do wonders," Mr Bingley finished cheerfully. "And upon my word, it seems he was right. You look entirely yourself again."

Elizabeth drew in a breath, experimentally. Her chest rose without protest. No dizziness followed. She pressed her fingertips together, half-expecting the familiar weakness to return, and felt only the ordinary stiffness of having lain too long in one position.

"Mr Wickham?" She blinked. "He… he has been a good friend to us, yes?"

"The very kindest," Jane agreed with watery eyes. "And he was quite right, though I've no idea how he understood what ailed you better than a doctor. Papa listened to him, though, and believed that Mr Wickham comprehended something that… well, quite frankly, I do not know how to credit, but it was true, I believe. It is only a pity he had to remain with his regiment, for one wants such a friend at a time like this."

Elizabeth blinked. "And Papa? Where is he?"

"He remains at Longbourn for now," Jane said quickly. "Mary's wedding is too near, and Mama—well." She smiled with effort. "Papa would not hear of you lingering and wasting away waiting for Mary's wedding when you could be helped elsewhere. He was content—well, perhaps 'content' is too strong a word, but he thought it best to trust us to see you safely settled."

Elizabeth leaned back against the cushions, absorbing this. The carriage swayed onward, the light at the window growing thicker, more grey. Outside, the road had begun to fill—more carts, more voices, a distant haze that softened the edges of buildings as they rose ahead.

"It is rather smokier than Hertfordshire," Jane observed, peering out. "Can that possibly be good for you, Lizzy? I had forgot quite how—"

"Nonsense," Mr Bingley said. "London smoke is a trifle compared to the country damp at this time of year. And see how well you bear it." He nodded toward Elizabeth with unmistakable satisfaction. "You have been awake these several minutes, and not a trace of faintness."

Miss Bingley inclined her head. "It is quite remarkable. One is always glad to see such *timely* improvement."

The carriage slowed. Stopped. There was a brief flurry of voices outside, the thud of hooves, the clink of harness. Elizabeth accepted a cup pressed into her hands and drank without difficulty, the tea sharp and warm. Someone offered her bread. She ate it, surprised to find an appetite waiting.

Horses were changed. The door closed again. The carriage rolled forward.

Elizabeth settled back, still alert, still clear. The motion no longer felt oppressive. For the first time in days—weeks—her thoughts lined up obediently, one after another, without slipping away.

At first, Elizabeth thought it was only fatigue returning—an ordinary thing, almost welcome. Then the warmth crept back, swift and unmistakable, flooding her limbs as though she had been wrapped too tightly. Her temples began to throb. Light flared behind her eyes, not painfully at first, but insistently, like fingers testing a bruise.

She closed her eyes.

The carriage lurched slightly as the road changed beneath the wheels. The motion tilted her stomach. She swallowed once, then again, but the effort sent the world sliding sideways. Jane's voice reached her—asking something, softly—but the words would not hold their shapes.

Elizabeth tried to answer. What came out was watered-down and wrong.

Jane stiffened, one hand rising to Elizabeth's wrist. "Mr Bingley?"

Bingley leaned forward, all his cheer falling away. "Miss Elizabeth?"

Elizabeth shook her head, though she could not have said why. The heat surged higher, blotting out the edges of the carriage, the faces before her. She meant to sit upright, to insist she was well enough—but her strength slipped from her grasp like water through cupped hands, and she sank back against the cushions instead.

Jane caught her. Miss Bingley drew back, her mouth tightening, her eyes sharp with something that was not fear. "A rather surprising turn, to be sure."

"She cannot go on," Jane murmured, and her hands trembled. "What can be done?"

Bingley nodded, already turning toward the door. "We are scarcely beyond London. It is as far to return as to press forward to where we meant to stay for the night."

"And London has physicians," Miss Bingley added promptly. "Proper ones. Lodgings, too—why, surely, we do have friends in London at this time of year. It would be foolish to continue on to Ramsgate."

Elizabeth heard this as though through water. The words reached her without urgency, without meaning. She did not protest. She could not have summoned the strength to do so if she wished.

The carriage slowed.

Then, with a long, careful turn, it changed its course.

Elizabeth felt the alteration—not as motion, but as relief breaking too soon, too sharply, like a breath taken after being held too long. She let it carry her, her thoughts loosening, slipping again into shadow, as the road bent back toward the city she had not known she was already longing for.

# Chapter Thirty-Eight

The clock had no mercy in it.

Darcy sat at the escritoire with a letter half-folded beneath his hand and watched the minute hand advance with infuriating composure. It was not late—by London standards, it was hardly evening at all—but the light beyond the windows had dwindled, and the fire had settled into that low, consuming burn which signalled the approach of quiet. He had already dismissed one footman. The house had begun, subtly, to draw inward.

The steward's letter lay unanswered. Figures blurred where he had tried to review them. Invitations—a bare fraction of the number he would have expected for December—had been stacked and restacked without decision. He had read the same paragraph twice and retained none of it.

He glanced again at the clock.

Harrowe had said a day or two. It had been one day and a half already. Darcy had told him *any hour*. Day or night. As if knowledge might obey urgency simply because it was demanded.

He rose and crossed the room, only to stop without knowing why. The house was too still. Even Brutus had settled on his pallet somewhere beyond the kitchens, where he liked to wait on scraps from Cook. Darcy turned back, drew up the poker, and adjusted the fire by a fraction that made no discernible difference.

The clock marked another quarter hour.

He had just opened his mouth to tell the servant to bank the fire when the sound came—not the sedate announcement of a proper caller, but a sharp, insistent knock that cut through the hall with improper force.

Darcy stilled, then glanced at the footman. "Admit them," he said at once. "It is likely the man I am expecting."

The door had scarcely opened before Darcy saw *her*.

Elizabeth Bennet—borne across the threshold in Bingley's arms, her head lifted, her colour high, her eyes alight with unmistakable awareness. For a fraction of a second, nothing else in the hall seemed properly placed.

Then the rest of it resolved: Bingley's coat askew, his breath still uneven from haste; Jane Bennet close behind, her bonnet undone, her face drawn pale with strain; and Miss Bingley entering last, composed enough to notice everything and approve of none of it.

"Darcy—" Bingley began, then broke off, adjusting his hold as Elizabeth stirred. "Forgive us. We had no intention of intruding upon you without notice, but—"

Elizabeth was pressing away from Bingley's chest with a look of faint chagrin. "Mr Bingley, you may set me down," she said, her voice clear, touched only by impatience. "I assure you, I am not an invalid. I am perfectly capable."

Darcy had not moved. He was aware of his own stillness only because it felt so unlike him. She looked... *well*. Colour warmed her cheeks; her eyes were bright, keen, unmistakably herself. For a moment, the memory of finding her outside Netherfield—the pallor, the pain, the collapse—failed him entirely.

Bingley hesitated, then obeyed, easing her to her feet with evident reluctance even as Darcy's instincts propelled him forward. He reached out to catch her hand as her feet touched the floor, but she shook her head and pulled at her cloak.

"I can walk," Elizabeth said at once, and smiled—faintly, determinedly—as though daring anyone present to contradict her.

Miss Bingley's gaze slid from Elizabeth to Darcy and paused there. "It is quite extraordinary," she observed lightly. "One would hardly believe she was nearly insensate two hours ago."

Darcy felt the words strike and pass him in the same instant. "You are all most welcome," he said, far too quickly. "Pray—come in. Miss Bennet, Miss Bingley—Bingley, of course. You must allow me to offer you rooms at once."

"Oh, yes! Thank you—Darcy, I cannot tell you how relieved I am you are at home," Bingley burst out, advancing as though the explanation itself might outrun him if he did not speak fast enough. "We should never have presumed, only there was truly no time, and Miss Elizabeth has been very unwell—*very*—for days now. Quite alarming, I assure you. Mr Jones could make nothing of it, and Mr Bennet was persuaded that she must be removed from Longbourn entirely, that the air—or the place, or something of the sort—was doing her harm."

Elizabeth's smile tightened, but she said nothing.

"There was, of course, the wedding," Bingley went on, with a helpless gesture, "and every wish to spare the family further distress, so it was settled—rather hastily, I admit—that we should take her to Ramsgate. Just for a time. Until Mr Bennet might join us and decide what was best. And truly, Darcy, she seemed so much improved upon the road—remarkably so—that we thought the plan answered perfectly."

Miss Bingley made a small sound of scepticism and examined the ceiling.

"But then—quite suddenly—she was not herself again," Bingley finished, lowering his voice despite himself. "So pale, so faint—I feared we should lose her consciousness altogether. It was as far back to London as forward to our lodgings, and with physicians here, and no house secured—my solicitor could not possibly have been reached in time—there was nothing for it but to turn back and come to you. I beg you will forgive the intrusion, and the want of notice—only I knew nowhere else to turn in such immediate need."

Elizabeth shifted slightly, as if to protest. The grimacing smile she offered Darcy was apologetic, almost rueful—*see how much trouble I have caused.*

Miss Bingley's eyes flicked toward her again. They rolled—only a little—but not so little as to escape notice.

"I would have it no other way," Darcy said, as though the assurance had been waiting for him. He turned sharply, already issuing instructions. "The south drawing room—see that the fire is built up at once. And prepare chambers for our guests. Draw baths, bring refreshments. Whatever is needed."

The servants moved. The house responded, doors opening, voices answering, the familiar machinery of order set abruptly in motion.

Two footmen came forward to relieve coats and hats; Bingley twisted out of his woollen sleeves, Miss Bingley turned, already assessing the room as if she might one day call herself the mistress of it all. Elizabeth moved, too—drawn forward in what appeared simple curiosity, her gaze on the footmen, the maids beyond, and then wandering back to fix on Darcy as she moved out of the way of the crush.

Her foot caught.

That was all Darcy saw—movement wrong, weight shifting—and his blood turned. He was on her before the thought finished forming, his hand catching her shoulder to hold her upright, his body braced as if to take her weight.

The touch emptied him. Not pain—absence. The contact hit him like a sudden hollowing, a swift, sickening sense of being emptied from the inside out. His knees threatened, just for an instant, to forget their duty.

She righted herself immediately, placing one hand on his shoulder as if to reassure him. "Mr Darcy? You need not look so alarmed. I was not faint. Just clumsy and distracted."

The room rushed back into him then—the servants hovering, Bingley half-turned in concern, Miss Bingley watching with a dark sort of interest—but Darcy's attention remained fixed where his hand still rested at her waist. Elizabeth stood perfectly at ease, her colour clear, her eyes bright, looking at him now as though she were the one steadying *him*.

He withdrew his hand. "Yes," he managed at last, and felt the word ring hollow even as he spoke it.

Her gaze lingered on his face, curious now, intent—and in that look he knew, with a certainty that made retreat impossible, that whatever she had gained by coming here, he was already paying for it.

The crash came from the back of the house—metal against stone, a pan knocked loose—followed by a shout that cut off mid-word. Darcy knew the sound that followed.

"Brutus—no!"

The passage filled with the drum of claws, the sharp, echoing bark that had scattered grown men more than once. Servants recoiled instinctively; one dropped a cloak outright. Miss Bingley gave a startled cry and retreated a full step, her hand flying to her chest.

Darcy moved without thought. "Brutus! Down—heel!" His voice snapped through the hall, sharp with command, and for a breath he expected the dog to barrel through regardless.

But Brutus had already altered course.

He skidded across the stone floor and stopped short of Elizabeth, the hair at his scruff raised in alarm, body taut with momentum. He thrust his nose forward, once—again—then lowered himself with abrupt peace and sat squarely before her, back straight, tail stilled, gaze fixed on her face as if awaiting instruction.

Darcy stared. His hand hovered half-raised, the reprimand unfinished on his tongue. The dog did not look at him. Did not look anywhere but at Elizabeth Bennet.

"Well," she said, after a moment—softly, not startled, more curious than anything else. "I appear to have passed inspection once more." She extended her hand, and Brutus permitted her to rest it on his head. "Hello, my good fellow."

Darcy found his voice at last. "Brutus."

The dog did not move. Did not even glance at him.

Darcy crossed the remaining distance, one hand reaching again for Elizabeth as if she might vanish the moment he turned away, the other gesturing sharply to the servants crowding the hall. "Bring refreshments," he said. "And clear this passage—at once."

He tried again, more sharply. "Brutus."

Only then did the dog break his stare, glancing up at Darcy as though surprised to be addressed, before rising with reluctant dignity and stepping aside—never taking his eyes from her.

Darcy lifted his hand again, not to command this time, but to indicate the way forward, his palm hovering an inch from her sleeve as though the space itself were treacherous.

Elizabeth glanced at him, a brief, searching look, then inclined her head and moved on.

Brutus followed at her heel.

Elizabeth had expected—quite foolishly, she saw now—that she would feel diminished by recovery. That she would wake to a cautious, borrowed sort of strength, like a guest using another person's good china. Instead, she found herself unmistakably well.

Her head no longer rang. The room held steady when she moved. She accepted the cup Jane pressed into her hands without bracing for nausea and drank it to the bottom, discovering halfway through that she was hungry enough to enjoy the offerings of Mr Darcy's excellent cook. This alone would have been miracle enough.

"It seems," she said lightly, setting the cup aside, "that I have made a very dramatic nuisance of myself for no lasting reason at all."

Jane smiled at her with a softness that hovered near tears. "You frightened us."

"I appear to have frightened myself," Elizabeth replied. "Though I must say, if I am to collapse again, I would prefer it not require the commandeering of an entire household."

Her gaze flicked, unthinking, toward Mr Darcy—and caught him looking at her already.

Not covertly. Not in the guarded, half-averted manner she remembered too well. He stood near the mantel, one hand resting upon it as though by habit rather than need, his attention so fixed that she felt, absurdly, as if she had spoken to him alone rather than to her sister. When their eyes met, he did not look away at once.

She lifted her brows, a silent inquiry.

He inclined his head—formal, restrained—and turned to answer something Bingley was saying with a care that felt... a little forced. A little distracted.

Elizabeth frowned, only a little.

Bingley, all warmth and relief, was recounting their journey with a great deal of unnecessary colour. Elizabeth let him have it. She leaned back against the settee, entirely content to listen, and even managed a small, genuine laugh when he described his terror at the thought of arriving at Ramsgate only to find her insensible again, with no doctors at hand.

"I should hate to think my constitution has developed a taste for seaside drama," she said. "I assure you, if I am to be ill, I would prefer it occur somewhere less inconvenient."

Miss Bingley gave a thin smile. "Yes, London is a terribly convenient place for a recovery. And what a marvel that Mr Darcy stood ready to receive us! Providential, I should say."

Elizabeth met the remark with an equal civility. "Perhaps that is the word, for it was certainly no design of mine. I should almost think I had been playing a part without knowing my lines."

Darcy's head turned at that, sharp enough that she noticed. His expression did not change, but something in his posture did—an attention drawn taut, as if he had heard more of her words to Miss Bingley than she meant for him to.

Miss Bingley, however, had heard precisely enough. Her gaze lingered between them, unhappily so, and Elizabeth felt a faint, unwelcome prickle of amusement. It was not the first time Miss Bingley had watched her in this manner. It was merely the first time Elizabeth felt no urge to defend herself against it.

Conversation flowed on. Jane was persuaded to sit. Bingley was prevailed upon to eat something. Elizabeth accepted a plate and discovered that she could eat without coaxing, without nausea. She caught Darcy watching this too—his attention slipping toward her hands, the careful way she lifted her fork, as though the act itself were proof of something.

It struck her then, not sharply but with a quiet surety, that he looked tired.

Not unwell. Not ill. But worn in a manner that did not belong to him.

She had known him long enough now to recognise the difference. Darcy was exacting with himself; fatigue usually announced itself only after the fact, when it could no longer be concealed. Tonight, it showed in the spaces between his movements. In the way he stood rather than sat, as if he did not trust himself to stay alert. In the cup left untouched at his elbow. In the pause—always just a fraction too long—before he answered Bingley's cheerful inquiries.

"You must have kept busy, eh, Darcy?" Bingley said, smiling. "You have been dreadfully mysterious these past weeks. We all wondered what had carried you away so suddenly."

Darcy's reply came smoothly enough. "Nothing of consequence."

Elizabeth looked up at that.

'Nothing of consequence' was not a phrase Darcy used carelessly. He named things specifically, or not at all.

Bingley laughed and put forth his own imaginings about what a single gentleman might find to amuse himself in London during the Season, but Darcy offered no elaboration. No anecdote. No person, place, or purpose. He spoke as though the intervening time had been empty, and Elizabeth found that she did not believe him.

Her father's words returned to her then, unbidden. The way he had watched Darcy across the library, his tone careful, his conclusions drawn not from speculation but observation. *"My eyes tell me that he is a... a shelter of sorts for you,"* he had said, as if it were a simple fact, like the weather turning or a clock striking the hour.

She had laughed at the time. She laughed less easily now.

For she had missed him.

The realization did not arrive with a sweep of butterflies or blushes heating her cheeks. It did not make her heart skip, as she might have thought it should. It simply took its place among other truths she had not quite known what to do with: that he listened more than she expected, that he bore disappointment without complaint, that when he looked at her now, there was nothing dismissive in it at all.

Trust, she thought, was perhaps not too strong a word. Sympathy, certainly. A sense that he would not turn away when things became difficult—even if he did not yet know how to meet them. And a hope he seemed to kindle in her—nay, an understanding that he was the one person to whom she never needed to explain herself.

Their eyes met again, briefly. This time, she smiled.

Darcy's response was not immediate. But when it came, it was unmistakable. His shoulders eased, only a little, and he inclined his head again—not formally now, but as if acknowledging something neither of them had spoken.

Elizabeth looked away first.

Miss Bingley noticed. She let her eyes rest on Elizabeth with a sort of offended horror, a fluttering of her nostrils, and a faint trembling at her throat.

Elizabeth, however, found that she no longer much cared.

THE MORNING FIRE IN Darcy's study had burned low, reduced to a red seam along the grate that gave more light than warmth. He had meant to have it built up again before the household stirred for the day, but the notion passed without action. The room was quiet in the particular way of early morning—not asleep, but waiting.

Letters lay open on the desk before him—his steward's careful hand, accounts neatly ruled, a request regarding winter stores that would ordinarily have been dispatched yesterday. Darcy read the same paragraph for the third time and found that the words would not hold. They slid away from him, leaving only the echo of another awareness entirely.

He had slept little. Not from labour, nor from wine, nor even from the unease that had driven him from his bed these past nights—but from the simple, impossible fact of knowing that Elizabeth Bennet lay beneath his roof. Close enough to speak to... touch, if she granted it. Sleeping under a coverlet embroidered with the Darcy initials in the corner and in a room with the portraits of at least three previous Mrs Darcys hung about the walls.

The knowledge would not be set aside. It followed him from room to room, into the small hours, into the grey light of morning, altering the house itself by her presence.

He set the page down and reached for another, then stopped, his fingers suspended. The clock on the mantel kept its steady measure. Too early for Harrowe. Too late to pretend that his attention was his own. He was listening—not for a knock, not for news—but for the sound of *her* moving somewhere in the house, for proof that she was there, and well, and untroubled by the things that had left him wakeful and unmoored.

He told himself—again—that this was foolish.

But a presence made itself known in the corridor beyond the door. Not footsteps precisely; something lighter, slower. He was aware of it before the knock came, as if his attention had already gone to meet it.

The knock was gentle. Considerate. It carried no urgency at all. Darcy was on his feet before he knew he had risen.

"Yes?" he said at once, the word leaving him too quickly, too unguarded.

The door opened. Elizabeth Bennet stood on the threshold, daylight at her back, her hair plainly dressed. She looked as though she had come down only moments ago—gown freshly pressed, eyes bright, the faintest suggestion of amusement already gathering at the corner of her mouth, as though she had caught him at something and meant to let him wonder what.

For a heartbeat, Darcy could do nothing but look at her.

She still looked very well indeed.

Not improved, not recovering—*well*. Standing easily, breathing without effort, the ailment that had driven her from Hertfordshire nowhere to be seen. The sight struck him with such force that his thoughts scattered, leaving behind only a stark, unreasonable relief that made his chest feel too tight.

"Good morning, Mr Darcy," she said. "I hope I am not intruding."

"No," he replied, far too quickly again. "Not at all. Please—come in."

He stepped aside without thinking, the movement instinctive, as though the room had always been meant to receive her. It was only once she crossed the threshold that he became aware of himself standing there, hands empty, heart misbehaving, the fire neglected, and the desk in disarray.

Elizabeth paused just inside, her gaze flicking briefly around the room. "I thought I might find you occupied here," she said. "But I could not sleep a moment longer—I have spent too much time abed lately. There was no one in the breakfast room, and I recall Mr Bingley back at Netherfield saying you would already be at work before the sun had properly risen. He spoke with great admiration, I need hardly add."

Darcy managed something that might pass for a smile. "Bingley's admiration is generous to a fault and entirely misplaced."

She turned back to him then, studying him more closely. "I hope our arrival last night did not—"

"It did not," he blurted without thinking. The denial came sharp, decisive, and he tempered it only afterward. "On the contrary. I was glad of it."

Her brows lifted, just a little. Not in disbelief—rather in acknowledgment, as though the admission had confirmed something she had already suspected.

"I wished to thank you," she said. "For your kindness. For your patience with such an unceremonious invasion of your household. I assure you, had I been fully myself—"

"You *are* fully yourself," Darcy said, and stopped.

The words had not been intended for utterance. They had simply escaped, carried on the same impulse that had opened the door too swiftly, that had stepped aside too readily to make space for her. He felt the heat rise at once and was dimly aware of wishing he could call them back.

Elizabeth, however, only smiled. Not playfully—something quieter, more considering. "Then I am doubly obliged to you," she said. "For indulging me even so."

She took a step farther into the room, her attention drawn to the desk. "I hope I have not entirely disrupted your work. There must be a reason you rose so early."

"No," he said again, more carefully this time. "I was not making much progress."

"Ah." She laughed easily. "Then I shall rather presumptuously consider my arrival an improvement on an otherwise dull room."

The ease of the remark, the familiar turn of wit, struck him more deeply than he expected. It had been this—this liveliness, this unforced animation—that he had found himself missing after he left Hertfordshire, though he had refused to name the absence as such.

"You are... truly feeling better, then?" he asked.

"Remarkably so," she replied. "Which is a source of no small embarrassment, I assure you. Miss Bingley has already suggested—quite delicately—that I have chosen a most artful moment to revive."

Darcy's jaw tightened despite himself. "No one could think you motivated by arts and allurements, Miss Elizabeth."

"I am glad to hear it. I should hate to think myself the object of suspicion." She hesitated, then added, more softly, "But my father will be relieved when he hears of it."

Something in her tone—quiet, unguarded—made Darcy's throat constrict. He gestured toward one of the chairs before he quite knew why. "Will you sit?"

She did, framing her skirt about the chair and casting a glance about his study as if she knew it already, and was merely reacquainting herself with it. She rested her hands lightly in her lap.

"I see," she said, "that your papers are all in precise rows. My father's desk resembles a battlefield after the troops have fled."

Darcy's mouth twitched despite himself. "Your father conducts his affairs by stratagem," he replied. "I prefer to know where the enemy lies."

She laughed—softly, but with real amusement—and the sound struck him with more force than it had any right to do. He felt it at once: that faint, draining pull, like a tide withdrawing beneath his feet. But he endured it gladly.

"I had thought," she chuckled, "that gentlemen who keep such order must be frightfully dull."

"I have been accused of many faults. Dullness is not one I often hear."

Her brows lifted. "Perhaps because everyone wishes for your good opinion?"

He leaned back slightly in his chair, pursing his lips. "Is that what you think of me, Miss Elizabeth? I am wounded."

"Wounded by a little tease, sir? I should think not. No, I think you rather fancy a bit of irreverence, though everything in your looks attempts to suggest otherwise."

Darcy inclined his head with a smile. "I shall never confess."

Elizabeth's smile came quick and unmistakably pleased, as though she had landed her point and meant to enjoy it. Darcy kept his gaze where it was, though each moment demanded more of him than the last. To see her thus—to hear it in her voice—was worth every fraction it took.

Her gaze drifted once more to the desk. "I imagine you must have been very busy these past weeks," she said. "It was quite a loss to the neighbourhood that you were called away so suddenly. Miss Bingley, in particular, felt your absence most keenly."

The familiar evasion rose—ready, reflexive. He had employed it all his life. But when he opened his mouth, it failed him. "I have been occupied," he said instead. "On... family business."

It was true. After a fashion.

Elizabeth studied him for a moment, then nodded, as though that answer—paltry as it was—had satisfied some private accounting of her own. "One cannot count you remiss in attending to your duties, sir."

The words were gentle. The meaning was not.

Darcy shifted, then said, too quickly, "You must permit me to offer my congratulations to your sister on her engagement to Mr Collins."

The smile she gave him this time was thin. Dutiful. "I hope she will be happy."

"You have your doubts?"

Elizabeth frowned, and for the first time, her eyes fell. "I... I am not sorry my family decided not to require my attendance."

He looked at her keenly. "You disapprove of her choice?"

She grimaced, just a little. "I disapprove of very few things absolutely. But I confess I should find it difficult to rejoice at a union founded entirely on obligation."

Darcy leaned forward with a question he could not hold back. "And if obligation were joined by something more?"

Elizabeth hesitated. It was no more than a breath's delay, but it was enough. Enough that he thought, for one reckless instant, that she might answer him honestly.

"Oh, there you are! I thought I should find you here, Mr Darcy."

Darcy blinked back to awareness to discover that Miss Bingley now stood in the doorway, her back arched to display the silhouette of her figure to best advantage. Her gaze flicked—once—to Elizabeth, then back again.

"How very comfortable the rooms are," she continued. "So tastefully arranged. I daresay you have done the most admirable job of redecorating them since I last saw them."

"They are precisely as my mother left them," Darcy replied, with a civility that held no warmth. "I may consider altering them one day, but I have not done so yet."

"Oh." Miss Bingley did not smile at all. She adjusted the fall of her skirt, smoothing one fold and then another, though they required no attention.

Elizabeth regarded the display with open amusement, her smile deepening rather than retreating.

The moment had begun to tilt in directions best left unexplored before coffee. Darcy rose and gestured toward the door. "Well, the morning appears to be advancing. Shall we go in to breakfast?"

"Oh, I am quite eager to see the breakfast room," Elizabeth said. "If it has been so comfortably established for years, I expect it will be perfection by now."

# Chapter Thirty-Nine

Evening came in due course in Mr Darcy's house, as though it knew better than to present itself too early or too late.

Elizabeth felt it in the way the lamps were lit before she thought to notice the dark, in the even cadence of the servants' steps as dinner was laid, in the curious strengthening of her own body as the day passed without the familiar ebb and surge of weakness. Nearly a full day under this roof, and she felt, quite unmistakably, perhaps the best she had ever felt in her life.

Which only made the awkwardness sharper.

She was keenly aware, as they took their places at table, of how well she must appear. Too well, certainly, for the trouble she had occasioned. She had apologised twice already; Darcy had dismissed it both times with a courtesy so firm it brooked no argument. Bingley, for his part, appeared delighted beyond reason to have them all gathered thus, as though illness, abrupt travel, and uncertainty were merely pretexts for conviviality.

Darcy sat nearest her. Not at the head—he had insisted on a less formal setting for this evening, a square table, of all things, with neither head nor foot. Close enough that she could see him clearly whenever she lifted her eyes.

It was then that she heard it.

Not loud. Not persistent. Just a brief interruption of breath, carefully smothered behind a hand.

She looked up at once.

Darcy's hand had already dropped back to the table. His expression was composed, almost deliberately so, but there was a faint tension about his mouth that had not been there earlier.

"Mr Darcy, are you quite well?" Miss Bingley asked. "You sound—"

"It is nothing," Darcy said, too quickly to convince anyone at the table. "A chill, perhaps. I went riding in the cold the other day."

Elizabeth watched him over the rim of her glass. She had never heard him cough before. Indeed, he seemed like a man whom illness would never dare to trouble.

Dinner proceeded, if not smoothly then at least politely. Jane spoke little, though she smiled often—mostly at Mr Bingley. Miss Bingley watched Darcy with narrowed attention, her appetite visibly diminished. Bingley filled the spaces with cheerful speculation—about physicians in town, about the weather, about how fortunate it was that Elizabeth seemed so very much herself again.

Darcy ate sparingly. He spoke when spoken to, but his attention wandered, his gaze straying now and again toward the sideboard, toward the door, toward nothing Elizabeth could identify with any clarity. And once or twice, she was sure she saw a muscle spasm ticking his cheek.

At last, as the servants withdrew with the first course, Bingley leaned back in his chair and said, with the mild curiosity of a man who had no notion he was touching upon anything of consequence, "Forgive my curiosity, Darcy, but I saw there was a messenger this afternoon. I caught the name of the sender, I think. Harrowe?"

The effect was immediate. Darcy did not cough. He did not speak. For the briefest instant, he did not move at all.

Then his eyes lifted—and found hers.

The look held no accusation, no appeal. Only a stark awareness, as though some private calculation had just been interrupted by the presence of an unanticipated variable.

Elizabeth's fingers tightened slightly on her fork.

*Harrowe?*

The name stirred something half-buried. She saw, all at once, her father's shelves, the slim, worn volume he had bought her when she lay delirious at Netherfield. She remembered the feel of that book in her hands. The lines she had quoted—lightly, carelessly—at the Netherfield ball.

And she remembered Darcy's face then. The exact moment his manner toward her had altered. Not in anger. In something colder. More guarded—and that had been the last time they spoke at all before he left for London.

She dropped her gaze to her plate.

Darcy answered Bingley at last, his voice now mastered enough to pass for boredom. "A matter of research. Nothing of present concern."

"Oh!" Bingley said, satisfied at once. "I wondered if it was something to do with that business you said called you back. Not that it's any business of mine, of course. I confess,

I had far too little to occupy my mind today. Perhaps we shall drive around Hyde Park tomorrow. What do you think of that, Miss Bennet? We might even try ice skating if you like. Caroline is an excellent skater, are you not, Caroline?"

Miss Bingley confirmed that last with a pride that seemed to seek Darcy's attention. Jane answered the notion with pleasure. Elizabeth did not look up again. She ate, she listened, she smiled when required.

The footman entered between courses and bent to murmur at Darcy's shoulder. A sealed letter lay upon the salver. Darcy glanced at it once—no more—and then, without comment, slid it to Elizabeth.

Miss Bingley's fork paused midway to her lips. "I beg your pardon," she said. "Was that not delivered to *you*, Mr Darcy?"

"It was," he answered evenly. "But it is not mine."

Elizabeth hesitated before taking it. The superscription was unmistakable. "An express from my father? Why would he charge it to your account, sir?"

"Pay that no mind," Darcy replied, already returning his attention to his plate. "No doubt a reply to the one Bingley sent this morning."

Elizabeth broke the seal with fingers that trembled only a little and unfolded the page. Her father's hand leapt out at once—firm, familiar, and oddly steady given all that had occurred.

She read quickly. Relief came first, sharp and undeniable. Then concern. Then something quieter, more complicated. She folded the letter again and laid it beside her plate.

"Well?" Jane asked gently.

"Papa is reassured," Elizabeth said. "He thanks Mr Bingley for his care, and Mr Darcy for his hospitality. He will come when he is able, but he is content, for now, that I am better."

"Indeed, 'tis a wonder," Miss Bingley said as she raised her glass to her lips.

A faint, involuntary sound escaped Darcy before he could suppress it—another short cough, quickly masked by the lift of his napkin.

Elizabeth's gaze slipped up to him.

He had gone still. Too still. One hand rested on the table's edge as though he had placed it there to keep from toppling over.

"Are you quite well?" she whispered, low enough that only he could hear.

"Perfectly," Darcy said. The word came a shade too quickly. "The air has been unkind to me, nothing more."

Elizabeth was not persuaded. She found herself watching him now without meaning to, aware of small things she would once have overlooked: the way he swallowed before speaking, the pause he took before lifting his glass, the careful economy of his movements.

She let her eyes fall again, but the letter lay folded beside her plate like a pall she could not ignore.

She waited. Counted the movements of the table. The clink of china. Miss Bingley's voice. Bingley's laugh. Darcy's silence.

At last, when no one was watching her—when Darcy's attention had been deliberately bent elsewhere—she slipped the paper into her lap and opened it again.

*My dearest Lizzy,*

*I am relieved beyond measure to hear that you are easier. That you are not merely easier, but yourself again; clear-headed, lively, impatient with fuss. That alone tells me more than any physician might.*

Her throat tightened. She read on.

*I cannot pretend I am easy in my mind about London. I am easier knowing you are not there alone, and easier still knowing whose roof shelters you. I confessed to you once before that I have long suspected (quietly, and without proof) that Mr Darcy's presence answers something in you that nothing else does. You will forgive a father for noticing such things, but I am gratified to hear that in this case, at least, it seems to be true.*

Elizabeth stopped reading long enough to take a bite, smile at Jane, and pretend to be entirely engaged with the meal. Then the letter pulled her attention once more.

*But ease is not cure. I have been consulting with Mr Wickham, whom I have found to be a sympathetic and rational ear. He is of the opinion (and I cannot dismiss it lightly) that whatever comfort Mr Darcy provides may be only provisional. He believes there is a reckoning bound up with that gentleman which, if delayed or mishandled, may cost you more than you now gain.*

Her eyes moved faster now.

*You must therefore be watchful. Not fearful, but observant. Attend to yourself. Keep note of what strengthens you, and what leaves you diminished. Be cautious of any moment that feels too much, whether of relief or of strain.*

She felt heat rise beneath her collar. She stole a sip of wine, but her eyes scarcely left her lap.

*Once Mary is wed, I intend to come for you myself. If at any moment before that you feel alarm or a return of your malaise, you are to go at once to your Aunt and Uncle Gardiner. I have written them and trust them entirely. You need not explain yourself beyond what is necessary.*

The page ended there. No flourish. No reassurance. Just the weight of his care, set squarely upon her shoulders.

Elizabeth folded the letter again with care and slipped it back into the folds of her gown.

Darcy lifted his glass, then set it down untouched. His hand returned to the table's edge, fingers spread, as though grounding himself by habit alone.

Her father thought him her shelter.

Wickham thought him her danger.

And Darcy—who met her gaze then, only for a moment—looked like a man bearing a cost he would not challenge and could not afford, yet paying it willingly all the same.

Darcy declined Bingley's invitation to sport with a civility so automatic it scarcely touched his mind. Billiards required motion without purpose, talk without consequence. He could not trust himself to either.

The study received him in lamplight and order. Books towering on the shelves. The clock upon the mantel marking time with a patience that felt, at present, almost offensive. Darcy shut the door and stood with his hand upon it a moment, listening through the oak for the sound of her footsteps.

But that was silly. The ladies had all retired for the night, and he had watched Brutus stubbornly following Elizabeth up the stairs himself.

He crossed to the desk and set his palms upon its surface, leaning there without sitting. His thoughts refused their accustomed discipline. They returned, again and again, to the shape of her presence in the house—so near it altered the air, so ordinary it seemed impossible that it should cost anything at all.

Darcy forced himself into the chair and reached for the topmost paper. His steward's hand. A sensible request for more funds from the coffer to cover the increased grain price he had negotiated. He read the first line, then the second, then found himself at the end of the paragraph with no memory of how he had arrived there. The page slid aside. Another followed it. Then another. Each failed him in turn.

At last, he abandoned the pretence and reached instead for the folded sheet Harrowe had sent that morning, already creased thin from having been opened, read, and read again. Harrowe's hand was heavy and uneven, the ink pressed deep as though he had not troubled himself with elegance.

*Mr. Darcy,*

*I have not come because I am still at the work, and because what I have found does not yet warrant the disturbance. I write only so you will not suppose I have forgot you.*

*Beyond the Liber and the Ballads, there are only scraps worthy of the name. Late marginal hands, a travelling bard's verse copied by a parish clerk, a death notice altered and crossed through. None of it would stand before a learned society, which may be the reason it endures at all.*

*One such verse follows Bedevere into old age. It claims he lived long, retained his name, and was spoken of with respect, but never again with honour. The bard dwells much on barrenness: of land, of house, of legacy. I send it for what it is worth, which may be little.*

*There is also this: several late sources describing the years after the Roman withdrawal record flooding, land loss, and sudden abandonment of settled places. The accounts disagree in detail and offer no explanation. Their only commonality is timing. That may signify something, or nothing at all. I cannot yet say.*

*I will come when there is something worth the hire of a hansom. Until then, do not wait on me. Such things were never kept to spare a man discomfort.*

*—H.*

Harrowe had offered no instruction. No safeguard. Only the same brutal narrowing of choice that had haunted him since Hertfordshire.

He set the note down and leaned back, one hand lifting to his mouth as a cough forced itself loose—short, controlled, dismissed as soon as it came. The effort left him momentarily light, as though he had stood too quickly.

Elizabeth Bennet slept beneath his roof again tonight. The knowledge struck him again—not as wonder, not as comfort, but as pressure. As demand. And there was little he could do but to answer, so he reached for the bell pull.

When the footman appeared, Darcy did not turn from the hearth. "Ask the upstairs maid whether Miss Elizabeth is still awake and dressed. If so, find out if she would do me the kindness of a few minutes' conversation," he said. "In the library. If she feels equal to it."

The footman bowed and turned to go, but Darcy stopped him. "Wait... if she desires to have her sister present, that will suit as well."

The wording mattered. He would have it so.

The footman went to do his bidding, and Darcy closed the study for the night, asking for the fire to be banked. Then he went to arrange the library to his liking. The fire built higher, the lamps burning brightly—not too intimate, no. This was not a seduction.

He studied the effect, then crossed to the chairs by the fire and adjusted them—not side by side, not too near—until they faced one another with a small table between, as though this were to be a discussion of books or weather or any of the other safe, ordinary things he had long since abandoned.

Yes, that would… no, there should be a third chair. In case she came with a chaperone. If she were wise, she would.

The fire flared and then dimmed while he waited. He stirred it, watching the embers catch and climb. The light shifted across the shelves, the spines of books rising and falling in shadow.

And then, footsteps sounded in the passage.

Darcy came to his feet, fingers lifting instinctively to his cravat before he caught the motion and let his hand fall. His throat burned; he cleared it once, softly, irritated by the sound. His heart had begun to miscount, and no amount of discipline seemed inclined to correct it.

Elizabeth entered alone. She wore a simple morning gown, not the one she had worn to dinner. So, she had been preparing for bed and changed to indulge him. Darcy's heart tried crawling up his throat at the thought, but it was the sight of her hair unpinned and twisted into a loose braid over her shoulder that made the moment seem… intimate. Nearly sensual.

No, no, this was not what he had intended! Pricks of heat sprang across his brow, his lip, and he looked away, letting his eyes be scorched by the heat of the fire rather than blazing at her. But he was weak… and he looked back.

Elizabeth's expression was composed but alert, as though she had been summoned for something she had already begun to guess. The warmth of the fire touched her cheeks like a caress, and that smile simmered on her lips.

"You wished to see me?" Her mouth curved, mischief tempered by kindness. "I comforted myself by recalling that the last gentleman who summoned me so gravely merely wished to explain my future and my moral failings to me. I trust you will require less temperance on my part."

"I promise nothing so trying," Darcy replied. Then, more evenly, "I must thank you for your time. If you are not too fatigued to stay a few moments, pray, sit." He gestured toward the chair nearest the hearth.

She did, then folded her hands in her lap and looked at him with that familiar, unsettling directness that had always made him feel as though he were being judged and assessed—not as he appeared, but as he was.

The room felt altered with her seated there, the firelight catching along the line of her hair, the warmth gathering itself into a halo about her as though it had been waiting to coronate her.

Darcy turned away abruptly and crossed to the sideboard. He opened one cabinet, then another, his movements disorganised and ill-matched to his thoughts, until he found what he sought. Sherry. His mother's, laid in years ago and scarcely touched since. He poured carefully. Two glasses, though he had no true appetite for his own. He carried one back and set it into Elizabeth's hand.

"For the chill," he said, though she showed none.

She accepted it with a look that held more curiosity than gratitude and raised it to her lips. Darcy remained where he was, his own glass untouched, the weight of standing preferable to the confinement of a chair.

Her eyes lifted from the rim of the glass to him, bright with a glimmer of humour he recognised too well. "Mr Darcy, do you mean to interrogate me or simply to intimidate me by looming so?"

Darcy coloured and took the chair opposite her at once, the motion a shade too quick to be graceful. The fire popped softly between them. He placed his untouched glass on the table and folded his hands as though they might be persuaded to keep still.

"I beg your pardon," he said. "I had no intention of—of hovering."

"So I presumed." She glanced down at the glass again and smiled. "It is excellent sherry."

"I am glad you find it so. My mother preferred it for evenings."

She nodded, as if this were an intimacy he had offered on purpose, and let her gaze wander to the shelves. The titles gave him a merciful moment. He opened his mouth, closed it again. Tried once more.

"What I wished to say—" He stopped. "That is—"

She waited, tilting her head and studying him with an earnest, open expression that seemed to permit patience without mockery. Thank Heaven for that. He felt like madman enough already.

"I am not practiced at..." He broke off and pressed his lips together. The fire leaned, just then, toward her skirts, a wavering curl of heat that should have singed the hem. It did not. It bent away, as if corrected by an unseen hand.

Darcy stared. Blinked. Cleared his throat and tried not to wonder what sort of woman this was, whom even fire seemed to worship.

Elizabeth set the glass down. "You may proceed at your leisure, sir. I promise not to faint at incomplete sentences."

He drew a breath. "You can be in no doubt why I asked to speak with you."

She considered him over the rim of her glass, then smiled—only a little. "On the contrary. I have entertained at least a dozen possibilities. As I believe you to be a gentleman, however, several of them may be dismissed out of hand. Most of the others are merely the product of a fanciful imagination, and I doubt you are a man ruled by fancy. So, there, I am entirely at a loss, sir."

He tried to answer her jest and could not. The breath caught halfway in, misfired, and tore loose instead. The sound that followed was not brief, nor decorous—something harsh and scraping that bent him forward before he could master it. He turned away, one hand braced hard on the chair, but the cough came again, deeper this time, dragging at his chest as though it meant to empty him of more than air.

Elizabeth was on her feet at once. "Mr Darcy—"

He shook his head. Tried to beg her to excuse him, wave it off as nothing. Perhaps a bit of sherry would do... but he could not cease coughing long enough to pick up the glass.

"Mr Darcy, you *are* unwell." She crossed the small distance and laid a hand on his shoulder, as if she could pat his back to loosen his cough like she would a small child.

The room tipped.

The chair bit into the backs of his legs as his strength fled him, not slowly, not politely, but all at once, as though a marionette's strings had been cut. He caught the edge of the table and missed it. The glass rang. His knees folded, and his forehead smacked the wood floor.

Elizabeth cried out and sprang back. "Oh—good Heavens, what have I done? Mr Darcy!"

He lifted a hand at once, palm outward, more plea than command. "Nothing. Pray—do not—" The words broke apart as another rasp seized him. He turned from her until it broke off, scrambled to his feet too quickly, and crossed the short distance to the hearth with a gait that betrayed him despite every effort at control.

She moved again, instinct driving her forward. "But let me help. Please, you are very unwell."

"Miss Elizabeth," he said hoarsely, gripping the mantel with both hands now, knuckles whitening against the carved stone. "Stay where you are. Please, I beg you."

She retreated, but not without a soft growl of protest. "Very well, sir."

The fire snapped softly behind the grate. Darcy leaned into the cool solidity of the mantel as though it were the only thing in the room that could be relied upon. His shoulders worked as he drew breath by force, jaw clenched, fighting the urge to cough again. A sound escaped him despite that resolve—low, ugly, gone as soon as it came. He shut his eyes until the world steadied into something he could bear.

"Shall I fetch... someone?" she offered.

Darcy shook his head. "I am quite recovered," he said, the words less broken now. He remained where he was, one hand still upon the mantel, the other easing away only after he was certain it would hold.

He could feel her behind him. Not by sound. Not by sight. By the same indefinable awareness that had plagued him since her arrival—an attention that refused direction, that would not be commanded.

"It occurs to me," he went on, carefully, "that it is a grand—if perverse—coincidence that we should both have been subject to so many... irregularities of late." He paused, choosing each word as though it might betray him if mishandled. "I wonder whether you have observed the same."

Elizabeth did not answer at once.

He felt her behind him—still, intent—before she crossed the small distance to the hearth. She held her hands out to the fire, not close enough to warm them, only near enough that the flames leaned subtly in her direction, restless in a way Darcy had learned to distrust.

She watched them for a moment. Then she looked away.

"Yes. I noticed it," she said, her voice almost matter-of-fact. "From the first time you touched me."

# Chapter Forty

He still stood at the mantel, one hand braced against the stone as though it anchored him there. The firelight caught the line of his shoulder, the careful stillness of a man who had mastered restraint by habit and now relied upon it too heavily.

Elizabeth crossed to the chair she had abandoned and sat again. She did not look at the fire again, but kept her eyes on him.

"At the Assembly. I blamed it on a spark, because it was easier, and because I have two… perhaps three very silly young sisters." She lifted a shoulder. "Everyone expects sparks at a dance."

"I recall something of that."

"And my injudicious words after, no doubt." She bit her lip. "But it was stronger than that. It struck through my arm—here—and ran down my back and nearly knocked the air from my lungs before I had time to decide how to stand."

His brows raised. "So fearsome as that?"

"There were other moments," she continued. "Small ones. Handing off a teacup, or when you would pass by me and accidentally brush my sleeve. Each time the same shock—less violent than the first, but still, like nothing I had ever experienced. As though something in me had been… rung."

She stopped, then toyed with the stem of her glass in thought. "And yet," she said, "it faded. Not at once, but over time. By the time you left Hertfordshire, it had become almost familiar. Rather pleasant, in fact."

"Pleasant?"

"More like a…" She frowned. "Like a humming. Rather like the purring of a cat. Except you probably think that nonsense, for I doubt you have ever kept a cat as a personal pet."

Then, her stomach dropped. Oh, dear, had she just told a man that her body hummed indecently at his touch? She half-lurched from her chair. "I am afraid, sir, that might not sound—"

"You need not explain further. I perfectly comprehend the intent. So, there *was* some… discomfort."

"Yes, but only at first. It has been some while since I found your presence… troublesome."

Darcy turned his head slightly and brought his hand to his mouth, as though to forestall another cough. When he spoke, his voice was level—but only just. "For me," he said, "I should say the opposite was the case."

She blinked, and her mouth dropped open slightly. "You…?"

"I felt nothing that first night. But since then, it has intensified. With time. With proximity."

Elizabeth did not answer at once.

She set her empty glass aside and rose, then checked herself, pacing two short steps before stopping. One hand lifted, then fell again. Perhaps she ought not to touch him just now.

"I believed it was only my own… peculiarity," she said at last. "That whatever occurred between us was something I must simply endure, or outgrow. I did not imagine it could move in the other direction. Do you understand any of it?"

He turned fully toward her then. "Some."

"And that is?"

"I know that it was not accident." He paused, then continued, choosing each word with care. "Nor imagination. Nor illness, in the ordinary sense."

He turned around to face her fully at last. "I know," he went on, "that it is bound to my family. That somehow, I was committed to this… all of it… before I was ever born."

"You speak as though it were some deliberate act of your father."

"Not deliberate," Darcy replied. "But not random."

He turned away again, one hand flattening against the mantel as though the stone alone kept him upright. When he spoke, the words came slower, each one drawn up as if from somewhere deep and reluctant.

"There are old accounts," he said. "Fragmentary. Incomplete. Preserved badly, if at all. They do not explain what is asked. They record only that there was…" he shook his head. "Some choice. Some moment of decision, and that something was refused. Or broken."

Elizabeth took a step toward him without thinking, then stopped. The fire bent slightly in her periphery, the flame drawing closer to her skirts before settling back into itself.

"And you believe," she said, "that we have arrived at such a moment."

"I believe we are approaching it. But I do not know... why you? What sort of foul luck chose you, Elizabeth Bennet, for illness and blight and this terrible curse upon you?"

Elizabeth moved instead to the chair she had abandoned and rested her hand upon its back. "It has happened before. I am not unique."

Darcy's brow furrowed, and he stepped closer. "But..."

"Aunts. Cousins. Women long before the Bennets came, who remained near the land around Longbourn too long." Her mouth curved, faint and unsmiling. "I never knew this until recently, but my father tells me it has gone on for as far back as he can tell, and for no cause anyone understands. They were said to have delicate nerves. Overactive fancies. A tendency to exhaustion."

"So..." He shook his head. "What happened to them?"

Elizabeth drew her lower lip between her teeth and turned away, wandering back to the chair but not sitting. "The lucky ones were married off, if they could be. Others were confined. Or hidden, passed among family who could bear with their predictions and strange visions and collapsing insanity."

"And you?"

"Oh, I am sure I was meant to be no different. Only I was struck by some sort of physical illness, not just..." She frowned. Dropped her eyes to the floor. "Madness."

Darcy stepped an inch closer, a strange light growing in his face. "You were chosen."

She shrugged. "I think I was just... next."

"No." He shook his head vehemently. "Nothing about this—any of this—is mere accident. Nor will it simply go away because we find it inconvenient. Something is expected... *demanded* of us. And I will be damned if I can find out what it is."

The words he had used—unvarnished, sharp with strain—still hung between them, at odds with the careful room and the gentleman who had spoken them. She had never heard him speak so, not even when provoked. It frightened her more than the admission itself.

Elizabeth folded her hands upon the chair's arm and found that she had gripped the wood hard enough to blanch her knuckles. She loosened them deliberately. Her mouth opened, closed again. Any comfort she might offer seemed barred from use, as though even sympathy would exact a toll he could not afford. And she could not touch him. She knew that much with an instinct she trusted.

"Well," she said at last, and stopped. Tried again. "I imagine—" Her lips pressed together, then curved despite herself. "I imagine Miss Bingley would give a great deal to be so thoroughly entangled in a mystical calamity with Fitzwilliam Darcy."

The silence that followed lasted no longer than a breath. He looked at her as though uncertain he had heard her rightly; something flickered across his expression—disbelief, then reluctant comprehension.

Then he laughed.

Not the restrained exhalation of amusement she knew so well, but a genuine sound, surprised out of him, as though it had taken him unawares. He turned his head aside at first, one hand lifting to his brow, and then laughed again—shorter, softer, until it broke on a cough he choked back manfully.

"I ought to have known," he said, when he could speak, "that you would find some means of making sport of even this. It was foolish of me to expect otherwise."

Elizabeth allowed herself a small, careful smile, relief loosening something tight behind her ribs.

He looked at her then—not as he had before, guarded or searching or braced against consequence—but openly. The firelight caught his expression and held it there: warm, intent, touched with an admiration she could not mistake. "At least, I am glad of one thing."

"And that is?"

"That you have recovered your wit. It would be a far darker business indeed without it." Darcy's mirth faded then, though the warmth did not leave his face at once. He studied her a moment longer, then let his hand fall from the mantel.

"You said yourself that you feel better here. Not merely housed and supped, but... altered. Have you any notion why London should effect such a change?"

Elizabeth's smile drew downward. "You have not discovered that already? Why, it is you, of course."

She saw his throat bob. "Me? But I thought... you just said—"

"Yes, but that was in the *beginning*, and I am not so certain it was you... directly. More like a sort of reckoning, or sensibility awakened. I puzzled over it for weeks, you may be assured. Then, when Mr Collins came to stay with us, I thought his voice alone should be the end of me."

"Mr Collins?" Darcy narrowed his eyes. "Interesting."

"But then I discovered that the proximity of certain company dulled it. I had narrowed that company to... well, what I thought was quite another person entirely, but all along..."

"But surely, you should have improved when Mr Collins left Longbourn."

"I would have hoped. But no. I grew worse by the day after the ball."

He swallowed, looked away. "After I left. I... egad, I was wrong. What does your father think? Surely, he must have some knowledge or opinion on the matter."

She dropped her eyes and, after a moment's hesitation, reached into the pocket of her gown. The paper she drew out was creased from having been folded and unfolded more than once.

"I supposed you would ask. And I did not wish to answer you unprepared." She held the express between them, offering it, but he made no move to accept it.

"My father writes with concern, as you may imagine. He is relieved—grateful, even—that I am improved under your roof." Her fingers tightened slightly on the paper. "But he has not been content to trust that alone."

Darcy's brow knit. "Meaning?"

"He has consulted Mr Wickham, the only man whose counsel has proved in the least helpful or accurate."

The name had scarcely left her mouth before Darcy turned away, a sharp sound breaking from him—low, involuntary, edged with disbelief. "Wickham?" he muttered, the word bitten off like an oath.

Elizabeth's hand faltered. She drew the letter back a fraction, her gaze lifting to his face. "You must forgive me. But that reaction requires explanation. What history have you with Mr Wickham? And what possible knowledge could he have of any of this?"

Darcy did not answer at once. When he did, his voice had lost its earlier heat and taken on something more guarded.

"He and I were raised on the same stories," he said. "The sort one hears at nurse's knee and thinks nothing of until one is too old to ask after them properly. Tales meant to frighten children into obedience. Warnings dressed as rhyme." He shook his head once. "An oath unkept. A charge deferred. A future claim laid upon my family. Wickham listened where I did not. He remembered what I dismissed. Valued it for the supposed 'honour' I would have gladly foregone."

Elizabeth glanced down at the folded paper again. "Then you will understand why his counsel troubles me."

Darcy's eyes returned to the express. "Tell me."

She hesitated only a moment longer. "He believes I ought not to be near you. That whatever passes between us is... poisonous. He calls my improvement here a false calm. A borrowed strength. He fears it will cost me dearer in the end."

Slowly, Darcy reached out. His fingers closed on the letter at last, easing it from her grasp. He unfolded it and read in silence, his expression flickering between feelings as his eyes moved down the page. When he finished, he refolded it once and held it loosely in his hand.

"And you?" he asked. "What do *you* think, Miss Elizabeth?"

She frowned, considering him with a seriousness he had rarely seen in her. Then she lifted her eyes and met his without flinching.

"I think," she said, "that whatever it is you have set in motion in me, the only relief I have known from it has been either in your presence—or in the thought of you, or of things bound to you."

THE NEARNESS OF HER was already undoing him—his balance gone subtly wrong, breath miscounted, the room narrowed to the precise distance between them. Want gathered where discipline had always held. He had lived his life by governing impulse. This—whatever this was—answered to no such governance.

"Define it," he said. The words came quietly, but they carried more than he meant to permit. He heard it himself: the edge beneath them, the demand sharpened by fear. "Is it fate you speak of? Affection? Or only the mind's last defence against something it cannot outrun?"

Her smile struck him before the words did. Not bright. Not teasing. Something inward, as though she had reached the end of an argument she had long been conducting with herself and had at last conceded the point.

"Perhaps all of them," she said. "Or none. It has a shape, but not yet a name. I only know that if my nearness did not wound you so plainly, I should be tempted to test it—to see whether what strengthens me might do so more completely, more... permanently. And whether there might come a point at which your strength returns, or if I am only capable of wounding you."

The sentence left him unmoored.

*Test it...* He drew in a breath and held it, bracing as though the floor might give way beneath him. His heart beat too fast, then stumbled, then recovered with a painful insistence that made his vision swim.

"Your touch does... wound," he said at last. "But not as you suppose."

Her brow creased. "Mr Darcy—"

"It *is* a weakness," he went on, forcing the truth past his throat. "It leaves me altered. Diminished, perhaps—but only because something of me has passed into your keeping ."His voice broke despite his attempt at composure. "And what returns to me is not loss. It is... attachment."

She did not interrupt him. Egad, he wished she would. Perhaps then, the words would stop tumbling from him. Perhaps she would force him to make some sense of them.

"It was so at Netherfield," he went on. "I lacked the sense to recognise it. I knew when you entered a room without seeing you. The house altered in your absence, as though it had mislaid some necessary proportion." His mouth tightened. "When you returned to Longbourn, I told myself it was relief to be free of disturbance. It was not relief. It was deprivation."

Her breathing shallowed... trembled, as her lips parted softly. He saw it. Felt it.

"Even when I resisted seeking you," he continued, "even when I was resolved to be sensible, I could not escape the knowledge of where you were. Reason availed nothing. Habit less. Duty not at all." A breath escaped him, short and without humour. "Even my dog defeated me."

Her lips curved in a reluctant chuckle. "Brutus?"

"He knew before I did. He would not settle. Would not be diverted. He dragged me from my books, from my explanations, from my resolve. There *was* a tether." He paused, then spoke the word he had avoided. "Not desire... not alone." His voice dropped. "Something far less governable."

She abandoned her chair then, slowly, as though any abrupt movement might fracture what lay between them. The motion pulled at him, hard enough that he had to brace his hand against the mantel to remain upright.

"What do you make of it?" she asked. "What is to be done?"

He met her gaze without evasion now. There was no strength left for it. "All I know," he said, "is that proximity has bred not only obligation, but... *want*—and I no longer know where one ends and the other begins."

"*Want*?"

Darcy lowered his eyes. The shame of confession—of such a complication to so many other matters which remained misunderstood and unexplained—how *dare* he lay yet another question over them?

He felt her move before he saw it.

Not a step—an intention. The space between them retreated, as though it had learned her shape and yielded to it. She approached with care, as if the floor itself might object, her gaze steady, purposeful, far too calm for what it did to him.

His breath broke loose from him, shallow and uneven. He leaned forward despite himself, drawn by the simple fact of her being nearer—too near—until sense struck hard enough to make him lift a hand.

"Wait."

The word came rough, torn from him. He held his palm up between them, not touching her, not trusting himself to. His fingers trembled. "I did not... when I asked you here, it was not for this. I meant only to speak. To learn what might be learned." A swallow, badly managed. "I would not—never—impose myself upon you."

She did not retreat.

Instead, she edged closer by a fraction that undid him far more completely than any boldness could have done. Her voice, when it came, was gentle—almost curious.

"And have you learned what you wished to know?"

He shook his head. He could not trust words now. The room had contracted to her breath, the line of her mouth, the small, dangerous certainty that she was waiting—not passive, not teasing, but present. Offered.

As though she had decided to see what he would do, and would not move until he did.

Something in him gave way.

The restraint he had built over a lifetime—duty, judgment, the careful governance of self—fell back as if it had been waiting for permission to fail. Hunger surged up, fierce and unreasoning, eclipsing fear and consequence alike.

Darcy reached for her. With no gentleness or caution, but the full, desperate claim of a man who had resisted too long and could no longer remember why.

He found her mouth.

Not fully—not cleanly. It was the barest collision, breath and heat and the ghost of contact, enough to scorch without satisfying. Her lips parted in surprise against his, and the sound she made—small, startled—cut straight through him.

Fire flared behind his eyes. Not metaphor. *Memory.*

The dream rose up unbidden: flame curling where it should not, light bending toward her as if it knew her name, his own hands burned raw from holding it back. He tasted smoke where there was none, felt again the terrible certainty that if he did not interpose himself, she would be consumed.

But not now.

He dragged his thoughts back with violence and pressed closer, as though proximity alone might banish prophecy. His hand slid to her waist, the curve of her fitting him with a rightness that stole what breath he had left. For one wild instant, there was only the exultation of it—of holding her, of knowing her real and warm and alive beneath his hands.

And then the cost came due.

Pain tore through his chest, sharp and immediate, as if something had closed its fist around his heart. His head reeled. The room tipped. He tasted iron and knew dimly that he was no longer entirely upright.

Elizabeth broke from him with a cry, hands fisting in his coat as she pushed him back to his feet, fear stark on her face. "Stop—Darcy, stop!" She stared at him, horrified. "You're—oh God—you are not well—"

The house answered.

Not with warning, not with a sigh, but with a brutal wrench, as though the ground itself had been seized and shaken. The floor lurched beneath their feet. The mantel gave a sharp crack as porcelain leapt and struck against itself. Somewhere overhead, something heavy shifted and fell.

Darcy staggered, his vision bursting white at the edges. Pain tore through his chest again—hot, blinding—and he tasted blood outright this time, copper and salt flooding his mouth as he fought not to fold in on himself.

The candle slid.

Elizabeth gasped—his name half-formed—and the flame tipped toward her skirts.

Darcy moved without thought, without balance. He lunged, caught her sleeve in a desperate fist, and dragged her back as the candle struck the carpet and flared. The motion wrenched another broken sound from his chest, but he did not release her.

Elizabeth tore free only to stamp the flame out at once, heel grinding wax and wick into the rug as the room continued to shudder around them. The fire died with a sharp hiss.

The shaking ebbed as abruptly as it had come.

What remained was wreckage: a chair knocked askew, porcelain scattered like bone across the hearth, the fire snapping too loudly in its grate. Darcy stood bent forward, one hand locked against his breast, breath coming ragged and uneven.

Elizabeth turned on him, white-faced and wild-eyed.

Darcy could not have said who moved first, only that suddenly she was there, solid and breathing and unhurt—and that the certainty of it struck him harder than the pain still clawing at his chest. His hand remained pressed there, as though he might yet fall apart if he let go.

The room felt altered. Not damaged—*answered*. That this had not been an accident of stone or weather. Something had heard the question he had asked, the test they two had attempted.

And it had replied.

# Chapter Forty-One

THE DOOR STRUCK THE wall hard enough to leave a mark. Darcy could only stare at it in a hazy sort of stupor—his hand had occasioned the violence, but his mind was still too sluggish to gentle his movements.

The sound echoed down the corridor, sharp enough to draw a gasp from Elizabeth beside him. She caught the edge of the door as it bounced back, glancing helplessly at the damage done to the wall. "Are you…?"

"I can walk."

The words emerged thin, scraped raw on the way out. His chest answered them with a tight, unyielding pressure that made each step an act of balance rather than intention. The floor had stopped moving, but he was not certain how he was connected to it. He reached for the wall, missed it, corrected.

Elizabeth's hand lifted in reflex, hovering near his sleeve before halting short. "Mr Darcy—"

"No!" He swallowed and forced the rest through more evenly. "Do not… Please, do not."

She withdrew her hand at once. The space between them felt abruptly colder.

Behind them, the library lay open and ruined: the overturned chair, the scattered porcelain, the darkened patch on the carpet where wax had been stamped and ground into the pile. Smoke lingered faintly in the air. Darcy forced himself to look at it properly, to take note. Evidence required attention.

A shout sounded from the stairs. Another answered it—this one sharper, alarmed.

Elizabeth gaped after the sound in some horror. "We… we have awakened the house."

"Yes," he said. "That is to be expected."

Footsteps pounded along the corridor. A door opened somewhere with a crack like a snapped branch. The house was coming apart into noise and motion, servants calling to one another, voices raised in the careful urgency of those trained to act without panic.

Darcy took one step forward and very nearly lost the second.

Elizabeth caught her breath, stopped herself again from wedging herself under his shoulder. He almost wished she would. Kill him with her mercy and have done with it.

Her face had gone pale beneath the flush left behind by the shock, her loose braid had begun to come undone at the nape. And in the light of the hall, he could see now how hastily done up her gown was, sleeves rumpled as though pulled on without care.

The realization struck him with a sudden, mortifying clarity. Matters did not look... innocent.

He straightened at once, though his spine gave way with a painful twinge that nearly buckled him. His hand remained pressed flat against his chest, fingers splayed, as though he could contain what remained unruly beneath them by force alone.

Voices rose nearer. "Darcy? Where are you?"

Bingley's, unmistakably. Footsteps hurried along the passage, then slowed, uncertain.

Darcy turned just as Bingley came into view, candle held high enough to throw light across the corridor in a wavering arc. He wore his dressing gown half-fastened, feet still bare, his expression shifting rapidly from relief to astonishment as his gaze took them in together.

"Thank God," Bingley began—then stopped. His eyes flicked from Darcy to Elizabeth and back again, polite instinct wrestling with a conclusion he was determined not to voice.

Elizabeth moved first, stepping back a pace, as though the space between them had suddenly become improper rather than dangerous.

"There was a disturbance." Her voice held steady, but her hands were clenched in her skirts. "The library—"

"I felt it," Bingley said quickly. "The whole house. Are you injured?"

Darcy shook his head once. The motion sent a sharp reminder through his ribs, but he kept his expression composed. "No. But there may be damage. I require the servants brought together at once."

Bingley blinked, then nodded, relief seizing eagerly upon the practical. "Of course. I'll—"

A crash interrupted him—glass, somewhere beyond the hall. A woman cried out.

Darcy did not wait. He moved past Bingley into the passage. Each step jarred, but he kept his pace sedate. Appearances, now, were necessary.

In the main hall, the house had transformed.

Candles flared in every direction, flames bobbing as servants hurried through the hall. A footman knelt near the far wall, brushing shards of glass into his apron. Water sloshed somewhere.

Darcy raised his voice. “Attend.”

It cut through the confusion at once. Heads turned. Movement slowed.

“Has anyone been injured?” he demanded.

A murmur of answers followed—no, sir; only fright; a fall; some porcelain shattered, one priceless vase toppled, but no broken bones. Relief flickered briefly through him.

“The west corridor must be examined at once,” he continued. “Chimneys first. Then ceilings. No one is to re-enter any room where stone has shifted until it is cleared. Bring lanterns. Secure the fires. If there is further movement, you will evacuate to the courtyard without hesitation.”

“Yes, sir.”

Miss Bingley appeared then at the foot of the stairs, pale beneath a hastily applied sheen of white cream that caught the candlelight oddly along her cheek. Her hair had been braided for the night and now clung to her greased temples. She took in the scene in a single sweep—and then her eyes found Elizabeth, standing just behind Darcy.

“What is the meaning of this?” she demanded, the civility she prized so carefully already fracturing. “Why are you here?”

Darcy made no response to Miss Bingley, but turned as a maid rushed up to him. “The library rug is burned,” she said, voice trembling slightly. “I know I put those candles out myself, but there is melted wax and a large scorch—”

“I will see it,” Darcy replied. “For now, have it covered. It was not your fault.”

Miss Bingley’s voice rose again. “A candle at this time of night? How could—”

“Caroline.” Bingley’s tone carried warning, gentle but unmistakable.

Darcy drew a careful breath, straightened, and spoke again to the servants, already cataloguing what must be done before thought could intrude where it was least welcome.

Behind him, he was acutely aware of Elizabeth’s presence—still there, still silent, still not touching him.

SHE STUMBLED ON THE last stair and caught herself on the newel before anyone else noticed.

"Elizabeth!"

Jane was there at once, her hand firm at Elizabeth's elbow.

"I am well," Elizabeth said, because Jane's face required it. "Truly."

Jane did not loosen her hold. "You look as though you have been dragged through the night itself. Where were you?"

Before Elizabeth could answer, Miss Bingley's voice cut in, sharp as snapped thread. "Yes, indeed. Where *were* you, Miss Elizabeth? *We* were all abed when the house decided to tear itself apart."

A servant appeared, breathless, lantern raised. "If you please, ladies, Mr Darcy requests you gather in the west withdrawing room. The walls are stone. It is thought safest in case there are more tremors."

"There will be no more tremors," Elizabeth said.

The servant blinked at the certainty. Jane tightened her grip.

"Hush," Jane murmured. "You cannot know that."

Elizabeth did know it. The knowledge lay quiet and immovable beneath her lungs, like a settled weight. She swallowed it back. This was not the moment.

They were urged forward together, a small procession shepherded along the passage and into a low-ceilinged room whose thick walls smelled faintly of cool lime and old hearth smoke. Lanterns were set along the table. Windows shattered open to the December chill. A maid tried to close the door, but the latch had broken.

Elizabeth sat because Jane pressed her down.

Only then did she feel the tremor in her hands—not fear, but aftermath. Her skin still held the echo of heat, of closeness gone too far. The memory of Darcy's breath against her cheek rose unbidden, and with it the awful, lucid knowledge of what her wanting had done to him.

She folded her hands together until the shaking ceased.

Jane knelt before her. "Lizzy. You frightened me."

"I know." The words came out thin. She tried again. "I am sorry."

"For the fright?" Miss Bingley interjected, positioning herself with intent near the lantern light. "Or for the impropriety?"

Jane looked up sharply. "Miss Bingley! What has my sister done to merit—"

"I think we may as well speak plainly," Miss Bingley said. "Since circumstances have already stripped us of every other comfort. A lady under my brother's care is found wandering the house at night, half-dressed, in the company of a gentleman not her relation. And during an earthquake, no less! One is forced to wonder whether the illness that so conveniently confined her earlier was not… exaggerated."

Elizabeth lifted her head. "You are welcome to wonder." Her voice surprised her with its steadiness. "But I will not answer it."

Miss Bingley's brows rose. "How very convenient."

Jane rose to her feet. "You forget yourself, Miss Bingley!"

"Do I? I think rather that I am remembering the obligations of hospitality. And propriety. And my brother's position, his rather convenient friendship with a single man of large fortune who seems to lose his composure whenever *she* is about! I believe that is twice now you have managed to throw yourself in his way with this strange ailment of yours."

Elizabeth closed her eyes for a brief instant. The darkness soothed her. When she opened them again, she looked not at Miss Bingley, but at the stone wall beyond her shoulder—solid, unmoved, unanswering.

"I did not fake my illness," she said quietly. "I would not know how."

"And yet you appear remarkably recovered. One might almost say entirely revived! How strange that Mr Jones could find nothing amiss."

Jane's hand found Elizabeth's shoulder.

Elizabeth did not shrug it off. She leaned into it instead, just enough to borrow strength without admitting the need. "Appearances are unreliable. I should think recent events have demonstrated that."

Miss Bingley drew a breath to reply—and stopped when a strange look crossed Elizabeth's face.

It was not pain, not pressure, but absence. Darcy was no longer near enough to warm the air. The hollow left behind was immediate and vast, as though something essential had been shut away without ceremony. She pressed her lips together until the sensation dulled into something bearable.

Jane was watching her too closely now. "Lizzy," she said softly, "you are cold."

"I am not," Elizabeth said. It was not true. She pulled her gown closer, all the same.

The door opened briefly. A servant glanced in, nodded, and withdrew again. Voices passed in the corridor beyond—all voices with purpose, a place to be and things to do.

Darcy's house, moving without him.

The thought struck with a pang sharp enough to steal what little breath she had. She fixed her gaze on the lantern instead, its light steady against the stone, and told herself—sternly—that this was as it must be. That she *had* wanted him—not only for the strength he offered, but for himself. That she had taken one step too far. That the cost had been exacted without mercy.

She had not meant to hurt him. But the wanting had not asked her permission.

Jane sat beside her and slipped an arm around her shoulders, shielding her from further comment without a word. Elizabeth let herself rest there, just for a moment, while the house creaked and settled around them.

No more tremors came.

Elizabeth knew they would not.

DARCY CAUGHT HIMSELF BY the doorframe and waited for the breath to finish misbehaving.

It did, eventually. The surge of strength that had carried him through the last inspection—chimney sound, hearths banked, windows shuttered—drained away as abruptly as it had come, leaving behind a dull pressure beneath his breastbone that made the world feel fractionally too near.

He straightened anyway.

The kitchen was serviceable. Fires reduced and contained, kettles shifted to the side hearth. The cook had been brisk, unflustered, affronted by the suggestion that her domain might fail under stress.

The stables were quiet; the horses uninjured, ears pricked in curiosity as they chewed their hay, stamping only at the unfamiliar hour.

Locks held. Doors answered properly. No cracks along the south wall. No fallen stone.

All of it ordinary. Reassuringly so.

Bingley hovered at his shoulder through most of it, offering assistance that was more presence than help, asking questions Darcy answered shortly, keeping his own observations to himself in a way that was meant to be considerate and was instead intolerable.

"You ought to sit," Bingley said for the third time, as they turned back toward the main hall.

Darcy shook his head. The motion sent a brief flare of dizziness through him—nothing alarming, he told himself, merely the residue of exertion. "There is nothing to be gained by it."

"You look quite ghastly."

Darcy spared him a glance. "You exaggerate."

"I assure you, I do not. You are pale, you are breathing as though you have run a mile, and you have refused wine, water, and food in equal measure. If this is not the beginning of a fever, I should like to know what is."

Darcy opened his mouth to dismiss it—and found, for an instant, that the words would not come. His chest tightened sharply, breath catching halfway in. He slowed his pace without remark until the sensation eased, then continued as though nothing had occurred.

"It will pass," he said at last. "I am merely fatigued."

Bingley watched him with a frown that had deepened steadily over the past quarter hour. "You said that earlier."

"And it was true then."

They reached the foot of the stairs. The house was quieting at last, the urgent motion giving way to cautious order. Servants moved with dignity rather than alarm now. Someone laughed softly near the scullery, and most were returning to bed. The familiar sounds settled around him like a garment he had worn all his life.

Darcy drew a careful breath. The air felt thinner than it ought.

There would be no more tremors. Of that he was certain—certain in a way that did not admit argument. The last shock had not been random. It had not been stone or fault or weather. It had been the wrench of separation, the land's answer to a question he had not finished asking.

If he did not approach her again, it would hold. At what cost, he did not yet know.

And if he did...

The thought did not complete itself. His chest answered it instead, a sudden, punishing throb that forced him to pause outright and grip the banister until the floor steadied beneath his feet.

Bingley caught his arm. "Darcy!"

"I am well," Darcy said at once, though his voice had come out rather garbled. He eased his arm free and continued upward, setting his pace by will rather than comfort.

At the landing, he stopped.

"The ladies may return to their rooms," he said. "The west withdrawing room has served its purpose. You might see to them."

Bingley blinked. "I—Darcy, that is your place."

"There is no need," Darcy replied. He kept his gaze fixed on the corridor ahead, on the closed doors that marked the upper rooms. "They are safe. Maids can be sent if they require any assistance. It would be better if I allowed them to settle themselves."

Bingley studied him for a moment longer than politeness required. "You are avoiding something."

Darcy's mouth curved into something that was not quite a smile. "I am prioritizing."

"Then allow me to be plain," Bingley said. "You are in no condition to inspect anything else tonight, and you are certainly in no condition to collapse in a hallway because you refuse to admit you are ill."

"I am not—"

"Darcy," Bingley interrupted gently, "may I have a word?"

The request landed with quiet finality. Darcy considered refusal—and found he lacked the strength to sustain it.

He turned instead and opened the door to his study, gesturing Bingley inside. Then he closed the door behind them. "What is it you wish to say?"

Bingley did not speak at once. He came to stand near the desk, hands clasped behind his back as though unsure what to do with them, his expression carefully arranged into something that might pass for ease if one did not look too closely.

"At the risk of being indelicate," he began, and stopped. Shifted his weight. Tried again. "Is there some… attachment between you and Miss Elizabeth Bennet that I ought to be made aware of?"

Darcy did not answer immediately. He moved instead to the edge of the desk and set his hand upon it, fingers splayed, as though the solid wood might anchor a thought that had begun to slip.

"I do not know what you mean."

Bingley winced. "Darcy."

"There is no attachment," Darcy said, evenly. "Certainly, none that concerns you."

Bingley drew a breath through his nose. "Then you must forgive me for being very nearly convinced otherwise."

Darcy lifted his head.

Bingley met his gaze squarely now, the discomfort he had worn so carefully set aside. "I found you together in the library tonight. Alone. Long after the house had gone to bed. Miss Elizabeth was not dressed for company, and you—" he hesitated. "You looked scarcely able to stand."

"That proves nothing."

"It proves more than nothing," Bingley said quietly. "It proves intimacy. Or at least the appearance of it."

Darcy's jaw tightened. He said nothing.

"And that is not all," Bingley went on, emboldened by the silence. "At the Netherfield ball, I watched you speak together through the whole supper. Why, you entirely ignored your tablemates. You were not bored. You were not quarrelling. You were... engaged. Happily so, it seemed, until some altercation. Whatever passed between you ended badly enough that you left Hertfordshire the next morning without explanation."

Darcy turned away.

Bingley followed him with his eyes. "When Miss Elizabeth collapsed in the fields and came to us to recover, one of the maids mentioned—quite by accident—that she had seen the two of you together on the servants' stair, late at night. I dismissed it at the time as confusion or fancy." He paused. "I am less certain of that now."

Darcy's hand curled against the edge of the desk. He loosened it again by force.

"And then," Bingley added, more gently, "there is her illness. I do not believe she pretended. Caroline's insinuations are ungenerous, and I told her so. Miss Elizabeth *was* unwell. That much was evident. But she is not unwell now. Not even a little."

Darcy closed his eyes.

The room felt smaller with them shut. He opened them again at once.

"You see the difficulty," Bingley said. "I am not accusing you. I am asking you—how am I to understand any of this?"

Darcy drew a slow breath. It did not go as deep as he wished.

He could dismiss it all as rumour. He could call it coincidence, misinterpretation, the natural consequence of nerves and proximity. He could even—if pressed—confess to some brief, ill-considered folly and insist the matter was ended. Forgotten. He could urge Bingley to remove the Bennets at once, to carry Elizabeth as far from London as possible, and leave him to recover in peace.

But he knew, with a clarity that admitted no evasion, that none of that would serve.

Elizabeth needed help. He did not know how to give it.

Her father did not know enough to see the shape of what was happening. Wickham knew enough to be dangerous. And he himself—he stood at the centre of something that grew worse the more carefully he tried to manage it.

Darcy turned back to Bingley. "I do not know how much to tell you."

Bingley's brows rose slightly. He did not interrupt.

"There are... histories," Darcy continued. The word tasted inadequate. "Family traditions. Matters long obscured by time and carelessness. I believed them—until recently—to be little more than metaphor."

Bingley's expression did not change, but something in his attention sharpened.

"What I know now," Darcy said, choosing each word with care, "is that Miss Elizabeth Bennet's health is not... entirely her own concern. Nor, it seems, is mine."

Bingley let out a small, incredulous breath. "Darcy—"

"I am aware how it sounds."

"Yes," Bingley said faintly. "You are."

Darcy waited for the laugh. For the indulgent smile. For the gentle dismissal he had prepared himself to endure.

None came.

Instead, Bingley leaned back against the desk, arms folding loosely across his chest. "If this were any other man," he said slowly, "I should think it a grand invention. The sort of tale people tell themselves to lend consequence to unfortunate choices."

Darcy said nothing.

"But you," Bingley went on, "are not inclined to invention. Nor to drama. Nor to indulgence in nonsense." He shook his head slightly. "And I have seen things these past weeks that do not sit comfortably with ordinary explanation."

Darcy stared at him.

Bingley met his gaze without flinching. "So—suppose I credit you this much. Suppose I accept that something is amiss, and that it involves you both. What, then, are we to do?"

Darcy turned away again, pacing the length of the study. The movement sent another sharp protest through his chest; he slowed but did not stop.

"I wish I knew," he said at last.

He halted near the window, one hand braced against the sill. Outside, the grounds lay quiet beneath the night sky, undisturbed now, as though nothing had ever trembled there at all.

"All I know," Darcy said, his voice lower than before, "is that I am bound to Elizabeth Bennet in a manner I do not fully understand. That my presence fortifies her. That hers undoes me." He swallowed. "And that whatever is required of us... is not something I can survive unchanged."

Bingley watched him in silence.

Darcy did not look back. “It is some sort of a union,” he said, because there was no plainer word that did not lie. “One my heart wants. My soul requires. And my mind knows will be my own ruin.”

He closed his eyes—not in despair, but in weary acknowledgement.

“That,” he said quietly, “is the extent of my certainty.”

# Chapter Forty-Two

Jane broke the roll neatly in two and passed the smaller portion across the table.

Elizabeth took it without appetite. The morning room was bright—too bright, perhaps—with winter sun striking the pale panelling and making the silver pot gleam as though nothing had happened in the night. The windows in this room stood intact. The walls bore no cracks. It was precisely the sort of calm that felt earned rather than natural.

Miss Bingley had not appeared.

"She sent word that she had a headache," Jane said mildly, pouring tea. "And that she preferred to take it upstairs."

Elizabeth's mouth curved despite herself. "How unfortunate."

Jane glanced at her, eyes warm and knowing. "I thought I heard raised voices."

"So did I," Elizabeth said. She buttered the roll with more care than the task required. "It sounded like a philosophical disagreement. Possibly involving propriety."

Jane smiled, then sobered. "Lizzy—"

Footsteps passed in the corridor beyond the open door. Elizabeth's hand stilled.

She had known he would come. The certainty had settled in her long before the sound reached her ears, the same quiet awareness that had lifted her gaze moments earlier, unprompted, toward the doorway.

Darcy paused there.

For a fraction of a second, his expression was not surprise at all, but recognition—something taut and searching, as though he had found precisely what he expected and was bracing himself for it. Then the look shifted, smoothed into polite astonishment.

"Miss Bennet. Miss Elizabeth," he said, inclining his head.

Elizabeth returned the courtesy. She was acutely aware of the distance he kept from the table, the careful placement of his feet, the way his hands remained occupied. A small stack of broadsheets was tucked beneath his arm.

"I did not expect to find you here so early," he went on. His voice held this morning, but there was a faint pitch to it that made her stomach lurch in answer.

Jane gestured lightly to the window. "The morning is agreeable."

"So it is." Darcy glanced down at the papers. "There is… a great deal of talk already about last night's disturbances."

He extended the broadsheets toward them—toward her—then hesitated, as though recalling himself mid-motion. The papers did not quite cross the space between them.

Elizabeth's fingers curled reflexively against her napkin. The thought of standing, of closing that distance, brought with it a swift, unwelcome memory of heat and breath and the terrible price of nearness.

"Jane," she said, too quickly, "would you—?"

Jane looked from her to Darcy, brows lifting in faint, amused confusion. "I am rather farther away."

"I know."

Jane's brows pinched together, but she rose without comment and crossed the room, accepting the broadsheets from Darcy's outstretched hand. Their fingers brushed briefly. Darcy did not flinch.

Elizabeth watched instead.

When Jane stepped back again, papers in hand, Darcy's gaze returned to Elizabeth's face. It held there—longer than courtesy required, longer than was wise. There was no warmth in it, no invitation. Only a quiet, searching hunger that made her breath feel shallow and ill-managed.

At last, he inclined his head once more. "I must see to other matters."

"Of course," Jane said.

Darcy turned and went down the corridor without another word.

Elizabeth remained seated, her hands folded tightly in her lap, the place where he had stood still warm in her senses long after the sound of his steps had faded.

Jane spread the broadsheets across the table, smoothing them with the flat of her palm as though they might settle into sense if treated gently enough.

"There are several," she said. "Different printers—*The Times*, the *Morning Chronicle*, the *Gazetteer*. And this one from *Lloyd's*." She lifted the first sheet and read.

"'*An Uncommon Disturbance Felt Across the Metropolis and Beyond.*

In the late hours of the night just passed, a tremor of notable force was felt throughout London and its environs, causing alarm among householders and damage to chimneys, glass, and masonry in several districts.'"

Elizabeth's eyes tracked the lines as Jane read. The words arranged themselves with unnerving calm.

"Read the next," Elizabeth said.

Jane obliged.

*"'Reports brought by express from the north speak to a more violent effect in the counties beyond the city, particularly Hertfordshire, where the shaking was said to be prolonged, and in some places severe...'"*

Elizabeth drew her breath in slowly and held it. The room felt suddenly too small.

Jane paused. "Lizzy? What about Longbourn?"

"I am sure the house stands." She forced a tight smile. "It is not plaster but stone. Surely, we will have word soon."

Jane nodded and went on.

*"'Walls were cracked in several villages. A bridge near St. Albans is reported damaged, though passable. Livestock were unsettled, with some fences reported broken. Wells clouded. No loss of life has yet been confirmed.'"*

Elizabeth closed her eyes briefly. *Wells clouded.* The phrase lodged and would not dislodge.

"There is another," Jane said, lifting a different sheet. "This one is less cautious."

*"'Some accounts suggest the tremor was felt as far as thirty miles from the city, diminishing toward the south but increasing in strength to the north. Several correspondents remark upon the unusual directionality of the disturbance...'"*

Elizabeth's fingers tightened together. *Directionality.* She could have told them that without ink or rider.

Jane hesitated, then continued.

*"'At the docks, confusion reigned for some hours. One merchant vessel was lost in the night, foundered at anchor under circumstances not yet agreed upon. Some attribute the incident to the swell that followed the tremor; others insist the sea was already restless and deny any connection.'"*

Elizabeth opened her eyes. "A ship sank in the harbour?"

Jane nodded. "It says the crew were rescued. The hull was not."

Elizabeth looked past the table, past the window, to where the house stood orderly and whole, as though it had not been the centre of anything at all. The quiet certainty returned, unwelcome in its power.

"It had everything to do with it," she said. "The quake, I mean. They are not distinct."

Jane lowered the paper. "Lizzy."

Elizabeth shook her head once, sharply, as if to clear it. "I do not mean—I only mean that people prefer separate causes. Perhaps the quake itself did not create the swell that wrecked the ship, but the same thing caused both."

Jane watched her closely now. "You sound very certain."

Elizabeth pressed her lips together. The certainty did not ask her permission. It sat where pain had once been and made itself at home.

"Read the rest," she said.

Jane did—but Elizabeth scarcely heard it. Her attention had turned inward, to the strange arithmetic unfolding beyond ink and conjecture.

London had felt it.

Hertfordshire had borne it.

And Darcy...

The thought stopped short, unfinished, as though even thinking his name might tilt something already strained.

DARCY HAD CHOSEN THE study for his conversation with Bingley because it was the one room in the house where he could plausibly expect not to encounter her.

That expectation failed him almost at once.

Not because Elizabeth appeared—but because the space she occupied elsewhere in the house pressed against his awareness with an insistence he could not dismiss. He knew where she was. The knowledge arrived without effort and remained without permission. He set his papers in order twice and abandoned the task both times, his attention slipping away before it could be completed.

Bingley paced.

He crossed from window to door and back again, stopped, turned, opened his mouth—and closed it once more. The restraint cost him visibly.

"You cannot simply avoid her," Bingley said at last.

Darcy did not look up. "I am doing nothing of the sort."

"You have altered your entire morning," Bingley replied. "You have taken your coffee here instead of the breakfast room, declined to accompany us, and given explicit instructions that messages be routed through the steward."

Darcy adjusted the stack of broadsheets on his desk. "I have work to do."

"You are attempting to outmanoeuvre your own house."

Darcy's hand paused. The faint pressure beneath his breastbone reminded him, sharply, why this was necessary.

"She is better," he said. "That is sufficient."

Bingley stopped pacing. "And you are not."

"Do not start that again."

"I am not starting anything," Bingley said, frustration breaking through his usual good humour at last. "I am standing in the middle of it. Caroline is upstairs composing a speech on impropriety and insult, and I am attempting to keep her from delivering it to anyone who will listen."

Darcy's jaw tightened. "You have my thanks."

"I should like more than thanks. I should like—" He broke off, scrubbed a hand through his hair, and turned toward the window instead. "Never mind."

The knock came then—sharp, peremptory, poorly timed.

Before Darcy could answer, the door opened.

The footman barely had time to announce the name before the man himself surged forward, coat askew, hat tucked beneath his arm, eyes alight with something that looked uncomfortably like triumph edged with alarm.

"Harrowe," Darcy greeted. *About time.*

"Darcy," Harrowe replied, already moving toward the desk. "You felt it. Of course you did. The whole city—no, farther—" He halted only long enough to drag the satchel from his shoulder and set it down with a thud. "I came soon as I could get these from the Archives."

Bingley stared. "Ah... Darcy?"

Harrowe did not notice him. He had already begun to unfasten the satchel, fingers impatient with leather and buckles, muttering to himself as he went. "I shouldn't've waited. I knew the delay was—ah. There it is."

Darcy rose. The movement sent a warning pulse through his chest, but he ignored it. "Harrowe," he said again, more firmly. "You forget yourself."

Harrowe looked up at last, taking in the room properly for the first time. His gaze flicked to Bingley, assessed, dismissed.

"Beg pardon," he said, with no trace of apology at all. "I didn't figure you had company."

"This is Mr Bingley," Darcy said. "My friend who has just arrived from Hertfordshire."

Harrowe inclined his head by a fraction. "Sir."

Bingley recovered himself enough to bow in return. "I am sorry. You appear—" He searched for the word. "Urgent."

"I am," Harrowe said simply. He reached into the satchel again.

Darcy held up a hand. "Not yet."

Harrowe froze, irritation flashing across his face. "Darcy—"

"Bingley," Darcy said, turning deliberately away from him. "My apologies for Mr Harrowe. If you would excuse us for a moment?"

Bingley hesitated. His gaze moved from Darcy to Harrowe and back again, curiosity warring openly with restraint. "If you are certain."

"I am. Thank you."

Bingley inclined his head and went to the door, pausing only long enough to give Darcy a searching look before stepping into the corridor beyond.

Darcy closed the door behind him and turned back to Harrowe. "Now," he said, "you may speak."

Harrowe opened the satchel on the desk with a decisiveness that bordered on reverence, drawing out a slim volume wrapped in oilskin so worn it looked more like habit than precaution. The cover beneath was dark, the leather cracked and rubbed smooth at the corners, the title stamped so faintly it had to be caught at an angle to be read at all.

"I was reading the Ballads last night," Harrowe said. "When it come on. The jolt. I felt it through the floorboards." He glanced up. "Would've come straight to you—but there was somethin' I needed to see first."

Darcy's gaze had fixed on the book. A pressure gathered behind his eyes that had nothing to do with fatigue. "Put that away."

Harrowe's brows lifted. "You'll want to see this."

"I wish to know," Darcy said, sharply now, "how you came by it. I was told books of that age could not even be removed from the Archives."

Harrowe paused, then smiled—not sheepishly, but with a small, private satisfaction. He reached back into the satchel and withdrew a folded sheet of parchment, yellowed with age but unmistakable in its authority. He laid it out carefully beside the book.

Darcy leaned forward despite himself.

The seal was real. The wording archaic, formal. The dates... *egad*.

"You cannot be serious," Darcy breathed.

"I am," Harrowe replied. "Entirely."

Darcy stared at the writ, then at him. "This grants your family complete access to restricted collections—indefinitely?"

"Correct."

"Across *generations?*"

"Aye."

Darcy straightened slowly. "On what grounds?"

Harrowe's expression sobered. "On the grounds that what was writ there was not to be lost. Nor to drift loose among those as couldn't tell record from rhyme. On the grounds that it was true."

Darcy exhaled once. "And the Crown agreed to such an arrangement?"

"The Crown," Harrowe said evenly, "*required* it."

Darcy's gaze fell to the page again. There were three dated signatures, and the top date was *1605*. The same year the Ballads were first printed.

Darcy's jaw dropped. "Then it was granted under James I."

"Oh, aye. James had a taste for antiquities," he said. "Lineage. Boundaries. What gave a kingdom its shape. He gave my forebear leave to examine parish rolls and monastic copies—quiet-like. Mind what I told you, he claimed to be descended from Sir Gareth? 'Twere a touch of the left hand about it," he chuckled. "No parson stood over that cradle, but James, he were proud of it all the same. Said such matters of inheritance were not to be neglected."

Darcy absorbed that. "And the later dates?" His finger moved to the last one, *1769*.

Harrowe's mouth thinned. "That was His present Majesty. Reaffirmed it, he did, and a good thing, too. My old man were turned away from the Archive one day, and His Majesty would have none of it."

Darcy hesitated. "You will forgive me if I find that difficult to reconcile with... the reports of his condition."

Harrowe went very still. Then, very quietly, he murmured, "No. I won't."

Darcy blinked.

Harrowe's voice did not rise, but it hardened. "His Majesty were raised on farming and ledgers. He reads land the way other men read faces. When the revision came before him in '69, it weren't madness moved him. It was memory."

He tapped the margin, the middle date. *1662*

"Charles II had renewed the licence after the Restoration—too many charters lost, too many boundaries muddled in the wars. Said records were to be kept close. James granted the first leave for the sake of order. Charles renewed it for the sake of stability. And George kept it for the sake of England."

Darcy said nothing.

Harrowe leaned back slightly. "A king as reads history proper knows what follows when keepings fail."

He looked directly at Darcy. "His Majesty weren't mad when he signed it. He was afraid."

Darcy sighed. "Very well, Harrowe. You have offered your bona fides. Now... what else do you have?"

Harrowe set the book down with care and reached again into the satchel, this time drawing out a sheaf of folded papers—pamphlets by the look of them, their edges brittle, the print uneven with age. He laid them beside the volume already open on Darcy's desk and began turning pages without comment, aligning passages with an instinct born of long familiarity.

"Listen to this," he said. "Not the verse—ignore the verse. That's there to hide it from the ignorant so it'd be kept in print."

He tapped a line with one blunt finger.

*When keeping fails and men give o'er,*
*The ground shall take the cry;*
*Not soft nor mild, but rent and torn,*
*Till breach be made reply.*

Darcy's gaze tracked the words.

Harrowe flipped the page of the Liber and found the corresponding passage, written in a firmer, more deliberate hand.

*When the keeping faileth,*
*flame shall rise before,*
*and waters answer in their turn;*
*the earth shall tremble betwixt them both*
*till breach be bound, or all shall burn.*

Harrowe exhaled once. "It's the same warning. Two tellings of it, that's all. This weren't speculation. They expected it."

Darcy closed his eyes briefly. The pressure beneath his ribs pulsed in dull agreement.

"It was always predicted," Harrowe went on, pacing now, agitation bleeding through his earlier restraint. "Not collapse—fracture. A tearing. A refusal to hold. But I believed"—he shook his head—"we *all* believed it would take generations. Centuries, even."

He stopped and looked at Darcy again. "'Least, I thought that until two-three months ago. Now, it is happening faster. So fast that one might believe the Lady herself had come to ruin. Or very near it."

Darcy's head came up sharply.

"Not ruined," Harrowe corrected at once, lifting a hand. "Not yet. If she were gone, the ground would show it plain. Worse than this. This is—" He hesitated. "—the edge of it."

Darcy swallowed and kneaded the palm of his right hand, for it had suddenly shot through with a fresh, stabbing ache.

Harrowe leaned forward, both hands braced on the desk. "You must tell me where she is."

Darcy did not answer.

"We *must* find her," Harrowe insisted. "Immediately. The longer she remains unrecognised—"

"She is down the hall," Darcy said.

Harrowe stared. His eyes widened. He made a sound that might have been a laugh if it had not caught so badly in his throat. "You're never serious."

"I am," Darcy replied.

Harrowe pushed back from the desk as though the wood had burned him. "She is *here*? In this house?" He ran a hand through his hair, agitation spilling over at last. "Darcy, what in God's name have you been doing?"

Darcy's patience snapped. "Everything!"

The word came out sharper than he intended. He drew a breath and tried again. “She was brought here because she was thought to be dying. Collapsing in fields. Failing without cause. London offered reprieve.”

“London?” Harrowe echoed.

Darcy’s mouth tightened. “No. *I* did. It was me.”

Harrowe crossed his thick forearms over his chest. “Go on.”

“When we spoke of it,” Darcy said, slowly now, carefully, “when we tested—”

“Tested?” Harrowe demanded.

Darcy turned on him, the movement sudden and ill-advised. Pain flared hot and immediate through his chest, stealing breath and sense together, but the words broke free regardless.

“I kissed her! It was a test. It failed.”

Harrowe froze, his mouth round with awe.

“It nearly killed me,” Darcy went on, the admission tearing loose everything he had held in check. “And when she drew away—when the bond was broken—the earth shattered.”

He stopped there, breath shallow, the room reeling faintly around him, and said no more.

Harrowe did not speak at once. He stood very still, eyes fixed on Darcy—not with disbelief, but with a sharp, searching intensity that made Darcy’s skin prickle.

“Of course,” Harrowe said at last. The words were almost reverent. “Of course it did.”

Darcy’s temper, already strained to breaking, snapped outright. “Pray, stop speaking of it as though it were *inevitable*!”

Harrowe looked up. “But it was.”

Darcy took a step toward him and had to stop himself from taking another. His chest burned, breath coming shallow and ill-managed. “You speak as though I invited it. As though I stood idle and refused discomfort, risk—”

“I speak,” Harrowe said, “having read what you’ve not yet laid eyes on.”

Darcy laughed once, harsh and without humour. “Then show it to me.”

Harrowe shook his head. “Not like this. Not in ink.”

“How? What shall I do? She nearly destroyed me! And...” Darcy swallowed, closed his eyes. “And I would do it again if it spared her.”

Harrowe’s gaze softened—not with pity, but with recognition. “That,” he said quietly, “is the problem.”

Darcy turned away, pacing the length of the study, then stopping abruptly when the movement sent a sharp lance of pain through his ribs. He caught himself against the back of a chair and forced the rest out, breath by breath.

"You come with warnings and confirmations and fragments," he said. "You tell me this was foreseen, that it is accelerating, that delay worsens fracture—yet you offer no remedy. No instruction. Only insistence."

Harrowe watched him closely. "I offer the only thing that's ever counted."

Darcy looked up.

"The Lady," Harrowe said. "Not the role. Not the verses. *Her.* You said yourself she were at the centre of it all. Mayhap you were right."

Darcy's jaw tightened. "You think to *inspect* her?"

"I only want to see whether what's happenin' now answers to what was once set down." He broke off, then continued more carefully. "If I'm right... then what it takes from you ain't where it breaks."

Darcy's pulse hammered painfully against his throat. "Then what is?"

Harrowe hesitated. It was the first time he had done so.

"It must be given," he said at last. "Not forced. Not proved by harm."

Darcy stared at him. "You speak in riddles."

"Caution," Harrowe corrected. "And I can't say more 'til I see her."

Darcy closed his eyes. The image rose at once—Elizabeth in the morning room, hands folded, gaze trusting still, despite everything he had done to unmake himself. The hollow ache answered it immediately, sharp and insistent.

"You may not alarm her," Darcy said.

"Wouldn't dare. But you've got to let me see her. Today."

Darcy's hand went to the bellpull. He hesitated only once—long enough to feel the weight of the decision settle fully into place—then rang.

The sound echoed down the corridor like a summons neither of them could take back.

# Chapter Forty-Three

Elizabeth did not wait to be asked to sit.

She remained where the footman had left her, just inside the threshold of the study, hands folded together so tightly her knuckles ached.

The man before her was nothing like she had expected. Harrowe was built broad and solid, shoulders hunched as though he had learned early to duck beneath low beams. His coat had seen better days. His boots bore the scuffs of long walking rather than polish. And yet the words he used—when he found them—came weighted and careful. The accent did not match the scholarship, which amused her. And she could not help but wonder what her father would make of the man.

He had been staring at her since she entered.

Not rudely. Worse.

With the fixed, intent regard of someone who had found a long-sought answer and was afraid it might vanish if he blinked. Almost like some sort of misplaced worship.

Elizabeth shifted her weight. Her gaze slid, unwillingly, toward the desk.

Darcy sat behind it, one hand braced against the arm of the chair as though the act of remaining upright required constant negotiation. His face had gone a shade lighter since she last saw him. A fine sheen of sweat traced his brow and darkened the linen at his collar. He did not look away when she met his eyes.

He did not smile. He watched her as though she were the only fixed thing left in the room.

Harrowe cleared his throat. "Miss... Bennet?"

She looked back at him at once, grateful for the interruption. "Sir."

He flinched faintly at the formality, then inclined his head. "You'll forgive me if I speak plain. Time is not—" He stopped, recalibrated. "Time is not likely to be kind where you're concerned."

Elizabeth's mouth tightened. "I find that is often the case."

Darcy's weight flexed against the chair until it squeaked.

Harrowe's attention flicked to him, then returned to her with renewed intensity. "You're aware," he said, "that the events of last night weren't... isolated."

"I am aware they were felt elsewhere," Elizabeth replied. "If that is what you mean."

"And more. The land's been groaning for some time. You're not the cause." He said it quickly, as though forestalling an objection. "But you're... the measure."

Elizabeth absorbed that in silence. The words settled uncomfortably close to truths she had not yet given shape.

Harrowe stepped nearer, then caught himself and stopped short, as though remembering propriety at the last possible moment. "There are accounts," he said. "Ballads. Marginalia. Notes dismissed as metaphor because they didn't fit doctrine. They speak of a meeting."

Darcy's breath hitched into a cough he could not quite restrain. He drew out his handkerchief and turned away as his shoulders shook.

Elizabeth tore her gaze from him. "A meeting?"

"A convergence," Harrowe amended. "Of place and time and persons rightly prepared. Not chance. Never chance." His hands lifted, shaping something invisible in the air. "The poets made it ceremony. The mystics made it ritual. I believe they were reaching for something they couldn't understand."

"And you can?" Elizabeth asked.

Harrowe hesitated. Just long enough for honesty to slip through. "Maybe."

Darcy made a sound then—low, restrained, edged with pain. Elizabeth turned despite herself, and she began moving towards him.

He shook his head once, imperceptibly. Whether in warning or apology, she could not tell.

Harrowe followed her gaze and softened his tone. "That weren't stray," he said. "Presence alone won't keep it. If you come to it without the right of it, it'll do harm."

Elizabeth returned her attention to him. "You speak as though this were a dance."

Harrowe gave a short, startled laugh. "Mayhap it is."

She did not smile. "You think," she said slowly, "that Mr Darcy and I must be placed somewhere specific. At a particular hour. To do... something."

"Aye."

"And you do not know what that something is?"

Harrowe's mouth opened. Closed. "Not... entirely."

Elizabeth exhaled. The sound was almost a laugh. "How reassuring."

Darcy shifted as he put his handkerchief away, and a bead of sweat trickled down his cheek. Elizabeth's hands clenched again, the familiar, unwelcome instinct to go to him rising sharp and immediate. She forced herself to remain still.

"You would have us attempt this," she said, "on the strength of verse and conjecture."

"On the strength of pattern," Harrowe replied. "And on the evidence of what has already occurred."

Elizabeth's gaze slid back to Darcy. He met it steadily, though the effort showed now in the tight line of his mouth, the careful control of each breath. He had not spoken a word since she entered. And yet she felt—unmistakably—that he was waiting for her decision.

"I will not be handled like some sort of a... a talisman."

"No!" Harrowe answered quickly. "I wouldn't dream of it."

"And I will not be frightened into obedience," she went on. "Nor persuaded by reverence. Whatever this is, it is not a performance."

Harrowe inclined his head, solemn. "Aye."

Elizabeth looked between them then—at the scholar who believed he saw the end of the road, and the man who bore its cost in his body already.

"If there is to be an answer," she said quietly, "it will not be found by injuring one of us to spare the other."

Darcy's eyes closed for a brief instant.

Harrowe studied her with something like awe—and something like unease. He drew a breath, slow and deliberate, as though checking himself before stepping onto uncertain ground. When he spoke again, the reverence was gone from his voice. What replaced it was harder.

"You misunderstand me."

Elizabeth held his gaze. "I do not think so."

"You think that because what it asks is hard, it may be set aside. It can't!" He gestured toward the window. "The fractures—the cracks in the fields, the wells run thin, the unrest you feel—that ain't threats meant to drive you. The land's already answerin'. And it's been left too long without reply."

Elizabeth's jaw set. "Then it may answer without us."

Harrowe shook his head. "It won't. It can't. Something must stand in the breach. "Somethin' has to bear what was once borne willin'. If not a man, then stone. Field. Tide." His jaw tightened. "That's the bargain."

The words settled over Elizabeth like ash. Her gaze slid, against her will, to Darcy.

He had not moved. Not when Harrowe spoke of strain, nor when the word *bargain* was uttered as though it were an ordinary thing. He sat in his chair now, with his shoulders squared, and his hands braced against the chair arms, accepting it—accepting everything—with the same silent endurance he had shown all morning.

Something inside her snapped taut. "I will not accept a *bargain* that requires his ruin!"

Darcy coughed again. The sound cut sharper than any word.

Harrowe's eyes flicked to him, then returned to her. "That's not a choice you have."

The inevitability of it landed heavy and suffocating, like a weight pressed suddenly to her chest. Heat surged up beneath her ribs, fierce and unmanageable—not fear, not sorrow, but a rising, desperate refusal that had nowhere to go.

"You speak," she said, and felt her voice tremble despite herself, "as though suffering were a mechanism. As though pain were proof that the answer is correct."

"Not proof," Harrowe said. "Payment."

The room seemed to contract around that word.

Elizabeth could hear Darcy breathing now—every careful, deliberate draw of air measured as though it must be rationed. The sound scratched at her nerves, dragged at something raw inside her that she had been holding together by will alone. She wanted to turn to him, to cross the room in two strides and put herself between him and this calm, scholarly certainty.

"You would have one of us answer," she said, and the words felt thick, difficult, "for what others failed to do. You would take what remains, and call it balance."

Darcy said nothing.

That was the worst of it.

He did not protest. He did not contradict Harrowe. He sat there as though the decision had already been made, as though his body were merely the instrument by which it would be carried out.

Harrowe did not retreat from her anger. He took it in—her clenched hands, the sharp set of her shoulders, the way her breath had gone tight and high—as though these, too, were data points, as necessary as any marginal note or brittle verse.

"Then hear it plainly," he said.

Elizabeth lifted her chin. Her heart was hammering now, hard enough that she could feel it in her throat. Darcy's breathing scraped on the air behind her, steady only by force, and the sound threaded itself through every word Harrowe spoke.

"There's a place," Harrowe continued. "Not a house. Not a church. Ground that was once marked and then forgotten. The ballads call it a meeting-ground. The *Liber* names it only by description—thorn and water, stone set where no stone should be."

Elizabeth's mouth went dry.

"I don't know where, but I think it's somewhere north of here," Harrowe said. "Near enough that the quake answered it first."

Darcy shifted sharply. Elizabeth felt it without looking.

"There'll come a time," Harrowe said. "Not marked on a calendar. Marked in the land. When the ground's already wearied, when the Lady's near spent, and the Witness has been drawn close enough that what lies quiet can't lie so any longer."

Elizabeth let out a short, incredulous breath. "So, we are to go there. Together. And then what?"

Harrowe hesitated.

The pause was small. It was devastating.

"*And then*," Elizabeth pressed again. "What happens to him?"

Darcy made a sound then—low, warning. "Elizabeth."

She turned on him at last.

He was worse. The sweat had darkened further along his collar now, his mouth set with a control that felt less like strength and more like surrender. He would go. She knew it with a clarity that made her chest ache. He would go wherever Harrowe pointed, stand wherever he was told, and call it duty.

The knowledge hit her harder than the quake had.

Harrowe spoke again, reluctantly. "The old accounts are clear in this. The breach won't mend for mere standin' near. Someone has to offer. Not in token. Not for a moment. But wholly. The land won't answer to a hand that flinches."

"You're describing some pagan sacrifice!" she said.

"I am describing a *choice*," Harrowe replied. "One that was refused before. One that left the land to tear itself instead."

Her pulse thudded painfully in her ears. "And if *we* refuse?"

Harrowe did not look away. "Then the fractures continue. They deepen. The Lady will weaken again—not first, but eventually. And when she falls, the land will not stop."

Elizabeth shook her head, a sharp, helpless motion. "You speak as though you are certain."

"I *am* certain," Harrowe said, and for the first time since she had met him, something like doubt cracked through his voice, "that failing will kill more than choosing."

Elizabeth closed her eyes. The place he had described rose unbidden in her mind—thorn and water, stone out of keeping. She had never seen it, and yet the image sat with a terrible familiarity, as though it had been waiting for her to name it.

She opened her eyes again.

"You ask us to go," she said slowly. "To place ourselves in the centre of something you do not fully understand. To let the land decide which of us it will take."

Harrowe's mouth tightened. "I ask you to answer before it decides for you."

Elizabeth turned back to Darcy.

He was watching her now with an intensity that made her breath stutter—not pleading, not command, but a quiet readiness that frightened her more than any prophecy. He had already accepted the cost. He had done so the moment she kissed him, and the world broke.

Her anger flared again, hotter and more desperate than before.

"No," she said—not to Harrowe this time, but to the shape of the future he was offering. "I will not agree to a plan that begins with his consent to be ruined."

Harrowe frowned. "Miss Bennet—"

"No!" she repeated. "You have mistaken my willingness to listen for consent. I will not agree to a solution that consumes one of us so the other may stand."

Darcy pushed himself upright despite the visible effort it cost him. "Elizabeth—"

She turned at last, and the sight of him—pale, drawn, resolute—hit her with a force she had not anticipated. "You have already taken enough," she said, more softly now. "You will not offer yourself as currency."

Harrowe's voice hardened. "Then you doom everything else."

Elizabeth faced him again. "If the only answer you can imagine requires sacrifice without choice, then you have not found the truth. You have found a story people told themselves to justify what they could not bear to change."

Harrowe stared at her. "The land does not negotiate."

She smiled tightly. "Then it will have to learn."

THE LIGHT HAD SHIFTED twice without Darcy noticing.

It lay now in a long, slanted bar across the rug, catching the edge of Harrowe's scattered papers and the spine of a book propped open by the weight of another. Ink dusted the desk. A candle had been burned down and replaced without comment. Somewhere beyond the windows, the house had resumed the ordinary rhythms of a day that refused to wait for clarity.

Elizabeth had gone upstairs, and he had not stopped her.

He could forgive her anger. He understood it too well to resent it. She had seen what Harrowe was proposing and named it for what it was. She had seen him sitting there, accepting, deteriorating, and had stepped away—not in abandonment, but in protection. Making space. Removing herself because her presence sharpened the cost.

It had been the hardest kindness of the day.

Harrowe sat hunched over the desk now, coat discarded, sleeves rolled, hair escaping its tie as he muttered to himself, fingers moving between margins and verses with a restless certainty that bordered on obsession.

"Boundary crossings," he murmured. "Always crossings. Never stillness—no, no, that comes later. Here—listen to this—"

Darcy did not.

He sat back in the chair he had not left since midday, one hand braced on the armrest, the other resting flat against his thigh as though to reassure himself that his limbs still answered. Each breath required attention now. He had learned how much he could draw without provoking the tight, clawing protest beneath his ribs. The knowledge came with an intimacy he would have preferred not to acquire.

Harrowe shuffled papers again. "If the Lady names the bond—no, not names—*acknowledges*. Acknowledgement precedes action. Always. Then the Witness—"

Darcy closed his eyes briefly and pinched the bridge of his nose. He did not know what else to do but remain.

Leaving would change nothing. Sending Harrowe away would only delay what was already advancing. And if there was a pattern to be found—some articulation of duty that did not require Elizabeth's consent to his ruin—then it would not be found without him there to hear it.

The door opened without a knock. Darcy's eyes opened at once.

Bingley stepped inside, already halfway through a frown. He glanced first at Harrowe—taking in the spread of books, the disorder, the man himself—and then back to Darcy, his expression darkening with quiet suspicion.

"I told the footman we were not to be disturbed," Darcy said.

"You also sent him away to order luncheon," Bingley replied. "I took advantage of the interval."

Harrowe looked up at last. "If you've come to object—"

"I have not," Bingley said pleasantly, and turned his attention back to Darcy. He crossed the room and tilted his head toward the far corner, away from the desk. "May I?"

Darcy rose. The movement drew a sharp line of pain across his chest, but he mastered it and followed, one step at a time, until they stood near the window where the light fell less harshly.

Bingley lowered his voice. "You have a guest outside. I told the housekeeper to show him to the drawing room."

Darcy's breath stalled. "You admitted someone to my house?"

"It is hardly a stranger off the streets, Darcy. It is Mr Bennet."

# Chapter Forty-Four

Darcy paused at the threshold of the drawing room long enough to master his breath.

The room was orderly, chairs set straight, the windows admitting a calm afternoon light that bore no trace of the night before. Mr Bennet stood near the mantel, hands clasped behind his back, his posture easy, his expression composed in the way Darcy had learned to distrust.

"Mr Bennet," Darcy said. He inclined his head. "You are welcome."

"Thank you, sir," Mr Bennet replied. "I hope I do not intrude."

Before Darcy could answer, footsteps sounded behind him.

He turned and found Wickham already crossing the room with an ease that suggested he had been there all along. The familiarity of his smile struck like a wrong note.

"Darcy," Wickham said warmly, as though this were a chance meeting rather than an arrival carefully timed. "How fortunate to find you at home today."

Darcy's gaze flicked back to Mr Bennet. He had been told of one visitor. Not two.

Wickham went on, untroubled. "Mr. Bennet's carriage and horses are being settled in your stables. I have given instructions that they be made ready again shortly, should Mr Bennet wish to depart without delay."

Mr Bennet nodded, satisfied. "Thank you, Mr Wickham. Darcy, your staff is remarkably efficient."

Darcy felt the questions rise at once—too many, too sharp. He held them back with effort and returned his attention to his guest. "I heard nothing about your intentions to come to London."

"I judged it necessary," Mr Bennet said. "After last night."

Darcy inclined his head slightly. "Indeed."

Mr Bennet studied him for a moment, then smiled faintly. "You appear surprised."

"That you came to see your daughters? No. At the timing? Perhaps. And your traveling companion…" Darcy glanced at Wickham. "An officer in the militia does not leave his company without notice."

Wickham took a step to the side, positioning himself to Bennet's right. "Colonel Forster was good enough to oblige me," he said lightly. "Given the disturbances in Hertfordshire, and the… temper of things at present, it seemed prudent that Mr Bennet should have an escort."

Darcy's eyes narrowed. "An escort?"

"One of his officers," Mr Bennet confirmed. "As I am, after all, one of the principal landholders in the district—and with Mr Bingley absent from the county, there is some concern that matters may go unaddressed."

"Unaddressed," Darcy repeated.

Mr Bennet's gaze held his now, keen and searching beneath the mildness. "There is unrest. Rumour. Fear, if you prefer the word. I have come to speak with the proper authorities in London and to see, with my own eyes, what is being said of my daughter's recovery."

Mr Bennet's gaze did not leave Darcy's face. "You will forgive a father," he said mildly, "if he asks why his daughter should improve so markedly upon leaving Hertfordshire."

Darcy kept his expression composed. "London offers advantages. Medical counsel. Rest from familiar pressures."

"And yet," Mr Bennet replied, "those same advantages were available to her elsewhere. Why is it here that she improves?"

Darcy did not answer at once. He chose his words with care, not because he doubted them, but because any truth he offered would not stand alone.

"I cannot account for every change in Miss Elizabeth's health," he said at last. "Only for what I have observed. She is, at present, quite well."

Mr Bennet regarded him for a long moment. There was no accusation in his look—only calculation.

"If you wish," Darcy added, "I would have her come down and speak with you herself. She will assure you of it far better than I can."

Silence followed. Wickham shifted slightly behind them.

Mr Bennet's mouth curved. "No. That will not be necessary. For the present, your assurance will suffice."

"I appreciate your trust, sir."

Bennet's smile tightened. "There is something else. Something I should like to ask you."

Darcy's attention flicked, unbidden, to Wickham. Certainly, there was nothing Mr Bennet could ask that he would wish to answer in Wickham's company.

Wickham met the look easily, his expression open, untroubled, as though there were nothing he would rather do than remain precisely where he stood.

Mr Bennet noticed at once. "Perhaps," he said thoughtfully, "your cook might be prevailed upon to produce some luncheon. We have travelled since early morning."

Darcy inclined his head. "It is likely already laid for the other guests of the house."

"Ah." Mr Bennet turned slightly. "Then I should not wish to delay them."

Darcy's gaze returned to Wickham. "You will know where that is."

"Of course," Wickham said readily. "I shall see to it." He moved at once toward the door, already speaking lightly of travel and appetite as he went.

Darcy waited until the door closed behind him. Then he turned back to Mr Bennet. "The broadsheets all report that the quake was felt—indeed, was stronger in Hertfordshire," he said, pacing around to stand near the mantel. "How do matters stand there?"

Mr Bennet's brows rose slightly, as though he had expected the question sooner. "Longbourn stands. Mostly undamaged."

"I am relieved to hear it."

"There was damage elsewhere," Mr Bennet continued. "Not ruin, but enough to unsettle people already inclined to fear it. The tremor was felt more sharply to the north. And Netherfield has sustained significant damage. I do not know the extent, or if it can be repaired. But sufficient that Mr and Mrs Hurst were preparing to remove to London this morning. They would have been here already, had they travelled as swiftly as I."

Darcy turned toward the door without thinking. "Bingley must be informed at once."

"No."

The word was quiet. It stopped him as surely as a hand at his sleeve.

Darcy turned back. Mr Bennet was watching him with a look no longer mild. "I did not come to speak of walls and roofs. And I do not give a fig for London authorities and what they can or cannot do to protect Hertfordshire at present. I came to speak of something more important."

Darcy held his ground. "You just told me Longbourn still stands. Miss Elizabeth is well, and I have already suggested that you see her yourself, but you would speak of other matters. Sir, I do not understand. She should be your first concern."

"She is," Mr Bennet replied. "Which is precisely why we must be plain with one another now." He stepped nearer, not aggressively, but with purpose. "You have known my Elizabeth some time."

"I have."

"You have observed her illness."

"Many have, yes."

"And you have observed," Mr Bennet went on, "that it retreated—quite suddenly—upon her arrival in your company."

Darcy did not answer.

Mr Bennet's eyes flicked over him, quick and unflinching. "You will forgive me if I remark that you do not look well yourself."

Darcy's jaw set. "Appearances can mislead."

"So can denials," Mr Bennet said mildly. "I have watched this for some time, Mr Darcy. I intended to ask you of it before, when there was leisure for speculation. Last night removed that leisure."

Darcy felt the question forming before it was spoken.

"Why," Mr Bennet asked, "is my daughter suddenly lucid in London? And why do you look as though you are standing only by stubbornness?"

Darcy drew a careful breath. "I cannot explain every circumstance that touches Miss Elizabeth's health."

"Then explain what you can."

"I can say," Darcy replied, choosing each word like foundation stones of a building, "that her improvement is real. And that I would not deceive you on a matter of such consequence."

Mr Bennet studied him. "And what of you?"

"You ask questions that suggest knowledge, sir. What is it that you know?"

Mr Bennet's mouth tightened. For a moment, he looked older than Darcy had ever seen him. "I know only this. My daughter was failing. Quietly. Persistently. No physician could name it. No remedy touched it. And then, a militia officer understood something no one else did. He advised distance. Removal. Separation from the land upon which she was raised." He paused. "Perhaps that advice saved her."

Darcy's breath caught. "That is not—"

Mr Bennet lifted a hand. "You asked what I know. That is all. I require an answer, Mr Darcy."

"What answer do you require, sir?"

"My daughter is well now," Mr Bennet said. "And I intend that she remain so." He frowned and drew in a long sigh before finishing, calmly and without heat.

"You will marry her. You *must.* That is the only way to save her."

Darcy did not answer at once.

For a moment, he stood as though the words had struck him somewhere deeper than offence—somewhere dangerously close to desire. The proposal Mr Bennet had set before him was, in another shape, the very thing his mind had reached for again and again since Elizabeth Bennet first entered his house: order restored, obligation satisfied, her presence made permanent and unquestioned.

Marriage.

Safety.

An end to uncertainty.

He drew a careful breath. "You believe," Darcy said at last, "that such a union would preserve her."

Mr Bennet's expression did not change. "I believe it has done so before. But... never in circumstances quite like these."

"No," Darcy said quietly. "And it will not serve now."

He moved a little nearer—not in challenge, but as one compelled to speak plainly where evasion would be a kind of dishonesty. "She showed me the express you sent. You think me dangerous to her."

Mr Bennet did not deny it. "I think," he said, "that my daughter began to fail when she met you, and that her failing worsened as your proximity remained... and then for whatever reason, she began finding a sort of relief whenever your name—or your presence—pressed too closely upon her."

Darcy paced across the room again. "I assure you, sir, it was not done with any intent of—"

"Have you ever known a man with a debilitating affinity for drink, Mr Darcy?"

Darcy's cheek twitched, and he regarded Mr Bennet in some askance. "Many. But that is a rather strange twisting of the topic at hand, sir."

Mr Bennet shook his head. "No, for the drink ruins some men. Consumes them from the first moment. They lose their way, lose themselves, until it comes to a place where they *are* the drink. They cannot manage without it. Some only seem rational after they have had four or five glasses."

He drew out his handkerchief and wiped it across a brow that appeared suddenly strained. "That, Mr Darcy, is what I am beginning to wonder about you and my daughter."

Darcy's jaw tightened. "And yet you ask me to marry her."

"I ask," Mr Bennet replied, "to see how you receive the question."

Darcy let out a slow breath. "Then allow me to answer it with equal frankness."

Mr Bennet inclined his head.

"There is nothing I should wish more than to secure Miss Elizabeth's future—her comfort, her protection, her happiness—by every means honour permits. And not for duty, but for my own... pleasure as well. If such a word is permitted me."

Mr Bennet watched him closely now.

"If marriage were assurance," Darcy went on, "if constancy alone were sufficient to quiet whatever afflicts her, I would not hesitate. I would welcome it."

"But you do hesitate," Mr Bennet said.

"Yes."

"Because you fear her?"

"No," Darcy said at once. "Because I fear myself."

Bennet's eyes narrowed. "Then perhaps I was correct. You are a sort of poison to her."

Darcy paused to frame his thoughts. "Not in the way you imagine. You believe that my proximity restores her. And in a narrow sense, you are correct. You have seen the effect. Others have seen it, too."

"And yet," Mr Bennet said, "*you* look almost as ill as she ever did. Another day, and you, too, may be insensate."

Darcy did not flinch from the observation. "Just so."

"Then tell me this, sir. If you did marry her—if you placed yourself always at her side, giving her life... what becomes of her when your own life fails?"

The question was not an accusation. It was a test. "That," he said, "is precisely what I cannot yet answer to my satisfaction."

Mr Bennet studied him for a long moment. "You are asking me to trust that you will discover it in time."

"I am asking you," Darcy replied, "not to mistake urgency for certainty."

"And I," Mr Bennet said, "am asking whether your reluctance arises from caution or from convenience."

Darcy met his gaze steadily. "If I wished convenience, I should have accepted your proposal at once. We would have the banns called tomorrow, or if that proved too long, we would be on the nearest coach for Scotland. But..." He swallowed and let his gaze wander to the window. "I do not know what becomes of either of us after that."

"You see the danger, then."

"I do."

Mr Bennet folded his arms loosely. "You understand that a father who hears this must wonder whether separation would serve her better."

"I understand," Darcy said. "I would wonder the same."

Mr Bennet regarded him long and thoughtfully. "Then you do not refuse me out of indifference. Nor out of want of regard."

"No! Egad, no. But marriage, in this moment, may bind her to the very thing that threatens her."

Mr Bennet exhaled slowly. "Then we are, it seems, asking the same question from opposite ends. And you have no answer yet?"

"No," Darcy replied. "But I am seeking one. There is one indulgence I would ask of you, sir, while matters remain thus unresolved."

Mr Bennet regarded him with mild interest. "Only one? What is it?"

"That you do not seek counsel from Mr Wickham."

The request was delivered plainly, without emphasis or retreat. Mr Bennet's brows rose slightly. "That is a singular restriction. And I cannot imagine it made lightly."

"It is not."

Mr Bennet studied him for a moment. "You must expect to be asked why."

Darcy hesitated—not from reluctance, but from the difficulty of placing the truth where it would do the least harm. "You know that Mr Wickham and I were raised together. He is familiar with certain family histories, but only in fragments, and always without the context that lends them meaning. He possesses enough knowledge to appear informed, but not enough to judge rightly."

"And yet," Mr Bennet replied, "when my daughter was failing, it was he who advised removal, and that advice proved effective."

Darcy inclined his head. "I do not deny the effect. I question the understanding that produced it. Mr Wickham has no stake in the outcome beyond his own sense of having been consulted. He is disposed to insert himself where he has no claim, and to do so with a confidence that exceeds his grasp."

Mr Bennet considered this. "You ask me, then, to set aside the only counsel that has thus far served my daughter."

"I ask you to weigh it cautiously."

"Caution," Mr Bennet said, "is precisely why I will not limit myself to a single voice. Until you can offer me a clearer assurance—one that does not rest upon uncertainty—I shall listen where I judge it prudent. And now, I should like to see my daughter."

Darcy inclined his head. "She shall be sent for."

He crossed to the bell and rang. When the maid appeared, he gave the instruction briefly and without elaboration. "Miss Elizabeth, if you please."

The maid withdrew.

Darcy returned his attention to Mr Bennet. "I will have a tray brought in for you. You will excuse me, please."

Mr Bennet nodded. "Of course, sir, and thank you."

# Chapter Forty-Five

The house had taken on the unsettled air of a place preparing to divide against itself.

Trunks stood open in corners where they had no business being. Cloaks were folded and refolded to better fit into overstuffed cases. Voices rose and fell along the corridor outside the morning room, their purpose clear even when their words were not: departure, separation, removal.

Elizabeth stood near the window with her gloves in her hands, watching the carriage being brought round for Mr Bingley. Jane was with him in the hall outside. Elizabeth could not hear what was said—only the cadence of it, softened, careful, and prolonged beyond what politeness required.

When at last Jane appeared at the door, her face composed and her eyes a shade too bright, Elizabeth felt a certainty settle in her that had nothing to do with conjecture. Whatever understanding existed between her sister and Mr Bingley, it was real—and, for the moment, unspoken by mutual consent. There were things, perhaps, that did not wish to be placed in the midst of upheaval.

Mr Bingley's voice sounded again, cheerful in tone if not in truth, as he took his leave of the household. He spoke of Netherfield, of damage to be assessed and repairs undertaken, of his intention to see matters settled in person. The words were those of a man returning to an empty house with no notion of how he might be welcomed back.

Jane stood very still as he went.

Elizabeth turned from the window as her father entered. "The carriage shall be brought round in a moment," Papa said, as though announcing nothing more consequential than a change of plans for dinner. "We should make Dartford tonight. With any luck, we ought to reach Ramsgate on Tuesday."

"Papa, I still do not understand. Why are we leaving London? And if you are so determined on Ramsgate, why not wait until tomorrow, when we could have a full day of travel?"

"Your aunt and uncle Gardiner will follow us," he replied, as if she had not spoken at all. "The air is bracing. The distance sufficient."

Elizabeth shook her head. "Papa, if you insist upon escorting me so far, we shall all miss Mary's wedding. You will not be able to give your own daughter away!"

Papa paused, the faintest crease appearing between his brows. "Your uncle Philips will perform the office."

"The office," Elizabeth repeated. "Papa—"

"Mr Philips is perfectly capable of giving his niece away," he said, with a weariness that admitted no debate. "The ceremony will proceed whether I stand beside her or not."

"But that is... why it is unjust. It is her wedding! Mary will wish—"

"Mary," her father interrupted gently, "will wish many things. This cannot be one of them."

Around them, the house continued its quiet preparations. A servant passed with a stack of folded linen. Someone called for a carriage rug. The sound of wheels on cobblestones carried up through the open window as Mr Bingley's carriage was drawn away at last.

Elizabeth turned back to her father. "This is about Mr Darcy."

Papa did not look at her at once. When he did, his expression held neither anger nor reproach—only a settled resolve that frightened her more than either. "It is about your health."

"And you believe," she said, keeping her voice steady, "that removing me from him will restore it."

"I believe," he replied, "that whatever ease you have found in his vicinity has come at a cost I am no longer willing to ignore." He shrugged into his coat and fumbled around for the gloves poking out of the pockets. "I wonder that *he* is."

Elizabeth felt the familiar protest rise—to argue, to insist, to explain—but found herself checked by the simple fact that her father was already turning away, issuing instructions with quiet efficiency, the decision made and set in motion.

Ramsgate.

Away from Hertfordshire. Away from Darcy. Away from the land that had begun, at last, to speak plainly.

Elizabeth looked once more toward the window, where the street had already returned to its ordinary traffic, and felt the strange certainty settle in her bones that distance, this time, would not bring the relief her father so earnestly intended.

Then something drew her back. Darcy stepped into the hall just far enough to be seen.

He did not speak. He did not beckon. He paused there, one hand resting against the doorframe as though he had gone no farther than necessity required.

Nothing passed between them that could be named. And yet she knew, with the same quiet certainty that had been guiding her all day, that he wished to speak with her—alone—and that the moment, once lost, would not be recovered.

She turned to Jane. "I shall return in a moment."

Jane's brows drew together. "Elizabeth—"

Elizabeth laid a hand over hers, briefly, firmly. "I will not be long."

Jane's protest died unspoken. She had seen the exchange. She had seen their father's resolve. And she saw now, too, that this was not a request Elizabeth could refuse without consequence.

Elizabeth stepped into the corridor. She knew where he would be. The library door stood ajar, light spilling across the threshold. Elizabeth crossed it without hesitation.

Darcy had turned at the sound of her footsteps. He stood near the hearth, one hand braced against its edge as though he had reached it only seconds before necessity intervened. The lamplight caught the strain in his face, the careful stillness of a man measuring every movement for its cost.

"You wished to speak with me?"

He nodded once and came to close the door behind her. The click of the latch sounded louder than it should have, final in a way that tightened her throat. He approached her slowly, though the distance between them was no more than a few steps. He only looked at her, and the look held so much unsaid that she felt it settle along her skin like pressure.

"What can be done?" she asked. There was no preface to it now, no restraint left for politeness. "What has he told you?"

"Harrowe?" A faint, humourless curve touched his mouth. "He has not left the study since he arrived. I expect we shall find him fossilised among his papers by evening." He drew a breath and let his eyes flick over her face before glancing down. "He speaks of ancient oaths and the manner in which they were kept. Of acts witnessed and costs borne in the body. Of rituals named and misremembered until nothing remains but endurance."

"And the answer?" she said. "How is *this* oath kept?"

"He has not found that. I am not certain he will."

The words struck harder for their simplicity. She took a step toward him without meaning to, then stopped herself, her hands tucking behind her skirts to keep her from reaching.

Darcy moved then. He closed the distance between them in two strides and reached for her as though restraint had at last failed him. His fingers slid down her arms and closed around her wrist, not tightly, but with unmistakable intent, and the contact sent a jolt through her that was equal parts relief and alarm.

"Darcy—" She let him drag her hand up to his mouth and then caught herself, her breath already altered by the nearness of him. "You must not."

"I know," he said, and yet he drew her closer all the same, his other hand coming to rest at her waist. The heat of him pressed against her, familiar and unbearable. He bent his head, and for an instant she thought he would kiss her outright, claim the moment without hesitation.

Her hand rose of its own accord, brushing his cheek, then the line of his jaw. The skin beneath her fingers was warm—no, feverish—and she felt the change in him almost at once. His breath shortened. The muscles in his chest sprang taut beneath her palm.

She pulled back sharply. "No. Please. You must stop."

His face had gone pale beneath the lamplight, a faint sheen gathering at his brow. "I need you, Elizabeth."

"You are worse," she said, the words tumbling over one another now. "You are always worse."

He did not deny it. He only looked at her with an intensity that made her heart ache. "And what of you?"

She looked purposely away. "What do you mean?"

"What becomes of you when you leave?" His hand had not fallen from her waist. "You speak of protecting me. But what does the distance cost you?"

Elizabeth bit her lip. She had not meant to answer that. She had not meant to think of it at all. The truth rose anyway, unwelcome and insistent. "I shall falter," she said, and the admission left her fighting tears. "The moment I am gone, I know it. Hertfordshire has never released me easily. The land—" She stopped, swallowing. "It will not cease simply because I travel."

He drew her against him then, not in passion but in something closer to refuge. Her cheek rested against his chest, and for one precious instant, she allowed herself the comfort of it, the solid familiarity of his presence. She heard it then—the faint, uneven stutter beneath her ear as his heart lost its careful rhythm.

She pulled away at once.

The colour had drained from his face. His breathing was laboured now, measured with conscious effort, and the sight of it made her own heart squeeze painfully. She could not help herself—she kissed the tip of his chin tenderly, then drew back slightly with a shuddering sigh.

"My father believes," she said, forcing the words into something that resembled reason, "that time and space may yet answer where nothing else has. That I may recover from this—this need for you, if I am not also pressed by the land that seems determined to draw upon my strength. And that you, freed of me, may be well again."

His expression did not change, but something in his eyes did, darkening with a quiet, unspoken refusal.

She reached up before he could speak and pressed two fingers to his lips. "Do not," she said softly. "I cannot bear it if you do."

He caught her hand. "Elizabeth..."

Elizabeth stepped back. She gathered herself, every part of her resisting the motion, and turned for the door. She did not look at him again. She did not trust herself to.

DARCY STOOD AT THE upstairs drawing-room window long after there was no longer any necessity for it.

The Bennets' carriage waited at the kerb below, its horses stamping with the restless impatience of animals too long held. Servants moved back from the door. The footman opened the door. Miss Bennet climbed inside, Elizabeth following a moment later, her figure briefly visible as she turned to arrange her skirts. Darcy did not see her look back. He could not have said whether she did. Mr Bennet mounted the step a moment later, and the carriage rolled forward.

It had scarcely cleared the corner when the sky broke.

Rain struck the glass with sudden violence, not the steady advance of a storm long foretold but a brutal, localised downpour, as though some unseen boundary had been crossed and punishment released. The street vanished behind a sheet of water. The outlines of houses dissolved. The carriage itself was lost at once, swallowed whole, as if London had closed its hand over it and would not give it back.

Darcy stood there until the windowpane shuddered beneath the assault, the sound rising to such insistence that sight became irrelevant. At last, he turned away.

The library, at least, was cloaked in silence. The fire had burned low, but the room still held warmth enough to make the air close. He crossed to the chaise near the hearth—the one he had occupied the night before, waiting with a patience he had not recognised as hope until it was stripped from him—and lowered himself onto it with more care than pride.

For a long moment, he did nothing but sit with his elbows braced on his knees and his head bowed, his hands hanging loosely between them. At least the house was *entirely* empty. Mr and Mrs Hurst had collected Miss Bingley and gone to open Hurst's townhouse near Bedford Square. And Wickham had taken a mail coach back to his regiment, but not without attempting to ingratiate himself as a "counsellor". Darcy had only nodded and watched him out the door.

The house creaked faintly around him, adjusting itself to the sudden weather. Somewhere above, rain hammered against the roof as though seeking entry. Darcy spread his hands, and his gaze traced the lines of his palms. Some said a lifetime could be read there. But he never believed that incidental creases of skin could dictate fortune. There were many things he never believed.

Then he drew a breath.

It went in without resistance.

He stilled at once, scarcely daring to test it. Another followed—deeper, easier. The tightness beneath his ribs, the rasp that had accompanied every inhalation for days, was gone. His chest rose and fell without effort, without the sharp edge of pain that had come to feel inevitable.

Darcy closed his eyes.

He might have laughed. He might have welcomed it as proof that separation had answered what proximity could not. Instead, the knowledge struck him with a weight so unexpected that his throat tightened painfully.

This was what it took.

Not resolution. Not understanding. Only her absence.

The breath came again, full and unimpeded, and with it the certainty that whatever had eased within him had not been healed, only unburdened—freed by the removal of the very thing that had sustained him.

His shoulders curved inward, and for a moment he remained there, motionless, the sound of the rain filling the room and the unaccustomed ease of breathing pressing hard against something that felt uncomfortably like grief.

HARROWE FOUND HIM THERE, with the fire burned down to coals and the rain still beating at the windows as though the house had merited God's wrath.

"I have it!" he cried, breathless with triumph. He had a sheaf of papers clutched against his chest and a book tucked beneath his arm, its spine cracked and swollen with damp. "The manner of it. The keeping. It was never only presence—never only waiting. It was a charge laid from father to son, answered by the heir as the work left unfinished."

Darcy lifted his head. "You have said as much before."

"And now I can say how." Harrowe dropped the papers onto a table nearby and spread them with hands that shook from excitement rather than cold. "Listen, this is no ornament. It's directive. The oath is sworn where the boundary was first laid. The heir names the failing aloud and takes it upon himself to amend. Witnesses are required—not to sanctify it, but to hold it in memory. The land is addressed as land. And the vow is borne in the body, or it is nothing."

Darcy rose. "You had best speak plainly."

"I am," Harrowe insisted. "The heir cuts the palm and lets the blood fall where the line was broken. Not to feed the earth—no, no, that's the French doggerel again—but to mark that the body answers for the word. He binds himself to finish what was not done before. The oath is spoken thrice. The witnesses repeat it back. Then—"

"And the Lady?" Darcy asked. "What of her?"

Harrowe hesitated. "Some records have her present as witness alone. The heir marks the oath in his own blood, names the breach, and binds himself to complete what was left undone. That would have sufficed for the later chroniclers. Very neat—too neat."

Darcy's jaw tightened. "That, I would endure, but I know there is more than that."

Harrowe looked up sharply. "Aye, there is."

Darcy narrowed his eyes and crossed one arm over the other. "Oh?"

"There are older rites," Harrowe continued, more carefully now. "Pre-Christian. Buried on purpose, I think. The monks would not copy what they could not sanctify." He paused. Shuffled a few papers and shuffled his feet.

"In those, the bond is not merely witnessed. It is... ah... claimed. Publicly. The heir answers for the breach with his blood, then validates it by... ahem... well, by *joining* himself to the Lady in sight of land and people alike."

*Joining?* Darcy mouthed the word. Harrowe could not mean...

Harrowe cleared his throat. "Aye... Fertility was not metaphor to them. It was proof."

Darcy's hand came down hard against his thigh. "Enough."

Harrowe gave a short, uneasy breath. "I do not say it lightly. But the land was bound through bodies as much as words. Blood alone marked obligation; union marked continuation. Without it—"

"Leave off!" Darcy thundered, his voice cutting through him at last, stripped of restraint. "I will bleed for any vow that is mine to bear. I will not dishonour her and call it duty. You will not reduce her to an instrument for your theories, nor dress violation as tradition, and expect me to listen."

Harrowe's jaw set. "I only speak of what was done."

"You speak of what was endured by those who had no better language," Darcy replied. "And you would have me repeat it because you lack the imagination to conceive of anything else."

"Well..." Harrowe sniffed and closed his book. "You did ask me to tell you what I found."

"Keep looking," Darcy said shortly.

Harrowe tapped his toe, scowled, then glanced about the room as though noticing it for the first time. "It's very quiet. Have I missed supper? I had thought—well. I've never eaten at a squire's table. Thought there might be a nicely turned haunch, at least. A hall."

"I am no squire, and there is no formal meal laid. The house is empty."

Harrowe frowned. "Empty?"

"The other guests have gone."

Harrowe's voice shifted, the scholar's cadence slipping, the Cockney edges coming through with sudden force. "Gone? All of 'em?"

Darcy did not look away. "Miss Bennet has left."

Harrowe stared. "*Left?*"

"Her father came for her. He thought it best. I did not disagree."

The colour drained from Harrowe's face. "You let her go?"

"I did."

"You let the Lady go when the land has been roused, and the line is open?" Harrowe's composure fractured. "That is dereliction! That is the very thing—"

Darcy jerked to his feet then, crossing the space between them with a controlled fury that made the room seem smaller. "You will not accuse me of cowardice in my own house! I did not chain her here to satisfy your appetite for precedent."

"You have chosen comfort over charge," Harrowe shot back. "You have chosen the body over the bond."

"I have chosen *her,*" Darcy said. "Which is more than your pages ever managed."

"You have chosen *comfort* and mistaken it for mercy. The land does not care for your tenderness. It remembers only what was left undone."

"Do not speak to me of mercy! You would have me bleed for a word and call it fidelity."

"It was never only a word! *Blood* marks obligation—but blood alone is not the keeping. The heir must claim what the vow was sworn to protect. And he must blend that blood with hers!"

Darcy's temper flared. "You truly expect me to claim her body? Publicly? You cannot even be sure that is the real intent of the passages!"

"I told you!" Harrowe said, unflinching. "The older rites were buried because they could not be sanctified. The monks copied what they liked and left the rest to rot."

"And you would have me resurrect that rot," Darcy said, advancing on him, "and call it necessity. I will bleed if blood is required. I will not dishonour her and dress it as tradition."

"You think the past was gentle?" Harrowe snapped. "You think vows were kept without cost? Bodies were the ledger. Union was of the flesh, not of the word. You would cast aside centuries of practice because you cannot bear the cost?"

"I will cast aside anything," Darcy thundered, the last of his restraint gone, "that demands I make her an altar and call my compliance righteousness."

Harrowe opened his mouth to speak again, but Darcy cut him off.

"No! You will not remain here and argue me into violence! If you cannot speak without reducing her to an instrument and me to a body to be spent, you will take your books and leave this house."

A knock came at the door—hesitant, then repeated.

"Not now!" Darcy bellowed.

The door edged open all the same, a servant's pale face appearing in the gap. "Begging your pardon, sir—but what are we to do with Lady Catherine while you are occupied?"

Darcy stared. "Lady Catherine?"

"Yes, sir. She is in the hall even now. We dared not refuse her. She is asking for you."

Darcy turned back to Harrowe.

Whatever fire had driven him moments before had guttered out, leaving something darker in its place.

# Chapter Forty-Six

Lady Catherine paused just inside the room, clearly expecting Darcy to advance. He did so, bowing and drawing out a chair for her before taking one himself. She glanced at the upholstery as if determining whether she could approve of it, then sat, her gloves arranged with deliberate care upon her lap.

"I trust," she said, adjusting her shawl, "that you felt last night's disturbance as plainly as the rest of London, and that you will not pretend it was the sort of inconvenience one may smooth over with polite disbelief."

"I would not," Darcy replied. "Nor do I think alarm useful where facts are not yet established."

"Facts," she repeated, with a faint, knowing lift of her brows. "Just so. And what facts have *you* established, Darcy?"

Darcy met her gaze evenly. "Only that it was felt widely, and unevenly. Reports are still fragmentary."

"Unevenly," Lady Catherine said, leaning back a fraction. "That is precisely what interests me. One hears of some houses scarcely noticing it, while others were quite shaken. Cracks in walls. Loosened stone. Chimneys crumbled. Have you heard anything of that sort?"

"I have heard rumours only," Darcy said. "Nothing confirmed."

"Nothing confirmed," she echoed. "And yet you would hardly deny that certain estates are more vulnerable than others. Older land. Improvident drainage. Houses placed for convenience rather than judgment."

Darcy inclined his head. "That is hardly unusual after such a quake. I would deny only that conjecture is useful before particulars are known."

Lady Catherine's fingers tightened on her reticule. "Conjecture becomes unavoidable when one hears that some houses were scarcely disturbed, while others were decidedly shaken. You have friends whose interests lie north of London, Fitzwilliam. Surely you have heard something of how matters stand there."

"I have heard that the shock was felt more strongly in Hertfordshire," Darcy said after a moment. "Nothing beyond that."

"And nothing of consequence?" she pressed. "No reports of damage? No cause for removal or repair?"

"Nothing has reached me to that effect," he replied. Then, as her gaze sharpened and lingered, he added, "If you are concerned for Netherfield in particular, I have had no intelligence to suggest it suffered more than any other."

Lady Catherine's brows rose, not in surprise but in pointed interest. "Netherfield," she repeated. "How curious that you should name it."

Darcy felt the faint rush of blood that always accompanied a misstep. "It is the largest estate recently occupied in that quarter, and therefore the likeliest to attract comment. Nothing more."

"And yet you spoke of it as though such comments had already reached you." She frowned and regarded him more narrowly. "Reports from Hertfordshire cannot yet have made their way through the usual channels. Why would you have such early notice of properties not directly connected to you?"

Darcy did not answer at once.

Lady Catherine inclined her head slightly. "Unless, of course, you *were* informed directly."

"I have received no formal report."

"But you have received *information*." She studied him a moment longer. "By express, I presume. One does not speak of 'intelligence' otherwise."

Darcy's jaw set. "Mr Bingley, who is the current master of Netherfield, was in London."

"Ah." The sound was quiet, satisfied. "Then he was here when the disturbance occurred."

"He was."

"And therefore learned of his property's condition without delay." She paused. "I should not have thought Netherfield's affairs would be your immediate concern unless its master were already under your roof."

Darcy's silence answered her.

Lady Catherine nodded once. "Staying with you, then."

"For a short time," Darcy said. "On his way elsewhere."

"With company, I imagine. One does not decamp to the seaside alone."

Darcy's expression did not change. "That is Mr Bingley's concern."

"Indeed," Lady Catherine said. "But when ladies are involved, concerns have a way of overlapping." She considered him with renewed interest. "Which ladies, Darcy?"

He did not reply.

She waited, unperturbed, as though silence were merely another datum. When he did not oblige her, she inclined her head again. "Very well. The names are not essential. My clergyman writes that he is even now travelling toward Hertfordshire for his wedding. He was disappointed to learn—some days ago—that his bride's entire family would not be present. An unusual circumstance."

Darcy frowned but made no comment.

"Families do not absent themselves from such a happy occasion without cause," Lady Catherine continued. "Illness, perhaps. Or some private necessity requiring removal. It is unfortunate when such necessities coincide with... disturbances."

Darcy's fingers tightened on the arm of the chair. "You did not come to interview me about acquaintances in Hertfordshire."

"No," she said crisply. "I came to advise you on inheritance."

"Oh?"

She rose then, crossing the room with purpose. Darcy was obliged, then, to stand as well, so he wandered closer to the mantel to wait on what she had to say.

"There has been, for some time," Lady Catherine said, "a pattern of imprudence in your conduct. You have permitted intimacy where distance would have preserved order, and indulged familiarity where discernment was required."

Darcy met her gaze. "If you refer to my friendship with Mr Bingley—"

"I do," she said at once. "And I refer to it as precisely the sort of attachment that leads gentlemen astray when it is allowed to deepen beyond its proper bounds. You have encouraged a degree of closeness entirely unsuitable to the disparity of your situations, and in doing so have ceded your judgment to a man ill-equipped to guide it."

"Mr Bingley is neither ill-intentioned nor incapable."

"He is a tradesman. A pleasant one, no doubt, but that does not recommend him as a counsellor in matters of consequence. Your father understood this. He approved your association with Mr Wickham precisely because such an arrangement preserved proportion—affection without influence, companionship without presumption."

Darcy's expression hardened. "Mr Wickham is not a standard by which I judge my companions."

"And yet," she said, "he was at least of the proper sphere. You have instead allowed yourself to be led into false assumptions, risky connections, and—inevitably—unfortunate entanglements. Such entanglements," she continued with a scowl, "are rarely singular. They radiate outward. One imprudent intimacy begets another."

Her eyes fixed on him with renewed sharpness. "My parson, Mr Collins, has advised me with some concern. He is soon to be allied with the Bennet family and has observed what others have chosen to excuse. Repeated indisposition in one daughter. Sudden collapses. Complaints of nerves and headache advanced with remarkable convenience. Conduct that invites attention while professing innocence of design."

Darcy felt the shift at once, like a draught across the skin. "You speak of Miss Bennet?"

"I speak of the entire family." Lady Catherine continued prowling across the room, her skirts lashing at her ankles as her pace increased. "And particularly of one young woman whose habits would be unremarkable were they not so persistently disruptive."

Darcy crossed his arms. "You will not speak of her in that manner."

Lady Catherine rounded on him. "I speak of her as a woman whose conduct has been remarked upon. Her cousin was at pains to correct her want of modesty when he perceived it. He was not thanked for the effort."

"You mistake illness for artifice," Darcy said. "And generosity for license."

"I mistake nothing. I observe patterns. A young woman falls ill with remarkable frequency. She recovers with equal suddenness. She exerts an influence that unsettles households and distracts gentlemen from their obligations. You yourself were altered, Darcy."

She gestured to him, openly now. "It is said you were pale when at Netherfield. Drawn. I should say overtaxed. One might suppose such proximity ill-advised."

Darcy's voice hardened. "Your suppositions are unwelcome."

"And yet, they are necessary! If a young woman is the cause of disorder—social or otherwise—then propriety demands she be removed from the centre of it. Either by distance, or by settlement. I am told she has now been taken away."

"Yes," Darcy said. "Her father thought it best."

Lady Catherine regarded him with a look of measured approval. "Sensibly done, then. It is always preferable when families act before matters are allowed to harden into impropriety."

Darcy narrowed his eyes. "And you believe her removal resolves it?"

"I believe," she replied, "that it removes the distraction." She settled once more in her chair. "You have allowed yourself to be misled by coincidence, Darcy. A young woman falls ill. You observe her with unmerited concern, unbefitting your connexion to her. Her condition alters, as illnesses often do, and you ascribe meaning where there is only fluctuation. Remove the object of attention, and the fancy dissolves."

Darcy's jaw tightened. "You reduce too much."

"I restore proportion," she returned. "And now that Miss Bennet is properly out of the way, you are free to attend to what actually requires settlement."

She paused, letting the implication take shape before she spoke it aloud. "There is a reason such matters have always been resolved within established lines. Not by indulging impressions, but by placing responsibility where it belongs."

"In Kent," Darcy said, before he could stop himself.

Lady Catherine inclined her head, satisfied rather than triumphant. "Precisely. Where order has been maintained, where precedent is preserved, and where there is no temptation to mistake novelty for significance."

Darcy shook his head. "You reference one source—only one, and it is likely suspect—to assert such a claim."

Her expression cooled rather than sharpened. "You have been speaking with Lord Matlock, I perceive. He has always had an unfortunate habit of mistaking antiquarian curiosity for authority."

Darcy did not answer.

"The Liber held at Rosings," Lady Catherine continued, "is the most accurate and most carefully preserved version in existence. It was copied under direct oversight, not left to the whims of scholars who prefer speculation to stewardship. It is unambiguous on this point." She leaned forward slightly. "The centre is where continuity has been maintained. Where responsibility has been inherited and upheld. Not in counties given over to fluctuation and neglect."

"Hertfordshire is not neglected."

"No," she replied. "It is indulged. That is far worse." She drew a measured breath. "Too many hands. Too many opinions. Too much interference from persons who mistake proximity for influence. That is precisely how disorder is allowed to masquerade as necessity."

"And who has given you this impression?" Darcy asked. "Surely not I."

"Do not play ignorant with me, Darcy," she scoffed. "I know very well you have dallied with that adventuress from Hertfordshire. Her arts and allurements—"

Darcy stepped menacingly toward her. "You have no business slandering a lady who is so entirely unconnected with you."

She straightened, her face blanching in some horror. "You already defend her! You see, you see what your carelessness has wrought! You invent meanings where none exist. Miss Bennet's removal has already clarified the matter. What you perceived as consequence will resolve itself in her absence. What remains is your obligation to place yourself where judgment is not clouded."

She rose then—not in anger, but with the assurance of a matter settled. "You will come to Kent, Darcy. We shall see this put right before further imprudence invites comment."

It was only when Darcy did not move, did not agree, did not even incline his head, that her composure faltered. He stared back at her, unblinking, watching her expectation crumble into silent rage.

Her voice cooled. "I see," she said at last.

She gathered her shawl with a whirl and a hiss of dismay. "You have refused my counsel. Very well. I shall know how to act."

The morning light at Ramsgate was gentler than she had expected.

Elizabeth sat near the window with her sewing laid across her lap, the needle resting idle between her fingers. The sea beyond the glass moved with a steady, almost deliberate calm, as though it had been instructed to behave itself. She found that reassuring in a way she could not have explained. The air carried salt and something faintly metallic, and though the windows were shut against the breeze, she felt it along her skin all the same.

Her father and Jane were speaking behind her in tones meant to be discreet. They had not mastered discretion well enough to escape her notice.

"I think," Papa was saying, "that we may congratulate ourselves. She looks—" He paused, as though selecting the least dangerous word. "—considerably restored."

Jane murmured assent. "She has colour again. And she slept. I was so worried that in taking her from London she might..."

Elizabeth smiled faintly to herself and kept her eyes on the stitching, which had gone crooked where she had last tried to guide it. The needle tugged once, not sharply, but with a small insistence, as though it wished to be elsewhere. She tightened her fingers around it until the sensation passed.

"It was the right decision," her father continued, more quietly now. "Distance has done what proximity could not."

Jane hesitated. "I only wish we could be sure it has done the same for him."

Mr Bennet gave a soft huff. "Darcy? If he was the cause, then his absence must be the cure. And if he was not—" He stopped, then added lightly, "—well, I am content not to speculate further."

Elizabeth kept her gaze steady on the seam. The fire in the small grate gave a low, companionable sound as it settled into coals. She had noticed earlier that it had burned higher when she first entered the room, though no one had stirred it. She had said nothing. She would continue to say nothing.

Jane moved closer at last and touched her shoulder. "You are very quiet."

"I am conserving my strength," Elizabeth replied. "It seems a shame to squander it so soon after its return."

Her father laughed, brief and genuine. "A sensible resolution, if ever I heard one."

"And a rare one," Jane added, smiling. "You will abandon it by luncheon."

"Almost certainly," Elizabeth said. She glanced between them. "Still, I cannot help but regret missing Mary's wedding."

Papa grimaced. "I regret only the sermon."

"Papa!" Jane scolded.

Elizabeth's lips curved. "I am sorry to miss Mary's happiness," she said, after a moment. "But I confess I am not inconsolable at being spared Mr Collins's raptures."

Jane laughed, then pressed her lips together. "You are both dreadful."

"And entirely unrepentant."

Papa shook his head, amusement and something more wistful crossing his face. "Your sister will forgive you. She always does, though I doubt you deserve it."

Elizabeth lifted a shoulder. "If I deserved it, it would not be forgiveness."

The room fell quiet again, the kind of quiet that settles only after shared laughter has passed. Elizabeth returned her attention to her sewing. The needle slid smoothly now, obedient beneath her fingers. The thimble at her hand shifted a fraction closer, though the table had not been disturbed.

She stilled her hand at once, the faintest prickle running up her arm. The fire gave a soft, sudden pop in the grate, and for an instant she had the curious sense that the room was listening.

Papa drew out his watch and squinted at it, holding it closer to the light. "Mary ought to be walking up the aisle about now."

Elizabeth kept her eyes on the window. The sea was unchanged. Calm. Proper. She drew a slow breath and told herself there was nothing required of her at this distance, nothing she could do but wish her sister well.

"Do you think," she asked, "that she wore the new lace Mama insisted on for her? I do hope she carried the blue handkerchief I made for her... a pity I was unable to finish embroidering it."

Jane crossed the room and touched her hand. "She will be very happy."

"I know," Elizabeth said. The words sounded correct.

A sensation had begun beneath her ribs, small at first and easily mistaken for restlessness. She shifted in her chair and tried to return to her sewing, but the needle slid oddly against her fingers, as though it resisted the path she set for it. The feeling spread, not pain, not weakness, but an insistence without direction, like an itch that could not be reached. She set the work aside and folded her hands in her lap, willing herself to be still.

Papa was speaking again, some gentle speculation about how Mary would find the weather at Hunsford, when the pressure sharpened. Elizabeth's breath shortened without effort, her chest tightening as though the air itself had thickened. She stood abruptly, the chair legs scraping.

"Elizabeth?" Jane cried.

The fire leapt from the hearth.

Not a settling flare, not a wandering spark, but a sudden, violent surge out of the grate, tongues of flame snapping forward as though drawn. Heat struck her skirt, and she cried out, the sound torn from her before she could stop it. She stumbled back, slapping at the linen as it smoked and caught, the sharp sting of singeing cloth biting through the layers.

Jane was there at once, hands flying, beating at the flames with her shawl. "Hold still—Papa!"

Papa was already moving, gone in a rush toward the kitchen. Elizabeth fought the urge to bolt, stamping and striking at the fire with clumsy hands, the room tilting as the pressure inside her spiked and scattered.

Her father returned with a kettle and flung the water on her. Steam burst up around her, the flames dying at once, the skirt sagging heavy and dark. Elizabeth gasped, soaked through, shivering now as the sudden heat gave way to cold.

For a heartbeat, there was only the sound of their breathing.

Then the kettle wrenched itself from Papa's grasp.

It lurched across the narrow space between them, metal screaming against air, swinging toward her head with a violence that stole what breath she had left. Jane cried out. Papa swore and caught at it, barely managing to wrench it aside before it struck her in the head. The kettle clattered to the floor and skidded, rocking wildly before settling at last against the hearth.

Silence fell again, broken only by the crackle of damp coals and the harsh rhythm of Elizabeth's breath.

Jane's hands were on her shoulders, steadying her. "Are you hurt? Elizabeth—are you burned?"

Elizabeth looked down. The skirt was ruined, blackened, and torn enough that she had to clutch it closed with one hand. Her skin, where she could see it, was unmarked. She nodded once, though she was not certain what she was answering.

Papa came closer, his face drawn and pale. "My dear... you are bleeding."

She raised her hand to her face and felt wetness there. When she drew her fingers back, they were streaked red. No one had touched her. No one had struck her. The blood had come all the same.

Elizabeth stared at it, her heart hammering, the room very still around her, and thought dimly that whatever had been building had not passed at all.

# Chapter Forty-Seven

The door was opened at Darcy's direction, and the footman stepped aside to admit the Earl of Matlock. Darcy had been waiting near the table and came forward at once, bowing as his uncle entered. "I am obliged to you for coming."

Matlock returned the courtesy and moved into the room. "Your note was explicit enough on that score." He paused, then glanced past him.

Harrowe stood by the table, one hand resting among the open books and papers spread across it, his dress plain and clean but hardly respectable before such an audience, his manner unembarrassed by the room or its owner. He inclined his head when Matlock's gaze met his, neither diffident nor familiar.

Matlock's brows lifted slightly. "I was not aware you were receiving assistance."

"I wished you to meet the person who has been advising me," Darcy said. "Mr Aldous Harrowe."

"Harrowe...?" Matlock repeated, the name slowing him now, his gaze lifting briefly before returning to the table—the annotated margins, the diagrams half-pinned beneath a paperweight, the signs of sustained inquiry rather than casual consultation. "The *same* Harrowe?"

"How old are you thinkin' I am?" Harrowe grunted with the ghost of a twinkle in his eye.

Darcy grimaced. "A relative," Darcy clarified. "His ancestor collected the ballads and the family has overseen the narrative ever since. Mr Harrowe has spent his life testing them against what survives outside the poetry."

Matlock looked again at Harrowe, this time with sharper interest. "I see. And in what capacity are you assisting my nephew, Mr Harrowe?"

"I know what no one else thinks is true," Harrowe replied. "And where to look."

Darcy turned back to Matlock. "He has knowledge of certain records not readily available, and a willingness to follow them where they lead."

Matlock regarded Darcy for a moment, then removed his gloves and handed them aside. "I see." He took the chair Darcy indicated, his expression thoughtful rather than disapproving. "You asked me here, Fitzwilliam, because you believe something is soon moving beyond speculation."

"I believe it has done so already."

Harrowe shifted as though to speak, but Darcy raised a hand and continued.

"There are several matters I must lay before you," he said. "Some of them will appear disconnected at first. I ask only that you allow me to finish before you judge them so."

Matlock inclined his head. "Proceed."

"I had word earlier today that Netherfield has suffered damage."

Matlock's expression altered only slightly, but it was enough. "Netherfield?" He glanced, briefly, toward Harrowe, then back again. "The estate leased by your friend? I was not aware it held any particular relevance to your affairs."

"Nor would I have thought so, until now," Darcy said. "The staircase has collapsed from the tremors felt three days ago. But the staircase is almost incidental, for the house has been cut through—cleanly enough to suggest a weakness already present in the ground."

Matlock frowned. "An old house settling poorly? Surely it is not unique."

"It is not old," Darcy replied. "And the damage is not settlement. Mr Bingley's steward reports a fissure beneath the foundation, one that follows the line of an old waterway. It appears the ground has been strained there for some time, and the shock merely finished what was already underway."

Matlock leaned back a fraction in his chair. "You speak as though you had anticipated this."

Darcy's mouth tightened. "I had reason to suspect it. I examined land records in November. There were inconsistencies—minor, easily dismissed—but persistent. Drainage altered, boundaries adjusted, and references to channels that no longer appear on modern maps. I did not know what to make of it then."

"And now you do?"

Darcy sighed. "I know it is not isolated. Mr Bingley has taken up the inquiry where I left off. The fissure aligns with others—subtle ones, but present—running through the surrounding land. They trace a pattern."

"And this pattern," Matlock guessed, "has led you to revise certain assumptions."

Darcy met his eyes. "It has confirmed them."

A smile crawled across Matlock's face. "You are suggesting that the *Liber's* references to place have, indeed, been misunderstood by your aunt."

"I am certain of it. I have been for some time."

Matlock exhaled slowly. "Then you believe the centre lies in Hertfordshire. And you believe this with sufficient conviction to summon me here. You are aware of what you imply."

"I am."

Matlock's voice, when it came, was quieter. "And the Lady? It must not be Anne, so who—?"

Darcy felt the words settle into place before he spoke them, as though they had been waiting for this moment to be acknowledged aloud.

"I know who she is. I… have known for some time."

"You have!" Matlock leaned forward, his face paling. "What family? Where does she come from, if not the Peredur or Bedwyr lines? Do others remain?" He glanced curiously at Harrowe, who only drew back, shaking his head. He would not answer.

"The records do not support a continuous family line," Darcy said, glancing at Harrowe. "Not in the manner Lady Catherine insists upon. She does not descend from a house of note, nor from one that has been preserved with any deliberate intention. If anything, her family history is marked by interruption—removals, marriages that break pattern, inheritances that pass sideways rather than down."

Matlock's brows knit. "Then you ask me to accept that the centre has shifted without stewardship, without preparation, without even recognition."

"I ask you to accept that it has endured… no…. that it has *chosen* without them," Darcy said. "Which is not the same thing as saying it has been preserved."

Matlock's expression remained doubtful. "It is a distinction without comfort."

"No," Darcy replied. "Nor is it one I arrived at lightly. You know how thoroughly I sought another explanation—how unwilling I was to accept a conclusion that upended both history and sense."

Matlock studied him for a moment. "And yet you are certain."

"I am," Darcy said. "Because the pattern did not begin in London, nor with theory. It began months ago, in Hertfordshire, before I understood enough to name it."

He drew a breath and continued, more steadily now, as though the ordering of events allowed him firmer footing.

"Miss Elizabeth Bennet suffered her first collapse near a fissure in the land behind her family's home—an old break, long dismissed as poor drainage. At the time, it appeared a coincidence: overexertion, cold, fatigue. But it did not resolve. Her health declined in ways no physician could explain."

Matlock's fingers tightened together as he laced them over his stomach. He did not interrupt.

"The closest house for her to recuperate was Netherfield," Darcy went on, "where her condition became more mysterious. Headaches, faintness, disorientation—always near the main staircase, which I now know sits directly above the same fault line that has since split the house."

"You are suggesting," Matlock said carefully, "that the Lady's illness preceded any conscious recognition."

"Yes," Darcy replied. "And that it tracked the land, not her blood. Which is why distance alone never cured her—only displaced the burden."

Matlock leaned back slightly. "And where do you place yourself in this account?"

Darcy rolled his eyes faintly to Harrowe, but there was no help there. He could not evade the question. "I noticed that her condition altered in my presence."

Matlock blinked politely. "I'm sorry?"

"At first, I told myself it was coincidence, or influence, or nerves. But the pattern held. Symptoms of headaches, discomfort with touch, dizziness and poor appetite. However, I learned that over time, my presence was what brought relief from those very same symptoms."

"I do not follow, Darcy. You occasioned pain, and then you were the remedy for the same?"

Darcy heaved a sigh. "We never spoke of... that, and so it was some while before I understood the entire nature of the matter. But the end of it was that her strength improved when I was near. Mine diminished. I could hardly lift her to my horse the day I found her collapsed outside Netherfield. There were strange sensations, odd occurrences. The exchange was not symmetrical, but it was consistent... rather, I should say, it was consistently evolving to a more... enhanced state."

Matlock was silent now, his scepticism recalibrating rather than resisting.

"I resisted drawing meaning from that," Darcy continued. "I told myself it proved nothing. But the land did not allow me that indulgence."

"And this is where conjecture ceased," Matlock said.

"Yes," Darcy replied. "Because there came a moment when acknowledgment could no longer be avoided. When the matter was put to the test—when the connection was recognised rather than merely endured—the response was immediate."

"You are still speaking in abstractions, Darcy."

Darcy inclined his head. "Then I will be plain. I kissed her. Or rather, she kissed me... I think it was both."

Matlock half-rose from his chair. "Indeed?" he breathed. "And?"

Darcy bit the inside of his lip and stared at the floor. "And she nearly killed me. I thought I was having a heart seizure. She saw it and ended the contact immediately. And at that instant, the ground answered."

Matlock was nearly falling out of his chair now. "You are not saying... the tremors?"

"There was no interval," Darcy said quietly. "No delay in which chance might be placed. The earthquake followed recognition as breath follows exertion."

Matlock was very still, blinking as his gaze grew unfocused. "And you survived."

"Yes," Darcy replied. "Though not without consequence."

"And the Lady?"

Darcy did not answer immediately. In his mind rose the image of Elizabeth as she had stood in the library, colour high, breath unsteady, eyes alight with something that was not weakness and not peace.

"Perfectly well. At least while she remained under my roof. After that, I do not know."

Matlock closed his eyes for a brief instant, then opened them again. "You have crossed further than you realise."

"I know," Darcy said.

"And yet you came to me," Matlock replied. "Not to confess, but to ask what follows."

Darcy inclined his head. "Yes."

Matlock did not speak at once. He sat with his hands folded, his gaze lowered to the table, as though turning Darcy's account over until it would lie flat. When he looked up again, it was not to Darcy but to Harrowe.

"And you?" he said. "You have followed these records longer than my nephew. Tell me what you believe."

Darcy felt the question land like a weight he had been holding at arm's length. He nodded once, giving permission he would rather not have to grant, and turned slightly aside, bracing himself against the back of the chair. Harrowe did not waste the opening.

"The accounts match in their shape, if not their words. Where the breach spreads, it's answered there. Not by stand-in. Not by sign alone." He tapped the page. "The Witness stands where the land's torn and sets the bond right by deed. Blood, at the least." He hesitated only a fraction. "And...uh... union with her. Proper. Witnessed. Meant to result in... issue to keep the line going." His gaze lifted to Darcy. "Because the Witness won't be walkin' away."

Darcy felt heat rise beneath his collar. He kneaded his brow, refusing to look at either of them, but he did not interrupt. He had learned the cost of doing so.

"Go on," Matlock urged.

Harrowe cleared his throat. "It holds together, if you look at it plain. The land don't answer to what you mean. It answers to what you do." He gestured toward the page. "She bears the weight. The Witness takes it back. They called it fertility because that's how folk once reckoned endurance. Children meant the line went on. Without it, the land keeps reachin' for what was sworn and never made good."

When he fell silent, Darcy realised his jaw had tightened to the point of pain. He forced it to ease and looked to Matlock, already prepared to see disbelief, or at least resistance.

He saw neither.

Matlock regarded Harrowe with a thoughtful expression that chilled Darcy more than outrage would have done. "It is inelegant," he said. "But not unreasonable. History has never been delicate where necessity was concerned."

Darcy stared at him. "You *accept* that?"

"I accept that it accords with ancient precedent," Matlock replied. "And with the failures that followed when men attempted to soften it into metaphor."

Darcy's hand tightened on the chair. "You speak as though that recommends it."

"I speak as one who recognises that systems rarely survive refinement," Matlock said. "If you reject this account, then you must have another to offer. What do you propose instead?"

Darcy drew a breath, slow and deliberate, and felt the familiar resistance rise again—this time not to speech, but to what speech would concede. "Lady Catherine has been explicit in her views."

Matlock's brows lifted. "I should be astonished if she had not been."

"She believes the matter may be settled by binding me in marriage and restoring the centre to Kent," Darcy said. "She is convinced the *Liber* supports her."

"Which it does not, according to you."

"No," Darcy replied. "It does not."

Matlock's mouth curved faintly. "She will not have been persuaded by that."

"She was not," Darcy said. "Nor was she dissuaded from 'acting.'"

Matlock snorted. "That has always been her favourite threat. But 'acting' how? What does she mean to do, truss you up and throw you in a coach for the Hunsford church?"

Darcy hesitated only long enough to know that evasion would serve nothing. "I would not put that past her, but she knows that I believe Elizabeth Bennet of Hertfordshire to be the Lady."

Matlock did not rise and pace, did not raise his voice, did not reach for outrage or denial. His uncle remained seated, hands folded, as though the weight of what had just been said required steadiness rather than motion.

"Then let us be plain," he said. "You are persuaded of the Lady's identity. You have evidence enough to convince yourself. You have dismissed Kent. You have rejected ritual as it is recorded. What, then, do you intend?"

"I intend to proceed with greater certainty," he said. "If distance alters her condition, if removal eases what has been drawn upon her, then perhaps the matter may be put aside long enough for—"

Matlock lifted one hand, not sharply, but with unmistakable authority. "No."

Darcy faltered. "No?"

"No more waiting. No more testing by absence. You speak as though you have the luxury of time, Fitzwilliam, and I tell you plainly that you do not."

Darcy straightened. "You speak as though the matter were already decided."

"I speak," Matlock replied, "as one who has been listening where you have not been permitted to go. I have been at the War Office. I have spoken with men who do not indulge rumour, and who have no patience for metaphor. What you call disturbance, they call collapse. Supplies have not merely been delayed; they have failed. Roads have given way where no flood preceded them. Grain has spoiled in sealed stores. Ships have run aground in fair conditions. This is not a season's inconvenience."

Darcy felt a chill that had nothing to do with the fire behind him. "And... the war? Richard?"

"Richard's last dispatch was already strained. The confidence of it rang false—too carefully shaped, too intent on reassurance. Since then, there has been nothing. And silence, at this juncture, is never neutral."

Darcy drew a breath that did not seem to reach his lungs. "Then you believe—"

"I believe," Matlock said, cutting him off, "that engagements we expected to hold have failed. Our infantry is losing ground. Not through incompetence or cowardice, but through attrition that no general can command. Roads washed out beneath supply wagons. Rivers swollen past their crossings. Men arriving to battle without boots because the stores never reached them. Blankets lost. Powder spoiled. Need I go on?"

He leaned forward slightly, and the controlled restraint of his manner only sharpened the force of what he said next. "There are regiments sleeping in the open, Darcy, because tents could not be raised on ground that froze solid beneath the stakes. There are wounded men who could not be moved because the tracks behind them were washed out by flash flooding in the night. And Napoleon—damn him—does not need to win cleanly when the land itself is doing his work."

Darcy felt something cold and inexorable settle in his chest.

"This is not rumour," Matlock continued. "This is not a matter of interpretation. The War Office is already scrambling to disguise losses we were certain would not occur. Parliament fears panic because they fear the truth. The public has not yet named what it feels, but it will. And when it does, it will not speak gently."

He held Darcy's gaze. "Whatever has been left unanswered has begun to demand payment at scale. And it is not content to take it from one house, or one county, or one woman."

Darcy's thoughts flew, already reaching for paper and ink, for names and distances. "If I write to Mr Bennet—if I learn whether Miss Elizabeth's condition alters with removal—"

"You will learn nothing that matters. Or rather, you will learn it too late."

Darcy's face fell from hope to frustration. "You cannot know that."

"I know this," Matlock replied. "Whatever balance existed depended upon proximity, not distance. You yourself told me that her condition did not improve in isolation, only in relation. You are not observing an illness that may be cured by rest. You are observing a force that has been displaced."

Darcy felt Harrowe's presence behind him like a held breath, but he did not look away from his uncle. "Then you would have me act blindly."

"I would have you act decisively," Matlock said. "You have spent months seeking to be certain before you moved. That caution may have been wisdom once. It is now indulgence."

"And if the cost is hers?"

"Then you must determine whether refusing the cost spares her, or merely postpones a greater one. I will not dress it more kindly than that. At this point," Matlock continued, more quietly, "you are no longer choosing between competing theories. You are choosing whether to answer what has already begun. The country will not wait. The land will not wait. And if you do not act, others will suffer for it—most of all the woman you are trying so desperately to protect."

Darcy closed his eyes for a brief instant, not in surrender, but in reckoning. When he opened them again, the path before him felt brutally clear.

"No more delay," Matlock said. "Tell me what you will do."

# Chapter Forty-Eight

The morning had begun too quietly to feel honest.

Elizabeth sat near the window with her sewing laid aside—she no longer trusted herself with a needle. At present, she was watching the light slide across the floorboards as though nothing in the world had shifted its course. The sea lay beyond the houses in a broad, pewter sweep, its sound softened by distance and walls.

She had slept. She had eaten. Her head did not ache. Her limbs did not tremble. If she listened only to her body, she might have believed herself restored.

Yesterday, after all, had ended *well enough*.

Mary had been married, as far as they knew. The hour had passed. The vows had been spoken. The world had not cracked open in church or swallowed the road beneath the carriage wheels. And Mary would be on her way to Kent by now.

There had been no cries, no fainting fits, no unseemly spectacle to force acknowledgement. Whatever had seized Elizabeth in that brief, terrible interval—whatever pressure had built until she could scarcely breathe—had loosened again. By evening, she had been declared merely fatigued. Overwrought. Excitable.

A wedding, her father had said mildly, was enough to try anyone's nerves. And so, the matter had been allowed to rest.

Her father sat with a broadsheet folded idly upon his knee, his spectacles lowered as he watched Jane move about the room. Jane had insisted on setting the breakfast things to rights herself, though the landlady had offered twice. There was a quiet satisfaction in her movements, a gentleness born of relief. Elizabeth knew the look well. It was the look Jane wore when she believed danger past—when a thing had *not* happened loudly enough to require a reordering of daily affairs.

"You see," her father said at last, glancing toward Elizabeth with a small, weary smile, "sea air and distance. I ought to have prescribed it years ago."

Elizabeth returned the smile because she must. "Do not let it be said that you neglect your children's health, Papa."

Jane laughed softly and crossed to the hearth, where the remnants of last night's fire still glowed faintly among the coals. "Shall I stir it up a little? It is damp this morning."

Elizabeth opened her mouth to answer—and stopped.

The sensation came without warning. Not pain. Not dizziness. A tightening, low and insistent, as though something deep within her core had drawn a slow breath and found itself cramped by restraint. The room felt suddenly smaller, the air thicker, charged with an expectancy she could not name.

"Jane," she said, too quickly, "perhaps—"

The poker rattled.

Jane paused, her hand still upon it. "How odd," she murmured, smiling as she nudged it back into place. "I must be clumsier than I thought."

Elizabeth rose at once. "Do not—please—do not stir it!"

Her father looked up. "Lizzy?"

The coals brightened. Elizabeth felt it then, unmistakable and horrifying: a pull, not toward the fire, but *from it*, as though the newly stoked heat had noticed her and leaned closer in answer. The warmth brushed her skin. Too warm. Too eager.

Jane had knelt and was reaching for a bellows when the flame leapt.

It did not flare wildly. It surged, clean and sudden, a tongue of fire snapping outward from the grate. Jane cried out as it caught her shawl, the wool blackening in an instant. Elizabeth was across the room before she knew she had moved, clutching at Jane's arm, beating at the flame with her bare hands.

"Jane—Jane, let go—!"

Her father was shouting, the chair scraping violently as he lunged for the cold pot of tea beside Elizabeth's chair. Jane stumbled back, her face pale with shock, her breath coming in short, broken gasps. The flame died as quickly as it had risen, leaving only the acrid smell of scorched cloth and the sound of Jane's breathing.

"Are you hurt?" Elizabeth demanded, her voice breaking as she seized Jane's wrist and turned it this way and that. The skin beneath the ruined sleeve had reddened fiercely, an angry mark already swelling across her forearm.

"It is nothing," Jane said, though tears stood in her eyes now. "Only a fright. Elizabeth, please—"

But Elizabeth had stepped back.

The room was wrong. She could feel it with a clarity that robbed her of breath. The hearth crackled softly, settling, innocent once more. The poker trembled against the stones, just once, then stilled.

Her father set the pot down with shaking hands. "Twice…" he murmured. "How?"

Elizabeth's gaze had fixed on Jane's arm. On the burn. On the undeniable truth of it.

"*I* did that," she whispered.

Jane frowned. "Lizzy, no—"

"I did." The words tasted like ash. "I felt it. Before it happened. I knew."

Her father stared at her now, truly stared, as though some long-dismissed notion had at last demanded attention. "Elizabeth…"

"I cannot stay," she said, the sentence tearing free of her before she could temper it. "Papa, you must take me away. At once!"

"Lizzy, you have only just arrived," Jane said, reaching for her with her uninjured hand.

Elizabeth flinched back as though struck. "Do not touch me!"

Jane froze, wounded more by that than by the burn.

Elizabeth pressed her palms to her skirts, suddenly aware of the heat still prickling along her skin, of the way the fire had answered her without command or consent. Jane had been injured… she had not. Her heart was racing now, not with weakness, but with terror so sharp it made her light-headed.

"I cannot be here," she said again, more urgently. "I cannot be *anywhere* like this! You see what happens. No, perhaps I do not faint. I do not grow ill. I make things—" She swallowed hard. "I make things worse!"

Her father crossed the room in two strides and caught her shoulders. She did not pull away from him. "Elizabeth! Stop this talk. You are merely overwrought. You have frightened yourself."

"No!" She shook her head, tears spilling now despite her effort. "I frightened *her*. And next time it will be worse. I can feel it! Something is building, Papa. I cannot stop it!"

Jane's voice trembled. "What are you saying?"

Elizabeth's breath came fast and shallow. "I am saying that if I remain, I will hurt you. I will hurt someone else! I do not know when or how, only that I will."

Silence fell, heavy and terrible. Her father removed his spectacles and rubbed his eyes. "Elizabeth…"

"Take me home!" she pleaded. "To Longbourn. I will lie in my bed and not move. I will be ill. I will be quiet long enough to die without harming someone. Or take me to London—to Mr Darcy! He knows what it costs. He would bear it. He could keep me from harming others, and he would not—" Her voice failed. "He would not be surprised."

"Elizabeth, you do not know what you are asking."

"I do." She met his eyes, desperate and resolute all at once. "I am asking you to choose the danger that can be borne over the one that cannot. I am asking you not to make me stay where I might kill the people I love!"

Jane sank into a chair, pale and shaken, clutching her burned arm as she watched Elizabeth with dawning fear. "But Lizzy, you said Mr Darcy, too, was... vulnerable. To you."

Elizabeth drew her hands together, as though she might hold herself in place by force alone. "But he knows. He understands the cost. *Please*," she said. "Please, Papa. Before it happens again."

And somewhere beyond the walls, the sea struck the shore with sudden, thunderous force, as though in answer.

DARCY DID NOT WAIT for dawn to soften the decision.

The house was still when he ordered the carriage, the lamps in the passage burning low and steady as though they, too, were holding their breath. He moved through the rooms with a deliberation that felt almost ceremonial—selecting the coat fit for travel, the boots already broken to his step, the papers he did not expect to consult and yet could not leave behind. Each choice was plain.

Each felt final.

Harrowe was waiting in the front hall, hat in hand, satchel already slung across one shoulder. There was ink on his fingers and a rawness about his eyes that suggested the night had been spent in argument with men long dead and was no closer to yielding.

"You're going to Hertfordshire. It won't work."

Darcy walked past him to the waiting footman. "And still, I am going."

"Without her? That's not courage, Darcy. It's blindness."

Darcy turned from him to be helped into his coat. "You have had your say. Repeatedly."

"You mistake me if you think I speak for comfort. I've studied this longer than you've borne it. And I've seen what follows when a man believes desire will answer for deed."

Darcy crossed to the door. Brutus already sat there, already alert, as though he had been waiting for the decision to be spoken aloud. Darcy laid his hand at the dog's neck, feeling the heat there, the life, the simple faith.

"Stay."

Brutus made a low, protesting sound and did not move. Did not even blink.

Darcy closed his eyes once. "Oh, very well. Come, Brutus."

The dog was on his feet at once, bounding for the door with a loud bark.

Harrowe's voice broke through the space between them. "You're not listening! If you mean to carry on like this—"

"I *have* listened," Darcy said, sharply now. "I have listened while Parliament dithers and men starve. I have listened while soldiers march barefoot into ground that breaks beneath them. I have listened while you tell me what pagan horrors must be done and my aunt tells me what is 'proper,' and all the while the cost is paid by people who never agreed to any of it!"

"Hold there, Darcy. I never said you oughtn't act. I only meant you cannot succeed alone."

He straightened, hand dropping from the dog's neck. "*I* am the only one answerable at present, and I will not wait for another failure to be recorded in your margins."

Harrowe shook his head. "But the land only answers blood—"

"It will not answer hers," Darcy cut in.

"You cannot substitute yourself!"

"I am *not* substituting," Darcy said, and now the restraint was gone. "I am presenting myself because I understand the cost. Her life is not mine to offer!"

"You don't know it wants hers. But she's *got* to be there—I don't know why, but she does!"

"Well, she is not here, and I am."

"Then you'll have to wait—call her back! I told you it was foolhardy to let her go."

Darcy clenched a fist at his side and slowly rounded on Harrowe. "At every turn, the answer has been delay. Study. Debate. Wait until the pattern is clearer. And while we wait, fields fail. Ships founder. Boys die in foreign mud. If there is anything I can give that slows this—if there is any weight my body can place against it—then I will place it there."

Harrowe stared at him. "You may make it worse."

Darcy nodded once. "I know."

Harrowe searched his face for hesitation and found none. "You may not return."

"Then at least I will not have stood aside." He reached for the door. "I am going. With or without your approval. If you mean to stop me, do it now."

Harrowe did not move, so Darcy opened the door.

Outside, the air had the sharp, rinsed smell of rain. The carriage stood ready, lanterns hooded, the horses shifting with a soft impatience that mirrored his own. Darcy mounted without assistance. Harrowe followed, less elegantly, the satchel wedged at his feet like a promise neither of them intended to keep. The dog sprang up after them and settled with a huff against Darcy's knee.

As the door closed and the carriage lurched forward, Darcy looked once—only once—at the darkened windows of his house. London lay quiet behind him, deceptively so, as though the night had decided to grant itself an alibi.

"North," he said, and the word felt like a vow made without witness.

THE ROAD NORTH HAD not changed.

Darcy had expected some visible sign—subsidence, fissure, water where there ought not to be water. He had expected the land to declare itself now that he came to it with purpose rather than conjecture. Instead, the hedgerows stood as they always had. The fields lay in their winter bareness, unremarkable. Even the air felt ordinary, damp and cold and wholly indifferent to his passage.

Harrowe rode opposite him in silence, satchel braced against his knees, fingers worrying at its strap as though he feared it might vanish if he did not keep hold of it. The dog lay at Darcy's feet, head lifted, ears pricked forward in a vigilance that had nothing to do with game or stranger.

Darcy ordered the carriage to take the western road that looped round Netherfield. Not the most direct route, but there was a place where that road branched and turned back, where one could stand on the rise and see Longbourn in the distance. Where a mere hundred paces or so could take him to the place he sought. They left the carriage where the lane narrowed and went on foot.

The fields here bore little resemblance to what Darcy remembered. The hedges were stripped raw by wind, their naked and broken branches clawing at the sky. The ground lay hard and pale, the winter having bitten deeper here than elsewhere, as though some protection long taken for granted had been withdrawn all at once. Darcy searched instinctively for familiar markers—a rise in the land, the shelter of a tree line—but the shapes had altered. Even the air felt different. Colder. Exposed.

He was already looking for the place where Elizabeth had fallen, but he found nothing.

The slope that should have cupped the hollow was flattened. The grass that did poke through the parched snow lay crushed and colourless, scoured down to soil in places, as though something had passed through and taken more than it left behind. Darcy slowed, his steps careful now, his eyes tracking the ground with an exactness born of memory and unease. This should have been near enough. He was certain of it. And yet—

He stopped.

"No," he said quietly. "It is here. Or it was."

Harrowe followed his gaze. "The land does not always preserve its scars where it is still bleeding."

Darcy exhaled and made his decision. "Brutus."

The dog had been straining at his side since they left the carriage, body angled forward, nose working the air in short, urgent pulls. At the sound of his name, he surged ahead at once, leash slackening as Darcy released it entirely.

"Find," Darcy said.

Brutus did not hesitate. He ranged outward in a widening arc, head low, movements purposeful rather than frantic. He passed once over ground that looked no different from any other, then doubled back sharply, circling, snorting softly. His tail stiffened.

Darcy followed.

The dog stopped where the frost lay thickest, where the earth beneath had sunk by inches into itself. Brutus pawed once at the ground, then sat back on his haunches and looked up, a low sound rising in his throat that was neither bark nor whine.

Harrowe grasped his hat and lumbered forward as if a dock crate were trying to crash over the ship's side. "This! This is it."

Darcy stepped forward.

The moment his boot crossed the edge of the depression, the sensation returned—not the hollowing of before, but a pressure from without, as though the air itself had thickened around him. The ground did not split this time. It simply... yielded. A faint tremor passed beneath his feet, too small to see, too deliberate to mistake.

He crouched and laid his palm against the soil.

It was cold. Not winter-cold, but... emptied. As though whatever warmth had once passed through it had been drawn away abruptly and with purpose.

"She was here," Darcy said, the certainty settling into him with a weight he could not dislodge. "Something... took from her. Attached itself to her, if you will. But when she left, it did not follow her."

Harrowe swallowed. "No. It followed you."

Darcy straightened slowly. The fields around them lay stripped and exposed, the winter having scoured them to their bones. Whatever quiet equilibrium had once held this place had withdrawn entirely. The land was no longer waiting.

It was reaching.

Brutus pressed against his leg with a whimper. Darcy rested his hand on the dog's head, fingers sinking into the familiar warmth, and for a moment the world narrowed to that simple, living contact. The dog trusted him. So did Georgiana. So did Bingley, with his open heart and unguarded loyalty. And Elizabeth—

The thought of her came not as ache, but as clarity. Her face as she had looked at him in the library. The stubbornness with which she had refused to let him be spent for her sake. The way she had left because she believed his life worth preserving, even at the cost of her own safety.

His breath shortened—not with pain, but with resolve. If this was the place, if this was to be the reckoning... Then it would be answered here.

The ground beneath his boots gave a deeper shudder.

Harrowe drew in a sharp breath and took a step backwards. "It knows you."

The hollow darkened—not with shadow, but with attention. The air thickened, pressing close around him, and the faint line in the grass deepened as the soil parted by inches, not violently, but with a dreadful patience, as though it had all the time in the world and intended to take it.

Darcy did not retreat. He loosened his grip on Brutus, laying his palm briefly against the dog's brow in silent command. "Stay."

The dog whined once, his body trembling head to tail, but obeyed.

Darcy stepped forward alone.

He felt the pull at once—not pain, not tearing, but a drawing away, as though something essential were being invited out of him without resistance. His chest felt hollowed, his limbs light to the point of unreality. He thought, with distant clarity, that this was how a man might feel when already half gone.

This, then, was the price.

His mind did not resist it. There was no panic, no reaching back. Only a swift, encompassing awareness of all he would leave unfinished—his sister's future, his friend's faith, the quiet life he had never expected to want until Elizabeth Bennet had made him imagine it.

He lifted his head. "If you want blood," he shouted, the sound tearing out of him raw and ungoverned, "then take it of me!"

The words vanished into the cold like breath.

He did not kneel. He did not posture. He stepped forward—into the seam itself.

The ground gave way beneath his boot and he did not retreat. The soil sagged and split, the dark line widening by inches, and a violent pressure seized him—harder than before, deeper. It was not pain at first. It was displacement. As though something inside him had been hooked and was being drawn out by steady, merciless increments.

His lungs emptied. He tried to inhale and found there was nothing to draw.

Brutus barked behind him, frantic now.

Darcy forced another step. If this was the price, he would pay it. If this was the reckoning long deferred, he would not leave it to her.

The pull intensified. His vision blurred into a dizzying swirl. His heart began to stutter—not the crushing agony he had known in London, but a slow, arrhythmic unravelling, like a clock slipping out of measure. He felt suddenly and sharply the shape of his own mortality—the hole he would leave behind: Georgiana at Pemberley, alone; Bingley nearly lost without him; Richard unmoored, trying to pull together a world unwound...

And Elizabeth. What happened to her now? Would she be doomed to a life without echo, without counterpart?

*Forgive me*, he thought—not to God, not to the land, but to her.

The earth shuddered beneath him. The seam widened further. Cold air rushed upward from the exposed hollow and struck him full in the chest, stealing what little breath he had regained. He swayed.

"Take it!" he demanded hoarsely. "If this is what you require—take it!"

He did not slice his hand. He did not perform ceremony or look to Harrowe—who was mute and stunned anyway—to recite old oaths. He simply stood there, upright by will alone, and surrendered the only thing he could—his own continuance.

The pressure on his lungs mounted. For one brutal, suspended instant, he believed it would take him whole. His knees buckled. His heart lurched violently once, twice. A roaring filled his ears. The world narrowed to a single, terrible point of surrender...

...and then it stopped.

Not eased.

Stopped.

The pull vanished as if cut cleanly away.

Air rushed back into his lungs, sharp and punishing. Darcy collapsed forward on his hands and knees, coughing up blood in his spittle. His heart slammed painfully into rhythm again, too strong, too alive. The seam in the earth did not close. The soil did not knit. The water below continued its indifferent shimmer.

Darcy tried to stand and only managed to stagger back, catching himself on his hands in the frozen grass. His palms burned with cold. His breath tore in ragged pulls. He was alive.

Alive?

The land had not refused blood because it was insufficient.

It had refused *him*.

The wind moved across the hollow, thin and barren. The crack remained—a wound without answer.

Brutus reached him first, pressing hard against his side, licking his hands, whining low and distressed. Darcy lifted his head slowly and looked at the unhealed seam cutting through the field.

He had offered everything, and it had not even wanted him.

"It answers you," Harrowe said slowly as he lowered himself to a knee beside Darcy. "But it doesn't accept."

Darcy swallowed. "Then what is wanting?"

Harrowe was watching the ground with an expression Darcy had not seen before—not triumph, not certainty, but something uncomfortably close to fear.

"In the old days," Harrowe said at last, "there were always two. One to pay, and one to receive."

Darcy straightened with effort. "You cannot have two!" he shouted to the ground. Any thoughts of what an idiot he must seem were nothing. "This is my offering. I am here!"

The seam in the earth widened another fraction. Not enough to swallow him. Enough to promise that it could.

He stood there, breathing hard now, not from exertion but from the sudden knowledge of what he had failed to do.

Harrowe did not look at him. "You cannot answer for her. And you cannot replace her."

Darcy closed his eyes.

He turned away from the hollow, already knowing what must come next, and despising himself for having hoped—however briefly—that it might not.

# Chapter Forty-Nine

THE COTTAGE HAD GROWN too small.

Elizabeth could not have said when it began—only that the walls felt nearer than they had the night before, the ceiling lower, the air too close despite the bitter cold that crept beneath the door. The grate stood dark and empty. No flame had been permitted there since yesterday. The poker had vanished. The kettle had been removed to the kitchen and kept there. Even her sewing basket had been quietly dismantled—needles gone, scissors 'misplaced,' the thimble nowhere to be found.

Porcelain only for her tea. Wooden spoons. Blankets upon blankets, until the three of them sat swaddled like invalids in a house that should have been warm.

The landlady's footsteps passed the door twice in an hour, and twice Elizabeth heard the restrained knock and the careful offer—coal for the grate, hot water for washing, broth to fortify the nerves. Papa declined with forced civility. Jane's voice followed, softer, apologetic. The landlady muttered something about sea damp and foolish Londoners and went away unsatisfied.

Jane no longer pretended. She watched Elizabeth openly now, her composure thin as glass. Papa held a book he had not turned the page of for half an hour, his spectacles slipping lower on his nose as his gaze drifted—not to the print, but to Elizabeth.

They no longer dared to believe the danger had passed. It had merely changed form. And Elizabeth knew it.

"I shall walk a little," Elizabeth said at last, setting aside the blanket that had begun to feel less like warmth and more like confinement. "The air is clearer by the shore."

Jane moved to rise, the quilt spilling out of her lap. "Lizzy, no."

Papa looked up sharply from his unread book. "Absolutely not."

Elizabeth remained standing. "I am not made of tinder."

"That is precisely what we are afraid of," Jane replied, the words escaping before she could temper them.

"I cannot remain here! You have removed every iron implement from the room. You sit in the cold rather than risk a flame. I cannot be the reason you shiver in your own lodgings."

Papa closed the book upon his finger and regarded her with grave steadiness. "We are only being prudent."

"You are being afraid," she said gently. "And you are right to be. So am I. Which is why I must go out."

Papa rose slowly. "Elizabeth."

"I have always walked when I cannot think," she said, holding his gaze. "If you deny me that, you deny me the only remedy I have ever trusted."

Jane's hands twisted in her shawl. "We will come with you."

"No." Elizabeth's voice sharpened, then softened. "No. If something occurs, it must occur with me alone. I will not risk you again."

Papa moved toward her. "You do not know that solitude is safer."

"I know that your own kettle was ripped out of your hands. And that Jane's arm is blistered from the fire that *I* caused."

Neither answered.

Elizabeth drew her gloves on and reached for her thick green cloak. "I shall walk to the shore. I shall not enter the water. I shall remain within sight of the houses."

Jane's lips trembled. "And if it begins again?"

"Then I shall discover whether it means to consume everything... or just me."

Papa studied her for a long moment, then stepped aside—not in agreement, but in acknowledgment that she would go regardless, and short of overpowering her by brute force, there was little he could do.

"Do not go far."

"I shall not." She opened the door before they could reconsider and stepped into the wind.

It struck her at once—sharp, salted, bracing. She drew it deep into her lungs, testing whether it would answer differently from the air within the cottage.

The sea lay ahead in a broad sheet of silvery light, the tide half out, its long breath drawing at the sand in measured intervals. Children ran near the waterline. A fisherman crouched beside a net, his knife flashing in the pale morning light. A small vessel rocked gently beyond the breakwater, tethered and patient.

Elizabeth descended the slope toward the shore. She folded her arms against the wind and gathered her cloak closer, more from habit than from cold. The sand was firm beneath her boots, ridged by the retreating tide. She kept her eyes lowered as she walked, watching the pale shells crushed into the surface, the threads of dark weed caught in the grooves.

*Marriage abates it*, Papa had said once, in a tone half speculative and half weary.

She had almost laughed then.

Marriage, or lack of it, does not charm away fire from a grate. Nor send kettles lunging through the air, spoons and needles trembling at her nearness, or a man's heart collapsing in his chest.

She paced along the wet line where the tide had lately been, her steps deliberate. If she could master her breathing, if she could still her thoughts, perhaps she could still whatever answered them. She counted her breaths—four in, four held, four out—an old habit from childhood when she had tried to quiet a racing heart before a difficult conversation.

The sea moved as it always had, withdrawing and returning in long grey sweeps. A fishing boat came into view from the fog, rising and falling on the water's roll as it traced the shore. The wind cut across her cheek and caught the edge of her bonnet.

She was being foolish to even consider it.

Darcy had nearly died when she was in London. That was the fact. Whatever stirred here could not be independent of him. Perhaps distance would thin it. Perhaps time would blunt it. Perhaps she had mistaken coincidence for design. But she could not escape the understanding that *she* needed him, and *he* needed...

She was not sure.

The tide crept closer to her boots. She did not notice at first. The wet sand darkened in a slow, encroaching band. The line she had been pacing retreated without announcement. She adjusted her path a step inland and continued walking, still staring at the ground, still counting.

*He anchored me.*

The thought struck her harder than the wind.

She saw again the library—the weight in the air, the strange relief that came only when he was near. Not ease, exactly. Not safety. But alignment. As though something wild within her had been forced into its proper channel by the mere fact of his presence.

And the cost of it had shown on him.

Colour drained. Breath shortened. That dreadful stagger in his pulse beneath her ear. She had believed herself the one being consumed.

What if *she* had been the one consuming?

Her breath faltered.

The next withdrawal of water seemed slower. The next return heavier. Not louder—just weighted, as though something beneath the surface pressed upward against it.

Elizabeth glanced up at last. The anchored boat beyond the breakwater tugged hard at its rope, snapping taut before slackening again. The fisherman repairing his net paused and looked toward the swell with a frown.

There was no change in the wind. Perhaps the tide was coming in.

She resumed walking, though more slowly now.

*He would come.*

If she sent for him—if she wrote a single line—he would come without hesitation. He would hold her when the fire leapt close. He would place himself between her and whatever force demanded... what of her?

He would call it duty. He would call it necessity. He would never call it love, but it would be that. Love of the purest sort.

*She loved him.*

The truth did not arrive gently. It did not bloom. It struck, complete and undeniable, like the tide against stone.

She loved him not for his endurance, nor for his rank, nor for the strange answering current that seemed to bind them. She loved him because he chose. Because even in pain, he would choose her safety above his own. Because he would bear what she would not ask him to bear.

And she *could* not.

She could not summon him merely to watch him pale and struggle and fight for breath. She could not stand again with her ear to his chest, counting the ruin she brought upon him.

Another wave drove farther up the sand, soaking the hem of her gown.

But matters between them had changed before... were continually changing. What if it was different this time?

And if she did not go to him, who would suffer instead?

The fisherman had risen now, shouting to someone else about the line of foam creeping toward his nets. A mother snatched her child back with a sharp exclamation. The anchored boat beyond the breakwater tugged and jerked, the rope straining against its post.

Elizabeth watched them with a detached sort of curiosity, then her thoughts consumed her once more.

If she remained here—if she remained *anywhere*—would the terrors follow? Would the fire leap? Would metal turn treacherous in innocent hands?

She closed her eyes against the glare.

*Is there a choice at all?*

To run to him would risk his life. To stay away would risk everyone else's.

Better to be destroyed together than to scatter harm among strangers. The thought was wild, desperate—and yet it carried a terrible coherence. If ruin must come, let it fall where it was understood. Let it fall where love stood ready to meet it.

*But love does not excuse destruction.*

Her breath grew shallow. The air tasted of salt and iron. "I must not think," she murmured, though no one stood near enough to hear.

But she *was* thinking. Of his face in the library. Of the way he had stood before her father and released what he might have taken. Of the knowledge in his eyes when she had left him—knowledge he had not spoken aloud.

He would receive her. Whatever she carried. Whatever it cost. That was precisely why she must choose carefully.

What if there was no version of this that spared him? What if she was not meant to be saved... but ended?

The next wave came higher than the last. Enough to send a thin sheet of foam racing farther up the sand. A child darted toward it, shrieking in delight as the water chased his boots. His mother laughed and called after him.

Elizabeth's heart gave a hard, involuntary beat.

The water surged again—farther this time, swift and gleaming, the foam hissing over sand that had been dry moments before. It struck the boy's legs and nearly swept him from his footing before his mother lunged and caught him under the arms.

The fisherman stood upright now, shading his eyes and pointing at the fishing boat heaving on the horizon.

Elizabeth did not move... and the tide paused.

Not as tides do.

As if awaiting instruction.

Her breath stuttered. The air seemed to draw inward with her, as though the whole breadth of sea had leaned close to listen.

*No.*

She took a step backward.

The water followed.

Not forward in a uniform line, but in a narrow tongue, a darkened channel threading through the broader wash. It slid across the sand toward her boots, and then broke—dividing cleanly, curling around her toes without wetting the leather. The foam eddied at either side of her feet and retreated.

A space remained where she stood. Dry.

The next swell rose more violently. It did not crest and fall in its usual rhythm but lifted as though something beneath it had thrust upward. The anchored boat beyond the breakwater snapped hard against its rope. Wood cracked. A man shouted from the pier.

Elizabeth's pulse hammered against her ribs.

*This is coincidence. This is terror. This is fancy.*

Another surge came. This one struck the small vessel broadside and flung it sideways against the stone. The rope gave with a report like a pistol. The hull scraped and listed. Two men on the quay ran for it, boots slipping on wet stone.

The fisherman's net, half-spread upon the sand, was snatched and dragged several feet inland as though seized by invisible hands. He leapt to retrieve it, cursing, and nearly lost his footing when the retreating water tugged at his ankles with unnatural force.

A woman screamed.

The sound of the sea no longer filled the world; it seemed to originate within her. Each swell corresponded to the spear of terror in her chest. Each withdrawal mirrored the pull beneath her ribs. She swallowed, and the water drew back. She inhaled sharply, and the next wave rose.

*It is me.*

Just like the fire. The kettle. The rot in the grain bins, the roses in the trellis, and the crushing winter storm that had nearly flattened Longbourn.

She turned her head toward the breakwater. The men there were bracing themselves, hauling at ropes, shouting instructions she could not distinguish. One slipped. For a moment, his body vanished behind the rising wall of green-grey water.

Elizabeth's heart lurched, and the sea answered. The swell bent. Not outward.

Around her.

The crest that had been driving toward the quay split as it neared the shore, its force shearing in two directions, racing along either side of the stretch of sand where she stood.

It left a long, trembling corridor in its wake, a path of relative stillness that widened and narrowed with the movement of her breath.

She took another step back.

The water drew with her.

She stepped forward—only a fraction, compelled by some horrid instinct to test it—and the foam rushed to meet her boots and then recoiled, as though rebuked.

The boy wrestled free from his mother's grip and darted again toward the waterline in wild delight at the spectacle.

"No!" Elizabeth cried, though she did not know whether she spoke to the child or the sea.

The next wave did not wait.

It reared—higher than any before it—shouldering upward in a heaving mass that cast a shadow across the sand. The anchored vessel slammed full against the stones with a sound of splintering wood. A mast tilted. Someone shouted that a man had fallen into the sea.

Elizabeth felt the surge build inside her, immense and terrible, pressing against bone and sinew as if her body were only a frail vessel for something that had no patience with flesh.

*Stop!*

The command formed without words.

The water hesitated. It did not crash. It hung, suspended in a grotesque arch, trembling, as though straining against a leash drawn taut. Every eye upon the shore was fixed upon the sea.

No one looked at her. Yet.

Elizabeth's knees weakened. Terror flooded her more violently than any tide.

If she lost control—if her thoughts fractured, if fear mastered her... what then? Would the harbour empty? Would the boats be dashed to kindling? Would children be dragged beneath the surf because she had walked too near the edge?

The suspended wave quivered.

A trickle of warmth slid beneath her nose. She lifted her hand and found it stained red.

The sea shuddered in answer.

She staggered backward, heart pounding, and the great wall of water collapsed—not forward, not inland, but outward, slamming back upon itself in a roiling crash that sent spray high into the air and left the shore in chaotic foam.

The man on the quay was dragged to his feet by another's grip. The boy was seized again by his mother. The broken boat thudded uselessly against stone, half-swamped but not overturned.

The water retreated. And once more, at her feet, it parted.

Elizabeth stared at the narrow, obedient channel, the way the foam curved in a perfect arc around the hem of her gown. She had not commanded it. She had not known how.

A sound rose from her throat—not quite a sob, not quite a prayer. The sea rose... began its assault on the land when she confessed in her heart that she loved Fitzwilliam Darcy.

# Chapter Fifty

Netherfield looked altered long before Darcy reached the drive. The façade still stood in proportion, the windows intact, the chimneys upright, but something in its bearing had broken. The gravel lay uneven in patches, as though the earth beneath had exhaled and not yet drawn breath again. A length of cord had been strung across the front steps to prevent entry through the main door.

Bingley was in the forecourt with a man in a dark travelling coat and another stooping over a ledger balanced on a courtyard stone. A third gentleman, older and narrower, held a measuring rod and kept glancing from the house to the ground with the air of one who mistrusted both.

Bingley saw Darcy before he had quite reached them and broke away at once, his expression brightening in visible relief.

"Darcy! Thank heaven. I did not expect you, but I am devilish glad you are here. You see how it stands. Or rather, how it does not."

Darcy took his hand briefly. "It looks far worse than your letter led me to believe. You cannot be lodging here."

"No. The inn at Meryton has surrendered its best rooms. Mrs Nicholls would not hear of my remaining within these walls, and I confess I was easily persuaded. Bixby and Mr Netherton's representative have been tireless. There is an architect—if you would like the particulars—"

"I should like them from you."

Bingley blinked. "From me? I am afraid I shall disappoint you. I have had the explanations twice and retain only half of them. The main staircase is the worst of it. The crack runs beneath the central span—clean through. One cannot risk a foot upon it. It is as though the earth decided to cut the building in half."

"The servants' stair?" Darcy asked.

"Entirely sound," Bingley said, almost apologetically. "Which makes no sense at all. It is not half so well supported. The architect swears it ought to have fared worse. But it lies on the east side, nearer the kitchens. The main stair is nearer the old drawing room."

"A different line in the ground," Darcy said.

Bingley gave a short, uneasy laugh. "If that comforts you, I will accept it. Though it does not comfort me. The ballroom floor has lifted in one corner. The plaster in the south gallery has fissured. The kitchens have lost a section of chimney, and the scullery wall shows daylight where it should not."

Darcy held up a hand. "I do not require the catalogue of rooms. I require the hour."

"The hour?"

"When did it fail?"

Bingley stared at him. "During the quake, of course. When else should a house decide to crack itself open?"

Darcy did not look away. "Nothing before that?"

"Nothing before," Bingley said, then hesitated. "Not to my knowledge. Though—"

"Though?"

"Well, there was some settling afterward. A shifting I cannot account for. It was not during the shock itself. We found it after we had all returned from the wedding."

"The wedding?

"Of course, you must remember. Mr Collins and Mary Bennet. A very respectable ceremony. The bride bore herself with admirable composure, though Mrs Bennet wept enough for the entire parish. I stood beside the aisle with the Lucases. It was all quite proper. Until..."

He paused, frowning at the memory.

"Until?" Darcy prompted.

"Well, the candles snuffed out. All of them. There must have been twenty at least—on the rail, at the altar, in the sconces. At the precise moment Collins spoke his vow, they went out. Not flickered or guttered. Simply out, every one of them."

Darcy glanced up at the broken beams. "Is that so?" he breathed.

"There was no draught," Bingley went on, shaking his head. "The church doors were shut. No one moved. They simply—whooshed. Mrs Bennet gave a little shriek, and then everyone laughed. The clerk relit them, and the ceremony continued. Mrs Bennet is a happy woman, indeed, and I hope the same can be said for the new Mrs Collins."

He looked up at the house behind him. "Anyway, as I was saying, when I returned here afterward, the steward met me at the gate. The crack in the stair had lengthened. Fresh plaster crumbles lay in a drift at the base. He swore it had not been so when he left for the church."

"How... singular."

"It is, isn't it? He gave me the time, and it must have happened during the vows." Bingley's expression shifted as he watched Darcy absorb the account. The nervous brightness faded; something more searching took its place.

"You were looking into this before," he said after a moment. "The fissures. The old watercourses. You had the steward pulling deeds from the last five decades past and muttering about culverts no one remembered digging. I thought you more thorough than reasonably necessary, perhaps even bored into scholarship because we did not amuse you well enough. I did not think you... anticipatory."

Darcy turned to glance behind himself.

Bingley followed his gaze toward the carriage. Harrowe had drifted away entirely and now stood with the architect near the south wall, gesturing toward the line where brick met soil. Brutus wandered amid the rubble, nose low, tail stiff, tracing the perimeter of the foundation as though the house itself emitted a scent.

"You have brought that fellow from London, I see. Care to tell me who he is? He looks as though he would measure the sky if given a ladder."

Darcy turned back. "Aldous Harrowe. The man I turned to for research."

"Research?" Bingley repeated, the word half incredulous. "Darcy." Bingley glanced round, then turned slightly, as if to block the sound of his words from other ears.

"You told me there was something you could not account for. That Miss Elizabeth's illness had some meaning. That the ground beneath Netherfield felt wrong in ways you could not articulate. I did not press you then because you seemed...troubled enough." His brow furrowed. "Have you revised that opinion?"

Darcy looked back at the house. At the main stair window, now boarded. At the faint, jagged seam running like a scar through mortar that had once been immaculate.

"Yes," he said. "I have."

Bingley drew a breath. "Then for Heaven's sake, tell me."

Darcy chose his words carefully, not to soften them, but to keep them from sprawling into the incoherence of superstition.

"There are several accounts I have been studying," he began. "Translations of ancient sources, held separately by my family and Lord Matlock's, and some obtained by Harrowe from the Archives. The persistent assertion that there is a place in this county where stewardship was once bound to something more than land and rent. A line in the ground, dismissed as metaphor because it proved inconvenient to credit it otherwise. And multiple confusions in the translations, some of which have been... attributed wrongly, prepared for in error by my aunt, Lady Catherine."

Bingley nodded slowly. "You did not say all that before."

"Because I did not believe it. Since then, I have become... persuaded. Moreover, I am also convinced that the descriptions did not refer to Kent at all, as she asserted, but here. To Hertfordshire. To this estate, to Longbourn, and the fields surrounding them. There are records of a culverted stream beneath this rise. A channel diverted when the house was expanded. The crack beneath your stair follows that course almost precisely."

Bingley's face lost what colour it had retained. "You mean to say this was inevitable."

"I mean to say it was foreseen. Not as an earthquake in particular, but as a fracture. A breach. The land answering a neglect long deferred."

Bingley let out a low breath. "And Miss Elizabeth?"

Darcy drew in a long sigh and drummed his fingers on his trouser leg. "Her collapses occurred at the very places the records mark as strained. The hollow where she fell. The stair where she faltered and could not pass—you have not heard that, but I was there, and I witnessed it. Each lies upon the same line."

Bingley swallowed. "You are suggesting," he said carefully, "that she was... what? Sensitive to it?"

"More than sensitive. Commanded, I suppose. Or possessing some control she did not know how to wield."

"By Jove!" Bingley breathed. "But what does it mean?"

"There is in the older accounts," Darcy went on, "a figure—styled the Lady in some versions. The one in whom the land's condition manifests first. Weakness in her precedes weakness in the soil. Recovery in her forestalls it."

Bingley stared. "And you believe—"

"I *know*," Darcy said, before he could soften it, "that when her condition altered in my presence, the ground responded."

Bingley's eyes widened. "Responded how?"

"When the bond between us was acknowledged—however briefly—and then broken again, the shock you felt in London was the immediate consequence."

"Bond... I do not understand."

Darcy sighed and grimaced. Bingley would force him to confess it again. "With a... a moment of intimacy. Call it... I do not know, affection, desire, the initiation of a union—"

"What are you saying, Darcy?"

"I kissed her!"

Bingley paled, and Darcy turned away from him to pace. "Darcy... I trusted you. I brought her to your house because I believed—"

"It was not a seduction, Bingley. I only wanted to talk to her, to see what she understood, to find out if we two could somehow, together, discover what was to be done. And the best answer we had was... well, it does not matter, because I was on the edge of a collapse when she pulled away. And that was the moment of fracture."

Bingley's mouth parted. "You cannot mean—"

"I do."

The wind stirred along the broken edge of the drive. Somewhere behind them, a plank thudded against brick.

Bingley's voice dropped almost to nothing. "Darcy. That was felt thirty miles away."

"I am aware."

"And I suppose you are going to tell me that the candles at the wedding had something to do with all this?"

Darcy's jaw tightened. "A vow was spoken that opened a line which had long been dormant. Not of inheritance, but of access."

Bingley frowned. "This is all... rather fantastical."

"And have you ever known me to be given to whimsy? Bingley, listen. Collins is not merely a bridegroom and not merely a Bennet cousin. He is her ladyship's instrument in Hertfordshire. When he bound himself to Mary Bennet in marriage, not mere maternal kinship, that bond did not settle succession. It granted proximity. It placed adversarial influence—however improperly interpreted—within the very household that stands nearest the fault."

Bingley looked from the house to the fields beyond, as though the explanation might be written somewhere in the frost-burned grass.

"And you," he said at last, "where do you stand in this?"

Darcy gestured vaguely. "Harrowe describes my role as the 'witness.' A sort of counterweight."

Bingley let out a long, unsteady breath. "And what is required of the witness?"

Darcy glanced once more toward Harrowe, who had crouched now to examine the foundation stone, oblivious to everything but the earth. "A vow kept," he said. "Fully. Not symbolically. Not in convenience. Kept at... cost."

Bingley's expression shifted again—no longer confusion, but dawning comprehension edged with alarm. "And if it is not?"

Darcy looked up at the cracked façade of Netherfield, at the stair that could not bear a single step.

"You have already seen the beginning of that answer."

THE INN WAS QUIETER than it had any right to be.

Darcy had taken a chamber overlooking the yard, though there was little to see beyond a lantern swinging in the wind and the dark line of the road stretching north. Bingley had retired hours ago, full of restless speculation and practical concerns. Harrowe had remained below with a map from Netherfield's library and a mug he had forgot to drink from. Brutus lay curled at the foot of the bed, breathing slow and heavy, as though the world had not split in two.

Darcy sat awhile in the chair by the hearth, coat discarded, cravat loosened, the fire reduced to embers. He had ridden hard that day, had walked the fields again until the frost soaked through his boots, had stood at the hollow and found nothing but silence where the earth had answered him before.

He closed his eyes only when they refused to remain open.

Sleep did not take him at once. It slid over him gradually, the room softening, the hiss of the coals blending with the wind against the shutters. He did not feel the moment the chamber altered.

He was standing in his chambers at his house in London. The fire burned cleanly. No smoke, no flare. The lamps were lit, but did not flicker. The air was warm, ordinary, untroubled. He knew the room as one knows a place by heart—the precise curve of the chaise, the faint sheen on the furniture where light struck polished wood, the shadow cast by the table upon the far wall.

*She* stood before him.

Elizabeth did not appear as an apparition or a vision half-formed. She was wholly herself. Her hair lay loose over her shoulders, not braided for sleep, not confined for propriety, but blown free—almost as a bride loosed her hair for her husband. Her gown was simple, pale, without ornament, and the sheer fabric almost looked like a living thing. There was colour in her cheeks, mischief on her lips, and a spark in her eyes. No tremor in her hands.

He did not question how she had come there. He did not question whether he was dreaming. The knowledge of her was so immediate, so complete, that doubt would have been absurd.

He reached, one finger curled as if to brush the whispery edge of her sleeve. "You are well."

She smiled. Not the brittle, determined smile she had worn when she refused to frighten him, but something quieter. "Am I?"

He stepped toward her, half expecting the air to thicken, the lamps to shudder, the floor to split. Nothing answered. The boards beneath his boots remained firm. The fire did not writhe. The windows did not rattle.

His hand lifted, hovered only a moment, then settled at her waist. Warmth met him. Real warmth. Not the burning pulse that had made his vision swim. Not the sharp, electric pull that had torn breath from his lungs.

She came into his arms as though she had always meant to.

He felt the weight of her there. The natural fit of her against him. How her breath brushed the hollow at his throat and his own did not falter. There was no stammering in his chest, no flicker of black at the edge of sight. His heart beat strong and even... a little faster now. *"Elizabeth."*

The first touch of his mouth to hers was unhurried. No shock split the air. No tremor rippled through the walls. The world did not recoil.

He waited for it. For the surge, the fracture, the wrenching pain that had followed the last time.

Nothing came.

Her hand rose to his collar. Not to push him away. Not in alarm. It twined there, fingers curving possessively into linen, and she answered the kiss with a softness that undid him more thoroughly than any violence could have done.

It was not fevered. Not desperate. It was what he had always imagined such a moment might be, had he ever permitted himself to imagine it at all—private, unobserved, chosen.

He drew back only enough to look at her.

"You see?" she said quietly.

He did not know what she meant, but the world had stilled around them. The fire burned as it ought. The bed was welcoming, and only steps away... All was as it should be if she belonged to him, if this was their claiming of each other in every natural sense.

There was only her.

He might have remained there—might have believed it a mercy granted too late—had the light not shifted. It did not fail at once.

The edges of the room lost their certainty. The clock upon the mantel blurred. The warmth at her waist cooled beneath his hand.

Elizabeth's gaze altered. Not in affection now. Not in ease. She glanced beyond him.

The fire guttered without sound. The chaise dissolved into shadow. The walls of the library retreated as though drawn backward into mist.

He reached for her, but his fingers closed on air. The floor dropped away. He was no longer in his house.

The motion struck him first—the lurch and sway of wheels over rutted ground. The air smelled of mud, horses, bodies, and unwashed leather. Voices crowded him, though he stood apart from them, unseen.

Elizabeth sat opposite a narrow window in a mail coach, rocking with the ruts in the road. Her hair was knotted tightly, but rebellious wisps of it had tugged loose. She had tugged a heavy green cloak fully about herself so that only her hands could be seen, folded tightly in her lap. The light was thin, grey with travel. Two children dozed against their mother's shoulder. A man in a rough coat and hat chewed at a strip of something salted. Across from her, a militia officer with loosened cravat leaned back with careless indifference, boots braced wide.

Elizabeth did not touch the seat beside her. She held herself aloof, leaving a gap as though the air were edged.

A child stirred and, without meaning to, kicked her ankle. She flinched, but raised neither hand nor voice.

But the metal buckle at the officer's boot gave a sharp, answering twitch.

The man beside her shifted closer, attempting to wedge himself more comfortably on the narrow bench. His sleeve brushed her wrist, and then he jerked back, snorting awake as if pricked.

Elizabeth's jaw tightened. She clasped her hands tighter still.

Darcy tried to step forward, to catch her hand. The coach rocked. He could not move within it. He could only watch.

The coach slowed. Lantern light bled through the windows as they pulled into a yard. Night had fallen; he could see it in the depth of shadow beyond the glass. Voices called out. Wheels ground against gravel.

The door was flung open, and Elizabeth rose with the others, careful not to brush against anyone more than necessary. She descended first, skirts gathered, boots finding the step as she held the handle on the coach, rather than taking the coachman's hand.

The yard was crowded. Lanterns swung. Men laughed too loudly. A horse stamped, foam flecking its bit. The militia officer jumped down behind her and stretched, sword hilt glinting at his side. He did not look at her, and she slid away before he could.

Elizabeth now stood uncertainly near the inn door, reaching into her reticule. She counted coins. Her lips moved faintly. She glanced up at the landlord, heard the price he named for a room, and looked back to her palm.

A man detached himself from a group near the stable wall. His hat sat crooked; drink had flushed his cheeks. "No need to fret, miss," he said, stepping too near. "Rooms scarce tonight. But I've one to spare. Plenty of space."

She shook her head. "I require only a small chamber. And privacy."

The man laughed and reached for her arm. Darcy felt the motion as if it had seized his own flesh.

The militia officer barked a sound of amusement. "She'll manage."

The drunk man's fingers closed.

In that same instant, the officer's sword tore free of its scabbard.

Not drawn by hand.

*Ripped.*

The blade flashed between Elizabeth and the man, slicing air so close that cloth parted at the drunk's sleeve. He staggered back with a curse. The officer stumbled as though shoved, staring at his own hand, which still hung empty at his side.

For a breath, no one moved.

The sword hung there—point angled toward the ground—quivering in the lantern light. Then it dropped. The clang against stone split the yard.

Laughter rose, loud and uneven. "Too much ale," someone muttered. "A fine trick, lass!" someone else called.

The officer bent, fumbling for the hilt, face gone pale. The drunk swore and backed away.

Elizabeth had not moved. The innkeeper's wife hurried forward, clucking in irritation, shooing the men aside with sharp words. "Enough of that. Girl, come along. You'll have the attic. It's cold, but it's private."

Elizabeth gathered her cloak around her and followed. At the threshold, she stopped. She turned, and her eyes met his. Not across a room now, nor across a field. Across a distance he could not measure. There was no sweetness in them. No illusion of safety. Just a word.

"Please," she whispered.

# Chapter Fifty-One

Darcy woke with the taste of salt in his mouth.

He did not start upright; he lay still for one suspended instant, staring at the low plaster ceiling of the inn chamber, listening to the absence of wheels, the absence of voices, the absence of surf or carriage wheels or rocking. The bed curtains stirred faintly in a draft that carried only the ordinary chill of Hertfordshire morning.

His heart struck once—firm, deliberate. No staggering. No wrenching pull. The evenness felt wrong. He sat up.

The dream clung not as a fancy but as memory: the pull of her hands, the heat of her kiss... then the lantern light on wet gravel, the flash of steel between her and the man who dared lay claim to her arm. And finally, her face turning toward him, not in illusion but in recognition.

*Please.*

There was no question of what she asked. Only whether he would answer.

He swung his legs from the bed and crossed to the basin. The water was cold, and he splashed his face, neck, arms, as if the chill could do more to rouse him than the dream already had.

Brutus was already awake. The dog stood at the door, not whining, not pacing, but braced. The muscles along his back were taut, his head lifted as though scenting something no human could perceive.

Darcy drew on his coat and opened the door. Harrowe was still in the passage below, arguing with the innkeeper over the quality of the ale and not enough lanterns. He broke off when he saw Darcy descend.

"What is it?"

Darcy set his hat on his head. "Elizabeth has left Ramsgate."

Harrowe's face altered—not with surprise, but with confirmation. "Inland?"

"Yes. She's coming for me."

"Alone?"

"Not entirely." He did not elaborate. The detail of the sword still rattled him in a way he did not yet understand. "She was in a coach. Traveling without her family. And she is afraid."

Harrowe's eyes narrowed. "Afraid of what?"

Darcy held his look. "Of herself."

Harrowe reached for his satchel and shifted it higher on his shoulder. "Then she'll trace the fault where it leads. She'll follow it to you."

Darcy turned toward the door. "I am waiting, and not tracing anything. I am going to her."

Harrowe blinked. "But *she* has to come *here!* Do you not understand? *This* is where the matter will be settled!"

When Darcy only pulled on his gloves and made for the door, Harrowe followed. "You do not even know where she is!"

Brutus was already bounding at the threshold, claws clicking against the boards, body angled eastward as if the direction were self-evident.

"I know enough."

THE FROST HAD NOT lifted from the hedges along the lane, though the sun climbed clear and bright. Fields that had once borne winter grass lay scorched pale, the earth hardened into a brittle crust. Darcy recognised landmarks only by distance, not by shape; hedgerows had thickened in some places, thinned in others, and the track that led towards the southeast felt narrower than memory allowed.

The horse beneath him breathed hard in the cold, steam rising in quick bursts from its flanks. They had changed mounts once already at a posting inn where the stable boy asked no questions and took Darcy's coin with wide eyes. Harrowe rode half a length behind, hunched forward, his satchel striking against his hip with each stride.

Brutus ran when he could, loping along the verge, falling back only when the frost cut too sharply at his pads. When he dropped behind, he did not wander. He kept the line of them, eyes bright, ears forward.

Where once there had been a sense—subtle but unmistakable—of held breath, of something watchful beneath the surface of field and hedgerow, there was now only absence. The ground looked spent. A pasture they passed bore a stretch of blackened earth where frost had not merely settled but burned. A farmer stood at the gate of it, hat in hand, staring down as though uncertain what he was looking at.

Harrowe urged his horse closer after a time, peering past Darcy at the road ahead as though something visible might explain their direction. The hedges had grown higher since they left the broader turnpike, the ruts shallower, the lane bending more often than it ran straight.

They had left the main road an hour earlier, where the sign for Hatfield leaned crooked on its post. The track they followed now bore no marking beyond worn earth and the faint memory of cart-wheels. It curved eastward, avoiding the distant haze that marked London's sprawl, keeping instead to open country and old boundaries.

Brutus ranged ahead, then slowed, circling once before pressing forward again, nose low to the ground. When the lane divided without warning between two hedged corridors of equal age and neglect, the dog did not pause. He veered left toward the narrower way, where the ground dipped slightly toward marshier air.

Darcy followed without hesitation.

Harrowe made a small, disbelieving sound. "Oughtn't we go back to the turnpike?"

"No."

"Then how—"

Darcy did not look at him. "She is this way."

It was said without explanation. As one states the hour. Or the direction of the wind.

Harrowe fell back a half-length, shaking his head. "As you say."

Ahead, the land lowered gradually, and the scent of water threaded faintly through the frost.

The frost thickened along the verges. At a bend where the road dipped toward a shallow rise, Brutus gave a low, sudden bark. He veered from the verge and crossed the road without waiting for command.

Darcy reined in sharply.

Brutus stood at the edge of a hedgerow that had not been there before.

Or rather—it had been there, but thin, disciplined, no more than a farmer's boundary between two modest fields. Now it rose twice a man's height, thick with hawthorn, the branches interlocked so tightly that the frost lay trapped within it like ash.

Darcy swung down. The horse tossed its head, uneasy.

Harrowe dismounted more slowly. "This was not so."

"No." Darcy stepped closer.

The thorns were new and hardly even firm. The wood still pale beneath its bark. They had grown not in season but in urgency, as though driven upward by pressure from below.

Brutus edged nearer and then stopped, tail low but not tucked. He did not growl.

Darcy extended his hand.

Harrowe snatched his arm back with one beefy fist. "Darcy! Do not—"

The branch nearest him inclined—not away, not toward, but aside. An opening no wider than a man's shoulders revealed itself between two cruel arcs of thorn.

Darcy's pulse struck hard once. He did not look at Harrowe. He did not question.

He stepped through.

THE COACH HAD NOT slowed once.

The horses had run clean and strong from the moment they quitted the last posting house... from the moment they left the inn this morning, for that matter. Their hooves struck the frozen road with a surety that bordered on unnatural. The coachman, who had begun the morning with habitual grumbling, had gradually grown almost jovial at the box. "Best team I've had this month," he declared once, half-turning to shout down through the window. "Road's clearing up like a bonny day in June!"

Elizabeth had not joined the other passengers' approval. For the road ahead might be clear, but the road behind them was anything but.

She had seen it first near midday. A hedgerow, brittle with frost as they passed, stood upright and ordinary in the pale sun. Moments later—she had glanced back only because the road curved slightly and allowed a view—the hedge seemed to sag inward, branches bowing as if a hand had pressed through them from above. The ditch beyond it caved softly, earth sloughing into itself in a slow collapse that no wheel had touched.

She had turned forward at once and folded her hands together so tightly her fingers ached.

*It is nothing. The ground is poor. The frost weakens it.*

An hour later, they passed a shallow stream that ran over a low part of the road, its surface filmed thin with ice. The coach rolled over the ice without incident. Elizabeth had nearly convinced herself she imagined the earlier hedge when she glanced back.

The ice had not cracked beneath the horses' weight. But it shattered after they had gone.

Not from beneath—but outward. The frozen surface burst in a sharp, spreading fracture, water that had not been there before thrusting up through the broken skin in dark, violent pulses that flooded the road. A boy who had been walking near the road leapt back with a cry as the water surged beyond the ruts, soaking the hem of his coat.

By the time the cottage door opened and a man called out, the water over the road froze into a smooth, hard glaze. No one looked toward the carriage that kept rolling away.

Elizabeth turned forward at once and pressed her hands together until her knuckles blanched. But by afternoon, she could not mistake it. The world did not break before her.

It broke in her wake.

The fields they passed lay wan and flattened, winter-stripped as any other in the season. Yet as the coach thundered forward, she saw in the glass's faint reflection how the furrows seemed to ripple and settle once she had gone by, as if some invisible hook had caught in the soil and ripped it up behind her. A copse of bare trees shivered in perfect stillness, though no wind stirred the coach's curtains. A stretch of road behind them darkened suddenly, the pale frost sinking into a dampness that had not been there before.

She pressed her forehead briefly to the cool pane and closed her eyes. Love and terror had braided themselves so tightly within her that she could no longer tell which pulled harder. She loved him. She loved him with a clarity that stripped away every former hesitation. But at what cost? How could she ask this of him?

The coachman urged the team on still faster as the sun lowered. "We'll make Dartford before dark at this rate," he called. "Good fortune at last!"

*Good fortune.* Elizabeth's stomach turned.

The town rose ahead in the late light, roofs crowding toward the road, smoke lying low in the cooling air. The Thames lay somewhere beyond, unseen but felt, its wide breath pressing against the edges of the place. Lanterns were being lit along the inn yard as they drew near; an hostler ran forward; another carriage stood already beneath the overhang, horses blowing steam into the dusk.

The coach slowed at last. The moment the wheels ceased their motion, the stillness rushed back upon her like a held breath released.

She did not wait to be assisted. She stepped down lightly, keeping her head bowed, her cloak drawn close about her. The inn yard bustled with ordinary irritations—trunks lowered, reins handed off, a servant scolding a boy for lingering underfoot. No one watched her. No one marked her passage as she slipped along the wall and through the open door.

Behind her, somewhere beyond the curve of the road they had just traversed, a dull cracking sound rolled faintly through the evening air, as though timber had given way under strain.

A man near the horses glanced back. "Rotten fence-post, I'll wager."

"Or frost splitting the rails," another answered.

Elizabeth fled indoors.

Inside, the common room was warm and loud, thick with smoke and the welcoming smell of broth. She kept to the edges, moving with deliberate quiet, a shadow among cloaks and benches. If she could secure a chamber quickly—if she could reach it unseen—perhaps the night would pass without incident.

She pressed her hand to her breast, willing the restless thrum there to quiet. No one must look at her too closely. No one must follow.

No one must guess at the ruin that trailed her.

THE ROAD BENT SOUTHWARD through lower country as the day advanced, the hedges thinning and the air growing sharper with damp. They had changed horses twice since dawn. The last ostler had eyed Harrowe with open scepticism.

"You'll want a sturdier beast if you mean to keep that gentleman aboard," he had muttered, tightening a girth with unnecessary emphasis.

Harrowe, already mounted, had leaned down and regarded the man with solemn interest. "It's not me wears out horses," he said. "It's horses that wear out me. Rough as an old rumble-wheel that last one was."

Darcy did not smile, but he heard the attempt. The country altered as they rode south. As if the entire road had been… arranged.

The hedgerows grew thick and towering along the lane without any clear reason. Hawthorn pressed inward from both sides, its branches interlocking above in places where winter should have thinned them. The thorns did not snag at Darcy's coat, nor scrape the horses. They simply leaned, then, most oddly of all… closed ranks behind them.

Herding.

At a fork in the road, the left-hand way lay churned and rutted, as if carts had recently turned back upon it. The right-hand track, though narrower, ran clear. No fallen branch blocked it. No stone lay out of place. Even the frost had withdrawn more quickly from that path, leaving it firm beneath the horses' hooves.

Harrowe squinted between the two. "Well. That's a choice made for us."

Darcy did not answer. He had already guided his horse to the right.

A mile farther, a low stone wall had partially collapsed across the verge, but not into the road. The rubble rested just shy of obstruction, forcing them inward toward the centre of the lane and forbidding them from taking any turn.

The pattern repeated itself twice more. Not hindrance. Correction.

Brutus moved ahead without hesitation, tail low, nose lifted, following something Darcy could not see but did not doubt. They reached a shallow dip where the ground darkened with old moisture. No standing water. Only a faint, straight seam in the frost that ran across the field beyond and vanished beneath a stand of thorn.

Harrowe shifted in his saddle and muttered, almost conversationally, "If this keeps on, we won't need to change horses. They'll think they're racing downhill."

Brutus barked once and bounded ahead toward the next bend in the lane. Darcy did not check him. He no longer had the impression of chasing anything.

He had the impression of being expected.

Elizabeth had not yet secured a place near the wall where she might remain unnoticed when a violent nausea seized her with such force that she caught at the edge of a table to keep from falling.

The scent of roasting meat, of heavy sweat and ale—not bothersome a moment before—now turned sharply metallic in her mouth. She bent without even a chance to catch herself and retched upon the rushes.

Dozens of feet scraped backward. Someone muttered in disgust. A bar maid made a sound of alarm and moved toward her with a basin, but Elizabeth scarcely registered it. The sickness did not linger, as it had with Mr Collins. It struck and passed in a single convulsion, leaving her breathless but upright.

The door opened again, as new bodies entered the room.

Elizabeth wiped her mouth with the back of her glove and straightened—too quickly. The room seemed to tilt, then right itself. She had not yet seen the newcomer's face, yet something within her recoiled as if from a blade drawn too near the skin.

The iron latch on the door shuddered.

It was a small sound—metal striking metal—but it silenced the murmur of the room at once. Tankards trembled where they stood. A fork leapt against a plate and rang like a bell. The poker in the hearth scraped forward an inch, though no hand touched it.

Elizabeth's breath shortened.

The lady who had entered had not spoken, yet the space around her felt compressed, narrowed by expectation. A younger woman followed meekly behind, her face shaped by the same crowded features and pinched expression. The innkeeper bowed low enough that his hair brushed his own boots.

"Rooms for her ladyship," a male voice voice declared. "The very best, at once. And her ladyship's carriage must be rolled under cover, not left in the yard."

The floor beneath her boots gave a faint vibration, not from weight, but like something pressing upward from below. She staggered half a step, catching herself again against the table.

The iron fixtures nearest her lifted.

The poker rose first, its tip dragging a thin line through the ash before it left the hearth entirely. The fender followed, tilting outward. A scatter of small nails leapt from the edge of a carpenter's satchel abandoned near the door. They hovered no higher than a hand's breadth before falling—not outward, not toward the door—but in a rough circle at Elizabeth's feet.

The tankards on the nearest table tipped and rolled, striking the boards and coming to rest against that same invisible boundary.

The inn fell utterly still, and all eyes turned in her direction.

Elizabeth stood at the centre of it, her hands clenched so tightly at her sides that her knuckles ached through her gloves. She had not raised her hands. She had not spoken. Yet the space around her had rearranged itself as though acknowledging her claim.

That was when a crack sounded behind her. The plaster between the door and the mantel split with a thin, decisive line.

Someone crossed himself. Others moved backward, tipping ale, colliding with tables and bumping against one another.

The lady who had entered stepped forward, her expression sharpening not with confusion but with cold recognition. Her gaze travelled from the disturbed hearth to the scattered ring of metal and finally to Elizabeth herself.

*"You."*

Elizabeth's stomach lurched again, though there was nothing left within it to surrender. The pressure in her chest squeezed harder—not illness, not weakness, but something defensive.

The hearth flame, which had burned low and obedient moments before, bent sharply away from her, curling toward the far wall as though driven by a wind no one else felt. The poker twitched where it lay and slid another inch—not toward Elizabeth but toward the hem of the lady's gown.

A murmur rose from the men gathered near the ale casks.

"Witch," someone breathed, half in jest and half in dread.

Elizabeth's heart pounded so fiercely she thought it must be audible. She forced her hands open, forced her fingers to uncurl, but the ring at her feet did not disperse. She had not commanded it, and she could not dismiss it.

The lady's eyes flashed. "What trick is this?"

"I—" Elizabeth's voice failed her. The air felt thick, unwilling to pass her throat. She tried again. "It is no trick. I did not do this on purpose! I beg you—"

The iron latch on the door slammed shut with a violence that shook the frame.

A woman shrieked.

Elizabeth stepped backward instinctively, and the circle moved with her, scraping against the boards. The sensation was unmistakable now: not random, not illness, not hysteria. Her body had recognised something in that woman's presence and answered it without consultation.

*Protect.*

The thought did not form in words; it manifested in the way the room had divided itself.

The lady advanced another pace, and the crack in the plaster lengthened, running like lightning toward the ceiling.

Elizabeth could not bear it. "Please!" she said—not to the lady, not to the room, but to anyone who would act without accusation. "Take me upstairs. Remove me from here! I do not wish to harm anyone."

The noble woman narrowed her eyes and pointed an accusing finger. "You have already done so."

# Chapter Fifty-Two

The innkeeper's wife seized her wrist before she could protest and drew her toward the stairs with urgent whispers about privacy and quiet and not alarming the other patrons below. Elizabeth did not resist. The iron had fallen. The hearth had breathed. The room had turned its gaze upon her as though she were spectacle and contagion in one. To be removed from sight seemed mercy.

The stair creaked beneath them, narrow and steep. At the landing, the woman did not pause to inquire which chamber Elizabeth preferred. She opened the nearest door.

"In here, miss," she said—too briskly.

Elizabeth was guided across the threshold. The door closed at once behind her. The latch fell with a clang, and there was the distinct scrape of metal set fast.

Elizabeth turned and tested the latch in panic. The handle did not yield at her touch.

The chamber was small and close, the single window latched tight against the cold. A basin stood upon a washstand, its ewer untouched. No fire had been laid in the grate. No bell-pull hung beside the bed.

The quiet was not kindness.

It was separation.

A ripple of sickness pressed against her ribs and rose into her throat—not nausea now, but something larger. Something that did not belong within the dimensions of a hired room.

She crossed to the window and lifted the latch. The casement resisted her hand, but when she stepped back to look at it again, to peer through the glass, the iron latch lifted, and the hinge gave a faint, complaining note. Then the window swung.

She was beyond questioning now. All that mattered was escape, not harming anyone else, and getting to Darcy. She leaned through, inspecting the casement, the shutters, the distance to the ground. At this height, she might break her legs. Or her neck.

Below, voices rose again. A command—female, imperious—cut cleanly through the murmur. Elizabeth still did not know the name of its owner. She knew only the sensation it produced in her: the same constriction she had endured when Mr Collins stood too near; the same crawling along her spine; the same violent recoil.

Elizabeth stepped back, glancing around the room. Would the door latch behave the same as the window?

The basin shuddered as she passed by, the water within trembling as though something beneath the floorboards had struck it. A hairline crack traced the plaster above the bed, running outward from the doorframe like frost spreading across glass. The nails securing the washstand creaked. The latch of the door rattled once, sharply, as if tested from the other side, but it did not release.

Elizabeth pressed both palms against her temples. What to do? That jump could cripple or kill her. But it seemed to be the only way out.

The boards beneath her feet gave a low, hollow thump. The iron hinge of the window screamed, glass shattering against wooden shutters as though it meant to tear itself free. The basin tipped, water sloshing against porcelain though no hand touched it.

If she remained here, the room would not hold.

Shouts were now ringing from below; feet struck the stair; someone called for the constable. The word witch sounded again, louder this time, emboldened by repetition.

Elizabeth moved toward the window and looked down again... to see fresh, green shoots of ivy climbing up the wall, still growing towards her open window.

The ivy pressed close against the wall, its stems thick and now reaching in, as if they would clock the window if she hesitated too long. She seized it with both hands.

It held. For a breath.

Her slippers scraped uselessly against the stone. The vine bent beneath her weight, its fresh tendrils wrenching loose from the stone in small, tearing sighs. She descended not so much by grace as by surrender, sliding, catching, lowering herself hand over hand as the wall rasped against her palms.

Behind her, the hinge shrieked. The frame tore free and struck the outer wall, hanging crooked, iron twisted like ribbon.

The ivy gave way at last. Not entirely, but enough to make her cry out in alarm.

She dropped the remaining span and struck the ground with a jolt that jarred her teeth. Pain flared sharp along her ankle and shot upward, stealing her breath. She staggered, one hand braced against the cold stone.

Voices rose within the inn—first a shout, then several, the sound swelling as the disturbance reached its crest.

She did not look back.

Elizabeth fled toward the road. She did not know who pursued her. She did not know why her body reacted so violently to the woman in that inn. She knew only that if she remained among walls and iron and confined air, something larger than herself would break free.

The road sloped toward the river. She ran toward it without knowing why.

THE FROST HAD BEGUN to lift where the sun struck full upon the road, but the air remained sharp enough to sting the lungs.

The road south into Kent narrowed as it approached the lowlands, hedges closing in and the soil underhoof growing darker, heavier, more prone to rut. He did not consult a map. He did not ask for signposts. When a fork presented itself without warning between two lanes equally plausible, Brutus veered without hesitation. Darcy followed.

Harrowe urged his horse closer as they descended toward broader ground, peering ahead as though the answer might lie in something visible. "We left Bingley asleep. Reckon he's put it together where you went?"

Darcy's gloves tightened on the reins. "I will answer to Bingley when I must. I will not answer to delay."

Brutus ran ahead, then returned, circling once as if to ensure they had not lost him, before pressing forward again with renewed insistence. The dog's movements were not wild; they were urgent. Darcy leaned into the pace, allowing his mount to lengthen its stride where the ground permitted. He did not pretend to himself that he rode toward certainty. He rode because to remain still had become intolerable.

The land warmed as they approached the river flats. The air carried the faint tang of brine, though the Thames lay yet some distance ahead. Once, as they crossed a shallow dip, the ground beneath the hooves gave a low, resonant thud, as if hollowed beneath, and Brutus halted, ears pricked, before darting onward again.

Harrowe shifted in his saddle. "You do not feel it as before. You look lost."

Darcy did not answer. He did not know what he felt. There was no pulling, no dragging ache in his chest as there had been when Elizabeth stood too near him in London. Not so much surety as when he had seen her fleeing Ramsgate, knowing she was coming for him.

There was only a gathering, a sense of proximity closing.

They rode in silence for another mile. Then Brutus stopped dead. He stood rigid in the centre of the road, head high, gaze fixed beyond a low rise where the lane curved toward the river crossing at Dartford. His hackles lifted, not in threat but in alertness.

Darcy drew rein. The horse stamped once, impatient.

Harrowe followed his line of sight and swore under his breath. "What is that?"

At first, Darcy saw nothing but motion at the far edge of the road where it met the yard of a coaching inn. Then the figure separated from the background—skirts gathered, hair loosened by wind or flight, running not with decorum but with desperation.

The road between them felt at once too long and too short.

Darcy did not think. He drove his heels to his horse's flanks and closed the distance at a gallop.

Harrowe shouted something—warning or question—but the words were swallowed by the pounding of hooves and the rush of blood in Darcy's ears. The figure ahead stumbled, recovered, and ran again, not looking behind her. Even at that distance, he knew the tilt of her shoulders, the line of her stride.

"Elizabeth!" he shouted, though the name was lost to the wind.

She faltered as she reached the open stretch before the ferry landing, one hand rising briefly as though to catch herself against air that would not support her. Her pace slackened. Her steps shortened.

Harrowe's voice cut sharp behind him. "Darcy, it's a devil! Hold hard, lad!"

Darcy had already swung down from the saddle before the horse had fully halted. The reins fell slack. Brutus streaked past him, reaching her first, circling once at her skirts with a low, urgent whine.

She turned at that sound, and her eyes, wide and dark with exhaustion, found his. For an instant, she seemed uncertain whether he were real.

Then her knees gave way.

Darcy reached her before she struck the ground, catching her against his chest with more force than grace. The impact jarred through his arms, through his ribs, but he did not release her. She weighed little, far too little, and her breath came in shallow pulls against his collar.

"Elizabeth!" he yanked his gloves off with his teeth, then his hands were at her cheeks, her throat, testing her pulse. Her eyes were not closed, but they looked glazed, as if she had spent the last of her strength reaching him.

Harrowe reined in hard a few yards away, staring at the stranger who had flown toward them on foot.

Darcy held her upright and felt, not the tearing recoil of pain he had feared, but something else—fierce and immediate and undeniable.

Dread.

SHE DID NOT REMEMBER the last yards of running. Only the tearing in her lungs, the cold air cutting her throat raw, and then—arms. Solid. Certain. Darcy's.

"They are coming," she gasped, clutching at his coat. "They are hunting me—"

"I know," he said, though his voice was not calm. It was thinner than she had ever heard it, drawn tight as wire. "I am here."

Behind her, the road roared. Not wind. Not sea.

Voices.

Brutus barked and charged the road, standing guard against the onslaught. Hooves struck the frozen earth. A carriage wheel shrieked as it braked too hard. Men shouted. Someone cried out, "There! There she is!"

Elizabeth twisted in Darcy's hold and saw torches swinging in the dusk, their flames bent sideways in the windless air as though unwilling to burn straight. The inn servants were among them. The militia officer. Stable hands. A boy from the yard. Faces she had passed without notice only an hour before, now sharpened by certainty.

Witch.

She heard it plainly now.

*Witch!*

Darcy shifted, drawing her slightly behind him, though he did not release her. She felt the change in him—the way his breath shortened, the tremor shuddering through his spine. He was not strong. Not as he ought to be.

"Do not hold me so tightly," she whispered. "I am hurting you."

His hand tightened instead.

A pistol fired.

The report cracked across the fields—and misfired in the same instant. The spark flared sideways, spitting harmlessly into the damp air. The man holding it swore and jerked back as though burned.

Brutus lunged… just as a second report split the air.

Elizabeth did not at first understand what had happened. The dog's bark broke into a strangled yelp. He stumbled mid-stride and crashed hard upon his side, legs scrabbling against the frozen ground.

Darcy's breath tore from him—not a word, but a sound she had never heard before. "Brutus!"

The name struck her like the shot itself. Heat flared through her chest, sharp and sickening, as though the bullet had found her instead. She tried to see past Darcy's shoulder—tried to move—but the world narrowed to the dark shape on the ground and the red already spreading against the dog's pale flank.

The man who had fired lifted the pistol again. He did not keep it.

Darcy slipped from Elizabeth's side and wrenched forward with a strength that should not have been left to him. The weapon was struck from the man's hand and flung into the grass. A cry rose from the crowd—anger, fear, something breaking loose.

Elizabeth stumbled forward, dropping to her knees beside Brutus. His body trembled beneath her hands. Blood slicked her fingers. His eyes rolled once, frantic, then found her. He was panting and whimpering, frenzied with pain and the desire to protect.

"It is nothing," she breathed, though her voice shook. "It is nothing. You shall not leave us."

A rough hand caught her shoulder—not cruel, but urgent. Harrowe. "Leave him to me," he said sharply.

Before she could protest, he bent and gathered the great dog into his arms. Brutus gave a low, broken whimper but did not struggle. Harrowe turned at once, carrying him clear of the advancing press as the crowd surged inward.

The space Harrowe had left closed at once. A militia officer forced his way through the front ranks, face flushed and set with a terrible certainty. He glared at Darcy, then the man whose pistol Darcy had flung off the road. Steel flashed in his hand, and he moved grimly towards Elizabeth.

Darcy stepped between them. "Stay that blade!"

The officer rounded upon Darcy instead. "Out of the way," he snarled, and there was no mistaking his intention. The blade descended with deliberate force.

Darcy raised his arm to turn it aside. He had no strength for such a contest. She felt that plainly in the tremor still running through him.

And yet the stroke did not fall as it should. The steel met something unseen and would not pass it.

A thin, unnatural sound threaded the air—metal under strain. Before Elizabeth's eyes, the bright length of the sword altered. It did not glance away. It did not shatter.

It yielded.

The blade bowed inward upon itself, its straight line curving as though pressed against a weight no one could see. The officer cried out and staggered back, staring at the weapon in his grasp.

Darcy reeled with the force of it, his balance failing. She reached for him, but he caught her first, one arm coming hard about her waist. The shock ran through him and into her, sharp as winter water.

For one suspended instant, the field held its breath.

Then the crowd recoiled. And surged.

"See how it turns!" someone shouted. "See how the torch flame bends? She's a witch!"

A sword flashed in another man's hand, and wrenched sideways as if tugged by an invisible hook. It tore free of his grip and struck the ground between Elizabeth and the nearest man, quivering upright in the earth.

Gasps and terrified shouts broke like a flock of birds taking flight.

Elizabeth felt it then—not outward, but inward. The pull. The answering.

The torches leaned toward her and away again. Water in a roadside trough heaved once against its boards and sloshed over. The iron buckle at her shoe warmed against her skin, and even the brass buttons of Darcy's coat popped free of their threads.

It was not unwanted obedience, like before. It was agitation.

Darcy's breath ran ragged against her temple. "Elizabeth," he said under his breath, and there was warning in it now. Not for the mob—for her. "Head down."

The crowd parted suddenly as another carriage forced its way through, the horses lathered, the coachman white with the effort of keeping them straight. The door was flung open before the vehicle had fully stopped.

That same noblewoman from the inn descended without assistance, rejecting the groom's offered hand with a motion so slight it might have been invisible to any but the man she dismissed. Her figure was rigid beneath layers of dark silk; the plumes at her bonnet trembled in the cold air, though she herself did not.

The nausea struck without warning. It was not fear alone, nor memory of Mr Collins's suffocating nearness, but something sharper—an internal recoil so violent she bent double, the contents of her empty stomach wrenching free as though expelled by force.

A murmur rippled through the men behind the carriage.

"See there… righteous judgement!"

"She cannot even stand—"

"It's unnatural!"

Darcy's arm closed around her waist. He ripped a handkerchief from his pocket and pressed it into her hand. "Breathe, Elizabeth. Breathe, love."

The word slipped from him without calculation. She felt it more than heard it, and leaned her head into his shoulder as her body shuddered.

He did not release her. She felt him gather himself instead—felt the line of his body lengthen, his shoulders square, as though some ancestral instinct had been summoned to meet what approached.

"Lady Catherine."

There was recognition in his tone, and warning. Elizabeth stiffened and looked up. So, *that* explained it.

Lady Catherine did not look at Elizabeth first. She regarded Darcy, and her expression did not blaze with temper, but settled into something far more dangerous: certainty.

"Darcy," she said, as though addressing a subordinate who had disappointed her publicly. "What do you here? You persist in compounding error with spectacle."

Behind her, the carriage rocked slightly as someone within shifted. Elizabeth caught a glimpse of the young lady seated inside—pale, teeth clenched so tightly her whole body trembled, eyes wide not with triumph but apprehension.

Lady Catherine's gaze moved at last. It struck Elizabeth like cold iron.

"And this," she said, taking in Elizabeth's bent posture, Darcy's arm around her, the circle of men pressing nearer, "is the… *influence* for which you would discard order. Fie! A sham and a temptress. You are a fool, Darcy."

A torch flared too high behind her. Sparks hissed into the damp air. One of the horses reared and was dragged back sharply.

"She made the water rise!" someone shouted from the road. "And the fire—you saw the fire!"

"The vines! I saw them at the inn—"

"Witchcraft!"

Lady Catherine did not rebuke them. Did not protest that "witchcraft" was not a mortal crime anymore, but it would not have mattered. The crowd were lathered to a panic, and it served her purposes.

She stepped forward, skirts sweeping over rutted earth, her gloved hand lifting as though to indicate an object for removal.

"I cautioned you, Darcy," she continued, her voice cutting cleanly through the rising agitation. "I explained to you precisely what indulgence would invite. Yet you choose to stand in a ditch, clasping the hand of a young woman whose very presence provokes convulsion and hysteria."

The iron fittings on one of the bridles gave a sharp metallic cry, twisting under strain. A groom swore and leapt to capture the horse, even as the bit fractured and fell from its mouth.

"There!" a man cried. "Look what she does!"

Elizabeth did not mean to move. She did not mean to answer the pressure building inside her. Yet the earth beneath her boots seemed to harden, then shudder, as if resisting something that demanded passage.

Darcy tightened his grip.

"You will cease threatening her, Lady Catherine," he said, and there was no politeness in it. "You are driving the crisis!"

Lady Catherine's chin lifted a fraction. "You mistake defiance for devotion," she replied. "The land does not belong to appetite, Darcy. It belongs to lineage and restraint. Stand aside."

The men behind her shifted again, emboldened by her presence. One took a step forward. Another reached toward Elizabeth's cloak as though to seize it.

Elizabeth felt the strange, wild forces that had shielded her before falter—no longer gathering around her in fierce defence, but scattering, confused, as though her proximity to Darcy had altered their allegiance.

The torches guttered. Then flared. Then bent sideways in a wind that did not touch her hair.

"She's doing it again!"

"Take her—take her now—"

The torches flared and guttered in the same breath. One dropped from its holder's grasp and hissed out in the damp grass. The sword embedded in the earth vibrated once more before toppling flat.

Another torch swung too wide and caught the sleeve of a man behind it. He shouted, beating at his own coat. A horse reared, nearly crushing a boy who stumbled beneath its hooves.

"Stop," Elizabeth whispered. She did not know to whom she spoke. "Stop—"

Darcy's breathing shallowed, and he coughed... blood.

"Seize her!" Lady Catherine cried. "Remove her from him! You see what she does! Stand idle, and she will ruin you all!"

Hands lunged. Darcy shifted to shield her, and she felt the cost of it in the tremor that ran through him. The ground beneath them gave a sharp, splitting crack—not wide, not deep, but enough to unbalance the men nearest them.

Then Elizabeth saw a child near the road's edge—fallen, scrambling as another horse shied.

If the surge came again... If it struck blind...

Someone could be killed. And she would destroy Darcy.

"No!" she cried aloud.

And something in the air collapsed. The torches burned straight. The water stilled. The iron lay inert in the mud.

The force withdrew.

Simply gone.

For the first time since the inn yard, she stood unguarded. Hands seized her arms, tore her sleeves, pulled the cloak from her shoulders.

Darcy tried to wrench her back, but the strength was no longer in him. She felt him almost withering beneath her fingers as they were torn from him. Someone struck him across the shoulder. Another shoved him aside.

"Do not!" she cried, twisting. "Leave him be! I am the one you want!"

Behind her, Darcy stumbled, caught himself as his knees hit the earth.

"Darcy—" she began, though she did not know what she meant to say.

You see it," Lady Catherine said, not to Elizabeth but to the men who held her. "You see the disorder she breeds. Even now, it falters and surges at her whim. Would you have this upon your fields? Your children? She is a demon. Unnatural!"

A murmur answered her—fear finding sanction.

"You will come to Kent," Lady Catherine informed him, as one pronounces a conclusion long settled. "You will restore what you have unsettled. This spectacle is the consequence of your indulgence. You will not compound it."

Elizabeth struggled, but the hands at her arms only tightened. Her sleeve tore further; something warm ran down her wrist. She felt Darcy attempt to move toward her, felt the effort through the air like a tremor.

He did move—rose from his knee to stagger one step, then another—but the colour had left him. His strength was draining visibly now. "Release her," he said thickly.

There was no force behind it. Only will.

A man struck him aside with the flat of his hand. Not a sword. Not yet. Merely the confidence of numbers.

"She near drowned a child!" someone shouted.

"She'll burn us all next—devil!"

"Bind her!"

Lady Catherine did not issue the order again. She did not need to. She had named the danger, and the men supplied the remedy.

Elizabeth was pulled backward in earnest now, her boots scraping furrows through the earth. She reached for Darcy despite herself—knowing the touch harmed him, knowing she ought to spare him even now—and he was able to lunge just enough that their fingers brushed once more before the grip was broken.

# Chapter Fifty-Three

Darcy did not remember crossing the distance between them.

One instant, Elizabeth was dragged backward through the press of bodies, her sleeve torn, her hair ripping across her shoulders; the next, he was among them, striking hands aside, driving forward with a force that owed nothing to prudence. The weakness that had dogged him for weeks fell away the moment she was dragged before Lady Catherine's feet. Strength returned—not kindly, not cleanly—but sharp and dangerous, like a blade drawn too quickly.

"Let her go."

He did not shout. He did not need to. The command cut through the nearest ring of men by the mere fact of his advance. One stumbled beneath his shoulder; another recoiled at the look in his face. He seized the wrist of the man who held her and twisted until bone ground against bone. The grip broke. Elizabeth lurched toward him, and he caught her again, one arm braced around her waist.

And at once the cost returned.

Her hand closed in his, and something inside him recoiled and gave way. The strength that had carried him through the mob thinned as though drawn through a narrow channel. His vision sharpened and dimmed in the same instant. The ground seemed less secure beneath his boots. He felt her pulse against his palm — too quick, too bright — and knew that whatever bound them was no longer dormant.

She wept into his collar, begging him. "No, Darcy! I will only make it worse!" He did not loosen his grip.

Behind Lady Catherine, her carriage stood at a perilous angle where the roadside had begun to fail. The matched greys plunged against their traces, iron ringing as harness strained. Anne's pale face appeared at the window, her gloved hand pressed against the frame.

Lady Catherine turned at the sound of splintering wood. For one suspended instant, her composure fractured; she saw the tilt, the sucking slide of earth beneath the near wheel, the black gleam of water below. Anne's cry pierced the tumult.

"Hold them!" she cried sharply to her servants, stepping forward as though command alone could force the road to obedience. "Are you blind? Secure the horses!"

The nearest horse reared high, forelegs striking air as its hind feet slipped. The second plunged sideways, the harness snapping taut between them. A torch fell and rolled beneath stamping hooves, scattering sparks against damp earth.

The soil beneath the near wheel continued to give, sloughing away in heavy clods and revealing darker earth beneath—a seam running along the roadside as though something long buried had shifted at last. One wheel dipped farther. A groom shouted. The carriage body groaned and began, impossibly, to twist.

Lady Catherine wheeled back toward Darcy, fury conquering alarm. "You observe the consequence!" she said, her voice sharpened by outrage rather than fear. "You feel what indulgence has purchased! This disorder follows her—follows you! Even now, you would persist?"

Elizabeth strained in Darcy's hold. "There is a woman inside the carriage! We must—"

Darcy blanched in horror. *Anne.* Innocent in all this, and endangered by her own mother's pride. He felt the pull in Elizabeth's frame—the terrible instinct to run toward danger rather than from it.

"No! Elizabeth, stay. Harrowe! For God's sake, man!"

A fissure traced itself along the road's edge, narrow as a thread before widening by degrees. The near horse screamed again. A trace snapped. The carriage lurched, one side dropping another inch toward the dark water of the ditch. Men who moments before had shouted for judgment now scrambled for footing.

Harrowe lunged, caught the dangling bridle of the nearer horse with both hands, and dragged its head sideways, using his full weight to turn the animal's panic away from the collapsing edge. A groom seized the other rein. Together they forced the team back a pace.

"Move!" Harrowe roared to those still clustered nearest the wheel. "Do you want it over on you?"

Darcy attempted to step forward to assist and felt his knees threaten betrayal. Elizabeth's fingers tightened convulsively in his. The contact burned — not in heat, but in depletion.

Behind Lady Catherine, Anne leaned from the carriage window, crying out in terror. "Mama!"

Another slip of earth answered her cry. The wheel sank deeper.

Lady Catherine glanced back long enough to quake in horror. Then she whirled, as if Darcy had the power to pull Anne from the brink.

"Do your duty, Darcy! Leave that temptress at once, and place yourself where continuity has been preserved and not squandered. Your father would be ashamed—*ashamed!*—that his son must be ordered about so, but this spectacle proves the necessity of it."

"To do what?" Darcy barked. "Lady Catherine, no matter the proper reading of events, this is neither the time nor the place. Call off this madness and let the matter be discussed with civility and decorum."

"Civility!" she cried back. "You would put off this reckoning for niceties in a drawing room? While Parliament trembles, while regiments starve for want of proper supply, while the stability of this nation hangs upon discipline and lineage, you would cast aside every established line in favour of fancy."

The onlookers glanced from one to another, boots shifting away from the uneasy ground as voices murmured confusion. Dismay. For want of direction and purpose.

"What would you have me do?" Darcy answered, in a voice so soft his aunt was obliged to step closer to hear him. "And why—" he dashed a hand toward her faltering carriage—"would you endanger Anne's health by dragging her from her warm hearth in winter? Let us look to her safety now!"

Lady Catherine's jaw trembled with rage. "Can you be so wilfully ignorant, Darcy? Your duty is upon you even now. You will attend her back to Kent, and complete the alignment so that the families might be joined properly!"

Lady Catherine's last words still rang in the air when Darcy felt Elizabeth flinch against him.

He thought at first it was only exhaustion—her weight sagging, her strength at last spent. Then her fingers closed convulsively in his coat, and he followed the direction of her gaze.

The mud at their feet was *moving*.

A slender green shoot pressed upward through the churned earth beside her slipper, slick and dark as though it had forced its way from a depth that did not welcome light.

Another followed. Then a third, and a dozen more sprouting in a perfect circle at her feet. They did not thrust wildly; they rose with terrible deliberation, coiling as they climbed.

Thorns caught the hem of her gown.

"Elizabeth!" Darcy dropped at once, one hand still locked around her waist while the other tore at her skirts, trying to tug her legs free of the thorny vine before it could wind higher. The stem resisted him. It did not snap like any winter growth he had ever known; it bent, flexed, and slid down her body only to fasten again, barbs hooking into silk and stocking with a precision that was almost intimate.

Elizabeth drew in a breath that never became sound.

The onlookers fell back in a widening ring. Someone crossed himself. Another muttered a prayer too quickly to finish it. The torches guttered in uneven light, and in that wavering glow the hedge seemed to gather itself—not spreading outward toward the crowd, not lashing in defence, but circling her. Claiming.

Harrowe swore under his breath and seized one of the thicker stems in both hands. He pulled. The vine strained against him, thorns biting into his palm, yet it did not release her. It tightened, inch by inch, about her ankles, then her calves, as though the soil itself had resolved to hold what stood upon it.

Lady Catherine stared.

For the first time since she had descended from her carriage, something unguarded crossed her face. "There," she said, though the word emerged without its former command. "There is your answer! She is a false offering!"

Darcy scarcely heard her. He had wrapped both arms about Elizabeth now, lifting her as best he could while the thorns scraped and caught. As he drew her upward, the vines stretched with her, rising from the earth in a twisting arc, refusing to break. One thorn scored across his wrist. Another pierced the back of his hand, bright pain blooming where blood welled dark in the cold air.

Elizabeth's head tipped back against his shoulder. "Darcy—"

He could not tell whether she meant to warn him or to beg him to let her go.

"No!" he cried, though he had no notion whether he spoke to her, to the watching crowd, or to the living thing fastening her to the ground.

A fresh rush of men pressed in, fear and righteousness indistinguishable now. One man, face white and eyes blazing, shoved forward with a pistol clutched in trembling hands. He did not level it properly; he brandished it, as though the mere presence of iron might master what he did not understand.

“Stand back!” he shouted. “Stand back, witch, or I swear I’ll fire!” The pistol trembled.

“Are you mad? Ignorant, superstitious fools!” Harrowe lunged for the weapon at the same moment the nearest horse reared again, hooves striking air, reins tangling beneath it. The ground split another inch. The carriage groaned, timber protesting under strain.

“This is no witchcraft,” he barked. “What do you mean to do, shoot at a thorn bush?”

The man faltered, but he was shaking so badly that his pistol discharged quite without intent.

The report cracked through the dusk and seemed, for one suspended instant, to tear the world in two. Smoke burst white and acrid between them. The ball struck not flesh but wood—splintering the sideboard of the tilting carriage—yet the shock of it drove a cry from every throat at once.

Elizabeth convulsed in his arms.

The thorn answered.

The slender stems that had coiled about her skirts climbed with dreadful deliberation. One circled her waist. Another slipped higher, gliding over the line of her stays as though seeking a truer purchase. A darker, thicker vine rose from the churned mud at her feet and passed, slow as a hand fastening a ribbon, across the hollow of her throat.

Her breath broke.

Darcy felt it. The instant of interruption. The small, helpless struggle of her lungs against a narrowing hold.

“Elizabeth!”

He dropped fully to his knees and seized the vine at her throat. The stem... yielded. It bent as living muscle bends, curling around his fingers. He yelped in surprise, and it slid from his grasp and wound higher, barbs catching in the curl of her hair, pressing against the pale column of her neck.

Around them, the murmur changed.

No longer accusation. No longer command. Someone muttered a prayer. Someone else fell silent halfway through one.

Harrowe caught a thicker strand about her ankle and braced his boot in the mud, hauling with both hands. The vine stretched. It did not break. Blood sprang along his palm where thorns bit through skin. He swore and pulled harder, broad shoulders straining, but the growth held as though anchored in stone.

A villager—young, white-faced, shamed by the pistol—darted forward and slashed at a coil with his knife. The blade skidded uselessly along the green surface, scraping bark that seemed too supple to be cut and too firm to be pierced. He stumbled back, crossing himself.

Elizabeth's fingers, still clenched in Darcy's coat, slackened. Her eyes met his.

Not in panic.

In apology.

The vine at her throat drew tighter. Closing out the world, taking her to itself.

He felt the constriction as if it were upon his own neck. The depletion that had plagued him flared sharper now, not merely draining but answering something in the earth beneath them.

He changed his grip.

No longer tearing. No longer fighting.

He slid his hand lower, to where one of the stems wound about her wrist, and pressed his palm fully against it.

The response was immediate.

The vine shifted beneath his touch. Not recoiling. *Turning.*

Elizabeth drew a shallow breath—no more than a thread of air—but it was breath.

Darcy stilled.

He did not look at Harrowe. He did not look at the crowd. He did not look at his aunt, though he felt her stare burn like frost upon his back.

He pressed harder.

The thorn rose along his wrist as though following a path it had long marked but not yet claimed. It climbed the span of his forearm, barbs pricking through cloth and skin alike. Pain shot through him—bright, precise—but beneath it ran something else. Recognition. The same answering he had felt in the hollow. The same terrible attention that had darkened the fields.

The vine at Elizabeth's throat loosened another fraction. She sagged forward, coughing against his shoulder.

Behind them, Lady Catherine made a sound that was neither outrage nor triumph but something nearer to disbelief.

"No," she said, and this time the word faltered. "No—this is not—"

Darcy gathered Elizabeth closer with one arm while the other remained fixed against the living coil. He could feel the root of it beneath the soil, a pull downward and inward, as though the land itself had fastened its grasp and waited.

He understood then—not by reason, not by Harrowe's arguments, not by his aunt's threats—but by the simple alteration of breath beneath his hand.

The thorn did not yield to strength. It yielded to inheritance.

He released her completely and shifted his hold from her wrist to the base of the rising stem and drew it toward himself. The movement was small. Deliberate.

The vine followed.

It unwound completely from Elizabeth's throat as silk unwinds from a spool, sliding upward and outward and onto him. It circled his arm. His chest. His shoulder. Each coil tightened with quiet inevitability, barbs sinking through wool, through linen, into skin.

Elizabeth fell completely free of its highest hold and gasped, drawing air in a broken rush.

"Darcy—no!"

The thorn climbed his collar. Wrapped once about his throat.

And held.

DARCY FELL RIGID BEFORE her, his eyes still locked on her face, though the rest of his body was no longer wholly his own. Vines coiled across his chest, across his shoulders, binding him with a dreadful sort of power. A longer spear of hawthorn had driven clean through the fabric at his side and pinned him to the ground as surely as if the earth itself had claimed him.

"Darcy!" Her voice broke upon his name.

Blood traced dark lines down his wrist and pooled on the ground where the barbs had pierced him. Another thorn pressed cruelly beneath his jaw, drawing a thin red thread that slid toward his collar.

She tore at the vines with bare hands. The barbs bit her palms; silk and skin gave alike. "Release him! Take me—take me back! Do not—do not touch him!"

The thorns only tightened.

His breath shortened. She leaned in to caress his brow and felt it against her cheek—shallow, strangled. She reached for his hand, but could not pull it free. There was only the crook of one finger, catching hers. Then it trembled once and then stilled in a way that frightened her more than any convulsion could have done.

"Elizabeth." He spoke with effort. The sound was low, scarcely carried beyond her ear.

She lifted her face to his. His eyes were clear. There was pain in them, yes, and effort, but not terror. Not regret.

"I chose this," he said. He coughed, and blood dribbled at the edge of his lips. "This is the answer."

"No," she whispered, shaking her head violently. "No, you do not know that—Darcy, please—"

"I do." His fingers pressed once against hers, deliberate, though the thorns had nearly encased his arms. "Do not grieve it."

The vine at his throat tightened again.

She saw the exact instant the struggle in his body ceased to be resistance and became surrender. His gaze did not leave hers. Not even as the breath failed in him. Not even as the strength left his hand.

His eyes went vacant.

"No!" she cried.

The world continued in dreadful fragments. Lady Catherine's voice, sharp and breaking, cried out behind them. "You see what she has wrought! That false woman, that pretender has killed him! You see—"

Harrowe's answering roar drowned her out. "Stand back from her!"

Somewhere, a horse shrieked again. A groom sobbed. The carriage creaked.

Elizabeth heard none of it in any coherent sense. She felt only the slowing beneath her palm.

She had pressed her hand to his neck, to the place where the thorn had cut him and where his pulse had beaten so fiercely moments before.

It faltered.

It shallowed.

It ceased.

The silence that followed was not quiet. It was absence.

Her own breath tore from her in a sound she did not recognise as her own. She fell to her knees in the mud, heedless of the rips in her gown, heedless of the blood upon her hands.

"No!" she cried, though there was no one left to bargain with. "No—no—"

And at once, without flourish, without spectacle, the thorn withdrew.

It did not recoil in violence. It did not lash or scatter. It slackened. The coils loosened from his arms. The spear that had pinned him dissolved as though it had never been more than a shadow cast upon the earth. The barbs that had pierced flesh shrank to green threads, and then there was nothing left of them at all but a faint ashen circle on the earth.

The soil stilled.

The fissure ceased its creeping.

Behind her, the carriage settled back upon level ground with a dull, final thud. The horses, still trembling, lowered their heads and looked nervously to their handlers.

Elizabeth scarcely marked it. She reached for him, for now she could.

She gathered his head into her lap, cradling him as though he were already borne to burial. His skin was pale beneath the streaks of blood. The wound at his throat was real—terribly real—though no thorn remained to explain it.

"Darcy," she whispered, bending over him. "Darcy, do not leave me!"

Her tears fell freely now, ungoverned, striking his face and the earth beneath him alike. She pressed her mouth to his brow, to the already cooling skin at his temple, heedless of who watched.

"I did not wish you to choose it," she sobbed. "I did not wish you to die for me!"

Around them, chaos struggled to resume its shape. Lady Catherine's voice rose again in horrified denunciation. Harrowe's broad frame barred her approach. Villagers muttered in tones that had lost their certainty.

Elizabeth felt only a hand, cool and trembling, come to rest upon her shoulder.

She lifted her head to find Anne de Bourgh standing beside her.

The girl's pale composure had been stripped away. Tears tracked unheeded down her cheeks. She did not look at her mother. She did not look at the crowd.

She looked at Darcy.

Then at Elizabeth.

Without a word, she sank down beside her and wrapped her arms about her in a gesture so simple and so human that Elizabeth nearly broke anew beneath it.

Behind them, Lady Catherine protested furiously as Harrowe and two shaken grooms drew her back from the road, toward the carriage that had nearly sunk into the black river only moments ago.

Anne held her tightly. "I am sorry," she said at last, her voice low and steady despite the tremor in her frame. "My cousin was a good man. He did not fail for lack of duty or will."

Elizabeth shook her head, choking on her own grief. "He did not act from duty," she managed. "Not from lineage. Not from—" Her voice failed.

Anne's brow knit faintly. "From what, then?"

Elizabeth bent again over the still face in her lap. She pressed her lips to his cheek, to the place just below his ear where his pulse had once beaten warm and certain.

"From love," she whispered. "And I—" Her breath broke entirely. "Oh, I loved him!"

Anne blinked. "What has love to do with any of this?"

Elizabeth's shoulders crumpled, and she choked on a sob so powerful that it stole her breath. She clasped a hand to her mouth, squeezing out the tears before she could master herself. "Love... love is the whole of it. Love..." She fisted her hands to push enough tears from her eyes to see, and words—older words than the *Ballads*, truer words than any myth—found their way to her tongue. "Love protects. It trusts. It hopes when there is nothing left to hope for. It endures past mortal strength."

She bent over him again, unable to bear the distance even of inches. Her fingers twisted into the wool of his coat as though she might drive life back into his chest by force alone. The fabric was sticky and slippery with blood. She did not care.

"Love..." The word fractured in her throat. She swallowed and tried again, her mouth brushing his temple, his cheek, the cold edge of his brow. "Love never fails. And neither did he."

Her voice broke entirely. She pressed her lips to his mouth, lingering there, as if warmth might pass from her into him by sheer persistence. One hand slid to cradle his face, her thumb tracing the line of his cheekbone, the hollow beneath it, the place just before his ear where his pulse had once answered her own.

"Darcy! Do not leave me, my love."

No one moved now. No horse cried out. Even Lady Catherine's voice had fallen silent somewhere beyond the edge of Elizabeth's awareness. The air seemed emptied of motion, emptied of sound.

And Darcy lay utterly still.

Elizabeth did not move. She did not lift her head. She could not endure to look upon his face and see nothing answer her.

But there, beneath her cheek...

Something shifted.

For one suspended instant, she did not lift her head. She did not dare. The world had already taken too much; she would not be made a fool of by hope. Her palm lay flat against his chest, fingers splayed over the torn cloth and his dear form. The air seemed to thin around her.

*There.*

A tremor.

So slight she thought at first it was only her own trembling. She lifted her head, stared at his chest. Surely not. No! It was only her longing, her agony and tortured imagination that—

Another pulse. Her breath caught—not in shock, but in refusal. She pressed harder, as though she could compel truth from stillness by force alone.

"Darcy?" The word scarcely formed.

Nothing.

She bent closer, her lips brushing the hollow of his throat, where the thorn had pierced deepest. Her tears fell there, warm against cooling skin.

And then his chest rose.

Not fully. Not cleanly. It hitched—as though some unseen weight resisted the motion—and fell again.

Elizabeth recoiled this time, a broken sound escaping her before she could contain it. She clutched at his coat, fingers digging into wool damp with blood as she caught him, tugged his heavy frame upwards.

"No," she whispered, shaking her head as if to ward off illusion. Her hand flew back to his chest. "No—do not mock me! Can it be true?"

Again. A breath, dragged in as though through bramble and ash. Uneven. Painful. Real.

Harrowe pushed to her side, drawing Anne away and bending over Darcy's body. She saw him only dimly at the edge of her vision, kneeling, one broad hand hovering uncertainly over Darcy's shoulder as though even he feared to interfere.

Elizabeth cupped Darcy's face between her hands. His skin, though pale, no longer held the chill of death. There was colour—faint, stubborn—gathering again at his mouth.

"Fitzwilliam Darcy," she breathed, the name trembling from her. "Do you hear me?"

His lashes flickered.

Not the full sweep of awakening. A twitch. A struggle.

She pressed her forehead to his. "You chose this," she whispered, her voice breaking anew. "You foolish, noble man—you chose it. And you were right. Now come back to me!"

His brow furrowed faintly, as though in distant confusion. His lips parted.

Another breath.

Then another.

Each one laborious, as if he were learning the mechanism anew.

And at last, his eyes opened.

They were not triumphant. They were not radiant with revelation. They were unfocused at first, searching, bewildered by torchlight and starry sky and the shape of her bent above him.

"Elizabeth?"

The sound of her name in his voice undid what little composure she had managed to gather. A sob tore free of her chest, and she lowered herself over him once more, careful now of his wounds, careful of everything.

"I am here!" she said, her hands moving instinctively to smooth his hair from his brow, to trace the line of his cheek, to assure herself he was not dissolving again. "I am here."

He tried to lift a hand. It faltered halfway, and she caught it, guiding it gently against her own cheek.

This time, when their skin met, he did not weaken. He smiled.

She felt it at once. No draining pull. No trembling collapse beneath her touch. Only warmth—human, mortal warmth—and the steady, fragile rhythm of a heart that had ceased and now persisted.

She drew in a shuddering breath and pressed his hand more firmly against her face. "Do you feel it?" she whispered.

He frowned faintly, still gathering himself. "Feel—"

"That you are not undone," she said, the words tumbling from her in relief and wonder. "That you are not lost, and neither am I."

His gaze focused slowly, recognition settling into place. Memory followed close behind. She saw the instant it returned—the thorn, the tightening, the choice. And the release.

Across the road, Lady Catherine's voice began again—sharp, disbelieving—but it seemed distant now, thin and impotent against the undeniable fact of breath.

Elizabeth did not look up.

She bent and pressed one more kiss to his brow, gentler now, reverent.

"Love requireth heart," she whispered against his skin.

And this time, he breathed without struggle.

# Chapter Fifty-Four

The house in Grosvenor Square did not know what had transpired upon a winter road.

Its doors opened to him as they always had — with elegance, a liveried footman waiting for him, with a warm fire in the grate and his mother's decor sweetening the hall. The door closed behind him with a solid click. No tremor followed. No answering crack ran through plaster or pane.

Darcy paused in the entry as though he expected one.

Nothing came.

Elizabeth stood not far from him, her cloak hanging loosely over her destroyed gown, her colour returned, though fatigue lingered beneath it. She had insisted upon walking unaided once they were within doors. He had not argued. He found that he could not endure the thought of her feeling confined again — by carriage, by hedge, by anything living or dead.

She touched the banister lightly as she passed. The wood did not darken beneath her hand. The iron brackets did not strain toward her.

It was over.

He removed his gloves slowly. It had been scarcely hours ago that his blood darkened the old Roman road, and already the punctures at his wrists had closed to thin, scabbed ridges. They stung faintly, but not with pain; rather as one remembers pain after it has departed.

Elizabeth stood in the centre of the hall as though uncertain whether she ought to advance or remain precisely where she was. Her hood had slipped back from her wind and earth-snarled hair. Dried mud darkened the hem of her gown. She looked impossibly slight against the sweep of marble and gleaming wood.

"Are you well?" he asked quietly.

She studied him for a long moment before answering. "I believe I am."

He crossed the distance between them, not quickly, not as he had done upon the road, but with deliberation. His hand lifted and hovered near her cheek before settling there at last, thumb brushing the line where a thorn had grazed her skin.

Nothing answered the touch. No tremor. No surge. Only her breath, warm against his palm.

Her hand came up and covered his scabbed wrist, and for an instant they both seemed to listen — not for rupture, not for crack or flame — but for the absence of it.

Her mouth curved, faint and incredulous. "It is quiet."

"Yes."

The word left him not as relief, but as certainty.

He drew her gently toward him. She did not hesitate. Her forehead rested briefly against his chest, and he closed his eyes as though memorizing the shape of her there.

"I thought I lost you," she murmured, voice muffled in his coat.

"You did."

She lifted her face at that. There was no coyness in her expression, no mischief. Only a depth that had not been there before. "I cannot lose you again."

"Oh, fear not, love. I am rather too stubborn to let that happen again." He bent his head and kissed her.

Not with urgency. Not with defiance of heaven and earth. The kiss was tender, almost reverent, as though both of them were testing a boundary that no longer existed. Her fingers curled into the lapel of his coat; his hand steadied at her back.

And the world did not fracture.

When he drew away, it was only far enough to search her face. "Would you be persuaded to rest?"

She laughed softly — a sound fragile and brave at once. "Only if you promise not to faint before I do."

"I shall endeavour to remain upright."

He did not trust himself to carry her—not because he doubted his strength, but because he doubted his restraint. The temptation to make her his, in every final sense, would be too much. What greater oath could he swear than the one he had already bled for?

But there were forms to be observed. Family to be honoured. The house, the servants, the city beyond—all of it would soon press upon them with questions and astonishment.

For a few moments longer, he would preserve what quiet they possessed and save the sweetest treasure for a moment that deserved it.

He rang for the housekeeper.

When she entered, she took in the scene in a single glance—the mud, the injuries, the intimacy that was impossible to disguise—and said nothing at all.

"Mrs Hodges, you will remember Miss Elizabeth Bennet?"

"Of course." Mrs Hodges bestowed a brief, welcoming nod on Elizabeth, then turned her attention back to him.

"Very well. Please see that my betrothed is made comfortable upstairs. A fire laid. Tea, a hot bath, fresh garments. Whatever she requires."

Elizabeth's eyes widened slightly at the word, but she did not contradict him.

Mrs Hodges inclined her head with grave satisfaction and the ghost of a most unprofessional smile. "Of course, sir."

As Elizabeth turned to follow her, she paused beside him. Their hands brushed — not by accident.

"Betrothed?" she asked under her breath.

"Unless you object."

Her answering smile was small, private, and entirely certain. "I do not."

He watched her ascend the staircase, each step steady and untroubled. Only when she had disappeared from sight did he allow his shoulders to lower fully.

He turned back toward the front hall and sought a footman. "Please inform the house that we shall be receiving company shortly. Miss Bennet's family will no doubt call without delay, and I expect Lord Matlock and Mr Harrowe as well."

"Yes, sir."

"Oh..." He had turned away, then stopped. "Mr Harrowe will be arriving with Brutus. He was shot, but has been seen by a surgeon and requires perfect quiet for his recovery. Please see that Cook has some broth ready for him, and make up a comfortable pallet for him... by the hearth in Miss Bennet's room."

The servant frowned. "Of course, sir."

The house resumed its rhythm around him — servants moving, doors opening and closing, a fire being coaxed to life somewhere above. Darcy remained where he stood for a moment longer. The world had not ended. It had merely altered.

And this time, the alteration did not demand blood.

Matlock stood waiting in the library, tall and grave, as though the intervening hours had been spent neither pacing nor arguing but merely considering. Harrowe occupied the window embrasure, his broad frame half-turned toward the square, as if London itself might offer annotation to what they had witnessed.

They did not speak at once.

Darcy crossed the room and laid the *Liber* flat upon the desk. The page he had last consulted lay open still, its margins crowded with Harrowe's cramped notes.

"It was never the county," Harrowe said at length, without looking away from the glass. "I've been arguing geography for twenty years. Fault lines. Watercourses. Inherited soil. But it were not the soil that required correction." Harrowe's mouth curved without mirth. "It was the vow."

Darcy remained standing. He had not yet grown accustomed to the simple miracle of a floor that did not shift beneath his feet.

"It awakened in Hertfordshire," Harrowe continued. "The fracture followed there. But it weren't kept there."

Matlock inclined his head. "No."

"It was kept," Darcy said, "where choice was made."

A contemplative, almost reverent silence followed.

Harrowe lowered the glass at last and turned from the window. "You rode south," he said slowly. "Not toward Kent in obedience. Not toward Hertfordshire in defence."

"I rode toward her," Darcy replied.

"Yes." Harrowe's voice softened. "And she toward you. How the devil you both knew..."

Matlock crossed to the table and laid his fingers upon the map Harrowe had so often annotated. The Thames curved there in ink, the old Roman road cutting across it like a scar half-healed. Dartford marked plainly enough. The ferry crossing. The raised causeway where marsh gave way to firmer ground.

"Here," the Earl said.

Darcy did not need to look. He saw it still—the churned earth, the ditch, the gathering crowd. The place where neither Kent nor Hertfordshire held dominion, where boundaries blurred, and road and water met.

"It *is* a crossing," Harrowe murmured. "Neutral ground. Neither inheritance nor estate. A place of passage."

"An ancient place of meeting," Matlock corrected quietly.

Darcy drew a slow breath. "We believed the question to be one of possession. Which land. Which line. Which steward had claim."

"And it was not?" Matlock asked.

"It was alignment," Darcy said. "Not of soil, but of will."

Harrowe let out a sound that was almost a laugh. "All my life, I've hunted proof of who the heir was, and that the Lady belonged to one county over another. That the fracture would close when the proper inheritance was restored to its proper seat." He shook his head. "I mistook symptom for cause."

"It was never to be enforced," Matlock said. "Nor coerced."

Darcy's hand strayed, unconsciously, to the pale ridge at his wrist. "It was to be chosen."

Harrowe's gaze narrowed. "And substituted."

Darcy met his eyes. "Yes."

Matlock folded his hands behind his back. "Lady Catherine would have compelled you to a church in Kent."

"And I," Harrowe said dryly, "would have compelled him to a ditch in Hertfordshire."

Darcy allowed himself the faintest curve of a smile. "And both would have been wrong."

"The thread was real," Matlock said, returning to the map. "It ran between the counties. That much none of us misread. But not as a boundary. As a path."

Darcy saw again the hawthorn rising in the hedgerows, the narrow lanes hemming them in, the sense—not of pursuit—but of direction. The dog's certainty. The way each fork had resolved without signpost or guide.

Matlock regarded him for a long moment. "And the moment you..." he cleared his throat and glanced uncomfortably at Harrowe. "Well, when you... expired... tell me more."

"The thorns withdrew," Darcy replied. "That is all I know."

"Because you placed yourself in her stead," Harrowe grunted. "Not as ritual. Not as lineage. As substitution."

Darcy met his gaze without flinching. "I chose *her*."

"And you knew," Matlock returned. "You *believed* you would die, even before you chose."

"Yes."

"And yet you did not."

Darcy's hand moved unconsciously to his throat, to the place where the thorns had closed with patient inevitability. The skin there was unbroken now. The memory was not.

"Something in me did," he said quietly.

He understood it now with a clarity that had eluded him even as the branches tightened. The certainty that stewardship required command. The belief that duty was a solitary burden. The conviction that love must be measured against consequence.

Those things had not survived.

Harrowe looked up from the map. There was no triumph in his expression. Only the exhaustion of a man who has watched the scaffolding of his life's work collapse and discovered, to his irritation, that something better stands in its place. "You're the luckiest bastard, Darcy."

Matlock's mouth twitched faintly. "And you, Mr Harrowe, will require a new occupation."

"I do believe so."

A discreet knock interrupted them. Darcy turned. "Enter."

It was Barlow, his London man of business, flushed from haste and still holding a folded sheaf of damp broadsheets beneath his arm.

"Forgive the intrusion, sir. Oh, excuse me, Your Lordship." He bowed to Matlock. "I know it is most irregular, sir, but I had to come at once. There are... reports."

Matlock arched a brow. "From the War Office?"

"From everywhere, my lord," the man replied, clearly uncertain whether he brought good news or madness. He extended one of the sheets to Darcy. "The afternoon edition. It will surely impact your estate and investments. I thought to bring you the earliest word."

Darcy unfolded it. The headline was not triumphant—London printers did not dare such language yet—but it was changed. Matlock stepped nearer. "Read it."

Darcy did.

"'In Suffolk, a warehouse condemned three days past for rot and blackening was reopened this morning at the insistence of the owner. The grain within, previously deemed unfit, is reported dry and whole. Similar accounts have arrived from Kent and Middlesex.'"

Harrowe let out a low sound that was neither laughter nor disbelief. "Kent as well, eh?"

Darcy's eyes moved down the column.

"'River levels along certain branches of the Medway and Thames have steadied despite continued frost. A millstream near Gravesend, formerly obstructed by silt and fallen timber, is said to have cleared overnight without further collapse of its banks.'"

Matlock took the second broadsheet. "And here—listen." He read aloud. "'A convoy delayed for want of sound flour has resumed its course, the casks having been found serviceable upon re-examination. Officers decline to speculate as to the cause of the earlier deterioration.'"

Harrowe leaned both hands upon the table, staring at the papers as though they might rearrange themselves into a map. "They will call it all an accident," he muttered. "Panic and public hysteria. Merchants eager to recover losses."

"Parliament will call it coincidence," Matlock agreed. "And that will be the end of it, in any official matter."

Darcy lowered the page. "And the War Office?" he asked quietly.

Matlock's expression sobered. "If supplies truly stabilize—if transport ceases to fail at every turn—they will not trouble themselves over the manner of it. They will be content that the thing is so. And perhaps we will have Richard home again by spring."

Darcy looked again at the lines of print. The language was cautious. Restrained. No hint of miracle or sensation. Only the slow correction of what had been unravelling.

He folded the broadsheet carefully and laid it upon the table. The three men stood in silence a moment longer, while outside the city moved on, ignorant of the hinge upon which it had nearly turned.

At last, Matlock spoke. "You understand," he said, "that no one will ever credit the truth of it."

Darcy allowed himself the smallest, private smile.

"They need not," he replied. "It is enough that it stands."

DARCY CLOSED THE DOOR himself.

The latch settled into place with a soft, definitive click, and the sound seemed to divide the world neatly in two: what clamoured beyond, and what remained within.

Elizabeth stood near the hearth, arrayed in a fresh gown, her hair neatly pinned up once more, and her hands loosely clasped before her as though uncertain what to do with their freedom.

He remained where he was for a moment longer than was strictly necessary. Merely drinking her in as a man parched. "You are certain," he said at last, "that you feel no ill effect?"

She turned toward him fully then. There was colour in her cheeks—not fever, not strain. Merely life.

"I feel," she said, and paused as though searching for a word that would not diminish what she meant, "myself."

The simplicity of it struck him more forcibly than any declaration could have done.

He crossed the room slowly. He had known courage in battlefields described by others, had admired composure in men who rode into cannon smoke, but this—this quiet approach toward her without fear of what might follow—felt more daring than any of it.

He stopped within reach. "May I?"

Her answer was not spoken. She placed her hand in his. He exhaled.

"I thought," he said, still gazing down at the miracle of her hand in his, "that I understood what was required. That I had made peace with the consequence."

"You had," she replied softly. "That was why your choice was accepted."

He lifted her hand and turned it gently, examining the faint marks at her wrists where the thorns had bound her. There were no wounds now. Only memory.

"I only chose it because I could not endure a world in which you were taken from me."

She searched his face, as though verifying the absence of exaggeration. "And if it had not restored the land?"

He considered that honestly.

"Then at least the choice would have been mine."

Her composure wavered at that—not into weakness, but into something far more vulnerable. "You arrogant, impossible man," she whispered, and there was no anger in it at all.

He allowed himself the smallest curve of a smile. "I have been called worse."

Her free hand rose then—hesitant at first—and touched his cheek. Not in testing. Not in alarm. In affection.

The sensation of it nearly undid him. He covered her hand with his own.

"I do not yet understand," he said quietly, "what portion of me was surrendered and what returned."

She regarded him for a long moment. "You were severed from fear," she said at last. "You thought you were born to repair something ancient. To answer for old men and older vows. But what was required of you was not obedience. It was choice over doubt."

"And you?" he asked.

"I suppose I was freed from being chosen."

His restraint faltered then—not in weakness, but in relief. He bent his head and kissed her. And his heart thumped, raced, but carried on. Beyond that, it was only the quiet, deliberate meeting of two people who understood the cost and chose one another regardless.

When he lifted his head, her brow rested briefly against his.

"We shall be obliged," she said with faint amusement, "to explain ourselves. To my father, to start."

"Explain? I daresay he will be relieved."

She laughed then, and it was the most ordinary, miraculous thing he had ever seen.

Darcy had not yet released Elizabeth's hand when the discreet knock sounded at the door. It opened to admit his housekeeper, who inclined her head and spoke with quiet propriety.

"Miss Bennet and Mr Bennet have arrived, sir."

"Well, now." Darcy chuckled. "It seems we have not yet exhausted our share of portents and manifestations."

Elizabeth patted his cheek with a teasing look. "That, sir, was coincidence. Nothing more." She stepped back, though she did not withdraw entirely from his side.

Darcy laughed and gestured to the housekeeper. "Pray show them in."

Miss Bennet entered first.

He had never before understood how much composure could resemble courage until he saw it in her now. She did not rush forward, though her eyes sought her sister at once and found her whole. There was no tremor in her step, yet relief altered her countenance in a manner too profound to disguise. "Lizzy," she sighed. "Oh, I knew… I *knew* when you left Ramsgate, you would have come here. You dear, terrifying thing, you!"

Elizabeth moved toward her with a cry that was more a sob of relief. They embraced—not fiercely, not with passionate tears and avowals— but with the quiet certainty of two who have endured enough to dispense with restraint.

Mr Bennet arrived at the door, and his eyes were arrested by the sight of his daughters. His coat bore the marks of travel. His hair was more disordered than fashion required. He paused just within the threshold, surveying the scene with that particular expression of thoughtful irony which had so often shielded him from the demands of deeper feeling.

He gazed fondly at his girls. Then, his attention went to Darcy.

"Well," he said at last, "I see that London's smoky air continues to prove beneficial."

Elizabeth drew back from her sister. "Papa—"

He lifted a hand to forestall explanation. "My dear," he said mildly, though his voice did not quite manage its customary lightness, "I have spent the better part of a fortnight suspecting that geography was not the true difficulty. It appears I was correct."

Darcy stepped forward then. "Sir," he said, with more gravity than he had ever employed in that address before, "whatever disorder has afflicted your daughter was not of her making. Nor of yours. If blame is to be assigned, it may rest with me."

Mr Bennet's brows rose. "That is a generous proposal," he replied. "One which I shall consider at leisure."

Elizabeth made a sound that was half protest and half plea.

Mr Bennet's gaze softened then, though only slightly. "Lizzy, my dear. You have frightened me sufficiently for one lifetime. I should prefer, if it is not too much to ask, to be done with mysteries."

Darcy did not hesitate. "You shall have none from me, sir. I love your daughter. I have loved her—imperfectly at first, and then entirely. Whatever passed between us was not obedience to old fancies or inherited pride. It was choice."

Mr Bennet studied him.

It was not the inspection of a social superior weighing an advantageous match. It was the assessment of a man who had nearly lost his child and would not hazard her twice.

"You appear," Mr Bennet said slowly, "to be in possession of your full faculties at last."

"I believe I am."

"And you do not look as though you are about to expire, despite my daughter's..." He cleared his throat. "Rather *close* proximity to your person when we were shown into the room."

"I am not."

Mr Bennet considered this a moment longer. "Then we must suppose," he said dryly, "that whatever threatened to consume the countryside has been persuaded to pursue another occupation."

He turned then to Elizabeth.

"And you?" he asked, and the quiet beneath the question carried far more than the words themselves. "Do you enter this arrangement from inclination?"

"Yes," she said simply. "From love, Papa."

Mr Bennet inhaled once, sharply, and for an instant his composure deserted him altogether. He pulled his spectacles from his pocket and held them in his hand, though there was no need to polish them or to put them on.

"Very well," he said at last. "I shall not oppose what appears already concluded by forces beyond my comprehension." He extended his hand to Darcy.

Darcy took it.

"You need not ask more, for you have my consent," Mr Bennet said. "On the condition that you never again require my daughter to wrestle hedgerows on your behalf."

A faint smile returned to Darcy's mouth. "I shall endeavour to keep future negotiations free of vegetation. And earthquakes."

Mr Bennet grunted. "Do not forget fire and the tide... oh, did she not tell you of those?"

Darcy's eyes narrowed, and he glanced questioningly at Elizabeth. "I expect I will have leisure to hear everything in time."

Jane crossed to them then, laying her hand lightly upon Elizabeth's shoulder. "I knew everything was well," she said quietly. "I knew before we left Dartford that we would find you well and healed and whole. The air changed."

Darcy glanced toward the window.

It had.

He could not have described how, only that the oppressive strain that had hovered over weeks of dread had lifted. The light beyond the glass seemed clearer, the winter sky no longer pressed low against the city roofs.

Mr Bennet replaced his spectacles in his pocket. "Well," he said briskly, recovering his usual tone with visible effort, "I presume there will be further explanations forthcoming. Preferably over dinner. And preferably without firearms."

Elizabeth's laugh—relieved, unshadowed—filled the room.

Darcy feasted his eyes on her. There was no answering tremor in the walls at the sound of her laughter. No quailing weakness in his limbs. No stirring thorn.

Only her.

And for the first time since that original fracture split the earth surrounding Netherfield, he felt no vigilance in loving her.

Only peace.

# EPILOGUE

*Pemberley*
*Michaelmas, 1817*

THE HILLS OF DERBYSHIRE lay burnished beneath an amber sky, the late sun striking fire from the stubble of harvested fields. Wagons stood in neat rows beyond the south lawn, their beds piled high with wheat and barley; garlands of oak leaves and red berries had been tied along the gateposts that morning, and ribbons fluttered lazily from the orchard trees where the tenants' children ran shrieking in play.

Elizabeth stood upon the terrace with a basket balanced against her hip, watching the preparations with a satisfaction that was no longer edged with vigilance. The air smelled of crushed apple and warm grain. From the lower meadow rose the lowing of cattle being counted and led, the murmur of men in cheerful dispute over measures and yields.

It was a good harvest.

It had been a good harvest everywhere, she had learned—though not everywhere equally. Only the week prior, when her father had arrived from Hertfordshire, he laughed about a letter he had from a magistrate inquiring, with polite bewilderment, how Longbourn's fields contrived each year to outstrip neighbouring estates by such a consistent margin. Papa had written back, she suspected, with a dryness that concealed more amusement than explanation.

Bingley and Jane, settled scarcely five miles distant at an estate newly purchased and cheerfully restored, had arrived that morning in high spirits, reporting that their own tenants spoke of the season's bounty with something approaching reverence.

Colonel Fitzwilliam, who had ridden in from Matlock two days earlier, declared that if Parliament sought proof of providence, it might begin in Hertfordshire and proceed northward. And then Mr Harrowe, who had been in Derbyshire only long enough to pass one dinner with them, had spent the rest of the evening arguing with the colonel over ale and army concerns and how ignorant politicians truly were about agriculture and history.

Elizabeth smiled at the recollection.

Below her, upon the sweep of autumn grass, her son's voice rose in fierce triumph.

Gareth William Darcy was five years old and entirely ungovernable in his energy—dark curls escaping every attempt at discipline, boots grass-stained, stockings perpetually sliding. He had claimed a fallen willow switch and now wielded it as though it had been forged for him in some ancient armoury rather than snapped from a hedge.

Colonel Fitzwilliam stood before him, coat discarded, sleeves rolled with exaggerated gravity. In his hand, he held a walking cane, which he presented with solemn ceremony.

"Guard first," the colonel instructed, dropping into a half-crouch. "A gentleman never strikes before he knows how to defend."

Gareth planted his feet with great care, jaw set. "Like this?"

"Wider," the colonel replied. "You intend to keep both legs, I presume."

Darcy, who stood several paces off with Bingley, folded his arms and called out mildly, "You may wish to inform him, Richard, that orchards are seldom stormed by cavalry."

Bingley laughed. "Speak for your own orchards. Mine have been threatened twice this week by Mrs Bingley's favourite pony."

Gareth lunged without warning. The willow switch whistled through the air and met the colonel's cane with a decisive crack. He staggered back dramatically.

"Well struck!" he declared. "But you dropped your shoulder."

"I did not!" Gareth insisted, affronted. "Papa, did I?"

Darcy stepped forward then, unable to prevent the faint curve at the corner of his mouth. "You did," he said. "Though you were very nearly victorious in spite of it."

Gareth frowned, considering this grave injustice. "I shall not drop it next time."

"That," Bingley said cheerfully, "is the proper spirit. One cannot conquer the orchard in a single campaign."

"Nor ought one to attempt it," Darcy added dryly. "Harvest is not war."

Colonel Fitzwilliam lifted his cane again. "On the contrary, cousin, harvest is precisely the reward for discipline. Now then—again."

They circled. Brutus—now grizzled, but stalwart in his loyalty to his young master—barked once in encouragement and trotted clear of the arc of combat.

Gareth advanced more cautiously this time, brows drawn in intense concentration. When the colonel feinted left, Gareth did not overreach. He recovered, adjusted, and struck with greater care.

The cane tapped his switch aside, but not cleanly. Colonel Fitzwilliam lowered his weapon. "Better," he pronounced. "Very much better."

Gareth's face broke into incandescent pride.

Elizabeth rested her hands against the terrace stone and watched them—the earned patience in Darcy's stance, the way Bingley leaned close to offer commentary no one had requested, Richard's theatrical flourishes, and at the centre of it all, her son, fierce and earnest and so very alive.

"May I have a real sword when I am grown?" Gareth called suddenly.

Darcy answered before the colonel could. "You may have one when you have learned first that strength exists to protect, not to dominate."

Gareth absorbed this with visible seriousness. "And if someone needs protecting?"

Darcy's gaze lifted, briefly, to the terrace. He saw her watching. The look that passed between them was quiet, unguarded. "Then," he said evenly, "you will stand."

Colonel Fitzwilliam clapped Gareth on the shoulder. "Which you have already done, sir. Though perhaps not yet against apples."

Bingley laughed aloud.

The willow switch lifted again, and Gareth charged away, towards the orchard with renewed vigour, shouting something about dragons that bore only a passing resemblance to horticulture.

Elizabeth smiled. The orchard was safe.

Darcy wandered from where Richard stood to say something to her father near the cider press. He, too, had removed his coat and rolled his sleeves in concession to the afternoon warmth; the sun caught at the faint pale lines that crossed his wrists and his throat—marks that had long since softened to memory. He laughed at something Papa said, the sound low and unguarded.

Elizabeth felt the old reflex stir—that instinct to test the air, to sense the ground beneath her for tremor—and then dismissed it with a quiet inward amusement. The earth lay firm. The wind moved only as wind ought. Nothing answered her nearness but the ordinary rhythm of life.

A cry of pain broke across the lawn. Elizabeth dropped her basket and twisted over the terrace, her eyes following the sound.

Her son stood frozen beside the orchard hedge, his switch fallen to the grass. Brutus circled him once, confused, before barking and stepping back. The boy stared at his palm as though betrayed by the world itself, and then his mouth trembled.

"Mama!"

Elizabeth was down the terrace steps before she registered movement, skirts gathered, heart lifting in instinctive haste. Darcy reached the child first, dropping to one knee and taking the small hand gently in his own.

"What have we here?"

"A thorn," Gareth cried indignantly, tears pooling without yet falling. "It bit me. I was just walking, and it caught me!"

Elizabeth knelt opposite them. A bead of bright red welled at the pad of his finger, stark against skin still dimpled with baby softness. One of the orchard's hawthorn branches had strayed beyond its trimming and caught him unawares.

Darcy examined the hedge with solemn gravity. "A formidable adversary."

The boy sniffed. "I did not see it."

"No," Elizabeth said softly. "They do not always announce themselves."

She drew the injured hand to her lips and pressed a kiss to the small wound. The taste of iron was faint and wholly human. She reached for her handkerchief and wrapped the finger with careful efficiency, binding it snugly but not tightly.

"It will mend," she assured him.

He searched her face for confirmation of this great truth, and, satisfied, allowed his father to lift him easily to his feet.

Behind them, the hawthorn stirred in the mild wind. Its branches were heavy with darkening berries, but no tendril coiled, no root shifted in the soil. It stood as it had stood all season—shaped by pruning, responsive to care, neither grasping nor retreating.

A thorn.

A prick of blood.

Nothing more.

Brutus nosed the boy's knee, as though offering an apology for having failed to guard him from such treachery. Gareth laughed—the injury already forgot—and wriggled free to resume his campaign upon the orchard, now armed with caution and bandaged finger held aloft like a badge of honour.

Darcy remained crouched for a moment longer, his gaze following their son before rising to meet Elizabeth's. "Are we to fear hedgerows now?" he asked quietly.

She held his look and shook her head. "No," she said. "We are to tend them. A thorn, sir, is just a thorn."

Music drifted from the lower field where a fiddle had begun its tuning. Georgiana's clear voice rose in greeting as she joined the circle of tenants, her husband at her side. Jane, luminous in the slanting light, called to Elizabeth to come and see the arrangement of tables near the great oak.

"Well, then. Shall we, my love, my Lady?" Darcy rose and offered his arm.

Elizabeth took it, bringing his hand up to kiss that sensitive part of his inner wrist before twining her fingers through his and curling herself under his arm.

As they descended together toward the gathering, she allowed herself one last glance at the hedge. The berries glowed deep and red against the autumn leaves, neither omen nor warning, but promise fulfilled in season.

Above the fields, the light lingered. And the harvest was secure.

GET SWEPT AWAY IN another Darcy and Elizabeth epic. Get your copy of *The Lantern Keeper's Promise* today!

# From Alix

Thank you for indulging with me and spending a little time with Darcy and Elizabeth.

I hope you've had a delightful escape to Pemberley. I'd love it if you would share this family with your friends so they can experience a love to last for the ages. As with all my books, I have enabled lending to make it easier to share. If you leave a review for *The Lady of the Thorn* , I would love to read it! Email me the link at **Author@AlixJames.com.**

Would you like to read more of Darcy and Elizabeth's romance? I have swoony Darcy and Elizabeth epic for you to try next. Get your copy of *The Lantern Keeper's Promise* today!

And if you're hungry for more, including a free story, stay up to date on upcoming releases and sales by joining my newsletter:

*Mr. Darcy's Fair Trade*

# ABOUT ALIX JAMES

Sweet and satisfying romance for busy readers.

Always on the go as a wife, mom, and small business owner, she rarely has time to read a whole novel. She loves coffee with the sunrise and being outdoors. When she does get free time, she likes to read, camp, dream up romantic adventures, and tries to avoid housework.

Each Alix James story is a clean Regency Variation of Darcy and Elizabeth's romance.

Visit her website and sign up for her newsletter at AlixJames.com

# Also By Alix James

**The Everbound Chronicles:**

The Lady of the Thorn

The Lantern Keeper's Promise

The Mirror at Northmere

---

**The First Impressions Collection:**

All Bets Are Off

Raising the Stakes

Better Luck Next Time

Make Your Play

**First Impressions Box Set: Winning Mr. Darcy**

---

## The Measure of a Man Collection:

The Measure of Love

The Measure of Trust

The Measure of Honor

**The Measure of a Man Box Set**

---

## The Mr. Darcy Collection:

Mr. Darcy Steals a Kiss

Mr. Darcy and the Governess

Mr. Darcy and the Girl Next Door

**Mr. Darcy: Swoonworthy Collection**

---

## The Heart to Heart Collection

These Dreams

Nefarious

Tempted

**Darcy and Elizabeth: Heart to Heart Box Set**

---

**The Sweet Escapes Collection**

The Rogue's Widow

The Courtship of Edward Gardiner

London Holiday

Rumours and Recklessness

**Darcy and Elizabeth: Sweet Escapes Box Set**

---

**The Sweet Sentiments Collection:**

When the Sun Sleeps

Queen of Winter

A Fine Mind

**Elizabeth Bennet: Sweet Sentiments Box Set**

---

## The Frolic and Romance Collection:

A Proper Introduction

A Good Memory is Unpardonable

Along for the Ride

**Elizabeth Bennet: Frolic & Romance Box Set**

---

## The Short and Sassy Collection:

Unintended

Spirited Away

Indisposed

Love and Other Machines

**Elizabeth Bennet: Short and Sassy Compilation**

---

## Christmas With Darcy and Elizabeth

How to Get Caught Under the Mistletoe: A Lady's Guide

The Scotsman's Ghost: Or How to Wreck a Yule Party

Mr, Darcy's Christmas Kiss

**Mistletoe, Magic and Mr. Darcy**

Mr. Darcy's Keepsake

---

## North and South Variations

Nowhere but North

Northern Rain

No Such Thing as Luck

**John and Margaret: Coming Home Collection**

Thornton's Christmas Clause

---

## Anthologies

Rational Creatures

Falling for Mr Thornton

---

## Spanish Translations

Rumores e Imprudencias

Vacaciones en Londres

Nefasto

Un Compromiso Accidental

Reina del Invierno

Una Mente Noble

Cuando el Sol se Duerm

A lo largo del Camino

Una Mente Noble

El señor Darcy se roba un beso

Cómo quedar atrapado debajo del muérdago

---

## German Translations

Tuscheleien & Tollkühnheit

Londoner Eskapade

Des Schurken junge Witwe

Die Werbung des Edward Gardiner

Wie man sich unter dem Mistelzweig erwischen lässt: Ein Leitfaden für Damen

Der Schottengeist

**Mr. Darcys Weihnachtskuss**

---

## Italian Translations

Una Vacanza a Londra

# The Lantern Keeper's Promise

## Sneak Preview

### Chapter One

THE OLD STONE COLUMN held the chill even in summer. Tonight, it breathed damp. Salt clung to the air. It lay on the tongue like memory.

He carried the oil can in one hand and the trimming shears in the other, balancing their weight as he began the ascent. The stair rose in its narrow coil, worn smooth at the center by generations of boots. He mounted without looking down, without testing the tread. There was little within these walls that had not already declared its temper to him.

Above, the lantern room muttered faintly as the wind pressed against the glass. Not a storm. That would come tomorrow. For now, it was only the low insistence of a tide turning beyond sight.

He emerged into the narrow circle of light at the top and set the can upon the small iron table. The lenses loomed around him—tall, faceted, clouded faintly at their edges where age had etched its claim. The brass bands that held them were dark with years of polish and salt. He had scoured them himself more times than he could number. The metal still remembered older hands.

He moved without haste. Wick first.

The old one had burned low through the afternoon watch. He lifted the glass chimney and eased the charred thread between his fingers. It left a smear against his thumb. He trimmed it evenly, careful not to cut too deep. Too little, and it smoked. Too much, and it faltered. There was a narrow margin between neglect and excess.

He set the wick straight again and poured the oil with steady hand. The reservoir drank it greedily. The scent rose—thick, mineral, faintly bitter. He wiped the lip of the can before replacing the cap. Waste invited failure.

Below, the sea struck the rocks with its steady violence. The sound reached the tower not as crash, but as hollow concussion—a pulse through stone. It had sounded thus long before he first climbed these steps. It would sound thus when he was gone.

He lowered the chimney and struck the flame. It caught at once.

A thin tongue of gold rose—wavering, uncertain, then strengthening as it fed upon the oil. He adjusted the wick carefully, watching for smoke. The glass brightened. The prisms answered. Light flared outward in a steady beam and turned across the darkening water.

He did not step back to admire it.

He listened.

The wind shifted against the panes, a hand testing the seams. The frame shuddered faintly. He laid his palm against the brass housing, feeling for tremor. All was well.

He circled once, examining the joints where salt crusted white in the creases. The mortar at the base had begun to flake again. He would attend to it tomorrow. There was always something to attend.

The beam passed over the black water and returned again in its patient sweep. Out there, beyond sight, vessels would mark it, correct by it, trust it without knowing the hand that kept it.

Trust was an odd thing.

He rested both hands against the sill and looked out across the wide, breathing dark. No moon. Only the faintest seam of pallor where sky met sea. The tide had begun its inward pull. He could feel it in the sound—the deepening undertow, the pause between surges.

For a moment, the tower was utterly still.

Then the flame trembled.

He turned to study it. Not unusual. That was why he always waited, to make sure it carried on as it ought.

A gust pressed the glass, but the chimney did not crack. The wick had been trimmed precisely. There was no reason for instability.

The flame dipped low, guttered, then climbed again. He adjusted it by a fraction, and it strengthened. He waited.

The wind eased. The beam resumed its long arc across the water.

Below, the sea continued its measured breathing. Above, the lenses gathered and released light as they had done for longer than any living memory.

Routine.

Order.

Endurance.

He stood beside the flame until it had burned an hour without wavering. Only then did he descend the spiral stair, each step answering the next, the echo following him down into the dark.

THE BREAKFAST THINGS HAD been cleared, though the scent of coffee still lingered faintly in the house. A small fire burned in the drawing room grate, more for comfort than necessity; London damp had a way of creeping more into the mind than the body. The curtains were drawn back to admit what little light the morning offered, and the grey of the street beyond lay flat against the glass.

Elizabeth Bennet stood at the escritoire near the window, sorting the morning's letters into two neat stacks. Trade invoices were set aside for her uncle; a narrow bill from the milliner she placed beneath the weight of a small brass paperknife. She paused over a third envelope, the seal already broken, and read once more the line she had read the evening prior.

Mary sat at the pianoforte, though she had not yet struck a key. A volume lay open upon the stand before her; she was tracing a passage silently with one finger, her lips moving as she considered it. Kitty occupied the chair nearest the hearth, her needle suspended above a square of muslin she had unpicked more than she had sewn.

"Will he come this morning?" Kitty asked, without looking up.

Elizabeth did not turn at once. "He wrote that he should."

Kitty nodded and bent her head again to her work, though her stitch went astray and she was obliged to pull it out again.

There was a chair near the window that had not been drawn forward since... too long since. It remained angled toward the light, as though its occupant had merely stepped away for a moment and might yet return. Elizabeth passed it without alteration and laid the letters upon the sideboard.

Aunt Gardiner entered quietly and took her place near the fire. "Your uncle will join us directly," she said. "His caller has come early."

Elizabeth raised her head. The words were difficult to find, but when they came, they were composed. Unemotional. "Very well."

There was a pause in which Mary finally struck a chord—soft, exploratory. The note hung in the air and faded. After two more notes, the drawing room door pushed open, admitting Mr Gardiner and another behind him.

Kitty started and had to smother a little cough. Mary's hand stilled upon the keys. Elizabeth crossed the room before either of them could rise.

The man who followed Mr Gardiner was a gentleman of middle years, plainly dressed, his coat brushed but worn at the seams. He bowed before Elizabeth with professional reserve.

"Miss Bennet."

She returned the courtesy. "Mr Hawthorne."

Mr. Gardiner closed the door. "Pray be seated," he said, indicating the chairs near the hearth. "We are obliged to you for your persistence."

The gentleman inclined his head. "I regret that I have little new to offer."

Elizabeth assumed her place, hands folded in her lap. She did not glance at her sisters.

The report was orderly, everything that could be expected of a professional. Mr. Hawthorne wasted no time in presenting his papers.

"The household at Lynwood had been re-questioned. The servants' recollections remained unchanged. The cliff path had been examined again in fairer weather. No further articles had been recovered beyond those already catalogued. No vessel had reported a sighting that corresponded with the date. No evidence of debt, correspondence, or private arrangement had emerged to suggest voluntary departure.

"I have spoken with the magistrate at Alnwick, and with two of the fishermen who assisted in the first search. The magistrate concurs," he said at last. "In such cases, Miss Bennet, when no disturbance of the ground is found and no sign of violence presents itself, one must conclude that the sea has claimed what it will."

The fire gave a small shift in the grate.

Elizabeth regarded the man steadily. "You have been thorough."

"I have endeavored to be so."

"And you believe there is nothing further to be done?"

He hesitated only a fraction. "Not within the bounds of reasonable inquiry. It has been... an extended investigation already."

Mary's fingers tightened on the keys until one of them accidentally rang out an E flat. Kitty's needle had ceased its motion entirely.

"Extended." Elizabeth's eyes wandered to the chair in the corner. "Yes, I suppose it has."

Mr Gardiner's hand flexed on his knee, a fist clenching and then, slowly, releasing. Mrs Gardiner was gazing absently at the floor with a faint hollow expression.

"What of the tenants?" Elizabeth's voice cracked. "You said there were some you might still interview."

Mr Hawthorne glanced at Mr Gardiner, but there was no help for him there. "Miss Bennet," he sighed, "I have re-examined every deposition taken at the time. The tenants along the southern road were approached again this past autumn, when memories might have cooled into greater clarity. Notices were circulated as far as Berwick and Durham. No account has been overlooked."

He paused, not for emphasis or evasion, but as a man measuring whether any further assurance might honestly be given.

"There has been... no report of a young woman matching your sister's description in any parish registry within a hundred miles. Nor has there been evidence of passage booked under another name. If there were cause to suspect concealment or coercion, I should pursue it. But there has been no such indication."

His gaze moved once more to Mr. Gardiner, then returned to Elizabeth.

"I would not withdraw were there ground upon which to stand. I remain at your disposal, should new information arise. But at present, I have exhausted the channels available to me."

Elizabeth's eyes had grown unfocused... distant. But she drew in a breath and rose, extending her hand. "We are grateful for your diligence, sir. And your sympathy is not unfelt, I assure you. If any new circumstance should arise, will you please inform us?"

Hawthorne was on his feet, and he took her hand almost gratefully. "Immediately, Miss Bennet."

Mr. Gardiner saw the gentleman to the door. The sound of carriage wheels on wet stone followed a moment later, then receded.

For a time, no one spoke.

Mary closed the piano cover with quiet care. Kitty bent over her muslin as though the pattern required sudden and urgent correction.

Elizabeth crossed to the window and drew back the curtain a fraction more. The street below went on in its indifferent business—carts, boots, a boy calling the hour. Nothing in it had altered.

After a moment, she folded the report the gentleman had left upon the table and placed it beneath the others.

"Thank you," her aunt said softly. "For trying so hard. You left nothing undone, Lizzy."

Elizabeth offered a thin smile. "Indeed, there is nothing further."

But she did not move away from the window.

The air held a thin brightness that promised neither warmth nor snow. Elizabeth drew her gloves more firmly up her wrists as she and Kitty passed beneath the bare branches that lined the walk. The Serpentine lay ahead, its surface a dull pewter beneath the pale sky, disturbed only where a pair of waterfowl cut across it in deliberate progress.

They had not spoken since leaving the house.

Kitty's step was bold, though she kept half a pace behind, as she had once done when Lydia's opinions set the direction of their walks. The habit had lingered; the influence had not.

"It is colder here than in the square," Kitty said at last.

"The water draws it down," Elizabeth replied. "It always does."

They turned along the edge of the lake. A nursemaid guided two thickly bundled children toward a bench; a gentleman in a dark coat stood reading near the rail. The city moved about them without intrusion.

Kitty sniffed against the cold's effects, and wiped discreetly at her nose with the back of her glove. "He sounded certain."

Elizabeth did not mistake the subject. "He sounded finished," she answered after a moment.

"That is worse."

"Yes."

They walked on.

For a moment Kitty seemed inclined to say more, then shook her head and bent it against the wind. "Mama will ask," she said instead. "She and Aunt Philips will write to Uncle Gardiner to ask what was said."

"She may," Elizabeth replied. "Uncle will frame it carefully."

Kitty glanced at her. "You know very well Mama has not slept since the latest round of interviews resumed."

"No."

"And Lydia—" Kitty stopped.

Elizabeth spared her a look. "Lydia is Lydia."

A faint colour rose in Kitty's cheek. "She says it is silly to keep chasing a shadow."

Elizabeth regarded the water. "Lydia has always preferred things that glitter plainly."

Kitty's mouth trembled, though she smiled. "She is certain Jane would have written."

"So would I be," Elizabeth said, gently.

They reached the bend where the trees thinned and the water widened. The surface seemed placid from that vantage, almost mild. Elizabeth rested her gloved hand upon the railing and looked across it, her expression composed.

"Do you believe him?" Kitty asked quietly.

Elizabeth considered before answering. "I believe Mr. Hawthorne has done all that may be done without conjecture," she said. "That is not the same thing as believing we know what has occurred."

Kitty drew a breath that was nearly a sob and mastered it before it formed. "I try not to think of—" She did not finish.

Elizabeth's hand shifted slightly upon the rail, not quite reaching, not quite withdrawing. "We do not imagine what we cannot see," she said. "It serves no one."

The wind moved lightly across the water. For a moment the surface altered—darkened, then smoothed again.

Kitty hesitated. "I saw that Mrs. Collins wrote last week."

"Yes. She asked whether there had been word. But you probably read the letter after Mary did."

Kitty sniffed and nodded. "I thought it was funny when she said the house is much the same. How could it be?" Kitty's mouth tightened faintly. "Though I was not surprised to hear the shrubbery has been cut back."

Elizabeth's gaze remained upon the water. "Mr. Collins is diligent in improvement."

Kitty glanced at her, uncertain whether she had been too sharp.

"Charlotte means well," Elizabeth added after a moment. "She always did."

"And Mr. Collins?"

Elizabeth's expression did not change. "Mr. Collins is attentive to his own concerns."

They walked a few steps in silence. "Will Mama come back in the spring?" Kitty asked.

"To London?" Elizabeth did not look at her. "No. She is content where she is."

The wind shifted again, carrying the faint scent of damp earth from the banks. Elizabeth drew her cloak more closely about her shoulders and at last stepped away from the railing.

"We shall walk once more around," she said. "It will do us good."

Kitty nodded, and they resumed their course around the smooth perimeter of the lake.

He entered the lower room and set the gathered debris beside the hearth, where damp rope and splintered timber would dry before being cut down for kindling. The interior would be warm soon—if that mattered to anyone, for it did not to him. He closed the door firmly behind him and crossed to the narrow table beneath the south window.

The letter lay where he had left it.

He did not sit at once. He removed his gloves, laying them parallel upon the table's edge, and brushed the worst of the salt from his sleeves. The floor bore the faint grit of the morning's walk; he swept it aside with the heel of his boot before drawing out the chair.

Only then did he unfold the paper again.

The seal had cracked cleanly. The impression upon it—an old crest, pressed without flourish—was still visible where the wax had cooled unevenly. He read from the second paragraph downward this time, as though to test whether the phrasing would alter upon repetition.

It did not.

Certain phrases drew his eye not for their emphasis but for their restraint. "Review." "Clarification." "Provision." The language was careful, and therefore dangerous.

He did not look up at once when he reached the final paragraph. His index finger tracked along the margin as though holding the paper in place against an unseen current.

When at last he lifted his gaze, it was not toward the window, but toward the stair. The tower stood above him, patient and unconsulted.

He folded the letter along its existing crease and set it beside the logbook. For a moment, his hand remained there, resting upon both. Then, he opened the logbook.

The previous night's entry waited unfinished, the ink dried to a dull brown along the margin.

"Wind E. by S. Moderate. Tide inward at first watch. Light steady."

He lifted the pen and considered the page.

There was nothing to amend.

After a moment, he added only the hour at which the tide had turned and sanded the line with care. The excess he tapped away upon the hearthstone. The movement was careful, unhurried.

Outside, the beam had ceased its rotation; daylight rendered it unnecessary. The lantern glass above caught the sun and returned it in pale fragments across the ceiling. His eyes found the shape of it upon the stone, the slow curve of brightness bending where glass had gathered it, and rested there longer than the light required.

He drew a fresh sheet toward him and began his reply.

"To the Trustees—"

The nib paused a fraction above the page before settling again.

"I acknowledge receipt of your communication of the tenth instant. The Lantern remains in sound condition, and no alteration has occurred in its function or maintenance. Should further clarification be required, I stand prepared to provide such particulars as may assist your review."

He stopped there.

The wind pressed lightly against the shutter. A loose latch tapped once and stilled.

He sanded the letter, shook off the grains, and folded it with the same deliberate care he had given the logbook. No flourish marked his signature. The ink lay dark and even upon the page.

He carried both letters upstairs before sealing his own, unwilling to leave the tower unwatched even for the length of a breath.

The lamps had been brought in and trimmed; their light lay soft against the ceiling, leaving the corners of the drawing room in a gentle obscurity. Outside, carriage wheels passed at intervals over wet stone, less frequent now than in the earlier hours. Mary had withdrawn with a volume to the smaller parlour; Kitty was at the table near the hearth, attempting a more patient hand at her needlework.

Elizabeth had remained by the fire with a sheet of heavy paper unfolded across her lap.

The seal bore no crest she recognized.

She read it once, then again more slowly.

"Uncle," she said at last, "have you ever heard of Blackscar Lantern?"

Mr. Gardiner, who had been reviewing a narrow column of figures in his ledger, glanced up. "Blackscar?"

"Yes." She held out the page. "It appears I am expected to have heard of it."

He rose and crossed to her, adjusting his spectacles before taking the letter. His expression altered only slightly as he read, though the alteration did not escape her. "So," he said quietly.

She lowered the letter. "Then, you are familiar with it."

"I am."

Kitty looked up from her stitching. "What is it?"

"A lighthouse," Mr. Gardiner replied. "On the Northumberland coast."

Elizabeth watched him. "And why should I be addressed concerning it?"

He took the letter she offered and scanned its contents. Then he frowned and folded the letter before answering. "Because, my dear, it pertains to your mother's family."

"Mama's?" Elizabeth drew her brows together. "I do not understand."

Mr. Gardiner resumed his seat opposite her. "It is an old settlement—older than your grandfather, and older still than his father. A trust attached to the Lantern property. It has, for generations, passed through the daughters of that branch."

"Through the daughters?" Kitty repeated. "Why, that is turning the matter on its head, is it not, Lizzy?"

Elizabeth glanced at her sister, then back to her uncle.

"Indeed," he said, passing the letter back to Elizabeth. "To the eldest unmarried daughter upon her majority," he clarified. "Provided she accept the charge."

"Why daughters?" Elizabeth asked.

Mr. Gardiner's mouth curved faintly. "Because the woman who first endowed the land intended it so."

"A woman?" Kitty said, leaning forward against the arm of the chaise. "Oh, do tell, Uncle."

"Oh, I do not know how much there is to tell. Your great-great-grandmother's aunt, if I recall the line correctly. She never married. The tower was raised upon her portion of the coast nearly two centuries ago, after a wreck that cost several lives. She settled the property by instrument, stipulating that its oversight remain in the female line."

Elizabeth considered this. "But why?"

"She believed," he said mildly, "that sons are too easily persuaded by profit. A reef may be cleared. A shoal may be charted differently. A light may be improved or replaced. But a promise, once attached to commerce, becomes negotiable."

Mary, who had re-entered unnoticed and now stood near the mantel with her book in hand, looked up at that. "It was an act of moral foresight, then."

"Perhaps," Mr. Gardiner allowed. "Or perhaps she simply preferred to see the matter entrusted to those who would not be tempted to dispose of it."

Kitty frowned faintly. "Dispose of a lighthouse?"

"It sits upon valuable... no. Desirable ground," he said. "And has done for many years."

Elizabeth lowered her eyes to the page once more. The language returned to her with altered emphasis: in light of the approaching attainment of majority... change in stewardship... formal acknowledgment required.

"Is there... income attached to it?" she asked.

Mr. Gardiner's mouth curved faintly. "No."

She blinked. "None at all?"

"None that would tempt your mother or your aunt Philips, I assure you. Were there, they would not have relinquished the matter so readily in their youth."

Kitty gave a small, startled laugh, which subsided when Elizabeth shot her a look.

"What, then, is the charge?" Elizabeth asked.

"The oversight of the Lantern's endowment," he said. "Certain responsibilities attached to its maintenance. Correspondence with trustees. Occasional presence, in former years, though that has grown less frequent. It is more symbolic than burdensome in these latter days."

Elizabeth's fingers tightened slightly upon the edge of the page. "It should have fallen to Jane," she whispered.

Mr. Gardiner did not answer at once. He tugged his spectacles off his face and dropped his hand to his knee. "Yes," he said at last.

Kitty's needle slipped from her grasp and fell soundlessly into her lap, sending her fumbling to find it again.

Elizabeth read the line again. ...attainment of majority... "Did she know?"

He inclined his head slowly. "A letter was sent to her at Lynwood, shortly before—" He paused, adjusting the paper in his hands. "Well. Shortly after she took up her post."

"And she meant to accept?"

"I believe she did. She wrote to me upon the subject. She wished first to complete the term she had agreed upon. It was her view that she ought not abandon an obligation once undertaken."

Elizabeth frowned and thumbed the edge of the letter; folding a tiny corner, then flattening it... folding it again.

"She would have come of age a year ago last August," Kitty said faintly.

"She would," Mr. Gardiner replied.

Elizabeth looked again at the neat, impersonal script of the Trustees' notice. In the absence of formal acknowledgment... alternate measures...

"And because she did not answer," she said quietly, "it passes now to me."

"Yes."

She did not immediately respond. The fire shifted; a small cinder fell inward upon itself.

"Is there penalty if it is refused?"

"Not to you," Mr. Gardiner said. "The settlement provides for succession. If you decline, the right passes in turn to Mary, then to Kitty, then to Lydia. Should none of you accept, the Trustees assume temporary authority until one of the line produces a daughter of age to receive it."

Elizabeth huffed. "Why, we could leave it indefinitely, could we not? If there are trustees who manage the property currently, and must have done since... how long, Uncle?"

"My mother accepted the charge. She married your grandfather the following year, but because she was unmarried when it devolved upon her, it remained with her thereafter. The Trustees' authority is limited. Their office preserves the property; it does not guide it. And I am told the structure is... in need of modernization."

Elizabeth's eyes lifted at that word.

"It is, I am told, a very old tower," he added.

The letter lay cool against her palm.

"Blackscar Lantern," she repeated, as though testing the sound.

Kitty drew her shawl more closely about her shoulders. "Northumberland is very far."

"Yes," Elizabeth said.

But she did not fold the letter.

HE HAD MENDED THE length of rope retrieved that morning from the beach, cut away what could not be saved, and set the rest to coil upon its peg. The oil had been measured and recorded. The wind had shifted northward, but not with force enough to trouble the glass. There was nothing to anticipate beyond the ordinary rotation of watches.

He prepared his supper with the same economy he brought to all things: bread warmed at the edge of the hearth, a portion of salt fish, a heel of cheese. He ate standing, as he most often did, one hand resting upon the mantel while the other held the plate. There was no ceremony in it. The room was warm enough now. He had built the fire because the air had turned damp and threatened his books, not because it comforted.

A sound at the door announced the only visitor the tower admitted without introduction.

The cat entered as though she owned the place, tail lifted, fur marked in irregular patches of grey and white that bore the evidence of too many past winters. She paused just within the threshold, regarding him without expectation. He set a scrap of fish upon the floor near the hearth. She approached only after he had turned away.

He did not speak to her. She did not require it.

When he finished, he washed the plate, dried it, and set it in its place. The cat had taken possession of the warm stone before the fire. By the time he crossed the room again, she had already closed her eyes.

He ascended once more to the lantern room at the appointed hour and examined the flame. The wick held true. The oil remained sufficient. The glass was clear. The beam moved in its accustomed arc across the darkening water, patient and unbroken.

He adjusted the wick by a fraction and descended.

Later, with the fire reduced to a low bed of coals, he drew a book from the small shelf near the window and seated himself beneath the lantern's residual glow that filtered faintly through the stairwell. It was not a novel; he did not favor them. The volume was worn at the spine and marked at intervals with slips of paper cut narrow and precise. He read without haste, one finger resting lightly along the margin.

The cat left as silently as she had come.

At some hour past midnight, his eyes closed upon the page. The book remained open against his chest, rising and falling with the steady rhythm of his breath.

He did not require an alarm.

Years of vigil had ordered his sleep as surely as tide obeyed the moon. At the hour he had long ago fixed in habit—when the oil must be examined lest it burn too low—he woke.

He did not stir at once. The room lay in its accustomed stillness, the embers faintly alive upon the hearthstone. But the faint thread of light that usually descended the stairwell at that hour did not touch the floor.

He was upright before the thought had fully formed.

The tower stood quiet about him. The sea moved with its steady concussion against the rock. Nothing announced disturbance. And yet the air within the room felt altered, as though a measure had been removed from it.

The ascent was swift but not reckless. His hand found the rail without searching. He took the steps two at a time where the curve allowed and reached the lantern room within seconds.

Dark.

The glass reflected only his own movement as a faint distortion against the night.

He crossed to the lamp and opened the chimney. The wick was intact. He touched it; it was warm, but not charred beyond measure. The reservoir held oil. He lifted it to be certain. There was weight enough.

He struck the taper and brought flame to the wick. It caught. For the span of a breath, it burned.

Then it narrowed, thinned, and withdrew into nothing, as though the air itself had smothered it.

He adjusted the wick lower and tried again. The same. He removed the chimney entirely and relit it bare.

The flame held for three heartbeats.

On the fourth, it failed.

He examined the draft vents, the cap, the seals around the glass. There was no crack. No breach. No sudden wind forcing its will upon the flame. The air in the room lay still.

He replaced the chimney and lit it once more, shielding it with his hand. The wick burned obediently until he withdrew his fingers.

Then it died.

He stood with his hand upon the brass housing, testing its warmth as though the cause might be discovered there. The mechanism lay in perfect order. Beyond the glass, the tide advanced and withdrew with its accustomed weight against the cliff.

The lantern, for all his knowledge of it, offered nothing.

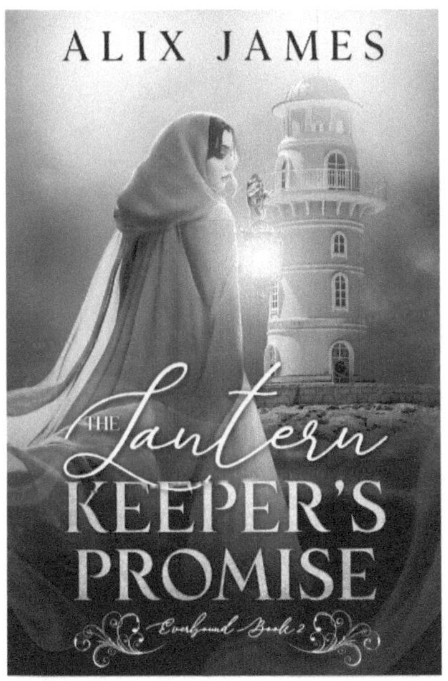


Get your copy of *The Lanternkeeper's Promise* today!

www.ingramcontent.com/pod-product-compliance
Lightning Source LLC
LaVergne TN
LVHW041051080826
845145LV00007B/1532

* 9 7 8 1 9 5 7 0 8 2 5 3 0 *